I0763601

THE HOUSE OF
GRAVES
TRILOGY

A NOVEL BY BARRY WOOD

ISBN 978-0-9971530-0-2
Library of Congress Control Number: 2016900881

The main protagonists in this novel are fiction. Any similarity to persons living or dead is coincidental. Of the actual historical individuals mentioned, every effort had been made to keep their words, intentions and actions consistent with recorded history. The endeavor was to follow chronological events as they relate to the narrative.

Editor, Author Gene Hull and Kenneth Victor Wood
Cover, Janet Sierzant

La Maison Publishing, Inc.
Vero Beach, Florida
www.lamaisonpublishing.com

Notes from the Author

This story is fictitious. It is a tale of actual places and incidents of the times woven into a story of people long since passed—or who never existed.

To my friends who have '*raved*' over my first two novels, I hope I can keep your curiosity here as well.
Your encouragement makes writing well worth the struggle.

I am deeply indebted to Gene Hull, my mentor and reviewer, who took my manuscript, ten and twenty pages at a time, to mark up and discuss. His friendship cannot be expressed without becoming too maudlin.

To my wife of 34 years, Christina, I thank her for the fifth time for her efforts in apprehending typos and amiably living with files, research books, charts, maps, yellow pads, Post-it notes, countless pens/pencils and miscellany spread across twenty feet of desk, tables and chairs—in our main living area!

Thanks to my publisher, Janet Sierzant, for expending every effort to improve my cover and manuscript.

PROVISO / Mea Culpa:
In publishing, the mantra is that one should not be their own editor. As I write for friends and their friends, the number of books produced are quite conscribed and friends accept the occasional blip in punctuation or spelling or nuance. At least I hope they do.

Table of Contents

PROLOGUE

***SEAWARD*, NOVEMBER 1846, SALEM, MASSACHUSETTS**

CAPTAIN RICHARD GRAVES was sure something was terribly wrong. The mounting squalls caused him to hunch his shoulders and brace his legs against the wind whipped sea. Hands cupped to his eyes from the stinging rain, he looked out over Salem Harbor from his estate *Seaward*, to the Atlantic Ocean and on to the Gulf Stream.

"What is it, father?"

"What is it? For Christ's sake, Jason! Did you not look to the weatherglass, feel the air? How long have you been a captain?"

Knowing the answer, yet disinterested, Graves continued, muttering, "The seas running too steadily north even at slack tide and whitecaps are breaking over Winter Island. The air's too heavy for November. There's weather south, well south—and intense. Damn!"

John Thomas, Graves other son came up, pulling his collar higher, his captain's hat tighter and caught some of his father's words, "That could mean a hurricane, father."

"Aye, yet we won't have much weather here. She must have spawned in the Caribe and our cold water is where she'll die."

"But don't you think our fleet should be safe in Cuba by now?"

"In Havana they should be, son—but safe?"

The three captains stared, each locked in their own thoughts.

They who go down to the sea in ships, and occupy themselves in great waters. These are the workers of the Lord; and his wonders in the deep...

Psalm 10

HOUSE OF GRAVES

BOOK I

CHAPTER ONE

1846 Salem, 1 September

THE ANNUAL GATHERING WAS CONCLUDED. The lawns of *Seaward*, the Graves family's massive granite estate looming over Salem's inner harbor, were now empty. As it had been for the past twenty-five years, the gathering was for the fall leave-taking of Graves Shipping's vessels, captains, and crews. Their goal was to make sail for warmer waters before the onslaught of another northern winter and, once there, work the southern sea-lanes.

On the day that followed the gathering, eleven great, wondrous windjammers and three whalers, comprising the Graves' oceanic fleet weighed anchor, cleared Halfway Rock to the leeward, and formed for their grand passage past the shore gawkers at Marblehead. Veering east by south around Race Point on Cape Cod's hook, they then eased westerly before beginning their southern run to lower their flags to half-mast as they passed the remaining inhabitants of Nantucket.

The ships then separated each according to their differing pace and made to rendezvous at St. Augustine, Florida. Further south, most of the ships would harbor in Cuba's warm waters, while three whalers, after their final refitting, would continue around Cape Horn and in to the whaling grounds of the north Pacific to hunt the Royal Fish. For the southern fleet, the next weeks and months would be filled with unloading ice, timber from Maine, textiles from the mills of Waltham and Lowell and other New England manufactured goods. From Havana, until early spring, the ships would transport southern products of rum, cotton, molasses and tobacco to England and Europe, whereas rice, beef, soybean and various other cargos would ship around the Caribbean as well as the southeast coasts of the United States and all of South America.

They berthed at Havana, northwest Cuba, with the exception of one vessel. That singular vessel, the fast clipper ship *Laurence Pike,* was moored to on-load sugar at Ponce, a town on the south central shore of Puerto Rico. By 30 Sept. 1846, the fleet was refitting in Havana.

Hidden in the Gulf of Mexico, a hurricane spawned in the dark Caribbean Sea, 6 October 1846.[1] There, it writhed into incredible strength and fury. Without forewarning, the tempest tore into western Cuba, devastated every structure in Havana and Cuba's eastern fishing villages, and left not one vessel afloat in Havana's anchorage. From Cuba, it thundered across the Florida Keys, obliterated every home, collapsed the twin lighthouses on Sand and West Keys, ravaged the island necklace, wrecked boats and brought death to scores of residents.

After the storm devastated the populace and buildings in mainland Florida, it moved along the warm Gulf Stream to strike the east coast again at Savannah, Georgia, crippling the seaboard with a storm surge that caused severe flooding and damage. The Northeast endured heavy rains and structural damage to bridges and homes then, by 14 October, the aging gale veered northeast, passed over Boston, Salem, Cape Ann and the northern Massachusetts' shoreline to perish in the graveyard of storms, the North Atlantic.

Captain Richard Melville Graves, his wife, Mary and his sons, Captain Jason Melville, his oldest at twenty-five, and Captain John Thomas, twenty-four, fretted over the weather. The father had experience enough to sense that New England's wind and rain were the remnants of a far more severe storm to the south. They waited

---

[1] To this day, the October 1846 hurricane is considered one of the severest to ever strike Cuba and the east coast of the United States. Barometric Pressure was recorded at 940mbar. Modern estimates rate the storm a terrifying Category 5.

for information that took two weeks to arrive and when it did, they were staggered. American Telegraph's repaired cables brought the news to New York and then over the trail of the Post Road to Boston; every Graves' ship had sunk in Havana's harbor or run aground and broken up while attempting to clear to open water. Their fleet now lay derelict.

The family, stunned at the loss of their ships and crews, realized that, without warning, they'd been brought to financial ruin. Aside from the loss of experienced crews, hurricane insurance was dearly bought and not considered, so it wore heavily on the father. Captain Richard Graves knew that if he had kept the fleet a month longer at Salem, the ships would have ridden out the sea.

Now, the empire he and his father before him had built was not simply in jeopardy, it was gone. The slight, solitary ray of hope arrived when it became known the clipper ship *Laurence Pike* at Ponce, south central Puerto Rico had only been brushed by the storm. At present, she was at Havana with her crew salvaging and awaiting orders.

Captain Graves ordered his youngest son, John Thomas, to use their coastal freight schooner, *Ocean Pearl* and take any paid consignment along the east coast as long as the weather allowed. After that, the Captain and his oldest son, Jason, went south by rail to find a southern vessel they could engage to reach the *Laurence Pike*. It was the loss of his ships that mattered to Graves more than their crews. He could easily get seamen—ships, he had to purchase.

2

CAPTAIN RICHARD GRAVES, having grasped the full extent of the disaster made his decision, and turned to Frederick Daly, Captain of the *Laurence Pike*.

"Fred, you know I'm in a tough position. I've made next to nothing on the salvage, so here's the story. I can only pay the crews for some of the time they worked—nothing more. They'll have to find jobs here in Havana rebuilding the town, or work their way north on their own. That includes you. My son and I will take over—wait, I'll tell you both."

The captain called his son over, "Jason, I've told Fred here that we're taking command of the *Pike*. The men are on their own, including Fred."

Jason Graves looked pained. They heard him cursing, yet only nodded to the now former captain of their clipper ship. Daly stood and without a word, walked off.

"That was a tough thing to do, huh, father?"

Richard Graves looked sideway to his son without warmth, "There are a lot tougher things to do; and that's being a Captain in this calamity for one. You should know that by now for Christ's sake."

"I do, still…"

Captain Graves was curt, "Drop it! There's more important subjects. The *Pike's* part-ballasted with distilled sugar. I've contracted for cotton here and then take on tobacco in Barbados. That will top us off and when that's done we'll set sail for Bilbao, Spain. We'll bring a good price—nowhere near what we need to keep *Seaward* going—but a good price, being one of the only ships around here that can make the Atlantic Passage, something you've never done."

Sailing across the Caribbean Sea to the Windward Island of Barbados, Graves found the plantation owner, Ian MacPherson was genial, pleased to have found a ship to move his cargo of tobacco leaf to Europe. Rum, iced from the old ballast from the *Laurence Pike*, refreshed them while MacPherson's overseer kept watch on the slaves to see that they balanced the cargo to Graves' instructions.

As the Captain and MacPherson settled on the veranda sipping rum, Graves kept staring toward the loading dock. MacPherson was curious, "What is it, Captain? Don't trust them to follow orders or never seen slaves before? You one of those damn Northern abolitionist?"

"You should watch your tongue, MacPherson. I don't take kindly to being called a damn anything. Then again, I'm your guest and I'll answer without rancor. I've seen slaves from India, China, Africa and everywhere else. I'm neutral to slavery, and don't have time to be a damned abolitionist. The reason for my staring is that big black buck you've got bossing those Negros."

Ian laughed, "Something, isn't he? Runs a tight ship, name's Monar. I bought him in Barbados when he was a pup, saw something in his eyes, I did. Had him taught proper English; brought him up with polite manners, but he knows his place in the universe. He also doesn't mind my using him for breeding, don't mind not one bit."

"You breed him? You're serious?"

"Of course. Mate him with the best females, gives me the best slaves. Not like our Maroons— blasted bush natives—always stealing and causing trouble."

Captain Graves shook his head, "I'll be damned. Wish ships could be reproduced like that."

"I bet you do, losing every ship but this clipper and that old schooner you mentioned." Ian appeared thoughtful, "Tell me, Captain, What's your next port after Bilbao?"

"Don't know. See what I can pick up along Europe or the Med. I don't mind admitting I'm at wit's end trying to recover my losses. Anything you can suggest for cargo over there, I'm listening, Ian."

"What do you mean by anything, Captain?"

"What do *you* mean by asking?"

"First, Captain, answer me a few questions—if you don't mind. You a hard-assed seaman?"

"Hard-assed? How could a good captain be otherwise? I went to sea when I was eight, under my father, a tough old bastard. Sailed most of the seven seas. Joined the Union Navy when the British started impressing our seamen into service in their warships. Fought in 1812 as a lieutenant on the *USS Chesapeake* with Captain Lawrence—bless his soul—he died fighting HMS frigate *Shannon,* bloodiest sea battle of the war against you damn Jack Tar Brits. Cutlass and knife. Our Captain was dead when we were taken prisoner to Nova Scotia and not one of us was without wounds. Yet five of us managed to escape, steal a boat, sail to Bangor, Maine. Does that answer your question?"

"I suppose it does. Yet first, Captain, I am not English; I'm a Scotty. Don't like the English any more than you, so I'll ask you again, what do you mean you'll do anything?"

"I don't follow you."

"Hear me out, Captain Graves. From what I see of your ship, she's narrow and sharp and a fine line. How fast is she?"

"She's from the McKay Yard, out of East Boston. I reworked her spars and sails. Give me passable air and she'll do an unbroken sixteen, maybe seventeen plus knots."[2]

Ian raised his eyebrows, "You're serious? So, in other words, what can keep up with her?"

"Haven't found another yet. Remember, she's a clipper, not a packet. Not as beamy, feels the sea better. Maybe a new McKay or Poole's clipper *Defiance* could keep up with the *Pike,* or the Brit's

---

[2] 17 knots=19.6 MPH

Yorkshire. She's real fast, but a packet too, so I doubt it. Add to that, I'm a better captain."

"All right then, my better Captain, let me lay out my thoughts. You can't make enough to clear your debts by running this cargo to Europe and then find some potential cargo back here and go back and forth time and again."

Graves took a quaff of rum, "Blast it, I know that, MacPherson. I'm just trying to keep going until there's something…"

"Captain, you've a passable cargo here for Europe. And I can get you a good cargo of textiles, rum and wood for a run to…*Africa*."

Captain Graves grew quiet, intent, "You're suggesting the triangular passage, MacPherson?"

"You mentioned you were indifferent to slavery Captain, not me, and would do anything."

Staring at his host, Graves did not blink. He thought he had standards, ethics. Yet, when it came down to it, he easily recognized he had his own world to save and keeping that was foremost. Standards, ethics? There and gone—there was no warning from Hector's Ghost.

For a moment, no sound escaped other than the slaves moaning some native songs.

"Lay it out; what do you have in mind, MacPherson, and what's in it for me? I'll listen."

"Bluntly, you pick up slaves along the Ivory Coast; deliver them to Barbados and your part ends. You don't deliver them to the States, getting through the British West Indies, or the Grand Bahamas is too dangerous. I'll sell them around the Caribe and the Deep South States from here. Anyway, Captain, you'll make a lot of money. Do it twice and you'll save your arse."

"I need more information than that."

"Of course you do. You'll get it if you say yes. Firstly, remember there's quite a few of your compatriots up in your Boston and New York, upper crust folk that invest in the triangular trade.

Newport's one of the worst. Then it's your Faneuil's, Cabot's, Easton's and even that Stiles gentleman, who traded—sorry, invested—in slave ships while he was President of Yale. Even Brown University's three Brown brothers used slaves to build part of the university—only hearsay of course. Their syndicated ships leave the northeast coast to Europe with legal cargo, then on to Africa with gold, silver and rum. After that, the big money cargo—slaves to the Caribbean or Brazil. That done with, the ships sail home scrubbed lilywhite clean to their owner's fancy estates in your Salem and Newport or New York. Then its pay off their investors and hobnob with the other rich who are actually doing the same thing— still on the sly of course. One year, round trip maximum, beats whaling for a three year stretch and a better return on their investment."

"But the British are hanging slavers along the African coast."

"Sure. They abolished slavery in '07 and take it seriously. Still, the length of the African coast is hard to cover and they're not permitted to board US ships—though at times they do."

"What about that new British screw propeller steamship I've read about?"

"That's the *Rattler,* but she's only good to a point. She can go when the wind doesn't and get further upriver. So the problem for sail is getting to the offshore winds before any steamship shows up. Once a clipper gets downwind, no stinking ten-knot steamer, even with sails, can catch you. That's why I asked you about the speed of the *Pike* before I brought up all this. To be frank, I ran slaves in the past, before I lost my Hermaphrodite schooner, *King of Edinburgh* to fire, so I know my plan works. Yet before I say more on the subject, what's your answer, Captain, yes or no?"

Captain Graves sat back, steeping his fingers, studying his options, "You say it will take three months. What's my return?"

"First, listen to what is involved. I would remove half your present cargo of distillery sugar and ship it to New England with my old topsail schooner. I can take that profit and send it to your wife at

Seaward; that should help her for a while. Removing that sugar gives us room for rum I've kept for just such a venture.

"Rum works a lot like money in Africa and I'll add gold as well. Now, if I recall the bilge of a packet ship, we can add another half-deck around the hull under the below deck…"

"Ian that would leave less than four feet in a damp hull."

"Believe me Captain, your cargo won't be standing, or there more than a month—if you and they're lucky. You want to know your yield so I'll try to arrive at a figure. Now, say the *Pike* can hold five hundred slaves…"

Again, MacPherson was interrupted. "Five hundred? For Christ's sake—how?"

"Damn it, Captain! It's been done. Trust me and let it go at that. Here's the numbers that will make you take the chance. A healthy male slave from Adansi or Kawhu will cost in American dollars, whether rum, gold, trinkets or whatever, around ten to twenty dollars. For every healthy one you deliver to Foul Bay here on the east coast—Monar knows it—I'll pay you one ninety dollars, gold if you wish, man or woman. That's all you do. Drop them off and come to me for payment."

Captain Graves did the math. "Five hundred times ninety dollars …."

"Make that four hundred, Captain. You'll have ah, shall we say, attrition at sea."

"Twenty percent losses? Christ. Still, four hundred slaves times a ninety dollars is thirty-six thousand dollars!"[3]

Ian smiled to himself, "That's right. Deducting your slave cost, crew costs, food for the cargo and miscellaneous bribes; you should clear thirty thousand. Now you see that while you are toiling away

---

[3] Due to variables, it is difficult to estimate the 1846 dollar for today's dollar. As a reference-it is estimated, the 1850 dollar to the 2010 dollar is a factor of X 28. One 500-slave trip, after expenses, could clear over $400,000 in gross profit in today's currency—with no taxes.

in honest commerce, your wealthy friends are sitting back laughing up their sleeves at you."

"What do you get out of this?"

"I warehouse them inland around Dash Valley, feed them Green Monkeys and mangos and sell them from Brazil up to the Carolina's. For that, I'll average a profit around seventy dollars each. I receive less because, straight out, I take chances, but you take the possibility of losing your ship. However, my plan will give you ninety-nine percent likelihood of success."

MacPherson made considerably more, he ran the auctions. However, not knowing the actual profits, Graves did not take long, "MacPherson, I'm in the game. Yet I'll need a crew."

"What do you mean by that? You have a crew."

"Think, man. I can't have any of my crew go back to Salem to squeal about what I'm up to."

"I see your point. I'll hire you a crew, but you'll pay them. Moreover, I'll loan you Monar to boss the crew where the nigger's are concerned. He knows about sailing over there, done it with me before. Hang on, Captain, I'll make him a deal."

Shouting his overseer to the veranda, MacPherson started, "Monar, I'll make a deal with you. I'll set you free right now; no strings other than you have to leave Barbados. You can go to Niger and stay there if you wish. Or, you could go with this here Captain Graves to Africa with my crew and boss you know what cargo back to here. You agree to that and I'll give you two hundred dollars and you'll be a freedman."

Monar showed no emotion and in unexpectedly excellent English responded, "I will agree to that, except I'd be a fool to go to live in Niger. I'll continue to work for you after—for payment of course."

MacPherson smiled, "You're getting to be as canny as a Scot, Monar."

"I've learned well from you, Master."

"All right, we've made a deal, Monar. This is Captain Graves."

Graves looked directly at Monar, "You know what our cargo will be, Monar?"

"Of course, I am without feeling about it, Captain Graves. It is my freedom *here* that matters, not in Niger. And the money? That matters much too."

Graves' shook hands with Monar, pleasing him. Ignoring the handshake and dismissing his slave, MacPherson started to turn to the Captain, but Graves continued speaking with the Negro, "Would you tell my son I don't want the spars all acockabill? Have him square them away."

When Monar left, Ian was irritated, "Listen, Graves, you don't *ask* a nigger to do anything. You order them. You'd better learn that quickly. Now, what do we do about your crew?"

"I've given that thought. I'll tell them I've sold the *Pike* to you and you have your own crew that I'll command. If you will forward me a sum to pay them a stipend and use your sloop to take them to Havana, I'd be obligated to pay you back out of my profits."

Shock ran through Captain Graves' crew. Yet in the end, there was nothing they could do to change the situation. With resentment growing and with only a few dollars, they were hustled by MacPherson's employees onto his other sloop, the *Laird of Glasgow* and sent off to Havana to the rest of Captain Graves' former crews. MacPherson and the Captain then retired to the plantation owner's main salon to review his plan for the expedition.

"Before we start, Graves, I'm a touch concerned about your son, Jason. What's coming up is not a pleasure cruise in the bay and to me, that chap doesn't look up to it."

Graves became irritable, "Don't you have concern about my son, he's my business."

"Back off and make sense, Captain. I've nothing against Jason. It's only that I believe he will be—shall we say, not in favor—of the coming excursion. And that could be troubling for us all."

Taking the offered crystal glass of rum and calming, Graves said, “I know why you brought it up, Ian, but Jason is dependable. He takes after his mother, has feelings for other people. Now my other son, John Thomas, takes after me, not a negotiator; makes a decision and carries it out. He wouldn’t like this either, yet he’d see the need and throw himself into it.”

“Well, that’s all well and good, but he’s north and Jason’s here. You’re sure about this?”

“Don’t bring it up again. I’ll handle Jason.”

3

EARLY MORNING, 3 DECEMBER 1846, SALEM

JOHN THOMAS GRAVES DROPPED into a leather chair exhausted. His mother, Mary, lit a lamp and brought him a mug of steaming tea with honey, then sat quietly for a minute.

"So, JT," she joshed him, "another one of your all night parties with the boys—and who else?"

"Don't I wish, Mother. We took the *Ocean Pearl* to Nantucket and hauled sperm oil to Boston and another consignment to Newburyport for transshipment down to Lowell…"

His mother interrupted him, "How are things in Nantucket? I heard the fire was dreadful."

"It surely was. Fire took the docks and warehouses, they're in tough shape and now that's there's less demand for whale oil, the whaling industry is dying and a lot of people are leaving, even old-timers like the Brant's. Can you imagine that?"

"My God, how the world is changing around us. Well, I wish them the best. Still, they have their sheep farms to help them."

"Yes, and speaking of sheep, there was a sheep storm and we had to layover a morning."

She smiled, "You had me going there for a minute, JT. I almost forgot they call fog a sheep storm."

He laughed with her, "Yes, but at least it helped stop the water from freezing over, just some of the rigging and that's good as the land roads are terrible, which helps us. I didn't tell you, our final run was dropping off some winches at Pickman's dock. If there hadn't been a full moon and their dock so long, we would have had trouble landing."

"Pickman's? Your father would be angry knowing you did something for them. They haven't spoken since old man Pickman himself put his bowsprit into the stays of the *James North.*"

"Good Lord, mother. That was years ago, plus Dudley died last April and his son, Jimmy and I get along great. He's helped find me cargo since our loss. Whether Dad is angry or not, it's too bad. He said take any consignment and I am. Still, when you think of it, Dad's been mad at about everyone, one time or another. So, what's the latest about Hawthorne and our docks?"

"Nothing new. As you know, since Nate Hawthorne's become Inspector of Revenue for Salem, it's been a running battle over the value of our waterfront and it won't get better until your father comes back. And then more than likely, it will get worse."

"Well, you actually can't blame Hawthorne. We've been getting milk from the cow without paying our fair share since grandfather put the docks in without permission."

"I know, I know, but your grandfather started here before most anyone, so he felt everyone else was an interloper and your father holds to that belief. And, don't let your father hear you supporting Hawthorne either."

"Don't worry Mom, I won't. Still, father should realize those days are long gone. Gramp's attempt to buy up most all of Salem still rankles a lot of people around here who remember."

"Yes, they're still not happy but least *you're* accepted by most, especially since you helped awhile back to find that poor Hunt girl after she drowned."

"Folks like you too, Mother, don't forget that. It's father who creates problems, but I always defend him. You know, strange you mentioned Lily Hunt. Only yesterday, I was thinking it's been three years since Jimmy Pickman and I found her. Never did find out how it happened. People who can't swim shouldn't go near the water, but you can't tell kids that. Still, she wasn't stupid, so it was strange."

John Thomas rose wearily from the chair and went over to kiss his mother.

"Here now," she laughed, "save that for all your pretty girls. I've been hearing things."

"Not lately you haven't, there aren't any Lorelei's in these waters. Now tell me, anything new? What's the latest from down south? I was so tired I hadn't thought to ask."

"Dear me; seeing you made me forgetful too—there is news. Some of our crews are filtering back. They say a number of the men are staying in Cuba to help rebuild and a few more are working along the damaged areas of the coast. Quite honestly, JT, they say father hardly gave them anything to help them…"

"Well how in hell could he, Mother? He must be broke!"

"There's no need for that kind of language, JT. Yet here's a strange part, two of the men were in the *Pike's* crew, Leonardo and Black Sam. They said that Father sold the *Laurence Pike* to a man named MacPherson in Barbados, and he's staying on to captain it."

"I don't believe that! Flat out, I don't believe it."

"Don't get worked up with me, I'm only repeating what I've been told. Nevertheless, more vital news; a check came—a thousand dollars. Makes me believe your father sold her."

"A thousand! That doesn't say he sold her, but it will help keep our heads above water a bit. Yet think, Mother. How can we keep going here if all Dad's up to is only being a Captain? "There's no future in that. If, for some bizarre reason he gave up the *Pike*, you can be sure he's set his goal to something vast, you wait and see."

"Well then, we'll just have to go about our business while we wait, won't we, Dear?"

«»

6 December 1846, Barbados

Captain Richard Graves was still studying the charts when Ian MacPherson returned from overseeing his slaves, "See anything wrong, Graves?"

"Not as far as you've informed me to date. Except for some of the rum, I drop my cargo at Bilbao, Spain, get paid, add textiles and on-load timber planks. Then make the run to Cape Verde. I've never dropped anchor at Tarrafal, so why there?"

"Tarrafal is because I didn't want your ship reconfigured for slaves at Bilbao since the British have agents there and other ports snooping around large windjammers heading for Africa. You know, they get a crewmember drunk, find out about the interior, any additional decks, chains, manacles and smell—stuff like that can give you away and they pass that along to the Royal Navy. So you go to Tarrafal to have the carpenters install all that's needed, away from the Navy's eyes."

"I follow, makes sense. However, it's your schooner that concerns me. A lot of water will pass under her before I see her at Tarrafal."

"The *Laird* left last week for Cape Verde and then on to the African Coast to scope the area and make contact with the chiefs. They'll start their collection parties going and warehouse them so they'll be ready to load as soon as you berth. Now, there's things I want you to know. The crew I'm giving you is mostly mulatto, white fathers, black mothers. Mulatto's don't like blacks because the black's treat them worse than the white men do. That means you won't have trouble with the crew other than they might beat the slaves more than necessary, so keep a lookout for that. Beat up or whipped slaves look like they can give trouble, so buyer's shy away from them and that means less money. And sick slaves are no use to you and they make others sick. Throw them overboard and maybe the ones chained to each side—and don't give me that look, just do as I say."

Ian took a mouthful of rum as he nonchalantly thumbed through his notes, "Any slave gives the slightest trouble, shoot him. That helps cow the others too. There's no such thing as sanitation. Below decks is foul enough to make you sick. Open the hatches when it's possible and bring slaves up twenty or thirty at a time. Keep the crew alert, slaves can get crazy chained up and try to jump overboard. There's netting you can have strung up to prevent most of that. No crewman goes below alone. One man stays at the bottom of the ladder and can carry a weapon or have others with him; but don't ever let a nigger get a weapon, not a knife, a fork—nothing."

Captain Graves got up and walked to the end of the veranda as MacPherson watched.

"Not getting second thoughts are you, Captain?"

"I never have second thoughts, Ian, just taking it all in."

"Very well then, just remember that slave mutiny on the *Amistad,* you can't be too cautious."

The Captain acknowledged the comment, "I will; did you know that those Negros were freed and went back to Sierra Leone to start a mission?"

"No, I was disgusted and lost track of what happened to them. Shows what can happen when the wrong people acquire power enough to twist the law. Nevertheless, Graves, the good part of your voyage is you'll have a crew who's done this before so there's no worry about a *crew* mutiny, or the American Navy. Your Secretary of War, Webster, agonizes more about preserving his fragile union with the south, than slaves. The Union wrings its hands, shows the flag in the eastern Caribe, mostly looks the other way, and lets England go it alone. That's fine with us. There's more, but I see your new Chief Mate coming up and I want to introduce you."

A lanky, virtually emancipated man climbed the stairs and stood unsmiling in front of Captain Graves. With little formality, MacPherson introduced the two, "Captain Graves; this is former US Navy Lieutenant, Toby Coffin."

The men only nodded as MacPherson began to laugh, "This is funny, Graves and Coffin. You two should get along great."

Quickly seeing his attempt at humor fell flat, he tried to salvage the situation until Graves cut in, "The ex-lieutenant and I are already acquainted, MacPherson. The *Cushing* wasn't it, Coffin? Port Royal, Carolina? Two sailors, one slashed with a bottle, the other knifed? You claimed self-defense, but got cashiered just the same."

Coffin's head lolled from side to side, but he was surprised, "That was way back, you've a good memory, Graves."

"It's *Captain* Graves." He turned to MacPherson, "Is this the best you've got?"

"He's the *only* person I've got with the experience you need."

Captain Graves' was displeased, "Then I guess I'm stuck with you, Coffin. Go about your duties and unless I call you I don't want to see your face again until we up anchor."

Coffin shrugged, mumbled a 'Yes…Sir' and shuffled off.

Graves turned to his host, "For Christ's sake, Ian, why did you wait until it was too late for me to dump that scoundrel?"

"How was I supposed to know he was cashiered? I didn't know him, a friend sent him over, said he knew his stuff. Anyway, what did you expect? An honest, unsullied Chief Mate? This is a bloody grim business and you need grim people who can handle themselves. You don't have to like them, just use them. Let's change the subject—where's Jason? I haven't seen him lately."

"I got to thinking about what you said, he could be a problem. I told him he could be more help at home than down here. Gave him a few dollars and sent him off on that inter-island ferry for Havana. He can find his own way home from there and tie up with his brother."

"What'd he think of that? Was he on to us?"

"What do you care what he thought? And no, I don't believe he knew anything."

"You should have sent him off before—with your old crew. Before all this started. Too soft."

Graves turned from the chart table, "I told you once, that's my business—not yours, damn it! Right now my business with you is about money and when do I get it?"

Ian smiled, "Come with me."

Down in the cellar, a cabinet easily swung aside and a safe, imbedded in concrete exposed. Hiding the dial, Ian spun it back and forth, turned the handle, and stepped back.

Captain Graves was shocked. Gold, Silver, English pounds and American paper money half-filled the space, "Your money's in there, Graves. So, as soon as I see the *Pike* on the horizon, I'll get it out. The rest is mine and in another year, I'll have enough to return to Scotland and live the life of the Laird in his castle, including the women."

"That's fine, MacPherson, but right now, how about sending another thousand to *Seaward* out of my share?"

"I've faith in ye, Captain, it'll be done with pleasure. Remember likewise, the *Laird* has some of my money to help buy the slaves."

4

"AWAY THE BOW LINES! Away stern lines!"

The rising sweep of the *Laurence Pike's* bow was pulled away from the dock by rowers in a dory. The clipper caught the offshore breeze, its sails luffing as they began to fill.

Gaining headway, the slumbering ship woke and the wisdom in the loveliness of her lines became evident. Main and foresails filled and ever so leisurely, the bow rose to cleave the sea. The clipper's body glided through the waters…again an ocean spirit. Vibrant, made for this, she was where she belonged. The wind gave her strength to rise through the churning waves and her rigging began to sing its ageless song.

Although alive, the enchanting clipper could not know…this time her rigging's song would be the weep of slavery.

«»

The crew was as competent as MacPherson stated. Even ex-Lieutenant Toby Coffin went about his duties efficiently.

With a following breeze, the clipper held an average speed of fourteen knots. Captain Graves' knew she was weatherly and he could get more out of her by carrying a heavier press of sail if he wished, but saw no need. In the evening, he thought of Seaward and the gamble he was taking to save it. Those thoughts then turned black, now that he had time to think.

The damn British. After the Slave Trade Act in 1807, they chased down slave ships by the dozen. At first, in the 1810s and into the '20s, the Royal Navy ships were slower than American sloops. But then the Royal Navy's *Sybille* caught the *Henriquetta*, a brig-slaver on her seventh trip. The Navy renamed her *Black Joke* and with the *Water Witch,* a former opium clipper, one slaver after another was caught—their captains hung. Then the *Black Joke* entrapped the Baltimore-built topsail clipper *Dos Amigos*, the British copied her lines and the race for speed, excellent weather boats and a Captain's cunning began. Graves' ship was fast, he crafty. He would need both.

«»

The British agent in Bilbao, Spain, was courteous in his request to inspect the *Pike*. Captain Graves knew the agent had no claims to board, yet he saw no reason to refuse, as at present, she was not a slaver, nor set up to be one. He understood the difficulty the Brit's had, Graves said to the agent and allowed him to look for false decking, check below and lockers for hidden chains, manacles, or excessive weaponry. Mainly, he used his sense of smell in the bilge and scuppers.

Finding no indication or stench of slavery and knowing the *Pike's* cargo, primarily rum, textiles, and being told she was taking on timber planking for Cape Town, South Africa, the agent found nothing suspicious. Due to this, he did not send any specific information down the coast other than a clipper ship, somewhat rare in those parts, named the *Laurence Pike* would be heading south along the Guinea coast. Next port Las Palmas, in the Canary Islands, then non-stop to Cape Town—or so the agent believed and passed on.

Actually, once underway the *Pike*, after clearing Cape Finisterre, Spain, altered course to Cape Verde.

Heaving to, the *Pike* dropped anchor off the beach at Tarrafal. Graves was curious when viewing charred skeletons of half a dozen ships and also noticed MacPherson's schooner the *Laird of Glasgow* was not there, a fact that was not bothersome. A longboat soon left from shore bringing a scruffy, little arrogant man, "You Graves?"

"I'm *Captain* Graves. What do you want here?"

"I'm here to fix up this here boat so she can stuff slaves to the gunnels. Call me Ishmael."

Captain Graves' grunted, "I see. Done some reading lately, have you, Ishmael?"

"Aye. And I'm from Melville's New Bedford and I was a once schoolmaster too."

"I wouldn't have thought you were well read by the look of you, Ishmael."

Without waiting for the man to respond, Graves turned, "Monar, come here. I want you to supervise this former schoolteacher—calls himself Ishmael. He's to reconfigure us."

"Yes, Captain, I'll watch him closely."

The scruffy, arrogant little man was quick to object, "I knows my job and I takes no orders from a nigger man—ever!"

"Ishmael, or whatever your real name is, if you were a teacher, it sure wasn't English. So I'm telling you, take orders from Monar or I'll order him to toss you over the side."

The man held his ground until Graves' gave Monar the order.

"All right, all right damn it," Ishmael started down the hatch, "I will—but I don't like it."

Indifferent to the comment, Graves turned to a stoic Monar, "You knew he had a knife?"

"Yes, in his belt at his back. No matter, he wouldn't have had the chance to use it."

After Ishmael brought aboard chain, shackles and weaponry, his carpenters and helpers were still at work a week later when the *Laird of Glasgow* hove to and rafted alongside the *Pike*. When the schooner's captain swung aboard, it came to Graves that he had never met him.

Monar, after the *Laird's* Captain greeted him warmly, did the honors, "Captain Graves, I have the dubious pleasure of introducing Captain Elmer 'Ghost' Gostman, formerly Master of Her Majesty's Royal Navy Frigate, *Holy Roller*."

Gostman let out a roar, “Why you big black bastard! I’ll have you keelhauled—defaming me like that.”

The *Glasgow’s* Captain slapped Monar on the shoulder, turning to reach for Graves’ hand, “Nice to meet you, Captain, sorry for the outburst. I once told Monar here about my time as a midshipman aboard the HMS *Hermés*. She would roll like a drunken Limey in the slightest breeze and I’d get sick as a dog until she hauled off from windward.”

“Good to meet you, Captain, I’ve been through that a few times in my years.”

Graves’ quickly sized up Gostman as an easygoing individual and liked his openness with Monar, a man who Graves had begun to appreciate more each passing day.

“Well, Captain Gostman—and please, call me Richard—shall we retire to my cabin to toast your success on surviving the deep and dark jungle?”

“With cheer, Richard, and call me Ghost, it sounds a bit more menacing than Elmer. Monar, you might as well as come with us, you’ll have to know the lay of the land better than us.”

They settled in the Captain’s quarters, Graves opening a bottle of rum. Gostman offered a mug to Monar who looked to Graves. With his Captain’s nod, he accepted, knowing whether black or white, a sailor needed his own Captain’s permission.

After a few sea yarns, Ghost was becoming expansive and started laying out his lengthy plan, ‘Firstly, Richard, as Monar mentioned, I’m formerly Royal Navy. After a series of escapades, including clashes with some quite unsavory Barbary pirates, I was skilled enough—actually, a combination of luck and family connections—to manage to become Captain of Her Majesty’s frigate *Prince*. This was roughly six years past and, I must admit, I was quite the cock-of-the- walk until the *Prince* and I were posted to Africa—Sierra Leone, in fact. That was when the ‘33 Anti-Slavery Act campaign got serious and we were up against most every damn flag in the Atlantic that travelled down the hump of Africa. We, the *Prince*, *Albatross* and *Rattler* and other ships—but especially the HMS *Rattler*—she's a screw propeller with sail, performed quite well along the Windy Coast. We ridded the seas of slavers, or at least most of them. In point of fact, my squadron was responsible for clearing a nest of them out of these very bloody islands. Cape Verde and her outer keys was a main slave terminus. We swept in here with five ships, wiped them out with a bit of gunpowder, let the American and French captains go, without their ships of course, and hung the rest."

Ghost stopped talking for a moment, visualizing. "You know, when you first see a couple of slavers hung, it bothers you some. Yet, when you hang a dozen, you start to become numb to it—until you lie in your bunk and the bile comes up. It's different when you're in battle, at least they've a chance, or it's quick. But when they're trussed up like a Christmas goose, and you see the fear, the pleading in their eyes it twists your guts and…"

He shook away the sight, "Anyway, we left them dangling, took the best ships, torched the rest—you can see their bulkheads bleaching out there—and these islands are now so clean the Royal Navy doesn't even stop here. I will readily admit we caught most slavers due to their captain's ignorance. They simply didn't have fast ships and they didn't plan ahead. However, to the subject, when I first saw the *Laurence Pike* in Barbados, I said to myself with a sheer like hers, she has to be a Boston McKay or New York Poole, and fast. That meant, handled well, the first part of our problem was solved."

While Gostman poured another round of shots, Graves asked, "So tell me, Ghost, what caused the evolution from catching slavers to wanting to become one?"

Monar interposed, "Wanting to be one? Ghost already is one. Had success until…"

"Until?" Gostman spoke up, "Aye, the bloody—*until*! Moved over two thousand slaves from Senegal to Dominica. Five trips, right up *until* the bleeding Danes caught me in my old two-stick schooner along the Ivory Coast. Took my ship, slaves, money, and threw me into a filthy gaol, a cage at Fort Christiansborg."

Graves asked, “Denmark was on the Ivory Coast? Are they still there?”

“Aye, Portuguese too, but barely. Rumor has it we British are bartering with the Danes for all five of their forts along the Ivory Coast. Who the *hell* knows what will happen then.”

Gostman was getting angry. Whether from memories or drink, Graves couldn’t tell.

“So, Ghost, you still haven’t said how you went from being RN to hauling slaves.”

“I mostly told you. When I started talking to the captains we captured. As I said, they didn’t plan ahead and didn’t have fast enough ships. The tipping point to convince me was when they disclosed how much they made each trip and how little the punishment if they were caught—at least at first. Moreover, I was in my cups a lot in those RN days. What else to do at sea along that stinking coast for months at a time? It sounded like a way to get out of the life I was leading.”

“So you retired from the RN and went slaving, made money, and lost it to the Dane’s. How’d you get out of prison?”

“My parent’s paid a ransom. Said that was the last bloody cent I’d get from them and so far, they’ve damn well kept their word. But at least it wasn’t indicated on my record at the RN.”

The comment about his parents excising him didn’t seem to bother Gostman. He shrugged it off and looked to Graves with a question. “Anything else you’d like to know, Richard?”

“One other. How did you tie up with Ian MacPherson? He seems a good fellow.”

Ghost was guarded, “Good fellow? I suggest you not judge a book by its cover.”

Graves’ thought the remark puzzling, glancing to Monar, who nodded in agreement.

At first, clarity to the comment didn’t come. The bottle of rum remained half-empty, corked and put away. It was time for Ghost to lay out his plan to seize the slaves and elude the British.

"A lot of this I knew from my past with the RN and for your benefit, I'll recite from memory right up to the present."

Captain Gostman then began a concise background to the problems the *Laurence Pike* and its crew were to face.

"When I headed from here to the coast, I met up with a warship, the RN brig *Warspite* out of Dakar. They rafted with us, sent a boarding party and checked us out. All I had on board was trinkets and some textiles to barter for food—Ian's money well hidden. It looked as if I was some useless wanderer simply drifting around the coast, nothing special, going nowhere yet with enough money for a tired schooner and short crew. In other words, looking just how I wanted. They fell in with it and when they learned I was former Royal Navy, we sat around drinking. You know, reliving the old days. It was an eye-opener. The Brit's are staying deadly serious regarding slavery. From what I'm told, they've over ten percent of their navy along this coast and considering they've the largest navy in the world, that's a lot of ships. And if you add Denmark and a few American, French and Portagee ships, that's a bloody lot of firepower."

Captain Graves was thoughtful, "Did MacPherson know all this?"

"Of course, or at the very least guessed it."

"Then what's this ninety-nine percent chance of success story he gave me?"

Ghost gave a rueful laugh, "You're looking at it, Richard."

"Excuse my ignorance, looking at what?"

"Ian spun that story out of whole cloth. I'm the reason he told you that—my background and knowledge of the area and slaves. I'm the only chance you've got. See what I mean by not judging a book by its cover?"

"Damn it! He spun a good story."

Ghost nodded, "Perhaps. But from what Ian told me, you must admit you were grasping at straws and open to any proposal that might save you."

A droll laugh from Graves, "He was right, I guess I was. Now what do we do?"

"You want to back out?"

"You think there's a chance we can pull it off?"

"Captain Graves, if I didn't think there was a chance, on my way back from the coast I'd have sailed right on by without so much as a wave. However, I would say the chances are only fifty-fifty. Yet if we go, let me warn you, I won't be caught alive only to be hung dead."

Silence descended between two captains who'd seen sea battles, been wounded, escaped alive and wondered if they had used up too many chances. Still, something else was surfacing. They were two aging sea dogs, sizing each other up, both confident in themselves and their abilities. What did they intend to prove, that they had the nerve to challenge the odds? There was that *unknown*, a journey into the evil of Africa—that foreign land with all its mystery.

Graves turned to the third person, "Call it, Monar. Your life is on the line too."

"I have faith in you both; Ghost from the past, you, Captain, from the present. I'm interested to see what your gods have decided for each of you—and for me."

The three, Yankee Sea captain, former Royal Navy sea captain and a black slave shook hands. The die now cast, except for one crucial subject.

Monar held up his hand for quiet, then went to the door. Opening it and satisfied no one was about; he closed it and moved near the two men.

"Now, Captains, seeing we're partners and the subject of Mr. MacPherson's reliability has been openly questioned, there is one thing more you should know."

By Monar's actions and his low voice even lower, the captain's quickly knew there was conspiracy afoot. They did not have long to wonder about it.

"If the voyage is successful," Monar began, "on the passage home, Toby Coffin has orders to kill you, Captain Graves and I think you too, Ghost."

SEAWARD **3 January 1847**

The bitter cold of a New England winter had settled in. Ice gripped the pylons along the docks, threatening to pull them from their hold in the ground. Hoarfrost spread its gnarled fingers across windowpanes and swirls of snow slipped through windowsills. Seamen shook the ship lines to clear them of rime and walked along beside their boats, hacking at the ice that pressured the hulls. Coastal New England hunkered down, a glacial tableau, frozen in time once again.

Nevertheless, this didn't matter to John Thomas and his brother Jason, for they were not there. When the bitter Canadian winds began to grip the coast, John Thomas decided to load their remaining goods of textiles and flee to the south before the hard freeze and there in hope of finding cargo for their schooner.

After carrying minor haulage along the coast, they at last found regular occupation carrying Cypress plank from sawmills by the Savannah River, in Georgia, down to Brunswick, mostly by cruising sections of the inland waterway.

On their sixth roundtrip to Savannah, while tying up at noon one Saturday, the sawmill owner approached, asking if they would like to join him for dinner. It was a welcome respite. The brothers were tired and ready to relax. Freshened up, looking smart in white shirts and pants with blue sailor's quarter jackets, with worn, yet dashing captain's caps, they cut quite the figures as they sat in the owner's carriage.

Gordon Carlton, their host, seemed the laidback, wealthy southerner as he ordered the Negro carriage men to their duties and then chatting with the brothers about the weather, his horses,

Graves' schooner and how hard the brothers worked and clearly got along.

"So, you two, what do you think of this area."

JT did most of the talking, "Well, Sir, we've not seen much of it really, Jason and I see mostly water, but that enormous fort on Cockspur Island as we come up the channel is something."

"Yes, isn't it. That's Fort Pulaski, nearly finished I hear. My wife's cousin, Bobby Lee, supervised most of the layout, dikes and foundation. She's quite proud of him. Second at West Point, you know, right now he's down in Mexico fighting bandits, already made Major."

The brother's nodded, as expected, although they found the information not particularly interesting.

The tang of the sea was still with them as the carriage turned off the dirt path and through a wrought iron gate held aside by two bowing Negros. The Graves' brothers entered into a world they had only heard about. Fields of cotton, not yet budding, lay before them. Negro's pruning, digging and turning the earth between the rows, a warm January sun burnishing their skin. The carriage traveled on, revealing acre after acre of cotton fields and scores of Negros, men and women, tending them.

The plantation home rose to their view under the arch of old oaks. In front of the house, two dozen carriages were parked in the roundabout, each tended by a black coachman. John Thomas and Jason glanced at each other, whispering this was not what they were used to in Salem and decided to be on their best behavior, at least for a while.

A vision in a hoop skirt glided down the stairway. The brothers' wilted as the vision reached up to kiss their host.

"Father! What have you brought home this time? Goodness me, aren't they beautiful!"

Gordon Carlton gave a weary smile, turning to the brothers, "I'm sorry, I should have warned you about my featherheaded daughter. However, it's too late, so now I'll introduce you. Jason and John Graves, this is my oldest daughter, Miss Charlene Lee Carlton. We call her Charlee…"

Charlee scolded her father, "How could you call me 'oldest', father? Why I'm only eighteen! What a thing to say!" Her eyes flashed, yet they could see she wasn't the least bit angry.

To continue with the interrupted introduction, Carlton said, 'These are the gentlemen I spoke to you about, Charlee, the ones with their own schooner hauling timber for me."

"Oh, father? Yankees? I can't believe they grow Yankees to be so handsome. Well, despite that, never mind. Come; let me introduce you to some fine southern ladies."

Carlton's protestations fell on deaf ears as Charlee took the arms of the Graves brothers and scampered them around the side of the mansion.

It was a family and friends get together. The brothers soon became the center of attention and politics about the North and the South took sway. Starting with President Polk, the men present carped over Polk playing both sides of the fence by acquiring the Oregon Territories, but allowing no slaves, while the annexation of Texas allowed slaves. President Polk was a North Carolina slaveholder himself they stated and not looking out for the land barons, the authoritative, who, with care, controlled the regions through 'Slaveocracy'.

The consensus being that Polk is sick and if he should turn over the reins to VP Dallas, then the barons could set everything to rights. The men then started once more on the brothers over the northern anti-slavery 'gangs' of Greeley, Palfrey and Quincy, until John Thomas and Jason were saved by Charlee and two lady friends.

"You men get away, you hear? We have two guests here who are not interested in your nattering on about nothing that's ever going to change."

Charlee took the brothers away but she soon left Jason with the other girls and took John into the drawing room. Alone together, a sea change came over her.

"Mr. John Graves, I hope you will excuse my featherheaded actions. I act that way as father's amused by it. Also, I can flit away from people I don't care to be with. However, I don't wish *you* to think me that way."

John Thomas now loved everything about her and although not a stranger with women, felt himself stumbling. "Please, Miss Carlton, don't apologize for anything…and, and, please call me JT, all my friends do."

"Oh? We're friends already? Fine, JT, then call me Charlee. Now, what shall we talk about? Slavery? No. President Polk and the Oregon Territory? I don't believe so. Let's talk about you and why I find you interesting without knowing a thing about you. Am I shameless saying that? Father would think so and mother would faint, so let's keep that our little secret, shall we?"

JT started to laugh; it was all he could think to do. He stopped, looked at her seriously, and spoke haltingly, "Charlee, you overwhelm me. Please, slow down or I shall want to run off and marry you not even knowing if you have already married three times, have seven children and a jilted beau coming through the doorway with a shotgun."

She laughed with him, "Would you still want to run off?"

"I'm not that glib with words, Charlee, yet I think I would still want to—yes, I think I would."

"Think is good enough. Now that we know where we stand, JT, let's talk about each other."

They were left alone for half an hour and the couple's conversation ranged from the desperate plight of *Seaward* for the Graves' family, to Charlee being tomboyish, loving horses and having difficulty with being the lady her mother wanted to help entertain her father's powerful southern friends.

JT had to know, "Why would your father ask two poor northerners here and, actually more important, why did you lay a course for me?"

"Lay a course? What an odd expression, must be some seaman lingo. It *is* a bit strange, about my father that is and why he asked you here. He said he met two intelligent young men, that they knew what they were about with a boat and weren't afraid to offer an opinion when they thought he was wrong on loading planks. He said you and Jason had good ideas that helped carry more cargo. Father appreciated that. And, you were independent when he offered to hire you as employees rather than as outworkers."

"That's because when our father returns, we'll set our minds to rebuilding our fleet and business."

"You mean back in New England?"

"Yes, Salem, that's on the north shore of Boston."

"Will you sail this far south?"

"I'll sail from Boston to the Caribe, to Europe if needed, but if you're asking will I drop my hook in Savanna, I'd imagine I'd have cargo for here quite often."

Charlee smiled, "I want you to know that my father also said he wanted me to meet real independent men. You and Jason. Yet, I think he somehow favored Jason."

"So why did you favor me? Jason is far better looking and more knowledgeable than I am. Or did you turn to me simply to differ with your father?"

"Well, Jason *is* better looking, although I don't know about his knowledge. Yet, I think father saw something in you, he wouldn't put his finger on it. He actually said intensity lingered behind your eyes, even when you smile. We're of Arcadian decent you know, Arcadians, from Canada's Maritimes. When the British kicked our ancestors out of Canada, they stopped here while the others went on to Louisiana. Down there they're known as Cajuns. Yet whether there or here, at times we see things that are not there, only sensed. I don't believe there's anything hidden behind your eyes, John Thomas, no matter what father says, nor was I drawn to you because my father wanted my thoughts on Jason."

Charlee took JT's hand. Her eyes seemed to glow, "Don't tell father I told you, but he intends to offer the two of you important positions with Carlton Import, Export. It would mean eventual control of all his shipping businesses if you both are as good as he thinks—and father is a good judge of people. This is really why you are here, for evaluation."

She was frank, honest. JT appreciated that in her, "Thank you for being straightforward, Charlee, and we like your father, but as I say, when our father returns, we'll head north. He heads our family and family means everything to him—to us."

"Does that mean no one else is allowed in?"

"Of course not. I simply mean we must get our house, Seaward, in order first. The Graves' empire, my father's domain is on the brink. Jason and I work to help keep the wolf from the door and food on the table until he returns."

"My father could help to pay…" Charlee stopped. She knew it was not the comment to make.

"Thank you for what you were going to say, Charlee, but that's not something we would consider."

I know, JT, I spoke without thinking. Mother says I do that far too often. So, where does that leave us?"

She was forthright and he smiled, "Well, with your consent, I will ask your father and mother for permission to see you."

It was Charlee's turn to smile, "You mean you intend to *court* me?"

"No. I mean that I would like to see you. When, and *if*, I decide to *court* you, I will ask them."

"Oh, my dear John Thomas, I do believe I'll have some say about that."

They considered each other; an unspoken acceptance formed.

Mrs. Gordon Carlton, Charlee's mother, entered quietly, took one look at this strong-featured, weathered young man and her daughter staring intently at each other and caught her breath. She was confused. This man did not fit the description her husband had made of a Jason Graves. This was more the portrayal of the brother her husband gave of John Thomas, the person with the darkness behind his eyes and, given Emily Carlton's Arcadian history, a chill crept through her.

She cleared her throat to make them aware of her presence.

"Mother!" Charlee's thoughts and eyes refocused. "I would like you to meet Mr. John Graves. Father asked him and his brother to come for dinner and I was just showing him around."

"Yes, I can see you were showing him around." She smiled, holding out her hand as JT rose.

"Captain Graves, please allow me to also welcome you to Hammersmith as much as my daughter appears to. I hope you will enjoy yourself here."

Before JT could respond, Mrs. Carlton turned to Charlee, "Dear, I know you are doing your best to entertain our guest; however, there are others…"

"Yes, mother. I'll be right along."

Emily Carlton turned to JT, "I'm sure you understand, Mr. Graves, and again, welcome."

She left the room, pointedly leaving the twin French doors open to the terrace and pool.

Charlee started to speak but they both heard her mother speak sharply to someone.

"Don't go in there, Logan! You've imbibed again!"

"This is my home! I go where I want!"

Charlee grabbed JT's hand, "God! It's my brother. He's…"

Before she could finish, Logan Carlton strutted in. "Ah ha, dear sister, Charlee. Having a quiet little tête-à-tête, are we?"

The words were surly, yet JT remembered they were guests. It was obvious to Charlee he was getting hot under the collar and she asked her brother to leave.

"Leave, Leave? Why we haven't even been introduced yet. That would be rude of me."

When Logan Carlton started toward him, JT noticed the man's walk was steady. He's faking being drunk, JT thought. Why? Be alert, careful. Charlee tried to be courteous, attempted to introduce them. Logan brushed her words off.

"Please, sister, don't bother with an introduction. Now that I see what he is, I don't associate with Yankees, much less sailors; I find they always impart a fishy odor."

Mrs. Charlton, standing at the doorway was mortified, Charlee started to protest, JT would not take more. He approached Logan Carlton, stood in front of him and planted his feet aggressively, "Better to smell of the sea than stink of liquor and act improper."

Logan was now aware a few people had gathered near with his mother at the French doors to listen transfixed. He had intentionally caused the scene to embarrass his sister, thinking it would not go this far, this quickly. Now, he had no choice. He reached to his belt.

Charlee shouted to him, "Don't!"

Nonetheless, Logan took a glove, said, "I'm a drunkard am I?" and struck JT across the face. There were gasps, as the glove was thrown to the ground. Angry, JT knew a challenge and there was no alternative other than to pick up the glove. Still, he said nothing. Thinking deliberately, he saw the silk glove was too small for his hand, yet he forced his fingers into it and over his knuckles. He held his open hand inches from Logan's face and made a fist. The glove split its seams.

Although Logan's eyes widened, they never saw JT's fist dart forward, impact his chin and send him stumbling backward.

The punch was not meant to knock Logan down, merely to stun and though he did not fall, in trying to regain his balance, Logan kept quick stepping backward. Step followed step until the sight became comical. Backward, he exited the room, past his mother and friends, still wrestling to regain his balance until, ten feet across the terrace—he tripped on the lip of the pool and pitched into the lily pads.

The decorum of the get-together disintegrated. Laughter, not meant as ridicule, simply at a humorous incident, flowed through the group. Gordon Carlton, his wife and family saw it differently. This story, gilded, would sweep the region, mocking the family. They all knew JT had not initiated the situation—he had been goaded. Nevertheless, the family's reputation was at stake and now the challenge their son had stupidly created had to be honored—or evaded.

Although the situation seemed nearly over, there was still confusion. In the end, Mrs. Carlton, chagrined, excused herself departing to her sitting room, Mr. Carlton ignored everyone and a sodden Logan took to horse. Worst of all, Charlee, her family's dignity in tatters, directed that JT and Jason leave.

Downhearted, the brothers walked around to the front of the mansion and asked one of Carlton's Negro drivers to take them to the waterfront. Meanwhile, Charlee, at the last minute, ran through the house, dashed down the stairs, ran to JT, kissed his cheek, whispered she would be at the marketplace by the docks at ten the next morning and dashed off calling over her shoulder, "Yellow parasol."

5

Tarrafal, Cape Verde, 7 February 1847

CAPTAIN RICHARD GRAVES was dumbfounded, "Kill me? Toby Coffin is to kill me? What are you saying, man?"

Captain 'Ghost' Ghosman was equally confused, "Yes, Monar, what in hell is this all about?"

Monar held up his hands, assuming a virtually spiritual pose, "Please my friends," he uttered softly, "the walls have ears, we must be quiet, then I shall tell you."

They hunched closer, the tension peaking. Monar whispered his tale, "Forgive me if I speak strangely, but there are events that you, as white men, do not know of and if you did, you wouldn't accept."

Monar's conspiratorial tone held them and he was correct—they did not understand his next comments.

"In the night, I am what white people call, a spirit, something there, yet not. The darkies say I am Vodou, magic—that I can withdraw into darkness and vanish."

Smiling, Monar broke the spell, "Of course this is not true. Still, even though I am black and can blend with the night, I am able to drift within the shadows of campfires and not be seen. And now, if you will believe this, I will tell you all I know."

The Captain's nodded. Monar held them. He had taken on an aura; his voice conspiratorial. They would not think to question whatever he told them.

"I sleep the way of the leopard, silently, yet aware of movement others are not, night sounds others do not hear. I wander after dark, feeling the night, the stillness encloses me. At the moment I speak of, a shadow moved within a shadow. It moved again and I began to hunt. I could feel the soundless step; see its shape at the rear of Ian MacPherson's house. I shifted quick enough to see a door open;

hear a hinge squeal. I took up my machete and slipped closer. Possibly MacPherson could be in trouble I thought, yet as I came near, a match and then a lantern flared and dimmed. The night was stifling; a window opened. MacPherson came to it and looked out, straight at me, yet though I was not five feet away, he could not see me."

Ghosman and Graves couldn't wait and interrupted, "Who was it, who went in?"

"I told you, Toby Coffin was to kill you, Captain, who else would you think it could be?"

Graves felt foolish, "Well you could have brought him up sooner, Monar."

"And lose the effect, the impact of the seriousness of the situation?"

"Mayhap you're right. Still, tell us—could you hear them? What was their plan?"

"Certainly I heard them, that is how I know their plot. If everything goes as hoped in Africa and Ghost here goes ahead to birddog us against Yankee and British ships near Barbados, Coffin will knife you and take over command."

"That's it? Simple as that?"

"Why make it complicated, Captain?"

Graves' scratched his beard, "I'm not so naïve not to see what MacPherson makes out of this, no risk and he doesn't have to split the profits."

Ghosman was quick to add that MacPherson would also get the *Pike*.

"Not if my son John Thomas found out the truth, Ghost. Although let's continue on regarding Coffin. Monar, do you really think he'd try it alone? He knows you or others might defy a mutineer. He'd be taking a chance."

Monar listened for sounds. Satisfied there was nothing but the ship's creaking, he responded, "He won't be alone. At night I have seen him with others, sly, whispering, planning. They do not see me."

Captain Ghosman had a ready question, 'Should we toss Coffin and the others overboard once we're underway?"

"Not right now," Ghost," Monar cautioned, "I feel Captain Graves is safe until we get near Barbados. Also, if we rid ourselves of them it would make us undermanned. Ian is always cheap with providing crew and a slaver always needs armed men when there are slaves aboard. We have only thirty-four, so no, it is best to keep our assassins until we don't need them."

Captain Graves was quiet. They could see him in thought and waited.

"All right, Gentlemen, add your opinions as I go through this. Our main goals are to get in, secure the slaves and supplies and then gain the open sea. Monar, I don't believe we, or rather I, am safe until we near Barbados. Coffin was navy and can navigate, so from the time we clear Africa, I'm in danger. Ghost will be in the schooner and of no value to help. I think that once we take slaves aboard it would be reasonable for me to carry a pistol for safety. That would make Coffin simply think I'm nervous, not raise any suspicions."

"What do you have for protection, Captain?"

"I've one of the five-shot Colt revolvers made in Patterson, New Jersey. It's called a Colt Patterson. Here, I'll show it to you."

From a velvet lined case, Captain Graves' lifted a long barreled, black revolver, "This is the newest model, number 5, rifled barrel, .38 caliber ball, not the old .28 and much more accurate."

Admiring the weapon, Monar, knowing little of guns, was confused, "Where is the trigger?

Graves partially cocked the revolver, "There, see? The trigger drops down as I thumb the hammer."

Monar was impressed while Ghost noticed the case for the Colts had depressions for two weapons, "Where's the other Colt, Richard?"

"When my son Jason and I left Salem, I entrusted it to my younger son, John Thomas. He'll be using our schooner *Ocean Pearl*. Right now, I'm glad I didn't give this one to Jason."

They saw the sense of the remark and Ghost added his own, "So, we go along with things as they are until the time comes to shoot Coffin and whoever else—correct?"

In accord, Ghost laid out his plans of leading off with the schooner to confirm the way in. He set down a scribbled note pad, "The schedule of the British ships is here. This indicates our goal will be unprotected by the Brits for two days before they overlap, starting nine days from now. We must hit that date. From that time, you'll have two days to get the *Pike* upriver and unseen from offshore. If we don't, the RN steamers *Argus*, she's a side-wheeler, heading south, and *Diligent*, with a screw propeller, coming up from the south, overlap off the Ivory Coast and you'll be in the middle. The *Diligent* is the one to worry about, Richard, with a head of steam she can pull over fourteen knots. Not as fast as the *Pike,* I know. However, she can get up to speed faster—providing her boilers are on line—and from what I know of her captain, they usually are."

Captain Graves was intent, "I recognize the problems. Just tell me when and where."

"Off Cape Palmas the sixteenth, as close to dawn as possible-you know it?"

"Cape Palmas? Yes, I'll recognize it."

"Good. From there, I'll take the lead. The river is about one hundred-fifty kilometers. As you know, the African coast runs close to west, east there, so stand off as far as you can see me with your glass. If the *Laird* comes about, or you see smudges of smoke, it will mean a British warship is there. I don't have to tell you to turn tail and run. If you're not followed, go back to Tarrafal. But even if you are caught, you've no slaves aboard."

Graves gave a wry smile, "Goes without saying, yet let's forget the 'buts'. Tell me, what river?"

"The Bandama Blanc. You'll see the village of Grand-Lahou first, then the mouth of the Tagba Lagoon off to port. The French have fortified outposts at Assini, to the west, and Grand Bassam, well off east, so you should have no difficulty slipping into the lagoon.

An old tugboat will meet you as you enter and take you in tow. After the estuary, the width soon narrows, so you must reef all sails and take up the lower spars. The tugboat will tow you about two kilometers upriver to a small lagoon off to starboard. It's a snug fit. The *Pike* has to be brought about, ramps mounted for the cargo and…"

"Damn, Ghost! A hell of a lot of things have to go right."

"That's right, and a hell of a lot more than I've said. But I've done it and it works."

"How long will we be there?"

"My schedule shows two weeks, Richard, and believe me, you'll need it to get the cargo aboard, bedded down, food and water stowed."

Studying Captain Graves, Ghost realized the Captain was only comfortable on the high seas. To be closed up in a steaming jungle was not to anyone's liking, although he hoped the time would pass quickly as there was much work— nauseating, horrid work—to be done. Time would pass slowly.

"Richard," Ghost wanted to be clear, "I won't be here much longer. I want to get well ahead of you to confirm the plan, pay out bribes and see the King for the slaves. We'll speak only briefly when you head in to the coast so anything that's not perfectly understood, let me know before I leave. Still, there's one thing I've put off until now. Your top-men must step the masts of your Main skysail and royal, Fore royal and topgallant and Mizzen royal. Of course, that takes down the spars and yards with them, but that's a necessity. And, you've got to bring the braces in tight."

"Ghost! You're serious? Do you know how much that will reduce my speed?"

"Yes, I do, but we need to do that. It lowers the profile of the masts to below the tree line so you won't be seen from seaward. The Brit's scan the coast; masts sticking over the rain forest are a beacon. Besides, you've short sail only for the way in. On the night before you leave, you'll reset the masts and sails."

"You'll sure keep us working, Ghost. That's one hell of a job re-stepping and rigging them."

"I'm quite aware of that, Richard, but you've got to be hidden from Brit spyglasses. I'll do my best to stay around the lagoon with the *Laird*, but remember, once there, you've two weeks. On the evening of the thirteenth day, leaving it as late as possible, have your boys reset everything I've mentioned. They *must* be ready and the towboat needs to have the *Pike* at the mouth of the lagoon with damn near every bloody sail unfurled. At this time of year, the offshore winds start at 0900. You've got to be there to catch them. As you clear the lagoon, be sure and throw out your stud'sails."

"You think you can warn us and give us a running start if we need it, Ghost?"

"I promise you, Richard, anything I can do, I will do."

Graves couldn't help a brief peek at Ghost, "Well, it seems you've covered most everything. Now let me add the icing to the cake."

Monar and Ghost couldn't imagine what Graves could possibly add. He pointed to the deck of his cabin, "Notice anything odd, former RN Captain Gostman?"

"No, other than the deck is scraped and scored from something heavy and strange holes."

"Very good, Ghost. Now I'll turn your eyes to the stern of my cabin—now what do you see?"

Ghost looked—and gradually understood, "There's a large hatch…block and tackle, cleats. That explains the scored deck. You've a Demi-cannon around here somewhere?"

Graves was grinning, "Excellent, Ghost. You're old RN training's come to the fore. Only it isn't a Demi, too heavy and takes too much crew. In the hold, I've what the US calls, a Long-nine, meaning long barrel, 9 pound shot. Not too formidable but quick, has some power and fairly accurate. I've used it twice to fend off privateers."

"And you mount it at the stern, why?"

"Simple. The *Pike* will out-sail anything, but there's times a stinger in the tail makes sure."

Ghost couldn't help find Graves admirable, "By the God above, Richard, the way you bloody Yankee's think, it's no wonder we lost the '12 war!"

"If you remember, you lost the one before that too." Graves couldn't help the gibe.

There was tongue-in-cheek laughter all round. Then Graves' turned to Monar, "I noticed you didn't seem surprised—about the cannon, I mean. You knew?"

"I told you, Captain, I roam at night."

"I see, but how in the devil you can see in the hold at night is beyond me. So I'm to assume you found the powder packs and shot as well?"

"Yes, Sir, all the gear is safe and dry."

Graves laughed, "Very well then, Monar. As you know everything, have that Pale Usher, Ishmael, rig a hoist and get the armament up here and mounted. Wait, on second thought, just have Ishmael bring it up—I'll have Toby Coffin rig it. He'll know how."

Graves' turned to Ghost, "He was US Navy, gunnery. It could turn out to be a good thing we didn't toss him overboard."

"It *could* turn out that way, Richard, but will it?"

"Well, it's my responsibility. Now, what have we left out?"

Ghost looked to his black friend, "Can you think of anything, Monar?"

Monar took the hint, "Nothing other than the box, Ghost."

Captain Graves had given thought that there must be a payoff, he waited.

Ghost looked to Monar, who listened to the ship. He nodded and Ghost lowered his voice, "Monar hid the main payment for the slaves in the bilge water in your ship. It's in gold coin, sealed in four packets. This is when you'll completely rely on Monar. He has a rough knowledge of the Kokonga language, although with a Zombo accent, yet they'll work it out. Monar will confirm the cargo is healthy and the agreed amount of men, women, children, and that the food is not rotten or the water fouled. In other words, that everything is bloody acceptable. When the slaves are shackled and you're ready to leave, the King will grace you with his presence. You won't mistake him. He's the most obese man you'll ever meet and still be able to walk—although he is carried practically everywhere. His name is Nganga and he's king, sorcerer, magician—you name it. If you think Monar has some strange powers, Nganga is the high priest of the occult. He's Juula born, hates the French because they killed nearly all the elephants for their ivory and now the Frogs are trying to subjugate his people. Nganga raids Sénoufo kralls to capture slaves to sell to people like us. Slavers are fewer now so he'll enjoy the gold and rum we bring. Nganga can't climb the ramp to the ship so you'll have no choice but to bring the gold down to him. It has to be you, the most important white man. Otherwise, Nganga will lose face. You lower your head to him and he'll make a big show opening the packets. If he's satisfied, he will make a bigger show of giving you back one token coin, which you will gratefully accept. Keep on his good side by saying we'll be back for more slaves—work it out with Monar. And for God's sake, stay alert. Keep in mind he's a headhunter. If he thinks we won't be back his attitude may change…"

Graves was terse, "Meaning?"

"Meaning, you may want a show of force on deck, bristling with weapons."

"Why do I feel your confidence in my success appears to be fading, Ghost?"

"Not that at all. Still, I always say being cautious is better than being beheaded."

Letting out a growl, Graves slapped Ghost on the back, "Then let us have a swig and toast to my keeping mine. Then again, the good part is, at least I won't need to be cautious about Toby Coffin for a while."

Monar and Graves walked Captain Ghosman to the *Laird of Glasgow*. Salutes and handshakes followed before Ghost jumped down to the gunwale of his ship shouting orders. The anchor chain clattered aboard and the *Laird* drifted away from the *Pike*. Gaskets securing the sails to the yards were removed while the clew and buntlines were hauled, unfurling each sail. The schooner tacked, dipped the Union Jack, the flag Ghost sailed under, and, close-hauled, gradually found the channel.

Captain Graves returned to his cabin. He needed time to think and there was so much to think over. The next journey now decided, no turning back, no sense to worry it to death. It was Captain Ghosman and Monar that entered his thoughts. They weren't simply partners in crime—for crime it certainly was—they had become friends. Friends in a cruel undertaking. In different circumstances, it would have been enjoyable to have them as partners, cronies, mates, to sit and talk with, laugh. Yet, that was impossible. He could never forget what they were about or what they would do. At least, Graves' thought, he wouldn't ever forget what he was about to undertake and he could never be friends with them afterward. They would go their separate ways. He, in shame. He had sacrificed honor to save *Seaward*—but at least it would be saved.

Graves' thoughts turned to his home. If he couldn't face Ghost or Monar, how on earth could he face his family? His wife, Mary or their sons? God, his mind screamed, I've got to keep this secret! Can I? Can I hide it and face them; lie with a straight face to my family?

A knock on the cabin door, his thoughts raced to the present, "Yes, who is it?"

"Monar, Captain. We've brought some of the gear for the cannon."

As Monar entered, saluting, Captain Graves' shivered. It was as if, by Monar's glance, he read Graves mind.

6

THE TWIRLING YELLOW PARASOL CAUGHT John Thomas' eye. With unconcealed haste, he and Jason moved through the crowded marketplace. There were grins all around, more so when Jason saw the girl accompanying Charlee.

Charlee could see pleasure in Jason's eyes as she introduced her friend, "Miss Emeline Laurie, this is Mr. John Thomas and Mr. Jason Graves."

Blond hair rustling in the breeze, Emeline had been told that John Thomas was not available, but that she was all to welcome to flirt and wander off with Jason. This Emeline did with an easy southern charm and the two were soon arm in arm, strolling the waterfront stalls.

Charlee watched them leave, then turned to JT, her blue eyes taking him in, "Well, John Thomas, you've certainly made yourself known, and I might add, exceedingly controversial in only one hour at Hammersmith."

JT was all at sea, it was not the expected welcome, "What is this? There was a little trouble, for which I apologized, and that should be that."

"A little trouble and that should be that? Are you serious? Please excuse my questions, but do you think you are in some Yankee backwater where you can ignore my brother's challenge by clouting him like you were some thug? My, Lord, but aren't you dense headed."

Startled by Charlee's remarks, JT was not inclined to accept her disrespect, "Miss Charlene, with all due deference to your femininity, I suggest you back off and take a different tack or this little chat will see an end before it starts."

Charlee appeared to pout. "Well, no wonder you're still single with that approach with the ladies, JT. She glanced around—no one was noticing— reached up and kissed his cheek, "But that's what I wanted to hear! Not some dandy's namby-pamby excuse."

JT, pleased yet confused, decided to make his position clear, "Charlee, listen to me. I won't play games with you, do not play them with me."

"I understand, John Thomas, I promise. Now what do you want to do?"

"I want to walk with you and talk to you and listen, and laugh."

"And after that?"

"Ah, another question. But this one I'll answer as it concerns you. I've been thinking of you; I intend to ask your parents if I may court you."

A moment to comprehend, another moment throw her arms around his neck. Her face lit up, "I've never been courted before. What should I do?"

"Still with the questions. A light kiss on the lips would be nice."

Her lips lingered a moment, then she pulled away blushing, "Really, JT, the things you make me do in public."

He laughed at her and then noticed how white she was, a China doll, "Tell me Charlee, are you ever out in the sun, do you ever feel it on you and get color?"

"Color? What crazy ideas you have! You mean a tan; do you want me to look like a Negro? For goodness sake, what are you thinking?"

"I should take you out on my schooner; let you feel the wind and sun on you. Watch you bronze, become even more beautiful."

"You're the most uncommon man even to think that, JT. You're bronze enough for both of us, so don't say another thing about my getting color. Goodness."

They laughed together until a thought took her concentration.

"What is it now, Charlee?"

"Logan, my brother. You have to apologize to him before you can court me, you know."

"Apologize…to him? That will not happen. I will apologize to your parents for the rumpus I caused, no one else."

"Please, JT, don't you see? You simply can't just ignore his challenge and you can't accept it! I'd die if you or Logan were killed. You must apologize—I'd understand why."

"There will be no apology from me to your brother and that is that."

Charlee was angry yet not sure at who or what. She threw her parasol down and stamped on it, "You stupid men! You have swordfights over nothing, hang Negros over stupid little slights, shoot each other over card games! I'd like to take a bullwhip to all of you!"

Tears came. He did not grasp how deeply she felt. His arms went around her; yet this was unfamiliar terrain, he didn't know what to say.

"Please, John Thomas, don't die…and I insist you don't kill my brother!"

"I can't apologize to him, Charlee, but as we talk, perhaps I have an idea. As the challenged party, I think I have the right to choose the weapons—am I correct?"

"Yes, although don't please don't accept the challenge."

"You have a carriage here. Let me go to my schooner and pick up something. Then we'll go see your father—right now."

Gordon Carlton was not pleased to see John Thomas. It was not that he didn't like him; it was the circumstances, which to say the least, were difficult. Added to that, his daughter going off without permission, to see the person at the other side of the challenge and her obviously being involved, complicated the problem. Carlton was torn, yet civil, "You say, John Thomas, you will not turn the other cheek and I am certain my son will not back down. Despite this, you feel there is a way out of this dilemma."

"Yes, Mr. Carlton, I do. If you would come with me and just listen."

"Very well, I must listen to any possibility you may present, nonetheless I hold little hope and blame myself for bringing you here in the first place."

With JT's request that they find an isolated area of the plantation, only he and Carlton took a carriage.

"Mr. Carlton, my choice of weapons will be pistols."

"So my daughter told me. I have a set of 1836 Johnson dueling flint locks you may use."

"We will not be using your pistols, Sir."

John Thomas then unrolled the bundle he carried.

Gordon Carlton stared at the weapon as JT spoke, "Mr. Carlton, this is the pistol I choose. It is a Colt, number 5 belt, revolver. It fires five .38 caliber balls and under stable conditions has excellent accuracy to sixty feet and a reasonable striking range of fifty yards. I intend to set our firing distance at twenty yards—sixty feet. I have fired this weapon numerous times to prove that accuracy. I am sure you will comprehend what that means to the life of your son."

Carlton blanched; his son lay dead before his eyes, "Why are you doing this? You said there might be a way out, yet now you're not giving my son a chance! After what I thought of you how can you be this cruel to me—to my daughter?"

"Please, Mr. Carlton, stop. All I want is for you to agree your son has absolutely no chance?"

"My, God, man, of course he hasn't."

"Good! Then now I believe you will go along with my idea."

«◊»

The time of the duel came all too soon. Mrs. Emily Carlton and Charlee were told was there is a plan—nothing more. Unsure, they fretted the time away in the house. It was imperative Logan see their concern.

Although dueling was banned in South Carolina, they continued in private, out of sight, with few people involved. Of course, John Thomas had Jason as his second. Logan, asked a Mr. Col Arceneau.

At nine in the morning, a small assemblage formed under a stand of cypress trees at the far end of a secluded, unsown field. Darkies, seeing the white men ride by, slipped behind brush cleared from the fields to the edge of the trees and there, well hidden, watched.

The duel judge, a Mr. E. Collins, asked Logan Carlton to withdraw his challenge. He refused.

John Thomas Graves, asked to withdraw, refused. The three witnesses, judge and seconds became uneasy. Their fears were coming true. Logan Carlton, though nervous, did not back down.

As soon as the judge stated the distance of sixty feet, Gordon Carlton blinked toward JT, who interrupted, "Sir, before I present the weapons for my opponent to select, it is only proper to describe the workings of the revolver and its capabilities."

The judge, witnesses and Logan agreed. With unexpected formality, JT paced off sixty feet.

There, he jammed a six-foot long, twelve-inch wide board upright into the ground. The distance, once stepped off, became appallingly short, due to older dueling pistols being notoriously erratic so the space was, in those days acceptable and never changed. Logan watched, steeling himself to the undertaking, firmly staying the course. While JT strode back, there was not one person who didn't doubt JT was acting out a pretense. A show for them. Yet why?

Taking the clothbound revolver from his brother, he showed it to the group. There were gasps. No one in this Savannah agriculture community had seen the like. Walking purposefully up to Logan, JT simplified the weapon's functions, "You thumb this hammer back, the trigger drops down, and," JT turned in one motion, sighted down the revolver, "squeeze the trigger."

The revolver roared and the ball splintered the wood. The hammer thumbed back, the trigger squeezed, the revolver roared again. The plank fragmented.

The group was shocked as the hammer thumbed back once more. Gordon Carlton rushed forward, "*Stop! Stop!* This is madness! This is not a duel—this is murder. I will not allow it."

Another roar and the wood shattered into pieces—then silence.

Mr. Carlton, outwardly in shock, turned to JT, "Please, Sir, I ask that you not…"

Logan, sensing an out, stepped forward, "Father, I will not shame you into pleading for my life. Mr. Graves, I was unwisely in my cups when I threw the gauntlet. For my family's honor, I respectfully ask that you allow me to withdraw my challenge."

It was done. Done virtually as Gordon Carlton and John Thomas planned. The women, having heard the shooting had been terrified, then elated when they saw the men, *all* the men, returning along the path. The darkies were delighted seeing the wood shatter, then snuck away forlorn that the board was not Logan.

A secret, yet nervous smile passed between JT and Carlton. Had Logan not been duped into retracting, he would have discovered there was only one revolver. The hell it could have raised with JT's reputation was worrisome to consider.

In Hammersmith's drawing room, John Thomas looked to Charlee. When she nodded, he stood and approached her parents as they sat on the divan. They easily guessed the reason for his nervousness.

"Mr. and Mrs. Carlton, I don't know the proper procedure for this, so I'll simply ask your permission so that I may court your daughter."

Carlton rubbed his forehead searching to the right words, "JT—if I may use your initials as my daughter does—my wife and I, after seeing the anguish Charlee has been through worrying back and forth between you and her brother, realized there was some…acquiescence shall I say, between you two.

"Let me explain our position. First, you have been nothing but honest in your business transactions with me. You are a hard worker, intelligent and, as you showed with this past affair, you can be quite Machiavellian—and I mean that in a positive manner—yet your using the revolver as the Deus ex Machina was a brilliant stroke for accomplishing our goal."

JT tried to concentrate on Carlton's remarks. Two years at Yale helped him follow the Machiavellian reference, yet he but vaguely remembered Deus ex Machina, as Greek gods' way of intervening. What this had to do with his request was beyond him and this was taking a long time to get an answer. And, experience told JT the longer a conversation lasted, the less was accomplished.

Charlee shifted with apprehension, Mrs. Carlton, exasperated; told her husband, "…would you please save your beloved Greek Gods for another day, Gordon? Get to the point or we shall all die of the tension."

Mr. Carlton tried once more, "Mr. Graves, my wife and I thank you profusely for your decency in the past affair and your proper conduct in coming to us now to request permission to court our only daughter. However—and I say this with substantial thought and melancholy—the point is that we feel the outcome of any arrangement between you and Charlee would lead to unhappiness for both of you. There, it's said."

Jumping to her feet, Charlee argued the answer with a succinct, "Why?"

JT awaited the reason and it was not long in coming, "To be honest, there a number of objections, Charlee. Firstly, JT's family is nearly destitute. Of course, he, Jason and their father could recover their losses and, to be honest, I could help them financially. However, that would take time and you, my dear, enjoy your life here and would not enjoy a husband who was at sea for months on end. That I am assuredly aware of."

Charlee started to protest, Carlton held up his hand, "Dispute if you wish, Charlee. Nonetheless, I know you. However, to settle this, let me ask JT one simple question. As a New England Yankee, what are your sentiments regarding slavery?"

Unexpectedly boxed in, JT could only express his thoughts, "It is wrong, Sir."

Carlton nodded, “Everything you see around you, this whole plantation, is the result of my hard work and my slaves. Would you stop slavery and see our life and their world destroyed? What would my slaves do? They have no intellectual capacity, whereas I am an honor bound to take care of them. Would you turn them loose into your freedom and starve? Tell me.”

“I don’t have an answer, Sir. I guess I’ve never been faced with that question. As you say, I’m a Yankee seaman. I go about my business of earning a living and expect others to do the same. I’m not involved in…”

Carlton interrupted, “You know that throughout the northern states there are radical abolitionists agitating for war against the south to free the slaves. And, our President Polk vacillates. He makes the Oregon Territory non-slavery; yet in the new Texas lands he reverses himself and makes it allowed.”

“Yes, sir, I’m aware of that, in fact I heard it here.”

“If there is—or perhaps I should I say, *when* there is a war, whose side will you be on?”

“Father! You’re unfair! How can you ask that of JT after all he’s done?”

“Charlee, think rationally, please. I know how you feel, but there are difficulties here that become insurmountable.”

Carlton turn again to JT, “John Thomas, I’m asking you straight out. Can you, with your principles, live in a house where slaves are all around you, working the fields, cooking your meals, tending your clothes, doing every conceivable service and happy to do so for the roof and food we supply? If this is against your beliefs, can you allow your wife to live here?”

Charlee watched JT’s face. She knew they had lost.

Shaking his head, JT focused on Charlee, “I don’t know how to respond, Charlee. I’ve got to be honest. I’ve never looked at slavery, I live in New England, it’s not part of my life. I’ve had Negros in my crew, but not as slaves. My belief is that slavery is not right. I don’t know what I was thinking, my feelings for you ran away with me—they still have. Yet your father has bared the divide between us. Unless you're willing to leave with me and…No, I won't ask that of you, I can't ask you to leave all this, your beliefs, your life, friends, family and for what…?"

Charlee took his hand, "I would, you know, go off with you right now. Yet father is right, we really don't know each other, we are poles apart, live in different worlds…" Tears sprung to her eyes, "…and we would lose each other. I would rather to think longingly of you…and hope that someday…"

"Charlee, you haven't seen the last of me, not by a long shot. I'll be back."

He turned to her father, "And, Sir, in truth I do not believe a slave is intellectually wanting and I think you are deluding yourself in thinking they want to stay here—rather than freedom."

With that, and a formality he did not feel, he kissed her cheek, found Jason, and left.

Charlee went to the window, touching the glass, "Pray, God, that you are right, John Thomas. As I will pray."

7

THE *LAURENCE PIKE* GHOSTED from the Gulf of Guinea into the Tagba Lagoon across from Grand-Lahou. As dusk descended, the old steam tug's mate looped the towline around her stern cleat and the struggle up the Bandama Blanc began.

The beginning of the plan proceeded as Ghost and Graves' hoped. No British ships along the Ivory Coast caused the *Pike* to come about and flee. The tug was on schedule and now, with gathering darkness and moving the ship further upriver into the Tai forest, she slipped from sight of the coast. All the while, the time consuming effort of lowering the topsails continued.

They moored the *Pike* in the river's channel. At first light, the tug would take up the ship's stern line and pull her stern first into a tributary. Until then, Captain Graves lay awake through the night, unfamiliar with the sounds of the jungle. Red Colobus and Mona monkeys shrieked their warning Krak, Krak, while leopards roared, then sought ambush of their prey. Yellow-billed Turacos and Black Goshawk's screeches added to the discord of the jungle.

In the dim light of a sultry, murky dawn, Captain Graves heard the tug's boiler fire up and rose to supervise the lugging of the *Pike* into the narrow waterway.

Monar came up beside him, a black apparition through the mist. "Sleep well, Captain?"

Graves' smiled, "No, as you probably know. I'll bet you were about in the night."

"Yes, I heard you tossing around. When you are new to the rain forest, it is hard to sleep. People think of the forest as silent, yet it is more alive, more deafening than Savannah when the paddle-wheelers are being loaded with cotton."

Graves' watched Monar as his eyes encircled the area.

"Everything correct, Monar?"

"Yes. There are many natives in the forest, but they are friendly, King Nganga's people."

"Is Nganga there?"

"I think no, one of his princes is, Vengoo or Zambem. Only one will be in charge until the slaves are aboard."

"How do you know this?"

"I have been into the dark and learn this."

A shout from the tug, "Which side do you want them to board, Captain?"

Graves' turned to Monar, who took charge, "Lay us up on the starboard, as close as you can without grounding when we're burdened."

"Aye, the current has scoured the bank here so if you keep your spars and booms clear, I can bump you in to ten feet."

Seeing Graves nod yes, Monar signaled the tug operator to proceed, then spoke to the Captain, "If you will order the gangway fixed, I will order the rum hauled up on deck and then get the gold from the bilge and bring it to your cabin, Sir."

When Monar left, and the *Pike* nudged close in to shore, Captain Graves' ordered bow and stern lines fixed and, unsure of any tidal effect, had spring lines fastened off to stout trees.

In the Captain's cabin, Monar patted the Long-nine cannon and unwrapped the sealed oilcloth holding the four packets. Only one-half packet would Monar take down the gangplank to whichever prince was there. At that point, Monar would find if Nganga was ready for him to inspect the food, mostly yams, dried fish and the water casks. If those were approved, following would be the examination and then handover of the slaves—if they were ready.

At the base of the gangway, Monar gave a slight bow to Prince Zambem and turned over the half packet. This accepted, natives started forth with thousands of yams, salted fish, assorted other vegetables and water casks which they would exchange for the *Pike's* empty barrels.

Graves' ordered Toby Coffin to supervise the stowing of the food and taste each water cask.

When Monar returned aboard, he conversed with his Captain.

"It is Prince Zambem, the King's favorite. There has been a battle with the French in the N'zi-Comoé region at the village of Dimbokro further up river. Nganga's soldiers had to go north and capture more slaves at Sakasso, very near Ashanti warrior lands. This means all the slaves are not here at present."

"And that means?" Captain Graves' concerns were for the timeline.

"If Zambem is correct—and there is no good reason to believe him—it will take another four or five days for the remainder to reach here."

"Damn! Remember, Monar, we have two weeks from yesterday. There's no option. We leave, whether we have all the slaves or not."

"I understand, Captain. I've told Zambem that. They will do everything they can, believe me. They need the money to buy ammunition."

"Ammunition? They have guns?"

"Yes, old worn out French rifles they've captured. A lot explode when they're fired, but better than nothing. You might not know that the French renamed the Ivory Coast the Cote d'Ivoire when they made it a Protectorate four years ago and the Baoulé hate them for that as well the ivory. Don't call it the Cote d'Ivoire when you speak with King Nganga-he is Baoulé."

"Not that I'll be speaking with him, but go on Monar, about the missing slaves."

"Half the slaves are here now, in baracoons—that's what they call warehouses. According to Zambem, the rest are coming down in coffles'—their expression for gathering them in herds. In other words they're chained all together with neck yokes and collars."

"Christ!"

"Captain, you should know this is only the start of the terror. If I may be bold..."

"What is it, Monar? Speak as a friend."

"As a friend? Thank you. I ask you to remember that. Captain, circumstances have forced this on you. To save your home and family you made a decision too quickly and I know you will not be able to tolerate your decision. I can see it in your eyes, read your mind. You are not going to be able to face what is to happen. It is not in your background, your upbringing. Still, it is too late. If we try to back out now, Nganga's savages—for that is what they really are—would kill us all. Do not doubt that we would never get out of this inlet and down the river."

"Monar, you underestimate me and are stepping over the line. I do not intend to back out, I can fight through this, I can..."

"No, Captain Graves. You said I speak as a friend. I can read your mind, it is true. Believe me, I know. You will not fight off the horror of the next weeks if you go on this way and we need you to sail us out of here, to get back."

"I'm as tough as you, Monar. Why do you think you can go on while I can't?"

"It is that I have two minds."

"What the devil does that mean?"

"It means I can shut out evil. I can shut out the murders, the whippings, curses and kicks. It means I use one mind to survive, to forget what I see. The other in me stores away the horror and revenge to take it out another time—if I wish. You can't do that, for you may be hard, but you are not evil. And, because you are not evil, if you continue as you are, you will perish."

Graves' pulled back, momentarily living a nightmare, "So you're saying you're evil?"

"Yes, one part of my mind is."

"And you think I will die, is that what you see?"

"Yes, my Captain. Only you can stop it."

"And how can I do that?"

"When the slaves start to come aboard, you must go to your cabin and stay. Block your ears. Come out when we need a captain and then look—but do not see."

"Yet you tell me you can bear it?"

"One part can."

"Monar, I will bear it."

"Sadly, you will find out you can't. Yet, remember, Captain Graves, I am in charge of the slaves. That was your agreement and that *may* save you."

"Yes, that was agreed. But I am in charge of the ship and will continue so."

The slaves came. The rattling of chains, their mournful sounds and the curses of the slavers gave the captives away as they seeped in along jungle trails and then coerced into the baracoons. Heat waves shimmered off the roofs, sweaty bodies, men, women and children, endured. Screams, moans, anger, fright, all the wretched emotions were there, bar one,—pity.

The slavers ruled by fear. Graves' heard the cries from the bullwhip; navy floggings of malefactors through the ships came back to him and he winced. He had to steel himself. He knew this was only the beginning of the slave's trial—and his. He felt he would not yield.

Three days later, the remainder of the slaves arrived. Toby Coffin and two Mulatto crewmen, chosen by him, acted as inspectors. They were no more qualified to inspect the slaves for diseases than any other crewmember, yet they went about their work with laughter at the women's humiliation and severe treatment of the men. After a short while, Monar took charge and one of the Mulatto's, tearing off a woman's top, was sent sprawling from being thumped on the side of his head with the flat of Monar's bolo.

"Do your job, mess with the women and I'll throw you below—to live with the niggars."

Toby Coffin was furious, "I'm Chief Mate! I run the slaves my way, Monar! Back off."

Angry, Monar started toward Coffin, who reached for his Navy knife.

The big black man's voice went deep, "If you want to keep that hand, Coffin, that knife should stay sheathed."

Coffin watched as Monar unhurriedly moved his hand to his bolo. Though the crew watched, the Chief Mate backed down. There will be another time, he reasoned. Now, two people will die before they reach Barbados.

Monar shouted to all, "Coffin controls the crew, I control the slaves. Anyone question me on that?"

With no takers, he continued, "Their lives will be bad enough without tormenting them. If someone thinks he can amuse himself with any of the slaves—he will *become* one of them."

Captain Graves' took the deck and watched the effect on the crew, "Coffin, Monar. In my cabin, *now*."

Once there, Graves' was brusque, "We're going to get this straightened out right now. Coffin, perhaps I have not made the chain of command clear. You're Chief Mate, in charge of the crew for the correct operation of this vessel. In this circumstance, your crew will also be responsible for the safety of this vessel with slaves onboard. The safety of the *vessel* only! You are to follow my instruction. Monar will control the slaves with the assistance of your crewmembers, which he will employ as he sees fit. In other words, you use the crew to run the *Pike*; Monar uses them to supervise the slaves. I expect the both of you to work together to that end. Make sure of this, it is *my* ship and there will be no unnecessary brutality on board!"

Graves stared at Coffin, "Am I clear?"

"Yes, Captain, can I say something?"

Graves nodded; Coffin spoke, "Captain, you have never worked a slaver. If the crew doesn't use an iron fist the slaves will riot. There's been mutinies by niggers on ships and you know the slaughter of whites when that Turner slave rose up and killed a hundred whites and…"

"Stop there, Coffin. I've told you Monar is in charge of the slaves. It's his responsibility. You will do as he says. There will be no wanton terror, period. You're dismissed."

Toby Coffin went to the hatchway, "Captain, I'll say one thing more. Shielding niggers may make you feel good, but you're—both of you— taking them to their deaths and you know it. In Brazil, their life span is seven years! Yet you feel good trying to protect them? You're…"

"Get out, get out or *you'll* be in chains!"

With the Chief Mate out of sight, Monar watched Graves' mood turn from anger into turmoil. He studied his Captain's hands as they gripped his desk.

"He's right you know, Monar. Coffin's right. We're trying to counterweigh what we're doing with some hopeless acts of kindness."

"You might feel that way, Captain. I don't. My goal is for our cargo to reach Barbados intact, with as little damage as possible and worth our effort. There'll be enough conflict with the slaves without Coffin and his gang adding to it."

Graves' gave a listless smile, "I know you're right, of course, and I'm sure you've been added to our Chief Mate's death list as well as me."

"If it wasn't already, that's to be expected, Captain. Except he doesn't know we're on to him. All we need to know is who will help Coffin when he makes his move and I've been stalking him at night; he's too smart to cozy up to anyone through the day."

"Good, but I've a thought on that. Coffin was a gunner in the '12 war. I'm going to tell him to pick a crew and train them for our Long-nine. I'd guess that as long as he doesn't suspect we know what he's up to, he'll use his gang to help man the weapon."

"That's a good idea—an excellent idea as I think of it. And another good idea, Captain, it's not too soon to start wearing that Colt."

Monar oversaw the inspection and the transfer of the slaves into the hold. There, the resistance to their fate grew. Fixed leg irons lined the deck area. Kicking and shrieks were met with wallops from belaying pins and whips until the captives were intimidated into lying down. The left ankle of each slave was then forced into a double manacle, the right leg of the next slave forced into the other side. After each two slaves were stretched out, an iron rod was slipped through eyelets and one leg was entrapped. A rod ensnared eight prisoners at a time and then locked in place. Eight more slaves forced down, another rod, more slaves, more rods. For some perverse reason, it was called the Rod of Justice.

Even in the first day, it quickly became a living hell. Males fastened on one side of the vessel, female, the other. Children allowed to roam unfettered. There was no sanitation. Fright loosened bowels. Screams and odors alone could drive people mad and often did. It was Gaol Fever.

Hour after hour, the gruesome trek went on. Slaves not considered healthy enough for the trip were worked as animals ashore or dragged into the jungle to have their skulls cracked. Up until that point, their begging echoed off the trees, alarming even the leopards.

Defiant slaves who refused to obey became a spectacle for the others with clubs, whipping or thumbscrews. The pain made the ablest of them as helpless and submissive as the weakest.

At the end of the second day, the supplies and nearly all the slaves were aboard. By Monar's count, however, they were fifty slaves short and he brought this deficiency to Prince Zambem who left after saying he would speak to Nganga.

Captain Graves' watched as Zambem left, "What do you think, Monar? Nganga's going to come for his money, are we going to pay the total amount?"

"It is a problem, Captain. We cannot fight our way out of here, so we may have to pay, that is showing a weakness I know, although Nganga has always been fair with selling us slaves."

"Don't you find it peculiar —Negro's selling Negros to be used as slaves by white men?"

Monar thought a little on the question, "There is no great value put on people here, Captain. Other than their value for what a king can get out of them— or for them. There are too many to feed and natives are not like whites, life is either there or…it's not. Actually, they're not better off here or the States."

Graves' ordered the crew armed and on deck. Unseen, Monar roamed the jungle's border while every one of the crew remained on edge and waited. Sweat trickled, bugs floated, they agonized.

Near noon, Monar came from the rainforest and was seen walking down the trail to the *Pike*.

"Your fifty slaves are coming, Captain, in good shape, with Nganga's wagon behind. Order the crew to bring the rum ashore, while I get the rest of the money packets."

The new slaves, better dressed and healthier than the previous, were funneled into the hold.

Graves' wondered about their condition until taken aback by the sight of Nganga progressing down the wagon's ramp to rest on a bench at the foot of the gangway. Standing with Monar, Graves wondered how anyone so obese could remain living, much more totter along.

Monar, speaking faulty KoKonga, managed to make the proper protocols as Captain Graves' bowed properly as he handed the packets one at a time to Nganga, who in turn shouted to Prince Zamben to come up and help. Handing the gold off, Nganga slapped Zambem in the head. There was further dialogue, which Monar found difficult to pass on to Graves.

"Ignore what is happening, Captain. It seems Zambem was too slow and not honoring Nganga's greatness with enough respect so Nganga cuffed him."

Graves' smiled at Nganga while commenting to Monar, "How can anyone honor this ton of fat?"

Monar listened intently to Nganga, then turned to Graves, "It appears that our fat greasy friend is pleased and *you*, who is almost half as great as Nganga, are offered some of his harem. It's not clear, but he is offering either six or sixty women for *your* sanctum, I'm really not sure which."

For a moment, Captain Graves was numb, "Tell this most exalted, glorious specimen of greasy, revolting manhood that I thank him. Unfortunately, I already have too many wives and more would only strain my relationship with my most favorite head wife."

Under his breath, Graves' said, "Besides, my head wife would *be*-head me."

Monar returned the smile, "I'll do my best, Captain, but if I come afoul, be ready to run."

Whatever Monar said, the King giggled and handed Graves' *two* gold coins. Nganga, seeing the rum now aboard, was then helped as he struggled up the ramp to his chair and, facing to the rear, he waved until the transport lugged him out of sight.

On board, Graves' ordered Chief Mate Coffin to ready the ship and re-step the three top- gallant masts just prior to dusk. He stood by the gunnel with Monar, looking into the rain forest.

"Well, my friend, that was an experience. I hope that fat pig drinks himself to death."

"I don't think he will have time, Captain. By my reckoning, I'd bet your gold pieces that Zambem was only waiting for the gold to come—before pulling a Palace Coup."

"I can't say I'd be sorry. Anyone would be better than that leech."

"Then what I tell you now will make you even more pleased with what I think will happen to him."

"You have more?"

Monar averted his eyes, "I really don't believe it will make you pleased, yet I'll tell you. The last fifty slaves we acquired were his own people. He sold them for the rest of the gold."

"His own people? God—damn him! Let them go, I won't take them."

"That's no good, Captain. He would kill all of them and consider your doing so an insult to his most royal highness and that could only be satisfied by blood. Needless to say, ours."

"Blast it! I wish he was still in sight, I'd give him a taste of the Long-nine…Damn!"

"Let Zambem do it, right now the tug's arrived to haul us into the Bandama's channel so we'll be ready for the early morning haul to the lagoon."

"Well then, Monar, tomorrow the eighth of March, will tell the tale."

Commander Keith Ramsey, of Her Majesty's Royal Navy screw propeller and sail Frigate, HMS *Diligent*, was fitting together pieces of knowledge, added to instinct. One, the former RN lieutenant of the *Prince*, Elmer 'Ghost' Ghosman was seen cruising in his schooner *Laird of Glasgow* for two weeks—apparently directionless—along the Ivory Coast between Sassandra and the French port of Grand Bassam. Two, on Ramsey's stopover in Gabon, he was informed by a RN Captain, that in Ghosman's past, he had been captured as a slaver by the Danes and freed when his family paid a ransom—'not on the documents, all very hushed up you know'.

Another piece to the puzzle was that British patrol ships had not caught one glimpse of that clipper ship *Laurence Pike* the agent in Bilbao had said would stop at Las Palmas before heading for South Africa. The clipper did not stop at Las Palmas, or anywhere in the Canary's. So, where was she?

Dusk was settling 7 March, when Commander Ramsey made the decision to solve the puzzle and ordered the steam up on the *Diligent* for a night run from his station by the British fort at Lagos. With the new faster steamship specifically built to stop any slavers, he hoped to intercept the *Laird of Glasgow* and find out just what game Ghosman was playing. To split the difference between the opposite ends of his objective's wanderings, Ramsey set a course for Grand Lahou.

8

10 March, 1847

JOHN THOMAS WAS at a loss. Go back to Hammersmith, try to work out a solution with Charlee and her parents, or sail off? The decision was not his to make or long in coming. Gordon Carlton arrived at the wharf and with every courtesy, handed him a sealed note.

"This is from my daughter, JT. I have not read it, yet I trust her word to me. Please read it and then we will talk."

JT walked off and leaned on the mainmast.

Dear JT,

I have agreed to leave for the 'Grand Tour' of the continent. Emeline, Jason's friend, will accompany me along with one of mother's older friends. We will be gone for two years. I am trying to be an adult about this, as I know my parents only want the best and I understand their concern. You and I acted on the spur of the moment without thought of the future and at present the gulf between us is impossible to bridge.

JT's heart ached; he could barely continue to read the next lines.

Now, with that said, don't believe a word of the last sentence! I believe time will prove our feeling were true and mother and father have finally agreed that if, after two years, you just happen to be sailing past and see a pretty girl standing on the jetty with a broken yellow parasol and heart, looking forlornly out to sea, you might 'come about' or whatever you call it and moor the *Ocean Pearl* beside a now smiling maiden and my parents will try to accept—whatever parents have to do to accept.

My, what a long sentence! A stream of thought, it is now called. Whatever, we must come to grips with our feelings and two long years will prove it to a doubting world.

I'm rushing this—father is tapping his foot.

To our life together, no later than December 31, 1849—

I implore you.

Yours, JT,

Charlee ≈

Folding the note, JT looked out to sea without seeing, "Two years." he mumbled, "An eternity. Still, better than no hope at all. And perhaps by then, father will be back and Seaward will be secure again."

John Thomas had no idea how long an eternity could last, or the great change life would bring to the both of them.

Mr. Carlton had an unusual look about him, not explained by his next words, "You're not alone JT, I still recall the yearnings of youth."

"Yes, Sir, thank you for delivering this note. Was there something else?"

Carlton nodded, "I've received an order for lumber, two by eight pine planking. Delivery to Havana, Cuba. The mills down there are still not running to capacity and they don't have enough seasoned wood to repair the hurricane damage. Do you want the shipment?"

"Definitely, Sir, when?"

"There's enough board feet ready at my mill in Brunswick. You know where. It's ready when you are."

"Then we'll leave now. Jason and I have enough money on hand for our small crew. If it's not too much to ask, would you please send the check for our transport to Cuba on to *Seaward*, our home in Salem? Make it out to Mrs. Mary Graves. And Sir, I ask that you do not overpay."

The comment was implicit and Gordon Carlton understood, "You're quite a person, JT, I'm truly sorry. It's just that…"

They stared each other down. Carlton wanting JT to leave before anything changed his plans. JT recognized that, and in truth wanted to be underway.

They shook hands and Carlton had no sooner stepped ashore than the *Ocean Pearl's* lines were hauled.

Heavily burdened with timber, the schooner wallowed against the Gulf Stream. After Saint Augustine and then southing past countless small villages dotting the Florida coastline, the brothers were glad to see the mainland slip to their stern as the schooner slipped west by south along the Keys and her last leg to Havana, Cuba.

«»

It was after the lumber had been unloaded and the brothers asking around for cargo they could take north when their plans took a turn as they ran into Fred Daly, the former Captain of the *Laurence Pike*. Daly was still smarting from being left beached by Richard Graves and having to find work as a shipwright in Havana. Still, he liked the Graves brothers and held no grudge with them.

After pointing out the sites where some of the Graves' ships met their doom and seeing the bones of the packet ship *Alice Murphy* and whaler *Astrid* bleaching in the sun, they continued their conversation about Richard Graves whereabouts.

Daly picked up from where Jason said his father told him, Jason, to head back to Salem.

"Well, I didn't catch up with you in Havana, Jason, so I didn't know you weren't with your father and that you'd come through here heading home. Where Richard is, I can't tell you. He's not here and the *Pike* hasn't been through here either. Why don't you head for Barbados and find that MacPherson fella? He should know where the *Pike* is—if he bought her like we've heard."

"We were just thinking that when we bumped into you. So I guess seeing we don't have…"

Daly interrupted, "Look, there's Johnny Bowen! He was part of my crew that your father put ashore in Barbados. He might tell you something more."

Bowen was somewhat hesitant to speak. Not knowing the two captains, other than from the remoteness of a deckhand, and realizing they were Captain Graves' sons, he indicated little.

"What's the matter, Johnny, cat got your tongue? These two boys is ok. You holding back on us?"

As soon as Bowen spoke, the brother's found the sailor was slowwitted.

"I don't knows nothing. But I hears things…strange, funny things…no, not funny…queer things."

"For God's, sake, Johnny, what queer things are you talking about?"

Bowen was nervous, "Before we left Barbados…there was this giant…big Negro. He come up to me…just me…he say he was gonna…he were gonna take my white ass to…to Africa and, and…sell it to the *cannibals*!"

"You let a niggar say that? You never told me that! Then what happened, Johnny?"

"You shoulda seen the size of that black…I, I hid…until Captain Graves said…he, he dun sold the *Pike* and for us to git."

The three men looked at Bowen thunderstruck. It took a moment for JT to speak, "You're sure, Johnny? Captain Graves said he sold the *Pike* and that darkie guy said he was going to take you to Africa?"

"Yes, sir. Cross…my heart…hope to die."

"Did you tell anyone? Any of the old crew?"

"I was afraid…afraid the Captain would…find me."

JT wouldn't believe it, "You were afraid my father would hurt you?"

When Bowen nodded his head and they gave it enough thought, JT said, "Father sold the *Pike* to Ian MacPherson—but why? So that

MacPherson could take it to Africa? That could only mean slaves! Father wouldn't knowingly sell the ship for that. Of more import, where is father? Something's wrong here, Jason and we're going to find out."

Jason agreed. Something seemed terribly wrong—but what? They copied the main markers for the run and set course for the Windward Islands and the eastern most island of Barbados.

«»

Ian MacPherson watched the schooner closely while it coasted up to his dock in Bridgetown. He didn't like strange ships or people, and took his spyglass to scan the deck. He held on one man, Jason Graves.

"Damn," he muttered, "what in hell is he doing back here?"

MacPherson hurried to the rear porch, shouting for his plantation boss, "Omar! I'm going to see who's at my dock. If it looks like I'm in trouble you come running with five more niggers carrying machetes. You understand?"

"Yes, Master."

"Good, now keep out of sight."

Taking deep breaths as he walked down the path, he watched his guests tie off the schooner and decided to let them start the conversation.

"Mr. MacPherson, you remember me, Jason Graves. This is my brother, John Thomas. We're here to find our father."

"Find him? I didn't know he was missing."

JT came forward, "Mr. MacPherson, where's our father and let's not dodge the issue."

"Hey, watch yourself, kid. Far as I know, he's somewhere on the high seas shipping cargo for me to Europe. I've sent money to your home for him—haven't I?"

JT ignored the question. "Listen, we've heard father sold the *Pike* to you and one of your Negros said they were going to Africa. Try answering that straight if you can."

MacPherson was thinking fast. They knew something, how much?

"One of my niggers said that? We only said that I bought the *Pike* to get rid of his crew, they were too expensive. My crews are cheaper—I own them."

JT, having just had a slave problem in Savannah, became heated, "I'll bet you own them. Where'd you get them—slaves from Africa?"

MacPherson decided he'd had more than enough and became belligerent, "I don't like your arrogance, kid. Where I got them is my business, not yours. Look, what do you want to know? Your father and I have a business arrangement. He works for me now. I've sent you money to support your home and… "

"Get off that subject. You're up to something. Tell us where our father is—or else."

"Who the hell are you with your—or else? Your father works for me. You don't like it? Too bad, get used to it or get out."

MacPherson looked down to Omar, then challenged the brothers, "You reckless young whippersnappers with your big captain's hats think you can sail in here and threaten me? Most of this is island is mine, understand? Now I'll teach you a lesson!"

Looking over MacPherson's shoulder, JT and Jason saw a half dozen Negros approaching with machetes. MacPherson's threat froze in his mouth as JT slid his Colt revolver from the back of his pant waist and pointed it at MacPherson's belly.

"We're not quite so reckless as you think—are we. Tell your Negros to sheer off."

MacPherson blanched, yet tried to hold his ground, "You shoot me, and those niggers will be on you so fast…"

JT looked around, "Maybe, but I could get three or four with this and Jason could get our crew from the boat. Father trained us pretty well you old fool. Still, thinking about it, I'd bet on your slaves not doing anything but cheer. But that wouldn't make much difference to you because you'd be lying on the ground with a ball in your gut."

MacPherson hastily waved the blacks away, "All right what do you want?"

"For Christ's sake! We want to know where our father is."

MacPherson wasn't trying to protect their father as much as himself. If these men reported him to the Brits or US Navy, their ships would cover these waters waiting for the *Pike*. After that would be the trial and if he didn't hang, he would never be released. Still, he did have an ace to play.

"Where's your father? Believe me, you don't want to know, but I'll tell you. Right about now his clipper should be in the Ivory Coast's Bandama River..."

The brother's knew, yet they had to hear and waited.

"He'll have four to five hundred slaves aboard. You're the fools; I said you didn't want to know."

It was the unspoken fear they'd held from Havana. Unspoken and not believed—until now.

"Look, I'll help you kids out here. Nothing mattered to your father, only your home. It means he belongs somewhere, or some foolishness like that. In other words, he said he'd do anything, and I guess this shows it."

"Shut up. You'll be dealt with later."

Smiling, MacPherson said, "You won't deal with anyone later you impudent bastard, so put that revolver away. You can't report this 'cause the Navy would catch your father and hang him from a yardarm. You won't do anything to me because I've got his money hidden away…"

"You think we'd touch your slave money?"

"You and your brother—maybe not. But your father sure as hell will. He sold his soul for that money and he's going to take it, that I know. And father is all that matters to you, isn't it?"

He had them boxed in. Jason was despondent, useless, turning to his younger brother, "What do we do, JT? We're not going to…"

MacPherson broke in, "Tell you boys what. You go back to Havana. Stay there, maybe you'll change your mind. Your father should be back within a month. You don't see any of what happens here. He gets his money. I'll tell him you know everything and you're waiting in Havana. He can go see you—or not go see you. That way what happens is out of your hands."

Jason wanted to be gone, beseeching his brother, "It's a good idea, JT, let's get out of here."

"It's not a good idea, Jason, just the only one at present. I need time to think. We'll go sailing, but not for two months. Maybe we find a cargo around Havana, or maybe we'll be back here."

Ian MacPherson also needed time to think and wanted the brothers gone. If they were in Barbados when the *Pike* returned and found their father dead, all hell would break loose. MacPherson could see it in the eyes of John Thomas. Anger—and the wildness to use it.

"I'm telling you boys, its best left to your father. Give him time to think before he meets you. As I say, maybe you'll have cooled off by then and can think more reasonably."

"This is not something you cool off about. However, we'll leave now and maybe give it two months. If father doesn't meet us, we'll be back—with a full crew."

Watching the stern of the *Ocean Pearl* round the headland, MacPherson cursed and then began to think. Those damn sons of Richard Graves can cause trouble. Fighting them wouldn't be worth the danger. Especially, the one called JT. He's the one to look out for and when he suggested my niggers just might not back me that made sense too. Well, it's near time to get out anyway. I've my money and by selling this next lot of slaves I'll be set up fine in Scotland. Still, I've got to be gone and quickly when the *Pike* docks. Put together a syndicate of buyers; sell off the cargo at half or three-quarter value. With Graves gone, sell the clipper. She's good and fast, they'll be plenty of buyers at the right price. If Coffin hasn't killed Ghosman too, I'll pay him off, slip over to French Martinique with the *Laird,* make her shipshape for one more run to Scotland and I'm home for the life the life of a Laird. I've earned it, working out here in this God forsaken place keeping these worthless slaves moving.

MacPherson relaxed. Talking to those brothers had been tense. Then again, it had helped put his life in perspective and aided him in making his decision to leave. Still, he was concerned that the brothers may reappear early and—totally irrelevant at the moment—MacPherson also fretted about the cost incurred with all the servants he'd need in Scotland. There were no slaves there anymore. Perhaps, he brightened; he could acquire indentured servants for his needs.

Now that, he thought, was another good notion. Forget the rest, it will all work out.

The brother's now knew that sick at heart was an old saying. Yet there was no better term they could express. Their father, a slaver. They must hide it from their mother and the town. Yes, but how? How could this be hidden or defensible? The more it sank in, the more morose they became. Jason went to the rail and vomited. As troubled as he felt, JT observed Jason closely. Jason was often moody, yet he was falling into a harsher mood than JT had ever known—and that was saying a lot, Jason had a reputation in the family and with other people for melancholy.

9

THE *LAURENCE PIKE* had scarcely enough steerageway to clear the Tagba Lagoon. All sails sagged virtually lifeless as she wallowed uncomfortably, trying to stay within the few channel markings. This morning, waiting for the breeze to liven, was painful for the whole crew and the slaves stifling below.

Monar, standing with Captain Graves, was stoic, "The wind either comes or it doesn't, Captain. It's in some god's hand."

"Well, I wish one of your gods would decide if it's going to blow before we see Ahanta war canoes or the British."

"Ahanta aren't this far east. More likely to see Denkera savages or as you say, the British."

"I don't find that comforting either way, Monar. Although if I had the choice, I'd rather be hung by the British, than boiled by the Denkera."

Monar smiled, "That some Yankee gallows humor I've heard about, Captain?"

Graves' didn't answer, staring intently to port through his Ross Binoculars, "There, Monar, off to port about four miles, it's the *Laird*."

"Is she underway?"

"She's sluggish; we'd get the off-shore air before her. They don't appear concerned though, only her mizzen is up. She's waiting, just like us."

There started a slight freshening breeze, Graves turned to the helmsman, "Let her off on a starboard reach; that will keep plenty of water under us. I'll give you a heading shortly."

The bow rose, slicing the waves; Captain Graves' spirits lifted with the ship as she climbed to eight knots, "Won't be long now, Monar. If we can stay on this tack, then run downwind, you'll see her come alive! Order the main top-man to get that damn luff out of the sails."

"Aye, Sir. If any British stink boat shows up we'll teach her a thing or two about sailing."

Aboard the schooner, *Laird of Glasgow*, Ghost Gostman saw the *Pike* and then a smudge on the horizon to the south. Signaling the *Pike*, to see Graves understood, Ghost frantically altered course and ran before the wind. To Captain Graves, the swing was implicit; Ghost was gone.

Graves was in full command now, knowing his ability, "Helmsman, ten points to starboard. Coffin, set the main and mizzen stud 'sails, now!"

Monar watched additional yards extended from the mains and auxiliary sails set, "First time I've ever seen that much canvas, Captain."

"I've done it in a few calms and now we need every sail set. Please leave the helm, Monar."

Graves' set the ship to the new heading. She had the bone in her teeth now. It had to be a British steam frigate chasing him and she might force him off the downwind leg. Yet there was no choice.

Commander Keith Ramsey, of HMS *Diligent*, had not seen the schooner *Laird* further out to sea, only the topsails of a square-rigger close in. Caring little of the wind, he drove the screw driven frigate above eleven knots and tightened the distance, but his problem were the severe rollers off his port quarter causing the ship to bury her bow. His other problem was that, with no forward weaponry, he must come broadside on his prey and order surrender or, with these seas, hope for a lucky shot to convince the captain to heave too. Ramsey saw the ship was a clipper and probably the missing *Laurence Pike*. More importantly, the ship was ignoring his signal. So, if there were slaves and they aren't thrown overboard—which wasn't happening at present—then Ramsey couldn't sink her. It was obvious to Ramsey the captain was trying to make a run for open water where the *Diligent* couldn't keep up. The major problems at present for Ramsey were the waves and critically, the wind, was increasing along with the clipper ship's pace.

Ramsey ordered the steam pressure up, the revolutions increased. The *Diligent* buried into the waves, shook herself upright and plowed on. This was the reason for his being here and Ramsey was not going to let it pass. He'd been too long on endless patrols to let a slaver steal away.

On the *Pike*, Captain Graves saw it was going to be a close thing; he needed half an hour more but the British steamer was gaining. Graves ordered Coffin to open the stern hatch and run out the Long-nine—a last resort. Coffin and his gun crew raced below as Graves knew he had to go directly downwind to escape but his foe was keeping him from that. Essentially, the gap between the two vessels was closing and the *Pike* needed to gain speed faster. The wind shifted and then slackened. Although the ship's momentum continued, it was not what Graves needed and helpless, he watched the British ship coming on.

Commander Ramsey ordered Beat to Quarters. He knew he had won. Even though his steamship was difficult to handle in the whitecaps he could slip pass the stern of the clipper and come up on her lee. At that time, if the captain refused to heave to, the *Diligent's* guns would dismast her.

On the *Pike*, there was next to nothing Graves could do other than shout down the hatch to Coffin that the British vessel would soon be passing their stern at about fifty yards. Perhaps a lucky shot would hinder her, giving the *Pike* time.

Crossing the *Pike's* stern, Commander Ramsey was shocked—a billow of smoke poured from the clipper's stern. There wasn't a chance to warn his crew and the nine-pound cannonball struck and splintered his ship's rail, careening into the funnel. With two marines and four seamen wounded, Ramsey was furious and ordered his portside guns readied but not run out. Keeping the gun ports closed until the last minute would prevent the seas from entering each time the ship rolled. He then ordered the Captain of Marines to prepare to fire a fusillade.

They passed the stern and the *Diligent* would soon begin its sweep to the *Pike's* port and the dismasting of her prey.

Ramsey smiled, "Fire on my ship will you?" He cursed. There would be no question—he would hang this captain from his own yardarm even if he was the Prince of Wales.

Monar, going to the bow of the *Pike*, stared forward in disbelief. Close ahead, bearing down on him with crowded sail was the schooner *Laird of Glasgow*. Monar frantically waved for Ghost to sheer off, get away, yet his schooner came on. Monar then rushed to the stern, shouting that the *Laird* was heading directly for them. Captain Graves, blind forward from his own mass of canvas, struggled to see as the *Laird* cut across his bow and glided close past the starboard. Fleetingly, Monar and Graves couldn't fathom the move. Then they abandoned gesturing the schooner to stand off—now realizing what Ghost was about to do. As he passed, former Royal Navy Officer Elmer Ghosman and former US Navy Officer Richard Graves, saluted. Monar, head down, turned away.

Ghost had masterfully used the cloud of sail on the *Pike* to hide from the *Diligent*. When the schooner rounded the clipper, Commander Ramsey gasped at his predicament. A schooner was bearing down on him and he was being forced away from the clipper and he had to avoid being rammed. Where it hell had a schooner come from!

Ramsey barked to his lieutenant and gunnery officer, "Hard right rudder! Open gun ports, guns run out! Fire as you bear on this schooner!"

The inexact order was to cost dearly. Instead of ordering the *port* gun ports opened, the gunnery officer ordered *all* gun ports opened, port and starboard.

The *Laird* was twenty yards away when cannonballs from the *Diligent* tore into her bow shattering the bowsprit and main mast, yet it was too late to stop her thrust. The *Laird* struck amidships, rose up over the *Diligent's* gunwale and drove her starboard side down, dooming the ship. Surging through open gun ports, cold seawater poured into the engine room, striking the superheated boiler. Ramsey's scream was unheard as the *Diligent* perished in a blinding explosion. The bow to mid-ship of the *Laird* was blown away. The crews of both ships died from the detonation and metal shards ripping through the *Laird.*

The breeze cleared the smoke to reveal the remnants of two fine ships as they wallowed for a few minutes before foundering and then slipping into the deep, leaving only flotsam and tattered canvas to show they once existed.

The crew of the *Pike* was in shock, yet there was no time to think. The explosion had hurled red-hot iron and blazing material onto the deck and sails. Captain Graves ordered crew into the rigging to cut away the flaming canvas as he brought the *Pike* into the wind to keep the flames from spreading. While the ship staggered, a lookout was ordered to the topmast. It wouldn't do to have another British steam frigate show up.

Monar appeared impassive, yet Graves knew, "He was your friend, Monar and I liked Ghost too. We'll circle the debris once our fires are out and make sure no one is left alive; you go below to see if you can quiet the natives. The hatches are opened to clear the air, but they'll be panicky over what's happened."

Monar shook his head, "Ghost was my friend, yes, yet there are more perilous things we must face at present. I watched Toby Coffin speak to his gun crew as they came up on deck. One was injured from the blast, but Coffin talked to the other three. I think he feels that with all the confusion they should make a move. With me going below, it would be a good time. I'll stay near the hatch at the helm. Now, order me below with anger, that will make Coffin think I wouldn't act to help you."

Appearing to direct the cleanup of damaged sections of the ship, Graves took notice of Coffin's gun crew moving into areas not in their duties. The Captain moved to the helmsman, "Tomas, don't change your expression, but there might be a bit of a tussle. You have your Bolo handy?"

Tomas, a mulatto and fully confused, nodded yes.

"Then stay alert to anyone coming up here who shouldn't, especially the First Mate."

"Ah, Captain, you begin to make sense. Even in Barbados, we do not like that white man."

Losing sight of two of Coffin's men, Graves moved to the taffrail, looking out to sea, apparently lost in thought. He turned and leaned on the rail, noting a man on each side of the helm and Coffin slowly moving amidships to the wheel. That left one person uncounted. Unnoticed, Graves loosened the Colt under his jacket and went back to the helm.

"Tomas, get ready. When I shout, watch out for the man to your right."

Coffin moved up the ladder toward Graves, "Captain, I want to ask you if…"

Graves' caught sight of the man on his left; shouted and dodged as he brought his Colt forward. The man stopped, knife poised. Graves shot him in the chest, then quickly turned to his right. Tomas, though slashed across the arm, more than held his own, swinging his bolo into his attacker's stomach.

Caught, unable to reach Graves, Coffin turned pale; the Colt now turned on him. He thought quickly, "Captain, I…I saw them attacking you and rushed to help!"

Keeping the revolver on Coffin, Graves' ordered Tomas to get help for his wound, then take some seamen and search for the unseen fourth assailant.

Monar rose through the stern hatch, "If you are looking for the other man, Captain, he is down below. He will not bother you. He will soon be going by the board."

Monar glanced at the attackers, "Why is Coffin still alive?"

“He said he was trying to save me.”

“Do you believe that, Captain?”

“Of course not.”

Monar grabbed Coffin, who struggled helplessly in the big man’s hands. Lifting him up, Monar went to the rail, “Your permission, Captain?”

Graves started to protest, yet said nothing. The screaming first mate was thrown overboard.

The crew was disbelieving of the killing until those who saw the attempted murder of their captain told the others and indifference at the loss of the First Mate settled in.

“Monar,” Captain Graves looked worn, “You know enough to be First Mate and hold this heading?”

When assured Monar could, Graves told him to assume deck command, trim the ship, take Tomas on as Second Mate and then come to the captain’s quarters.

10

NIGHT CLOAKED THE SHIP by the time Monar finished his duties and knocked on Captain Graves' door. Receiving permission to enter, Monar stepped into a cabin barely lit by a sputtering oil lantern rhythmically swinging in its gimbal.

Sitting on the Long-nine gun carriage, the Captain scarcely was seen in the shadows casting about the room. Silent, he simply stared through the stern gun port at the waves, iridescent in the half moon.

"Captain?"

Graves' turned, Monar eyes met a face masked in sorrow, "Yes, Monar. What is it?"

"I'm reporting the ship is trimmed, sailing well and the slaves are supervised. Also, Sir, you asked that I report here when I had carried out your orders."

"Yes, I did…I recall that now. Very good then…thank you."

Monar delayed his leave-taking and waited.

"Are you still here, Monar?"

"Yes, Captain."

"Then don't leave. Pour us a drink, would you? Come and sit awhile."

Graves first few words weighed on him, although not surprising to Monar, "I'm stripped of my illusions, Monar."

"I can't imagine why you had any in the first place, Captain. It is past the time you should be rid of them. You have taken an albatross around your neck and you cannot free yourself. You can only accept—and go on from there."

"Is there no way I can rid myself of this—what I've done?"

"I can only speak truth, Captain. There is no balm and that you must face. Think, Captain, what could there be? Return the slaves? If you did, you'd be killed by King Naganga. Take them to Nigeria? You'd be hung by the British. Would that help your family? No, you can only go forward. You must face you are a slaver, your ship a slave ship. You must face that Ghost died to save you and English sailors died because of you. This you will never escape, nor should you."

"You know this, don't you, Monar? Somehow, you see it or feel it, don't you? I have no dignity left."

"Your mind has entered a bleak place my friend, there is only a dark ahead that you cannot avoid and that leaves you with only two choices—that is truth."

"What do you mean…how could you know what is truth?"

"I will not tell you, for my secrets are my own. Yet I know your choices. You can either put a gun to your head…or…"

Graves' did not wince at the comment; Monar now sure it was on the Captain's mind.

"Or what, kill myself or…?"

"Or you can rid yourself of your Christian morality to endure the blackness in your soul."

Shoulders sagging, the Captain was lost, "I don't understand you, Monar. Is that how you survived your lot—by accepting the diabolical?"

"Yes, it is what people call wickedness and I have it without guilt. Every man has evil thoughts, Captain. Call them wicked, foul, or immoral, yet they loom in everyone, unknown, until there is a need. You, the tough, Christian seaman, were like the rest, unwitting. Yet once tested, the evil came forth. Your hidden wickedness now exposed because you did not want to consider the consequences. Your only thought was to save your way of life and those around you, so evil swiftly emerged. I am different. I use evil as a device, a weapon; you used it simply as a way to keep that you had built. The hurricane destroyed your secure world and you're using the backs of slaves to restore it. "Yet even as you continue to use them, you can't accept what you have done—that will be your downfall."

Graves was mystified. Sitting there, enfolded in the night, he accepted Monar's assertions without doubt or rancor. In the near past, the Captain would never have allowed anyone to speak such words to him.

"If you're so wicked, Monar, why did you tell me that Toby Coffin had a deal with MacPherson to kill me?"

"Note, Captain, I told you only *after* I gauged you and saw Ghost's opinion of you. If I did not think you were the better of the people, I would not have told you."

Graves' grunted, "That's rather blunt, still I suppose that is self-preservation."

"Every action, every thought one makes is for self, one way or another, Captain."

"That's not true. Some of what I've done here is for myself, yes, but more is for my wife and my two son's legacies."

"Ah, that is true. Yet why you do it for your family is because it makes *you* pleased. Therefore, you do it for *your* pleasure. Everything, from a doctor who helps a patient, a priest who blesses a sinner or a mother who hugs her child, is done for self-pleasure."

"That is cynical and not true."

"Yes, Captain, sadly it *is* cynical, yet even more sadly, it *is* true."

Graves rose, paced back and forth in the dark cabin, "I can't argue the point right now, but I swear I will not take gold for what I've done."

"You *will* take your gold and use it. You will earn every bit before your life is over. Captain, listen to me. Refusing it will never free you and you'll need me to get through the future. I am your deeper self and I do what you cannot, but must be done. Don't you see your failings? You couldn't shoot Coffin; you couldn't say to throw him overboard. Why did you hesitate? What were you saving him for? He was a mutineer, he would have been hung by every court—except, ah yes, except, he could have claimed he was fighting you against slavery. And then, my friend, Coffin would be a hero, while you would swing on the gallows. White court's love to hang people. White slaver or black nigger, it matters not. As long as someone wobbles in the wind, it means the court is upholding the law."

"Monar, how do you think along those lines?"

"Very simple, Captain. It is ingrained. I've hung many people in my thoughts. Don't say you haven't. Despite your Christian beliefs, or should I say, superstitions."

"I'm troubled and dread you are right; my tomorrows are no longer mine to control." Graves went to his bunk, "I am weary, good night, First Mate."

Instead of his bunk, Captain Graves reverted to studying the infinite whitecaps. Confused in his life and mystified with Monar, he reflected on Poe's poem The Raven[4] and how the narrator wished to rid himself of the allegorical bird—yet never could, for it was his own creation.

---

[4] Edgar Allen Poe's, The Raven. Published to great success in 1845.

11

18 April 1847

"I'M TELLING YOU, JASON, we're returning to Barbados, so stop your carping!"

After leaving Ian MacPherson at Barbados, Captain Graves' sons, still appalled by the news their father was a slaver, returned to Havana. On the surface, they tried to doubt MacPherson, yet in their hearts, knew it true. John Thomas, resigned to that truth, gave more awareness to watching Jason descend, bit by bit into melancholy. Not having the vaguest idea what to do for his brother, and with what little patience he had, JT, despite Jason's opposition, paid off their crew. Discouraged and shorthanded, the brothers sailed the eighty-three foot schooner back into the Caribbean, laying over at Jamaica.

After even more weeks of waiting and with barely a modicum of forethought, JT set his mind on another run between the Windward Islands of St. Lucia and St. Vincent to Barbados. Once there, his singular thought would be to force a more passionate confrontation with Ian MacPherson.

Again, JT set the *Ocean Pearl's* course due east for Barbados.

« »

At the same time, plowing west for Barbados with a bone in her teeth, the fast clipper ship *Laurence Pike* roiled the seas into a tumult of foam tossed waves. Captain Graves breathed in the briny spray, memories streaming past while he struggled to live with the present.

Monar broke the spell, "Woolgathering, Captain?"

Graves' response was a wry smile, "In a way I suppose, yet I only hope to get these final few days out of the way without further menace."

"Actually, Captain, it's been a fast trip. These weeks may set a record."

Graves said nothing. Time meant naught compared to loss of slaves and crew from the black vomit, dysentery and small pox that ripped through the ship. Overripe yams, fetid water and poorly dried salted fish triggered sicknesses that led to dying and death, which in turn saw forty male, female and young slaves discarded overboard. Following that, twenty slaves, obviously having planned an uprising during their deck exercise, managed to kill four of the crew before shot or hacked down. So many dead or injured thrown overboard from this trade created the story of sharks shadowing this ship and countless others.

"You know something, Monar? The total loss of slaves to this point amounts to around twenty percent, just as Ian MacPherson had predicted. I thought that ridiculous, insane, and swore I'd do better…yet…I don't know…"

"You were used to commanding events, Captain; yet things happened beyond your control. When you think of it, given the few crewmen we have left and only a few more days to get through, we should think ourselves lucky to make port."

"Lucky? Perversely I suppose. But speaking of making port, no further thoughts?"

"Without Ghost and the *Laird* to birddog ahead, Captain, you've agreed we're without eyes so sail on regardless—correct?"

"I can't think of anything better and you said you could find Foul Bay if I find Barbados, so it all comes down to avoiding the Brits and possibly the American Navy."

Monar did not reply to the observation, there was another matter to deal with.

"Captain, now that we're close, we've got to discuss MacPherson."

"Yes, MacPherson. Won't he be surprised staring down the barrel of my Colt."

"I agree, however, we must make a plan, get him in a position where he cannot escape with the money, or call his Negros—not that I believe they would help him."

"Well, you know the lay of the land better than I, what do you think?"

"First, I get the slaves over to the warehouses in Dash Valley. That is halfway across the island and the mulattos at Foul Bay will help. Then, here is where I want you to decide what to do next—what do you think of my continuing on to Bridgetown and meeting with my Master telling him it went as he planned and Coffin killed you, but Ghost died?"

"That's no good, Monar; he'll wonder why it wasn't Coffin who reported to him and get his money. Let's not get bogged down on this. The main thing is to catch MacPherson unawares. Too much can happen 'twix the cup and the lip as they say. If we can get near him, my Colt will do the rest."

Monar "You'll shoot him?" Monar imparted a wicked smile, but was doubtful.

"No, I hope it doesn't come to that. We only want him frightened out of his wits enough to open that safe—and that gives me a simple idea. You say his slaves won't help."

"A little gold will assure that."

"Fine. So without them warning him can you get us to his house without his seeing?"

"Of course."

"Then it's settled." Graves gave a rueful laugh, "You go ahead to see that nothings out of the ordinary. If clear, our plan becomes straightforward. Smash in and demand our money."

Now all that remained was to hopefully reach Barbados without being tripped up by anti-slavery warships.

What Captain Graves and Monar didn't know at this time was the British Navy's attempts to stop the slave trade was extremely costly, yet unsuccessful overall. Due to this, Parliamentary action favored withdrawing navy ships from African and the Caribbean Islands. While there remained patrols of sorts, they were significantly conscribed in the West Indies and, as Barbados was the easternmost island, the *Pike* was virtually unchallenged by any British or American warships.

The result was their concerns were needless. Coming up on Barbados, Monar spied Ragged Point, avoided the coral reefs to the south and found Southeast Beach. After that, Foul Bay came up to the north and there they dropped anchor.

Monar's Mulatto's formed at the Bay and offloaded the slaves with whips, chained them to neck collar locks and led them toward Dash Valley. Monar then ordered the crew to work stripping the *Pike* of all indication of her past journey—slave decks torn out, chains and iron fetters thrown overboard, bilges pumped repeatedly, all while the hatches remained open for ventilation. Monar also took care to see that no one left the *Pike* and inform MacPherson of their arrival.

Drawing a map of the road west, Monar told Graves the distance across the island was only eleven or twelve miles as the crow flies, but the wandering dirt paths would make it more like thirteen to fourteen. It was a laughingly short trip after their thousand-mile journey, yet it could be fraught with as many snares and hazards. This point they both grasped and prepared as best they could.

« »

Leaving Captain Graves in a cabin in Weymouth, two miles east of Bridgetown, Monar continued on horseback to Bridgetown Port, north of MacPherson's docks. Wanting to find if there had been any changes since he had left, Monar talked with friends who commented only that there seemed to be more activity around MacPherson's manor than usual. Specifically, the slaves were concerned over wealthy people invited to view the house, slaves and plantation.

Knowing nothing of the problems MacPherson had with Graves' sons, Monar could not understand why there was increased activity at Ian's plantation. Finally putting it down to perhaps the British Authorities were mounting pressure on Ian concerning the failure of eliminating slaves in their territories.

With no other information of importance, Monar proceeded down along the Cheapside Docks toward MacPherson's home, which stood little more than a mile away. He casually noted ships tied up from Brazil and Argentina. Former slavers he thought. Then, stopping in mid-step, a chill ran through him. His gaze focused on a well-rigged schooner, obviously recently berthed, with two young men busy putting her in good order. One of the men the spitting image of Captain Graves.

Walking to the ship's stern, he wasn't surprised. **OCEAN PEARL SALEM, MASS. USA**. He started toward the two sailors.

« »

Captain Graves' mood grew blacker with each hour. Monar was due back by morning and here it was after noon and still no sign of him. Why? All he had to do was to check the lay of the land that nothing had changed and come back so the two of them could plan the next move. Yes, MacPherson could have been away or some such thing and if Monar had to wait until late and did not want to travel after dark due to the Maroon bandits, it could all take time. And, another terrible thought—what if Monar made a deal? He himself admitted he was diabolical. What if, at this very moment, he was coming with others to kill him? Well, Graves' knew, there wasn't the slimmest chance to escape if that were to happen. All he could do was sweat in the heat and wait.

He saw them coming, three men on horseback. Graves checked his Colt and slid it under the back of his belt. He recognized Monar and loosened the revolver. Then his knees buckled. He grabbed the porch railing. Countless thoughts jumbled around in his mind. His sons, home, the collapse of his empire, slavery, death, family, Seaward— diverse thoughts, yet they blew into the wind. Only one crystalized—Slavery. Then another—he whispered the words he hoped he never would. "My sons! Christ on a cross, my sons *know*."

He sat on the top step, head down, cradled in his hands. The riders stopped thirty yards away, spoke between themselves, after-which Monar came forward and dismounted.

"You recognize them, Captain?"

"Of course, you think I can't recognize my own sons? Why in hell did you bring them here—did you tell them what I've done?"

"MacPherson told them weeks ago and I *had* to bring them here—there was no choice. They were going to face Ian down about you and that would have been a disaster. Who knows what could have happened, but it would have destroyed our plot."

"What on earth caused them to come to Barbados?"

"Captain, it is too long to tell. Why they came to be here doesn't matter, the point is they're here. The other point is you have to face them, call it a fragment of your purgatory."

"How have they reacted?"

"They are your sons, Captain, how do you think they will react to you?"

"God, I don't know. Jason will be upset, but he will accept. JT? I don't know. I'm fearful."

With that remark hanging between them, Monar returned to Graves' sons.

"You must realize your father is upset at your being here and learning of his deeds. I'll warn you again, what happens next between the three of you will set the cardinal points for the rest of your lives. I ask you to understand the pressure he was under when the hurricane struck. You must remember the life he gave you and your mother before all this."

JT looked to Jason, who closed his eyes, saying nothing, "I won't speak for Jason, Monar, but we could have started over, rebuilt our fleet, made another life for our family instead of a deal with the devil."

"No, John Thomas, you could not have. Perhaps if you had his experience, but not now. Your father is too old. When you speak with him, you will hear it in his voice. It is easy to speak of starting over when one is young; yet age adds difficulty to every challenge and makes the simplest task a struggle. His mind failed him, told him what he had to do. He lives in purgatory, yet does not ask forgiveness, only tolerance. You do not have tolerance at present, for you are too young to grasp its meaning. But try, for as sure as you turn from him, you will regret it."

"It's because of slavery the girl I love is gone, Monar, and now you want us to forgive our own father for being a slaver?"

Monar stood to his full six feet, five inches, well over JT.

"It is because he is your father. Stop thinking of *you*, as all youth do. Hear my words. *I* don't ask you to forgive anyone, Master Mariner John Thomas Graves. That is up to you. Yet if you do not forgive—I do not say condone—simply forgive, then this day will bring you shame in your old age. This is a certainty."

JT tried to accept the words, knowing them to be spoken by a man who, even in the short exchanges they had with him, saw things they did not and knew the thoughts of others before they spoke. Still, JT thought him wrong.

More words would be useless, Monar sensed. He took the reins from the men; led the horses to a shed and then, too far away to hear, turned to watch the tableau unfold.

It was awkward, and never stopped being so. In his son's eyes, the Captain read all their lives were changed forever. He had hoped that…well, what had he hoped? Forgiveness, compassion? Fleeting, foolish thoughts. His only possibility to endure—they are his sons. If respect was past, then perhaps the blood tie remained.

Jason stepped up to his father, lunged forward and hugged him, "Dad…I'm sorry, I'm sorry for what you had to do…what happened. We can, you know, work it out…somehow."

"Thank you for saying that, Jason. I'm sorry for what I undertook too." He turned to his other son, "Do you feel the same JT? Can we work it out somehow?"

"The only 'somehow' I see, father, is for you take them back."

"Take them back? To Africa? That's too insane to even think it! What are you saying, is that the only way you and I can work it out? I've been through too much to do that."

"*You've* been through too much, father? *You?* What have those poor devils you stole been through?"

A spark flared in Graves, "Damn it—who in hell are you to judge me? The only way you've been tested is in an angry sea! You've had everything handed to you! Never struggled, fought and clawed to get ahead like your grandfather and I. Yes, I'm disgraced; I have no illusions on that score, but don't look at me like I'm evil! I lost everything, everything I built for your mother and you two. I'm not going to leave my life a meaningless, worthless blank. Do you understand me?"

"Think of what you're saying father, and don't blame us for your failings! You'll never be an honorable captain again! You've lost that and much more. We could have rebuilt it all, but you've failed *our honor*, the *family's* honor. Do you think what happened ends here? Everyone will know. Mother will be humiliated…"

"I'll kill anyone who insults her."

"That's right! Kill some more—and the next person and the next—where will you stop?"

"I won't listen to you! I saved *Seaward,* not you*!"*

Struggling to make his father understand, it suddenly became clear to JT, "No, father, Seaward will become a pile of stone."

The words grew louder. Monar came up and stood between them scowling, "Stop now, stop this for Christ's sake! You speak sharp words that will never be forgotten!"

They went silent, each enclosed in their own fears. Monar took in the minds of each in turn, "Gentlemen, we have but one problem here. Jason, you are ready to accept your father. Captain Graves, you feel you have done wrong, yet you will not stop until the bargain is completed. Jason will go along with that. It doesn't matter to me as long as I get my freedom and money. So…the one problem is you, John Thomas."

JT looked at each one. Jason eyes were pleading, his father's, angry. Monar was amused. Childish white men he thought, "Well, John Thomas, what will you do?"

"I'll leave."

"Leave, John Thomas? How? To where and with who? I doubt you have much money. You've no crew, or ship really—it's your father's, not yours. Are you going to swim away? It's fine to have ethics, yet don't let them blind you to your dilemma. Even angry, you're surely not that foolish."

JT was being boxed in. He wanted to lash out in frustration, yet couldn't, "You seem to know all, Monar, what do you suggest?"

"For the moment I'll hold off on that. Right now, Captain Graves and I have an overdue meeting with Ian MacPherson. You two go back to your ship and wait there. If I don't miss my guess, there's weather approaching and it is best you go there to safeguard her. When we collect our payment, we will meet you at the Cheapside Dock. Then I'll suggest what to do."

JT stared at his father, "You won't come with us now, father?"

"No."

Wind driven downpours lashed the trees and interrupted the conversation between the two men heading to MacPherson's plantation.

"Damn, Monar, we don't get torrential downpours like this in New England."

Monar turned his slicker's collar to the slashing rain, "We're used to it down here, but don't think we like it any better than you. Still, for now, it hides us."

The rapidly passing storms left in their wake sodden vegetation steaming in the sunlight. They confirmed their plan.

"All right, Monar, if you feel the slaves will not do anything until you tell them, I'll go along."

"As I said before, Captain, gold will work wonders with the slaves. Then we barge in, confront the bastard and demand your money—and mine—and my freedom."

They smiled to each other, "When my Master takes one look at your Colt I think he will be most agreeable to any offer where he survives."

They both were grim, although by this time Monar had devised another step in the plan. A step he knew Graves would not go along with.

MacPherson had been busy the past two weeks. The plantation and its slaves—which had evaded the eye of the British anti-slavery mandates by practiced application of bribes— were sold and he had received a considerable down payment.

After that, he had arranged to sell whatever amount of slaves coming off the *Laurence Pike,* sight unseen, at half price. If there were more than four hundred, they were a gift to their new Brazilian owners.

He was near ready. All that remained was to hear from his spy that the *Pike* and the *Laird* had dropped anchor at Foul Bay without Captain Graves. He had British purchasers lined up for the *Pike* and secretly arranged to have the *Laird* refitted at St. Kits. This way, if Graves' sons came back with fire in their eyes he would be gone, with no one knowing where.

Smiling to himself, MacPherson wished he could see the look in the son's faces when they returned to find him gone and their father feeding the fishes. Perhaps, he debated, could Toby Coffin—and Monar too—meet with accidents? Those savings alone would surely allow him to have all the servants he needed.

The rain was easing. Early, but get cleaned up for the prospective buyers he thought. He spoke into the shaving mirror, "Any day now my good fellow, the *Pike* will…"

The door hurtled open, the knob punching a crater in the wall. In his fright, Ian slashed the razor blade across his cheek. Dropping the razor, he fell against the wall, struck dumb, staring into the barrel of Graves' Colt —and the two men behind it.

Captain Graves and Monar grinned wickedly. Ian was dizzy, quickly seeing his world crashing around him. Wide-eyed, MacPherson still couldn't utter a world.

"Seeing the dead, Ian?"

He couldn't find his voice and hadn't noticed the blood trickling down his chest. Graves grabbed a towel off a rack, tossing it to him, "Here, we don't want you bleeding to death before we get our money."

They pulled him into the parlor, checking his boots for a knife—Ian gazing around helplessly.

"Don't look for any slaves to help, Ian, no one's coming to help you. You're all alone in your tight little world, not a soul to help."

MacPherson found his voice, "Why…why are you doing this to me, Graves? We had a *deal*!"

"Ah yes, you're right. However, you had two deals—didn't you? And the second would cancel the first very nicely. Toby Coffin kills me, and perhaps Monar. Then you get the slaves and the *Pike*. Very profitable deal indeed."

"Where did you get that crazy idea? You're making this up to rob me!"

Monar cocked his head, "I heard you scheming with Coffin before we left."

"You're making that up too!"

Graves spoke up, "Monar told me of the plot and Coffin tried to kill me. Nothing more need be said other than he and his gang are shark fare now. Let's go to your vault—*now*!"

Panicky as he was, MacPherson knew he could lose everything and that couldn't be allowed. He thought quickly. There was a Deringer[5] .45 Caliber flintlock in the safe.

---

[5] In those years, Derringer spelled his name with one 'r'.

If he could grab it quickly, he could shoot Graves and maybe get his gun before Monar could react. If the Deringer fired that is. Take the chance. Yes, it could work. Surprise them, get…

"Open it."

"I will, give me room, I'm nervous." Ian spun the dial, opened the door and reached in—too hastily.

As he pulled out the pistol, an incredibly sharp pain seared his hand; Monar's knife had pierced it through to the palm. MacPherson fell back dropping the weapon, agony spreading throughout his body. He was beaten; there must be something he could do, but what?

"Another trick, *Master*," Monar grinned, removing the knife, "and you will join Toby Coffin."

The safe disclosed a bounty of U.S. bills in all denominations, British Crown notes, some jewelry, and coin. The U.S. coin was in silver dollars, although most the Spanish doubloons, pesetas and reales were all old, and all gold. Salvagers had evidently discovered the wreck of a Spanish treasure galleon and paid for slaves in gold. None of that mattered to the three men; what did matter was the safe held a fortune.

Gritting through his pain, MacPherson tried to put a good face on it, "All right you two, I'm trapped. Take what I owe you and be gone."

Graves was ready to do that but a sly smile slipped past Monar's lips, "What you owe us? Come now, Master, just how much *do* you owe us? You kept me a slave for thirty years and then tried to have us killed. I'm sure you can recall that, we surely do. You would have killed us just now if I hadn't stuck you. In other words, we decide what you owe us."

Monar was as good as his word. Finding musty sacks some of the coins originally came in; he stripped the safe of its American coin, then divided the Spanish gold equally among the sacks.

Captain Graves said nothing, was there a right or wrong here? The line wasn't simply blurred, one didn't exist. He no longer knew the justification of their actions. Or, he wondered, was it he simply didn't care?

Monar held sway and it was to acquire what was there and devil take the hindmost. Nevertheless, he was not frantic in his conduct and did not deem his behavior the deeds of a thief. It was more the acting out his deeper thoughts of revenge for his time under MacPherson, the man he had to call Master for the years he was owned.

MacPherson, meanwhile, was in tears, whether from the pain of his stabbed hand or loss of his fortune, the men didn't care. In his greed, he had taken a chance of gaining more by killing Graves and now the price for failing was too much to bear. Damn Toby Coffin, he thought, damn this Captain, but mainly damn Monar. By some instinct, MacPherson knew that the first time they crossed paths the boy would be trouble, yet he felt compelled to buy him. Now, it wasn't merely trouble, now this big black bastard was his nemesis.

Monar, whose handsome mother was long deceased, was the result of breeding Negros in Georgia. Five years old was Monar, when MacPherson saw him and even then, smart as a whip. Still, it was the lash that never brought tears, the never blinking unfathomable eyes and the wrath prowling behind them that intrigued MacPherson. Still again, something more. Nothing one could put their finger on; as if he was possessed of a certainty others couldn't envision. It was bothersome and MacPherson bought him as a challenge. Educated him like a white man, however always made him remember he was black, made him utter Master. Bred him as a prized stallion and taught him his status in the universe—and to never expect to escape it. That succeeded until now and now this, Ian winced, this black bastard was giving him orders, towering over him, taking away what wasn't his.

MacPherson swore a great oath under his breath, "Once this is past, no matter the cost, I will hire thugs to track this black down, bring him back in chains—chains never to be removed. Yes, settle with Monar first, then Graves." The satisfying thought kept MacPherson intent on the thievery. Remember what he was seeing and use revenge to survive the sight.

Leaving Graves to watch MacPherson, Monar found the Mulatto boss and ordered him to bring a horse and wagon to the door. Giving the man four gold sovereigns, Monar left orders that the Mulatto would carry out once he and Graves left. The man's eyes went wide, but Monar assured him all would be well and the slaves would be legally freed and cared for by British.

Heading back to the basement, Monar was satisfied. He had relived this scene—with variation—countless times and now, it finally came to fruition. Deciding with Captain Graves it was time to leave, Graves took the third, and last, sack to the wagon while Monar said he would tie up MacPherson, then they could get to the Cheapside Dock, the *Ocean Pearl* and open water.

Graves' sons were curious, though saying nothing as the sacks were secured below. They reluctantly obeyed their father's order to cast off and follow Monar's bearings to round the south of the island, then north to Foul Bay.

While Jason and John Thomas attended to the schooner, Monar got Graves' attention and pointed to the shoreline. A plume of black smoke drifted over the trees.

The Captain was puzzled, "What's that? It looks to be near MacPherson's."

Monar, amused, asked Graves to sit down, "Captain, I am going to ease your conscience of a great burden so that you can begin to live again. That *is* MacPherson's manor burning and with it, I have undone your sins."

"What riddles do you confound me with now?"

"Listen, Captain, sit quietly while I explain. MacPherson is burning in that house as he will assuredly burn in hell…"

"What? You're saying he is dead in there? You killed him—are you mad?"

"Stay calm, Captain, your sons are looking."

"Damn it, Monar, don't tell me to stay calm. You've killed him and all *my* sins are undone?"

"Captain, think clearly. I killed MacPherson, not you. Therefore, I'm the sinner here and I'll go to whatever hell may overtake me. You however, are off the hook."

"Are you making a joke of this?"

"No, I'm trying to have you keep your sanity. So, please be quiet and listen."

Captain Graves settled down and Monar continued, "Think it through. MacPherson would have hunted us down like dogs. We would never have rested easy. Therefore, he had to be removed. I did it; you had no part in it. Do you see? You have no guilt. Next, I told the boss man, Keebe, to burn the house down. Let the authorities figure out what happened. MacPherson will be nothing but charred bones—especially so with the house falling in on him."

Graves winced, "Good, Lord, Monar, I've seen war, but no one who thinks like you."

"Yet I am right—right?"

"With your twisted logic, possibly. Curse me, but I somehow dread you are."

"Then I'll continue. You are unlikely to know, as I, that our departed friend had bribed the British agents here to look the other way, right under the nose of their Government. When rumors that MacPherson's slaves had not been freed as ordered, the agents falsified the reports for money. With Ian dead, there will be no further bribes, so now the agents have no reason not to report they found slaves and have them freed. The next item on my list to help you was to have Keebe inform the British there are other slaves held captive in Dash Valley. They'll be freed and the British have to take care of them as well, so they're probably better off than in the jungles of Africa waiting to be sold again. That means your problems are almost over."

"My problems are almost over? I see two major ones working here this very moment."

"Your sons?"

"Of course. Plus the slaves who died and we threw overboard."

Monar ignored the dead slaves, "Only one son will be a problem; Jason will do as you wish."

"You see that do you? That's more than likely true, but it still leaves JT, and he'll be a trial to bring around, if ever."

"Captain, he needs time. He's been wounded. He must have looked up to you very much and that makes his hurt that much the greater."

Graves didn't want to hear this and glanced from the smoldering fire on shore to the clouds scudding along the horizon, "You know Monar, it sounds strange for me to thank you for killing someone, yet you were right in doing it. He was not a just man."

The Captain returned to scrutinizing the clouds, "Christ, listen to me, after what I've done who am I to judge who is and isn't just?"

"You're going to have to reach inside to answer that, Captain. Anything further I might say to justify it would be meaningless. For now, I'll leave you to your thoughts and go help our crew."

Monar stopped a moment, "With your permission, Captain, I'd like to have a few words with John Thomas."

"You certainly may. If you could bring him around, you'd be a miracle worker."

"I've been called many names, Captain, but never that, for there is no such person."

For a while, there was no time for conversation. Thinking they would be longer at MacPherson's, the Captain and Monar had ordered the shipwrights at the bay to careen the *Pike* and check the hull planking below the waterline. The waters of the West Indies were notorious for the Teredo, a shipworm that rasped into wooden hulls and destroyed them.

Captain Graves had the foresight to use expensive copper sheets to clad the hull and used copper and zinc for the planking bolts to prevent corrosion. As it turned out, the *Pike* wasn't fouled as it was known some action between copper and seawater causes a poisonous film.[6]

Two major decisions came to a head while at Foul Bay. Surprisingly, Monar mentioned that he considered himself a freedman, no matter the legalities and he wanted to continue on to Salem with Captain Graves, if the Captain would like. There was no surprise when Graves readily concurred. Aside from an affinity for the Captain, the past events that transpired on the east side of the island were another good reason Monar decided to leave the Caribbean.

The second decision came after rancorous dispute. JT was not about to accept his father's deeds and every discussion between them was strained. Added to this, the Captain and Monar had to be careful in all their conversations, for both sons had no knowledge of the encounter at MacPherson's, his death, the money or the fire.

They believed their father had received money for the slaves—nothing more. This payment alone, JT considered blood money and even after learning the slaves would be freed did not ease the fact his father had been a slaver. Monar, arguing the Captain's case, could offer no solution to ease the tension.

As far as John Thomas and Monar, they tolerated each other for what they were; nevertheless, JT would not be swayed. Whether his father's reason was for family or Seaward did not matter to JT and the truth reared its ugly head each time they spoke.

Eventually, it was Monar, acting as intermediary, who struck upon an agreement. With the *Pike* renovated, she and the schooner would sail to Havana, the Mulatto crew would be paid off and a new crew procured from any of the *Pike's* former deckhands or other sailors. Past this point, only one other matter was certain; come hell

---

[6] The action of electrolysis was not known to seamen at the time-only that some process prevented fouling.

or high water, hurricane season or not, the goal was Salem. At the moment, what would happen there was not clear…or considered.

«»

15 July 1847

The *Laurence Pike* stood well offshore, north by east. Newly refurbished and under shortened sail, she lifted her bowsprit and burst through each surging wave, glorying in her newfound freedom. Old salts on fishing-boats watched, they knew a good ship possessed a soul and the sight of the two hundred-twenty foot long, black hull ghosting silently past held them in awe.

Only fifty yards away, she clove the sea, whispering to them. Those who heard as she passed felt a shiver run deep within. Leaving boats unsettled in her wake, men stared until the *Pike's* sun-bleached sails were lost in the haze of the horizon. Reverently, each wished her long life.

«»

Jason Graves chose to stay with his father on the *Pike*, while Monar, surprisingly, said he would crew on the schooner *Ocean Pearl*, notwithstanding John Thomas stating that while heading north he was going to tie off somewhere along the way.

Once in Savanna, and his reason for the diversion not given, he offhandedly mentioned he would return after dark. Of course, his purpose was to visit Charlee, although after that, JT had no idea what would follow. His lax plan soon dissolved.

Gordon Carlton spotted the schooner tied off at the wharf, "JT, over here! Hello, nice to see you looking fit."

JT, caught off-guard, noticed Carlton did not appear upset seeing him, "Hello, Sir. I've just come up from the Caribe on my way home. Thought I'd stop by and…well…you know…"

“I understand, JT, yet I’m afraid I must disappoint you. Charlee left for Europe three weeks ago, first port of call, Southampton, England.”

JT stared at Charlee’s father, “Is that the truth, Sir?”

“Please, JT, I ask you to not question my word.”

Carlton was being straightforward, “My apology, Mr. Carlton. I spoke rudely. I can only use my feelings for your daughter as an excuse.”

“I accept your apology without reservation, JT. I’m not so old that I can’t recall young love and all its impulsive acts. Yet, I again implore you to find your own life without my daughter. You knew her for a few hours; don’t let that fleeting time ruin your life. Charlee is flighty; you would know that if you knew her longer. Don’t expect her to wait, please, for your own sake.”

JT ignored the plea, “She will be back in two years?”

“That is the arrangement as far as known; if you want to call it that. London, Paris, Rome, the Greek Islands and wherever else strikes them.”

“Then you’ll see me in two years, sir.”

“I’ll be honest with you, JT, I don’t look forward to that—and you shouldn’t.”

“She was not there?” Monar’s remark startled JT as he returned aboard.

“How on earth did you know I was intent on seeing a woman?”

“Not supernatural I assure you, John Thomas, merely perceptive. Your gaze and thoughts the last few days could only be over a woman. Your dejection when you returned so abruptly renders my guess a reality. Also, you mentioned before a girl you loved once and lost.”

“Your way of reasoning is quite simple when you explain it.”

Without prying further, Monar asked if JT wanted to slip their lines.

“No, we’ll layover. I know this leg of the Savanna, yet I don’t want to run it after dark.”

"Hello on the *Ocean Pearl*."

Groggy with sleep, JT stumbled to the main deck in the dark. He saw Monar glancing toward the dock and pointing to a darkie holding a lantern.

"What the devil do you want at this hour?"

"Sir, this here's a message from my Massa, Mr. Carlton. He say I not to wait."

JT returned below, lit a lantern and broke the seal to the missive.

My Dear John Thomas,

Firstly, let me apologize for neglecting to ask of your father. I hope you and your brother found him in good health and spirits although, as we spoke, it appeared there was something more than Charlee troubling you.

Be that as it may and certainly not meant to pry, I wish to offer to employ you and your vessel for the next few weeks hauling planking from Pennyworth Island, just north of Savanna, down to Brunswick.

The plank will be herded down from upriver at Tillman, South Carolina and you would have to take a trip up there to explain the volume of plank you want delivered for each shipment, and when. I'll explain all this if you are interested.

I do hope you will accept my offer. I need a dependable shipper and I estimate you will be kept busy for six to eight weeks.

If you are interested, I will be just south of the docks at Winslow Ironmongers—ask anyone— around 10:00 tomorrow morning. Hope to see you then.

Sincerely Yours,

Gordon L. Carlton,
This 18th of July 1847
At Hammersmith

Monar, who had assumed the position of First Officer, poked his head into the cabin, “Everything all right, John Thomas?”

“Yes, we’ve been offered cargo for a few weeks from Savanna south to Brunswick.”

“I really don’t know what that means, where are we and what cargo?”

JT smiled, “I guess I really haven’t been too forthcoming, have I? We’re in Savanna, Georgia. If I accept the offer, it will be a few weeks of on-loading lumber here and dropping it off down in Brunswick, that’s Georgia also. Still, it will mean we won’t see father for a while.”

“It matters not to me, Captain. When we’re to see Captain Graves, that time will come.”

“Well, I’m thinking about it. Might be best if I stay away from Seaward for a while.”

“Why is that?”

“Let father and Jason talk with mother without my getting into the argument.”

“That could be best, you do have a temper.”

JT shook his head, “You do realize you’re speaking to your Captain?”

“Yes, and I’m black, as well. Two sins, John Thomas.”

“That’s not a sin and you don’t feel sinful at all, Monar. Another thing, after all our conversations on the way here, why do you still call me Sir or John Thomas? I’m called JT.

“From what I’ve heard, only your friends call you JT.”

“Then when we’re off deck or alone, call me JT. That is, if you’d like to.”

12

THE NEW PROPELLER DRIVEN tugboat wrestled up-bound to Tillman against the current of the Savanna River while JT and Monar inspected every aspect of the propulsion system.

"What do you think, Monar? Noisy and stinks, not really sailing in my book."

"True, yet it is taking us where we couldn't go with the schooner without a lot of trouble and a long time, same as when your father and I were on the Bandama Blanc."

The reference bothered JT and he shut it from his mind, "I suppose this is the coming thing, but I don't like it and its good the mill owns woodland because this thing sure is gobbling it up."

"That is the truth, Captain. There must be a better way to feed that boiler because you'd have to tow acres of trees to cross an ocean. Maybe they could feed it cotton."

They were still having a good laugh when a sign in bold letters hove into view along the east bank of the river—ADAMS LUMBER & COTTON ENTERPRISES, Tillman, SC.

As the steam tug's captain tied her off at the pier, a heavyset black man greeted them on the dock, "Welcome to Adams Lumber, gentlemen. The post rider said someone would be moseying up here sometime."

JT looked about, admiring the area, "Thank you. Is Mr. Adams about?"

The black man turned jovial, "I can see Gordon didn't say anything. I'm Adams, Samuel Adams, no middle name to be exact, just like the real Mr. Adams. This is my establishment."

Monar guessed that already—no slave would have acted as offhandedly to a white man as Adams.

JT flushed, "My apologies, Mr. Adams. I feel foolish."

"No need for that. I assume you are Captain Graves and that Gordon didn't tell you about me—his sort of joke I suppose. Anyway, let me show you around while we discuss business."

JT introduced Monar, which told Adams that the big black was not a slave and was to be treated as an equal.

The property Adams owned covered nine hundred acres of fertile riverbank and timberland. It was an efficient and thriving business, with blacks everywhere, falling trees, stripping and hauling trunks on sledges to the three mills positioned strategically about the forest.

JT also noticed the plantings of hundreds of sapling. He was impressed although he did not see cotton plants.

"I thought I'd see cotton fields—to go with your sign."

"Ah, yes, cotton. Well, to tell you the truth, I grew up in the cotton fields, Gordon Carlton's in fact. To try to keep a long story short, I had a mechanical-like mind, so Gordon and I copied one of Eli Whitney's cotton machines and used waterpower to run it—worked half-assed, but it worked. Still, Gordon didn't have to pay no rent to Whitney and that partner Phineas what's-his-name. Course, lots a people done the like and those two went broke. Eli made a fortune later on muskets but that's no mind to my story. Anyway, Gordon was pleased with me, give me books, had me teached, so when I become freed he knew of land up here and loaned me enough to buy a piece. I pays him back, with the extra he charges, he gets business for me, loans me more and here I am, ready to buy more land. And to finish my story, the reason for 'cotton' on the sign so's I not forgets my past."

By the time the story been told, they were sitting on the veranda of a neat two-story house drinking Juleps. The noon sun sparkled the river, Wood storks and old growth oak hunched together over the water like weary men and JT found he was relaxing, yet the humidity hung heavy on him. Neither Monar or Adams were bothered by it.

"You've a nice place here, Samuel, but the heat gets to me."

"You're from the north, way north by the sound. We're used to this, but when that happens Captain, you sweats and when you sweats you needs more liquids."

With that, he called into the house for more and a fine-looking black girl soon appeared carrying a laden tray. JT started to rise, Monar held his arm down. Adams saw the Captain didn't understand, "Captain, I see that Monar recognizes, yet perhaps I should have made myself clear from the beginning. Other than the white bosses, I'm the only freedman here, the only one. Not even Sara here's free."

JT was confused, "I'm not following you, Samuel. Who are these people then?"

"Why they is slaves, like I was. Bought them at auction just like fine white folk do. I own them; treat them like I learned from Mr. Carlton. Fair and firm."

Stunned, JT struggled for words, "I can't get a handle on what you're saying. You're a Negro and yet you have Negro slaves? How could this be? How could you do this?"

Samuel couldn't prevent a smile, "Young man from the north, you needs a lesson."

JT sat back, too confused to do anything else.

"Now, Captain, I'll tell you why I can do this. I'm sure you've seen all the northern papers and anti-slavery crackpots spouting off about all us poor beaten slaves—and it's all true. There are terrible happenings here. Hangings, whipping, burnings, runaways torn up by dogs and even worse. But not here. Here a slave's treated fairly, not kindly, no. I can't afford to coddle and survive. My slaves know that if I go under, they'll be on the block again and then they doesn't know what will happen to them. That's why they work hard here, because that threat is always hanging over their heads. Better the devil they know than an unknown white devil."

"But despite that, they are still slaves! They're owned by you."

Adams called into the house, "Sara, come out here!"

"Yes, Mr. Sam?"

"I'm going to give you freedom, a fifty dollar gold piece and I want you to leave—now."

She shrank back, frightened, "What did I do? I'm sorry. Please don't send me away!"

"Then how about I sell you to the Captain here, he offered me a hundred dollars."

JT started to protest, Monar shushed him.

"What have I done, Sir? Please—I won't do it again!"

"I'm only teasing, Sara. Testing my friend here. He patted her bottom, "I would never give you away—not to anyone for any amount. Now you run along."

Sara beamed, ran her hand along Adam's shoulder and slipped back inside.

"You're missing the point, Samuel. No matter how well you treat them, they are still slaves. Don't you follow what I'm saying? I mean…"

Of course Adams understood; he was once a slave. JT felt the fool. He fell back into the chair, "I…I can't explain the moral…"

"Of course you can't, Captain, so don't try to enlighten me, 'cause you can't. If these people, people the white man brought to this land and made slaves of, were ever set free, what would they do? Where would they go? Back to the jungle? Blacks here were born here. They have no family; doesn't know where they came from. Who would take care of them? You? Would you support one of them? Ten, twenty of them? No, course not. You'd run from that. So you see, you condemn this, which is noble of you, yet offer nothing to replace it. I support and protect them."

"You protect them? From who—white people? How could you possibly protect them if some whites decide to take over here?"

"If you would like to know, I will tell you. They, the whites, were warned. Funny isn't it? Me threatening white folk. Yet it's really quite simple. They believe someone they love will die if they so much as look crosswise at me. They think I keeps a band of red painted Caribe Arawak's in the bayou, the swampland, to protect me. They think they give me trouble and one or more Arawak's will slip into the white Massa's home and slit his throat or some loved ones. That is how I protect my people and runaways. White folk fear."

"Why should they believe that?"

"Why? Because, my white friend, it has happened. Not by Caribes, but it has happened."

The shipping program agreed on, the steam tug moved easily downstream while Monar watched JT, gazing without seeing, into the gnarled old-growth woodlands.

"Lost in thought, JT?"

Returning to the present, JT was lethargic, "Yes, guess I show it. Then again, perhaps I'm not thinking at all."

"You are thinking. It is that your thoughts are all jumbled, too many of your values—or should I say principles—are challenged all at once."

"I would like to say only that I was thinking about this ship, Monar. That I'm fascinated by this propulsion system and let it go at that. Still, you're right; it's this trip, Samuel Adams, Gordon Carlton, my father—everything is muddled in my head."

"Do you want to talk about it?"

"I don't think talk will do any good."

"Then when you do, we will, JT."

With that statement, Monar moved over to focus on the jiggling needle of the steam pressure gauge. JT stayed put, rubbing the stubble on his chin, "Hey, Monar, now's a goodish time as any. Let's go aft."

Monar smiled. JT, he thought; if something bothers, get it out, as he should. Yet this, Monar knew, would not be trivial.

JT scrutinized the wash from the propeller, "You know, I don't follow what's happening in this world. I hardly ever had much contact with black people. Oh, sometimes talk with them on the ship, especially the young ones. They'd want to know why a tiller goes one way and the ship goes the other, or why the flag flies forward when the ship moves forward. Innocent stuff like that. The older ones I never asked what they did in life, never asked what they did at home, or even if they had a home other than the sea. In other words, didn't know them. They were as good as the rest of the crew, so I simply didn't treat them any different from the rest. That's the way father taught us."

"Your father was a good teacher."

"Perhaps. Too bad he didn't practice what he preached."

"Things happen, JT, events can overwhelm some people."

"I know, but what's right or wrong here? A man like Gordon Carlton, I really liked him—honest, straightforward, his handshakes his word. Yet he sees nothing wrong with keeping slaves," JT dropped his head, "and his daughter doesn't see anything wrong with it either. Then take Sam Adams. He was a slave, became a Freedman like you and now buys slaves. How can that be condoned? How can any man, never mind a black man, own someone?"

"What an insulated world you lived in, JT. What is it with you? Slavery didn't touch you so you didn't give a fig? And now, now that your family is involved, you get upset. There's always been slavery and it will continue way forward from here and us. You know that."

"That's not necessarily going to be true, Monar. Look at the Brits, they're wiping it out. There's also anti-slavery talk up North."

"JT—don't fool yourself. The British have *officially* stopped slavery in their country but they still have enslavement with indentured servants and look at child workers—that's just another form of bondage. Up North, Yankee land? They have child labor they do nothing about. And do they think the South will set their slaves free without a fight? The South would go broke. Do you think the Yankee's will fight to free them? It's easy to *talk* war. From what I hear, the country had enough of it in 1812. You think anyone's going to war over slaves. My God, that would be a disaster—for both the North and South."

At this moment, when the conversation was getting deeper than JT could discuss with conviction, the tug grounded into one of the ever-shifting sandbars along the Savanna. Naturally thinking the captain would be angry, they were surprised he had no particular response. The tug's transmission, was shifted into reverse while he muttered, "…where'd that blasted bar come from?"

Gears clunked. The propeller reversed its rotation to thrust the water forward under the hull. The captain smiled at the two wind sailors, "See? The propeller's enclosed in an iron cylinder to protect it. When we runs aground, we reverses, and the propeller pushes water forward under the hull and scours the sand away."

Backing off from the bar, the tug's captain was smug while the two sailors' shook their heads, holding more respect for screw propeller stink-boats. Thoughtlessly, they failed to go back to their initial subject, choosing instead to consider the ramifications of powered ships.

«»

By the look of things, the contract with Gordon Carlton would finish up in two weeks. It proved to be a lucrative agreement for both parties. The arrangement with Carlton, kept on a business level only, meant that JT was not asked to Hammersmith. The two were cordial, yet strangely, the gulf between them grew each time they met. Even more strangely, Logan Carlton, Gordon's son, became quite affable and would stop by the Savanna docks or just happen to be at Pennyworth Island to ask how the work was progressing. One reason for his interest became known when he asked to actually work as a deckhand on the journey to Brunswick.

Curious about such a request, JT agreed and once there, Logan helped unload plank and generally worked as a plain laborer for the ship and around the wharf. These were hard jobs, especially so for someone, although physically strong, was using muscles not conditioned for the work at hand. Yet Logan never complained and that was peculiar.

It became obvious there was something on his mind when he approached JT and Monar at the end of the day. Instead of wages, which had never been discussed, Logan asked if they could go by way of the Gulf Stream on the return leg to Savanna. JT knew the Stream was hours off Saint Simon's Island, quite out of the way, yet he consented. Logan had an unstated reason and JT and now Monar wanted to hear it.

JT's crew added sail and with a stiff following breeze, the schooner roused the aquamarine waters of the Gulf Stream. Even tired sailors lifted their heads to the spray and came alive as the port gunwale came level with the water line. The *Ocean Pearl* thundered along—called 'wet foot sailing'—they all loved it. Observing Logan closely, JT saw him nervous at first and then, realizing the schooner was not going to roll over, he began to enjoy the sight and thrill of an unladen ocean schooner on a dash downwind, its sails radiant in the evening sun.

Turning to find JT watching, Logan smiled, gave a carefree salute and moved up to the bow as it collided with the waves to send billowing spray high over the bowsprit to soak him.

At twilight, JT eased off the wind, gave up the helm, calling to Logan and Monar to sit with him, "Well, Logan, did you find what you wanted?"

Logan, a mist of salt still upon his face and blond hair, flushed, "Yes, John Thomas, I did and I'll tell you why I wanted this experience. My father is friends with men named Bancroft and Upshur. George Bancroft is Secretary of the Navy and he started a Naval School in Annapolis two years ago. Have you heard of it?"

JT knew of Bancroft, as he was from Massachusetts and knew but little of the school. Monar had no knowledge of either man or the school.

Logan continued, "Well anyway, father asked Mr. Bancroft to be my advocate to Mr. Upshur. He became Superintendent of the School in '45, and I've been accepted on father's word and my record at Princeton. Princeton's in New Jersey, but I went there for only two years—it was too damn cold. Anyhow, to be honest, I haven't known what to do with my life and I don't see myself as a plantation owner. What I'm trying to get to is, I've been accepted to the Naval School and as I've never even been on any ship other than side-wheel riverboats, I wanted to see if I liked the deep sea. I find it all quite rousing."

JT couldn't help but laugh, "I can understand liking this," JT swept his hand around, "this is glorious, yet there are many more times that it's simply boring or terrifying." Looking to Monar, JT asked, "What do you think? Think Logan would make it in the Navy?"

Monar studied Logan, who was not used to a black boldly scrutinizing him and surprised that JT would ask advice from a Negro man, freed or not. When Monar finally did speak, he was blunt, "It seems to me that Mr. Carlton here has all the physical requirements to be a handsome naval officer. The rest, well it's hard to say, my knowing him such a short spell."

Monar stopped, appeared lost in thought, "There are two roads open to gentlemen such as you, Mr. Carlton. One, sit back and have slaves help you lollygag around the rest of your life."

Logan bristled, yet remained discreet; he knew JT viewed Monar with regard. For his own part, JT felt that as he had asked Monar his opinion, he had the right to state it—although Monar was edging along the margin of disrespect.

Monar went off on a different tack, "The other road, is more fraught with unknowns. Most especially, employed by his country to go and fight its wars—such as in Mexico right now. If you so choose, Mr. Carlton, it could lead you to glory, perhaps to being viewed a hero in some war. Or worse, a hero in a lost war."

JT and Logan were puzzled, "You see a hero in a lost war being worse than being dead?"

"Yes, think it through. The rest of your life you'd waste spent cursing those who failed you."

JT pondered this answer, "I'm beginning to follow your point, though it be harsh. Still, this humble sailor doesn't want to go down that pathway and start discussing it—because you see life with a curious perception, Monar—one an ordinary person doesn't comprehend."

Logan Carlton was mystified. His studies in the classics included the Greek, Latin and the philosophers—although he considered them more dreamers than thinkers. Now however, here was this black Freedman acting like an equal—or worse, an intelligent, pretentious black. Still, Logan wasn't stupid, not by a long shot, he decided not to enter the fray and take the chance of losing any debate, "John Thomas and Monar, I'm afraid the sea air has tired me. I'll retire now."

«»

The contract was completed, JT paid off; it was time to leave for home. Gordon Carlton said his farewell the previous day and, at the final moment before casting off, Logan, on a gray stallion came clattering onto the dock and reached for JT's hand, seemingly repentant, "One last thing before parting. My father told me how you and he tricked me regarding the duel that didn't happen and you having but one revolver. I was angry until I realized your doing so saved my honor and my life. This is a thank you from an impulsive, foolish person. To you Monar, I'll consider your thoughts, yet believe this; one thing I will not do is sit about letting my slaves wait on me. You know, I have the strangest feeling we three will meet again—and it has nothing to do with my sister."

The stallion pranced back and vaulted off the dock. Logan was gone with a wave.

"He turned out to be not such a bad sort after all, eh, Monar."

Monar didn't answer directly, "He may be right—about meeting again, that is."

« »

Salem 4 September 1847

Salem's inner harbor slid into view, then the long Pickman wharf and finally, the Graves' dock. They berthed behind the *Laurence Pike* where two rather shabby looking men took their thrown lines, yet did not tie the schooner off. One of the men shouted, "You the *Ocean Pearl*?"

"We are. Who are you?"

"You John Graves?"

"Yes damn it! Now tie her off."

Clumsily, obviously not seamen, the two did so and then went back to the *Pike* as Monar and JT busied about setting spring lines. The crew, already paid off, hurriedly disappeared up the ramp leading to town. "Not too much of a welcome for us from these two dimwits, Monar."

Monar murmured that was true, and looked about carefully, "Something's odd, JT. You pointed out Seaward on the rise as we came in, ample time for them to see us and come down. Yet they did not and these two ratty looking men make me ponder. Is this your usual homecoming?"

"Of course not. I was so glad to be home and then meeting those two blockheads on the *Pike*, I overlooked no one was here from Seaward. You're right, let's see what's going on here."

As they approached the *Pike*, the distinct odor of burnt, wet wood was noticeable and now there were four men, two of whom casually held clubs.

"Who's in charge here?"

One of the men stepped forward, "I am, you the Captain's son?"

"Yes, what the devil is going on? What's that smell?"

"Well, it was this way. One of my men fell asleep on watch here. Someone tosses a bucket of whale oil and a torch onto the forward decking and we fought it as best we could without no goddamn fire brigade to help. Got it out, we did. Weren't too much damage and I kicked the watchman's ass off the boat."

JT was speechless and Monar asked, "Why would anyone try to set fire to the *Pike*? Where were the firemen?"

"It's the damned town folk, who else? No one wants to help." The speaker stopped, a thought struck him, "You ain't been in touch with the Captain have you? He ain't told you. Come on, I'll shows ya at the bow."

The two travelers stood in shock for there, on the black hull in white paint was one word—SLAVER.

Taking a step back, JT realized the secret was out and the fire and paint were responses by outraged townspeople, their revulsion being played out. His coming face to face with the shame was obvious to the *Pike's* guard as he continued, "It's been in that Boston paper, the Herald. Said something like 'Clipper Ship Salem Slaver'. And you thinks that stinks? They burned your dock-way one night and broke some windows up at Seaward. 'Course the Captain's men caught some o' them and that warn't pretty for them, it warn't."

JT became furious, "Seaward? Some bunch attacked Seaward? Is my mother all right?"

"Oh, you don't even knows that? She'd left afore then, for her folks weeks ago I thinks—right afore your brother left."

The news, piling worse on the top of bad, somehow strengthened JT. Watching JT's bearing straighten, Monar admired the change and waited. It didn't take long.

"You, whatever your name is, get me a carriage to take us to Seaward."

"We've a wagon one of my men can take you up in."

It was dusk by the time they passed through paint-spattered columns at the entrance to Seaward. JT was lost in thought over the news they had received at the dock and Monar remained silent, knowing what anger and grief must be going through his friend's mind. In the darkening sky, JT was returning home on the rear of a dray to a house now guarded like a fortress.

Two more strangers met them at the entrance door. "Where's my father?"

The guards anticipated his arrival, "The Captain's in the great room, he ain't well."

Draped windows and walls soiled from flickering oil lamps added unnecessarily to the murkiness. The stink of tobacco and dank sea air assailed them as they approached the Captain. They couldn't hide their shock, "Father, what on earth's happened?"

"Hello, my son…come here, you too Monar…it is good to see you both well."

Monar was saddened and he knew, "You have jungle fever, Captain."

"Aye, Ague Fever…worse ever…in the Philippines years past…sweating, fever chills. It's God's way of…of punishing me. Monar, do you know…I hear their screams? I see them...I…"

Monar quickly saw in a moment, it was not solely the Ague Fever. The Captain's unforgiving mind had devastated him and there was no sense arguing his beliefs. His guilt from being a slaver had trampled the mind and fever ravaged the once sturdy body. Monar did not question the progression; JT would not accept it.

Not to be denied, the illness was progressing. The townspeople and the New England Anti-Slavery Society picketing Seaward made the Captain hide. The appalling loss of respect and prestige cut him. Unable to endure his wife leaving and the disappearance of his son, Jason, compounded his tension. Reduced to a shell of his past, the word *slaver* snaked into his brain and distorted his beliefs. Without spirit, a lost man, he no longer was interested in living.

Three people had made his life. Mary, now gone from it, Jason disappeared, God knows where and John Thomas, his favorite son, who still could not tolerate his father's deed.

Speaking with his father, JT was at a loss, every question brought a negative response.

"Where has mother gone?"

"I think…to her family. You knew she's a…Lowell."

"Does that mean she's back in Boston?"

A shrug, nothing more.

"What's happened to Jason, Where'd he go? Did he just up and leave?"

"No…I think he was…kidnapped."

JT was stunned, "You're serious? Why do you think that?"

"I'm told…rumor. I don't know why, he took…not a thing."

While JT and Monar considered this, Captain Graves fell asleep, snoring loudly. Monar saw the scotch bottle lying empty on the floor and took JT aside.

"There's no sense trying to find out more right now, JT. Let us go and have a drink."

Brooding after attempting to get more from his father and failing, JT sent two letters to his mother's family asking when and where he could meet his mother. He waited futilely.

Only one trip to town told him he was not welcome, due to the sins of the father. It took Monar to set a course for him. Where was his brother? The guards only knew he went down to town one evening, or at least headed that way, and never returned.

Jimmy Pickman, JT's only remaining friend, privately tried to help but the sole concrete fact he could pick up was the last time anyone saw Jason, he was drunk and alone as he left Rope's End Tavern on Derby Street. The constabulary was indifferent, stating officially that Jason ran away as a direct result of his father's sins.

Monar, unknown and not tainted by the Graves' name, wandered the taverns for nights on end, always agreeing with the tenor of the disgust for the family on the hill. Ultimately, one night in the mostly vacant Rope's End Tavern, a drunken patron—and a hint. Monar offhandedly mentioned Jason was as bad as the father and he hoped Jason wouldn't return. The drunk laughed, "Oh, no worry, he won't return, unless they lets him."

As sly prodding brought no further rejoinder, Monar finished his drink and tossed a coin on the table for the drunk. Wandering out into the shadows, Monar was patient, waiting. The drunkard, now stalked by Monar, shuffled past the last gas lantern into the darkness.

A heavy hand gripped the man's shoulder. The grasp shocked him so much he staggered into a picket fence, after which he stood rigid with fright, exactly as Monar wished him.

"You know where Jason Graves is. Don't bother to say no my dear fellow, for if you do I'll carve you from neck to belly and leave you to die."

With that, Monar held his bolo so that the blade shown in the moonlight, "Tell me you believe me."

The man nodded franticly.

"Now, where is Jason? I will not ask again."

The blade terrified the drunkard and the truth hurriedly emerged.

"They was only going to scare him, you know? Only going to chase him off. They wasn't…"

"That's not what I'm asking. Now I told you quietly I was not going to ask again." The knife glinted.

"He's in a fort being built on Georges Island. Please, don't hurt me!"

"That remains up to you. What fort and where?"

"Fort Warren. It's in Boston Harbor, on Georges Island. Please don't..!"

"I don't believe you, you're lying and I told you not to. Why would anyone take him down there? You're not making sense with all the people who must be around."

The blade swung, barely missing the man—it all came out in a rush, "There ain't no work there right now, it's done in fits and starts. The islands deserted. One of the people who done took Jason worked there, that's how they knew it was empty. I've been down there to bring Jason food. There's cells underground, that's where they keeps him."

Monar mulled the story over. It was so stupid; he felt it to be true. It was most of the information he wanted. Just a little more and then threaten the informant.

"What's your name?"

The change of questions so unnerved the man he blurted out, "Ephraim Coffin."

Monar smirked as the memory came to him, "You have a brother, Toby?"

"Ya, he's older than me, ships out as First Mate in the Caribbean."

Monar couldn't help showing a wicked grin, "Not any more he doesn't. Now I'm going to ask a few more questions, Ephraim my friend. How you answer them is very important to *you.* Are you following me, you understand me?"

"Yes…Sir…sir."

"Good. Now, how do you and I get into this unfinished fort when we get on that island?"

The drunk wet his pants, but he went gamely on, "The dock and sally port is on the leeward of the island. To get in, the doors ain't on the sally port yet. You go along what they call the Corridor of Dungeons, that's a two story granite wall. Then there's a stairway going down on the left. After that, I'm not sure, I had a guide with a torch and didn't pay no attention…"

Monar screamed, the blade flashed, "You're lying!"

"Dear, God, No! I'm not. Please, I swear on my mother's grave!"

"How many people are there? Quick now!"

"There's always a man stays on the dock to keep people away, tell them they're trespassing. Then there's always two with Jason. That's all."

"How many kidnappers altogether?"

"Seven, seven in all. They takes turns."

"Including you?"

"No, no. I weren't in on what happened. All I done was bring them food."

"When do you go again?"

"Day after tomorrow."

Monar had all the information he needed, "Answer me one more question. What do they expect to do with Jason at the end of all this?"

"I don't know. They don't neither know what to do. I'm scared for him."

“I’ll bet you are, particularly now. You don’t know who I am, do you?”

“No, but you is surely big.”

“Well, now my friend, I’m going to be honest with you. Go home and forget all about this meeting. I know your name and I’ll tell others to find where you live. If you open your mouth about this, you will be what we call in the Islands, walking dead. Your life depends on saying nothing and if you do as I say, no one will ever know you told. Remember what I tell you. One thing more, don’t bother delivering food there in two days.”

«»

The fort and its half-finished ramparts were reconnoitered with binoculars as they sailed the channel waters surrounding Georges Island. As dusk approached, they watched three people roaming the dock until two walked away through the sally port.

At present, the *Ocean Pearl* lurked to seaward of the Island where their chart showed five fathoms. At slack tide, they pulled in the dory’s painter and waited. Then, with only moonlight as a guide, they rowed easily on the incoming tide.

Pulling the dory across the shingles to above the high tide line, they began to walk halfway around the steep embankments of the seaward side of the island until, once near the dock, Monar took the lead. He signaled to stop upon seeing the glow from a lantern up on the dock. They had agreed to a ruse that, if they could not surprise the lookout, Monar would hide and JT would call out for help and as the lookout came near, Monar would grab him from behind. It now became apparent even Monar couldn’t surprise the guard, for the dock was long and the three-quarter moon and lantern foiled that.

They went to the second plan. “Help, help, I’m hurt.”

The man got a fright, then took up his Deringer and oil lantern. He stepped to the end of the dock, looked around, then started along the shore while JT stayed kneeling and crying out.

"Who the devil are you? What's your…" He held out the lantern, "By Christ! Your John…"

The pistol rose as Monar's bolo slashed into bone at the nape of the man's neck. The lantern fell from a dead man's hand, rupturing oil that flared on the rocky shore.

Monar pulled JT to his feet and hurried him behind an inshore berm while the flames sputtered and died on the damp shingle.

JT was in shock, he had never witnessed a man being killed, "My, God, Monar! I, I didn't think it would…"

"Be quiet! We must wait to see if anyone comes."

Monar moved to view the entrance to the sally port. No one, no boats seen offshore, all remained silent.

He spoke to JT, "So now, my friend, do you have a problem with my killing that man? I had the choice you know, kill him, or let him kill you. I thought you'd prefer it this way."

JT was awkward, "I realize that, Monar. It was just so quick…so shocking."

"The first time I saw a man killed, it was slow. He was flogged to death over two days."

"I'm sorry, Monar. I know we agreed this might happen, yet it was so unexpected."

"Did you know him? He knew you."

"I knew the voice, but can't place it."

"Whatever, it is best not to let anything else surprise you, you have the Colt."

There was no one by the sally port or along the granite wall. The stairway heading down took them into the dark where JT stopped at an open doorway.

He whispered, "This is no good, Monar, we can't see a damn thing to know where we're going."

"I can see; I have cat eyes."

"You're serious, you can see in this?"

"Not well, but enough. Now we must become quiet and listen for sounds. We're in a large room. Put your hand on my belt and follow, if something is in the way I'll tell you."

Sliding his hand along the wall and looking ahead, Monar went on for a few yards, then whispered, "There is another stairway down. What do you smell?"

"I don't…wait…oil, lamp oil."

"Yes, it's venting up the stairwell. Yet there's barely the slightest glow, JT. Come, follow quietly."

They went down the second base of stairs; Monar strained to see and found they were at the edge of a corridor and turned the corner. Now, they saw a glimmer along the walls, but more than that, they became aware of raucous voices. Echoing off the walls were vulgar shouts they couldn't make out, yet were frightening, jumbled sounds of taunts and amusement.

Monar restrained JT, "Carefully my friend, we must not rush into the unknown. Just a few more yards and I will look."

Keeping JT behind him, Monar glanced into the room and pulled back trying to remain unemotional although the spectacle was shocking.

Jason behind a cell door, praying, an iron collar around his neck. A rope from the collar leading out to a sitting man jerking on it and laughing. Another man sitting, yelling obscenities. On the table to the side of him, a glowing lantern, a knife and a revolver.

"JT, you must listen. Jason is behind bars. There are two men with weapons sitting at a table. The light is poor, so do not see anything other than two men to the right. Don't think—see nothing else. Shoot both; there's no other way to save your brother. You must do this, can you?"

JT didn't hesitate, "Yes."

"Then we do it—now!"

It was over quickly. JT took in the scene; men gaping dumbfounded, an instant later their laughter drowned out. The chamber exploded twice from the Colt booming out their fate.

The reek and pall of gunpowder furthered the chaos. The jailors lay contorted for eternity.

JT's anger at the sight of his brother enveloped him while Monar ensured the two men were dead. The gun shots had made Jason cower in a corner of his cell.

Leaving JT to wrestle with his conflicts, Monar found the keys to the cell and Jason's collar. His appearance was frightening. He shrank back—terrified at the black man's approach.

"Jason, you're safe now, it's me, Monar."

Disheveled, bearded, unwashed, Jason said nothing and Monar had to assure himself it was truly Jason, "You are Jason, right? You must be."

Without a sound from the bedraggled man, Monar shouted to JT, bringing him out of his trance. Remaining in a trace of shock at his own actions, he hurried to his brother, "God! Jason, are you all right?"

A flicker of recognition, "Don't, John Thomas, don't come near me." Jason cringed in fear.

"Jason, for God's sake…"

"Don't…don't say, God to me, John Thomas. I'm evil, evil! I've fallen into hell's inferno along with father! This is God's torment and I must endure—to save my damned soul."

JT turned to Monar, at a loss, "What's going on, what is…?"

Monar put his finger to his mouth, "Quiet, JT. We must be calm. I've seen this in the islands. These men were wicked and must have infested him with the devil."

JT wouldn't accept that, "No, I don't believe you. Jason just needs time to realize it's us."

Reaching out to his brother, Jason pulled away, "Don't touch me! Don't you understand? Demons possess me. I must suffer for my sins. These men were helping and you killed them!

They told me I must have a tribulation before Jesus's Fifth Coming. Now what will I do? I..."

His jaw slackened, he started into convulsions, forcing them to hold him down. Glassy eyed, his struggling stopped; he went limp and lost consciousness.

Making sure Jason was still breathing, their apprehension eased for the moment. Yet Monar was leery, “It’s not good, what is happening here, JT.”

“I’m worried too. Let’s hope he’ll be all right when we get him home.”

“That’s my worry. I’m fearful—he may be possessed.”

“Possessed of what? You believe what he’s babbling?”

“Yes. Still, the more important point is, *he* believes it and that’s what I mean—it may be the devil’s work, the devil’s words. I’ve seen it in the Islands. It is a sign.”

Monar stared at Jason then to JT, “He calls you John Thomas instead of JT. He has turned from you as his brother and denies you. That is what happens. It is known to white men as Island Vodou, witchcraft. The religious there call it Satan, the Accuser’s work, demonic possession…”

“Demonic possession? Monar, come off it! Please don’t tell me you believe that rubbish. I’ll bet you all my brother needs is rest and recognize his nightmare’s over.”

“I hope you’re right and won’t argue with you. Yet it is dangerous if zealots find this out.”

Deciding to leave the shambles as it was, Monar picked up the emancipated and insensible Jason and then followed JT who carried the lantern through the maze. They were tempted to bring the schooner around to the dock, but thought better of it and so carried Jason around the island and placed him in the dory.

At length, after hoisting the dead weight of his brother aboard and the anchor hauled, JT allowed the schooner to drift on the outgoing tide. The offshore breeze rose. Setting the main, JT picked up Black Rock Channel and glided between Lovell Island and the Brewster Spit as the clouds consumed the moon. The two men were obsessed with their thoughts.

Georges Island was gone, save for its terrors.

13

10 October 1847

SEAWARD HAD BECOME A SANITARIUM. Captain Richard Graves, although somewhat in remission from the distress of malaria, was still unwell. He did nothing to help himself, given to brooding most of the day and drinking until unconscious at eventide. The Captain was too ill for travel and having doctors pay a quick visit in a closed carriage required cajoling and money in equal amounts. At times, it was necessary to threaten a doctor's wellbeing should he disclose his patient's condition.

The only reaction to the Captain's disinterest in life was the infrequent visits of his son, Jason. Strangely enough, on those occasions, the Captain came as close to wrath as he could muster by raging at his son for allowing some fools to kidnap him and seduce him into believing he was possessed by some idiotic demi-devil.

After it became apparent Jason's meetings with his father were without value and actually an added aggravation to all those present, the visitations ceased.

Jason hovered on the verge of madness. He possessed temperament deviations for no perceptible reasons other than his kidnapping. One moment he would be malevolent, manic, holding JT and Monar in contempt and the next moment he'd be in dread. He shrieked he was a fallen angel, held by evil spirits, calling for the angel Chaos to take him. Yet succeeding each seizure he would become cognizant of his surroundings and sit serenely, nodding, always nodding, as though agreeing to some inner voice. He wouldn't answer when spoken to; when fed, most was thrown toward the fireplace. Never looking out a window, he walked the inner rooms, forever nodding to his voices. Worst of all, while the weeks overtook them, he never improved, in turns vindictive then frightened then implacable, malicious.

His moods made Monar, reading a line in the poem *The Raven*, mention it to JT one evening.

"JT, listen to this from this fellow Poe, this is your brother's mind. 'And his eyes have all the meaning of a demon's that is dreaming'. JT, I'm telling you, that's Jason, face it."

Not responding at first, JT continued to stand on the bluff, looking down on the town by the sea. How he wished he were behind the wheel of a brigantine only now clearing the harbor and standing out to sea. She was the *Blue Star* he knew, outbound with cargo for Rio de Janeiro and Montevideo and then around the Horn and on to the Hawaiians. Three years she'd be gone. That's what he needed he thought, Savanna, Charlee, the sea.

The *Blue Star's* sails filled, JT's eyes misted—the evening sun shimmered her wake in gold.

His nomadic reverie drifting off, JT put his foot up on the stone seat and answered Monar.

"Perhaps you're right. Father wants to die so he can burn in hell for his sins. But, Jason? I don't know what Jason wants any more than he does. You're out of ideas as well, aren't you?"

"I told you from the beginning, I'd seen his like in Haiti. Once Vodou seizes you, there's no chance to elude it and none of those know-it-all doctors you've brought in from God knows where has the slightest idea what to do—because there isn't a thing they *can* do."

"I know, I know, you told me from the beginning. But can you blame me? You and your damn Vodou! Demons creeping into your brain. Nothing scientific, demons in the brain—too late for Jason; we're sending you off to some insane asylum."

"That is right. Send him off to some home intended for his kind. Look, JT, I understand how you feel. Jason's your blood; the Captain's your father. You've tried, done your best but you don't have the vision, you can't accept what's in front of you. Stubbornness is not going to cure either one of them. Send Jason away to where people may be able to help. You're losing your life for nothing—so send him. Do you know what this town would do if they had the chance?

"What do you mean by that? Jason had nothing to do with the slaves."

"That doesn't matter! In the taverns here, I've heard the history of this town. Do you know they hung witches? And worse? They brag about it! They'll show anyone the sight where it happened, like it was some amusement. That's the nature of this town, it has no shame. I know the Captain will never leave, but at least get your brother out of here before they find out the truth of Fort Warren and want to hang Jason along with us. Your father can well afford to put him somewhere."

It was true, JT was at wits end. It was also true it continued to take a toll on him. Yet at the moment he was rankled by the mention of money, "Right, use the money father earned shipping slaves."

"For god's sake, JT, what better use? For that matter, some of it was for honest work—the shipment to Bilbao for example."

"It will be hard to separate that money from what you and father took from MacPherson—and don't look surprised. I thought something wasn't quite square. One of the *Pike's* crew informed me that father didn't make a straight run to Salem. They berthed in New York for three days and took some heavy satchels off, came back without them but with a strong box and three guards…"

"Who told you this?"

"Doesn't matter who—let me finish. There may be parts even you don't know. The guards stayed with father right up to Seaward, then left by train. I'll bet you know where the box is and how much is in it, don't you? You must, I've seen you whispering with father when you thought no one was around. How'd you get away from MacPherson's with it? You didn't tell Jason and me the whole damn story about him—did you?"

Monar was indifferent to the question, "You seem to know so much, JT, why don't you tell me what you think? Or is it you're afraid you really don't want to know the truth?"

"I can take the truth—if it is."

“Then I’ll give it to you. MacPherson hired the First Mate on the *Pike*, name of Coffin, to kill your father. But I warned your father and at sea, when Coffin tried; I killed him.”

“Are you telling me true?”

“Yes. And, when we got back and demanded the money—some of it mine—MacPherson tried to pull a gun, but I was quicker. He died, we took the money and I gave some to the blacks. I’m not going to try and justify it, especially to you and your closed mind, but MacPherson tried to kill us; your father had nothing to do with his death. However, work this over in your mind, JT, if MacPherson had his way, your father and probably me, would’ve already been given the deep six when you went back to MacPherson’s and if he was there, he’d have laughed up his sleeve at the two of you.”

There were elements in Monar’s story JT wanted to argue, yet the last remark stifled any protest.

Most of the story was true. The other parts, Monar justified as he felt the need, “So, now you have the truth.”

He’d been foxed, JT knew it. Now he was indebted to Monar for saving his father’s life—not once, but twice. Yet this wasn’t how the conversation started. The question was over Jason and his future. That was what Monar wanted decided and Monar always worked out the cleverest solution.

“We were speaking of Jason and none of this answers what to do with him, does it?”

“No, it doesn’t. I can give you my advice, or not.”

JT nodded, Monar looked around to make sure no one was near, “I say this as the only person here with a clear mind at present. One of the Captain’s old sailors is leaving the sea. Said it is too hard on him. He has relatives in New Hampshire, wherever that is up north, at the end of some 10th road, up there in a notch. Says his relatives live there and they’re going to build a stage coach inn. I offered we pay him a stipend if he took Jason up there, far away from the sea, I thought that might settle him down, perhaps give him something to do.”

“Who’s the seaman?”

"Joshua Crawford."

JT frowned, in thought, "He's a good man, hard worker, honest. If we did something like that, you couldn't have picked a better man. Have you told him what my brother is like?"

"Yes. He's actually been to see Jason. To me, Joshua does seem to have a calming effect on him."

Monar had his say; JT would need time to chew on it.

Another subject Monar had to bring up, which JT knew nothing about, "I want to talk about the *Laurence Pike*."

"The *Pike*? Monar, you can burn her to the waterline for all I care."

"JT, you can't blame the ship for being a slaver, only her captain."

"Whatever you say. Father can do what he wants with her."

"He has. It's written in his will. As of last week, the clipper is yours."

JT knew nothing of it, "No, do not say that. I haven't heard a thing about father's will. Damn, you seem to know everything."

"As you say, it's one of the things we whisper about. Look, JT, The *Pike* was earned with hard, honest work. Your father, Jason and you bought her long before what happened. She has always been yours in the will. It is just that your father knows he will never sail her again and as you will not accept his money, you're going to need a source of income—and the ship is all you'll have."

He quickly recognized he was boxed in again. Still, he had helped pay for her and she was bought honorably. And now, God, she was his in his father's will! JT would not be giving up his honor. His mind expanded; twenty-four years old and the owner of a clipper, a fast clipper! It got the better of him, "God, Monar, I *can* accept her."

"Good. Would you like to have her given some sorts of rites? You know, a priest or minister or witch doctor to sprinkle holy water on her—something like that?"

"Of course I wouldn't. Why would you say something like that?"

"I just thought that would help in case the *Pike* creaked one night and you'd think it was some dark spirit creeping along the deck after you."

"There's only one dark spirit creeping along the deck I'd concern myself about—and you know who!"

A moments silence and then laughter from both.

Dusk settled and the New England October chill sent them inside for a whiskey by a fireplace. The thoughts of owning the *Pike* became real to JT. The thoughts were both exciting and concerning. Monar knew why.

"Your face is easily read, JT, you wonder how are you going to afford the operating costs."

"You're right. I'm just beginning to work those out in my head. It's a big challenge."

"You'll need a partner."

JT took a firm line, "I'll not go to my father, Monar. I'll thank him for the *Pike,* of course, but I will not ask him for a cent, even as a loan."

"We knew you wouldn't. Yet *I* want to make you an offer."

Surprised and not believing where Monar would raise the kind of money required, JT speculated it would come from his father in a roundabout fashion.

Monar forestalled that, "The money will not be from the Captain, JT, I've earned it."

"I don't mean to sound rude; but you were a slave." "JT, let's speak of how this slave earned something. I was born a slave. From the time I was five to the time your father and I went back to MacPherson's, I was his slave—thirty years. I worked fourteen hours, six days a week and if you think I didn't earn what I took from him, perhaps this will convince you."

With that, Monar turned around and lifted his shirt. Ribbons of scars crisscrossed his back, their rosiness emphasized on the dark skin. JT flinched while Monar pulled his shirt back down.

"I never cried, that made MacPherson even more furious, but the worst part? I had to call him Master. I earned my money."

"All I can say is I believe you. Make your offer; I'll accept whatever it is."

"All right then. We checked the lower hull at Foul Bay so that's fine. However, we don't want the *Pike* to be refitted here because a group of people will want to make her a rallying point for abolitionists or whatever the devil they call themselves. There's a small ship building company in Bath, Maine, we should take her there for refitting, new decking from the fire, painting and a lot of new canvas…"

"By the sound of you, you've gone over this with father."

"Yes, he's fairly knowing, mindful at times, more so when you're not around. Yet make no mistake, he is easily confounded when the goblins assail him."

"And the malaria?"

"He's weaken from it, mending somewhat. It's his outbursts that mostly bother me. However, right now, let me continue about the *Pike*. I will assume the cost of what I mentioned and insurance, supplies and crew for one year plus odd expenses…"

"Jesus, Monar, that's a hell of an outlay."

"Yes, it is and that is why I want ten percent interest in the *Pike* and twenty-five percent of her profits."

JT couldn't help laugh, "You've definitely had a talk with my tightfisted Yankee father! Still, I'll say it's a deal."

Monar had one last comment, "You have to rename her."

14

JASON GRAVES WAS PASSIVE about the decision. More than anyone, Joshua Crawford did have a calming effect on him whenever there was an outburst. Due to this and the fact the Captain could not have cared less about that son's condition, it was agreed, with even JT's consent, that Crawford take Jason into northern New Hampshire for an unspecified period.

During the stage of Jason leaving, and moving the *Pike* for repairs and new sails in Maine, Monar was given to roaming at night. In Boston he took in the words of the black speaker, Frederick Douglas, publisher of the *North Star.*[7] He also found a periodical named *The Hangman* mentioning, 'The slaver, Captain Richard Graves'.

A different occasion took him as far as Weymouth, on Boston's South Shore to listen to a recently formed anti-slavery, militant group calling themselves the Wide Awakes. Monar had read of them in the *Olive Branch* newspaper, although they were not offering the olive branch to any slaver they came across.

Revenge took him to Marblehead, and there in the graveyard hour, he tied a Mister Covey to his oxen gate and truly whipped him until he cried out for mercy. Monar ceased and loomed over the pitiable creature, "If word comes to me again you've whipped another person on this gate, or anywhere, I will come for you, and that will be your last night on God's green earth."

«»

---

[7] On seeing a ship haul her anchor, Frederick Douglas once wrote, "You are loosed from your mooring and are free. I am fast in my chains and a slave

Thinking over the past few months, Monar was perplexed. In truth and owing to Ian MacPherson, he had naturally developed a hate for every white man—and indeed, he felt that only fitting. Born from breeding an intelligent, handsome black woman from Niger and a formidable black from the Cote d'Ivorie, he was the last of the ten children she bore. Of them, he knew little, for each was auctioned when young.

Monar's time for auction came when he was five. He still evoked the memory of being taken from his little friends and sold like a domestic pig. It was the last time he cried, and from the anguish of clawing for his only friends, he toughened.

His new master, tobacco planter Ian MacPherson, wanted to amuse himself and used Monar as an experiment, educating him as a white man with the best tutors informing him of the world. MacPherson's goal was to prove a black man—even a bred black man—was incapable to absorb more that basic thought, unable to equal a white man's creativity.

MacPherson was proved wrong, absurdly wrong. Monar was an empty vessel that absorbed and retained nearly every morsel of information. From the King's English to mechanical theory, from sailing to the history of the white European, he learned, and learned to be quiet about it unless tested.

MacPherson foolishly bragged to other planters about his infantile research with Monar. The planters however, found MacPherson wrong and joshed him until his ego, greatly stung, left him with no other recourse other than to bully. It came to be there was nothing Monar could do right, which brought the lash. It was as if intelligence could be driven from him with the whip. Yet Monar did not run, he endured. He realized the fate of slaves who ran. They were hunted down with hounds and suffered inhumane treatment. There was no cunning plan to escape from the island, this he understood. The satisfaction of snapping his master's neck also glimpsed a terrible fate. Some power deep inside made him wait. He schemed and even though the whippings stopped after fifteen years, the respite that came between them was one sided. Monar waited. A silent, controlled hatred encompassed his rage. Nonetheless, it was the all-encompassing word Master, the word MacPherson insisted Monar utter, that would manifest one opportunistic day and give vent to his wrath.

Extraordinarily in his conceit, MacPherson never fathomed the hatred. Why should he? Far too many were sure a black was not truly human, no matter how well educated. Monar was an aberration, yet still a slave—and slaves were whipped. Not enough to cripple of course, that would be a waste. A whipping was to instruct and make clear to a slave that he or she had incurred their master's wrath. The southern slave owner believed the bible indicated this to be universal law.

However, after all his years of weighing his considerable hatred of whites because of one, Monar grappled with second thoughts—was it possible not all white men were wicked? This reflection began with Captain Graves who, after Ghost Ghosman, was the one remarkable white man with whom Monar had prolonged conversation. At first, he thought Graves predictable. Buy and sell humans, make money. Yet the more they spoke, the more Monar realized Graves held no distinction to color, that he was a man with minor arrogance. Graves only concern was could a man do his job. Color did not enter into a man's value, a judgment Monar rendered and the reason he decided to warn the Captain of the plot against him on the *Pike*.

Monar lamented none of the deaths then or since, only the Captain's insanity, which would lead to the same end.

For now, the Captain he came to respect was lost. Need had prevailed over ethics, humans were sold for immoral gain. It came to the failing man he paid an exorbitant price—his honor and he found no path to justify or endure his behavior. Only the bottle brought fleeting comfort.

This Monar knew, but kept his own counsel, no one would understand. If people wanted to and believed him, Monar could have told them the Creoles of Haiti had an adage for a man consumed by his faults—manje tét litou vivan—a a man eating himself alive.

Cognizant at intervals, the Captain allowed he was creeping toward the beckoning madness, yet was unable to impede it. He wished to speak only with Monar and hurried his thoughts. His will was revised; he directed his fortune to the maintenance and safeguarding of Seaward in perpetuity, or until such time as his son, John Thomas, accepted ownership. Other funding went to the keep of Jason and a significant sum to his lost wife, Mary, as well as to 'that church on Essex Street'. With the exception of the *Laurence Pike,* her wharf and all relevant equipment being left to JT, the Remainder passed through to '…Monar, no last name. A freed black man, former slave, assumed born in Cuba, formerly of Barbados'.

Waiting until Graves had a somewhat lucid period; the family attorney witnessed and filed the will. No one, other than the Captain and Monar knew of the chest locked away in the basement. If others ever knew of it, they would not have believed the wealth still remaining after the will was honored. The chest and contents became the *Remainder* to Mona.

15

"Tell me, JT," Monar casually tossed out the question, "What do you think of the possibility of adding steam propulsion to the *Pike*?"

"Have I been talking in my sleep, or have you been reading my mind again?"

"Neither, I've watched you scribbling and thinking aloud, JT, so it was simple, because I wanted to bring this up to you. Is it feasible?"

"Anything is feasible if there's enough money. The steamboats of the British, like the *Great Britain* or that foolish side-wheel monstrosity *Great Eastern*, were explicitly built for steam propulsion. The *Pike* would require being refitted with a lot of iron framing and along with the propulsion unit, it would increase weight and area needed, and both reduce quickness."

"We could offset the loss of speed by taking less cargo."

"True, Monar. Still, that's the tradeoff. We should find a marine designer first to see if it's feasible and the cost. Then work out if it will be profitable."

"I'm not a captain, yet to me, the fact we could go when there's no wind and in and out of harbors when we want without waiting for the tide is a major factor."

"All right then, partner, we're agreed. We'll dig into it."

«»

The desk in Naval Architect John W. Griffiths' office in New York was strewn with sketches, estimates and models of ship hulls detailing steam systems. Griffiths was the renowned designer of the *Rainbow*, built in New York 1845 and *Sea Witch* built in 1846. They were two vessels celebrated for their beauty, yet more so for their speed—the *Sea Witch* became the ideal slaver. The letter

Griffith received from JT concerning the alteration of his McKay clipper to add a steam driven propulsion system interested him to the point where he had begun conceptual designs and proposals. His first meeting with JT and Monar encompassed the positive and negative judgments.

"Can it be done Captain Graves? Of course. However, the key word that you must remember here is compromise. To be honest, to convert a classic McKay vessel and see a smoke stack protruding amidships is not a sight I wish to envision. With that said however, without question steam power is here and will be the coming thing for most vessels. Converting—or I should say augmenting—sail by power-driven means is acceptable. Nevertheless, adding steam power as an adjunct to an *existing* vessel—one not specifically designed for it—creates load and that merges with other difficulties."

"Mr. Griffiths, my father knew some problems with hull pressure is the past and had the frames strapped with iron right back to the keel to add strength, but retain flexibility."

"Yes, and that's all to the good, Captain Graves, but let me add more to that. You'll need diagonal bracing as well. The upper and lower deck stringers and beams must be rebuilt with iron and fastened to the beam-ends. Same goes for the lower deck plates, 'tween deck pillars and keel plate. We'll have to add a new iron keelson, from mid-ship to stern and reconfigure the rudder. That's only to give you an idea of what's ahead. This doesn't include the framing for the Watt horizontal steam engine, coal bunker, through hull fittings and so forth. You follow?"

"The gist of it, yes. Therefore, assuming as you say, it can be done, let's look at performance. What have you come up with for estimates?"

"I believe you'll lose a knot or two, but gain in what you're after—functionality. If you square the cargo fore and aft properly, you shouldn't feel that difference but it will be there. I'll give you final weights of the system, including coal, so you can adjust deadweight tonnage."

"We were wondering about the drag of the propeller."

"That's been solved. A screw propeller has been developed where the blades fold when not in use. In other words, when not under power, the blades fold back from forward motion through the water. When torque is applied, centrifugal force pushes the blades out. Not as efficient as solid formed propellers, that I'll grant you. But as you said it will be secondary propulsion, you're not going to cross the Atlantic with it."

"What is required as a crew for steam?"

"The main concern is safety. A boiler explosion can, and will, destroy a ship."

Monar moved away, remembering Ghost and the British frigate, *Diligent*. JT didn't notice.

Griffiths went on, "That's a rare occurrence here on land as well at sea now, because we have eccentrics, that is, safety valves, they release excessive steam pressure buildup automatically…"

Monar interjected, "Right, it's safe as long as the safety valve is working properly."

"Quite so, Mr. Monar, quite so, and the operators alert. Yet first, to answer the question of a steam crew, for the amount it will be used, the captain, first mate and someone with mechanical talent and dependability will be enough. We'll train whomever you want," Griffiths laughed, "but he better love to shovel coal."

The questions and answers went on for another hour. Boiled down, there were downsides but the positives outweighed them. Two questions remained.

"The cost and when, Mr. Griffiths?"

"Estimate for a single screw is, seven thousand dollars, subject to revisions. Time to completion, four, five months. If you chose my builder, he will warranty workmanship, not performance."

JT asked if the completion date could be tightened.

"Captain Graves, northern builders plan for winter weather to slow the outside yard work by a third. I could say perhaps, however, they would charge a premium."

JT looked to Monar, who nodded; it was after all, his money. Griffiths' hid his surprise—the black man oversaw the money—at least for the reconstruction.

Most of the discussion over, there was one last item on JT's list, "If I understand you correctly, Mr. Griffiths, if we were under both sail and steam, sparks could at times fly from the smokestack, so I assume the main sail of the mainmast and crossjack of the mizzen will have to be furled."

"It's best. You'll never be sure which way the wind will carry the cinders."

"Then I want you to bulk up and lengthen those spars two feet on each end. I'll have the sails sized to match when you give me the dimensions."

Griffiths pondered the statement, "I see what you're after. You know your trade, young man."

"With respect, sir, I'm twenty-four. There are younger clipper captains."

"I did not mean to slight you, Captain. My comment was to point out that there are few captains who would think that far in advance for a compensating element to average out your Rate of Knots."

JT accepted the compliment, "Thank you. Now, to continue, I don't believe you mentioned the builder's name."

Griffin appeared uncomfortable, "Mr. Graves, this is a difficult subject to broach. In your initial letter suggesting an interest in augmenting a clipper with steam, you mentioned her name being the *Laurence Pike*. I thought it strange you would come to New York when there are so many worthy designers and builders in New England. I admit I inquired around and…well, it seems the reputation of her has preceded you…"

"Mr. Griffith, if you have reservations over this…"

"No, no—that's not it at all. I'm not pro or anti-slavery," Griffiths looked to Monar, "it's simply that I could not be sure of any builder in this vicinity doing a first rate job and…I presume you know what I mean."

"I understand what you're trying to say, so let me respond. My father made an unwise decision, a decision for which he now pays dearly. I do not believe in slavery and my father and I have parted company, something I consider a tragedy. My friend here, Monar, is a freed black and as I say, my friend as well as partner. Now, with that said, do you want the commission?"

"My answer is a quick, yes. What I was trying to get to—quite awkwardly I admit—was that I feel your clipper should be taken further south for the work. I contacted Kennard and Williamson in Baltimore; they have done work for me in the past. They've built Baltimore class clippers, the precursors of your Yankee Clippers and I'll vouch for them. Being in Maryland, a southern state, you won't have to worry about deliberate harm to the ship. A plus would be a warmer port to shorten the projected time."

There had been no change in his father when they returned to Seaward. Monar reported to Richard Graves the revisions planned on the clipper and the Captain's depression dissolved for a while when he heard the *Pike's* name would be changed as well.

"Let me tell you when I made first mate, Monar. Laurence Pike was my skipper. He was one of those people you'd call a remarkable human and astounding navigator—could thread the needle through the Straits of Magellan at night—that's how good he were, I'm telling you. Saved all our asses in storms many times he did. Sometime later, he was lost at sea, all hands. I had become captain by then and bought my first schooner, the *Hattie's Camp* out of Newfoundland. She wasn't good enough to rename her after him, so I waited until my father gave me permission to have McKay build a fast clipper down in East Boston. That's how the *Pike* got named, after Captain Laurence. The man deserved it."

Then, in the instant it would take to snap ones fingers, Graves' kindly memory of Captain Pike and the ship dissolved. Rheumy eyes, the color of the fireplace embers, closed and the Captain reverted to the edge of the abyss, "You know, Monar, after what I did to that good ship and Captain Pike's honor, I think it is a good thing to rename her."

"JT doesn't know what will suit her, Captain."

Graves' slouched, the shadows were oncoming, "She's ill-starred now, he can name her any God damned thing he wants—it won't help."

"Don't lay a spell on her, Captain, you failed, not her."

The captain did not hear and it didn't matter—he'd slipped over the edge once more.

«»

11 November 1847

The skeleton crew on the *Pike*, supplied from New York by John Griffiths' office, was happy to leave the onset of another cold New England winter. As the clipper turned the point and on into the entrance of the Chesapeake, sails were shortened for the lengthy slog up the Bay to Baltimore. Close-hauled against the prevailing winds, the ship passed Cape Charles, Virginia to starboard, then the islands of Tangier and Smith where the ship moved into Maryland waters.

It was a long haul to the point the Chesapeake narrowed by Hooper and Barren Islands.

"Damn! Captain," Monar finally stated, "this is one long blasted Bay."

JT erupted with a laugh, "Jesus, Monar, I think that's the longest sentence you've said since we've been underway."

"Do you blame me? My lips were frozen stiff. They've only just now thawed. Damn, how, or why, do you stand that miserable weather up there? At least here it's a little warmer clime."

JT couldn't help laugh, "We're New Englanders. We wear the weather as a badge of honor"

Monar gave the statement some pause, "Then you had damn well better be wearing more than a badge if you want to survive that life."

JT took pity on Monar, "Sorry, I wasn't thinking, you being from the south all your life. I guess we'll have to take southern cargo only, or wrap you in blankets."

"That won't be enough. I'm only now able to move my fingers again too."

JT saw a chance for a jibe at his friend, "So that's why you didn't lift a finger to help the crew trim ship the whole way."

Monar didn't take the taunt quietly, "Hold on there, Mr. Captain. As minor partner, investor, first mate as well as the price I'm paying this crew of misfits—I'll stay supercargo. That way Maritime Law says I don't have to work the ship and I'll be damned if I'm going to do anything more than shout orders—which I might add, I have to do time and again."

JT responded in kind, "Maritime Law? From now on, I forbid you to read any more of my books. And another thing, the only reason you have to repeat yourself is no one understands you due to that damn deep lilting accent you have—or is it a drawl?"

"It's the bleeding King's English as spoken in the islands for God's sake! And don't get me started about the English language as interpreted by New England Yankees."

JT did not respond. Monar was right, at least about the cost of the crew. Hiring New York sailors instead of Salem seamen was costly, yet necessary. For fear of publicity, neither JT nor Monar wanted anyone from the north shore to know where the *Pike* was headed.

His mind wandered. How much this passage had bonded his friendship with Monar. JT had never had such a close friend as the black man, not even Jimmy Pickman and, of all things; the man was more intelligent than any friend. Added to that, he knew or sensed *things*. Even when JT asked about changing the ship's name, Monar listened, gave thought, then simply said JT would come to recognize whatever was best.

JT had the ship's port and starboard quarter-boards, as well as the stern-board, all stating the ship's name, removed. Away from the crew, he and Monar, without a word spoken, nailed the three boards together, wrapped a length of chain around and, confused sentiments aside, slid the bundle over the side. The *Laurence Pike* no longer lived.

JT did not regret his decision. Years past, when advancing from apprentice seaman before the mast to midshipman, he began thinking of one day having his own ship. Not an apple-cheeked brigantine like the English, but a clipper. As a boy, notions such as *Queen of the Seas, Warlock, Master of the Ocean Gale, Black Wind,* and many other names struck him as elegant, much more impressive than *Laurence Pike*. Yet, his grandfather and father bought the clipper and named her after Captain Pike and now, leaning on the bulwark, JT was sorry, sorry for the need to change her name, sorry for his father and mother and Jason. What wouldn't he give up to have everything back. Father, mother, Jason—they had the world, or as much of it as they wanted. Then, a fleeting thought, he still had no name for his ship.

Thinking a moment about Logan Carlton's navy career as they saw the Naval School, JT eased the ship off beating into the wind, turned to port and tacked on a reach up the tidal waters of the Patapsco River. Baltimore beckoned.

With Fort McHenry to port, they came abeam the wharfs as described in their instructions and furled sail, allowing the ship to drift on the slack tide. There were a few vessels berthed along with a commercial steamship and they waited. After a time the sound of a tugboat's engine firing up and then chugging away from a dock came to them.

"Are you the *Laurence Pike*?"

"Aye, that we are."

"We had to guess, you know. We didn't know when you would be here and saw no name on your vessel."

JT laughed in his embarrassment, "Sorry, thoughtless of us. We'll throw you our tow."

"No need, we'll raft alongside and lay you in to starboard."

Berthed, they met their host.

"I'm Joseph Wright, Chief Engineer and Boatwright for K and W. I'll be responsible for the work you've commissioned with us."

Chief Engineer, Wright, wasted few words after that introduction as he and his assistant laid out designer Griffiths' plans, as well as their own, on a hatch cover. The New York sailors left immediately, anxious to acquire tickets on the steamship *Pocahontas* and the day trip up to Norfolk and rail lines back to New York.

With the plans and ideas understood all around, Chief Engineer Wright straightened up and was frank, "Griffiths' plans are quite clear—on paper. However, until we look below we're blind men describing an elephant. So let's start in the bilge and work our way topside."

Although not a young man by half, for the next three hours, Wright climbed ladders, waded through bilge water, moved ballast and wormed his way into the deepest bowels of the keel right through to the stern. JT and Monar listened as he described to his assistant how the rudder's gudgeons, pintles and skeg would have to be reinforced to support the propeller shaft and a bug shield needed against worm damage.

With these last remarks, even JT was over his head, and with Monar, simply nodded as Wright concisely listed the requisites. They did learn one important point however; Chief Engineer, Wright earned his title.

"Very good, gentlemen. You've a sound ship. We'll get these notes down and be back tomorrow to start dimensioning for the ironmonger. And before you ask, I would say the cost is bang on and three months, plus or minus—subject to your revisions of course."

With that, Wright was up the last ladder to topside, across the deck and gone along the wharf— pursued by his assistant.

JT was baffled, "Well, what do you think of him?"

Monar was somber, "If the rest of his people worked his speed, I think we'd be out of here in three weeks, not three months."

Monar poured a scotch for them each and rested on the stern, looking across at the *Pocahontas* arriving, "How long do you want to stay here, JT?"

"Depends. I was thinking a month, just to be sure of the work, but with this Wright fellow, I'm pretty confident. Let's give it a week and take it from there. If the harbor isn't frozen over up north, I'll take the *Ocean Pearl* to Nantucket and sign a crew for the beginning of the year."

"Why there?"

"Edgartown's a whaling port and whale oil isn't in as much demand now, so I thought there would be some good sailors looking for positions."

While he watched the steamboat move away from the dock stern first, Monar heard the screech of the whistle as the vessel turned and departed. He then noticed one person, his back to them, remaining on the dock. Dressed in black and unmoving, the man gazed out over the harbor.

"Well, I'll tell you, JT, I'm in no hurry to go back to the Salem and see polar bears."

The individual fascinated Monar, "JT, see that person there? He hasn't moved since the ferry left. He's like a statue, motionless."

Looking to the man, JT wasn't that curious, "Is he bothering you? You're acting as though he's a wraith or something. Probably some drunk or poor soul doesn't know where he is. Every harbor has them."

"Sadly true, I suppose. Yet it's his appearance, I find it compelling."

"Please, Monar, don't take me on one of your cabalistic voyages again, believing that man standing there involves us."

"Well," Monar smiled, "we're already talking about him, aren't we? Yet then again, think of it, aren't we supposed to be our brother's keeper?"

"To sound wary, Monar, at present there's enough problems with my own brother. Come on, Wright's assistant said there's a tavern with good food at the north end of the wharfs."

Returning to the clipper after a full meal and beers, they scanned an empty wharf.

"See, Monar, he's gone. Another lost soul, one of too many. Nothings to be done about it."

The following morning found Kennard & Williamson employees throughout the ship. At first, JT was kept busy fielding questions about her, then moved aside, but not without being handed a sheaf of papers—the top one entitled, Mechanics of the Brougham/Watt Reciprocating Steam Engine System. Theory, Process, Function, Diagrams, Installation and Employee Instruction/ Testing Methods.

JT flipped the pages, noting steam pressure, fly-ball, cube root, drop cut-off, piston speed—and tossed the packet to Monar, "Here, you're so damn smart, read this and explain it to me."

"Read it? The devil you say!" He looked at the cover, "I can hardly pronounce the word, 'reciprocating', never mind know what it means."

That evening, they were so engrossed in their reading; they did not see the man in black until just before dusk. The man remained, seemingly captivated, unmoving, facing the river.

"If he comes one more time, JT, I'm going down there and find what he's about."

JT faked concern, "I'll bet he's one of your Vodou apparitions, and as I think of it, you haven't been foretelling things lately and now it bothers you that you don't know who this fellow is. Run down there and offer him a drink, bet he follows you around the rest of the night."

"Go ahead and make fun if you want, but I'm telling you, there's something puzzling here."

Through the next day, Monar kept glancing to the wharf and JT kept kidding him—kidding him right up until the man appeared once more that evening. Now, even JT thought it strange that a person would come to stand—to stand, to stare and nothing more.

Monar approached in the failing light, looming behind the person, "Excuse me, Sir?"

The figure did not turn, nor was he disquieted, "Yes?"

With the scarcity of a response, Monar became embarrassed, "Ah, I was wondering about you. I've seen you here for the last three nights and was curious about…well…"

The man turned to look up to Monar, "Your voice seemed so distant above me, I thought it might have been someone from the Almighty."

Monar stifled a laugh. A clever comment, the voice southern, cultured. The man held a delicate smile, but it couldn't veil a once handsome, yet now gaunt, visage.

The man focused on Monar, "I'm sorry, I was deep into intellection and only now have I regressed to the present."

The voice disclosed no unease with the bulk or color of this stranger as the man continued, whispering, "I was unmindful; I seem to manage that state more each day. Now, how may I be of service to you?"

Monar was taken by the man's dignity that manifested in a charisma he'd never known. Though his frock coat had seen better days and buttoned to the neck by a frayed collar, the man still commanded deference. He was dressed entirely in black from scuffed low boots to slouched hat. He stood patiently, waiting for Monar's answer.

"My partner and I arrived three days ago, that's our vessel right there…"

"Ah, that mysterious ship."

"Mysterious?"

"Certainly. A clipper ship without a name? I imagine there is a fascinating narrative ascribed to her for plunging to such a loss of majesty. Tell me, is there an intrigue?"

"Yes, although not one the owner would want me to repeat."

"Then it shall not be written—or come to pass."

Was that from Genesis, Monar wondered his senses on edge. It was the man's choice of word and phrase, "May I ask your name, Sir?"

"Of course, pardon my poor etiquette. My name is Poe, Edgar Allen Poe. And yours?"

Monar thought it so. Still, to meet the author of stories he had read—*The Gold Bug*, *The Fall of the House of Usher*, *The Black Cat* and of course, quite recently, *The Raven*—was an honor.

"Mr. Poe, I've had the pleasure of studying some of your stories and poems. I'm most pleased to meet you. My name is Monar, formerly of the Caribe and only recently down from Salem in Massachusetts."

"Ah, Salem, where they pride themselves for hanging sorceresses. I do not envision their character having changed even a modicum through the passing years. However, that matters not.

"I was born a little south of there in Boston, although taken away when I was five."

Poe regressed to looking over the harbor, seemingly forgetting Monar was there, while Monar sought to keep the chat going, "I recall that you were an editor in New York. Are you only visiting here?"

"I am, for memories. I lived on Wilks Street in West Baltimore off and on. My wife and I were happy there...before moving to New York."

"Does she like it there or rather be back here?"

"I do not wish you to feel apologetic my friend, yet your question is an exemplar of one that should not be asked. You see, my Virginia died of tuberculosis the beginning of this year, January 30, 1847 to be precise. She was twenty-four."

Poe walked closer to Monar, "I did not wish for you to be discomfited, yet there are some sorrows the heart cannot veil or withhold. The heart, you know, is a frightful master."

“I’m truly sorry for your loss and sorrow, Mr. Poe. Come; let us have a drink to loss and a memory that will not diminish. I’ll call my friend and we will have a meal and wine.”

The floor of the Witch’s Delight Pub, covered with sawdust, was salvaged from a beached windjammer and if the three men sitting in deep discussion had given it thought, they would have decided that when the floor was laid, it was the last time the pub was cleaned—if indeed then.

Poe’s attire, though tatty, was out of place, the other patrons considering him a dandy, if not a poseur. Whatever they thought, they kept it to themselves, Monar’s mass and their noting the bolo wedged in his boot when he sat, kept them tightlipped. Poe noticed none of this; busy regaling his hosts with tales of prose and editing some of “the most atrocious, ghastly, grim, wretched and appalling English” authors could put to paper.

The wine was unpleasant, yet not the reason for his refusing another glass—as he explained.

“Thank you for offering, but please let me enlighten you gentlemen for the reason of my declining another. I can be quite pleasant with one glass of any liquor. A second however, causes my temperament to inverse and I curdle to an obnoxious, insufferable buffoon, one you would not wish socialize with in any way, form or manner. I would not care for you to see that.”

Saying this, Poe reached into his coat and withdrew a vial. “To compensate however, I take a few drops of Laudanum—you may know it as opium.[8] Would you like a few drops?”

Not concerned, aware opium had a calming influence, that even babies were given a drop or two when fretful—they declined and continued listening to Poe.

---

[8] In the 1800s and early 1900s, Opium was accepted for medicinal purposes much like aspirin today.

Now he held the floor and people within earshot stopped to eavesdrop while others moved close by, "…and the silken, sad, uncertain rustling of each purple curtain thrilled me—filled me with fantastic terrors I had never known before…"

This was from *The Raven,* spoken only as its author could. Soaring with passion and emotion, his poetic verses flowed in cadence "…wondering what this ominous bird of yore, what this grim, ungainly, ghastly, gaunt and ominous bird of yore meant in croaking…*nevermore*."

He held every drinker spellbound for two hours, reciting "*To Helen, Song, To My Mother* and other poems. Snifters and pints filled their table and overflowed to others. Poe kept to his vow to not drink another glass, although the Laudanum did appear twice more.

Eventually, sadly, the recitations concluded, the brilliance of the evening dispelled, the customers drifted off, many in tears. The three men sat, two awed by the other.

He was relaxed now, but serious, "Now tell me, have I earned the right to one question?"

They were perplexed, yet ready to answer any request he might propose.

"Your vessel is without name. She is not new, what dishonor must she have performed?"

Monar dodged the query by turning to JT. It was, after all, his family, his ship.

JT had not expected the question, yet he agreed to answer. He looked about, it was late, few remained and they drunk, "She once had a name, which now makes her a pariah."

JT faltered. Poe, dissipated in his Opium miasma, waited serenely for JT to resume.

"She was a slaver."

Unmoved, Poe sat with his hands folded, "You cannot reproach a *ship*, for she cannot sin, aside from fable."

"You're right about that, Mr. Poe; I came late to being reconciled to that truth."

"So then, what have you decided to name her?"

"I, we, haven't."

Taking a piece of paper and writing on it, Poe said, "Monar, you mentioned you liked the cipher in my story "The Gold Bug" and you both enjoyed my recitation tonight," without their taking notice he scribbled briefly away, "so here is her new name, in a very simple cipher. Now, however, it is time for me to take my leave. There is another world, one not near so congenial, for me to enter."

They asked to pay and were told there was no payment necessary; the Witch's Delight would never know another night as this again. Poe whispered it was just as well, "I had but little to put toward the cost."

Monar presumed this to be the case and slipped two gold coins in Poe's coat pocket.

Outside, the cool air refreshing, Poe was expansive, turning to them, "Our time together draws to a close. To paraphrase Omar, the tent maker, 'The moving hand writes, and having written, moves on. Some little talk of me and thee, and then—no more of thee and me'. Thanks to your warmth and courtesy, I now go into this dark unrelated to the way I entered, for you have reminded me to retain a fragment, a fragment that is all I have left of my dignity. We will not chance here another time, yet eternities could glide past and I will still recall this precious, single tick of the clock. Now you go to your unknown destiny, I have already seen mine."

He shook their hands. As he walked into the gloom, they knew it would be of no use to argue him to stay, or meet again.

Out of the shadows, unseen, they heard a friendly laugh, "It is not in cipher, good gentlemen, simply hold the paper to a mirror."

Wandering along the dock, each was lost in their recall of Edgar Allen Poe. They had been in the presence of a literary brilliance and knew this was an interval in their lives never to be relived.

"Tell me, Monar, did you follow that 'moving hand writes' or 'no more of thee and me'?"

"Some of it. He was sort of rendering thoughts of a Persian poet, name of Omar Khayyàm, although Poe misquoted him somewhat. Khayyàm, among other endeavors, wrote the Diwan Rubàiyàt. From the segment Poe excerpted it would seem he's holding to the belief that fate takes trifling notice—if any—of a person, them writes them off or simply ignores them."

"If that's what you think concerning him, it's sort of depressing—or have I had too much to drink?"

"No, you're right. Poe's writing is often on that path. Now? His peers avoid him, other than for the brilliance of *The Raven*, and then if you add the loss of his wife, I wonder if his mind, his sensitivity can cope with the future."

"Could we help?"

"I don't see it happening, I really don't. In that very same Rubàiyàt, Khayyàm wrote something like 'once a flower blooms, it forever dies'. An allegory for one's life. Tonight, Poe's eyes were the door to his spirit, JT; He must have read that quatrain at one time or another and feels his life is past flowering."

"You think that, or is that what you *see*?"

Other than a nod, Monar didn't respond.

"Well then, if you do see that, what do you see for us?"

"Yours is yet to be told. Mine? For that you will have to wait to know." [9]

Holding Poe's note to the mirror, they read the clipper's new name.

THE GOLDEN RAVEN

---

[9] Edgar Allen Poe never attained a success he so richly deserved. Found unconscious in a Baltimore gutter, he died one day later, 7 October 1849. He was forty years old.

16

30 January 1848, Baltimore

The wait for the ship began. Christmas and New Year had come and gone with little notice by JT and Monar. Having never celebrated the occasions, Monar was indifferent about them, while JT, although missing the days, did not want to stop and give thought to his transformed life.

After the train to Boston, JT then went on to Salem. He felt an obligation to his father, yet was still unable to forget the past and nothing between them had changed. With no word of his mother, he then went on to Nantucket to contract for crew. With New Bedford becoming the new center for whaling and the demand for whaling ships with Nantucket sailors dwindling, a crew was easily found. These were men willing, with little thought, to go to sea for one to three years as long as the pay was reasonable and the captain just and fair at the ship's locker. Nantucket, though dying, was an island that few men left, except of course to live on ships—smaller islands.

Monar's journey took him to Salem after JT. Captain Graves was lingering on and needed to pour out his soul to Monar, the only person who did not judge. Actually, Monar felt the old Captain was doing his penitence before he died—although in truth he was simply breathing, one could not call it living. With unforeseen and beneficial information from the Captain, Monar returned to Baltimore with heavy heart.

Once back in Baltimore and while JT was still away, Monar took charge. The *Golden Raven* gained a new interior and her innards pulsated from testing the latest Brougham-Watt Steam Engine—although this blemished her exterior with the addition of an unsightly white funnel. Monar found it offensive, and accordingly, insisted the stack be sectioned with a friction fit, bolted if necessary, yet able to be removed and stowed.

Still following JT's written instructions, Monar supervised the carpenters work on two gun ports on each side of the top deck and the mounting of four, twenty-pounder carronades. These short, comparatively lightweight cannons were devastating at close range. The heavier, extended range, 32-pound, Long-nine remained in the captain's quarters, and breech-loading swivel guns, mounted topsides fore and aft, and eventually to be charged with grapeshot, meant that an experienced gunnery officer and crew could protect her from any mischievous brigands.

JT sent ahead sailors who were experienced in gunnery, steam propulsion and the general workings of a clipper ship. Two bow and one transom boards, engraved *The Golden Raven* and burnished with gold leaf, were mounted as Monar hoped—although he had one more figurine commissioned without JT's knowledge.

«»

In Salem, anyone who ever gave thought to John Paul Gould, found he wasn't too difficult to define. A sallow countenance, pockmarked from the scars of smallpox and a body giving all the manifestation of rickets without actually being so, would be a precise description. Boring to speak with, there was little to redeem him, other than he had money and was happy to spend on beer for bootlickers—in addition to anti-slavery causes.

John Paul Gould was a cousin, some number of times removed, of the revolutionary war hero, John Paul—the Jones surname affixed years later in America by the Scottish hero.

Part of John Paul Gould's knack as a braggart was his boundless knowledge of his cousins' undertakings, from the whipping of a sailor who later died, the killing of a mutineer and on to Jones' heroic command of the American Navy ship, *Bonhomme Richard* during the triumphant battle with the HM *Serapis* off Flamborough Head, England.

Gould never tired of quoting the famous words "I have not yet begun to fight", although John Paul Jones often stated he never uttered the words—he was more worried at the time, he said, by the fact his ship was sinking.

Wanting to be a hero in his own right, Gould belonged to the Wide Awakes and found in the wrathful abolitionist group those people needed to carry out his plan, a plan focused on punishing the slaver, Captain Richard Graves.

Gould had carefully scouted the lands to the west and north of Seaward as the acres of the estate itself were well guarded by roaming sentries, along with Captain Graves' two mastiffs. When Gould found elevated wooded acreage with a swampy intervale between the wood and Seaward, he gathered his little army and laid out his battle strategy.

"Simpson, you said you were a navy gunner in the '12 war, I want you to come with me to estimate the distance between some wooded land I've found and Seaward."

The five men of Gould's assemblage looked at each other until one had to ask, "What are you talking about John Paul?"

"We're going to get a cannon to bomb Seward and end Salem's shame!"

«◊»

JT could not believe his eyes. A hand-carved, oversized golden raven, its head and part of the upper body were fitted into the bow, the wings spreading up around the bowsprit. Staring ahead, beak open, the one sable eye JT could see, glared down at him.

"Damn, Monar, damn! There's never been a figurehead like that! That looks like gold leaf! This must have cost you a fortune."

Monar enjoyed JT's reaction, "It did, so don't bump it into anything."

Putting his hand on Monar's shoulder JT told him, "It's fantastic, damn! That's all I can say, other than thanks. *The Golden*

Raven will be known everywhere. Monar, this is just like I dreamed as a kid—something special! Thanks again."

He looked around, everything was shipshape, nearly all the work finished, Monar had seen to it. Then, JT saw the ten-foot high, two and a half-foot wide, round, white, funnel.

"Yee, gods and little fishes! It's even worse than I pictured."

Monar couldn't stop laughing at JT's anguish. When he could speak he was happy to respond, "No question, JT, but we can take it down when we get sick of looking at it. However, let me tell you this, we've given the *Raven* a few tests in the Bay and steam screw power is terrific. We can come about in her length."

"I'll believe that when I see it."

"I'm serious, JT, the engineer you sent down showed me. You put the rudder full over, then give the screw brief on and off power. The forward water resistance on the bow and the sudden pressure from the propeller wash on the rudder makes the stern kick sideways just a bit. Keep doing that and the ship turns within her length."

"I guess I'll have to believe you, because the principle is sound."

They walked about the ship, Monar explaining the various changes and minor problems until they came to the stern.

JT gazed across the wharf, "Ever see our friend again?"

"No, unfortunately. But a letter was delivered from him—for both of us."

'What did it say?"

Monar reached inside his oilskin and handed over Poe's note.

To Two Gentlemen from Salem,

It is eventide. The time to depart is near. Night airs waft through the ship that is destined to carry me away.

While I wait, I stand with my eyes damp, my mind charmed and captivated by a stern board √ Golden Raven

John Thomas, the eternal sea foreknows and proposes noble endeavors by you.
Monar, I make no pretense. In your eyes, lurks the graveyard of faith...for you see beyond the cloak.
May Galnen give calm sea
Aeolus, fair wind
&
Hera, starry night
To remember me.

With Memory of a Treasured Evening and two golden coins,
E. A. Poe   23 Feb 1848

"What do you make of it, Monar?"

"I'm not sure; I've had longer than you to think on it. If it's cipher, it's well hidden. Yet by the Greek gods he mentioned, he certainly wishes us well."

"It's peculiar for him to see noble events for me. God knows why and it's surely a guess on his part, probably to make me feel good. But of you? I don't know if you had faith or not—he thinks at one point you did— and at times it does appear you see what others do not."

"Actually, JT, you can read into the note whatever pleases. I think that was his intent. For now, put it aside for another time. He is a brilliant man and it was a stroke of luck we met him."

"True, we were lucky. So, where do we stand? When will we be ready to up anchor? I thought we'd head south, give the *Golden Raven* a shakedown and find some cargo."

"We already have a cargo waiting, JT—roundabout thanks to your father."

«◊»

John Paul Gould was excited. His plan was coming to fruition. After a few pints, Harvey Simpson, the former Navy gunner, had fallen wholeheartedly into John Paul's plan to bomb Seaward. Drinking ale with the plotters on the edge of the wood John Paul had picked for the deed, Simpson estimated the distance to Seaward at a half mile.

As usually happens when a person with some knowledge speaks to those with none, Harvey Simpson wanted to take charge of the expedition.

"The ideal weapon to make an impact", he stated, "would have been a 42 pounder but the damned thing weighs in at 2.5 tons, so we have no choice other than to settle for a 24-pound carronade. It's a lighter barrel, yet even with that we'll need a solid wagon and strong backs. Who can borrow a brace of horses?"

One of the five schemers, little understanding the commitment he was making, volunteered his draft horses and hay wagon.

Simpson continued, "I can lay my hands on an old 1812 carronade and gun carriage. We can swab out the barrel and cock mechanism with no problem and I'll find a quoin somewhere."

He had thrown the word quoin out, knowing no one would be familiar with the marine idiom. To blank stares, he smugly explained, "A quoin is a screw type device that adjusts the angle of the barrel thereby adjusting the trajectory of the missile."

With the four other men present, including John Paul, now trusting they were in the presence of an expert, Harvey Simpson was voted Gun Captain.

Assigning positions for gun crew, Simpson gave each man a number. Number 5 would be the powder monkey, number 4 would load the powder charge and number 2 would ram the ball down. Of course Simpson was number 1, he would give the orders, sight the gun, pour the fine powder into the priming hole, cock the firing mechanism and pull the lanyard.

"One thing you've got to remember, a 24-pound carronade is notoriously inaccurate. It's rated for over half a mile, but that simply means if all things go to plan the ball will reach our target. However, what part of the target is the question. So don't ask me to blow the front door off its hinges, only a Long-nine or Paixam's exploding shell would be that accurate. But believe me, this gun is known as The Smasher, we'll damage a lot of granite and windows on Seaward—they'll know we came calling."

"How many shots can we get off? What if the guards see us and we have to skedaddle?"

"Well, even in the dark, they'll more than likely see the gun smoke, but that swamp in the intervale will delay anyone as well as there being no real roads into here. So, when I'm done training you, I'd guess we'll get off three rounds. And when we jump in the wagon, nothing goes with us, including the gun."

They realized the plan was moving forward and it became exciting. Additionally, it had become nerve-racking.

John Paul Gould saw the tension build and took over the floor, "This is a moment in history men, be not of weak heart. We strike a first blow to end slavery. This will rouse the citizens of Salem and the surrounding countryside. It will be another shot heard round the world and we will all be heroes for the cause of…"

Simpson, as Gun Captain, considered that made him leader and leaders do not care for being intervened, "Forget that stuff! Right now, there's more important things. Here's an inventory for each person listing what they need to get. We'll meet two nights from now for practice—same place. Remember to keep your mouths *shut*! That's it, dismissed."

The three men left—John Paul was furious, ""Who the hell do you think you are? You don't interrupt me and *I'll* tell them when to leave. I'm the leader here and don't you forget it!"

"Forget it? I never knew it. All you're here for is to supply the money and be number 3. When I order, you use the wormer to swab the barrel out. You're just a number and if you don't like it, take your money and leave; we can do it without you."

Actually, Simpson did wish John Paul would take his money and leave. Being half-drunk and amused when agreeing to the attack, Simpson had more time to think and now he couldn't imagine a more dim-witted undertaking. Nonetheless, he was stuck. To back out would be the smart thing to do, although doing so would expose him to ridicule—and that, his ego could never endure. Moreover, what if Gould was wrong? What if they were not considered heroes, but fanatics? That could mean jail—his modest Navy pension taken. Simpson realized that even if he wasn't jailed, he might have to go back to sea.

John Paul saw the turmoil and lashed out at him, "Second thoughts, Harvey? Afraid for your reputation? The great gunner on the *Wasp* in the war? All your bragging about your gunnery and boarding the HM *Reindeer* and being wounded? Everyone knows the Brit ship was under- gunned and undermanned. If we knew why you were put ashore at Lorient and if the *Wasp* wasn't lost with all hands in the South Atlantic, I'll bet her captain would have been a different story about you. And now—second thoughts? You'll be the laughing…"

"Shut your bunghole, Gould, you're a damnable fool to think this up. We'll see who's afraid when they unleash the Captain's dogs!"

With that, Simpson stomped off, leaving John Paul the victor of the argument—but wondering. Dogs? The Captain has *guard dogs*?"

«»

Saturday, 3 March 1848

"What do you mean by that, Monar—thanks to my father we have a cargo?"

Monar knew his remark would get JT's attention, "I'll keep this short, if I can. When we were following the *Pike* from Barbados and left them to go to Savanna, your father did not sail straight to Salem—as you've surmised. He moored in New York, met people he knew and exchanged most of our, let me say, wages from MacPherson, for US currency…"

JT cut in, "I knew it! That's how Father has enough money for everything! And you! No wonder you've enough to carry the *Pike*—I mean *Raven*!"

"Calm down, for Christ's sake." Monar smiled as JT flopped on a chair, irritated. "Look, JT, the money we took was earned from MacPherson and he made it from tobacco."

"Right, on the backs of slaves."

"Damn it, JT, this is the last I'm going to listen to this! We can go round and round over slaves and money until the cows come home. I'm tired of it! Your God damned conscience is infuriating. I'll not be devious; I'm giving you the truth—straight out. You're the captain and it's your call. Yet we had an agreement. You want to break it? If so, go ahead. But remember, I've poured more than seven thousand dollars into this vessel on your handshake…"

"I know, but…"

"Don't *but* me. I told you all about MacPherson months ago. Furthermore, you're not trying to put it aside and get on with your life. So let's get this on the table and finish it once and for all. Yes or no? Incidentally," Monar was firm, "if you say no, you'll lose this ship, because I'm not paying for the work without our agreement in place."

"Are you threatening me?"

"Take it any damned way you want. I'm just telling you, no agreement—I leave. You pay for the shipwrights and the iron construction which, by the way, you haven't even inspected."

A split was looming edge, neither man giving quarter, yet neither man wanting it over.

At last, Monar made one last effort, "JT, I know you can go to your father and get the money. Why don't you?"

"I'll never do that."

"Even if it means you would lose the *Golden Raven*?"

"Even that."

"I know it's not pride that makes you this way, JT. I think you're the first principled man I've ever met who ever kept to them. I admire that—despite the fact you're dead wrong."

"That's your opinion, and call it what you will, I will not accept money from my father."

"Adamant with your own blood—yet you accept it from me."

JT nodded, "Yes, and why? Because I believe your past gives you justification—my father's past does not."

"You're making yourself judge and jury, you know."

"Perhaps…yet there is nothing I can do, my mind won't change."

"Your mind won't change? A peculiar way to put it, yet I believe you. There *is* nothing you can do, that's you and I'll just have to learn to put up with it I suppose. Let's go on as we have, we know each other too well to have this come between us."

The black cloud forming between them dissipated, JT held out his hand.

"One request, JT and I'm serious about this. Your father is on the brink, nothing I can do helps. As we'll be gone for who knows how long, he is sure to be dead before we return, or you have a change of mind. See him one last time before we go."

JT hesitated, then nodded, "All right. Now, what is this valuable cargo he has found us?"

"There's a New York federation of financiers who want to transfer a cargo to Southampton. They need a trustworthy, meaning silent, non-governmental way to carry out the transfer and they trust your father and through him, us. Of course some of their people may accompany us."

"And the cargo?"

"Gold bars and US currency, Five-hundred thousand dollars' worth."

17

THEY HAD STRUGGLED MIGHTILY with the cannonade. Axing trees to stumps enabled the overloaded wagon to reach the edge of the knoll. After that, they dragged the gun to a point where only a few juniper and wild blueberry bushes hid it.

John Paul Gould had fallen into line, acknowledging Harvey Simpson as Gun Captain and leader. John Paul did have other worries that he hid from the other men. He was anxious, only for himself of course, when he considered how the authorities had not solved the death of three Salem men on George's Island and that a few other Salem men suddenly lay back to sea, or otherwise left town. Who had been responsible for the deaths and departures he wasn't sure, but he tied those events together with the abrupt return of the missing Jason Graves to Seaward. This accounted for John Paul's cagey idea that, once the deed done, he would leave town and wait to see which way the wind blew before returning. If some of this group disappeared, John Paul was certain he'd be on any list.

Inside, he knew John Thomas and that black man were involved with the dead and missing sailors so with them gone, perhaps it was worth staying if there were glory—but be able to run.

Stakes were driven and block and tackle tied off between the gun carriage and trees to reduce recoil so that after each firing the gun would be hauled back into firing position. The powder charge inserted, the cannonball rammed home. They waited, fidgeting until dark.

Simpson was ready, "We're set. You know your jobs once I fire. Don't freeze up—I'll bash anyone who does. John Paul, clear the bushes away so I can check my alignment."

More nerve-wracking minutes passed as Simpson screwed the quoin to the final adjustment. The fine gunpowder was in the primer vent. Simpson removed the vent apron protecting it and cocked the mechanism. He looked at the men and saw excitement, fright, fear, and foreboding.

"I'm ready, stand clear!"

All took a deep breath. He pulled the lanyard, the cannonade thundered, belching flame, smoke, and a 24-pound cannonball. Except for Simpson, every man jumped at the sound. One man did not stand clear enough. He screamed as the recoil of the weapon caught his leg, snapping it like a stick.

Simpson ignored the man, shrieking at John Paul, "For Christ's sake—swab it out, you fool!"

The aim was true. It struck Seaward center, by the colonnaded doorway. The column shattered and granite shards ripped into the dark, blowing out windows and striking down one of the guards.

Inside, Captain Graves felt the tremor. Rising, his mouth widened in anger. He was back at sea—the blasted British were attacking again!

"Assault! We're being attacked! Beat to quarters! To the guns, raise the gun ports, run out the guns! Prepare to repel boarders. Hard right rudder! Marine snipers aloft!"

Grasping a cutlass off the wall, the Captain raced through the rooms—rousing his sleeping men to battle stations. Outside, the remaining four guards were baffled, mouths agape, staring at each other while the two mastiffs raced in different directions—neither to the sound.

At the gun, confusion held sway as well; swabbing the barrel took too long, hauling the gun back into position, difficult. At last, the powder charge and cannonball shoved home, the gun primed the lanyard yanked.

No two cannon shot land in the same location. The second ball tore through a window frame and bored into a wall— but not before striking down Captain Graves.

It became frantic at the gun. When the first shot went off, the horses raced away with the wagon. With the wagon gone and one man severely crippled, the men wanted to run. Despite them, Simpson was after one more shot. When they saw no one appeared to be coming, he cajoled them to their jobs by sheer anger. Haul the gun forward, swab, powder charge, ram the cannonball, prime.

"Fire!"

The aged barrel of the gun exploded. Killing shards from the detonation slashed out the life of four men. Only one man, Sylvania Browne, lying on the ground behind the gun carriage with a shattered leg, survived to tell the tale.

«»

"Stand off about fifty yards from that rip-rap coming abeam the port, Monar, then lower the revolutions, the onshore breeze will ease us to our dock."

The onshore breeze against the Golden Raven's freeboard nestled her to the Graves' wharf. Monar shifted the transmission into reverse. The ship shuddered a moment, then came to rest.

"Strange, Monar, no one here and where's the Ocean Pearl? No gear around either. The dinghies are gone, no line to tie off, what the devil's going on here?"

The crew used ship lines to secure, while Monar blew off steam pressure.

"Well, at least the power worked as we hoped, eh JT?"

"Yes, it sure did. I can't get over how sturdy the ship felt with the additional framing."

He looked around, "Release the crew for two days. Until the morning of the fifth at six am."

JT's befuddlement turned to concern. The deserted dock was stripped of all gear. He paced the boards waiting for Monar to finish shutting down the engine, then saw a figure move along the quay staring at him. The man came down the gangway and across the wharf. JT now recognized him.

"Jimmy Pickman, how are you? Long time."

"So it is you, JT! I wasn't sure, I looked across the harbor and saw that stink boat funnel and enormous bird on the bow and said what in hell is that? Still, I knew the Pike's line and she was at your dock so I decided to come over in my carriage."

"You were right, Jim, she's the old Pike reworked for a single screw. But tell me, what's going on here? Where's the Ocean Pearl and all the dock gear."

Pickman was apprehensive, "Hear me out, JT. There's been trouble here. As far as your schooner, she's safe at the far end of my dock. Here, the dory and everything else has been stolen."

"Damn it! Who had the nerve to steal from us? Where were our guards?"

"Actually, it could have been the guards who stole the stuff—among others. Still, there's greater crisis I have to bring up, JT. I'm sorry, but there's no other way to couch this—your father's dead. JT, I'm terribly…"

"Wait, just give me a minute to get my wits about me, Jimmy."

JT walked to the rail. Disbelief mingled with a thousand jumbled thoughts, all without form tugged at his brain. Monar, wordless with his own feelings over the loss of the Captain, his friend, left JT there alone, going up to Pickman and introducing himself.

"What happened? The Captain's heart just give out?"

Pickman stepped back from the man, "No, Mr. Monar, in truth, it comes down to murder."

JT heard and came back intense, "What are you saying, Jimmy, father was murdered?

"JT, five men got a cannon and fired on Seaward. From what I've been told, your father went berserk—I'm sorry, that's the word the guards used—your father thought he was aboard ship, at war. He ran through the rooms shouting orders and a cannonball put him down. I'm sorry."

Monar's face was as stone, "The men, you have them?"

"Not really, the gun exploded, four died."

"You said there was five men, what happened to the fifth?"

"Lost his leg, crippled for life—if he lives, that is. Blood poisoning."

"When did this happen?"

"Last week," turning to JT, Pickman said, "but there's more I'm afraid, JT. The guards took off, leaving Seaward unprotected. It's been vandalized. When I heard, I had some of my men go up to protect it. I'll be honest, they weren't too concerned either…well, your father…"

"I know, Jimmy, let it go at that. Thanks for all you've done, I couldn't have asked more. Where's father now?"

"No one claimed him. I had him on ice but wasn't able get in touch with your mother and then the ground thawed enough so I had him buried at the cemetery. I didn't have a marker put in because I didn't want that vandalized as well; I've a drawing of its location in my coach, I'll to give you. Oh, and before I forget, I've got your father's two dogs at my house, I'll keep them if you want."

"That will be fine. I'm indebted to you, Jimmy, but aren't you taking a chance yourself? You can't be too loved by the residents."

"I'm like you and your father, JT. Anyone crosses me will regret it."

"All right then, we'll head on up to Seaward now. You've been a good friend, Jimmy—could I ask another favor?"

"Of course, but first, your schooners at my dock and you can keep her there as long as you like and I'll have a few of my men watch over here. So, what do want me to do?"

"Give me a minute to think." They waited. When he spoke again, it was with finality, "Jim, we won't be here long and I don't know when we'll be back. This wharf is financed along with Seaward. I'll get another agency to patrol it and the house. What I'd like to offer you is the use of the Ocean Pearl and our wharf as long as you want. I won't have that many ships again."

Pickman was taken back, "JT, that's a tremendous offer. Believe me when I say we need the space. Let me lease them at some figure."

"No, they're yours until whenever. If the time comes to sell the wharf, it's at your price."

Jimmy Pickman loaned his coach. As they wound their way up the road to the granite home on the hill, the onshore breeze was bringing a warm spring to New England. Neither man cared.

JT, locked in his own thoughts, didn't notice Monar was quiet, moody. When he spoke it was heartfelt and intense, "A great man is lost, JT. He was great because he descended into a self-imposed torment from his one flaw; he wanted to keep what he had built, for himself, yes, but also for his wife and you children—and his legacy. He spoke with me as an equal even when I was a slave. We became close friends when no one else would help, when no one else would understand the pain, the agony over his deeds, deeds that made him so troubled. His real legacy, JT, will be how one error, one dreadful episode, can erode a mind—can prey on an honest person and destroy every other good he had done…"

He turned to JT and met the moist eyes that saw nothing, "I'll not go easy on you, JT. You wronged him, you wronged your father. You wouldn't let him into your heart and comfort him. And the profound thing of him? He understood and forgave your unkindness, something you were not capable of doing. I'll not go on, I've had my say over this, but you'd be a better man by remembering you failed your blood."

The silence between them was unbroken.

The two men Jimmy Pickman had posted to guard the site recognized JT and let them pass the paint-splashed columns of Seaward. Still without words between them, they stopped at the front of the building. Broken windows and the door were boarded up; one bombed and broken column lay scattered across the entrance. Monar ripped off the board blocking the door and entered the hallway and noticed a cannonball embedded in the wall down the corridor, and then caught sight of the red stain defacing the wall and carpet.

He was infuriated, seething within. His friend was dead—he wanted revenge. Yet against who? The fools who did this? They were dead. There was no way to wreak vengeance. One crippled man left and even he will more than likely die of blood poisoning. Well, Monar thought, he'd let that happen, it was a pain-racked way to die.

In an attempt to ease his grief, needing some release, he took the bolo from his boot and threw it the length of the hallway. It sliced into the far wall and stuck there, yet there was no relief. He went deeper through the rooms, alone.

Regret. Monar's words were as a knife coursing through JT's very being. He wandered unseeing along the trash-laden floors, past broken furniture, smashed sculptures and ripped paintings of ancestors. At the great room, someone, some nobody, had taken an axe to his father's chair—the splintered, oversized ruin of it became too much. JT dropped to his knees and wept. Monar's words had taken their toll on him. He had denied his own blood, his own father.

Following Pickman's drawing through the cemetery, they found the fresh mound under an aged oak. Telling JT to go on ahead, Monar stood, his back to the grave, patting the horse, whispering to it softly.

JT was lost, his mind in tatters. He could only ask his father to forgive. Repeatedly he asked, yet there was no answer, "I'll make it up to you, father…someway, somehow."

When JT returned to the coach, Monar approached the grave and sat crossed-legged under the oak, "There is little I can say, Captain. I'm sorry I couldn't help save you from yourself, but what happens when a person dwells on their behavior too long is never pleasant. You know how I feel, I would rip out the heart of those who did this if I could, but they died before I could get to them. They are lucky. Aside from losing you, that is my soul regret. After helping JT, I was going to tell him I thought I'd stay with you, but…well, I won't go on with you about him right now—it will give us something to debate in hell…my friend."

Traveling back to the *Raven*, Monar spoke up, "I'm not going to take back a word I said, JT."

"Why should you? Your words were true. You showed your love for my father in what you said on the way up to the house. I was callow—blind."

"You are honest in that you can recognize you failed. Yet you know it's too late—don't you?"

Later that night, Monar went off in the coach, stopping at the Essex Street Church. Being refused his request, Monar drew to his full height and said Captain Graves had bequeathed the church a sum of considerable value. Still rebuffed, Monar, with a maniacal look then whispered he would snap the parson's neck. "…like the worthless, withered old twig you are."

With that impetus, off they went at the witching hour to the grave for benediction.

When returning to the church, Monar threatened the parson by shouting a malediction on him of demons from hades and then roughly pushed the poor man out of the coach, laughing manically and pounding his feet on the floor of the coach, he watched the good reverend, muddy nightshirt a-flying; scamper off across the lawn. That man knew that this night he had seen the very devil up close.

"Where have you been?" JT was curious, although knowing Monar was given to being nomadic after dark.

"I thought your father should have a final blessing, so I took a parson up to him."

"And the parson went?"

"Do you think he really had a choice, JT?"

Looking to his friend, JT could only murmur thank you, "I should have thought of that."

"You were too busy pitying yourself."

They looked hard at each other. Two pensive smiles, understanding between the two men.

"I'll try to do better in the future, Monar."

"I believe you must and will. There will be times to prove your mettle."

Damn, JT thought, another one of Monar's dark perceptions?

«»

Everything was done. The countless little things and more. Guards hired from Pinkerton's Agency, a new company from Chicago, the crew returned aboard. The Boston attorney, named Richard Dana, who, Jim Pickman said, spoke Brahmin, hired as Power of Attorney for Seaward, Jason and JT's mother, Mary. Attorney Dana said he would make every effort to find Mary Graves, despite her failure to attend her husband's admittedly vague, funeral. A headstone was ordered. There simply was nothing left to do, no reason to stay in Salem.

JT leaned on the gunwale, having relived memories with Pickman, "Well, Jimmy, those were some good larks we went off on. Some not so good times as well."

"You're thinking back on Lily Hunt, aren't you?"

"I guess I was. Sixteen years old, to find her drowned like that, doesn't make sense and how some feeling I had kept me wanting to go up along that feeder stream—you remember? You wanted to go downstream, but something nagged me to keep going up. It was so strange; I don't know why, yet some premonition made me go that way."

"I don't want to remember, JT. That was the first time I saw a dead person. But let's drop the subject, you're leaving is sad enough. Think you'll be back?"

"Certainly no plans, but you never know. Perhaps you'll see the Golden Raven race in here someday and anger the good townsfolk again."

Truly, JT thought, his only predestined plan was to see Charlee by the end of 1849.

Jimmy interrupted JT's thinking, "Just rein her in before you hit my quayside, that's all I ask."

JT returned to the moment, "I'll try to remember that. Well, old friend, it's time you abandoned ship unless you want to go New York and England and Savanna or God knows where else."

"Thanks, I'd like to, but I've a company to run and money to make. Just don't stop in Canada. The Irish immigrants from the potato famine have brought a Typhus epidemic to their ports and stand well off Ireland's ports as well, same problem."

"Thanks, I wasn't aware of that."

As Pickman walked down the ramp, he turned and only somewhat joked, "Be careful with your engine, bear in mind the steamboat Pulaski—that was God awful."

"I know, but that was back in the '30s. Lot of safety been added since then. You'll see, someday you'll be putting around here in a stink boat, fouling up the atmosphere."

His wave returned, JT then turned to Monar, "We shipshape and ready to slip the ties that bind us to Salem, Chief Mate?"

"Yes, Captain, even the lockers are full. Want me to get steam up?"

Looking about the busy walkways, JT decided not to, "No, we'll leave under full sail, and I mean full sail, goose-wing her. Order the men to the yards and have the bow drawn out. We've a fair offshore breeze and it'll give the gawkers something to see. And don't put up that damn chimney! "

The Golden Raven shivered, purging her shackles to shore.The sails began to fill; gawkers came from everywhere, out of shops, from side streets, children ran along the wharfs. A two-hundred foot Clipper ship leaving her mooring in full glory was a sight seldom seen. The Golden Raven's figurehead, burnished by the sun, softly rose to assume its task of guiding the way. Though a seafaring town, the people, despite their hate of the Captain, couldn't help but stop in their tracks in awe. JT threw the wheel over to catch the breeze, then eased the clipper off to run downwind. He caught sight of Jim Pickman, his workers and a throng of townspeople gather at the end of wharfs—clapping furiously. A massive mountain of white duck canvas cloaked the harbor's entrance as the fast clipper ship glided majestically through the harbor. The moment was bittersweet. Salem would never see such a sight again—for the *Golden Raven* would never see Salem again.

18

Saturday 22 April 1848

"DAMN THIS FOG, MONAR, I can barely read the chart, never mind see from one marker to the next. Keep this heading until the next red buoy, then draw off to starboard to find that ship basin. We'll drop anchor when I give the word. Keep your revs down to where we can barely hold steerageway."

"Yes, Captain, I've two men on the bow. Good that we have steam power, eh?"

JT laughed with Monar, "Yes, handy, but not too much good in this pea-soup."

They had made the turn into New York's lower bay and were straightaway blanketed in a fogbank hugging the shore. With sails furled and under power, they picked up markers by compass bearings until it became too chancy. Now, proceeding off channel to where the chart defined a ship basin, they crept to where they could lay to until the fog lifted.

"Back off the revs, Monar, there's a good chance some other ships may have done the same."

As they inched along, they heard someone shout, "...Bloody hell! Hey, there mate, sheer off to port! Don't stove in me ship, she's bunged enough!"

The broad hull of a packet ship rose through the mist. Without waiting for the order, Monar stopped the propeller while JT threw the rudder over. The *Raven's* bowsprit cleared the packet ship's rigging and drifted alongside. Monar then reversed the transmission, the *Raven* juddered and, abeam the packet ship, went dead in the water.

Again they heard the unseen speaker, "Nice piece of sailing, mate. I was sure you were going to thump that pretty little bird of yours on me gun'al. You're lucky that gold glows even in this filthy muck."

The speaker came into view, a round, flushed little man, whiskers down to his captain's jacket, clenching a meerschaum pipe in his mouth.

JT tossed off a salute, "We thank you, sir, for your warning. Our bow lookouts must be asleep." JT looked around the man's deck, littered with debris, "What happened to your ship?"

As if by rote, the man spoke, "Me name's Gideon Boyle, Master of this vessel the *Black Watch* out of Newcastle on Tyne—England to you. We were knocked down by a monster wave; we were broached, went up on our beam-ends and lost our main and mizzen sticks. God help us—we lost all but…five of the crew and…one passenger… I, I…"

Monar came up to JT, "Talking about it makes him begin to fathom what happened."

"I see that." JT spoke to the Captain, "Are you all right, Sir? How can we help? Do you have injured?"

"Yes…yes we do. Would you please…raft alongside…yes…

raft alongside—and help a bit?"

"Of course." JT looked to Monar, "We'll make us fast to his ship and drop our stern bower to be sure. You get some men and supplies, including brandy, and go over and do whatever you can. Make sure to check the injured and see that she isn't going to founder."

"Yes, Sir, we'll do all that we can."

The ship looked sound, Clyde built and not taking on more water than any other ship. Yet, from below decks to topside was a calamity. The *Black Watch's* mizzen and mainmasts were by the board, their stays and rigging cut away to stop her from floundering. Her topsides were another matter. Two of her four cannon had broken their mounts and shattered three or four sections of the top deck bulkheads. The other two cannon would have rolled loosely except for fouling in the stays and broken decking. Unless he was mistaken, JT though the ship had hogged. The wave must have hung her amidships and her fore and aft, unsupported, sagged and fractured her spine, probably at the scarf joint. JT figured the *Black Watch* would likely never go to sea again.

Jumping down to the ship's deck and seeing that his crew was doing a good job in helping, but not seeing Monar, JT went over and kneeled beside Captain Boyle.

"Captain, my name is John Thomas Graves; I'm master of my ship The Golden Raven. You say there was a monstrous wave—where was this?"

Captain Boyle, on his third swig of brandy, was calming, "Aye, Captain Graves, we were near becalmed, little steerageway. The bloody wave, come out of the fog, hit our stern port quarter…broke right atop us. Methinks an earthquake somewhere. Must a…been fifty feet or more if it was a foot. Took away our lifeboats, two masts and…God, most of my crew. We were further off-shore; I'd say ten leagues."

JT calculated the now seldom used distance marker, "More than thirty miles? How the devil did you do it? This ship is little more than a hulk." He was sorry he used the term.

Boyle looked up with red eyes, "Well, this hulk and a jury-rigged foresail got us here."

He gave further thought, "Do ye think her back is broken? Somehow I heard a cracking sound."

When JT nodded, Captain Boyle cast an eye about to the five remaining crewmembers—five out of twenty-five.

JT realized the stress the captain must have endured and was obviously still under and gave Boyle another mouthful, "You must have done a hell of a bit of seamanship, Captain. It's surprising you didn't turn turtle and lose everyone."

"It wasn't me, sir; Lady Bunting was at the tiller."

"You had a woman at the helm—why or earth would you do a thing like that?"

"Because she's as good as any Captain—and navigator too. And aside from that, she owns the *Black Watch*. It was she who heard a kind of hissing sound and, and she…asked what the devil it was. I never heard the like before…I looks about and there was this bloody great mountain of water. I couldna speak—it crested and come roaring down on us."

"It broke right on you?"

"Yarr, there must a been a shoal…a shoal under us that made her break right there."

"Then what did you do?"

"I dinna know, I found meself halfway down the blasted ladder coughing me guts out and Lady Evelyn with blood on her face shouting bleeding orders everywhere to almost no one."

"You're telling me that after that this woman got you into here?'

"Dinna you ken me, laddy? A lass but not just any lass, that she isn't."

JT could tell that Captain Boyle was quickly three sheets to the wind.

Boyle recalled something else, "Lady Evelyn, hit in the eye, she was."

"Where is she now?"

"I sent that…black bloke of yours below to her quarters. She's banged up."

"Yes, you said that. You sent Monar down to her? She'll be petrified."

"Not her, she's a tough old Jack-tar, never you doubt that. Her father give her this ship, one of more than thirty."

JT was surprised and curious, "That seems strange, all that wealth and his daughter owns a packet ship. You'd think she'd have a fancy decked-out schooner."

Captain Boyle was fading but stiffened, "Not strange…this was me ship for thirty years. Thirty years with Lord Warfield Bunting's, Black Moon Line, I was. The best captain I might add, the best—despite what you sees. Lady Evelyn…God bless her…wanted to visit friends in America and his Lordship doesn't want her to sail without another captain along. And this ship? Well, you'll see the *Watch* is a right comfortable and quick vessel—or she was. Made in Greenwich for the Lord to travel in style before he give it to his daughter. God…she had three servants aboard, they're gone—washed away by God."

Captain Boyle started to fade; the brandy just what he needed, "It's odd, do you know?" he started, "This was to be my…last voyage, round trip. Drop me Lady off, wait 'till she returned. Go back to Newcastle. Planned to move inland, we was…Cambridge with me wife…guess it…will…be my last…"

Setting the bottle down beside the captain, JT leaned him back on the wheelhouse, "Sleep it off for a while old timer, you're going to wake to the shock of it all again."

JT checked on the help his seamen were giving to the five other survivors and saw Monar coming up the ladder, "You find our last survivor?"

Monar was unusually brief, "Yes."

"And?"

"And I helped bandage the eyebrow."

"That's an extremely brief report, First Mate."

By now, Monar was grinning from one ear to the other, "JT, you won't believe who's below."

"I already know; some woman captain named Bunter."

"Not Bunter, Lady Evelyn Bunting, Warfield Bunting's daughter. I met them before! Spoke with them years ago in Barbados. That was when Lord Warfield was sailing the Caribe looking for land, Saint Kitts, or Nevis, I think, doesn't matter. She was very young then, around eight or nine. She must be twenty-seven, twenty-eight now—but damned if she didn't remember me."

JT smiled, "Who the devil wouldn't remember you, you big oaf. And I never knew you to be so happy to see a white person."

Monar spoke seriously, 'JT, my friend, this isn't just any white person. When I met them in the islands, she was an unruly, independent girl. Now? Well now, she's a vision, a beautiful, beautiful person."

JT chided him, “A beautiful English woman? You’re making her into too much, aren’t you? I’ll bet you’re putting me on about some dowdy little frump.”

Monar smirked, “Go below and introduce yourself. She has a bandage on her eyebrow, yet you’ll agree. And try not to make too much of a fool of yourself— I’ve already warned her about what a buffoon you are, so she’s not expecting much.”

Starting down the ladder, JT shouted over his shoulder, Monar! If you’re kidding, I’m going to keelhaul you— I swear.”

Looking to the bottom of the ladder, JT gaped, struck dumb by a wan smile from a stunning woman. He heard her low accent as if from afar, “That’s something I’d like to see.”

Startled, then finding his voice, “What, what would you like to see, Miss?”

“Why you—when you attempt to keelhaul Monar, what else?”

He was struggling, captivated by her grey eyes, “Oh, that’s… that’s, you know…sort of a joke between us, yes, only a remark between seamen, of course—jokingly.”

JT then appeared to have swallowed his tongue and watched Lady Bunting make a face, a lovely face, “I assume you’re to be our savior, Captain Graves,” JT nodded wordlessly as she continued, “and I would like to speak with you once you know what you’d like to say. When you’re sure, I’ll be in my cabin. Simply knock, Captain.”

The door closed behind her tussled blond hair while JT stood, mouth agape, listening to Monar at the top of the ladder, laughing… laughing…

Going back on deck, JT was shamefaced, “Why the devil didn’t you say how pretty she was?”

“Me? Weren’t you listening? I said she was beautiful woman, a vision.’

“I thought you were putting me on! Damn near made a fool of myself!”

“Damn near? That you did, JT—in spades.”

Monar went up to JT, putting an arm around his shoulders, "Ah, youth, what laughingstocks you be compared to we older, more worldly men. So now, with more knowledge, do you think you can go back into the fray without embarrassing me again—Captain, Sir?"

By now, JT was shaking his head in disbelief. It was apparent he had shown his few years and he determined to—to what? "What should I do, Monar?"

"Advice? My Captain wants my advice so he doesn't hang up on the rocks again? Come on, JT, stop making so much of it; you got caught off-guard, that's all. Why not just try to be yourself?"

"What if that was my real self?"

"If it is, then I'd hop back aboard the Raven and go hide in the chain locker. Look, JT, that woman is so far above you, above any of us in every way, why worry? So for Christ's sake, until she goes ashore, try to string a few sentences together and not bore her to death."

"I just don't get it, Monar. I wasn't this way with Salem girls, or Charlee."

"JT, listen to me. The girls in Salem and probably even Charlee, no offence meant, were girls. Nice girls, pretty girls—whatever—but girls. Lady Evelyn Bunting is a woman. Now you know the difference. And, if you're smart, be courteous, help her if asked and stay out of her hair."

Monar was still smiling as JT walked off, cussing. He then steeled his spine, went down the ladder, hesitated in the companionway, then knocked. There was no answer.

Turning to leave, the door opened, "Captain Graves?"

He was ready now and firm, "Yes, Miss Lady Evelyn. I'm just checking to see that you are all right and if there might be anything we can help you with."

She was beautiful, undeniably so, even with the patch on her eyebrow. She smiled at the Miss Lady Evelyn, "I'm fine, Captain."

Yet he saw something in her eyes, "May I come in? I'll try to make sense this time."

She was wearing, of all things, jodhpurs, boots and a long-sleeved leather jerkin, all of which were formfitting,

"Please excuse my attire, Captain, my dress clothes are ill fitting for the circumstances and I've toggled together these riding pieces as they're all I have left, until more dry that is."

"You look fine; the outfit surely looks fine to me, Miss." He could have kicked himself.

Starting to speak, Lady Evelyn smiled, then caught herself and looked away. Awkward, JT struggled for something more levelheaded to say, "Is there anything I could get you? Some food...Brandy? I'm terribly sorry about the loss of your servants."

Another engaging smile, "They weren't my servants, Captain—they were my friends. We had planned to meet up with other friends in New York, travel to your Virginia for dressage and perhaps a hunt..." Her eyes glistened, her voice dropped, "Please excuse me, Captain. I don't mean to make you feel discomforted, but I find I'm not ready to accept company yet—would you please excuse me?"

JT started to leave; Lady Evelyn walked to him and gave a sisterly kiss on his cheek. He felt touched by a spirit when she put her hand on his arm, "Thank you, Captain. I understand you only wished to comfort. Please return this evening and I'll try to be a courteous compere. Oh, and bring some of that brandy you mentioned, that would be nice."

With that, Lady Evelyn opened the door for JT to ease through, "Of course," she whispered, "be sure and bring my old friend, Monar."

That evening, a radiant smile sought to hide her sadness at the loss of her friends and crew, "Welcome, Captain and Monar, to my most humble abode."

Lady Evelyn nodded slightly as the two men entered while she continued, "I went to ask Captain Gideon to join us but I'm told he couldn't be woken. I was also told it was something about his being under the weather. Either of you gentlemen know anything about that?"

JT was sheepish, “I’m afraid that was my fault, Lady Evelyn…”

She interrupted, “One moment, if you please, Captain. Under these circumstances, I think it would be best if we deferred the usual courtesies to the proper time. For the present, simply call me Evelyn and I will call Monar, Monar. What do you propose I call you, Captain?”

“My name is John Thomas. Friends call me JT; I’d be pleased if you considered that.”

“Then I would like to please you…JT. Now, tell me about Captain Boyle, he seldom imbibes and never to this point.”

“Well, Miss, I mean, Evelyn, we felt he was going into shock from the wave and his fall, so I suggested he have a nip or two and well…”

“I see,” Lady Evelyn fixed a stern glare on JT, “and did you also know that before a fall that rendered Captain Boyle unconscious for a bit, he still managed to tend the remainder of the crew—God rest their souls—and still help me?”

Guessing Lady Evelyn was not as stern as she appeared, JT offered his response, “No, I didn’t know, yet I’m not surprised. Any Captain should do that. But the reason I gave him the brandy was simply because I thought it the best medicine.”

A smile creased her mouth. She asked them to sit and noticed their gift, “Ah, I see you brought the brandy…JT,” she laughed, “and mugs also. Very thoughtful, I afraid my crystal set was a causality of that frightful wave.”

Lady Evelyn’s eyes glazed, reliving the incident. Monar hastily spoke up, “I can’t tell you how surprised I was to see you again…Evelyn—and that you remembered me from twenty or more years past.”

“Remember you? Please, Monar, I think you were fifteen or sixteen at the time, yet even then, you were taller than anyone and from my little girl view, you were a sight to never forget—even more so now. When I saw you come into my cabin, my heart jumped, my knight in shining armor had come to rescue me. Well, perhaps not shining armor, but seeing that burnished bolo you still carry in your boot brought you back to me. Tell me, how is that nice Mr. MacPherson doing? As I recall, father said he had an eye for the women."

Monar appeared dismayed, "My master unfortunately died in a house fire. I knew he was in his cups—I'm sorry to have to say that and I should have taken more care of him. He must have fallen somehow. The next we knew his house was a tinderbox. No chance to save him. All we slaves were sad."

JT looked away, unable to keep from smirking. Monar's poignant story of MacPherson's passing appeared so sincere it was difficult to reconcile it with the actual event. Lady Evelyn didn't quite swallow the story either, "I'm sorry about Mr. MacPherson's passing, but really, Monar, 'the slaves were sad'? That's rather gilding the lily, don't you think?"

As they chatted on, she realized her nerves were causing her to go on too much about the wave, "Excuse me, gentlemen, I do believe I'm nattering on and not being the proper host—I apologize."

Not that they knew it, but her speech was southwest Cornwall and both men hurried to deny her any need for any apology, they simply loved to hear her voice.

The brandy was measured out into mugs, the oil lantern swung listlessly, they made small talk of the lapsed years.

Lady Evelyn's past was written in the sailor clothes she wore. Long-legged blue navy trousers of coarse spun cloth, loose white blouse buttoned to the neck. A waist-length blue jacket with narrow lapels and two brass sleeve buttons overlaid the blouse. She appeared quite comfortable in the clothes and, of all things, a worn captain's hat lay on a whaleback trunk, which they both noticed.

Lady Evelyn smiled, at their expressions, "Yes, gentlemen, even though I'm only a frail woman, I have my British Maritime, Master Mariner papers."

Simply stated, both men knew those papers meant she had unrestricted license to sail any type of ship, anywhere a ship could be sailed. They knew of no woman who had such.

Despite that, JT had to ask, "You've commanded a steam vessel?"

Blond hair fell over gray eyes as she nodded, "Aye, among others, I captained the side-wheel steamship *Hope* to Malta, for the Royal Navy and I was Master and Navigator on the armored steamship *Ghazna*, delivered to the Dardanelles for the Turks. She was a screw propeller—like your system, only twin screw."

She knew her way around ships; that was apparent. Yet her answers brought more questions causing Monar to query, "You commanded an armored British warship? I don't follow what that means, and where are the Dardanelles?"

Lady Evelyn was unexpectedly forthcoming, "Let me back up. I'm immodest, it must be the brandy, yet I wanted you both to know—especially you, Monar. You must remember how I was when we met in Barbados."

Monar's blush, even within his dark skin, was clear, "I remember quite well, Evelyn."

She gave him a side-glance, "I was afraid you did. I guess that is why I want to explain how I've changed. Now, to explain how I became a captain. I have two mental peculiarities that few women have—probably because they don't get the chance in a man's world. One, I love mathematics, hence navigation. Two, I learned to sail dinghy's in the squalliest water imaginable off Penzance and the Isle of Wight—literally on a servants' knee. Mother left when I was five and in truth, I remember little of her. She was rebellious; father told me when I was older. She would be gone for weeks and leave me with nannies—in fact anyone who would put up with me for that matter. Luckily, at least for me, the servants' found I would shut up, at least for a while, if they took me sailing. Now, father didn't exactly ignore me, but he was building his empire and I wasn't a son—as males, you know what that means."

She took another sip of brandy, it was clear it was affecting her, yet it helped release the anxiety within. Her eyes darted about the room, seeing snippets of her life unfold.

"Let me shorten this up, Gentlemen. At about the same time mother left once again, father found I loved sailing. It was as if, for the first time, he realized salt water flowed in my veins as it did in his. From that time forward, there was nothing he wouldn't do to help me achieve my hope of becoming a merchant captain. And here I am, end of story."

She had been telling only one element of her becoming a captain. There were the battles, sometimes physical. One argument in the Balearics led to a duel with a Spaniard. It was with pistols—she, barely grazed in the arm, her opponent, severely wounded.

Then, began the struggles to acquire her marine licenses. Her constant failures in tests, it turned out, were due specifically to Board Members falsifying her answers. That was the sole time her father stepped in. He had influence in government, with the power to hold up funding the massive merchant fleet budget that was England's lifeblood. The Board relented, allowing oversight to her evaluation. She passed easily; her father then forced every Marine Advisory Board Member off the Board.

Of this, neither JT nor Monar knew a thing. JT, however, could easily imagine the difficulties a woman would have to overcome in the era of iron men and wooden ships. This was the first time, that he'd met a woman who was his equal at sea. His equal, he thought. Whom did he think he was kidding? He had to admit she had done more, sailed more years, and to distant ports he had hardly even heard about. The capper was she had the all-round experience, from sail to power, that he had yet to acquire.

"Now, to finally answer your questions, JT. About the ironclad steamer *Ghazna*—and this can get confusing. She was the former RN ship *Constant*, a seventy-four gun, Ship of the Line. She was built in '28 and getting old. We, England that is, had her converted to iron clad hull and started an analysis—in other words—an ironclad warship first, and then steam power screws added. But before a true evaluation she was sold to…

"Let me start again. The British government believes there is going to be a war in the Dardanelles or the Crimea because Russia is starting to infringe on the remnants of the Ottoman Empire. England is adamant that Russia not gain entrance south into the Gallipoli Peninsula or any warm water port in the Baltic. Therefore, we and the French—the bleeding French of all people—intend to stop them, but covertly, at least for now. With a civilian crew and my having nothing to do with the RN, I was engaged to deliver the steam ironclad, *Ghazna*—reduced to fifty guns to help compensate for the additional plating I might add—to Canakkale, a Turkish port near the Dardanelles. And I'll say this, making it from Southampton to Canakkale, through the Med with the *Ghazna's* new iron incasing was one chancy trip. Her weather keeping is little better than a sieve's. Anyone who takes her into battle had better keep a life vest handy—or wear one, because she is one top-heavy, unstable ship."

JT was enthralled, never had he heard a woman speak with such knowledge of the sea. Quite simply, he was in love with her aura, beauty, ability, intelligence, language and, let's face it—her position in life—all of it wondrous to him.

Monar saw JT's gaze and shuddered, trying to ignore him, "So, Evelyn, on the morrow. If the fog lifts, JT and I plan to raft the *Black Watch* further into the bay until we make contact with a harbor pilot. Captain Boyle will have to tell the pilot what he thinks about your ship, but JT's afraid she's hogged and the pilot will designate the wharf. But wherever he assigns, be assured we'll get you safely ashore before we're on our way."

She squeezed her eyes shut, hurting her eyebrow, "I was hoping the best for the Watch, yet I believe JT's right. Let's proceed the way you said, Monar, and take it from there. And now, I'm feeling tried, gentlemen, if you'll excuse me, I've some sad letters to write."

After they left, Lady Evelyn took up pen, ink and paper. Yet she was tired and admitted to herself, a bit tipsy. Sitting back in her chair, reviewing the meeting and the interaction between the two men, she thought it strange. They seemed quite close. She had heard Monar laughing at JT earlier on the top deck—when JT was tongue-tied on first meeting her—and that was certainly not something that would happen in a normal captain to subordinate context aboard ship, or anywhere, actually. She would not have allowed it, yet the more she gave it thought, it seemed the two of them were more partners, rather than captain and mate. Then, another thing, what really did happen with Ian MacPherson? Monar's description was too pat and too offhanded. His 'all the slaves were sad' comment was too much to swallow. Whatever happened, Monar had grown mentally, physically and apparently, financially. Yet more than his size, she recalled his eyes back then, and how they glared at Mr. MacPherson. There was no love lost there. Even though she was young at the time, she could easily remember that.

Lady Evelyn saw the bottle holding the remainder of the brandy and sipped on it. And the young man, John Thomas-JT. Handsome, she mused. Probably made all the girls go silly. She could see why. Rugged, clearly rough about the edges, yet decent—that characteristic caught her eye. And smart, anyone as young as he and owned and commanded a fast clipper had to be intelligent in many ways. She lay down on her bunk, beginning to doze. Lady Evelyn's last thoughts were of when she was that young girl and how captivating Monar was then—and still is.

After the meeting with Lady Evelyn, Monar tried to convince JT that his feelings for her were not love, but infatuation. Having no success with that and while JT was doing last rounds, Monar went to the modest library in the Captain's quarters, found an 1843 edition of Noah Webster's dictionary and looked up the word he wanted. He bent the book's binding back, underlined the words and kept the book open with a set of dividers.

Going back up the ladder to the top deck, he called out to JT, "Ho, Captain, left some reading for you on your bunk. Something to sleep on. See you in the morning."

JT was curious and finishing his rounds, retired to his cabin. The dictionary was open, he saw the underlined words.

Infatuate… to affect with folly...

Infatuated… made foolish by love, blindly in love…

Infatuation…foolish or all-absorbing passion…

And then, he read the next underlined word below.

Infeasible…not feasible; impracticable…

JT laughed aloud. At just what, he wasn't sure. He dog-eared the page and then slammed the volume closed. Perhaps Monar was right. Stay with your own class, less hurt. Yet, there was Charlee, was he even in her class? Was there to be hurt there as well?

The fog bank dissipated with the early morning sun. Lady Evelyn Bunting had her father's Black Moon Line pennant flown at half-staff from the remaining mast while the *Black Watch* was made fast to the *Golden Raven.* Under steam power, the journey upriver began.

Captain Boyle was depressed and stayed in his cabin while Lady Evelyn toured topside, checking the rafting lines and suggesting the rudder be kept two points from midpoint to compensate for the drag of the Black Watch. The Hudson River was strange water to JT and Monar and they paid attention to her and the chart.

They said hello to Lady Evelyn as she came up to the helm, "Gentlemen, how are we this morning?"

Nodding they were fine, JT asking how her eyebrow felt and then if this was her first visit to New York. She answered the last query, "Actually no, the one other time I was here was in '43, five years ago. It was the maiden voyage of the Great Britain. She was iron hulled, Bristol built and it was exciting; father was with the Maritime Commission Board and had pushed to have her built, so he managed to have me included in the festivities."

"It must have been exciting, going from wooden ships and iron men adage to the start of iron ships and wooden engineers."

She smiled in agreement, "I guess you're right, JT. The *Britain* was something; three-hundred-twenty-two feet of iron hull, a thousand steam driven horsepower, and twin screw.

Of course there were other steamships visiting New York but they were side-wheelers. With the Britain, you couldn't see the propulsion; she simply glided through the water. That surely brought the crowds out in amazement."

"And here we are," Monar observed, "two wooden ships wrestling against the Hudson River's tide with one propeller between us. The times are changing for us old salts."

Lady Evelyn looked across the littered deck of her ship, then back into Monar's eyes, "I much prefer the old days, Monar, my friend. Iron men, wooden ships."

The harbor pilot's boat slipped alongside. The *Black Watch*, after the pilot went below to assess the damage, was towed by the pilot boat to the wharfs holding derelict vessels. So that Lady Evelyn would not hear, the pilot whispered to Monar that the ship, as she was not leaking too badly, would be utilized as a prison ship for New York's various scoundrels. If Lady Evelyn had the slightest thought her beloved *Black Watch* would become a prison ship, she would have had her towed to sea and burned.

Storage containers were made available for most of Lady Evelyn's belongings and a last offer for the ship as she lay, accepted. These funds and more were given to Captain Boyle and the remainder of the crew along with a letter from Lady Evelyn that the captain would present to Warfield Bunting for additional funds for the families of those lost.

JT and Monar admired Lady Evelyn's expertise in handling the transactions and firmness in the dealings. The sharp salvage dealers soon learned she was not above the fray or shy in calling them out if she felt a shrewd or deceitful practice was attempted. She learned well from her father, she said.

When the harbor pilot informed JT and Monar of their wharf location and number, Monar paid his respects to Lady Evelyn. She took his hand, saying a few words quietly to him. Monar brows arched slightly, was then he was off, per written instructions from certain Boston financiers, to Middleford and Kent, Esq., Attorneys for the Second Bank of New York.

Zachariah Kent, Chairman of the Second Bank was, in point of fact, the person who exchanged Spanish reales and British Crown notes for his old friend Captain Richard Graves when Graves and his son Jason sailed the Laurence Pike from Barbados to New York. Since that time, Kent and the senior Graves stayed in contact and when Kent wrote needing a confidential shipment of gold and silver transported to England, Graves, though slipping away mentally, recommended his son, John Thomas and Monar.

The reason for confidentiality was two-fold. One being the Second Bank of New York, including Attorneys Middleford and Kent, along with other US consortiums of financiers, wished to invest in a proposed offering of stock that bore the imprint of the privately held and mighty, British East India Company. This offering was for a major railroad undertaking that would link Madras, a seaport on the west of India, with Calcutta, the capital, in the Bengal, to the northwest. Further expansion of the railroad would drive it across India to Bombay, another seaport in mid-western India and then on to Delhi in the north. Buried deeply in the prospectus, was that the agreement would maintain a private territorial army to bowl over any bothersome peasants or Maharajahs along the way. The railroad was a major undertaking, with millions to be made for the investors.

The other reason for secrecy had to do with the United States' banking problems. After the Bank Panic of 1837, President James Polk had not been able to rein in what was known as the 'wildcat' banks. These were banks whose own paper currency—issued without federal oversight and no central banking institution guarantee or government insurance—caused fifty percent of the banks to fail. Speculation fever that could lead to inflation then began. For this reason, foreign countries, banks or corporations would not accept US paper currency and they required the physical transfer of species—in the Second Bank's situation, gold and or silver—to England's banking system and England, in turn, would guarantee the portfolio.

Monar's meeting with Zachariah Kent, who'd previously been informed by Richard Graves that Monar was both black and big, went predictably. That get-together led Kent and Monar to another encounter, for encounter it became, with JT in an old, isolated warehouse further up river.

Once there, JT and Monar were stunned as they looked down at open wooden crates to see bars of gold intermingled with machine parts.

The obdurate Zachariah Kent began, "Both of you listen carefully, as I will tell you only once. What you will be carrying is seven-hundred, fifty thousand dollars in gold ingot and two-hundred-fifty thousand dollars in silver bar."

Kent turned to JT and Monar, patronizing them, "That is more than stated previously to your father, yet I see no reason to adjust your commission."

JT became edgy, speculating what Kent would say next. It didn't take long, "There will be ten wooden crates in all. They will be similar to these with nailed wooden covers and then wrapped with heavy canvas stenciled Atlantic Power Weaving Loom Company to account for the weight. After that, they will be secured with rope and each knot sealed with wax. Before closing, you will inspect each crate; note the quantity and bar number in each, then witness the wrapping and wax seal. Understand, one of my employees will be with you during this procedure to confirm and sign off on your number. I will then sign that and two copies made. I will keep one, insert one and wax seal it for you to hand to the receiver in Southampton."

Kent's whiney voice was wearing on JT as he asked, "And the third one?"

"I have not finished, Graves." The response was superior, condescending.

Monar could see JT becoming goaded and spoke up, "Mr. Kent, your manner is difficult to accept. Just as you are Attorney Zachariah Kent, JT is Captain John Thomas Graves, and we both would hope you remember that."

Caught unawares, Kent was far from apologetic, "Dear me, are you actually comparing a New York financial attorney to some boat captain from Boston? He ignored any answer, "Now listen, the both of you. You are in my employ, I will speak and you will listen…"

Monar caught JT's eye, they pushed past the two guards and started for the door.

"Where do you two think you're going?"

JT turned angrily, "Find yourself another ship, you pompous ass."

Monar added, "And we'll be sure to let the lumpers know what's in those boxes!"

"You can't do this to me you bastards—come back here!"

They reached the door, Kent chasing after them, justifiably worried, "Wait! All right, if you're so damn touchy, I'll call you Captain Graves!"

JT stopped, "Fine. Now there will be an additional twenty-five percent commission for the additional cargo—and as I feel you're proving untrustworthy, all to be paid in advance."

They didn't know, but Monar's mentioning he would tell the lumpers—who Kent knew as roustabout dockhands—about the gold brought the usually high strung attorney to near panic, he could never get enough guards quickly and that made him instantly contrite, "Yes, yes, all right. When can you take shipment?"

JT laid out his plan, "I'll be here first thing tomorrow morning. Have your men here and ready. When my part of the counting and sealing is done, I'll go back to my ship and bring her and my crew around. I want a winch set up here and your own men gone. I also want forty bales of cotton on the wharf…"

"Forty bales of cotton? Where am I supposed to get them?"

"How do I know? Ask around for Christ's sake! Cotton accounts for fifty percent of our country's exports, New York is a chief port—they must have some. Find some nabob you can buy them from."

"What do you want them for?"

"That's my business, just get them here."

Kent hurried off shaking his head. Monar smiled after him and asked, "What do you want those bales for?"

"When I was in Savanna, Mr. Carlton mentioned that a cotton bale weighed around four-hundred pounds. So I thought we'd use a belt and brace approach with the gold. The crates are mislabeled and sealed and now we'll surround them with heavy bales to discourage any of our crew from poking about. And, I might add, I think cotton is bringing a good price in Europe, so it will be a little bonus for us."

Monar couldn't keep a straight face, "Very nice idea, JT—got us a twenty-five percent increase and a cotton bonus. You might bring us a profit yet. But tell me, what does belt and braces mean?"

"An old expression, my friend. You use a belt—in this case the mislabeled crates—to safely keep your pants up, then add braces—you know them as suspenders—that's the weight of the bales for additional security. See? Makes sense when I explain it—doesn't it?"

Monar left, smirking, "Does make sense, but I wish I hadn't asked."

The plan proceeded as expected, accept Zachariah Kent himself shared the gold and silver bar count and oversaw the sealing of the crates. New guards, having no knowledge of the crate contents, were then posted and JT left with Monar, going back to the *Golden Raven* to get ready and bring her to the warehouse for on loading the crates.

At the *Raven*, they were in for a surprise.

"Lady Evelyn!" JT didn't hide his pleasure, "Nice of you to come to say goodbye."

Captain Gideon Boyle, who appeared in better attitude than they had last seen him, accompanied her, smiling wanly. Acknowledging him, they returned their attention back on Lady Evelyn. Monar and JT took note that she seemed distracted, uncertain as she spoke.

"It is quite nice to see you two again. We were here yesterday but you both were gone."

"I wish we'd known." Monar offered, "Yet we're glad you came back today."

Monar sensed something was troubling her, "Evelyn, is there something we may help you with?"

Lady Evelyn straightened, "I've a great favor to ask you both…"

"Anything, simply ask."

"We wish to return to England—with you, with you both."

Moistness edged her eyes, yet she maintained her poise, "I have found there is no possible justification for my ingenuously writing letters of remorse to my friend's families and then simply continuing on with my holiday. I have an obligation to my lost crew as well, and it was insensitive of me—I can only hope the blow I took wobbled my brain and…and there I go again speaking too much. I'm asking you to allow me—us, to return on the *Golden Raven.* We will pay any fee you ask."

Listening to her, JT and Monar had not the slimmest doubt they'd say yes. The only concern was the Captain's berth was not designed for a woman, much less a Lady. They knew, however, that come hell or high water—they would work it out.

JT had one issue, "Of course you'll come with us, but one thing, Evelyn, weren't there five other surviving crewmen, what about them?"

"I asked. None of them will go to sea again. They gave me letters; they want to start a new life here, in your country and two men are writing to ask their families to come over here."

With grins all around, Lady Evelyn's belongings were retrieved from storage and she was escorted to the Captain's quarters—

formerly JT's. It was then Lady Evelyn had her first true laugh since the wave struck. She found she had to share the cabin—with a Long-nine cannon.

One thing both JT and Monar could agree on was Zachariah Kent's efficiency. By the time the *Golden Raven* hove to and tied off at the wharf's bollards, Kent had dockworkers ready, the hoist mounted and exactly forty, four-hundred pound bales of cotton sat on the dock, lined up behind the ten sealed crates. Kent also handed over a wax-sealed envelope.

The workers set to it under the watchful eyes of Kent and JT, while Monar, below, supervised the positioning and balance of the cargo.

Captain Boyle and Lady Evelyn scrutinized the undertaking, "An exceptional amount of supervisors for a relatively small consignment, don't you think, Gideon? To me, the lumper's boss seems to know his business, but JT and that Kent chap are following him about like hawks."

Boyle agreed, it was strange, "Aye, it is odd. Perhaps Americans here don't trust their dockworkers. Oh well, Lady Evelyn, it is not our concern to worry over."

JT and Monar were satisfied with the packing. Kent had few words, "The letter I gave you is the sealed Bill of Lading. This lock-box is our agreed payment, plus our settlement for the off- contract, in gold coin. This envelope contains the instructions on who to contact in Portsea."

"Portsea?"

"Yes, south coast of England, part of Portsmouth, near Southampton. It's on the chart."

Without another word, Kent sniffed and toddled off.

Laughing, Monar couldn't keep silent, "Good Lord, JT, not so much as a going away present. Don't think you made a friend there!"

JT joined in the laughter, "Can you imagine him? Not even a cheery goodbye. Still, by the look of that lock-box, you really can't say he didn't leave us a present."

As they stood smiling, Lady Evelyn came up, "You gentlemen look quite pleased with yourselves."

Focusing on her, JT was pleased, "Yes, we are. Well paid, a good ship under us and a beautiful woman in company. Who shouldn't be pleased? We're off to Portsea! Wherever the devil that is."

Lady Evelyn was surprised, "Portsea? That's wonderful! My father's main office is right across the bay in Gosport."

Then she was curious. Why Portsea, she wondered. That's a Royal Navy Base.

The rounded moon's glow had glistened on the misty bay. Now, at the dark of night, breezes dissipated the haze and filled the sails of the black clipper. With Sandy Hook well behind them and her bow spearing into the deep sea, the *Golden Raven's* eyes searched for the Gulf Stream. Before them rolled three thousand nautical miles to England.

19

10 May 1848

TWO DAYS OUT from New York they had a new navigator. Lady Evelyn had shown JT and Monar, the latest guide of Matthew Maury's, *Wind & Current Chart of the North Atlantic.*[10] They had no knowledge of the guide and when she mentioned she'd been navigator of the *Black Watch* on the voyage to New York, the partners elected her. Next, she stood duty watch and took the helm at times, spelling JT, Monar and the second mate.

The only clothes she wore on deck were worn, loose blue trousers, gingham blouses and a floppy merchant cap with a brim to protect from the sun. Every man aboard could see she was comfortable at the wheel, at home on the sea.

"Tell me, JT," she asked, "you ever think you'd be interested in selling the *Golden Raven*?"

He knew Lady Evelyn was already in love with his ship, "No, I never will. My father owned her and left her to me."

"Oh? I didn't know that. Still, I really don't blame you for not wanting to sell her; none of our British packets looks so elegant or feels the sea and respond to the helm like the *Raven*. Tell me, has your father been gone long?"

"No, not too long."

JT's short answer made her quickly realize he did not want to speak of his father and then she saw Monar coming aft to take the helm, "Relieving you, Captain."

"Thank you, Chief Mate, maintain this heading; at 0900 I'll give you a new bearing."

---

[10] Matthew Fontaine Maury 1806-1873. Referred to as the 'Father of the US Weather Service.

"Thank you again, Captain." Turning to JT, Monar continued, "Hello, Captain JT, tow log indicates we're gaining on seventeen knots."

Stretching, JT looked at the sea, estimating the waves at four to six, "I'm not surprised, that feels about right."

Lady Evelyn expressed satisfaction at the pace and then excused herself to go below to her cabin while the two men chatted on.

"What are you thinking, JT?"

"About Lady Evelyn?"

Monar glanced sideways at him, "Is there anyone else you think about?"

"As a matter of fact there is. I've been rethinking my feelings and realizing you were right about me, I was infatuated. Oh, I still am a little I guess, how couldn't one be? But I think you'll agree, I not going too overboard about her now. It's Charlee, except for my brief stumble over Evelyn, I know its Charlee."

"I hope you're right, yet…"

"What do you mean, yet—what?"

"It isn't because Evelyn's changed?

"Changed…in what way?"

"You haven't noticed that she's less casual than when we met her and how different—once she takes the wheel?"

JT acknowledged but justified that comment, "All captains are different once they take the helm. When you're in charge, you naturally become changed, that's a given. You're god and the men know it. Even though she's a woman, they respect her, but it's that captain's cap."

Monar took exception, "I think it's more because she's beautiful and knows what she's about. They know Evelyn's the navigator and a Master Mariner. When she tells someone to trim sail or whatever, they step right to it—even quicker than when I shout at them. However, I'm off my point. She's beginning to assume a façade like a few British I knew in Barbados."

"I don't see it."

"Then you're not looking. You don't agree Evelyn's more aloof? No not that— detached, distant. You know, the Brit's believe they're special."

"That's not like you, Monar. I thought you liked her and she has a lot on her mind. Besides, the Brit's weren't special in 1812—at least to our navy. Although, as I think of it, they do own most of the world that's worth owning."

Captain Gideon Boyle ambled up and Monar let the subject drop. He liked Lady Evelyn and he now grasped he liked her a little too much. Perhaps that was making him more sensitive.

She tossed her captain's hat on the Long-nine and loosened the neck of her blouse. She loved being at the helm, the wind, the standing rigging's song, the men's chatter—it all came together with the skill and power of commanding a vessel—but more so, on the *Golden Raven,* this wonderful ship.

Now, however, in the near hush of the cabin, with barely the sound of rushing water passing the hull, she had time to think.

Her closest friends were not here. The three who understood her life of wandering, who wished they could be the same, yet marriage and children kept them from it.

It was the one trip they planned together. They laughed and whispered deepest thoughts; fell asleep to the lapping of waves and woke to iridescent waters and moon brushed seas. The crossing to America was a dream. Then—they were gone.

How could she accept…gone? How could she bear their loss and explain to others the massive wave that took them—yet she survived? Her guilt at their loss haunts, never to pass.

Her father will help. No one in England knows; it will be up to her and her father to assist in telling the tale. She must be strong, that much her father would demand of her—and she will.

0845. Nearly time to give the new bearing to Monar.

Monar, she smiled, father will remember him. Especially father will remember how she followed him around, a young girl in awe of the big youth who had a bolo in his boot even then. Even now, she admitted, there was still something, something that attracted her.

She didn't want to delve deeper and knew, or believed, or hoped, that once they were safely back in England, Monar's aura would return to the recesses of her mind. Still…

Moreover, what of JT? He was enjoyable when he was himself. Rough on the edges, like all Yankees, but certainly likeable and intelligent. Still, far more important than anything else, of any man she had ever known, it was JT's love of his ship and the sea that made her smile when she thought of him. They truly had that in common. Simply thinking of it brought a smile. Yet what is the story about his father? Perhaps she'd ask Monar, or would that be snooping?

Then she thought of the very idea of introducing either man to the society that she and her father, Warfield Bunting, associated with ashore. That gave her second thoughts—yet she'd be damned if she'd let that bother her, and if anyone didn't like it, they could be damned!

0855. Time to set the new bearing.

«»

The compass rose needle indicated true ninety degrees west. Lady Evelyn was tired from the long days at a sea that were now behind them. They were nearing her homeport.

JT turned over the helm to Lady Evelyn, who knew these waters; she was borne near them and learned to sail here and had actually raced her schooner against others for the Cowes Cup.

After the *Golden Raven* glided between Milford on Sea to port and Yarmouth on the Isle of Wight off to starboard, she then eased two points to proceed up the heart of The Solent. After that, she brought the ship back easterly, now between Cowes off to starboard and Gilkicker Point on the mainland. The ship maneuvered southeasterly into the waters of Spithead and she smiled at the stares and waves from passing crews; few English had even seen a Yankee fast clipper, never mind one under full sail, breezing past.

Monar and JT studied the chart, yet watched fascinated as Lady Evelyn, still without one glance at the chart since sighting southwest England, aligned between Monckton Fort and Southsea Castle, brought the *Raven* dead north to spill wind from the sails while ordering main and mizzen sails reefed and had Monar's steam crew to bring up pressure. One mile later, the ship guided through the narrowed mouth of Portsmouth Harbor basin and past The Point. Lady Evelyn ordered all sails furled and revolutions to maintain headway only.

JT was impressed, "Evelyn, start to finish, one fine bit of navigation and seamanship."

She knew it was, "Why thank you, kind sir." She laughed, "Now, let me orient you. To port is Gosport, where my father's administrative center is located. There's a slip right there, where that packet boat is tied off. To starboard is…"

JT interrupted, "What's that old warship moored over there?"

"She's England's pride and joy, JT. HMS *Victory*, Nelson's flagship at Trafalgar. She's over a hundred years old."

JT couldn't help kid her, "Oh, that's right. Trafalgar was a sea battle you Brit's won, wasn't it?"

Lady Evelyn gave a frosty glare and the merest of smiles, "You, sir, are not a gentleman."

She was pointing out Portsea and the main pier of Portsmouth coming abeam to starboard when launch flying the Union Jack came alongside ordering they heave to. A young naval officer climbed the ladder and asked permission to come aboard. JT nodded to Lady Evelyn. Standing at the helm and knowing the lad was a midshipman by the white square of material on his collar, she gave permission, "Certainly, Midshipman." He was now confused—a woman, a civilian—yet she knew he was a midshipman. What next? Nevertheless, a captain is a captain and he had his orders, "Madame, I mean Captain, you are approaching the Royal Navy Dockyard. I must ask for your Authorization Certificate."

Lady Evelyn was not surprised at this—after all, it was a military base—and how did JT expect to enter it? She turned to him and for a moment, he seemed perplexed.

Remembering the letter Zachariah Kent handed him when leaving New York and producing, then unsealing the envelope, he found three pages. The shipping manifest, his British contacts, Hoare, Henderson, and the Certificate to Enter the Royal Navy Dockyard, Portsmouth, restricted to South Jetty, signed by Commander, Sir William. T. Hoare.

While he handed the papers below to the launch, the midshipman listened to someone, an officer apparently his senior. Evelyn whispered to JT, "Nothing like knowing where you're papers are, Captain."

Embarrassed, JT didn't have time to respond as the midshipman returned, appearing somewhat uncomfortable, "Captain, you have permission to enter the Royal Dockyard and you are redirected to Troopship Jetty where you may tie off. In addition, you, your crew and any supercargo are not allowed to disembark until notified. Do you know where that Jetty is, Lady Bunting? It's on Watering Island…which really isn't an island."

It became evident someone in the launch had recognized Evelyn and enlightened the midshipman as to who he was addressing. By this time, Evelyn was baffled by the circumstances. Why on earth is this, an American merchant ship, entering a Royal Navy base? She kept it to herself.

"Yes, thank you, midshipman, you've been most helpful. I'll pass that on to Sir William."

"Thank you Lady Bunting. My name is Moore, Midshipman Harry Moore. And may I say this is the most lovely clipper ship I have ever seen in my life?"

Lady Evelyn melted the sailor with her smile, "Thank you for that also, Midshipman Harry Moore. She was built in the Americas by our American cousins," and with a dig back to JT, "not surprising that they've learned from us how to build ships."

Moore made no response, other than stating he had been ordered to keep the Certificate, after which, he would proceed to notify personnel at Troopship Jetty that an American Clipper ship, named *Golden Raven,* would be abeam the jetty in short order.

While the steam launch headed to the jetty, Moore couldn't help but wonder how an American vessel, just in from the States, could have an undated, barely limited harbor clearance signed by the Royal Dockyard Commander. Yet again, it was not his to wonder. Another thing, looking back over the gunwale as he went down the Jacob's Ladder, Moore saw another Captain—who he recognized as Gideon Boyle—approach the helm. One ship, three captains, what was the truth about that? Must be some secret plot unfolding, he conjectured to himself only. He was not far from the truth.

The Royal Marine Captain was adamant, "Sir, as stated, I was ordered to post my men here, allow no one ashore and make three drays available to remove crated machinery from your vessel. The orders were clear; pending further orders, I was not to remove the cargo. I expect those orders shortly and that they will reference you and your crew. For now, we will wait."

For half an hour, while Lady Evelyn and Monar remained patient, JT paced around the deck until a coach pulled up to the jetty and the Royal Marine Captain hurried to it as a sergeant opened the coach door.

The Captain spoke loudly enough to be heard on the *Raven*, "Sir! Situation as ordered."

A softer voice, "Very good. Have your men stand easy. I'll speak to the ship's master."

With that, the speaker and two other officers began walking across the jetty while JT ordered the gangway lowered.

Lady Evelyn's eyes went wide and she whispered, "My word, JT, you're either getting the royal treatment or going to be hung. The tall officer is Rear Admiral Thomas Henderson, the middle one is the Dockyard Commander, Hoare—he signed your Certificate—and

I don't know the captain with them. Just what have you been up too? Whatever it is, you better get organized."

Rear-Admiral Henderson requested permission to board, and without waiting for a reply saw Lady Evelyn, "Lady Bunting, they mentioned you were aboard." The Rear Admiral took her hand, continuing, "How are you? Is that a scar over your eye? How in heaven's name did that happen? I've notified your father, he was quite surprised you were back—and without the Black Watch. He'll be over shortly, said to say welcome."

He turned to Hoare, "You know Lady Evelyn, doesn't she look marvelous? Come, introductions can wait. This ship must have a Master's cabin, let's all retire to it for some privacy."

So it went, the three officers, Lady Evelyn, Monar and JT squeezed into the Master's cabin. Henderson breathed something about damn Yankee's when he saw the Long-nine cannon taking up space, but after introductions and some answers given to his questions, the Rear Admiral became introspective, glancing between JT and Lady Evelyn. He was about to speak when the sergeant knocked and entered, "Sir, Lady Bunting's father has arrived."

Startled, not ready for the meeting, Evelyn knew she had to tell the tale, "Excuse me, gentlemen, I will meet my father on deck."

They rose, keeping bent over due to the low ceiling. After she left, Rear Admiral Henderson asked, "So, tell me, why was she on this ship and where is the Black Watch?"

JT and Monar gave the account of loss and tragedy and the three officers displayed the proper concern, noting to one another that one of Lady Evelyn's friends was the daughter of Lord Charles Guy and another woman the wife of Sir Sheffield Goodman.

The Rear Admiral spoke for all, "A total disaster for the families all round, including the seamen's. I'm sure Lord Bunting will make things right. Were no bodies washed up?"

"Not that we heard of, although we left not too long after it happened."

"Very well, then. We'll have to put that aside for the moment. Lady Evelyn has no knowledge of what you carried?"

With agreement on that from JT, "Then good, tell us, Captain, is the cargo intact?"

"Yes, Sir, it is. We did have a slight difficulty when one of our crew was a bit of a snoop and tore the canvas corner of a crate, so you will find that, but nothing's amiss."

"You weren't guarding it?"

"We had protected the crates with four-hundred pound cotton bales all around. Somehow that person pried some away so he could crawl to the crate and cut the canvas."

"Still, you had no guards?"

"Sir, we put to sea directly following the loading and every crew member has a duty. Other than our checking now and then and those cotton bales we felt no guards were necessary."

"Then how did you find the man?"

"My partner here, Monar, is given to—shall I say—wandering at night, he caught the fellow."

"You have him in irons now?"

JT didn't answer, Henderson waited, "Well, tell me, man, you clap the sod in irons?"

Monar leaned forward, glaring at the Admiral, "He is in the sea."

The Rear Admiral raised his eyebrows and asked nothing further, ordering the captain to take five naval seamen, clear away the bales and check the crate count and condition with the manifest. If there is no discrepancy, winch the crates out and load the drays. After that, the captain was to use to the Marine guard to take the cargo over to Admiralty House. "And, be bloody sure not to drop one flaming crate!"

The Dockyard Commander, Samuel Hoare, then took over the questions, "My assumption is you both know what is in those crates—correct?"

JT and Monar nodded, Hoare continued, "You're both to be commended, not everyone outside the military would have been so moral with five-hundred thousand dollars in American gold and silver in their hold."

JT was annoyed, "Well, here we are and there's another two-hundred, fifty-thousand as well, an amount you don't appear to know about."

Both officers were shocked, asking for the manifest. Monar turned to JT, laughing, "See? If they didn't know, I told you we should have kept that silver as our bonus."

Flippantly, JT agreed, then asked "All right, you were listed as my contacts—what now?"

Rear Admiral Henderson mulled over the question, then motioned to Commander Hoare, telling him to leave and oversee the transfer of the cargo to Admiralty House and check the security, after which Hoare was to await him at the Royal Naval College next door.

The Rear Admiral spoke quietly to JT and Monar, "Gentlemen, you have done yeomen's work in bringing this cargo. I can only tell you that it is going to a good cause to further the Crown's influence overseas…"

He knew he was muddying the waters. Americans didn't give a fig about extending the Crown's influence and the Admiral certainly couldn't reveal information that he and other upper echelon naval officers were investors in the British East India Company, a private entity group, exploiting the riches of India under the guise of facilitating England's commerce.

He did however; want to thank them some way. "Forget what I was saying. Tell me, do you have other plans? By that, I mean do you have freight here in England for other ports?"

"No, nothing in sight. Any thoughts that might help us gain a consignment?"

"Quite possibly so. It may take a week or two to firm up, but I'll tell you what, the navy will issue a retainer for you, your ship and crew, up to a month. That way you can see a bit of England and ease off after your voyage. I should also think Lord Warfield would be most pleased to come up with some plan, now that you've returned his daughter. How's that sound?"

"We'll take you up on that, Admiral; we can use the rest and cargo."

"Then it's settled! I'll find Captain Wells and he will have a navy tug tow you to a quay off the Naval Dockyard to where you may tie up. Your time is free until we speak again and I'll have an officer be in touch. Thank you again, gentlemen, let us repair to the weather deck."

Lady Evelyn and her father stayed at the offside rail trying to hide their pain. He had come up to her with concern for her eyebrow, yet that became secondary for it was clear something terrible had happened. Learning of the loss of the Black Watch shook him for its crew had been his crew, he felt their loss. That and his daughter's friends were children of his associates. There would be untold sadness for the times ahead and he knew his wealth could only ease the ache so much.

To lighten the matter, if only for a short while, Lady Evelyn mentioned the journey home with JT and Monar, "Father, you must remember Monar, the big black boy we met in Barbados."

"Monar? My word. You mean that young man over there you followed around like a puppy?"

She smiled for an instant, "No I did not…well, I suppose, maybe I did…just a bit."

Her father forced a smile in return, "Yes, I suppose you did—quite a bit. Yet tell me, where did you meet him, not in New York?"

"It was New York; he's now the partner with the owner of the ship that saved us."

"I'll be damned. Even though he was a slave at the time, I thought that boy would make something of himself. That man MacPherson must have given him his freedom. So tell me, what is his partner, your other savior, like? Is he black also?"

"No, John Thomas, he's called JT, is a New Englander. Good looking, about twenty-five I should say. He was confounded by my indescribable beauty."

They shared a needed laugh before she continued, "He's a good captain, well-liked by the crew and certainly he and Monar are quite good friends. The way they interact is amusing, nice to see. Certainly strange partners, but yet nice."

Evelyn and her father saw the men coming up on deck. However, before the introductions began, Rear Admiral Henderson asked Lord Bunting if they might have a private word together.

"Well, Henderson, what is it?"

"Lord Bunting, our cargo arrived on this ship."

Warfield Bunting thought as much, "Once I saw an American ship in a RN dockyard that was not too difficult to ascertain. The question is, does the captain know of the cargo's contents."

"Yes, the captain and that big black chap. In fact, they knew about the gold and silver and actually aware there was more than we thought."

Bunting shook his head, "I see. It would seem our American investors do not quite comprehend the meaning of the word secrecy. So, I assume we will just have to work around it."

"There's a bit more, it seems one of the crew was found sneaking a look at the cargo and when I asked if they had the miscreant in irons," the Rear Admiral paused for effect, "the big chap said the man was in the sea."

"Bunting laughed, "My word. Well, from that and the fact my daughter said nothing of it, I deduce no one else is aware of the cargo. Although I'll make sure. For now, inform our other investors and stress they remain quiet—it's their necks sticking out. That means you, Hoar, as well as Henderson and the other naval shareholders. You know damn right well that if Prime Minister Russell learns Royal Navy personnel is entangled with the East India Company and reimbursing Black Moon for crews and ships—to say nothing of munitions—to promote personal profit in India, we'll all go down with the ship. And, if it's found Americans are involved there'll be holy hell to pay."

"We know that, Sir. Yet what about these two chaps? Should something be done with them?"

Bunting was exasperated, "And what do you suggest—drop *them* in the sea? Come man; put your thinking cap on. In fact, as I think of it, I'll take care of them. Now be a good sort and get that funereal expression off your face and act the Honorable all knowing, Rear Admiral."

In reality, Lord Warfield was pleased to see JT and Monar. They had brought his only child back safely and for that alone, he was grateful. Moreover, the fact they had also delivered the consignment was icing on the cake. To Warfield Bunting however, his daughter was all-important in his life. His fortune had long been secure; the game he was playing was simply for annoyance. It was political one-upmanship to chide Prime Minister Lord John Russell and Lord Palmerston. Of course, the government in due time would discover the complicity and the shadowy investment in the powerful British East India Company.[11] Yet it mattered not, for by then the new investors, Americans at that, as well as Bunting's other holdings in the Company and its people would make him near impossible to dislodge. So now, as Lord Bunting approached his daughter, JT and Monar, he couldn't help but think of the political game he was playing. A pox on then all—on Russell, Palmerston, the Corn Act, Factory Act and the Health Act as well. Take care of the Irish, resolve the Potato Famine, for God's sake; even the Turks are sending food. We're a country of merchants, so get out of the way. Let us be charged with England's well-being and if we make a profit while doing so, so what?

Lord Warfield warmly and sincerely welcomed his daughter's saviors. He relived his meeting with Monar in Barbados and teased Evelyn, to her distress, over her fascination with the lanky black

---

[11] The Royal Charter of 1600, held by the British East India Company with its private armies, was not arrogated by the British Crown until 1858.

youth. There were smiles, although Evelyn and JT did not smile quite as much as others.
Insisting the two sailors stay at his estate on Church Path, Landport, Bunting stated a carriage would pick them up before dusk. That would allow time to move the *Golden Raven*, as requested by Captain Wells and allow the crew some pub-crawl wages.

Saint Leo's Abbey nestled on a rise in Landport, a sector of Portsmouth. Built in the Gothic Strawberry Hill style of Horace Walpole by the Church of England, it was originally a bishops' retreat. Down through the decades the Church's property, unused and sadly decayed, was eventually vended. Multiple owners buckled under the cost of striving to restore the property until a Mrs. Cheveau sold it to an up and coming merchant named Warfield Blackwood Bunting. Bunting didn't give a fig that the property was known throughout the area as a white elephant and renamed it Blackwood Abbey. With money and his Architect friend, Decimus Burton to help with the design and renovations, the Abbey was charmingly restored. He loved the home despite the fact that his wife, Blanch, enjoyed life on the continent more than an English Abbey, or for that matter, Warfield and their daughter. He never divorced his her; in fact, he kept her with funds enough to manage a comfortable living entertaining on the fringe of Paris' social untidiness.

Eventually, it came to Lord Bunting that he didn't miss his wife. He was married to his work and, once learning his daughter had seawater running in her veins, brought her and tutors back from another estate in Cornwall. He doted on her as his only child without a mother's love. Yet mainly, he sensed she needed her own life and the vivacity to live it as she pleased, rare for a woman in the 1800s.

Warfield, nonetheless, loved and indulged Evelyn and easily supplied her with tutors for navigation, seamanship and, indeed, when she was ready, a ship. They had that singular bond, a love of the sea. That, he felt was natural; they were after all, British. The only issue he had, which he kept to himself, was that he would like a grandson. Yet with Evelyn now twenty-eight, he began to wonder.

Aside this, and work, there was only one other person in his life—Lily.

Gas lamps lined the roadway to the home of Lord Bunting as his Hansom carriage, drawn by two matched bay horses carrying JT and Monar, came to a halt at the entrance of Blackwood Abbey. Bunting waited at the base of the steps with another person. JT and Monar had fully expected that person to be Evelyn, but were startled to find a lovely woman, her hand through Warfield's arm, smiling up at them as they stepped awkwardly from the carriage.

"Monar, John Thomas, welcome to our home, Blackwood Abbey." Bunting turned to the woman, "May I introduce you to Miss Lillian Fields?"

Miss Thorne, dressed in a deep green gown, offered her hand, both men struck by her loveliness and grace, "Welcome, my American sailors, welcome to our shores. Warfield has told me so much about you I feel we are already friends. So please, call me Lily, our friends do."

Her welcome gave JT an opening, "Thank you, Lily, we will, and please call me JT, as my friends do." JT was a bit put out that Evelyn wasn't there, or that she hadn't told Lily about him.

Sitting on the veranda, a mild July evening breeze soothed them. As servants attended with wine, Evelyn Bunting walked in from target shooting, carrying a lantern and two Purdey pistols.

Monar was the first to react with feigned unease, "Good Lord, Evelyn! Shooting in the dark? What have we done to incur such wrath?"

Warfield was bothered that Monar was informal with her name. She turned with a false smile to Monar, "One for each of you just to make sure you do not tell tales of our voyage home."

Adding to the scene, JT asked, "What on earth do you mean, Evelyn? We would never tell your father about your unladylike language and lack of manners when ordering everyone around on the *Golden Raven.* Now then, what are you doing with those two antique pistols?"

Again, during the laughter over Evelyn's alleged lack of manners, Warfield noted she showed indifference to not being called Lady Evelyn and chose only to respond to JT's comment over her pistols, "Antique? I'll have you know the Queen, herself, has a pair exactly like these."

Lily was surprised, "Really? Victoria, our queen—has pistols?"

Warfield ended the rambling exchanges by taking up his goblet and standing, "A toast, Americans included! To the Queen and her pistols! And with that, let us now relax."

Everyone was comfortable in the amusement of the moment, and by dinner, the five were not unlike old friends. Yet Warfield still gave thought to their nonchalant responses to Evelyn.

During the evening, it was agreed by the people around the dining table, that they would take Warfield's private rail car for holiday and give JT and Monar a tour of London. Of course, the trip would have to wait until after Evelyn and her father had completed their condolences to the families of their friends, and fund the other sailor's wives and children.

Neither London nor the repose was to be. While JT and Monar were treated royally at the Abbey, Lord Bunting had convened a closed meeting with the East India representatives and the naval investors—in civilian attire of course—and approved the investment offering. It was at the aftermath of this meeting and on a completely separate subject that Rear Admiral Henderson mentioned the next covert shipment of supplies for the vague 'Varna Task', so referenced, was at the naval depot and must be moved before any inspectors stumbled upon it.

The simple fact was the British were stockpiling non-perishable war supplies at the port of Canakkale, on the Turkish, Ottoman Empire's coast along the Dardanelles. The supplies would then be transshipped to the port of Varna in the Black Sea. This move was to thwart any future attempt by Russia to force their way south from the Crimea, into the Bosporus and Dardanelles Straits and acquire a warm water port on the Aegean Sea.

Although this was a covert effort by the Royal Navy, it had the arm's length, yet full support of the government. However, no British warships were to be engaged in delivering these supplies and that required the clandestine use of privately owned shipping. It was here, Lord Bunting helped. Not only did he supply ships and crews, a great percentage of the cargo was from his manufacturing plants. In sum, all of this would benefit the Lord of Blackwood Abbey—and at a premium.

Rear Admiral Henderson suggested the *Golden Raven* could be one of the two vessels needed. This served two purposes, he felt. The *Golden Raven* was not British and a suitable stipend would reward the partners for a job well done concerning the gold shipment.

Warfield thought the suggestion worthwhile, yet held reservations, "Those waters are strange to the Americans, who do you have for a navigator?"

Here, the Admiral appeared awkward and it took but a moment for Warfield to reason why.

"I see, as there'll be two ships, you're contemplating my daughter as captain on one and navigator for both, because she's been there previously."

"Please, Lord Bunting; think it through before you say no. As you say, she's been there with the *Ghazna*, knows the waters as far as Canakkale and we couldn't find a more qualified person—or one who would be more quiet about it. Besides, we must be prompt in moving the cargo."

Warfield knew the Admiral was right. Evelyn did know the waters. More importantly, there was no war, only the 'Eastern Question', the term for the Sick Man of Europe—the Ottoman Empire. Yet Warfield still had one concern about his daughter—her fascination with Monar.

«»

In one week, they were ready. The *Golden Raven* provisioned and burdened with war supplies along with the *Vixen*, a new Bunting packet ship. She was more along the lines of the American clippers although not as fast and lacked steam power, yet still able to hold her own with Lady Evelyn at the helm. The *Vixen* did have one up on the Raven however. She had originally been fitted out by Bunting for the China trade and due to that, she carried a complement of fourteen, thirty-six pounder guns. This was unusual and as his daughter was captain, to insure her safety, Bunting had seen to it that most of her crew was former Royal Navy, all without Evelyn being aware.

As it happened, the navy had only now finished utilizing non-descript merchant ships to graph the waters leading to the Gelibolu, or as the British knew it, the Gallipoli Peninsula and, as much as possible, they'd scoped the Dardanelles Strait to the entrance of the Sea of Marmara. After that, there was little in accurate charts for reaching the Bosporus Strait, through into the Black Sea, or, for that matter, to reach Varna, Bulgaria on the western end of that Sea. The British felt the need for this information and more to facilitate plans of the Royal Navy.

Although the latter sector was sketchy for the RN and they wanted enhanced charts, that fact did not bother Warfield, as the two ships were not to enter the Black Sea—known as the Russian Lake—only to proceed to the Narrows at Cannakkale, the coastal city along the Dardanelles.

Considering the *Vixen* was the slower vessel and Lady Bunting more experienced, it was decided that she should lead. With the two crews together, still keeping the actual port of call unsaid until they were at sea, she spoke to the sailors.

Her summary was specific, "We will be delivering supplies to the eastern Med. As most sailors know, it's an unfriendly sea and the gunnery officers of both ships must be sure you men know your job. Captain Graves' crew and mine must be sharp; I do not want even one brigand having a chance to board us. As the *Vixen* is the slower vessel we will lead, if we are becalmed the Raven will tow us. I know my British crew will do their duty to ship and Queen, just as Captain Graves' knows his crew will do their duty. Captain, do you have anything to add?"

JT had been listening intently. He had never heard a captain give a discourse like this before and he had certainly never given one. With JT, it was merely 'we're going to such and such' and off they would sail. This was different; Lady Evelyn was acting as one would expect from a naval officer— not a captain of a merchant ship and he wondered if this was a British tradition of some sort. Monar, caught off guard as well, watched JT and nodded for him to get up and speak.

JT rose awkwardly, as awkward as he felt, "Don't have much more to add to Captain Bunting's speech—other than I hope the Lord watches over all of us."

An enigmatic smile touched across Evelyn's lips and gone, "Very well, the crew of the *Vixen* is dismissed. Captain Graves—your crew?"

"What? Oh, yes, my crew is dismissed." Then quietly, "You could have done that, Evelyn."

"She tilted her head, "No, Captain, I could not. They are your crew." She moved closer to him, "And, unless we are alone or out of earshot, please address me as Captain, or Lady Evelyn."

Though few had heard, he'd been hastised on his own ship, JT rejoined in kind, "Come off your high horse, Your Ladyship. In fact, please remove you and your high horse from my ship!"

No one had ever spoken that bluntly to her and it stung. It was not an auspicious beginning, "JT, we must maintain tradition to assure order in the crew. Even Yankee informality must understand that simple fact!"

There was no common ground, JT summoned his boat crew, "Please escort Lady Bunting to her ship, or anywhere else she may wish to be escorted."

Leaving her standing there speechless, JT went to the helm, "Steam up, Chief Mate. Prepare to haul anchor once the *Vixen* gets around to finally leave the harbor."

Passing JT to order the steam crew to stations, Monar couldn't help whisper, "What a pleasant cruise this is going to be with you two lovebirds squabbling."

If looks could kill, Monar would be stone-cold dead before he took another step.

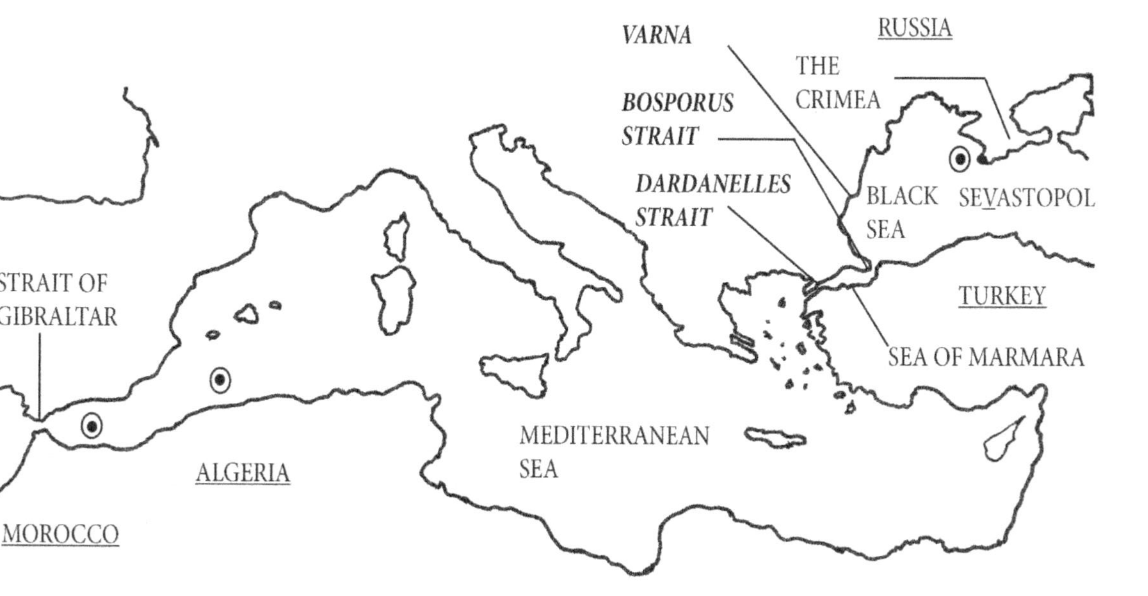

THE MEDITERRAEAN, MARMARA AND BLACK SEAS

20

18 August 1848

THE *VIXEN* AND *GOLDEN RAVEN,* sailing in tandem, passed the coast of France and Spain's, Bay of Biscay, Cape Finisterre and Lisbon, Portugal, eventually rolling eastward toward the Strait of Gibraltar.

In the faint breeze, the *Vixen* led the way, as she was a better light air ship. In order to keep pace, the *Raven* ran on low steam power, which, as it turned out was a fortunate circumstance after they cleared Gibraltar's great rock. Moving into the Mediterranean and coming abeam of Algiers the first Barbary corsairs appeared. Ahead of *Vixen,* coming directly at her, two swift boats, single sail Xebec's, divided to either side of the *Vixen* and began to close on her. JT saw the enemy vessel's approach and assumed Evelyn did as well—his assumption confirmed when her gun ports opened, yet the guns not run out.

Watching the event unfold through his glass, JT ordered the steam pressure raised and the *Raven's* four guns readied. Both captains' knew the crews of the overloaded Xebec's would try to board quickly and slaughter everyone other than those valuable for ransom or slavery.

The lead enemy vessel began to close on the *Vixen's* starboard and JT could only imagine the feeling of the Xebec's crew when, inside fifty yards, the *Vixen* turned to port, rolled out her seven starboard guns and sent a five cannon broadside of grapeshot into the vessel. The Xebec reeled under the onslaught as the *Vixen* started back on course. The smoke cleared, and while reloading, the *Vixen* shot off her last two unfired starboard cannon into the same vessel.

JT was stupefied by the carnage. In one broadside the sixty-foot Xebec was reduced to a floating hulk, her sides and sails shredded. He saw barely a person moving aboard her.

Now it was the *Golden Raven's* turn. The remaining Xebec, seeing the disaster, tried to veer off in front of the *Raven* to make a run for it. JT ordered full revolutions, quickly brought his ship broadside to the enemy and shouted through his speaking trumpet, "Gunner! Grapeshot?"

Everyone ducked as countless wild shots from the Xebec tore through the sails.

The gun captain nodded to JT and then shouted to the gun crew, "Keep your shot low—we don't want to overshoot and hit the *Vixen*! Fire as we bear."

The first cannon fired and recoiled, the Xebec disappearing in the smoke. Through the smoke, the gunnery officer estimated when his next gun would come to bear, then gave the word and the second gun roared.

Painfully slow, the Xebec drifted from out of the haze, the bow shredded, amidships a shambles. A goodly number of men wounded, others tottered about or fell overboard. The sail, mostly untouched, carried the listing vessel unsteadily away.

Coming back to course and finding Monar staring over the rail, JT found his voice, "Have you ever seen anything like this, Monar?"

"Never, never in my life. It's unbelievable the damage done with grapeshot."

He came out of his disbelief and passed it off, "Then again, it could have been us on the other end—so why the hell should we be concerned?"

JT shuddered at the thought, "Think we should finish them off?" He then decided against it.

They came alongside the *Vixen*. There'd been no cheering as the ex-navy crewmembers on her had been through it all before. On the *Raven*, Monar and JT kept a restrained behavior to match them. It had been so simple, so incredibly simple to snuff out eighty lives.

Lady Evelyn called over JT, "Hello the *Golden Raven.* I thought your US Captains Decatur and Bainbridge ridded these waters of these riffraff! Anyway, good show! They thought they were going to seize two ripe merchant ships. Nice bit of work you had with only two cannon."

"Why thank you, Captain Bunting. We Americans cleaned them out way back in 1815. They just keep coming back like bad pennies I guess. Nonetheless, I want you to know your volley inspired us. Good lord, what a sight."

"No one was more surprised than me. It would seem my father filled my berths with navy and marine pensioners and they picked up where they left off—didn't miss a beat. You didn't have that advantage. Just shows what all the practice can do, but I was surprised you didn't finish those corsairs off."

"We thought that possibly the remainder might tell others to think twice."

"Perhaps, however it's their chosen vocation. Yet honestly, I wasn't really surprised you let them go. Enough is enough. And thank you for not hitting us with your broadside."

"Pleased you understood our concern."

"Then I thank you once more. Anyway, JT, the night should be clear and we'll hold this new heading. If you have any trouble following my stern light, just signal. Cheerio."

JT watched as the *Vixen* eased four points to port. Monar couldn't resist a kidding, "Well, well my hero, it appears you two lovebirds have made up — not kissed—but at least made up."

JT was flustered, started to say something, thought better of it and ordered, "Take the Watch."

And, the strangest thing of all, found himself thinking of…Charlee *and* Evelyn.

The island of Crete slipped far off to starboard, their heading changed to near true north as the two windjammers cruised through the scattered islands of the Aegean Sea. There, Captain Bunting ordered drop anchor. They had been sailing day and night and the anchors made fast was a welcome interval. Lady Evelyn and her chief mate were rowed to the *Raven.*

As she tossed her captain's cap on JT's bunk and leaned back on the Long nine's gun carriage introductions were made.

"JT, Monar, this is Harry Griffin, former Chief Gunner's Mate, Royal Navy and now mine. Harry, meet Captain John Thomas Graves and his Chief Mate, Monar."

Handshakes, polite conversation and chitchat soon gave way to the reason for Lady Evelyn calling the meeting, "Right now, we're moored on the lee of Rabbit Island. Just so you know, northeast is Cape Helles and the mouth of the Dardanelles Strait."

She got up and on the chart, pointed to their location, "I was going to hold off on this until we reached the Narrows at Cannakkale, well into the Strait, but I was told to open this message from Rear Admiral Henderson when we neared Cape Helles."

JT and Monar knew nothing of any message and were intrigued. JT smiled, "I'm guessing we're going to hear something quite interesting."

She returned the smile, "You guess right, JT, and I might add my father will be furious when he eventually finds out—as he's bound to. We have another mission it seems. It boils down to the Admiralty wanting us to chart the waters from the northern end of the Dardanelles to Varna, Bulgaria in the Black Sea. If we decide to enter the Black Sea, Varna is our new discharge port. However, we don't stop there. After that, we're asked to chart from Varna to Sevastopol on the tip of the Crimean Peninsula, chart east to the Kerch Strait and then back to the Bosporus Strait."

This was a significant codicil to their agenda. Initially, they were to deliver the supplies to Cannakkale in the Dardanelles—well within Turkish waters. The letter from the Admiralty requested they enter the Black Sea—essentially a Russian lake.

It was a major undertaking. None of them had been in the Black Sea and Monar and JT did not know the significance of Sevastopol.

JT asked, "All right, if we agree to do what they're asking and make Varna our discharging port, why all the interest in this place called Sevastopol and that Kerch Strait?"

"Well first of all, the two requests are tied in together. You may remember that in the past I mentioned there could very well be difficulty between Russia and England. Czar Nicholas is using the pretext of protecting Christians in Turkey in an effort to prevent British interference with any conflict between Russia and the Turkish Ottoman Empire. The Empire's vulnerable. It's going through what they call a Tanzimat, a reformation, to the point of even abolishing slavery. But when going through this, the previous Sultan, Mahmud II barely improved their army and navy and then to a limited degree."

Evelyn glanced about to be sure they were following her. With their looks, she continued.

"All right. Now, with their military weakened, that leaves them corruptible and weak-willed. If the Czar decides to lean on the Ottoman Empire to try and get a warm water port, England will not allow that—and here I'm assuming things by looking at the chart—it's apparent the best place to bottle up the Russians would be in the Black Sea and north in the Sea of Azov. Here…look at the chart. See, there's a choke point at Kerch, called the Kerch Strait. Blocking that Strait would stop more of the Russian Navy ships from getting into the Black Sea."

JT interposed, "I understand why they want us to chart the course to Kerch, but where does that place Sevastopol come into the picture?"

Lady Evelyn vacillated, then spoke frankly, "Sevastopol was a major Black Sea port for the Roman Empire, once known as Chersonesus, it pokes into the sea and controls the sea routes. It's on the southern tip of the Crimean Peninsula. It's a base for the Russian Navy; they took it from Turkey in the past."

JT and Monar had the same questioning expression, "The Russian Navy? Evelyn, that means their navy is already *in* the Black Sea. We're to sail right up to their base, in between Russian warships, while we plot a course so the Brit's can bottle them up—is that all? Wouldn't it be simpler to stop in and ask for a chart?"

"JT, follow me here. To my mind, there's no question the Royal Navy could beat the Russian Black Sea Fleet and put an army ashore at Sevastopol or Yalta. After that, they'd block the Kerch Strait at its southern end and prevent any more of their warships from entering the Black Sea from the north. The only little detail missing is to know where the channels and shoals are at Sevastopol."

She caught her breath, studying the chart, the men amazed at her analysis and grasp of events.

She seemed to know so much—that is, if she was right and there came a war.

"Gentlemen, let's not get ahead of ourselves. We don't know what's occurring where we're headed, that means this whole conversation may be moot. We're to meet with the British Ambassador in Constantinople—or Istanbul, whatever they call it now—and he should have knowledge of what's happening up north of there. But, my point is this, even though the Black Sea is probably open to most shipping, of course we can't be seen going our merry way charting the sea lanes. If there is any chance of being spotted, then our taking soundings becomes very chancy. Father would go insane if his only child is shot as a spy. I'm not too keen on that and neither are you. In other words, this won't be a doddle in the park."

Pensive, JT thought for a moment, "You seem to know quite lot about the navy's plans and this area, Evelyn. Did you know about this beforehand?"

"Honestly, JT? No. My father told me before that events have made the Admiralty need to know these waters, but I didn't think they'd have the nerve to ask *me* to do it. That's why I said my father would be furious if he found out the Admiralty was using me. However, let me stay on the subject. Remember, we don't have to sail right up to the Crimean Peninsula. The Black Sea is over a hundred seventy-thousand square miles; we won't bump into the Russian Navy often."

"Once will be one too many, Evelyn. This could start a war."[12]

She was agitated, not used to having to explain her decisions, "Let me put it this way, with or without the *Golden Raven*, the *Vixen* is going. This isn't a threat, simply a fact."

The answer wasn't what they wanted to hear and Monar laid it out, "We're not going to let you go alone if we can help it, Evelyn. However," He looked to JT, who agreed and Monar continued, "we have a potential problem. This is a British, Russian squabble — America doesn't have a dog in this fight. You have a Brit crew, we've an American crew. JT can't ask them to take this on without them agreeing."

Lady Evelyn expressed surprise, "You have to ask your crew's permission?"

"Understand, my crew is not ex-Royal Navy or Marines. They didn't sign on to get involved in someone else's quarrel — especially on the side of a country that was our enemy in 1812."

With that, JT went topside.

After glancing to Harry Griffin, who simply shrugged it all off, Monar whispered to Lady Evelyn, "You know JT wants to go, Evelyn, yet he's right. It is only fair to ask the crew."

"I can see that, Monar. As you uniquely said, you American's don't have a dog in this fight. Nevertheless, no matter what your crew decides, the *Vixen* does what the Admiralty asks."

---

[12] The Crimean War, known in Russia as the Eastern War, did start-5 years later, October 1853 and ended in March 1856. Major battles were fought on the Crimean Peninsula, although the war ranged from the Balkans to the Baltic to the Far East. Notable incidents include the first war reported by electro-telegraph and photography, the Charge of the Light Brigade, Florence Nightingale and the Thin Red Line of British history. Significantly, as it turned out, the war was the first naval action by self-propelled ironclad gun batteries, that later led to ironclad warships.

Half an hour later, JT returned, "Most agreed to go. I told them that if we saw action, I'd double their wages. Five of the crew backed out, we'll drop them off at Cannakkale and pick them up on our way out of here. I'll note all this and names in the Ship's Log, Monar."

Lady Evelyn was relieved, "I'm glad the *Golden Raven's* coming, it should be interesting."

At Cannakkale, near the Narrows in the Dardanelles Strait, they laid over for provisions, coaling and information as this was the farthest Evelyn had been along the Gallipoli Peninsula. While there, they were shocked to learn the *Ghazna*, the former warship the British had converted to steam propulsion, fifty guns and ironclad—the very ship Lady Evelyn had sailed to this port for the Ottoman Empire— had been pilfered by the Russians with the connivance of her Turkish captain. This was only one such example, the Harbor Captain told Lady Evelyn, of the shifting sands of loyalty in the Balkans and the Anatolia.

She gave a rueful smile at the news, "Actually, Captain, knowing the lack of sea-keeping of the *Ghazna*, it's probable one of your Turkish crews have been saved from drowning."

27 September 1848

They decided each ship would enter separate soundings, bearings, times, estimated distance covered each six-hour period, weather conditions, visual sightings, descriptions of landmarks and general observations. These conditions would then be compared between ships and with an old chart of the Anatolia region Evelyn had discovered at Cannakkale. It would be their test.

Gallipoli was the last port before the Sea of Marmara. With only an inexact length of one-hundred miles, this relatively smaller leg of their expedition was unchallenging yet it would prove or disprove the old chart.

The preconditions agreed, at first light the *Vixen* moved off, followed shortly afterward by the *Golden Raven*. JT was to keep well distant to port, yet retain visual contact. The spread was to assume there would be a fleet tracking this course and the ships would not necessarily be in line.

Keeping to port, the coastal lands of Macedonia and Bulgaria were nothing more than miles of sand, trees and a few villages scattered along the coast. To starboard, islands the chart called Marmara and Avsa were seen, and off in the distance another land mass[13] or island that was missing from the chart.

Noting there may be shoaling, Evelyn stood the *Vixen* well off shore until the islands were well astern and both Captains were rewarded with open water as far as the horizon, about five miles. The waves were constant, no sign of shallows. Soundings revealed nothing less than eight fathoms at mean low—plenty of water for Her Majesty's warships.

Estimating ten to twelve knots, the two ships converged after sighting Istanbul. The lookout on the *Vixen* sighted unmarked islands[14] below the city and the ships eased southeast until they saw Turkish ships moored and decided it was safe to anchor there for the night.

As they rounded the point to enter the lee of the first island, they came face to face with the largest warship they had ever seen. In fact, she was the largest warship in the world, the one-hundred, twenty-eight gun, Turkish warship, *Mahmudiye.*

Although Evelyn had seen countless large Royal Navy warships at Portsmouth, she was still awed by the sheer size of this ship, yet she had the presence of mind to dip her father's Black Moon Line pennant. JT, seeing that, lowered and raised his father's red burgee with its white G.

---

[13] Kapidag Peninsula.

[14] The four Princes Islands, ten miles SE of Istanbul.

They saw scurrying on the warship's top deck and, shortly afterwards, twice came saluting cannon fire. Although knowing of it, JT and Monar were not used to hearing that formal salute, but looking over and seeing Evelyn smile, eased their concern.

The Ottoman Empire's Star and Crescent Red Ensign flew from the stern of the *Mahmudive* and most of the sailors aboard knew the *Vixen's* Union Jack. They were especially inquisitive of the lines of the clipper ship, her gold figurehead and flying a flag with thirty stars and thirteen red and white stripes.

After dipping her Red Ensign twice, a speaking trumpet from the warship announced, in English, there would be tea served in one-half hour and the ship's launch to be sent for them.

Dressed in the best outfits they could find, Lady Evelyn, JT and Monar were piped aboard the great warship. To their surprise, the entire ship's company was at attention on the forestays and yards with the officers in line abreast to greet the three sailors. They realized someone was putting on quite a show, but why? Theoretically, they were only merchant sailors.

A captain stepped forward; welcomed them to the ship in perfect Eton English, asked their names and escorted them to the admiral's cabin. There, the captain introduced each by name to Kayhserili Ahmet Pasha, Koradmiral of the Ottoman Empire's Black Sea Fleet. The Vice Admiral was in his finest, dark blue, knee length coat, shoulder boards woven with gold lace and three silver stars. Along both lower sleeves were four gold stripes, the upper with curl, and the lower a broad band. The three visitors, impressed by their reception, failed to notice another person, who, although not acknowledged at present, sat quietly on a settee at the rear of the cabin.

Vice Admiral Ahmet Pasha now took over the meeting.

"Lady Bunting, I schooled through your Naval College and knew your father. I see you have another ship. Is she to replace the—the *Black Watch* wasn't it? The one so tragically lost. By your coming this far, I want to thank you for agreeing to carry out both our country's needs."

Turning to JT and Monar, "And you two gentlemen, Captain John Thomas and partner Monar, I wish to thank you both as well. I know this problem does not involve your country, but we will remember your efforts in our behalf, I will see to that."

They were dumbfounded into silence. The Admiral knew so much, and even more, so soon.

Laughing at their confusion, Admiral Ahmet Pasha turned to the man on the settee, "Lord Stratford, our young friends seem to have lost their tongues. Come, enlighten them."

Lord Stratford the most recent British Chargé d'affaires, replacing Hugh Rose in Istanbul, informally nodded to each.

"To enlighten then. Our familiarity with your past events is quite simply explained. The Electro-telegraph is now complete from France through the Caucasus's and down into the Anatolia. Admiral Henderson informed us of your past tribulations in America and Captain Bakr, the Harbor Captain at Cannakkale, knew of the corsairs and contacted the British Legation at Istanbul about you by that telegraph, henceforth on to me, as Ambassador."

Lady Evelyn found her voice, "You're the person we were to seek in Istanbul."

"Yes, we heard when you left and planned to sally out to meet you, but one of our people saw you turn toward these islands, so we waited. We thought it better here, away from prying eyes. Yet actually, prying eyes are everywhere. Istanbul is a breeding ground for intrigue these days."

Orderlies entered with drinks and later, dinner, while they spoke quietly of the request from the Admiralty. It became all too evident the *Mahmudiye* was in the Sea of Marmara to protect her from the Russian Navy. True, there was no war. Yet powerful as she was, she would be too splendid a trophy to resist, war or no war. If the Russian Navy even *thought* they could seize the *Mahmudiye* and overwhelm her, they would make the attempt. The few Turkish ships in the Black Sea were not worthy targets to start a war over—at present.

JT was mystified, "Then if you can't go into the Black Sea safely, what do you intend to do with the *Mahmudiye*?"

"Our navy will never be strong enough again to take on the Russian Navy alone. After the Tazimat, the takeover, Sultan Mahmud II's decision to reorganize the government was central, and though they built this ship, the navy was weakened. As to your question, we save our ships and wait."

"For what, Admiral?"

"For the British and the French, to make up their minds—no offence meant, Lady Bunting."

"None taken, Admiral Pasha, we do take our time. However, I'd like to go back a bit in the conversation. You mentioned prying eyes and that *your* people saw us. Are we to assume *other* people saw us as well and that our expedition will be tracked and reported to the wrong people?"

The Admiral and Lord Stratford exchanged glances. Stratford answered, "Probably, yes."

She was thoughtful for a moment, then spoke to JT and Monar, "Perhaps this is not the time to mention this, but to say the least, this news is not good. I believe you should rethink our agreement in view of the information. I suggest you deliver your cargo to Varna and head home. I won't forget to thank you then for all you've done."

JT had to ask, "You're going to go through with this, despite what you've just heard?"

"Of course. We'll be out of sight of land and if anyone follows us, my crew will blow them out of the water." She laughed at her remark.

"Then we go with you."

"Seriously, both of you, why would you do that?"

"Because you're too irresponsible to be left on an ocean by yourself."

She laughed again, but thanked goodness.

Dinner and the end of the evening were over. As they were leaving, Vice Admiral Pasha spoke quietly to JT, "You may not think too highly of our navy at present and yes, we are getting rusty, yet if war comes, the *Mahmudiye*[15] will do her duty, I will promise England that."

Overseen by the two Turkish Forts of Rumeli on the western, European flank, and Fort Andolu on the eastern, Anatolian flank, they passed from the Sea of Marmara, into the Bosporus Strait, the narrow, serpentine gash of waterway separating the Marmara and Black Seas.

Moving into the Black Sea, the town of Kumköy came up to port. Evelyn studied the chart Admiral Pasha had given her of the southwestern Black Sea and set a bearing that would take them north, north by west across the one-hundred, fifty miles to Varna. Varna, and then what?

Daydreaming the hours away, thinking of various issues, she knew JT and Monar agreed to go with her because they admired her. Not, she reflected, in the loving sense of the word, more that they respected her, recognized her for what she could do as a woman. JT, she smiled each time thinking of him. At first, he was enamored.

Yet, as with all sensible young men, he recognized it for what it was and reverted to his first love, that Charlee woman he mentioned. She shook her thoughts, went to the wheel, checked the helmsman's heading and then returned to watch the towed taffrail log, used to judge the *Vixen's* speed.

Now she mused over Monar. A fairytale of another color. *She* was the one who'd been enamored. Her Black Knight from the past.

---

[15] With a figurehead of a Roaring Lion, the *Mahmudiye* had three gun decks with lengths of 200 feet each, bearing a total of 128 cannon. Built on the Golden Horn of Constantinople in 1829, she carried a crew of 1,280.

In addition to other naval conflicts and while under command of KorAdmiral of the Fleet (Turkish), Kayserili Ahmet Pasha, the warship, strictly sail, fought valiantly alongside the British and French navies at the siege of Sevastopol in1855. She was broken up in 1874.

Of course that was back then, when she a child, easily fascinated by something new, or extraordinary. That was Monar then and Monar still. Her father saw her attracted long back in Barbados and saw it once more at Blackwood Abbey. Yet in Barbados, it was a silly girl's attraction. Is it that now? God knows. And Monar's feelings? He's puzzling, mysterious. She cannot see past his eyes or know his thinking. He never lets on….

Evelyn stopped, cleared her mind of him—or rather overrode those thoughts and heeded to another vexation. Guilt. She had seized on their feelings for her and by that, manipulated them into continuing. Given the recent intelligence, it could, and very well would, be a risky enterprise. She gave them the chance to refuse—yet it was false, a pose on her part. She already sure their answer would be yes, or she would not have asked. They couldn't say no to her and that was her guilt.

Had she wished, she could slip the *Vixen's* anchor tonight and drift away in the gloom, go off on her own. But that was a mindless, asinine thought. Monar never seemed to sleep and that was to be her excuse. She knew it was just that—a pretext not to abscond, to save her pride.

Angry within, standing at the rail, she forced herself to admit she needed them, their strength and their minds. Yet more so, the revelation came to her, it was their companionship that she needed and wanted to be part of.

Varna, Bulgaria, once the Roman port of Odessus, was as they expected. Dusty, dirty, sweaty and raucous. The British Navy's harried civilian agent valiantly tried to keep order above the hubbub of the natives, all of whom struggled to earn a few shillings at the Briton's expense.

He stood back from Lady Evelyn, knowing he smelled, "My name's Hastings, Albert. Here's my identification. My dock-walloper is late, so please forgive this rabble. It may not look it, but we'll have you offloaded in a jiff."

Although not quite true to his word, the dockworkers became a little more organized once Hasting's Arab manager, obviously suffering from whatever cannabis he absorbed the previous night, ambled in and set about thrashing his laborers into some sense of order.

Evelyn shook her head, bewildered at the clamor and looked back to the *Raven.* She laughed aloud watching JT shouting—she assumed— some Yankee cusswords at the natives, then throw his hands in the air and walk off, apparently still cussing.

For all his being harassed, Hasting was a fount of information. Evelyn, at first annoyed he knew where the ships were headed, found he could assist with the local sea channels and the number of the close-in islands, The Saints he called them simply as every island's name began with 'Saint' this or that. The one island he warned she stand well off from was named Snake or Serpent. It was well north, he said, but in 1829, the Russian's took it from the Turks and in '42 built a lighthouse there. Evidently, the lighthouse would not be the problem; it was the fact the Russian's had recently installed a high-powered telescope in the tower and that its lens reached well into the sea-lanes.

"So, Hastings, what you're saying is, we will be seen."

"Not necessarily, Captain Bunting, look at this map I acquired a while back."

The misnamed map turned out to be a rough drawing of the alleged course to Sevastopol.

There were no distances or markers, no allowances for windage, drift or tides. It was simply a slightly concave charcoal line from Varna to a spot labeled Sevastopol, and only one heading.

Evelyn was not pleased, "Hastings, even to call this a map is a bit much. Who drew this?"

He was defensive, "I got it from a Russki deserter, got him drunk, paid him two shillings."

"I think you overpaid." She tried to smile, "I gather neither you nor this Russki chap is a navigator."

He missed the cynicism, "No, I'm not, but he said he used to swab the wheelhouse on the Russian battleship *Gromovnik* and now and then glanced at the charts and compass. And look, this concave bend in the line. The deserter drew it so we'd avoid the telescope on Serpent Island. So he did know about that."

She thought it more likely the line's sag was due to the condition of the person drawing the line, "You mean to tell me there's not a better chart of the Crimea than this?"

That's the point I'm trying to make, Captain. The Tsar has had the Black Sea area deluged with false charts for years. Wrong information of what is where, shoals, ledges, latitudes—even added in islands that aren't there to fool a navigator."

She wondered if she could swallow all this. Was it the Russian's were that crafty, then again, was the drunken sailor right or a spinner of tales for two shillings?

"Would you stake your life on this piece of paper if I gave you vast odds, Hastings?"

He dodged the question, "I'm a Scot, Captain. I wouldn't stake my life on a sure thing for any odds. Yet I wouldn't discount this until it was proved wrong."

She had to be frank, "Hastings, I know you're only trying to help, but you see, following this curve means nothing at sea. And if the bearing is followed, we may arrive at mainland Russia, the Crimea, or miss everything and wind up on a ledge."

Deflated, Hastings apologized, I'm sorry Captain Bunting." He then seemed enlightened, "I just thought of something else. When are you casting off?"

"Later tonight, if we're discharged. Why do you ask?"

"I've another idea; don't leave until I return—please!"

JT shook his head at the scribble, "Hasting's threw away good money when he bought this piece of…paper, Evelyn."

"I know and I did a little more than just imply that, JT, but he tried—more than most of the others it seems."

Monar looked up, "It's difficult to believe no one knows more than this."

"I agree with you and JT, Monar. Yet I'll bet the Russian's planned to carve up the Ottoman Empire for decades—they took some of it years ago—that's why they've kept the northern Black

Sea closed. We British didn't care; charts were of no interest to us until we saw the Russian Bear clawing to get a warm water port. By then, it was too late for charting…"

JT spoke up, "Right, and now the Brits left it for a woman to bail them out."

Evelyn put it another way, "No, they left it for the best non-navy *captain and navigator* to bail them out."

Monar laughed, "Who just happened to be a *woman*—and don't you forget it, JT."

He chuckled with them. There was really nothing else he could do.

Near dark, the cloud cover lowered, the offshore breeze diminished. While waiting for Hastings to return, they plotted his information on the many 'sainted' islands and did their best with the pitiful information supplied on Serpent Island and the charcoal drawn 'bend'.

By 2300 hours, tide and darkness were full and, as they slacked the lines of the two ships, a lantern was seen swaying down the wharf.

The same lantern's light shone down on them as they gathered around a table in the *Vixen's* cabin. The table held an old often-folded chart—in Arabic.

"A lot of good that will do! Who speaks Arabic?"

Hastings was surprised no one knew he did, "Why should you be amazed? My speaking Arabic was the requisite for this God-forsaken posting. If I'd been smart, I would have kept my mouth shut when the Foreign Office visited Cambridge for trainees."

Monar spoke for all, "Too bad for you, Hastings, good news for us. Now, let's get to it."

"I just found this in the house of Ghalib Hajjar; he was an old Arab sea captain before the turn of the century. Let me look at it more closely. Damn—excuse me Captain Bunting—for some reason Captain Hajjar penned it in Tamil. People around here don't know that language."

"What about you?"

"Well, not really…of course the numerals—you know 1 2 3 4 5 and so on, are the same as ours," Hastings laughed at himself, "they should be, we got them from the Barhmi numerals in the first place—except for the zero—but I don't know the algorithm to change Tamil to Arabic."

JT walked in circles, Monar stared at Hastings, Evelyn gazed at the chart, "Look, we're got numerals we can read, let's start from that point."

Hastings quelled even that, "Just because we can read the numerals, doesn't mean we can decipher their value because there are no zeroes. Actually, I think this might be in cipher."

JT cut to the quick, "So, we have a chart of sorts, which may, or may not, be of this sea, it's in Tamil, which few people can read, of which you are *not* one—Correct, Hastings?"

"Correct, sir, I cannot read Tamil."

"So to continue, even the numbers we have can't be read properly, and they may be in cipher."

Monar summed it up better, "JT, Edgar Allan Poe would have loved this."

Hastings tried to develop a procedure to decrypt the chart. At the end of an hour, he tossed his pencil on the chart, "I give up, I'm sorry but I'm wasting your time. Although as I worked on this, I do remember that Russki drunkard said it was five-hundred and sixty miles—no wait; it was five-hundred and sixty-*nautical* miles to Sevastopol. He seemed sure of that."

Hastings scribbled a while longer, "I can't correlate that figure with numerals on the chart."

Hung on the well-known horns of a dilemma, and assuming the number was somewhere near correct, in landlubber miles that was three-hundred plus miles as the crow flies. Yet, even trusting the drunkard, did that include the questionable bend in his chart? If it did, at an average sailing pace ten knots, or less for soundings, they should see the Peninsular after fifty hours or so. That would put them in position the morning of the day after next, plus or minus whatever happened along the way.

JT had enough, "In the time we've spent worrying this to death, we could have been halfway there. Ten knots is slow as death, so let's get underway and get this over with—fifty or sixty hours more or less, what difference does it make?"

Hastings tossed another fly into the ointment, "The Russki also mentioned the waters around Sevastopol held a beehive of torpedoes."[16]

"Christ!" JT said it, thinking he was speaking for all of them, "Are there any more tidbits you wish to recall this drunken friend of yours mentioned?"

Evelyn wasn't the least surprised. She wouldn't have thought otherwise. When not at sea, she'd lived around a navy port most of her life.

"JT, calm down. Hastings' did his best. You're acting as if he should have everything laid out. That's what *we're* here for—remember?"

She was right, that was what they were there for, "All right then, Evelyn. Like I said before, let's get underway."

With the coalbunker topped off and a faint offshore breeze, the sullen, moon-shrouding clouds obscured their ships as they cleared the Saints. They feinted south, extinguished all lights and then came back to an easterly course. Unfortunately, the subterfuge only amused to the person behind the telescope in a third story window. After the course correction, she was off to the telegrapher in Burgas.

When Hastings said goodbye, Evelyn watched JT closely. He was courteous, even thanked Hastings for trying his best. She knew, however, that JT was tense. It wasn't fear, of that she was sure. It was only the vexation, the uncertainty of whatever lay ahead. He

---

[16] In the early/mid 1840s, mines were referred to as torpedoes.

wanted it done, or at least, started. Get into it, confront it was the bravura of his youth. She still considered JT young, young yet in a remarkable, inexplicable way. Still, if it came to a mêlée with a Russian ship, how would he react? She had no doubts of herself…or Monar.

She couldn't prevent a grin. Speaking of inexplicable, Monar was certainly that. Baffling, enigmatic fit as well. He sat in that meeting saying little, or perhaps all he said was something or other about an Edgar Poe. Yet his eyes drifted to each person. She could feel he was listening, thinking, judging, always vigilant, prepared. She would never get behind that thick black skin—that she knew.

They began the soundings even before the bearings became vague on the southern Black Sea chart Admiral Pasha had supplied in Istanbul.

Dark merged into dawn and brought rain and wind making the sextant useless. Evelyn had learned at Istanbul that the restrictions of the Bosporus Strait along with wind caused an oscillation in the mass of water in the Black Sea. This oscillation created a tidal current uncommon to oceans. Compounding the problem of position was the inability to find any landmarks, if there were any, through the intermittent rainstorms.

Evelyn was left with no choice. With these variables, she would have to depend on dead reckoning. Plainly stated, conjecture. Experience, knowledge, feel—yes. Use any word, yet it still came down to guesswork. Exactly that which the Royal Navy did not want. Still, she had no alternative and felt they could backtrack to Varna later if her bearings turned out erroneous.

When they passed merchant and fishing ships, the only curiosity of those ship's crews seemed centered on the *Golden Raven* and its figurehead. The *Raven* being the only clipper ship ever seen in these waters, the stares she received continued long after she passed.

The rainfall became unrelenting. Darkness once again descended on the ships making it impossible to keep in contact as they crept into the night. At midnight, gale force winds struck from their port quarter. With all visual contact lost, Evelyn knew their whole agenda—timetable, bearings, soundings had become moot. They would have to start over. Right now, however, scud along; under double reef and try to hold course. JT tried the same—as best as possible.

The weather eased off before dawn. A freshening breeze hounded the clouds away and filled the *Golden Raven's* canvas. There was not another ship in sight. Monar climbed twenty feet up the stays to increase his offing line, and saw a sail to their stern. He nodded to JT and continued looking until he could recognize Lord Bunting's Black Moon Line pennant on the mainmast. JT spilled the wind from their sails, letting them luff and waited for the *Vixen*.

The two ships wallowed in the swells while their captain's spoke through speaking trumpets. Both knew their position on an empty sea was questionable at best and after a short discussion, they agreed their whole plan was a shambles. They settled on proceeding due north on the assumption that the first land they caught sight of would be some segment of the Crimean Peninsula and the decision made was to stand well offshore in case of torpedoes. Yet some reference point on the coast was needed, following which the ships would retrace their bearings to chart their passage back to Varna. Evelyn knew the importance of this and convinced JT and Monar of it.

This entire new plan, such as it was, became wasted effort. They never saw the Peninsula.

The *Vixen* had to beat to windward, so the *Golden Raven,* under low steam and mainsails furled, took the lead as the *Vixen* fell astern. The weather held; a moderate sea gave way to a four-foot swell, the *Raven* carved into it, gliding through the sun-lit morning.

"Smoke on the horizon, Captain. Dead ahead."

The lookout, forty feet up on the foremast, estimated the distance at eight miles. JT allowed the staysails to luff, barely keeping steerageway while telling Monar to lower shaft revolutions and allow the *Vixen* to change tack and come up. At the same time, the steam pressure was increased. Until he knew who the other ship was—and of course he knew it couldn't be good—he stayed cautious.

The *Vixen* came abeam. The *Raven's* sails had blocked the *Vixen's* lookout from seeing the approaching ship and now, looking to where JT pointed, Evelyn climbed the stays with her spyglass, "Damn! It's the *Ghazna* and she's coming on full bore!"

Tense now, JT had to ask, "Are you definite, you sure?"

"For God's sake, yes! It's rare for masts to be all the same height like the old *Constant* and I saw the sun glint off her iron sides. She can't be five miles off, there's no time to waste—she's powered, remember? She has a full head of steam—we've got to make a run for it!"

Even as he watched Evelyn lower the Union Jack, JT was thinking fast, recognizing the *Vixen* could never outrun the warship, "Come about and run downwind, I'll try to stall her!"

"Stall her? That's crazy talk, you know she's fifty guns. She'll run you down!"

He ignored her, "Monar, we're in deep trouble!"

"I heard, what do you want?"

"Give me all the steam you've got!"

He could hear Evelyn yelling at him as he centered the helm and felt the slow heave of the ship as the screw bit. The two steam powered ships were heading straight for each other until JT threw the wheel to port. Minutes later, judging the distance at one-mile, he hauled the *Raven* around to starboard. It was a bold move; he was heading directly for the *Ghazna's* midship. Unfortunately, this move gave the *Ghazna* the weather gauge and brought the warship's starboard cannon—thirty of them—to bear when she passed the bow of the *Raven*.

With the Long-nine useless in the stern, JT knew his attack appeared suicidal, yet their only chance. He was depending on details Evelyn had mentioned about the *Ghazna*. If she were wrong—the *Golden Raven*, he and his crew, would not survive.

Monar came topside and saw the broad beam of the *Ghazna* less than a half-mile ahead, "Jesus Christ, JT! What in hell are you doing?"

The forward cannon of the warship began to bear, JT's crew running for cover, "Every one, down, *now*!"

The *Ghazna's* cannon began firing one after the other. The first ball missed, bursting the sea. The warship rolled, the second ball struck and shattered the *Raven's* foremast. The third struck the bowsprit, splintering it, tearing off the bobstays and smashed the right wing of the raven figurehead. The forth cannonball crashed into the bird's golden face, obliterating it. The fifth and sixths balls tore into the bow stem at the waterline, fragments shredding the foresails.

At this moment, the captain of the *Ghazna*, seeing his enemy was not going to sheer off was now frightened his ship would be rammed and veered off under full power. The ship yawed to starboard and her next two cannonballs went short, blasting into the water. The warship, instantly off the vertical, top-heavy and unstable, brought the gunwale's edge close to the waves.

JT gritted his teeth as he rolled the *Raven* away to port. He had done what he intended; force the *Ghazna* to veer sharply away. Evelyn was right! That ship is *unstable*!

Her cannon, now slanting downward, couldn't fire and their weight, along with the iron cladding, dragged the warship over further. Listing at almost thirty degrees, her mainmast spars began to drag in the sea as her captain stopped both propellers, feverishly hoping the *Ghazna* would right herself. Immobile, she wallowed in the swells, her sailors on the slanted deck valiantly continued to fire grapeshot from swivel guns. The grapeshot and snipers in the yardarms causing turmoil in the *Raven's* crew.

"Go over, Damn you! Turn turtle you big bastard!"

Monar grabbed JT's shoulder, spinning him around. A mass of white sails filled his view as the *Vixen* interposed between the *Raven* and the *Ghazna.*

"What the devil is she doing, Monar? We'll be clear soon."

"She's going to stop those blasted snipers and finish her off!"

The *Vixen* had tacked and, under full sail, came abeam the *Ghazna*. Evelyn never looked to the *Raven*. Intent to the task, she ignored the musket fire from the warship.

Two of *Vixen's* cannons, loaded with grapeshot, roared and ended the sniping. Following that, her five cannon, discharged a pointblank cannonball broadside that tore into the partially submerged rail. The *Ghazna's* starboard freeboard went under, followed by the port cannons breaking loose and crashing into the starboard guns. The additional weight doomed her.

She went on her beam-ends, foundering as seawater spilled over her gunwale and poured in through her gun ports and hatches. With her deck awash, the port screw propeller breached the surface. A moment later, her boiler exploded underwater and blew out her bottom. Timber filled air burst through her deck hatches. It proved to be her last breath.

"JT, I thought you'd gone off the deep end and then I saw what you were doing. You guessed the *Ghazna* was top-heavy."

"No, Evelyn said it was—all I did was to prove it!"

Monar slapped him on the shoulder, "What a great trick…" He looked at the red dampness on his hand, "What the devil?"

"What's the matter with you?"

"What's the matter with me? Look at my hand JT. Christ—look at your shirt!"

Looking at the stain, JT shook his head in puzzled, "Damn, Monar, I have no idea how that happened."

"Well it's damn evident a sniper caught you. Move your arm around, feel anything wrong?"

"Can't say that I do."

"Then it's probably only a flesh wound, let's get below and take a look."

There were a few items ahead of a wounded shoulder. They moved the *Raven* away slowly. There were at least four-hundred men from the *Ghazna* in the water or climbing into lifeboats and the lifeboats had sails. If the enemy decided to be heroic, there were more than enough men to overwhelm the two crews of the *Vixen* and *Raven*. While Evelyn came abeam, lookouts were ordered to the mainmast.

There were three dead in the *Raven's* crew with four wounded. The foremast stays and bobstays were hacked away to help the mast and bowsprit to be pushed overboard. The greatest danger at present was the damaged bow. The *Raven* was taking on a serious volume of water.

"This doesn't look good, Monar. We're far enough from the *Ghazna's* crew now, heave to; we're driving more water onto us. Get our pumps working and we'll see what the *Vixen* has."

The *Vixen* rafted and Evelyn swung aboard. She had mixed feelings. It was obvious JT had committed himself completely to her previous comments about the *Ghanza*. It was a terrible, irresponsible chance he took. He would have had a decent chance to escape, yet he went on the attack and that gamble had undoubtedly saved her ship. On the other hand, was it solely *she* he was trying to save and gambled his crew? What should she say? Thanks, you irresponsible God damned fool; do you need your brains examined? Perhaps she should simply say thanks.

Told they were in JT's cabin, she headed below after ordering her medical officer to help topside. Monar had given JT his studied opinion it was just a scratch. Although a bullet had skived across his shoulder and left a four-inch long gash that luckily missed bone.

"You poor boy, JT, let me get this covered up before Evelyn sees it; God, she'll want to be your nurse all the way back to Portsmouth."

She heard from the cabin door, "Before Evelyn does what? What in blue blazes has he done now?"

Her eyes swept across his bloody chest to his shoulder, "Damn, JT! Don't you know you're supposed to duck when people shoot at you?"

He appeared embarrassed, starting to put his shirt on.

Evelyn took charge, "For heaven's sake! What are you thinking? Don't put that bloody mess back on. Monar, get him another shirt, while I take a look at this so-called scratch."

It was ragged, but Monar had done a good job of cleaning and trimming the edges.

"Very nice, Monar, you've debrided it nicely. You want me to stitch it up, JT?"

"Stitch it? You? Why, what's to gain? No, don't."

She laughed at his confusion, "If I do, it might heal more quickly, leave less of a scar—or do you want all the pretty girls to be impressed?" She bandaged it, "Now put that shirt on."

He turned his back while tucking the shirt in. Evelyn rolled her eyes at Monar, "For God's sake, JT! Are you just out of the priesthood?"

Blushing, JT said he had to check the forward planking.

Evelyn stopped him, "Wait a moment, JT. I'm sure you know what you did was a foolhardy thing to do. With that said, it was also a heroic thing to do, and I," tears formed, "and I want to thank you," She quickly wiped her eyes, "and you too, Monar—for letting him do it!"

She hugged them both, then collected herself, "All right then, let's go see what we can do about the shattered beak of this bird."

It wasn't good news. Shipwrights from both ships agreed the *Raven* was in poor shape. Three pumps could keep up with the inflow of water while the ship was drifting, but with her cutwater fractured, it prevented a firm fastening of the planks to the bow stem. Forward movement, even with tarred canvas sails covering the damage, was at best two or three knots.

After two days, it was time to make a decision and Evelyn presented the facts, "JT, it's your ship and your decision. I'll go along with whatever you decide, you deserve that—yet we've the crews to think about. So, I've got to tell you what you already know; we've hardly made headway. I think the southern Regale Winds have swung around from the southeast and are going to give us constant headwinds. With the *Raven* in this shape, it will take weeks to reach Istanbul. There will be survivors from the *Ghazna* and when the Russian's find out what happened we'll be sitting ducks if another warship…"

JT stopped her form going further, "I know, Evelyn, I've endangered everyone here, I'm sorry. Memories, I guess. We'll transfer what we can to the *Vixen* and get it over with."

When she left, Evelyn was halfway along the passageway when she heard a loud *damn* from JT and started to return. She froze, upon hearing him speak to Monar, *"I tell you, Monar, it hurts to lose the Raven, yet it's for the best. Let's bury this slaver under fifty fathoms in a foreign sea. She deserves it."*

A slaver? She thought. The *Golden Raven* was a slaver? Evelyn could not believe it true. She heard Monar's voice in response, *"She deserves it? JT, you know better. Remember Poe said a ship cannot sin—only people sin."*

Evelyn slipped away.

Waiting until the transfer to the *Vixen* was completed, she found Monar alone. She ignored the strongbox he carried, "Monar, I need some answers. I overheard you and JT talking about…about the *Raven* being a slaver. Was she? It certainly sounded like it and I can't believe JT would be involved in slavery."

Her concern was electric, how much did she hear? Still, she deserved the truth.

"Evelyn, this is a private matter, yet you deserve to know. The *Raven* was once the *Laurence Pike*. She was one of fifteen ships his father owned. A hurricane wiped him out and he turned the *Pike* into slaver to survive. JT's father, Captain Richard Graves was a good man who evil tested—and he failed. Still, he was once my friend and that, I cannot forget."

"Your friend? You're a black man! How could that be?"

"Because he couldn't live with evil and it destroyed him, that's what I mean by a good man."

She hesitated, yet had to ask, "Was JT with him—when she was a slaver?"

"No. In fact, it drove the two apart and his father died before they could put it to rights."

"Thank you, Monar. I couldn't believe otherwise. However I have one other question that's bothered me for some time—what happened to Ian MacPherson?"

That surprised him, although he did answer, "He wasn't a good man and I killed him."

She blinked only once, "I somehow thought that. It doesn't change anything with me. Knowing you, there was a reason."

He had started to leave, then came back, "Since we're being honest, you should know that when we attacked the *Ghazna*, I was in the engine room; I didn't grasp what JT was up to until I came topside. It was strictly him and his intent to save *you*—so you didn't have to thank me."

"That's quite frank, Monar. Nonetheless, you went along with him once you knew."

"Of course I did, although you're missing the point."

JT leaned on the *Golden Raven's* rail, his back to the *Vixen*. All for naught, he thought. He lost his ship and they never caught even a glimpse of Sevastopol[17] or the Kerch Strait. [18]

---

[17] The British and French did use Varna, Bulgaria, as the staging port against the Crimean Peninsula. They did not, however, directly attack Sevastopol, instead landing an army north, at Eupatoria, and advance south. It required the Battle of Balaclava, the Battle of Inkerman, the Battle of Mamelon, the Battle of Tchernaya and the Second Battle of Balaclava before Sevastopol was under siege by land and sea. In an effort to maintain a 'Fleet intact', the Russians kept the Black Sea Fleet in harbor at Sevastopol. It was a blunder like no other. The fleet never ventured forth. Stripped of her guns and sailors, the vaunted Black Sea Fleet was scuttled. Sevastopol surrendered in 1855.

[18] In 1855, during the invasion of Kerch in the Sea of Azov, the first battle between ironclad floating vessels took place at Kil-Bouroun. This was seven ears preceding the American Civil War battle of the ironclads, USS Monitor and CSS Virginia, (formerly the USS Merrimack).

With the *Golden Raven* lost, his last hold on Salem would be gone. Of course Seaward was there as a house, not a home. Where were his mother or Jason and would he ever know?

The canvas used to slow the water pouring in was removed. As the mainsail was set, the wheel lashed, his memories revived. The last recollection had been of his father, Jason and he laughing as their ship, then named the *Laurence Pike* out-sailed the topsail schooner *Lorelei* and left her in their wake.

The ship had been stripped of any value when he tossed a torch into his oil soaked cabin and then jumped to the *Vixen* with the Ship's Log. The *Golden Raven's* restraining lines were cast off— he didn't take a backward look. The trip home began. Yet, the mind behind the wet eyes wondered, where *was* home?

She hadn't missed the point, only wanted to avert it.

21

27 Sept 1848

LOGIC MADE IT CLEAR. One-hundred men, in a ship designed for fifty, was a toxic brew and cause for concern. Compounded by the fact that the War of 1812 between the United States and England was only twenty-six years earlier and in both crews, many of the Yankees and Brits had been in that war. All needed was an incident to ignite—or some deterrence to prevent.

Evelyn and JT, with Monar, designated to all as Keeper of the Peace, intended to ward off any smoldering resentment, bitterness or bile—hopefully without force—although Monar wasn't adverse to it. They settled on the carrot and the whip approach.

First, the whip. Lady Evelyn, with the quality of leadership she seemed to effortlessly muster, quite simply laid the situation out to her crew, "I will remind my crew that nearly all of you are former Royal Navy and that this ship is under a Royal Navy Diktat."

They didn't know its meaning, yet it sounded important and though not quite true, truth is in the eye of the beholder, when avowed by a Captain.

She continued, "I would also remind you of two factors. One, the *Golden Raven* was not under the RN; it was their captain's decision to accompany us. And number two, if her captain had not sacrificed his ship to save the *Vixen* and her crew, the *Ghazna*, with her sixty guns and twin screw propellers, would have drowned us like dogs. Every one of us would be floating—face down in this sea—if it wasn't for the *Raven* and her American sailors. *And*, because this was a secret undertaking, no one, not your mother, your wife or sweetheart would ever know what happened, or why you never came home."

She had them in the palm of her hand, "Which leads me to state that, anyone found fighting will be confined to the chain locker, limited to bread and water, docked their complete wages and given over to the Naval Court. I respect you all and expect your unbounded cooperation."

Then, the carrot, "One other note. I can understand your cramped quarters will now be even more so, but if there is peace between our crews, or at least restraint for the long trip ahead, there will be a bonus for each man. However, one person, one fight, and consider all bonuses cancelled. I would not want to be the person who caused everyone to lose their bonus."

Her meaning well taken, Evelyn handed the gathering over to JT. Before he spoke, he whispered to her, "No fighting? That include you and I too?"

"Right now, it would be best if you just worry about your crew."

JT surveyed his men, "What Captain Bunting said goes pretty much for me as well, accept for one little issue. Anyone gives us trouble will answer to me, and trust me, I fight dirty. Aside from that, if I'm not tough enough, Monar would love to help me."

The *Vixen*, with two crews comprising one-hundred seven men and, of course, one woman, surged through the southern Black Sea and then labored through the Bosporus Strait without trouble. Moored off Istanbul, Evelyn, JT and Monar were once again asked aboard the Turkish warship *Mahmudiye*. They reported their success in landing the materials to the port of Varna and their catastrophe in the Black Sea before even reaching Sevastopol.

After listening to the story, Lord Stratford, expressed surprise and concern while Vice Admiral Ahmet Pasha, stunned at the story, began the questions, "You mean to tell me that the *Ghazna* just came straight on? There was no recognition signals asking who you were?"

JT responded, "Nothing, they came at us full bore. To my mind, they knew who we were."

The Vice-Admiral started thinking aloud, "So, it would seem that there's spy in Varna who must have telegraphed on to Sevastopol who you were. What flag were you flying?"

"We weren't, both Lady Evelyn and I had lowered them."

The next question began to reveal where the Vice-Admiral was heading.

"So, as you said before, you removed your bow and stern name boards from the *Golden Raven* and set her on fire, plus she was sinking. Was there anything the Russians could find to prove she was an American vessel? Could they read the *Vixen's* name?"

"That's correct, we stripped the *Raven* bare and the *Vixen* was too far away –at first that is. However, she was a private vessel anyway. The US government was not involved in this."

The Ahmet Pasha responded, "I'm sure that's true. Yet it is better there is nothing that would boost this into an international incident—since the Bear is trying to help pay their debts by selling off Russia's Alaskan Territories[19] to the United States."

Lord Stratford looked to the Vice-Admiral, "I see that what you're saying, Ahmet, is, that we just deny any knowledge of the whole affair and I'm comfortable with that approach. However, how is the Russian Navy going to explain to the Czar the loss of the *Ghazna* and a few hundred men?"

Ahmet laughed, "We know there was a storm. They could blame that or they could say the British built a shoddy vessel and sue your Admiralty for reparation." They both laughed at the thought, "That is, after they explain how they came to acquire the *Ghazna* in the first place!"

Becoming serious, Vice Admiral Pasha stared at JT, "What you did, John Thomas, was very heroic, it also shows the truth in Lady Evelyn's judgment of you and the instability of ship the British sold us—although that does not lessen your deed. From what you have said, it was either leave her to the Russian fates or do what you could. In other words, you saw no choice. As you do not deserve to

---

[19] It wasn't until after the American Civil War, 1867, that Russia sold her Alaskan Territory for $7,000,000, or 2 cents an acre. Known then as Seward's Folly, the United States grew by over 560,000 square miles.

bear the loss of your ship, we, the Turkish government that is, will do what we can. I expect to get back to you before you leave."

Ahmet Pasha then turned abruptly to Evelyn, "Tell me, Lady Bunting, the British Empire is your country, what is the Queen doing to help the starving people of Ireland?"

It was an unexpected query, totally off the matter at hand and decidedly disrespectful to a guest. Lord Stratford, ever the diplomat, intervened, "Ahmet, please, you're asking an answer from a person who has nothing to do with the British Government and should not be expected to respond with profundity to your question."

"Then I shall ask you, Lord Stratford, what are the mighty British doing? They, who rule the seas, control the world from Canada to India to China—why can't they help a backward little island next to them—people whom they dominate—why can't they stop them from starving? Even we, Turkey, are sending ships, laden with supplies to help them."

Evelyn was not going to be quiet and have Lord Stratford protect her, "With respect to your position, Admiral, let me tell you a thing of two. The Irish used to depend on wheat and greens, now they depend solely on the potato because it is easier to grow. There was potato blight in the 1700's that caused famine and this one now and in the future there probably will be another. This hits England and Europe as well, but they developed other crops to survive. Ireland should have done the same, but didn't. And, if you are sending ships there, you'd better warn the crews not to land at the port of Larne or any port in Northern Ireland for that matter. Plague is sweeping the landscape and your ships will end up as coffin ships."

"My crews worry not of plagues or coffin ships, Lady Bunting. It is written in our scared Quran, we are a land of plagues, yet undeterred, our Five Pillars of Faith sustain us."

It was beyond Lady Evelyn and Lord Stratford's fathoming why the subject of England's response to Ireland's famine was broached, but before they could continue, the Admiral abruptly changed focus, addressing JT this time, "It's come to me that your two ships had a skirmish with some religious Muslim sailors when you came through the Mediterranean."

JT, who had said nothing during the difference of opinion between the other parties, now felt himself in the limelight, "That's true. Yet religious or not, we were attacked, we won."

"You won, yes. Was it so necessary to win so convincingly? I'm told seventy martyrs men died."

Lady Evelyn interrupted again, "That was not his doing, Admiral. My ship, took the brunt of the assault and we responded and caused the most damage. John Thomas had only four cannon and would have been overwhelmed. In fact, at the end, he let some of your so-called martyrs escape."

Ahmet Pasha was angry, yet kept his face soft, pleasant. A *woman* was interrupting between men. It had been amusing at first. She was beautiful, in a foreign way, but disruptive and needed a strong man to slap her and put her in her place. Infidels were hopeless, weak where women were concerned. It annoyed him to think it was she, this *woman*, who destroyed so many of his fellow true believers. However, he had to keep in check. The Ottoman Empire was going to need the British Lion to combat the Russian Bear and no incidents between Turkey and the British must occur. No matter how maddening, Ahmet Pasha knew he was overstepping his bounds. Moreover, what to make of the American, John Thomas, who they call JT? He had let some believers escape—a weakness. Knowing that about the man, Admiral Pasha thought, could be of value someday. He decided to keep his promise, at least to the American.

The Marmara Sea lay before them and they stayed strictly to their charts and test the plots made during their voyage from Gallipoli to Istanbul on the outward journey.

As requested by Ahmet Pasha, they laid over at Cannakkale, there to find three Turkish officials' wishing to meet with JT. In full view of the crews, and respecting proper form, they presented him with an honor signifying the Order of the Medjidie and Hero of the

Ottoman Empire. The officials, apparently unaware of the basis for the Edict, simply awarded it by fixing a ruby incrusted starburst with crescent on JT's right breast. Next, JT was then handed an envelope without explanation and the two officials saluted and left the wharf.

Alone, except for Lady Evelyn and Monar, JT opened the envelope and began to read. He was puzzled, "US Sea Captain, John Thomas Graves, five thousand dollars...No! *Fifty,* fifty thousand American dollars! What the devil is this?"

They stared long and hard. An international note, underwriter and guarantor—The Ottoman Government, made out to John Thomas Graves. Fifty-thousand dollars. Signed in English, ***Sultan Abdülmecid*** **I.**

Written, again in English, along the lower edge: *May this cover the expense of a new Golden Raven. Koramiral Kaysherili Ahmet Pasha*

When it sank in, JT took his black friend's hand, "Partner, we're going to help the families of the men who died and then we're going to own one of the fastest, most beautiful clipper ships in the world!"

Lady Evelyn was pleased for both men and admired JT for first thinking of those lost and then including Monar in the compensation. Another nuance in her diverse thoughts on JT.

Cannakkale lay in the *Vixen's* wake. Soon they would be through the Aegean Sea and on into the eastern Mediterranean. The history of the Mediterranean is rife with pillaging and crews killed or sent into a lifetime of slavery. The Barbary Corsairs of the past were mostly destroyed or diminished by the Treaty of Morocco in1830. There were, however, pockets of resistance, pirates who hid in waterways and backwaters who refused to give up their right to prey on commerce for gain—mainly the sale of men and women in the marketplaces of Algiers and Salé. They would try their luck again.

The *Vixen* and the *Golden Raven* had an example of these corsairs when they entered the Med from Gibraltar, and even though they were dispatched without difficulty, that was only a minor example, the corsairs, in smaller ships, were caught off-guard by an experienced crew. Also, the *Vixen's* Chief Mate, Harry Griffin, a former RN Gunner's Mate, had traded broadsides with Berber Corsairs in the late 1820s and knew and respected their power—diminished or not.

With his suggestions, both captains' gave Griffin leeway to pick out experienced members from both crews to head-up gun teams and tactics. The workups became intense. More so than prior training on the voyage and Griffin, not surprisingly with Monar's backing, seemed to look into the future and dislike the view. The British crew, with mostly RN pensioners, picked up on their Chief Mate's and Monar's unease and helped train some of the inexperienced Americans.

JT, when seeing the concern, spoke to Monar about it, "What's going on here, Monar? Griffin is really driving the crew and you, you seem the same."

"There's something out there, JT, I sense it. When I spoke to Griffin about it he said the Berbers are Muslim, and Muslim's always seek revenge for anything they take offense to."

"So you're saying it was Muslim Berber corsairs we beat off Algiers and they're waiting for us to come back this way for revenge?"

"That's what he thinks might happen. He says they call it Jihād—their duty. And, if they die doing their duty they think they go on to some sort of ecstasy."

"I find that hard to believe in this day and age, more like they're still fighting the Crusaders."

"All I'm saying is that something is out ahead, JT, and it is not good, and Griffin is right to drive the crew as he is."

"Well, from what I've seen, the way this crew looks, if any Muslim's mess with us they're going to go on to their ecstasy sooner than they expect."

JT then caught up with Lady Evelyn to discuss the same subject, "What's your thoughts on this Muslim thing, Evelyn—concerned?"

"Well, yes and no. No, because when I delivered the *Ghanza* to the Dardanelles before, I wasn't concerned. She was sixty guns and we also had the HMS *Humphries* chaperoning us through the western Med. With another eighty-four guns, no corsairs were going to challenge that much firepower. And, yes, I'm concerned because the *Vixen* is only fourteen guns and no steam power. If there are enough bad people out there, they might take a chance. Our saving grace is we've got twice the crew, although any enemy wouldn't know that until they attack. And I've heard they are fanatical, ready to die in battle."

"That's what Griffin says, they think they go to paradise or some such thing."

Evelyn appeared disdainful, "Well, Chief Mate Griffin does have empirical knowledge of this region and his squadron was on station here for three years, so I've heard that from him before. But what in heaven any man would want with seventy virgins is beyond me."

JT blinked, befuddled. Evelyn began to laugh, "You don't know that's what they think?"

He was embarrassed, "I…I never heard that."

"My word, JT. Well, perhaps you're to be forgiven, being from *New* England. In England, we're closer to the near east and more aware of that… ah, phenomena…in some Islamic sects."

JT sidestepped further talk on the subject, "So you think it's possible, that they may attack, I mean…not the other thing."

Evelyn smiled, "Possible, probable. That's the only prudent way to look at it, JT, considering their beliefs that is, and we being only one ship."

As she finished speaking, Evelyn looked to the south and the movement on the distant shore, "Put your glass to that bit of dust over there, JT."

"There is something moving, Evelyn. You must have the eyes of a hawk." He focused in his spyglass, "It looks like three men, on camels and they're moving west, damn fast."

He put down the glass, "You thinking what I'm thinking?"

"Can't help but think that, can we. Let's meet with Monar and Griffin."

Past Benghazi without anything untoward, other than dust dervishes and heat waves roasting the parched land. Past Tripoli, they seldom saw more than a few drifting dhows along the shore. With Pantelleria, the old Roman banishment island, far off to starboard, the *Vixen* now eased more westerly, ready to enter the expanse of the Alboron Sea in the western Med.

They spoke of the new ship, and where to build it. JT had naturally thought of the McKay yard in south Boston, yet there were other shipyards and nothing really held them to the States any longer. JT's father purchased the plans when he bought the *Laurence Pike* and JT did not forget them when the *Golden Raven* was set adrift. Evelyn said to speak with her father, he knew the best builders, not just the average, or cheapest.

Algeria, where they were on alert for trouble, went abaft the stern. They close-hauled against the prevailing wind off the coast of Morocco and that brought them within seven miles of the shoreline, closer than desired. With hope, before long, the Pillars of Hercules would loom and they'd be past the massive rock pinnacle of Gibraltar, then into the freedom of the Atlantic.

Yet they were without illusion. To their port, lay miles of Berber territory that still held the remnants of the fierce Muslim nomads of the Barbary States.

Monar had stayed at the rail two days and nights. At dawn, he asked where along the coast they were while taking up the spyglass.

JT looked to the chart, "As an estimate, seeing that point of land, I'd say off a place named Melilla. Why?"

"Does the chart show river or inlet?

"Maybe, it shows what looks to be a bay a bit down the coast and a town called Nador—why are you asking?"

Monar handed the glass to JT, "See where I'm pointing off the port quarter? It looks like the topsails of a square rigger flying a green flag with a red band at the top."

JT's heart leapt, "Damn, Monar, you're right! Moroccan flag, rigged as a brigantine and she's put to sea. Can't be five miles off. Call Griffin and Evelyn."

When Chief Mate Griffin arrived, JT handed him the spyglass, telling him the vessel was square-rigged on the foremast and rigged fore and aft on the main. In other words, more than likely a quick brigantine—if handled correctly.

Griffin stared through the glass, "Thunder and lightning! This is a bother all right," he looked to the *Vixen's* pennant, "and she has the weather gage. Upwind, she can maneuver and come at us from any direction—my guess she'll cross our bow first and rake us."

JT spoke up, "That's what happened to the *Raven*! If we fall off being close-hauled, that would mean moving closer to her and any shoals or sand bars."

While Griffin studied the difficult position facing them, JT studied the enemy ship, "Ten guns to a side, my guess about twenty-four pounders, sails look like hell, ship looks tired, but there must be two-fifty, three-hundred men crowded onto her."

Evelyn glanced to JT and Monar, "Ok, Griffin, it's your call."

He nodded; his mind made up and shouted to the gunners mate, "Reload with grapeshot—*now*! First mate, have your marines prepared to repel boarders—*on the double*! Second Mate, lower the starboard anchor thirty feet and stand by! Captain Graves, see that your men are armed to the teeth." Griffin grabbed a seaman, "Raise the RN Battle Ensign and the Stars and Stripes."

It was improper, however Griffin wasn't concerned—he wanted to inspire the men.

Monar left, leaving JT and Evelyn standing in a swirl of activity, trying to make sense of it all, "Griffin, why grapeshot? We're not close enough. And why the anchor?"

Looking to be sure he knew the enemy's intention, Griffin rushed his answer, "We're in a bad position! That ship is going to cross our bow and rake us at close range where our guns can't touch her. That's called crossing the 'T'. It's the same thing as the *Raven!* We'll go dead in the water and be worse off ..."

Evelyn saw he was tense, hurried, "Can you stop that?"

"Yes, if," Griffin gritted his teeth, "as Nelson, said—every man does his duty. Now please, for your sake, go below."

She did as asked, went below, grabbed her pistols, a short sword and returned to the helm.

Chief Mate Griffin's gamble—for it was surely a gamble—was to stop the enemy from crossing ahead of the *Vixen*. With his ship's steerageway at best three knots and no chance to tack off on another bearing, he knew of only one possible way to prevent the bow from being destroyed. First, he must turn the ship as quickly as possible and second, come alongside the foe—not grapple, that would be disaster—yet close enough to enfilade that ship with grapeshot.

He braced himself. The brigantine came on. Wait…wait. Every eye watched the enemy ship, every man steadied, fearful yet steadfast. Wait, wait, time dragged, but don't commit too soon—that would mean death.

The brigantine began its turn to cross the *Vixen's* bow from her port side. Griffin hastily saw that ship had no gun ports, no protection for the shrieking gun crew.

"Thank God for small favors," he mumbled.

His second mate, at the anchor chain stood unblinking at his chief mate—he knew the drill.

"Now! Griffin shouted. As the wheel was thrown over, he raised his hand and with a chopping motion shouted, "Away the anchor!"

The chain rattled through the hawser-hole and, moments later, the second mate felt the anchor thump on the seabed and signaled the crewmembers to trap the chain on the capstan. The anchor seized, the cable went taut, barring the *Vixen's* headway. The ship strained against the force tethering the bow and with the rudder locked, the ship began slowly rotating in an arc around the anchor cable.

This change in direction surprised everyone on the enemy vessel and brought the *Vixen* near parallel to the enemy, now only thirty yards away. That vessel's gunner became confused. Having been told to fire on the *Vixen's* bow when ordered, he hesitated, awaiting the order.

The enemy's leader, mystified at how the *Vixen* turned so suddenly, froze and it was all Griffin needed. His next signal instantly obeyed; a seven-gun broadside of grapeshot spewed forth across the distance. The enemy gunners never fired as they and masses of Berber warriors screaming at the gunwale disappeared in a cloud of gunpowder. After the roar there was a hush, then came the cries of the wounded being thrown overboard followed by the howls and screeching of the fanatics.

Griffin ordered the anchor chain slipped and relief showed on the *Vixen's* crew. Yet, the battle was just beginning. The *Vixen* had only won the opening maneuver.

The leader of the enemy vessel, whose bow now conveyed worn paint stating *Princess Kathleen*, still had the weather gage and veered his ship within reach of the *Vixen*. Grappling hooks thrown from the *Princess Kathleen* had the *Vixen's* crew racing to hack the rope lines, many men dropping under withering fire from snipers in the Berber ship's rigging.

Without additional grapeshot canisters, the *Vixen's* crew quickly rammed home seven, thirty-six pound cannonballs and, though they were now too close to aim at the top deck, Griffin gave the order to fire. The iron balls tore through the deteriorating sides of the *Princess Kathleen* and devastated the below deck, killing dozens more.

Yet the enemy ship couldn't be stopped, the grapples pulled her closer and the two vessels locked together. Block & tackle hauled up anti-boarding netting as twenty former RN Marines formed two lines and fired volleys of powerful .70 caliber slugs from Brunswick muskets at the warriors who hacked at the nets. The marines then rushed forward with fixed bayonets as the enemy broke through and all of *Vixen's* sailors rushed into the hellish cauldron.

Insanity began in a mêlée of sabers, short swords, cutlasses, dirks, double-barreled shotguns, belaying pins and muskets used as clubs. JT's revolver emptied as well as Evelyn's. Monar's bolo slashed. Shrieking Berbers, death cries, the wounded's screams, hacking scimitars, skulls cracked and streams of blood, the deck awash, causing men to slip. If they went down, they were dead. Life-blood flowed to the scuppers and ran down the *Vixen's* side.

JT and Monar stayed by Evelyn as the dead and dying fell in front of them. Monar was a colossus, enemy warriors stumbled to get away from his bolo and short sword. Covered in enemy blood that blended with his own he fought tirelessly, unyielding, as JT and Evelyn protected his sides and back.

Nonetheless, the crew was gradually overwhelmed, driven back, valiantly giving their lives. Their day had come. A collective fear spread.

Evelyn was the first to accept, "I won't be captured, JT! I won't be a *slave*!"

"Don't say that—don't!"

"There's too many, God damn it all to hell—and you know it! Stay with me, JT."

He did, yet couldn't bear the thought of what could happen.

The unrelenting attack beat them back until, barely heard over the clamor, the sound of a horn, a high-pitched screech, repeated three times. From an enemy so blood-crazed, there was actually a respite. At first the warriors hesitated, angry, and then drew back grudgingly. Slaves to obeying the sound, they stepped on the bodies littering the deck until returning to their own ship.

The *Princess Kathleen's* leader held up a white flag for a truce and stepped forward.

"Very well done and fought, Englishmen. Oh, I see an American flag, so I do not wish to slight you foolish sailors either, yet you should chose better friends. I am Emir Murat Hizir the Younger, of Morocco and you have entered my sea without consent or a tithe to travel my waters. You did the same with impunity and death as you travelled to the east when my followers wanted only to barter fruit with you. And now, you see what that impudence has cost you—and is yet to cost you."

The Emir glanced over to the *Vixen's* deck, distain curling his lips, "Yes…what is yet to cost you. Many of my men have died and that matters little as they will enter paradise. However, you have mightily affronted *me*. Still, despite this insult, I will be generous. I'm sure you will acknowledge you have no chance to survive my next onslaught. That means, should you not surrender, there will be no quarter given and my men will have no restraint in how they take revenge."

Emir Hizir pondered his words like a cat pondering its next move with a mouse; both the Emir and the cat knew the ending.

"Now, you have a woman aboard, a woman who struck down four of my men with her pistols and sword. For her boldness, I shall reward her by allowing her to live in my harem, once she has been taught servility of course. Your big black man is a miracle from Allah. He shall be allowed to live with my Royal Sentinels once he is gelded and agrees to obey Islamic Law. The white infidel trying to protect that woman was valiant and is permitted life as a slave with a chance for freedom. The rest, the uninjured, will be sold as slaves." The Emir held out his hands, palms up, "The wounded have no value to Allah and must bear the immutable fate of all infidels."

While the Emir ranted on about the fate awaiting them all, Monar, standing on the raised helm saw, over all the fanatical faces, his fate in the clouds. Yet, another sight fixated him—the weatherworn topsails of a square-rigger. He whispered to JT, "Don't look, but do you think the Berber's have another square-rigged ship?"

Monar saw his fate was not to be decided this day, but JT was baffled at the question, "Why the devil are you asking that at a time like this?"

Monar gave a sly smile, "I'll take that as a no. Don't look, but I can see a square topsail past their ship. Just trust me in what I do next. We need to keep their attention, so I'm going to play for a little more time."

He separated himself from the sailors around him and waved his bolo in the air, "Emir whatever your stupid name is. You think so much of me? Then I challenge you to combat, or any three men you choose. If I win, we go free. If they win, we will surrender with no more killing."

There was murmuring among the crews of the two ships and Lady Evelyn started to protest, but JT shook his head for her to hold her tongue.

The Emir gave pause, considering the bargain, asking his aides their advice. There was not a chance of his losing the enemy or their ship, even *if* Monar won the challenge.

Emir Hizir's made his decision, "An interesting offer, my African foe. Regrettably, I must refuse it. You'll understand that I have plans for you and I do not wish you to be injured. I am now bored with all this talk. Allah has decreed your insult to his love has come to an end."

To prolong the delay, JT stepped beside Monar, "Same deal, only we'll take on six men!"

Not to be left out, Evelyn shouted out, "Add me in—only we'll take on ten of your scum!"

Monar was stunned. He couldn't believe either of them and laughed raucously. The Emir took the laugh as some sort of trap and signaled to his warriors to prepare for the final slaughter.

Monar had already judged the distance between him and the Emir at about forty feet. Time and the need to act converged. Seeing a puff of smoke emanating from the strange ship, he shouted to the Berber crew to look behind them. Distracted, all heads turned. Monar gripped his bolo with two hands and hurled it with all his strength at the Emir.

Monar's bolo flew as a cannonball struck. A section the *Princess Kathleen's* weather deck and rail vanished in a devastating explosion. A score of men went down from splinters as the base of her mizzenmast split.

Outright shock enveloped the both crews. The Berber's frantic shouts were drowned out by another detonation blowing away men and segments the ship's freeboard planking. Everyone dropped, tense, no one there had ever experienced an exploding cannonball. They awaited the next impact—yet it didn't happen. Monar looked for the Emir, unable to see him. The Berber's were frightened, leaderless, milling about. JT found his spyglass and clambered into the stays.

"She's American!"

The Emir was found unconscious, lying under one of his aides. That aide had stepped in front of his Emir to see the other ship and for his curiosity had a bolo embedded in his back.

Leaderless, the conflict was over, though not the aftermath. US Marines from the fifty-gun frigate USS *Cumberland* stormed the *Princess Kathleen,* shot anyone who resisted and chained Emir Hizir and the remainder of her crew. For the *Vixen's* crew, most of them traumatized, there was little elation and, too exhausted to cheer, they said their prayers and lay about in exhaustion.

USS *Cumberland's* Captain Breese, and Executive Officer Foote, stepped aboard the *Vixen*, "My God," Breese commented, "It's like stepping into hell. Is the captain still alive here?"

Lady Evelyn, Monar and JT had been attending to the wounded and JT nodded for her to speak to their savior. Blood-spattered, Lady Evelyn stepped forward.

Another shock for the Captain as she introduced herself, "I'm Captain Evelyn Bunting of the *Vixen* and over there are Captain Graves and Monar, our Chief Mate. Talk about arriving in the nick of time, Captain, thank you. And you are?"

"Captain Steven Breese at your service, Captain Bunting, and this is my exec, Alastair Foote. By the looks of this, it's a shame we didn't arrive sooner. May I undertake the clear up here? I have four hundred men who, once they see you, would be most pleased to pitch in."

"Then please have them see me." She managed a smile, "But, be sure to separate my wounded crewmen from the enemy's."

"I will be sure to do that, although it does seem that you had a very large crew against these bastards—if you'll excuse my English."

"Under the circumstances, certainly, Captain. I'd call them the same to be frank. We had perverse luck. There were two crews aboard. We lost our other ship in the Black Sea."

Captain Breese and Foote were baffled as to why an obviously British ship was in a Russian lake—where the two offices had never been.

But first things first, "Foote, have Lieutenant Dahlgren get work parties over here. I want this vessel ship-shape as soon as possible. Throw the Berber dead and seriously wounded overboard. Send the medical team over and have the sail maker cut up enough of our spare sails for winding sheets for Captain Bunting's dead."

Aye, aye, Sir. The *Jamestown* and *Erie* have hove to."

"Fine. Have Captains Wallace and Reston join me here at their convenience." Breese looked to Evelyn, "Those two ships and my *Cumberland* form my Western Mediterranean Squadron. "When their captains arrive, we'll need an analysis of this event for my report. However, for the moment, Captain Bunting, I suggest you take a breather, by the look of you, you need it."

Pointing at her bloodstained shirt, Evelyn signaled to JT and Monar that she was going below to change. Monar watched her unsteady step.

He wanted to run to her, hold her. Instead, "JT, go to her."

"Go to her, me? Why?"

"For Christ's sake, are you blind? She's a woman. Women aren't supposed to go through this sort of hell. She needs someone and sadly you're all we've got—so go!"

"Why don't you?"

"Sure, all I'd need is for some sailors to see a black man comforting a white lady and sure as the devil I'd be found hanging off our yardarm in the morning. Now get down that ladder."

What Monar didn't think through was JT was on the verge of breaking down as well. He had stood firm, killed six men. Yet his fear was not for his own life, but that of Evelyn's and what would have ensued should they lose. That had driven him into an emotional frenzy. Now, with the descent into aftershock creeping in while heading for her cabin, response to the insanity started shivering within his very soul.

He knocked, no answer. Again, nothing. Pushing the door slightly, he saw her in tears.

"Evelyn, are you all right?"

"Go away, JT. It's only now come to me that Chief Mate Griffin is dead…he saved us and now he's gone. Please—go away."

He stepped into the cabin, "Evelyn…"

"God, JT…leave me to myself! Can't you see I'm *crying*?"

He walked over to her, "Evelyn, look at me—*look at me*!"

Lifting her head, she saw his face, "JT…you're crying."

"Don't you think what happened, what could have happened, distresses me too?"

Evelyn saw he hurt as much as she. She stood and they moved together, finding comfort in each other's arms. Then a kiss, a soft, light kiss that brought, not relief, but conflict.

The kiss lasted too long. She was alarmed and eased away from him, yet took his hand, then remembered, "Enough of this, JT. You're beholden to another, aren't you?"

He shrugged his shoulders, befuddled by her transformation, "I guess I am…yes."

Evelyn took her hand away, "And you're just that damn honorable, aren't you?"

"I guess I am."

Her tears turned to anger, anger directed to herself now, "Well then, damn it, I *guess* we should get back to helping our crews and stop muddling around down here."

«»

The aftermath was overwhelming. Out of fifty-seven American sailors, twenty-four were dead, thirteen seriously wounded. On the

British side, all twenty former RN Marines died. Added to those, ten other crewmen died, resulting in their total of thirty dead and seven seriously wounded.

Of the Berber warriors, the estimate was one-hundred-fifty dead—not including the gravely wounded thrown overboard—and one-hundred-thirty in chains. It was a frightening thought to comprehend the outcome if there had been one more enemy assault.

Captain Breese summarized how the American Squadron came on the scene, "Most people think the Barbary Corsairs are done with and they're mostly right. However, despite our treaty with these blasted countries along the Med, there's no compliance, so there still remains sanctuary, rivers where pirates slip out and attack shipping. This time we were in the right place."

JT was curious, "Those two explosions, how can a cannonball explode like that?"

"We now call them shells; it's a cannonball but hollow. It's a shell, developed by a Frenchman name of Paixhan. Ours were filled with gunpowder and a primitive impact type fuse and, well…you saw what happens when they hit properly."

"We certainly did, everyone was belly down on the deck."

"Well, Captain Graves, you have an example of why it's now said soldiers will become cannon fodder."

"At least it makes it harder on corsairs like these."

"In this case that's true, but it's very lucrative when they get away with it. An example is this Berber ship. Three years ago, she was the *Princess Kathleen* out of Belfast, Ireland, carrying textiles and immigrants escaping their famine. For the two years we've been here on station, we couldn't find her, thought she'd sunk. How many died on that ship from these scum, I don't know. Yet figure the textiles were worth a small fortune and the crew and passengers will have brought a good price when sold into slavery. And, of course, they had the value of the ship if they'd chosen to sell her."

"Tell me, Captain Breese." Evelyn had to ask, "Do we have any idea how many people have become slaves to these vermin down through the years?"

"I've heard well over a million. Sounds a lot and it is. Nonetheless, you've got to remember that so far, it's figured there's been well over six-million Africans sold into slavery to the Americas—and it's still going on. Why do we stop slavery here and not there? Is it because we were fed up with paying tribute so here we fight them? I don't have the answer. Still, one day, and I believe it will come; we'll do a better job of putting an end to the African traffic and Pacific Blackbirding as well. We've got to, our honor's at stake."

It was sobering, yet they had no answer either. They were still caught up in their recent tribulations and with no comment forthcoming, the Captain continued, changing to another matter.

"Even though we're the Eastern Med Squadron, the Navy is short of first class Ships of the Line, so these past two years we actually patrolled from Anatolia and the Levant in the east to Gibraltar. We were only now going off-station and west of you…"

"How did you see us, Captain?"

"We didn't see you, we *heard* you. You were over the horizon line and after the first cannonade, I sent lookouts to the top of the main, then we heard a second cannonade and he saw the gun smoke. We came about, ran downwind and found you."

"Thank, God, you did."

"Yes, thank, God. And now, I have duties to execute."

The sea burial of the American and British sailors was performed quickly, yet with honor. A canvas shroud for each, a cannonball at their feet. The Captain's last words, "At last, it's as should be, American and British sailors fighting side by side and now, united in death as friends. Let us pray both will be united in life as well, from this point…evermore."

One more official duty. "Emir Murat Hizir, the Younger, of Morocco, by you actions, you have been convicted of Piracy on the High Seas. I have been charged by my country to eliminate this piracy by hanging pirate principals and conveying any cohorts to the Dey of Algiers for punishment. Section one of those orders will now be carried out."

The Emir was ferocious, then frantic and at the end, reduced to whimpering. Sailors from the *Golden Raven* and *Vixen* volunteered to take part. A block and tackle hung off the mainsail spar, a stout line passed through it and fashioned into a noose while six sailors took up the line. The Emir, gagged to stop his sobbing, was dragged forth. Too weak to stand, he was held upright for the noose to be snugged around his neck. Barely noticed, Lady Evelyn walked to the line, gripped it tightly for a moment, whispered Chief Mate Harry Griffin's name and walked away.

Seeing the fear on the Emir's face, Monar smiled cheerfully, "What's that bastard complaining about—isn't he going on to meet those virgins?"

One of the *Cumberland's* sailors responded, "If that's true, I hope they never give the son of a bitch a moment's rest."

Every crewmember watched as the Master at Arms nodded to the Captain, the captain nodded in return. A drumbeat began.

"Haul away!" Emir Murat Hizir the Younger of Morocco, kicked his way to paradise.

Captain Breese had one further thought. With only topsails set on the derelict *Princess Kathleen*, the Captain had the wheel lashed and sails set for the ship to close haul off to the southwest—the approximate direction from which she came. With her deck coated with pitch, normally used to seal the hull and sails, the *Kathleen* drifted away. A strong-armed sailor hurled a torch onto her deck and all hoped she would burn to the waterline near Melilla or Nador.

The *Cumberland, Jamestown and Erie* led the *Vixen* through the Strait of Gibraltar. The three United States Navy vessels dipped their flags in a parting salute and there was barely a dry eye on the *Vixen* as she fired three blank charges in return— gestures of thanks for each American ship. The American squadron headed back to Algiers with her prisoners chained on deck. The British ship started her long convex curve past Portugal, Spain and France to the jewel set in the silver sea—England.

As the *Vixen* carved the Atlantic due north through a sailor's sea, Monar was amused by the new courteous and formal interaction between Lady Evelyn and JT. Monar would wait. Something had happened between the two when he told JT to go to Evelyn, but Monar was damned if he was going to ask. JT would tell him in his own good time. Monar guessed what transpired, but waited. The subject never arose in any fashion, they had other cares to face not only the loss in lives, but also the replacement cost of the *Golden Raven*.

JT was adamant, "I'm not going to claim it. The insurance on her covered the Atlantic Ocean from Greenland south to Tierra del Fuego and from the east coast to Europe as far as the western boundary of the Strait of Gibraltar. You knew that before we entered the Med."

"Yes, I knew it. However, you're the Captain, you had the say, go or not go."

"Oh—so now you're going to blame me for losing the *Raven* and everything else?"

"Probably."

"You son of a bitch."

Evelyn, listening from below, couldn't believe the next sounds she heard were the two of them laughing. They're thick as thieves, she thought. For a woman to comprehend how one man could call the other a son of a bitch and then both laugh themselves stupid, was well beyond her comprehension. She did however, have intelligence enough not to try and still intend to continue listening.

JT was committed to paying the crew twice their wages and a death sum for the men who died as well as another amount for the wounded. It would be costly. Add in another massive cost of buying a ship and there would be precious little left of the $50,000 from the Turkish Bearer's Note for operating expenses.

Monar flatly stated that it didn't make sense for JT to act against his own interests and posed his theory that all crews took chances when signing up and JT's sense of obligation was excessive. Failing to convince JT otherwise, Monar then did an about face and offered to dip into the chest he kept, but JT said that money would continue to be the last resort. They bantered back and forth until the subject was beaten to death and buried.

Overhearing them, Evelyn took it all in and admired JT's standing firm to his indebtedness to his crew. And Monar? He favored a different direction, but agreed in the end. Yet what was his comment about dipping into his 'chest'? Was that, Evelyn wondered, the same chest she had seen him take from the *Golden Raven*? It didn't matter. The two of them saved her life and she knew that once she explained their heroics to her father, he was not one to forget.

JT. The more she knew, the more she liked—rough edges and all. Then again, perhaps those rough edges attracted her. He had none of those pretentious manners in the circles her father and she associated with in London. Still, as she gave more thought, actually her father's formal meetings and socials were expected of him and in truth, he attended primarily to burnish his image, more than enjoy.

Back however, to JT. That moment with him in her cabin. That could have been a step forward, or perhaps a leap forward, until she remembered JT's sweetheart—thank goodness. He said he only met that girl twice, both for a short time. Charlee must be quite the Siren, Evelyn thought, one of those American southern belles she'd heard about, honey dripping from their lips—allegedly.

"Well, listen to me," Evelyn said to the lantern as she turned it low, "the green-eyed other woman." She laughed it off, although being the other woman for once was not to her liking.

22

31 Oct 1848

MIDNIGHT WATCH. Sailing north, the weather turned cooler. Bundled against it, Evelyn piloted the *Vixen* past the Channel Islands into the southern English Channel. Sliding through the long following seas, they would soon slip to the east of The Isle of Wight, then north to Portsmouth Harbor.

"How come you're standing Watch, Evelyn?"

JT had come up on deck, shivering as he handed her a mug of steaming coffee.

"Thank you, JT, I needed it. We're in my home waters now; I took the Watch because of my wanting to see dawn kiss my country."

"No matter how much you go aroaming, this little island's still home, is that it?"

"Being overly poignant, I live on two islands, my poor scarred ship, and England. I love to be with both. Still…"

"Still…what?"

"I don't know. After losing my friends and crew and the *Black Watch* in America and now the disasters in the Black Sea, plus the Med…so many people lost…"

"You're not thinking of staying ashore? Seems that more than the ship is scarred."

"Perhaps that's true. Yet being ashore for a while may help. And my father could use some company, although I guess he has Lily for that, but I know they both would like me around more. What about you, JT? What are your plans from here?"

He laughed, "My plans are definite— utterly undecided. We have responsibilities to the crew, both living and gone. After that, well, whether to buy a ship here, find a crew and freight, or take passage home…although I'm not sure where home is right now. But getting back to you, Evelyn, I've never seen you indecisive, so unlike you."

"Forgive me, JT. These last few days have given me too long to think, with no shoulder to rest my head on." She wished she hadn't been quite so blatant, but at least he took the hint.

JT put his arm around her, "Here, rest your head on this shoulder."

"OK, just for a minute—OK, JT?"

"OK, just for a minute."

Nothing said, withdrawn into their own thoughts, they stared as dawn tinted the low clouds pink as they scudded along the horizon.

"You smell of the sea, JT."

"Sorry."

"I don't want you to be, I loved the smell of the sea…still do, it seems."

It was longer than the agreed minute. Long enough in fact, to see the sun's rays edge the green trees in gold across Evelyn's country. Curiously enough, the two parted; neither uttering a word. She reached her cabin hatchway, knowing it was their last night together.

"Fair thee well, JT."

"We'll still see each other on shore, Evelyn."

"Not like this, John Thomas. Not like this."

Lord Warfield had received a signal from the Coastal Watch Station at Bembridge, on the east coast of Isle of Wight that the *Vixen* had passed, obviously heading for Portsmouth Harbor. He first ordered a tug out to meet them, then climbed to his third floor office on North Wharf and waited until his daughter's ship passed Blockhouse Fort. After focusing his telescope on the Black Moon pennant, Warfield scanned the deck.

"What the devil is this?" He mumbled to no one, confounded, "The ship's tatty, only see half the crew, what's Evelyn thinking about, coming into port in this condition? Something's got to be wrong—and where is she?"

At last, he breathed in relief after spotting his daughter at the helm, speaking with persons Warfield now recognized as John Thomas and Monar. At least she seemed well. Still, if they're on the *Vixen*, where in hell is the *Golden Raven*?

Seeing the steam tug approaching, Evelyn ordered shortened sail while she continued her conversation with JT and Monar.

"It's the best approach, believe me. My father is going to blow his stack—and don't doubt it. So it's better if both of you are not there. Lily and I are the only ones who can calm him and he'll be embarrassed if you saw that. Just give me an hour to lay out what happened and if anyone will help you recover what's lost, he will—especially when I tell him you two heroes saved my life."

They tied off on the Black Moon Line's Gosport pier. Lord Warfield waited impatiently until the gangplank was in place. Before he could board however, Evelyn hastened down to him, giving a brief kiss along with a few well-chosen words. Seemingly perplexed, Warfield then gave a wave to JT and Monar, as Evelyn took his arm and they walked off.

Leaning on the taffrail with Monar, JT absentmindedly pulled his navy coat closer against the bitter wind. He stared across to the HMS Victory and the Guard Ship in the middle channel.

"Well, JT, your thoughts?"

"I've given up trying to understand her and it's the same with this. She's more than likely right, it's her father, let her speak with him. Yet it's the worry over the state of affairs we're in that gets under my skin."

"She'll work it out for our benefit, you'll see."

"I suppose."

JT had other concerns, seemingly on a subject other than the present. Noticing, Monar had to ask, "What's up with you, something else bothering you?"

"Bothering me? Something else? Yes. Stupid I know with all that's happened, but something else is bothering me, but I've been having damn near the same dream most every night."

"I know you have."

"You know, how would you know?"

"Don't mean I know what your dreaming, JT, it's that a lot of nights when I come in, you're tossing and mumbling the same way. It's become obvious the dreams are not pleasant, to say the least. Once or twice I thought to wake you."

"Do you ever sleep, Monar? You never seem to, always wandering the ship. I can't recall ever seeing you asleep."

In the darkened cabin, JT couldn't see Monar smiling, "Of course I do, I take catnaps, two or three minutes at a time. You don't see it because I can sleep with my eyes open if I wish."

JT forgot about his dreams, "Come off it, what are you handing me? Sleep with your eyes open—I'm to swallow that?"

"All right, perhaps sleep, as you know it, is the wrong word. I consciously trance, rest, where I see and hear everything around me, yet don't respond unless necessary. It might bother you to know I often man the helm when I'm that way. Think about it, JT, have you ever seen me even tired?"

Try as he might, JT could only think of the aftermath of the clash with the corsairs and even then, Monar, though weary was ready for more. In fact, rather than tired, JT reflected on Monar looking as if he reveled in the conflict—although JT never mentioned that to him.

Monar's question wasn't answered and he brought JT back to the subject of his disquiet, "We were talking about your dreams."

"Yes, the dreams. Always the same, never clear, dark like in a fog, a big man, blurred, captain's cap and bulky naval jacket—he simply stares at me. Kinda nervous or…scared look."

"Your father?"

"It's not clear. Father was never scared about anything, so I doubt that, yet who else could it be? And why so often now?"

"When did this start?"

"I think it started around the last time we were in Salem. At first it was only now and then, you know, once or twice a month, now it's three, maybe four times a week."

"I don't know your past, JT, I can't help. Tell me about your other dream."

"Well, it's probably the same dream. The man, or as I talk about it, maybe a big boy, fades away and a woman, maybe a girl, appears. Same thing, dark, not clear, scared, or a hurt look."

"And neither says a word, JT?"

"No, not a sound, except when I wake, the word 'think' is on my lips. What do you make of that?"

"I'm no soothsayer, JT. Yet I imagine some forgotten incident in your past has come to the surface. Bear in mind however, you secreted it for a reason and there be things best not harkened back. Yet don't misunderstand one thing, JT. You're not being haunted, you're haunting yourself. Still, when you come down to it, do what was on your lips—think."

Monar was not telling JT the truth. He knew one can be haunted by unknown powers. He had seen it in the Caribe, the black witch, black as coal, blacker than the ace of spades she turned over and spoke a majestic curse—a curse the slave owner laughed at. Yet the *thought* of the curse haunted him and he worried himself sick and died. Monar thought it amusing—the slave owner was a black man.

After sending employees to find lodging for the crewmembers of the *Vixen*, Lord Warfield and Lily sat with little apparent emotion, listening as Evelyn continued her lengthy tale of deceit, battles, heroism and tragedy. After she concluded, he rose, released a great blasphemy and without another word, picked up his fluted glass tumbler and threw it vehemently into the fireplace flames.

Lily smiled her patient smile. She knew his moods. His reaction to his daughter's story was a needed physical outlet to his wrath.

"All right now, Warfield," Lily's voice unruffled, "the main thing to remember is Evelyn's home and safe. Now you've had your little, shall we say 'fling', so let's sit back down before, as you sailors say, you go off the deep end, or down the hatch, or whatever it is I shouldn't repeat."

A sheepish smile curled his lip, "I'm angry, Lily, sorry, but I'm angry…"

"I know, Warfield, and you've every right to be. Nonetheless, please remember how angry Evelyn and I will be with *you,* if you give yourself a stroke. Let's calm and work this out."

Then Lily revealed an impudent smile, "I'd gladly get you another scotch, dear, but it seems you've accidently dropped our only tumbler in the fireplace."

"Damn you, Lily…" Still, Lord Warfield was vanquished. He groused about, apologized for damning her, found another tumbler and returned to his chair.

Evelyn hid her smile watching her father, a man well known for titanic outbursts, and Lily, honeyed oil spread across agitated waters.

"All right then," Warfield brusquely asserted, "Let us see if any wisdom may be taken from this calamity of Americans saving my daughter's life."

"Only JT and Monar, Father."

Oh? And what of this American warship *Cumberland* and its four-hundred American sailors tripping over themselves to help you? Where was a British warship, having her bottom scraped and patted?"

This was the only amusing moment after the otherwise dreadful story. Warfield could see how the retelling unsettled Evelyn and yet, for the encounter he foresaw, he needed all the information he could gather. He fixed in his mind the fright and heroism against the Russian's *Ghazna*, JT's sacrifice of his ship to save Evelyn, the savagery of the Corsairs and Monar's challenge to the Emir and, when all thought lost, the American warship saving them. However, it was the letter that most infuriated. The letter from Rear Admiral Henderson asking that Evelyn, Warfield's only child, put herself in peril by voyaging far into the Russian lake and the possibility—no, the likelihood—of exactly what happened. The letter had caused it all. If it hadn't been for JT and Monar…he shuddered to think of the ending.

One of the Lords in the Admiralty was behind this. Warfield was sure. Someone who knew his daughter would honor it as a duty to country. Henderson was only a *Rear* Admiral. He wouldn't have the nerve to go behind Warfield's back and ask her to help on his own account. The first thing to do? That would be unearthing who authorized the letter—and punish them.

Well, Lord Warfield at length smiled; whomever, it was going to cost the Admiralty dearly.

By dusk, as the chill evening settled on the harbor, Evelyn returned to the ship. JT and Monar had also settled in, it had been a long travel to a safe harbor and relaxing with a bottle of whiskey was a reward. Evelyn was only too happy to join them. Each had lived through horror and seen their mortality. By rights, they should have gone to a watery grave with so many others. They were not murdered or slaves, that was a miracle—supplied by the US Navy.

Not jovial, each knew the close thing it had been, Monar even confessing he had expected only another ten minutes of life and now that thought was sobering.

JT, asked his feelings when it appeared the end so near, said his mind refuses to recall. They said that was a dodge until Lady Evelyn said only that she would go to her cabin. She would say no more. Monar, realizing the depth of the melancholy steps they were descending, called a halt to the conversation. They would honor the dead, they agreed, by helping those left behind.

While resolving that, footsteps heard on the ladder proved to be Lord Warfield's and he entered their closed world. Not for a moment or a word, did he hesitate to accept the offered bottle and take a long swig.

Gasping the whiskey down, near tears from the drink and emotion, he shook the men's hands, choking out inept words of gratitude and acknowledging he had a debt to pay. They did not argue his words; it would be disrespectful to him.

The bottle drained, the banter buoyant, it was agreed they would meet in the morning. While Warfield and Evelyn went to his carriage, JT and Monar waved them off, conscious this evening was the last they would spend aboard with her.

«»

Lord Warfield Bunting, knocking about in his study at Blackwood Abbey, awaited the arrival of the five Royal Navy officers he'd ordered to appear. Bunting's furious reaction had eased into a scheme and the remainder of his anger was kept in check. Each moment he gave thought to what could have happened, he placed his daughter's past peril in perspective and replaced it with resolve. It was Warfield's approach to problems. First anger, then thought, then the idea, then a scheme, which in this case would forward his company and help those few who survived.

Bunting had the upper hand. He was a civilian, not answerable to the Admiralty, thereby not subject to their code of conduct. That gave him the hammer. The RN officers were unquestionably subject to naval codes and thus they became the anvil and he would give them a sound pounding. They were investors, dedicated investors in the privately held East India Company which, if by itself not misconduct, supplying ships and naval personnel gratis to forward that company, certainly was. If discovered, the Crown would descend on them like the proverbial ton of bricks, stripping them of rank and pension.

Still, Warfield had made sure his friend, the 1st Earl of Ellenborough, Edward Law, was not involved. The former Governor-General of India, recently from there to assume the position of First Sea Lord of the Admiralty, had no knowledge of Evelyn's journey into the Black Sea.

Lord Warfield's friendship with the Earl of Ellenborough was on a first name basis, Warfield having initially supplied, at cost only, merchant ships with cannon, for the Earl's military excursions along the Gulf of Cutch in India's Western Sind. The two men formed an understanding whereby the British East India Company—of which Lord Warfield Bunting was a significant partner—and their private army would in no way hinder the advancement of the British establishment with respect to the government of all India. Of course, at times East India directors did interfere by exploiting India's Caste System to The Company's advantage. Still, overall it evened out, as the British Raj and East India's private armies did crush any number of rebellions, thereby helping the Earl, Edward Law further his agenda. At this point in its history, The Company had not seriously overstepped their Charter. They would…eventually.

Evelyn watched her father, his hands supporting his head, eyes darting over a page on his desk.

"What's got you so studious, father? You've been scribbling for over an hour."

"Just putting the finishing touches on tonight's meeting with some naval people over you and your friends Black Sea travels. It should be intense; I forgot to mention that previously."

"Oh, and this is one of those times you would like me to flee and not seen or heard?"

"If you don't mind. Still, you could listen at the keyhole."

"No thank you, father dear, Lily and I will adjourn to the wine catacombs until liberated."

Evelyn knew, despite his liberalism toward women, he was Chauvinistic in his business conduct on certain issues. When Evelyn was at home, he always kept her up to date on his business dealings, from ships to shipping, land holdings, manufacturing output and so forth. Yet, when it came to difficulties, difficulties which required quite some manipulating, browbeating or coercive 'coaxing', Warfield kept his daughter at arm's length. That way, should some of his dealings receive excessive scrutiny, she could honestly declare no knowledge on the matter. Such was the reason he did not want her, or Lily's, presence for this night's meeting.

"One thing before you leave, Evelyn. Be sure to send a thank you note to the Secretary of the United States Navy, John Young Mason, concerning your trials and tribulations in the Med. Mention the *Cumberland's* Captain by name and thank his crew as well. Add my name."

"Father, I've already done that and don't think I don't know what you're up to tonight."

"And don't try to fool me into tattling, although you'll find out about some of it soon enough. It's all for the good of the company and your two suitors."

"Two suitors? Good lord, father! Is that what you think? Monar is inscrutable and JT is committed to someone else."

"Then JT is a fool." With that, Warfield busied himself with his papers. Covertly, he was pleased. Evelyn now appeared to consider Monar simply a good friend and, whereas JT was remarkable, he was nevertheless, American. As much as Warfield believed in hands across the sea and all that, it would be too much of a stretch to picture JT directing the Black Moon Line. Although, as Warfield thought more of it, new blood wouldn't be a bad thing. Yet the American seemed a touch too straightforward—and worse, too honest. He needed to add a dash of Monar.

They arrived, the five upper ranks of the naval establishment, all investors in The East India Company. If they for one moment thought they would be able to gloss over the difficulties surrounding the Black Sea debacle as well as the slaughter off Melilla, they were sadly mistaken and quickly brought to task. Although, at first, they did their best to dance around the salient point of the meeting, Lord Bunting laid it out with a distinct undertone of menace.

"Gentlemen, enough of this tangential prattle. Unless we come to a firm agreement this night, I have here the communiqué that will be delivered to the London Guardian and Lloyd's Weekly tomorrow. The banner states that officers of the Royal Navy—and here I list your names and rank—did request a civilian merchant captain, a *woman*, to enter into the Black Sea, a known Russian lake, to—and I quote myself here—deliver military goods to Varna, Bulgaria. From there, she was to chart the course to Sevastopol, Russia, as a preparation for a war."

There were gasps followed by protestations that Warfield ignored, "Furthermore, its known these same officers are shareholders in a privately held company with the word 'India' in its title and by themselves, did sanction naval ships and crews to be utilized by that company without reimbursement."

The officer's saw their careers and pensions dangling throughout Warfield's letter. He then cut them to the quick, "I swear I will go to Eddy Law and lay out the essence of your involvement."

Warfield used the First Sea Lord's given name to make them aware of his link to the Lord and that became the tipping element in the conversation.

"And now gentlemen, I've completed an analysis of the danger you put my daughter in and will brook no variance to your cost of that excursion."

For effect, as much as anger, Warfield slammed his paper onto his desk. They had no recourse other than to listen to list of demands. As he read, his voice was inflexibly severe and brought muted torment.

1-All pensioned off Royal Navy sailors or their survivors will receive full death benefits.

2-The pensioned 20 Royal Marines will receive posthumous awards of some sort and full benefits to their survivors will be paid.

3-Survivors, including wounded, both British and American, will receive triple wages for the duration of that voyage and continuing medical care.

4-The Navy, or its assigns, will refurbish the Black Moon Company's *Vixen*.

5-The Navy, or its assigns, will replace in its entirety, the fast clipper known as the *Golden Raven*.

1 through 3 will be activated and finalized within one month from this date.

4 will be completed in 60 days.

5 will be started and completed concurring to American Captain John Thomas Graves' plans and agenda. To be constructed at the Thames Ironworks and Shipbuilding Company.

The officers were stupefied. Those who could find their voices proclaimed everything to be impossible and too costly. It wasn't feasible, they said, to find the money.

Warfield hid his ire, smiling through it all, he knew they would find the money in various naval slush funds and actually write off the ship as a needed research vessel before it slipped off the Naval Research Ship listing.

It was only when he heard one officer mumble Lord Warfield wouldn't dare—that he had too much at stake to make such statements to the papers that Warfield's face went scarlet, "You foolish bastard! *I* don't dare? We'll see who doesn't dare!"

He called to Evans, his valet, while jotting down on an envelope the names of the newspapers he'd mentioned. When the valet arrived, Warfield folded his letter, placed it in the envelope and ordered the valet to leave immediately to the addresses listed.

Silence. They heard horses being limbered up to a carriage. Warfield said, "Gentlemen, goodnight." He reached the door before they appealed to him.

"For God's sake Bunting, stop that man!"

Warfield turned, "*You* stop him, I refuse to!"

He started for the stairs. Bewildered, after hurried nods all around, the lowest ranked officer ran for the door. Warfield had won another battle.

After every officer signed what Warfield called the Letter of Intent, they sullenly filed out into the frigid night. He had made enemies, yet what could they do? He knew that as soon as they needed him again, they would be back asking favors from his company and he'd help them and all would be smoothed over. That was the way things work and overall, worked quite well.

Evelyn met him as he left the officers at the door, "Things go as planned father?"

"Quite, although Evan's came in handy."

"Who was that man running out the front door a little while ago and stopped our carriage?"

"A man who thought he could out-bluff me.

"And were you bluffing?"

"My God, yes. Oh, remind me to give Evan's a spot of cash tomorrow."

"Ah, that's a surprise; you needed an assistant this time."

"Afraid so, I must be getting old, needing my valet to outwit five Admiralty officers."

Warfield had one more task he would let slide for the present. He had found the Fifth Sea Lord was the author of the letter Rear Admiral Henderson gave to Evelyn. That person's misstep would be rectified in the future and unexpectedly—for him at least.

Looking over the agreement, Warfield was pleased. Death benefits or pensions for all the crews, American and British. Wounded were taken care of as well as the repairs to his *Vixen* and a new clipper ship for JT and Monar. In truth, Warfield had felt an obligation for all of this and would have paid the cost, including the new vessel out of his own pocket. However, saddling the Admiralty with the expenditures was so much the better for the bottom line. His crafty moves saved those expenses and Warfield would see to it that JT's new vessel would have the best English shipwrights, none of those damn India built vessels shoving their way into British ship trades by cutting costs.

14 Nov 1848

"Cholera."

Lily, Evelyn, JT, Monar and Lord Warfield had just ordered drinks at The George Inn before a night out at the Portsmouth Theatre when Evelyn dropped the word.

Lord Warfield stared at Evelyn, "What are you saying, Cholera in Portsea—again?"

"You're surprised, father? For years you've fought with the city council to drain the marshes and start a refuse collection in the old town. That you would help financially if they would move the poorer classes away from the industry there—it has certainly cost you enough and it didn't get done."

Turning to JT and Monar, both of whom seemed puzzled, Warfield tried to be brief, “If you don’t know; one reason for cholera is from industries fouling the water and not giving a damn about their own employees. Added to that, there are too many people who don’t seem to care about themselves and expect someone else to help them when they don’t take care. There’s no reason for them to be ignorant of what happens when they allow farm animals to run free. Nevertheless, they still drink fouled water and their intestines get infected, they start vomiting, have diarrhea, dehydrate, shrivel up and many die.”

“I know a little about it, they had it in New York, but how bad is it—is it just in Portsea?”

Lily answered, “God, no. We’ve had these outbreaks in Portsea and other areas of Portsmouth just this past February. It was so bad that Warfield was able to convince the council to flush the water lines and boil the water to try to stop it. Then there was an outbreak north in Newcastle-on-Tyne, and another in London. London is still dreadful around Westminster and Waterloo Roads, that’s the Lambeth area. It began in London a few years back when the population tripled and no one gave a damn about sanitation, so they did nothing to clear the filthy streets. With no drainage, industries are still contaminating every bit of water in sight. It was bound to happen, even the Thames is polluted. Here, Doctor Engledue said Portsea is one huge cesspool. Warfield does what he can, but…”

Warfield broke in, “Yes, we all do what we can. For now however, I think the reason Evelyn mentioned this is because you’re heading to the Thames Ironworks in London shortly. You’ve got to be very careful what you drink and if there’s any question, boil the water or only drink liquor and understand you might also have a shortage of skilled workers due to this outbreak.”

Evelyn turned to her father, “Do you think it would be better to have the ship built in Liverpool or Birkenhead, maybe even on the Clyde?”

“No, we all want oversight, and the best way to do that is building locally. Besides, the area around the Liverpool docks is a cesspit and now there's talk that Birkenhead is ripe for cholera. As far as the Clyde, she's too far north in this weather, so we'll stay with Charles Mare. Once the yard's ready, Monar and JT will stay at our London home to make sure their plans are followed."

JT looked up, "Thank you for that, Warfield. We've already sent a few revisions to Mr. Mare and James Ash, he was a Naval Architect before going with Mr. Mare, and they made some suggestions in return. Also, the yard's name been changed to C J Mare."

"Then sending that was a good start in getting to know them. What were the revisions?"

"There a number of minor changes, but three major ones he brought up we've agreed on. We're going to go with wrought iron for the framing and bulkheads, but the ship will have wood planking. Mr. Mare said the best steam engines were by Napier, so even though he used Brougham and Watt engines with the HMS *Trident*, we're going with twin Napier engines that have three-hundred-fifty shaft horsepower each. It's only an estimate, but with the clipper, we may reach fifteen knots[20] under steam power alone."

"Amazing what those new engines can do, JT, but why wood planking? You're going with iron framing and bulkheads; why not iron all the way?"

"I know it's true that iron framing will help prevent hogging in a major sea, but I'm old school I guess, sir. To me a boat is wood, it has flex that steel doesn't and I simply think wood feels the sea better. Aside from that, Mr. Mare said that below the water line he'll use Malabar teak first, with an alloy of brass with copper sheeting and that alloy works against Teredo shipworm. That made my decision easy."

---

[20] 17.3 MPH

Warfield grasped JT's thoughts and approved, "Very well, then. So you've spoken of wood and the Napier's, what was your third major change?"

"We're going to rake and lengthen the masts."

"Lengthening the masts is one thing, but you'll really rake them? That can give you a problem with the windward helm if you angle them back too far."

"Yes, sir, I know that can cause a tendency to sheer off, yet it allows us to point up more. I worked it out with Mr. Ash and an old shellback sailor Mare employs as works supervisor. He was lead shipwright on that new Aberdeen clipper *Stornaway* and he'll get the few degrees I want."

Warfield was pleased JT knew so much, "Well, JT, it's your ship to do as you please."

"She will be the fastest clipper in the world Warfield, that I promise you and thank you again."

Hesitating for a moment, Warfield then mentioned the next subject, "JT, I'm sure you recognize the First Lord of the Royal Navy had no knowledge of the letter sending Evelyn into the Black Sea and that he most certainly doesn't go around giving out ships to Americans."

JT had gathered there was a little subterfuge going on apropos the Navy buying him a new, first-class clipper and nodded that yes, something did seem a bit odd.

Warfield continued, "We've, myself and five naval Officers, have worked out a stratagem whereby they will, among other points, repair the *Vixen* and build a new ship. When you actually *speak* with Charley Mare, it's important for you to profess to be liaison between unspecified US Naval personnel and the Royal Navy's Experimental Squadron. I know that's a peculiar name for a supposedly clandestine group within our Navy, but that is its name. They're developing, among other things not to be mentioned, all steel warships such as the recent HM *Trident*."

Clearing his throat, Warfield still looked uncomfortable, "One last detail. Your ship will have the very best workmanship, however, don't act surprised when your new ship is finished she'll have a full complement of twenty-six, thirty-four pounders."

"Are you serious, Warfield? Twenty-six cannon!"

"Unfortunately, yes. To keep up the deception, we have to make it look bona fide right down the line, and cannon are on the itemized inventory for experimental warships."

JT shook his head, "So, if I understand this clearly, I represent—covertly—the US Navy and there will be a vessel, again covertly, built mostly to McKay clipper ship plans and my sail plans, built for the Royal Navy and, once again, covertly documented on the RN inventory. Now tell me, how does this ship *covertly* disappear and wind up with me?"

"Ah, that is artifice spun into art. My naval associates —who will visit the yard now and then to make it all look so damn official, have a delightful ruse. They've registered the ship with the RN Experimental Squadron. As I say, it's an actual squadron and, as with any number of other experimental ships, this one won't prove out in sea trials. Then papers will be generated condemning her to the breakers along with her allegedly burned out engines. At that point, certain officers will detach her from the active roll—I'm not sure about the cannon —but the ship, engines and all will be yours—and where you got that ship is no one's business."

Lord Warfield's townhouse in Westminster was an island of warm comfort. It was difficult for JT, and hell for Monar, to leave it every other day to venture into the frosty weather to Charles Mare's Shipyard on Bow Creek. Added to the temperature difficulties were the facts they were in and out of the shipways cradle enclosure, mast houses and carpenter's workshop that were forty degrees. From there it was the blacksmith's shop and kiln, generating heat around ninety degrees, but the sail and rope loft stayed little above the outside temperature of the day.

While Evelyn decided to winter over at Blackwood Abby, she arrived in London once each week and she, JT and Monar would drink, eat and converse at such pubs as the Lamp and Flag at Covent

Garden, or up at the Nag's Head in Belgravia for drinks or attend the theater. Each of those evenings, no matter how late, she would stay at Brown's Hotel in Mayfair or at some friends. They were three, not so old companions, reliving past and sometimes difficult remembrances. Yet at other times there was a lingering *something* that no one spoke of, seemingly afraid to break a spell—or bond—between them.

The following day, after visiting the shipyard, Evelyn would travel by train back to Portsmouth and report to her father on the ship's progress.

It was in the early part of December when Monar resolved to leave.

23

17 Dec 1848

IT CAME AS A SHOCK.

"You're sure my friend?" JT never expected his words, "You're sure I can't talk you out of heading south?"

"Absolutely, this bloody weather is taking a toll on me. I'm going to head down to Cape Town. I'm sure Lord Warfield will let me be supercargo on one of his ships heading around the Horn, I can be left there and find a ship back in three or four months."

"If you must leave, why not head for the Caribe? At least you know people there."

"Aye, and they know me. Who can tell the reception I'd receive? Ian was fairly well known, remember."

"I suppose you're right, but damn, even though they've ended slavery by name in Africa, I hear whites still rule in the Cape Colony, that's not your cup of tea."

"I know, Massa. I'll behave."

"Practicing up by calling me Massa?"

"Yes, Massa."

JT slapped Monar's shoulder, "You'd be better off sailing to hell, you get uppity in Africa."

When speaking about Monar's plan at Blackwood Abbey with Lord Warfield, he held the same thoughts as JT expressed—only more so and with more reason.

"Look, Monar, I know you can take care of yourself, but I think it's best you avoid the whole of Africa, especially the south, you're the wrong color. My captains have led me to think the new Cape Governor, Sir Harry Smith, is instituting military rule and taking charge to a degree unheard of. The Boers, meaning the Voortrekkkers, are up in arms and there's been pitched battles between the Boers, whites and probably five native groups who have been driven out of their ancestral lands. That's why I don't invest there. So please, Monar, for our sake if not your own, stay away from the Cape Colony."

Lily and Evelyn had come into the room and heard Warfield's assessment of Monar's plan.

Both agreed, "You will *not* be going to Africa!"

It was strange for Monar to hear the concern for his safety; in his life, no one had ever expressed worry over him. It warmed him, yet he hid it, "Then where do I go to get away from this blasted weather?"

Warfield thought for a moment, "Well, there's Spain, or Cape Verde, or the Canary Islands."

"No, I want nothing to do with anywhere along the West African coast. I need a change."

Warfield was ready and casually suggested, "India."

They looked at him in unison, "Really everyone, I mean it—for a number of reasons."

Monar was doubtful and the first to ask, "And the number of reasons are?"

"Well, it's a long story, Evelyn and Lily know most of it, but now I want to involve you and JT in it."

Few people could piece together Warfield's substantial involvement in India and China and the two women were surprised he brought those countries up with Monar and JT.

When Warfield structured his thoughts, he began, "Since I met you two gentlemen, I've been impressed with your ethics, intelligence and personal conduct. From delivering more gold than we expected from America, up to the way Lily, and Evelyn feel about you both."

Here, Warfield cleared his deliberations and spoke frankly, "Monar's wish to leave our bitter weather has initiated a subject I want to broach to you. So let me lay out the background to the subject. First, India. I export numerous products to India such as steel rails for railroads, steel drums, wheels, cotton machinery, and cloth from my mills in Lancashire. I import the cotton, which by the way, most of it comes from America. Can you see the cycle unfold?

Raw cotton from the States and Australia, converted into finished cloth from my English mills then to India and then on to the States and Australia. However, when selling to India, I buy back finished clothing and colors as well as dyed cotton textiles, jewelry, diamonds, pepper, rice, wheat, indigo dye, jute, leather goods—it's an endless list and, importantly, my ships work both outbound and return.

All those products, I then sell through a division of my Black Moon Line, called Warfield's Shoppes and Merchants Limited. We're a nation of shopkeepers you know—and I'm happily one of them. Warfield's Shoppes makes the product, ships the product and sells the product. We have five-hundred shops in England and Western Europe. Remember, this is separate from the thirty ships of the Black Moon Line or my naval contracts, or East India or China."

That the man was wealthy was now fully understood. And, it was the reason he told the tale.

"This all may be boring to you."

The men shook heads, the women nodded, bringing a laugh from everyone, until Warfield continued, "I've laid this out simply as a lead into what's on my mind. I will now be brief, believe it or not, as going in depth would take far longer than I already have. Monar, I want you to go to India. You will be taken care of by my Agent, who is called a Resident over there and he'll help you get around. You can learn the area, scope out more markets, import and export; find more efficient methods for us—by us I mean you, JT and me—to develop. I want you to mostly observe what companies other than the East India group—I know their pursuits—is importing and exporting. Especially, who is shipping opium to China and receiving tea in return. JT, I would like you to see to it that your new ship—do you have a name yet?"

"No, sir. I'm working on it."

"No matter. If you're interested in my offer, when I'm finished that is, I want you to get your clipper shipshape and Bristol fashion as soon as possible—most likely late spring. It looks like my ships will be frozen in this winter from Southampton to Plymouth, which is a waste. Ships that do not move drop like dead weight to the bottom line. So, JT, I want you to find a warm water winter port, or ports, for next year, like your father had. Despite that freak hurricane, it's the thing to do. Next item, JT, there is a full payload waiting for your new clipper as soon as she's prepared. The cargo's for India where you'll meet up with Monar for the next step in my strategy. If you both agree, you will receive full captain wages from this day forward as a start, after which we will sit down for a serious discussion. But I'll hint, India is the gateway to China."

Warfield took a breath, stared intently at Evelyn with a twinkling in his eye and then turned back to the two men, "Interested, gentlemen?"

It didn't take long. One look at each other, then a nod in agreement. JT had one question, "Warfield, it's more than a fair offer, yet I'm curious about the East India Company. What will they do when we're poking about, in direct competition for them, when you're a senior investor in their own company?"

"JT, the EIC is numb. They're so top heavy with partners, supervisors and company men right down the line, that with all their competition, it would take two years for them to even hear of you, if ever. And should they, I'd quash anyone in that organization who says a word."

A goodly measure of how Warfield conducted business was revealed in that statement.

"Now, Lily, Evelyn, would you please get us businessmen a drink while we still have our wits about us enough to enter into one more piece of business?"

The women smiled as they responded. It was now obvious that Warfield had one or more scotches before the conversation even started and the drinks had loosened his tongue. They had no idea of what was to come next.

"JT, Monar, this is the most important part of this conversation. I run my businesses by myself. Oh, you may be sure I ask Lily and Evelyn their advice often, and I often take it. Nonetheless, other than these two lights in my life, I have no advisors and no partners. I know I am archaic, yet there is a simple reason, and the reason is that, up until meeting you both—and since—I have never trusted a soul in business. Accordingly, this is my second offer—the opportunity to join the Black Moon Line in some fashion."

It was the first offer Warfield had ever made and four of five present were shocked.

Lily and Evelyn went to Warfield and kissed him, Lily expressing her pleasure, "At last, Warfield, you're getting on toward sixty and you've finally found someone, or rather two 'someones', to take a bit of the pressure off you. Can a holiday be far behind?"

"Well, and believe me when I say this to all here, I'm putting a lot of trust and effort into these two men. If they perform as I expect, I *will* have a little freer time and there will be two prosperous employees added to Black Moon."

They celebrated the evening away until the hour was late. Warfield, remaining in his book lined, mahogany and garnet leather study, sat deeply into his chair, absentmindedly staring into the flickering shadows of the fireplace. He had revealed a portion of his plans and everyone, including himself, was pleased. Or rather, he was *mostly* pleased. His ideas were grandiose, too great for the typical person. Too great even for exceptional people, such as JT or Monar or Evelyn or Lily, to absorb all at once. It had to be done piecemeal.

He was wealthy, he made Lily and Evelyn and many others affluent and given away more in charitable deeds. Anyone, if knowing his intentions for the future would say why, why try for millions more? Yet, Warfield understood what drove him. It wasn't money for the sake of money, it was the challenge…and the power it bought and would continue to bring.

He sipped the scotch, his mind drifted to a long past moment. New Castle-on-Tyne…an orphaned nine-year-old, nostrils black with coal dust, staring at a blind donkey while it pulled its coal cart along the track at the bottom of the mine. The mule was blind for it never saw the sun and the youngster, going into the mine before dawn and leaving it at dark six days a week, unexpectedly thought of himself as a blind, dumb donkey…

Years later, when the boy became a man, he learned the meaning of the word 'epiphany' and realized, at that long distant, precise moment, he would become a blind donkey, like the other miners. He let fall his coal hod and ran…

Warfield waved his hand, attempting to scatter the persisting ghosts, the years before the mast, bullied by first mates, trained by fair captains and, most of all, the infinite and unrelenting sea. Yet, the sea he learned to love. He thrived, so when chances arose to enrich him, he took them time and again and…

Once more, Warfield eased back to the present. He had much to do. If JT were correct, his clipper would be sharp bowed and perhaps as he said, the fastest in the world. Twenty knots, conceivably twenty-two and that was the swiftness he needed.

Put first things first however. The plan Warfield had laid out mentally, nothing in writing of course, would bring untold wealth. His plan first began to form eight years past, back when the British first won the 1840 Opium War with China. That war forced the warlords under Daoguang, the Qing Dynasty Emperor of China, to cede Hong Kong to the British for one-hundred and fifty years. This method of Gun-Barrel Diplomacy, so often successful by the British, also opened trade rights to five other coastal towns—Foochow, Canton, Ninpo, Amoy and Shanghai. Trade then flourished, but there still remained one major problem that Warfield and all traders couldn't avoid—gold or silver for tea, the demand for which made tea dreadfully expensive for lower and middleclass Englishman. Of course, bringing opium from India and Pakistan, then bartering that for tea helped reduce the cost of exchange, but Emperor Daoguang, always wanting an excuse for one more war, frowned on the western barbarian. His displeasure could lead into another opium war, another war of death, destruction and perhaps—a frightening thought for the British—China could win this one, and where would tea addicted Britain be then?

Afghanistan had a monopoly on opium, this the British consortium controlled. Yet of more importance, China had *the* monopoly on Camellia Sinensis—tea. To say she guarded that plant with jealously and force was a profound understatement. The plants, hidden from the world, were near sacred and any attempted theft of a single plant was punishable by death—and enforced.

For eight years, Warfield frequently gave thought to bringing tea to the British and European masses. Accomplish that, he knew, and vast profits would result. Yet it couldn't be done—in China. He had the solution. What he didn't have, up until now, were people he could truly trust to keep a secret...

"Still at it, Father?"

Warfield, his mind deep into China, hadn't heard Evelyn enter, "What? Oh, yes, dear, merely tying a few loose ends together."

"Anything I can help with?"

"Not really, it's something for the future. You run along now, see you in the morning."

It was Warfield's way of saying to leave him alone and Evelyn took no offence.

Lest she read his mind, he waited until the door closed behind her. Evelyn was the last person he wanted to know his thoughts. The definitive scheme. The strategy to steal one-hundred tea plants from China and grow them in India—with the aid of JT and Monar, whether they knew it or not. Of course, others had tried it many times and either failed or died, which amounted to the same thing. A Doctor Campbell stole away a few seeds five or six years ago, but seeds would take years to grow and more years to get worthwhile leaf. Another problem for the good doctor was rumor held that the Hai San leader, Hok An Keow pursued him. No, Warfield must be sure only mature, leaf-bearing plants were pilfered, quickly and in secret.

It could be done. He could have the able assistance of that longhaired, God worshiping, Sleeping Dragon Society Lord and out-and-out brigand, Mr. Archibald Feng Yün-shan. Archie Feng could get the plants to the coast, of that, Warfield was certain. The certainty being that Archie Feng was the only person who had stolen from Warfield and absconded, scot-free—more or less.

Warfield concluded his thoughts. Monar will carry two sealed letters to Ashley Ealing, the Black Moon Line's India Resident. Ealing was to read the letter addressed to him with, among other notes, instructions to train Monar in the purchasing and trading procedures, barter system and how cargo for China, Australia, the United States and England is prepared. At no time, was Ealing to forget Monar was an important person. After he had an overview of all this and familiarized with key people, the two were then to hand-carry the letter marked 'Feng', whom Ealing knew, to Canton. After Archie's response, it was to be sent back to Warfield. *It is crucial*, Warfield stressed, that his *letter not be seen by anyone other than Archie!*

After those events unfolded and he received Archie's required time frame for the plant delivery, Warfield felt JT's clipper would be near finished and his part in the drama would begin.

With the British ceded Hong Kong, most European ships used that harbor or Shanghai. It was tea for gold, silver or—secretly, through dozens of corrupt officials both European and Chinese —opium. With Canton exclusively British and Archie's haunt, Warfield's plan required he use that port and his Resident would lawfully pay one more time in silver—not opium— for the tea. That transaction would be to keep up appearances with the Chinese authorities that the Black Moon Line was law-abiding.

It would be after that last cash deal at Canton, when one-hundred, small leaf, black tea plants or shrubs or whatever they were, Warfield smiled, would be delivered to his ship, in this case, JT's ship, and transplanted on his land estate in Darjeeling, the Bengal, India. Give him five years, Warfield knew, five clandestine years, and China's stranglehold on the tea trade would come to an end. He could still find excitement in international competitiveness and the holding of the prize; *this* prize would bring millions of pounds tea to the masses and millions in gold to Warfield. Although years away, he planned to create another company, Warfield's Tea. Then he would retire and build another racing schooner for the Cowes Regatta and...beat the Royal Yacht Squadron at their own game.

«»

"I know you didn't sleep last night, where'd you wander off to?" JT heard Monar slip out early in the night and only now wandered back in.

"I went to Limehouse. It's a section in East London; Chinatown and the dock basin."

"And..."

"And there's a lot of Chinamen there."

"If it's called Chinatown, one might expect that."

"Only too true, JT, there's a lot of opium there as well."

"Is that bad? Opium is not against the law; they give it to babies to calm them if they're fussy. In fact, I recall Mr. Poe using it, only he called it Laudanum."

"I won't say I'm against it; then again, after seeing its use in Limehouse, I'm not so sure. There are scores of dens and cubicles where they smoke opium and I'll tell you, they're in a state of dreams, stupefied, can hardly move. It's worse than the drugs I've seen deep in the Caribe."

"Any worse than the drunks we see in the hovels around here?"

"Quite possibly. Or maybe it just seems worse because they're more bunched together."

"Well, ignore going there then. Why don't you visit the British Museum instead?"

Monar laughed, "Thanks, I don't think I'll use you as a guide." He was thoughtful, "By the way, I haven't heard too much about your insipid dreams lately. They stopped?"

"Yes...well those dreams have, now they're about Charlee and Evelyn—they're fighting."

Monar stifled a laugh, "Surely not over you?"

JT shouldn't have answered, "It seems so."

The servants in the upper quarters might have woken from Monar's thunderous bellow, "My, God, JT! You really do have outlandish dreams!"

He would not wait. Monar said Christmas meant nothing to him and on 22 December, he waved goodbye from the cold while standing on the deck of the Black Moon merchantman, *Captain John's Spirit*, one of the last ships to depart before the inner harbor froze.

Before leaving, Monar divided the contents of his chest with a protesting JT, who agreed to the move solely due to Monar agreeing the remainder could be returned to him in India.

Prior to Monar's departure, Warfield had been pleasantly surprised, during a confidential meeting with the black man. Warfield began giving a mere overview for acquiring tea plants and found Monar enlisting in the idea unequivocally. With that, anxious to articulate the concept to someone, Warfield disclosed the far-reaching intrigue and found a willing accomplice, one more than ready to follow the concept. After easing over this hurdle, the two men debated how JT would receive the idea, for after all, laid bare, it did not exactly fit in the legal activities category. Monar's answer was they must be truthful with JT—not overly truthful, just somewhat. That was considered good enough for the present, for after Monar and JT met up in India, there would be adequate time to discuss the clandestine element in the trip when sailing to China.

However, Monar felt Lord Warfield had something more on his mind and at last it came to light, "Monar, I'd like to ask you straight out, do you think there's something personal between my daughter and JT? Lily thinks it."

Monar thought hastily, then spoke calmly, "If you mean physically," Warfield winced, as Monar knew he would, then continued, "no, there's nothing going on. If you mean emotionally, Lily's right. I know there is, yet I'll add *they* don't admit it, or else are doing their best to ignore it."

"Why? If I'm not too old to recall, they've been through enough experiences not to know there might be some, ah, feelings for each other."

"Honestly, Warfield, I think they both have those feelings, but both are holding back."

"Because of that Charlee woman my daughter mentioned."

It was a surprise to Monar that Evelyn had mentioned another woman to her father, "Yes, I think that's the story. JT is honorable and in my opinion, foolish. He only met Charlee twice and I doubt if it was for more than three hours total. And she's not a woman, I think she's only eighteen, so who knows how flighty she may be. Anyway, she left for Europe before he saw her again and also her father owns slaves. For his own good reasons, that's against JT's principals. Still, he gave his word that he would see her by the end of next year, '49. So, there you have it."

Apparently decided, Warfield measured his next words, "I have a reason for my next question, so please bear with me. If JT wasn't this honorable, do you feel he would be, shall I say, *interested* in Evelyn? Be straightforward."

Perplexed, Monar could see the direction the conversation was taking. Of two minds, one of which was his own, unattainable feelings for Evelyn, while his other thought presumed why the question was posed, "Warfield, if that Charlee or JT's self-imposed honor weren't at hand, it would be evident he is madly in love with Evelyn, I'm sure he's fighting with himself."

"That's what I want to hear, and now I'll tell you the reason."

Warfield glanced around to be sure Evelyn and Lily were out of earshot, "I'm fifty-seven, Monar, and like some men my age, I'm thinking of my legacy. Of course, Lily and my wife are well taken care of now and in my will, but I mean my legacy, my holdings. Evelyn will inherit it all. However, it is too much for her to handle. This isn't to say she is not smart enough, because she is, except for the devious elements one needs to be successful that she has trouble with."

After their previous discussion about stealing tea shrubs, Monar and Warfield couldn't keep straight faces before he started again, "That is except for the *dubious* elements, she could handle it. The problem is, she doesn't want to. She often helps me and she can see the toll it takes on keeping it all together. What I'm trying to say is, my life is not the life Evelyn wants and I have no other heir. However, if she marries, then there's a chance there could be a son and…well…"

"Two questions occur to me, Warfield. One, hasn't Evelyn had the opportunities to marry, and the other difficulty I see is, do you think a Yankee is the best choice for your daughter?"

Warfield appeared reflective, "To answer the first, yes, Evelyn's had many offers, some of them quite titled. I know that for a fact, as suitors must come to me first and ask permission to court her. No one has interested her. If she weren't so level-headed, I'd think she believes those books that Miss Austin or Edgeworth woman prattle on about."

"And the other matter, Warfield? An unrefined American?"

Embarrassed, Warfield plunged on, "I'm the first to admit I was against it. Still, I've watched JT and come to realize, to my chagrin, that he is much more to my liking than any number of her possible suitors—titled or not, English or whatnot—with whom I've come in contact. I'll go a step further; JT has very much the ideals and intelligence I wish for Evelyn."

"And for yourself."

Warfield couldn't help laugh, "And for myself, to be sure. Now, tell me, what do you think?"

Monar had no scruples discussing JT's private life; it was for the best he thought, "You're right of course, Warfield. Yet the question remains, what to do about the other woman?"

Warfield had obviously given the problem thought, "You've said JT's supposed to see that Charlee woman no later than the end of '49. So, as the end of this year, is coming up, let's work out the timing. Even with the two work crews, JT's new ship won't be ready before spring. Then there's the masts to be stepped and rigged, sails, guns mounted, engines and crews broken in, provisions, cargo and everything else. That means May at the earliest before the ship's ready, if then. Then, he's to meet you in India and after that, on to China and back to India. All of this together says he can't do it—he'll never make it back to see that girl by the end of next year."

The two conspirators had been immensely pleased with themselves. By keeping JT busy, they hoped he would forget the date. That was all it would take, make him forget to keep his word.

With Lord Warfield's letters safe in his trunk and instructions in his brain, Monar sailed off for Bombay, India to find life's next design for him.

«»

The workers at Mare's Shipyard, including John Mare himself, had to be patient. With Monar gone, JT's efforts to improve his clipper became ever more forceful. Copper boilers instead of iron, shaft alleys strengthened, the deck of the Master's cabin reinforced to support a Long nine 36-pounder cannon. Comparing McKay's plans with those of the smaller British built clipper, *Scottish Maid*, JT further extended the bowsprit and strengthened the dolphin striker to counter increased jib volume, lengthened the mainmast to one-hundred twenty feet, redesigned and extended the spars and booms on the diagrams. During this, he reshaped the topsail-plans to allow for moon-sails, and fashioned or restructured a dozen other areas. Mare and former Admiralty engineer Ash, made JT justify each idea before approving. However, the few proposals JT could not justify, he added as personal requisites.

Strangely enough and without knowing, JT's tapering of the forward hull foresaw by years, the evolution of the *fast* clipper into the *extreme* clipper.

He agonized until eventually deciding to name his ship, *The Raven*, simply because he couldn't come up with a better name. With that decision, he roughed in a design of the figurehead with only a raven's head and no wings. The final carving, painted black, with yellow eyes, was near frightening. Whether this was intended or not, the ship's carver was not told.

The freeboard of the narrowed hull above the red waterline would be completely black with no color delineation for the gun ports. The sole color break would be the bow and stern boards carved with the name of the clipper and inlaid with gold leaf. Charles Mare considered these modifications outside Royal Navy praxes, but Lord Bunting's naval officers made official visits of approval and the payments kept to the agreed schedule. Believing the ship was disguised as a cross between a merchant ship and a fast warship, a decidedly secret concept, no questions were asked by J C Mare Company.

Christmas and Boxing Day passed with little change in the weather. Modest gifts passed around between them; a sterling, J Johnson Fusee pocket watch with a feature JT's timepiece did not have, a sweep second hand. Engraved to *John Thomas Graves from Warfield, Lily & Evelyn, 1848 Safe Voyage/Safe Return*. A thoughtful gift, although JT wished it was from Evelyn alone.

JT's gift to Warfield and Lily was an early Great Qing Dynasty vase Lily had admired, while to Evelyn he gave the book *Wuthering Heights*, by Emily Brontë.

He had signed it '*To my Friend in Conflict and Peace*'— *JTG, 12.25.1848*.

Lily, in mentioning she wished they thought of some gift for Monar before he left, was pleased when JT informed them that he had given Monar gifts. Gifts of books on *The Atlantic Pilot, Navigation and Seamanship Rules, Celestial Navigation* and *Royal Navy Ocean Charts*.

They looked bewildered. "You see, up to '45, a captain didn't need a Certificate, but now, Monar will need one to receive his Master Mariner rating to captain a ship. And let's face it, if he's to be in charge of a ship, he really should know how to get where he's supposed to."

"To my Friend in Conflict and Peace." Speaking aloud to no one, Evelyn smirked, "Friend—how does he mean that? Like a pal or perhaps a chum? Could he have engraved anything frostier?"

She closed the book, thinking to herself, 'Well, I guess I can stop wondering if I have serious feelings for him, it doesn't seem to matter. I hope he's very happy with his southern belle. Then again, damn it, he's so nice, more of a man than I've ever known and would have liked to know better…'

Warfield and JT entered the drawing room; she was flustered. Had she been talking aloud? They didn't seem to notice anything untoward and she quickly collected her wits.

Her father was distant, something other than her on his mind. That was good.

"Would you mind, Evelyn, if I have a private conversation with JT?"

As JT began to say hello, she took her book, fleetingly nodded to both and left the room.

"What was that departure all about, Warfield?"

"Damned if I know, she looked like she thought we were reading her mind."

JT laughed, "That's one thing about her I can't do."

"Perhaps you should try." Before JT could probe into the comment, Warfield continued, "Enough about her right now, we need to talk. JT, I'm going to give you a short—well as short as I can—history lesson because it's important to your future with my companies."

It was a profound understatement the 'short' part.

"JT, the reform of Parliament in '32, gives this period in our Empire's history incredible opportunities for someone who has the intelligence and nerve to grasp it. In spite of themselves, Parliament, industry, commerce and the Royal Navy have, quite accidently mind you, molded a structure of governing so strong that no other country can compete. We are a naval power and control the sea-lanes. Our worldwide commerce comes from the industrial revolution Britain started. Our success is with powered machinery and each new invention or improvement keeps us ahead of everyone.

To get to the point. My ships bring in raw material such as cotton; my industries convert that raw material into textiles that we ship around the world on my ships. And, Warfield's Shoppes sells all of the products we either make or import. That's two pillars, commerce and industry. The government backs us financially, not that I need it, and the Royal Navy protects us. Those four pillars and the ability to maintain them is the key to keeping us successful."

JT could see where Warfield was leading, yet not the reason for the lesson. He didn't think it was to impress, "I follow your account of how all this came about, Warfield, still, with all you've got to handle it makes me wonder—how much more you want to grow?"

Warfield smiled, "JT, the principle I've held fast to is, grow and diversify with the times, or wither and die on the vines. England has the largest naval fleet in the world and I intend to have the largest *merchant* fleet in the world. And, the largest shopping facilities in the world."

JT could see the man wasn't bragging. It was, simply put, his goal. A rather sizeable goal. Yet there was more to be said and JT waited.

"And here's how I'm going to do it, JT. I've just bought a shipyard on the Firth of Forth, that's a river in Scotland. I've ordered four British clippers, sail and steam—no damn slow India built packet ships for the Black Moon Company. Along that same river, I'm also building my fourth textile mill solely for fabrics and, another engineering factory. Aside from those moves, I'll be contracting for seven more merchant ships with Charley Mare and another Thames shipyard at Deptford. This is a large order, mainly because I've closed a contract with the Admiralty to build, from the keel up, four fast, iron-hulled, sail and steam warships for the High Seas Battle Squadron. Mare has five slipways and three wet docks as well as their old larger wet dock, so I know they can handle it if he gets enough riggers and shipwrights."

Warfield took a breath, "So to finish up on this subject, I've won the overseas mail contract, with Government subsidies, to America, South Africa, India and Australia. And lastly, the Admiralty is generating, at this very moment, the contract for the Black Moon Company to build slipways, wet docks and coaling stations in Madras and Bombay, both coasts of India."

JT thought silence was the best rejoinder. If he spoke, he knew no comment could possibly encompass his thoughts on the magnitude of Warfield's holdings and undertakings. However, at his host's reticence to continue, JT had to ask his primary question, "Like I said, how on earth do you keep it all together, straight in your head, Warfield?"

He didn't respond at first, letting his thoughts organize, "JT, I told you awhile back I wanted to open a serious discussion with you and Monar. Well, because of all these ventures coming to a boil at the same moment, I'm not premature. I like the way you've supervised the building of your clipper, no element is too small for you. So, when you're satisfied with your ship and head to India to complete the task I've written out for you and Monar in China, I want you both to return here. Study and learn about everything you see, for unless I'm mistaken, my decision will be for you to assume the position as Director of the Black Moon merchant fleet. Monar will, I believe, become Director of Overseas Trade and Management."

JT's jaw nearly went slack, "Warfield, that's a tremendous undertaking. Honestly, I'm not near ready for that position."

"Of course you're not, neither is Monar. The question is, do you want it? You both have two things going for you—brains and integrity. You can learn all the rest and," Warfield laughed, "I can teach you how to not be *overly* ethical. One more thing. Before he left, Monar agreed in the fundamentals, if you agree, after two years, you both can expect minor Partnerships in the Black Moon Company as well as sit on the board of Warfield's Limited when it's formed, that is."

It was the chance of a lifetime and JT knew it. In spite of this, he had to tell him, “I must say something first, Warfield. Please don’t think I’m not appreciative with what you’ve offered. Still, I gave someone my word; I’ve an obligation to keep it and that might interfere with your plans.”

Knowing what was coming, Warfield was undecided whether to mention that fact or wait. He decided to see how JT handled it, “Something you can’t ignore JT, or don’t wish to ignore?”

“Doesn’t really matter which. I gave my word.”

“Then, tell me, how will this interfere?”

“This is awkward for me, Warfield; I gave my word I would meet a girl in Savanna, Georgia, by the end of next year.”

This opening gave Warfield the chance to carefully pry into JT’s relationship, “When was this, JT, when did you say this?”

“It was March of ’47.”

“’47? That’s getting on for two years ago. You think she still feels that way?”

“I believe so, yes.”

Warfield had to be careful; not wanting to let on that Monar had informed him.

“Why did you leave her for two years?”

“She lived in Savanna. As I told you, our family lost everything in the hurricane and there was no way I could support her in the life she’s use to having.”

“JT, I don’t mean to pry, I simply want to understand why we can’t come to an agreement right now. Tell me—how old is she?”

“Eighteen, she said then.” As he spoke, JT could see the doubt forming about his judgment in Warfield’s mind and wanted everything out, on the table, which only made things worse, “There’s another reason I left, her father has slaves and she see’s nothing wrong with that.”

“JT, let me be honest. I’m dead against slavery, and you’re against slavery, and she apparently, is not. On top of that, you hardly know her, yet you think an eighteen year old *girl*, who believes in slavery, will still be waiting for you after two or three years."

"Yes, I know it sounds foolish, but yes, I do think so."

Warfield knew the answer, yet asked, "Do you at least write?"

JT was by now recognizing how foolish he sounded, "No, sir, we don't write. Back then I spoke with her father and he said she left for the continent soon after I first met her."

"JT, I just don't know what…"

"May I try to put into words what I feel, Warfield? A lot has happened since I saw Charlee—to *me* I mean. I became alienated from my father, my mother has gone God knows where and my older brother…well, he's not right in the head from… from a severe shock. I don't want to get into my father and me, but he left me a clipper and I met your daughter when she was very distressed and then there was meeting you, and the Black Sea, and the battle where I lost my ship…"

Warfield could see JT was nervous and let him ramble on. What he had to say was important to them both.

JT continued, "…after that was the battle with the pirates and seeing how brave Evelyn was and sailing with her…her strength…her intelligence and…"

He stopped, clearing his thoughts, "Lord Bunting, I can't say how I feel, I have no right to. I have to do what I must, keep my word, even if it may not be what Charlee wants to hear… I just can't say any more until once I see her, sir."

Warfield said nothing, going to the fireplace and kicking at an ember. He listened between JT's words and found what he wanted. He would say nothing more on the subject, nor would he reveal his beliefs to his daughter. What happens will happen.

"JT, inasmuch as you've told me, I think we should continue along the path I've mentioned until such time you feel you must decide a different path to your future. At that time, if you wish to leave, I'll call it all square."

"Thank you, Warfield. You're most fair. I wish I could say more."

As JT left, Warfield was pleased, to a point. That woman Charlee was going to be a nuisance, a problem that was going to take a year to resolve. Well, until JT leaves for India, Evelyn and JT will see each other often. Warfield would see to that, but say nothing to either of them, just let nature take its course and that southern belle, that *girl*, would be a thing of the past.

However, if she were not, the position Warfield planned for JT was not workable.

SOUTHERN INDIA AND CHINA

24

27 March 1849

MONAR FELT THE SPRAY on his face as the *Southern Star*, a Black Moon packet ship, labored through the eastern Bay of Bengal. Turning his back to the spray, he saw Ashley Ealing, Bunting's Resident for India, vomiting over the taffrail, "Feeding the fishes again, Ashley?"

"Afraid so, blast it. Begins every bleeding time I set foot on a ship's deck it. If you haven't suffered seasickness, trust me, it's a misery; all I want is to feel terra firma again. I'm sicker right now than last year when that blasted cyclone in the Bengal killed hundreds and I almost drowned."

Warfield's letter introducing Monar and his assignment in India—omitting his true China undertaking—had gone smoothly. The letter had also stated that Monar only needed to have an overview of Warfield's holdings; that he was being groomed for other endeavors and was not assuming Ealing's position. Understanding that helped the Resident and Monar become friends. Ealing knew his trade, speaking both Nagari Hindi and Cantonese and Monar came to respect the other's position. As for Ealing, he was especially wary of Monar when he casually referred to Lord Bunting as Warfield; there was obviously a close tie there for Ealing would never think of referring to him that way. To everyone Monar met, it was Lord Bunting, and to be less conspicuous, Monar then did the same.

He found Calcutta, India, alien and dirty, a sweaty land. Yet after meeting the poor as well as the mighty, he saw deeper into the beauty of the people and land and its monuments and began to accept it for what it was, a beautiful, tired land. Yet he wasn't sorry for a run to Canton,[21] China.

Ashley's account on the depth of the East India Company's tentacles reach into India and the power of foreign Regents astonished Monar. These men, mainly British, more commonly known as the Raj, short for Rajah or Prince, were key in helping the East India Company's private army's win battles at Plassey and Buxar in the Bengal and break the numerous Maharaja's control of the land, thereby assuring gradual rule by the EIC over an autonomous nation-state.

In addition to the British East India Company, or anywhere their paramountcy did not reach, the French, Dutch and Russians were struggling to thrust their way in. Yet at this time, it was not the East India Company that concerned the British Government—it was the Russians.

Their competition was called The Great Game, whereby the Russian Government would make a grab for a Knight—such as India or Turkey—in the geographical chess game and England would check them, more often checkmating. Yet, there was the Russian foothold in the brutal, untamed northern mountains of India and Afghanistan that kept the British Army constantly on alert and their Sepoy infantry, led by British officers and non-com's, fought to keep the Bear at bay.

Ashley Ealing was emphatic that Monar make Lord Bunting aware that brigands and spies were not only to the north, but also among the southern shipping ports and solely for one reason—opium. From the poppy valleys in the Great Central Highlands of Afghanistan, the milky juice from the unripe poppy seed pods was collected, dried and converted to opiate that was then trekked on pack animals by way of the Khyber Pass. From the Pass, it then travelled over sections of the old Silk Road and from the Road it

---

[21] Also known as Guangehou. The name Canton is generally used here.

wound transversely along ancient paths through the Punjab and Sind. The drug continued along a dozen trails past Lahore and Jodhpur in India or down the Indus River and further south into the shipping lanes.

Danger lurked in every mile. Afridi or Pashtun clans from the Khyber, and tribesmen in the south learned opium was another word for gold in the British, China trade. Throughout the regions, gunfire and death were common night and day.

Monar learned the extent of Warfield's far distant authority when Ealing mentioned Lord Bunting owned a remote militia, a militia called—if only whispered amongst the Raj —'Lord Bunting's Brigands'. This militia, stationed just south of the Khyber, assured he received his quota and the best product, even before the East India Company Regents were aware.

Basically, Monar already knew the reason for all the subterfuge. There was no question the British had found—many whispered actually developed—a demand for opium in China. Without that demand, private companies would have to pay for tea in Coin of the Realm and the contrary thought was that those same companies created the demand for tea in England in the first place.

The Canton voyage was, as far as Ealing knew, for that very reason; trading opium for tea and silk from corrupt officials. This, Ealing had no problem with, yet he was kept unaware there would only be this one last trip trading opium for tea. This last trip that is, if Warfield's letter to Archie Feng was accepted. With that acceptance and Monar's opinion prove positive; concerning the likelihood of success in stealing tea plants, the next and last payment for tea would be in gold. Immediately following that—thievery. And if caught—death.

«»

The five-hundred mile Strait of Malacca separating Sumatra from Malaysia, beckoned them—the Strait, and Malacca pirates—although little was expected from the pirates considering the

Southern Star was protected by the forty-four gun, Blackwall Frigate, HMS *Prince of Wales.*

With no sign of the pirates other than a few sailing craft, they were into, through and past the Strait and Singapore in a few days. Later, the bows of the *Prince of Wales* and *Southern Star* breached the waves north into the South China Sea.

The Chinese mainland islands of Hainan and Hong Kong passed from sight and eventually the Pearl River Delta led the way up river to Canton. There, a forest of masts greeted them along with a one-gun salute to the *Prince of Wales* from the armed sloop, HMS *Volage*. The *Southern Star* was warped in to the Black Moon pier by sampans and coolies shouting endlessly at each other while the *Prince* lay in to the RN docks.

Monar took it all in, the masses of people, hundreds of sampans, scores of foreign ships and, the noise. One thing, however, stood out more so than the rest; Chinese war junks.

"Aren't they something?" Ealing mentioned on seeing Monar stare at the ships.

"Damn, Ashley, I can't believe their size."

"It is surprising when you first see them. That three-decker over there probably goes over 800-tons if she's a pound."

"I've never seen a ship with five masts, they're formidable."

"They may look it, yet not really, Monar. Big, yes, but not agile. Actually lumbering would be the proper word. If they had the weather gauge, it would be a bit of a problem although that's neutralized by their being so slow and with pitiful weaponry. We just don't let them get close in; if it's a battle, they carry four or five-hundred warriors."

"You sound like you know, Ashley."

"I'm Royal Navy, retired. Before I went with the Black Moon, I was with the British East India Company as sub-lieutenant on the BEIC frigate *India*. We and the HMS *Nemesis* whipped a few war junks at Chuenpee. They fall apart, although one of their type did make it from here to England and America in '46, '48. Didn't you see it?"

"No, guess I was somewhere else."

Ealing looked down the dock to a weighty figure in an orange, silk hanfu, or robe, as he waddled down the dock.

"Ah, I see our Mr. Yin is honoring us with his presence once more."

Monar asked, "And our Mr. Yin is?"

"Mr. Yin is what we would call a fat peacock, but we address as his most honorable customs agent. He's come to pick up his stipend, otherwise known as a payoff."

"And if we don't pay his stipend?"

"Then he finds opium in the burlap packs labeled textiles and we all get executed."

Monar was impressed at Ealing's indifference, "You don't seem concerned."

"Not at all. If he was going to find contraband, he would have half the Empire's army down here in front of him. In other words, Monar, I haven't found a Chinaman yet, who couldn't be bribed. And why shouldn't they be? Look around you, humbled people, beaten down by their own damnable corrupt rulers."

While Ealing excused himself and went below, Monar continued watching Mr. Yin when he went to sit on a hatch cover. Ealing returned, carrying a small sack and Yin, in plain sight to all the crew, waited while the sack was placed on his lap. The fat man separated the coin into gold and silver stacks, counted them out as he dropped them back into the sack, seemed satisfied, said something as he handed a paper to Ealing and waddled back up the dock.

After he left, Monar went up to the Resident, "What did the orange peacock say to you?"

Ealing laughed, "Chinese idea of humor—said he hoped I wasn't cheating him."

It was humorous; it was the only way to look at it. The paper Yin handed off was a release for the cargo and soon coolies from the Black Moon warehouse were swarming through the hold removing the 'textile' packages.

"All right, Monar, Captain Walsh and I have to go over to see Charley Elliot; he's Chief Superintendent of British Trade in China. I'll take Lord Bunting's letter and track down Archie Feng. After that the Captain and I will check the shipping manifest, then I'll be back."

"What are we loading beside the tea chests?"

"No people. Just porcelain, spice and lacquer-ware, as far as I know. One thing more, Monar, unless Feng sends for you, don't leave the ship without some old China hands along."

Monar walked the ship's hold, watching the coolies sweating away as they stacked the tea chests tightly to prevent shifting in a rough sea. Few workers had seen a black man, fewer still had seen a black man this large, and murmuring Cantonese, they were sure Monar was painted black to scare them into working harder—so they did.

A rickshaw, pulled by a wiry little man, rattled along the wharf before it stopped by the *Southern Star's* gangway.

"Moorah, Moorah."

It was close enough to his name, so Monar went down to meet the runner who handed him a note. In one sentence from Ealing, it stated that Archie read the message and the rickshaw driver would take Monar to him.

Trying to convince Monar not to take the trip alone, the first mate glanced at the frame of the rickshaw and saw a painting of a coiled, slumbering dragon.

He pointed it out to Monar, "My mistake, you'll be all right, sir, you're protected by the Sleeping Dragon Society. Just don't wander away from the rickshaw."

Monar had heard a little of the Sleeping Dragon from Warfield and didn't question. He then squeezed into the seat and caught the pained look from the driver as he struggled under the heavy load to give the vehicle motion.

Through streets and alleys teeming with sailors from a dozen nations, Chinese coolies and hooligans' glares, and then along the length of refuse reeking lanes the rickshaw runner's braided queue never ceased its tempo. He knew the pathways and alleyways, yet it was dusk by the time the rickshaw stopped beside the façade of a tired building on the outskirts of Canton.

Three Chinamen stood about— thugs was the first notion that sprang to Monar—while he stepped down and the driver kept nodding. Before he could reach for a few coins however, the rickshaw was clattering away down the cobblestones.

The three thugs eased apart and then waited as one of them shouted through the doorway. Two more thugs arrived, this time with spears, while the others drew knives. It was obvious they were playing it safe given the size of their guest.

Monar stood his ground, aware of his position, "Feng? Archie Feng?"

One of the men nodded and pointed to Monar's leg, then held out his hand palm up. Knowing they wanted his bolo, he was certain that giving it up was the sensible thing to do. Yet he wasn't going to be intimidated. In one motion, he eased the blade out of his boot, hefted it and threw it full force into the door the two men had just exited. Monar let out laugh as the men jumped aside and then angry, began to come at him.

A voice from above, "Well struck! Good show, do come in—presuming you are Mr. Monar."

The men fell back as Monar went to the door, made a show of working the bolo out the wood, returned it to his boot and passed inside. To his surprise, he wasn't in a room, but on a short wharf, under a house built on stilts. At the end of the wharf, Monar noticed two more thugs, staring back with indifference, cutlasses by their side and unkempt, like the others.

A trap door above opened, giving light to a stairway, "Be a good chap won't you and come up this way, Mr. Monar?"

A rather large, well-built longhaired man, worn more from life than age, loomed at the head of the stairs. Scarred eyebrows, broken nose—many times—a gnarly face.

"I'm Archibald Feng Yün-shan, leader of the Sleeping Dragon Society and I'll state what is obvious; I can have you killed at any moment Mr. Monar. I won't, however, as long as you behave as my guest, but more so because Lord Bunting wrote me not to kill you."

The room reeked of opium and the unwashed, Monar feigned indifference, "Good of Warfield, I'll thank him the next time I see him. And my name is Monar, not Mr. Monar."

Archie Feng was impressed with his guest's casual use of Lord Bunting's name as well as a seemingly unruffled bearing. Considering the surroundings, he should be at least, unnerved.

"Tea…Monar?"

"Yes, I'll try it, I never have."

"Not in England? Quite an odd thing to hear."

Feng, with two fingers, rang a tiny bell—Monar kept from smiling—as two young, attractive Asian girls entered with a tea setting, the tea steeping in a container under a padded silk cozy and two rice cakes on petite porcelain plates.

Waving away the girls, who, frightened at the black man, couldn't leave quick enough, Feng acknowledged. "You're an uncaged tiger to them, they've never seen a man your size, much less painted black."

He then caught Monar off guard, "I hear you do not sleep."

"What on earth is this about?"

"Just trivial talk. I saw Ealing this afternoon and ordered him to tell me about you and one of the things he mentioned was you—as he said—*stalked* the *Southern Star* night after night and were awake all day as well. I am fascinated by that."

Monar was going to deny, but decided on another tactic, "Do you know of the islands, the Caribbean, Feng? No, of course you don't, or you wouldn't have thought that strange. I lived with a Vodou priestess for years, deep in the jungle of Barbados. After a decade of preparation and her guidance, I found several feats the mind could achieve. I become close to an Incubus, however, staying solely within the concept of sleep, I created a subterfuge whereby I deceive my mind into believing it has rested. By that deception, my mind never conveys to my body that it is tired—so I don't sleep."

Of course, it was all imagery Monar was creating. There was no priestess or living in the jungle or never sleeping. True, Monar slept only in brief cycles, yet Feng said he was fascinated, and a touch of mysticism could go a long way with a person who could be frightened of it and he was worried by Monar's offhand mention of the word Incubus—a male demon.

"Could you teach me, my friend?"

My *friend*, what a turnabout, Monar thought, "Only if you're willing to spend five years in a jungle with a not-too-attractive priestess, Feng."

Crestfallen, Feng wasn't going to stay five *days* with an ugly woman—be she priestess or whatever—to learn not to sleep. Nevertheless, slipped into his words, Monar implied he had other mysterious powers and Feng decided to be careful around him. For like many other Chinese, he was afraid of the black arts—my god, he thought—a male demon. Was there such?

"What about you, Feng, do you have any unique traits?"

Before Feng could answer a scream issued from the stairwell, interrupting their exchange. Monar looked up, but Feng smiled as he shouted to those below. Two men came, dragging a bound man to the top of the stairs and then pushed him to kneel in the middle of the room.

Archie explained, "This man was caught stealing from another man's rice bowl. He said he was hungry, yet didn't think that the other man might be hungry also. I now deliver the sentence."

It seemed a sham to Monar. A different trapdoor opened, the man's scream filling the room as he was pulled over to the opening by his queue. Feng removed a revolver from the folds of his hanfu, placed it to the nape of the man's neck. Fleeting pleads, blocked by the gun's report, a splash in the water below.

"You asked if I have any unique traits, Monar. Yes, but only one. I am coldhearted."

Feng spoke callously, yet he was again concerned. Monar had not so much as blinked throughout the incident. There should have been some response, some reaction to seeing a man shot like a dog.

However, Feng knew nothing of Monar having seen blacks shot for the wrong look, walking on a sidewalk, bowing, but not low enough, or something so inadvertent as breaking a glass.

In truth, Monar deduced what was going to happen the moment the man was dragged into the room. He was also aware Feng was going to watch his reaction. With that in mind, Monar steeled himself against any emotion, and so not pity nor even concern shown on his face.

This greatly bothered Feng. Any normal man would respond in some fashion. Monar, by being indifferent to the incident, meant he wasn't a normal man. And *that* was worrying.

With his guest's cold disinterest, Feng's first thought was to kill him. Anyone that impersonal, as impersonal as Feng himself was a danger. Yet, could a demon be killed? He was leery of Monar, that he might have occult powers—he implied as much—and could be an assassin hired by Lord Bunting. No, that wouldn't be it. Bunting desperately wanted those tea shrubs, so that didn't make sense. Then again, would Monar dispose of him once the shrubs were safe? If it wasn't for Feng's craving for the payoff Bunting promised, Monar would now be dead—if that was possible. Feng decided to wait until the shrubs were aboard. He would watch Monar closely and at the slightest indication, Feng's men would be ready to strike.

It was hard to keep his voice level, "What do you say, Monar, ready to talk business?"

Monar gave a half smile, "Before we start, Feng, Warfield didn't tell me your business. Just what is it—or shouldn't I inquire?"

"I've no problem with the question; I'm the private executioner for the Lord of Guangehou. I help him keep order throughout the foreigner's prefecture."

"And by private you mean?"

"I eliminate people who talk too much or the Lord feels could somehow become a problem. More tea, Monar?"

The arrangement between Lord Bunting and Archie Feng was guileless to write, difficult to accomplish. Originally, one-hundred adult and healthy leaf bearing black tea shrubs would be supplied. Feng decided to increase that to one-hundred fifty, for some reason he said it was a favor to Lord Bunting. Feng would also train Black Moon employees in the continuing care of the shrubs on Bunting's land in Darjeeling.

In return, Bunting would present Feng with an estate in India, financing for some commerce he might wish to establish, a Chinese junk, and a minor percentage of the net tea profits.

"I know that Lord Bunting will be fair, Monar."

Then came the difficult component, the removal of the shrubs from China. Feng said he would deliver them, roots in moist soil, bound in burlap to Gangmencum, a village on the northeast coast of Hainan Island, any time after the leaf gathering season—past June of this year. There must be a six-day notice, accurate within one day, so that there was time to remove the dormant shrubs and hope in that week they would not be missed. Six days was the time needed to transport them from the mainland to Hainan. Once they were missed, Feng said, it is inevitable that no matter how many people are killed; they will find who stole the shrubs and track them to Hainan.

"It is crucial you are on time, Monar, and we must have a fast ship."

"Feng, if we have a minute's head start, I'm certain the ship we'll have will never be caught."

"Then it is in your hands, Monar, all our lives depend on you being there. So, shall we have a shake of hands and have hot tea to seal it?"

"I'll shake on it, but no tea. I'm baffled, what's all this fuss over tea about? It's so damn bitter. If China was the sole source of whisky, I could understand the thievery."

25

30 April 1849, Portsmouth

THE *RAVEN* WAS READY in record time. Before the masts were stepped, sea trials for the engines proved exceptional. The estimated full powered, sprint speed of seventeen knots[22] more than pleased everyone involved. After those tests, the masts were stepped and rigged and with an entire complement of men, weaponry and provisions, she again proved sea worthy and ready for her final trial. Warfield, Lily and Evelyn accompanied JT on the final evaluation on the Solent. Warfield had made a few modest wagers with London, Southampton and Plymouth yachtsmen and hearing this, countless people lined the south shore, making their own bets with bookmakers that came from everywhere along England's southern coast. Over twenty-two knots, consistently for five minutes or more was the bet, and the stakes were high. but when the bookmaker's saw the ship, the odds narrowed.

A stiff breeze, following sea and a good captain was all the *Raven* needed. The course started at Limington in the west, then along the Solent separating the Isle of Wight from the mainland, through Spithead waters at the entrance of Portsmouth Harbor and then past Southsea to Selsey in the east. The black hulled clipper, its snow-white sails billowing, looked to be gliding over the whitecaps. The *Raven* whispered its song to the sea and under a press of sail in variable winds, for more than thirty miles, she peaked and held over twenty-four knots.[23]

---

[22] 19.5 MPH

[23] 21 MPH

It was felt by every sailor onboard the *Raven* could be good for more. Everyone involved with the ship was satisfied with the results of all his revisions. JT felt vindicated.

Three cheers for the *Raven* went up, *'The swiftest ship in the world*' was the catchphrase. Unofficially, of course.

With a feather in his cap, only one thing bothered Charles Mare—there wasn't a naval officer in sight. All part of the Navy's inept attempt at secrecy he then supposed.

From Portsmouth to London, the American sea Captain, John Thomas Graves was the talk of the moment. The Swiftest Man on the Ocean newspapers called him. Offers to buy the *Raven*, or for JT to speak at parties, or even simply appear at functions were requested. He became the must have guest at any formal event in the spring social calendar.

He turned them all down, except where Lord Bunting's reputation, the Black Moon Company, or Warfield's Shoppes could be enhanced.

Warfield was stimulated by the events unfolding. Business across the board in Europe, India, China, and the States continued on the upswing. The key to the Warfield's future was the positive news from Monar concerning Archie Feng's tea 'movement'. Warfield knew the expression Old King Cotton' from the States, some day he would be 'Old King Tea' of England—he knew it in his bones.

JT's modesty was honest; he wanted only to be gone to India and China and see Charlee. And this was the single factor where Warfield had failed. He and Lily had done everything short of ordering Evelyn and JT to marry and both had resisted.

JT wanted desperately to say he loved her. Yet that wasn't right to do so and then leave her to tell Charlee he loved someone else. What would Evelyn think of his doing that? What a mess he'd created for himself. He was forced to wonder—was he utterly mad or majestically stupid?

For Evelyn, JT was, if not stupid, then at the very least, maddening. His giving his damn word to that woman. Well, she had put up with enough. Did he really expect her to wait? In the end, she decided to leave. Captain one of the Black Moon merchant ships and be gone.

That's what she'd do. It was now Tuesday. Father said JT was leaving Thursday, the day after tomorrow, and he intended to say goodbye to her before he left. She'd leave right now, except she'd promised her attendance at tonight's affair to hostess, along with Lily, for Lord Bunting's social friends.

And, that would be *it*! This one last evening in London, tell father she was leaving, go by rail to Portsmouth and be gone—a goodbye from JT or not.

At this affair, JT was once again surrounded by the socially connected, all trying to get in a word. An American Yankee in British upper crust circles was singular and the fact he was the Swiftest Man on the Ocean added to his uniqueness.

Lord Bunting and Evelyn stood to the side, amused by JT's popularity. It hadn't changed him, he was anxious to get back to sea. Truly, they both admired him, in different ways, of course. Evelyn was about to tell her plan to Warfield when a couple rudely began pushing their way to JT, "Who's that brassy couple, father?"

"Oh, good Lord, it's Jack Woodley's son, Stewart. One of the endless Earls of DunDonald. Hopeless womanizer. That must be the latest paramour he's rumored to have. No wait, I correct myself, I believe he's engaged to this one, it will be his third marriage—that is, if he goes through with it."

They came within earshot. "…come on, Stewart, dear. I told you I knew him! JT, JT! Over here, it's me—*Charlee*!"

Warfield's and Evelyn's eyes went wide wondering if they'd heard right.

Hearing her voice, JT's jaw went slack.

Charlee overwhelmed the group, "JT, so nice to see you again! I *told* Stewart I knew you! Aren't you surprised? Imagine us winding up in London, England, at the same time. Oh, this is my *fiancé*, which means my husband-to-be—he's an *Earl*. "Stewart, this is John Thomas, JT to his friends. We knew each other in Savanna, in the States."

JT was in shock, first at seeing her, now this, "Your *fiancé*, Charlee? You're engaged…you?"

"Yes, silly. You're probably thinking of our silly little vow way back about seeing each other in the future—or something silly like that. We were so silly! I met Stew—I mean *Stewart*, he likes to be called Stewart—over here and he swept me off my silly little feet—so here I am, silly little me all engaged to a real English noble, an *Earl*!"

Evelyn turned to her father, both with the same thought. '*This* is why he was keeping his word—is he senseless?'

After his initial shock wore off, JT thought he was going to soar. She's engaged, Charlee's engaged! It was hard for his mind to absorb the fact he was no longer committed. His word meant nothing; written in sand, washed away with the tide. Gone. Thank Christ Almighty! Now, all he wanted was to leave and see Evelyn—but Warfield first.

"Charlee, so good to see you happy, I couldn't be happier for you. I'd like to stay and talk but I've a million things to do before I shove off. Please excuse me."

It was rude of him not to be introduced to Stewart, one of the many DunDonald Earls, but he saw Warfield and Evelyn and headed for them, "Would you please excuse me, Evelyn? I would like to speak to your father."

Warfield knew, "Well, JT, after seeing that spectacle, what could possibly be on your mind?"

With his most solemn mood, "I feel so stupid, Sir. But now I would like to ask you for permission to court your daughter."

"The answer is yes— and it's damn well about time!"

"I know it is, Warfield, it's just that…"

"I know, I know. Now stop fumbling and go find her."

Evelyn was nowhere to be found. It was going to happen; he was going to ask her. After all this time of hiding emotions, acting like no more than friends, it was going to *happen*.

How, she asked herself, should she react? She decided just before he found her.

He was amusingly formal, she thought.

"Lady Bunting…Evelyn, your father has given his permission for me to court you and it would please me if you will allow me the same."

"JT, you've put me through hell, you've made an emotional wreck of me, I'll admit it…hiding my feelings while you, you and your damn word of honor, kept us apart this whole time…"

He was shaken, "Evelyn, I'm sorry…I didn't mean …" He trailed off.

"You didn't mean what? Do you see how foolish, how absurdly crass, asinine, you've behaved. And for what? That immature little girl, that *silly* little girl I heard in there?"

JT tried to stop her, "Evelyn, she wasn't like that before…I…"

She held up her hand, "John Thomas, I'm looking at this objectively; I think it would be best for both of us if you simply sail off in the *Raven* the day after tomorrow as you planned and we meet again in a year or two. That is if you don't give another one of your sacred words to some *silly* little China doll first."

She fumed back into the room, apparently furious, leaving his dream in tatters.

Warfield was speaking with the UK Secretary of Foreign Affairs when he saw Evelyn return alone and flushed. Excusing himself from Mr. Peel, he hurried to his daughter.

"What's the matter with you? He must have asked you!"

"Yes, father, he asked."

"And you said yes."

"No, father, I said no."

"How could you say no?"

"Father, stay calm. Think. Think of all he has put me through, put *us* through. You know how you like your little revenges? Well, I'm your daughter; I'm having a little revenge!"

Warfield relaxed. She *was* his daughter, "I don't condone it, but I understand. But remember, I'm not going back to Portsmouth, so JT and I had our goodbyes. So however you play it dear, just keep in mind he shoves off this coming Thursday."

Before she left, he took her by the arm, "One more thing, Evelyn. Confucius once cautioned something like-*before you go and seek revenge, dig two graves*."

"I understand, father, yet I never knew you to follow that advice," she laughed, "and they'll be no need to start digging. I'm sure he'll get what he's after by tomorrow evening."

"Very well, I warned you. Just be careful that you haven't overplayed your hand, dear."

Flummoxed. That word, among others, certainly fit. Yes, he had been foolish, and yes, on the face of it how absurd he must look. Nonetheless, for Christ's sake, it was his word that was given, why won't she understand that?

JT left the gathering, ignoring everyone. The railway station was closed; only a watchman to tell him the night train to Portsmouth wouldn't depart until dawn.

"Then find me a carriage to take me there."

"Sixty miles, at this hour? That would be quite a cost, mate, it would indeed."

He sat back in the Hansom cab. It would be a long, uneven and dark journey. It befitted his mood.

As she thought JT would stay at her father's London home that evening, Evelyn overnighted at Brown's Hotel. She hadn't slept well, in truth, hardly at all. She'd begun to regret her stand and by dawn, decided to go to Warfield's house and see JT. One night, she felt, would be long enough to make him wait. Not wanting to go too soon or look anxious, she held off until ten in the morning.

Lily met Evelyn at the door. She knew what had transpired from Warfield, "He didn't stay here last night, Evelyn. So perhaps he went back down to Portsmouth."

"At that hour? Damn! Now what should I do? What do you think, Lily?"

"Well, it would seem there's a little pride swallowing due here, Evelyn. Wait a moment."

Lily came back with a Railroad timetable, "You've missed the morning train but there's another leaving Waterloo Station at one o'clock. Where's the *Raven* now?"

"She's at the Black Moon wharf in Portsea."

"Then you're all set. Take the train to the Portsea Extension and on down to Harbor Station, then the ferry across. I should think you'd be there by three or four in the afternoon at the latest. A day early and time to square things away."

"Thanks, Lily. May I take your carriage to the station?"

"Of course, Evelyn, good luck! Oh, and if there's a next time, don't be quite so vengeful."

Warfield came up after Evelyn dashed off, "Why didn't you say something to you daughter, dear?"

"Lily, I was afraid I would have reminded her she should have dug two graves."

Once Warfield explained, Lily agreed.

The train crept, that's all she could think. It wound its way southeast, seemingly to linger at every hamlet and byway until finally leaving behind the Fratton and Goods Stations. Passing Gun Wharf, the rail snaked to the dock and the train lastly hissed to a halt in a billow of steam at Harbor Pier.

Evelyn looked across the channel, past the Guard Ship and HMS *Victory* to the Black Moon wharf. Then, she frantically stared up and down the harbor.

It was no use, the Swiftest Ship in the World—the *Raven*, was gone.

HOUSE OF GRAVES

BOOK II

How often they are likened as straw
before the wind...
Like chaff swept away by a gale…
Job 22:18

CHAPTER ONE

18 May 1849. The Roaring Forties, Southern Ocean.

THE EXTREME CLIPPER SHIP *RAVEN* was the essence of man's quest for speed. Running before the wind, the two hundred-twenty foot, black hulled clipper carved the ten-foot swells, hurling sheets of seething blue water gloriously into the air.

Her American Captain, John Thomas Graves, had put his heart, soul and every trace of his expertise into designing this craft and she had returned his efforts by being the swiftest clipper ship in the world. With an experienced crew of former Royal Navy sailors, they had wrung every knot out of her on the shakedown voyage from Portsmouth, England and under Cape Agulhas, South Africa.

Here, where the mighty South Atlantic collides with the typhoon prone South Indian Ocean, the *Raven* well proved her physical power by weathering the ravaging storms of the misleadingly named Cape of Good Hope.

With the gales of the Roaring Forties and the oceans great rollers pushing her headlong south and east of Madagascar, she would soon haul northeast into the expanse of the Indian Ocean, and point up for India's southern point.

Captain John Thomas Graves, despite sailors all about him, had finally found time, time to find some solitude. In his aft cabin he set his feet on the carriage of the Long-nine cannon and stared without seeing into the *Raven's* wake.

"Organize your thoughts, you damn fool!" He blurted out and looked around—no one heard him.

Had he overreacted to Evelyn's taunts about his keeping his word to Charlee? God, what a fool he must have looked, when Evelyn and Lord Warfield saw how childish Charlee was and, of all things, she was *engaged*—engaged to some blue-blooded fool of an

Earl while he, JT, was honoring his word to see her by the end of the year.

Since he had given his word, he was prepared to chance everything offered by Lord Warfield to honor it and—great Christ—only to have Charlee show up engaged, making fun of their pact. *Silly,* she had called it—*silly*!

Then afterward, it proved another silly—no—*stupid* step to take when he idiotically rushed to court Evelyn who, in truth, was the one he anxiously desired.

After the spectacle he made of himself, no wonder Evelyn was angry. No, maybe not so much angry, perhaps hurt was the better word and she hid it with anger. Could someone get over hurt? Of more importance, could *she*?

Should he have stayed, he kept wondering. If he had waited, given her time to…to what? He'll never know now. Instead of understanding, he was headstrong and had fled to Portsmouth, roused his crew from their lodgings and sailed off just after dawn, a day early. Like some embittered, jilted lover would do. No—more like a naïve, witless boy.

JT didn't know that Lady Evelyn, vexed with him over Charlee, decided on a bit of vengeance for his slighting her in the past and meant it only as a brief put-down before granting his request to court her. She then regretted her taunt and hurried to Portsmouth Harbor knowing the *Raven* would not leave until the following day—as was planned.

Unfortunately for both parties, the *Raven* was gone.

Well, *to hell with it;* was JT's fleeting thought, yet that was it, fleeting. At twenty-seven he was bound to a relentless mental hurt, an appalling sense of loss. She was gone.

For days he wallowed in self-pity until—and he didn't quite know at what point it happened—it came to him that he had to stop and at least *act* the part of skipper, instead of thrashing about like some gasping cod.

Still, at long last—when coming topside one morning to the sound of 'sail ho'—he half wished it was some Arab corsair's ship where he and the crew could let off steam with some excitement and test themselves in seamanship and gunnery. Then again, the last time that had happened, it took the United States Navy to save Evelyn, him, Monar and what was left of their crews. He soon rid himself of the wish.

So it was just as well the westbound ship's home port was Southampton, leaving JT and his crew disappointed. Yet it was an opportunity for him to pass over two envelopes; one to Lord Warfield Bunting stating how brilliantly the ship behaved and the other letter addressed to Lord Warfield's daughter, Lady Evelyn.

After that, John Thomas was done with it. He could do nothing more than have hope about her now and there was an assignment to offload Warfield's Manchester steel railroad track at Bori Bunder, India, for the inauguration of the Great India Peninsula Railway. It was another plum for Lord Warfield; the British East India Company paid for his steel, transported on his ships, all for his new investment.

The chart markers John Thomas required were picked up; Reunion Island, then Mauritius, formerly the French islands of Ile De France and Ile Bourbon, taken by the British in 1810 to finally eradicate the marauding French Corsairs.

After the long run to the Maldives, they labored north, upwind, along the west coast to Bombay and Bori Bunder.

After offloading, they hauled around the southern tip of India, passed Devil Point and on into the Gulf of Mannar, the strait between India and Ceylon. After standing well off the fringing reefs to port, the *Raven* cleared the Palk Strait, transiting into the Bay of Bengal and set course to the various mouths of the Ganges River and Calcutta. There he would meet up with Monar.

Monar, his massive body easily seen towering above the Indian dock workers, hurried down the wharf.

Holding out his hand, JT gripped it firmly, "Well, my good friend, how are you? You're looking pretty relaxed."

"Relaxed? Well, JT, compared to the way you look, I probably *do* look relaxed. What's the matter with you?"

"That can wait; tell me what you've been up to."

"First, let me look at your ship. I knew it had to be you, the moment she cleared the point everyone looked up. Damn, the *Raven's* beautiful, JT. Is she as fast as she looks to be?"

"Aye, I'd put money on her to beat anything afloat."

Monar smiled inwardly, the *Raven* was going to need every bit of her quickness for what he and Lord Warfield Bunting had in mind.

JT continued, "And another thing, with this crew Warfield supplied me, I'd give odds on her. They're former Royal Navy and believe me; they know what they're about."

Monar was half-listening, already knowing that was Warfield's intention when hiring the crew. Yet, at this moment, he was counting the guns. Twenty-four, thirty-six pounders and obviously the latest in exploding shell cannon. All the better for his plan—*if* he could get JT to go along.

"But the guns, how on God's cruel earth did the navy supply you with them?"

JT couldn't help laugh out loud, "If the Admiralty ever knew how Warfield hoodwinked and threatened naval officers into building me this ship they'd go bonkers."

"He does twist the rules past the point of breaking, yet he has the nerve and gets away with it—that's how he succeeds."

"That, brains and money, Monar."

Monar closed the subject, "His brains and nerve brought the money."

"True. So, back to what you've been up to."

"Christ, JT, it's been one trip after another. All over South Asia. To China, Singapore, Saigon, Bangkok..."

"You learning anything?"

"Sure, but the main thing I've learned is that our benefactor has a tiger by the tail—as they say over here."

"How about a brief overview, for now."

"I'll tell you, but brief will be difficult. Just take everything he told us at Blackwood Abbey about his empire and double it. His Resident here, Ashley Ealing, has filled me in and said that Warfield is known as a Nabob over here and from what I'm told, a Nabob is an important person who made his wealth in the Indian subcontinent."

"That's to be pretty much the story I should think."

"Yes, but Ealing said that it also could mean a partner in the East India Company with dubious ethics."

"Well, once again, that could fit Warfield."

"That doesn't bother you?"

"Frankly? Standing here on the deck of the finest clipper ship in the world that didn't cost me one penny, makes it difficult to condemn him."

"I'm glad to hear you've eased your standards a bit."

At JT's failure to respond, Monar continued on about Warfield, "And it's not just his shipping empire. Here, I'll give you an example; he has his own army by the Shagi Fort near the Khyber hills along the Afghanistan, India border. They're called Lord Bunting's Brigands…"

"That doesn't surprise me either; why should it? For one man to create the domain he has, I suppose he needs an army to safeguard it—especially in these territories."

"That's a given up on the Afghan, India border when the product is opium which, in this region is like gold."

"Huh—it means that much here?"

"Not here, JT. Opium comes from the poppy fields next door in Afghanistan, but it's not used much in India. It's China where the western nations use it as underground currency to buy goods, and I'll include Warfield and particularly the British East India Company. The Chinese customs agents are all thieves. Really, it all started with the BEIC. It's just like I saw in Limehouse on the London docks, they hooked the Chinese on opium because the Brits didn't want to pay in silver for Chinese product so they're becoming a nation of addicts…"

“You’re serious about this, Monar, you’re sure?”

“Damn sure. And the British Government gives more than just a wink and a nod. It’s the old ‘can’t see it from my house’—making believe doesn’t involve them. And not just them; all the western governments have a hand in carving up China, or the Celestial Kingdom as they call it. But the Brits got the upper hand. I’m telling you JT, someday, there’s going to be hell to pay if all those Chink warlords unite.”

“This Ealing fellow is giving you quite the lesson.”

“He sure is, and let me tell you, the East India Company, of which our Warfield is a principal, controls and I mean this—*controls* most of the India trade here as well as in China—with the connivance of the Brit Crown.”

“How do they do it? I mean that little tin pot island controlling countries that are ten, twenty times their size?”

“I don’t know, I really don’t—other than their sea power,” Monar laughed, “or something’s in their blood.”

“Well, my friend, I guess we’ve simply got to go about our work and not worry about the rest.”

Monar laughed again, “I’m not telling you this so you can worry about it. I just want to give you background so you’re not surprised at what the BEIC and Warfield mean around here. In India, the British used the East India Company’s own army, to win a war last March against the Sikh Empire at Gujarat and they annexed the Punjab. In China, back in ‘42 and now ‘49 they won the Opium War against the Sikhs, Qing Dynasty, and the Canton Merchants. The resulting Nanking Treaty with the Qing’s gave the British five ports and the Island of Hong Kong. Brits have beaten out the Dutch and French in the whole subcontinent and where the Brits are, the Brits control. But, a note of caution, the Qing’s are rickety and that could be testy.”

Monar’s brief background failed to include the dozens of small and good-sized wars, the great number of dead, and the weakening of the Indian caste system which, whether good or bad, was dependent on whose ox was being gored. And there were more wars and goring to come.

In the time it took JT to digest most of this information, Monar decided to slip in a casual remark that could lead to the subject he wanted broached, "Except tea, JT, that's where China has them over a barrel or rather a tea chest— by charging outrageously for it."

JT responded exactly as Monar sought, "Why's that? There seems to be enough tea in England."

"That's because of the circles you travel in. You know, the highbrow type can afford it, but not the lower classes—or like us, the middlebrow types."

"It's that expensive? It's only plant leaves and the tin it comes in must be cheap, so why the high cost?"

"The why is because China has a monopoly on what's considered the best tea and charges a fortune and that makes the British bleed gold and silver or turn to opium.

"No other country grows it?"

"From what I've learned, a few others, but not near as good a leaf and the Qing's kill anyone who tries to get their tea plants. They did the same thing with silk generations ago; kill any person after the silk worms. So you can be sure of that, it's been tried and it's happened."

Monar wished he hadn't said it quite so bluntly. Nevertheless, JT was disinterested in silk, yet bothered by China's tea dominance and demand for precious metals for something that came from a plant. This was exactly what he wanted JT to feel, but Monar then blundered, "This is how Warfield felt about it when he made plans to…"

"Wait a minute, Monar! Hang on, you're up to something here—you and *Warfield* are up to something. What do you mean, he *made plans to…*? You deceiver! Trying to hoodwink me, leading me down the garden path?"

Embarrassed, Monar could only nod and attempt an explanation, "I apologize, JT, I should have known you couldn't be fooled for long…"

"More sweet-talk!"

Yet by now, JT was laughing and it was but a few seconds before Monar joined in.

"All right, all right damn it, JT, I could have been a touch less subtle and bit more direct but this is important for us and I wanted you to see the need."

"Important for us and the need for what?"

"The need for us, you and me, of course with Warfield's backing, to borrow some tea plants."

"And by 'borrow', you mean…"

"Steal, two hundred and fifty of them.

2

12 May 1849, Blackwood Abbey, Landport, England.

WHEN EVELYN, FOR HER own good reason had, in irate but bogus words, told John Thomas that he would *not* be welcome to court her, he had abruptly left. Then, when she went to Portsmouth Harbor to apologize, he had sailed off early. Bewildered at her blunder, she had departed—or rather fled—to her father's estate in Cornwall to quietly admit her foolishness. Failing to find a solution to her self-inflicted wounding, she returned to Blackwood Abbey.

Lord Warfield Blackwood Bunting, his companion, Lillian Fields and his daughter, soon found time to sit down together and reason out the challenging position into which Evelyn had placed herself.

"I told you before father; I only *acted* angry when I told him not to court me—it was only for a little revenge. It was what he deserved, you know that, and I've seen you do the same thing to people."

"Yes, but I know when and when not to do it. To do that sort of thing to JT, knowing he had to honor his word to that foolish little girl, was the wrong thing to do. I told you that at the time. And, for nothing more than to hurt him, you told him that perhaps you would see him when he returned, that is 'if he didn't give his sacred word to some little China doll first' was uncalled for. That was so unlike you Evelyn, He's a decent man. I'm at a loss for words."

Warfield definitely wasn't at a loss for words and Evelyn had never heard him to be quite so troubled at her remarks to JT. That he had wanted her to fall in love with JT, was a given, yet she could see there was something else going on, something he was keeping from her.

Well, that didn't matter at the moment. What did matter was her next move—and she stated it flat out.

"I'm going to India…"

Warfield put his hand up to stop her next words, "You are not. Mainly because he may not be there."

"What do you mean? I thought you said that's where he was going. You up to something father?"

"I'm not necessarily up to anything, I'm simply saying JT may be in India or he may be in China. Nothing more nor less."

"Then if he's not going to India, I'll go to China."

"You'll do nothing of the sort and I'll tell you why. I'll be going to India myself. I'll take you with me."

Both women were surprised and Lily spoke up, "Really, Warfield? Then count me in as well."

"Lily, my going was a good possibility, yet due to Evelyn's impatience and being so hellfire bent on going, I think its best we all go. I've a project started over there that could need my help getting off the ground."

"Another project, Warfield, what now?"

"Oh, just a little something. Something that might make JT and Monar quite wealthy."

«»

"Steal, Monar—two hundred-fifty tea plants?"

JT's gaze was fixed on Monar and his words, "Well, JT, I could say *purloin* if it would make you feel any better."

JT started to comment, Monar cut him off, "Just hold on, let me finish. Warfield has tried to buy, rent or whatever it took to acquire Chinese tea plants for years, but they've refused any transaction. I just told you, it's gold or silver and that makes it too expensive for the average person. The Brits love their tea and all Warfield wants is to end the monopoly and bring the price down so the lower classes can afford it."

"Right and help Warfield make more money."

"So Warfield creates it so that anyone can afford to have a little enjoyment and he makes a little money—when did you decide to turn your nose up to profit?"

A memory struck JT at this moment. He recalled the workers at Mare's shipyard this past winter, during the building of the *Raven*. Huddled around they were, shivering by the fires, with hands around mugs of steaming tea as they sipped and shivered. Likewise, he recalled how the workers kept pouring more hot water on the same soggy tea leaves because fresh tea leaf was too expensive. And here was Monar, laying out the reason.

"What's Warfield's idea?"

Monar laid out Lord Warfield's plan. His contact would get the plants; take them to an island off China. There a ship would carry them to India where they would be grown.

JT couldn't prevent a grin, "Sounds simple to me. Someone hasn't tried this?"

"Others have, didn't have much luck."

"Not among the living I presume."

"That would be a good bet; the Qing Dynasty doesn't put a high value on life."

"Why'd they fail?"

"No plan—but mainly, they didn't have a fast ship."

"Ah, I see it now, Monar, the *Raven* is the answer."

"Correct, but I'll hasten to say Warfield didn't think of her until the end of last year when you convinced him she would be fast. However, he was committed to some plan whether you agreed or not—but he wants us in, and I am."

"Well, before we go any further, I've a letter for you from Warfield; let's see if he's changed his mind."

Monar, private.

Monar, hope you are well and I'm going to assume you have convinced JT to agree to our plan or soon will. The ship is ideal. JT's done a wonderful job,

Tell Ashley Ealing to prepare a few acres at my Darjeeling estate in the Bengal for 'Fruit' trees. Do not give any indication otherwise.

Now, you know where the gold and silver is and this will be the procedure.

I'll assume you have contacted Archie Feng by now and made him ready. Go back to Canton for a cargo of tea and lacquer ware. Pay in silver, not opium. That will reduce suspicion with Chinese Customs or at least the higher ups.

Contact Archie, he always said he needed a week to acquire the plants. Tell him everything is in place and make a schedule—time and place—to meet. If he requires a week, then before the transfer, some of that time can be used to on-load the *Raven* with the 'legal' tea chests. If that does not use up enough time, take the *Raven* out of sight of land until Archie's ready. You may have to dump the lacquer ware at sea to make room for the plants. That can't be helped. For the rest, use your wits.

And now, the last bit of information. I'm coming to India, but not by way of the Horn. I'll take ship to Alexandria, Egypt, then to Cairo, then land travel across Egypt-around a hundred miles I should think- to Suez at the top of the Red Sea. That should reduce my travel time to Madras to plus/minus fifty days. I want you to send a good Black Moon ship to Suez with instructions to wait for me or until they hear otherwise-no matter how long.

After you acquire the plants, we'll meet at Fort St. George, Madras, on India's east coast. Archie should be with you and tell him our agreement is in place and I will have the monetary portion of it with me.

Monar, success in this endeavor will prove to be the most important and valuable of my career and shares of that success will flow to you and JT.

We are going to market the Culture of Tea to the masses here, Europe, India, the Aussies and US States-in fact, why not the world? Believe-we're on the cusp of great events.

Good luck to you both.

Lord Warfield Blackwood Bunting

One more thing to the both of you-be extremely careful around Archie-he's too clever by half. Also destroy this letter immediately after it is fully understood. wbb

Monar handed JT the letter, waiting until it was read.

"Well, JT, your thoughts?"

"Warfield assumed I'd be with you on this."

"Yes."

"Interesting. Ashley Ealing is his Resident for India and Warfield doesn't want him know any of this?"

"Correct, and he is our China Resident as well, though there are other, shall I call them, sub-agents in both countries who he manages."

Monar was leery; JT appeared unconcerned about anything he was being told.

"Whose is this 'Archie' fellow?"

This wasn't what was troubling JT, but Monar answered him, "I'll give it to you straight, Archie is the person who will get the plants and deliver them to Hainan Island off the coast of southern China. His real name is Archibald Feng Yünan-shan and he's the leader of a Society called the Empire of the Sleeping Dragon, some degenerate gang I imagine. He's also the executioner for the Mayor of Canton. I've met him; he's not one to be trifled with."

“He’s an assassin? Is Warfield aware of this?”

“I presume so, there’s not much he doesn’t know.”

JT made no comment. Monar burned the letter, paused, and then asked, “What’s up with you, JT? You seem detached, indifferent to all this. What happened back in England? It’s got to be something to do with Evelyn. Let’s talk that out first so I know what in hell is going on.”

JT wavered, then recognizing it would eventually come out. He loved Evelyn he said, but had given his word to Charlee. Then Charlee arrived in London, silly and engaged. JT’s eagerness in now having the right to court Evelyn was clumsy and then the disaster of her refusal dumbfounded him, he lost himself and fled in the *Raven*.

Monar listened, silent to the end. He also had feelings for Evelyn, but knew them hopeless and so was honest when asked what he thought, “JT, plain and simple, you’re a damn fool, at least where *that* women is involved. You should have stayed there, put up with the verbal battering—which, I might add, sounds like you richly deserved—and then got on with your lives, *together*.”

“All right, let’s say I agree I should have stayed. But what can I do now, so far away over here?”

“There’s little you can do. She said perhaps in a year or two when you returned to England she’d see you—although her saying, ‘if you’d not given your sacred word to some ‘China doll’, was amusing. But anyway, you wait, wait and complete your commitments in India and maybe, just maybe, you’ll grow up here. I can offer other advice but you’re not going to take it, so why bother.”

“I’m glad you find her comment amusing.”

“For Christ’s sake JT, you need either a mental or physical kick in the arse to stop your whining and I’ll gladly supply both. Otherwise, look in a mirror and decide what you’re going to do with your future.”

JT had thought he’d worked things out on the passage to India, but evidently that was proving wrong. Yet he came to understand it wasn’t solely Evelyn bothering him. He wanted to be a different person, in a different place, a different time. That time before his father became a slaver to save his estate and family, yet also to maintain his loftier position in life and the world around him and more importantly, his standing in Salem along with the other admired captains. JT had known that life. The son of Captain Richard Melville Graves meant something then. The secure, assured, preordained world that his grandfather and father had created, he assumed he'd live it—everyone thought so. Yet look at it now, everything was lost. His mother was gone, to where, no one knew and his older brother Jason in a home, no longer right in the head. Possessed by demons, Monar claimed, and who could possibly dispute Monar.

The hurricane had caused all that havoc in one day; turned his father into a slaver and caused the rift between them. Now, father was dead, too late to reconcile. JT's world was torn apart. With the Graves' last clipper, the *Golden Raven*, he and Monar struck out on their own only to see her destroyed by a Russian warship in the Black Sea, off Sevastopol in the Crimea, of all the damnable places to be for Christ's sake. How did that happen? Lady Evelyn, of course. To save her. Even back then, he would have given his life and his ship for her and, despite her hurtful words, he still would. Infatuation, then enchantment that turned to love, that turned into…loss. What comes after, despair?

Thanks to her father, Lord Warfield, JT owned an up-to-the-minute, sail and twin screw, steam powered clipper, the fastest in the world they believed, and he knew. He'd been peculiarly lucky, so many people have died around him and Monar and Evelyn.

"Why did we live and so many died." He spoke aloud, "Well, it's time to put all this behind…"

"For Christ's sake, JT—get over it."

Monar had come topside from below, "I'm beginning to lose faith in you—blast it! What's done is done and past. You've the future ahead of you—make something of it or you'll wind up like your brother."

JT held up his hand, "Hold on, leave Jason out of this! I was about to get going when you jump on me."

"Jump on you? I should have smacked you over the head with a belaying pin and tossed you to the fishies. But if you mean what you've said, then well and good. I'm tired of doing everything around here as well as babying you while you wail away at the moon."

It hadn't been as bad as Monar indicated, but JT's melancholy did engulf him at times and that angered Monar. It was over Evelyn—of course, but Monar also came to realize JT's past had caught up and near overwhelmed him. Now, if as he said, he was coming out of his dark moods, then the nexus, the bond forged between them would continue. Monar smiled to himself, he would help JT through it. Much had been done and soon enough there would be danger lurking. And that required a clear mind.

JT unexpectedly asked, "Where's this Madras place Warfield mentioned he'd meet us?"

"Well, at long last showing some interest. You sailed past it on your way to Calcutta. Turns out it's the first outpost the British founded in India and a not too clever a choice at that."

"All right, I'll ask—why?"

"It's a seaport without a port; plenty of waves though. You and cargo, ride shallow draft native boats called massulahs in on the surf—there's some crazy rides."

"That doesn't make sense."

"Regrettably, no one pointed that out to the British."

Ashley Ealing, Warfield's Resident for India and China was suspicious. Monar's partner and friend had come from England and, just as evident, from Lord Warfield. This JT person had seemed in poor spirits for quite some time, yet now, now the two were in constant discussion and Ealing felt he was intentionally kept uninvolved in their meetings. There was no sense in pretending, they were thick as thieves, plotting something, and, it was a good bet Lord Warfield was implicated or rather behind it all.

Ealing had seen JT hand Monar a letter from the Lord, and then, after JT's spirits improved, they were often pouring over a chart of the South China Sea for some undisclosed reason. The Resident would have loved to see it.

Ealing, had only been told to go to Archie Feng's estate in East Bengal, and see to it that a few acres were cleared and prepared for 'fruit trees'.

So, what was going on and what did he know? Precious little. There was a letter from Warfield that he couldn't read, a new person close to Monar and now he, Ealing, being ordered by Monar to clear land for trees.

But Ealing did know something more. He knew, before Monar's friend arrived, back when Ealing and Monar were in China, that Monar had a letter from Lord Warfield to Archie Feng Yü-Shan, and Feng was notorious, known to do the Mayor of Canton's biding, including assassination and, for that matter, every other scheme that brought him riches.

These thoughts bumped around in Ealing's head until one more piece of past knowledge was recalled to almost complete the puzzle. Lord Warfield once groused to Ealing that he was fed up with Chinese demands of gold or silver for tea. He was fed up as well with Chinese Customs agent's demand of opium for tea. Someday he was *'going to beat the slant eyed yellow men at their own game.'* Or so he said.

And the final piece for Ealing? It took only a moment to evoke the sight of the *Raven*, sleek, fast, steam driven and over twenty cannon. Put together, far too much there for a common merchant ship.

"Lord Warfield hasn't assembled all this for fruit trees." Ealing whispered into the darkness, "It's shrubs he's after, *tea shrubs*. Now, the question comes—how do *I* benefit from this?"

Ashley Ealing knew the answer—all he had to do was figure out Warfield's scheme and get ahead of it.

3

15 July, 1849 West of the Spratly Islands

THE CLIPPER CARVED into the South China Sea. After passing to the lee of the Paracel Islands, the *Raven's* eyes turned north by northwest to scope out the eventual objective of their quest—Hainan Island.

Ghosting along the coast, under sail in light air, they followed their chart past Changpi Port, then a tiny village called Yimencun, and finally the cavity of Gaolong Bay.

"This is where Warfield expects the plants, Monar?"

"The tentative plan calls for us to meet Archie Feng at Gangmencum, but the chart says that town there on the point is Nangangcum, so I'm not sure what's where."

"Maybe it's a misspelling, but whether or not, we'd better get it damn well straightened out with your Archie Feng when we see him in Canton. Right now there could be prying eyes, so let's not show too much interest in the area."

Monar scanned the deck, "You're still concerned about Ealing being aboard, eh?"

"Aye, of course, yet he said the Registered Agent for the Black Moon Line must be present and sign off on shipping documents, so as I said, we had to bring him."

"You still believe him, about the Resident thing?"

"I told you, I couldn't argue the point. It would cause him to get suspicious and we couldn't take that chance."

"He's probably already suspicious, he's no fool."

"You know, Monar, I still wonder why Warfield didn't want him to know our plans."

"True, I wish he'd told us. He said only that Ealing was former Royal Navy and after that with the French East India faction and then Black Moon for twelve years, but we're to keep him ignorant of our intentions, that's orders."

As he watched Ealing conversing with some of the crew, JT couldn't come up with anything more, "Well, you haven't seen him when you've prowled around at night and he's given us no hint that he's up to something, so we'll simply have to keep our eyes peeled."

"What I think *he's* up to is finding out what *we're* up to and if he does, he won't be with the Black Moon Line long enough to make it thirteen years, JT."

"I've a thought, Monar, when there's a chance, casually ask some of the crew what he's been talking to them about. Perhaps we can get an inkling of what he's questioned them on if anything special, because I'm getting less and less of a good feeling about him."

"I follow you, but at least the crew can't help him, they don't know anything."

"And keep it that way. However, when we make a run for the shrubs, watch him closely."

"He gives trouble, trust me; he'll be deep sixed."

For his part, Ealing was still developing his strategy. The crew was of no use in confirming his beliefs, but that didn't matter, there were too many other signs to ignore. Monar and his friend were keeping him in the dark, but why was there no opium loaded to trade for the tea chests? Without opium, they must have gold or silver aboard, still, to prove that he'd have to snoop about, although that damn Monar never seemed to sleep and wandered the ship at all hours.

That needn't stop Ealing from presuming coin was aboard and go from there, yet where was the *there* to go?

He could be sure the *Raven's* cruising close offshore past Nangmencu and the Gaolong Bay was no sightseeing tour. So if stealing tea shrubs was the goal, it would then follow that the Gaolong Bay area could be the pickup point. Tea wasn't grown on Hainan Island however, so, how would it get there? It took but little conjecture before the solution sprang to mind. Of course! The last time they were in China, Monar had met with that shrewd, cunning bastard, Archibald Feng Yün-Shan—he and his Sleeping Dragon Society assassins. So, Ealing believed, Monar was the emissary from Lord Warfield to Archie, to tea, to Hainan.

"It's coming together," Ealing reasoned aloud, "but when and how? I still need more to go on to make it all jell and worthwhile for me."

«»

Lord Warfield Bunting and Lily watched Evelyn closely. The Black Moon merchantman, the *Christina Louise*, was only now passing the vicinity of the Moroccan Coast where Evelyn's ship, *Vixen,* had been stormed by hundreds of corsairs bent on the death or enslavement of her, JT, Monar and the remainder of her crew. It was only at the miraculous, ultimate moment when the arrival of the United States warship *Cumberland* saved their lives—and those who were left.

Her memories flooded back; she and JT fighting to protect Monar's sides while the towering Negro, with his bolo, cut down every man within his arc. He owned the deck where he stood and dared anyone to enter—many trying, and failing. Their lives should have ended there, for they had chosen death before slavery. Their lives should…

"Evelyn, you all right?"

Tears filled her eyes as her father took her to him, "Is this where it happened—those God cursed bloody pirates?"

She nodded, too choked up to speak.

"I've never seen you this way, dear. I'm afraid I haven't appreciated the close thing it was for you."

When she could speak, "It's difficult to put into words, father. Have you ever seen death? I mean in the face, eye to eye?"

Warfield *had* seen death eye to eye, more than once. Momentarily back to his youth, in a coal vein under the North Sea, seeing the sun only one day a week. And, the blind donkeys—ah indeed, again the donkeys. In the mines they *never* saw the sun. Yes, he had looked death in the eye, only in another form; the slow lingering death revealed in the eye of a blind donkey. In that one moment, the coal dust coughing boy glimpsed his existence—and escaped to sea.

Once he achieved growth in his self-made world, he returned to Newcastle on Tyne to find his family. Mother gone from exhaustion, father and friend Jock dead from black lung and siblings condemning him for leaving. Jock had once said the soot from the mill made 'even the moon turn black' and that had stuck in Warfield's memory…the Black Moon.

He rallied to the moment, "Sorry, dear, me mind wandered. Must be getting older than I thought. I feel terrible you had to go through that frightful time."

Evelyn had seen him shiver and observed he said '*me* mind'. He'd unconsciously reverted to his poor Scots roots. It told a lot about his past, yet that was something of which he not ever spoke, and she shifted to another matter.

"So, now that we're both back in the present, father, you've told me Alexandria is next and then some foolishness about going by camel to Suez on the Red Sea and after that on to India," she looked intently at him, "but what you still haven't told me is *why* we're doing this trek. Let me be correct; I know *I'm* doing this to see JT, but why you?"

"What I've planned should be done by now, or will be shortly, so it's harmless to tell you. I'm taking a few tea shrubs from China and planting them in Archie's estate."

Both women were brought up short. Lily was intent, questioning, "*Taking* Warfield? It's prohibited to *take* even a tea twig in China, and dangerous, you well know that!"

And then Evelyn understood, "*This* is what you have JT and Monar up to—isn't it? You've got them involved in this thievery."

"Now dear, a piddling bit of pilfering will hardly be noticed and it's going to make them very rich."

"The devil it won't be noticed! You're sending them on a dreadful errand, father. Get me on that damn camel!"

«»

Hainan Island was in their wake, their eyes set toward the still distant Pearl River and Canton. On midnight Watch, JT's mind wandered. Each passing wave brought them closer to the start of their mission. Thievery. There was no other word for it. Oh, one could call it pilfering, taking something without consent or unsanctioned, yet it still came down to theft.

Monar saw him, could almost read his mind, thought after thought. The straight arrow, JT, was wondering how all this had happened, his being in on the attempt to steal tea shrubs in China. Monar couldn't help but smile, pleased as he went below to roam in the night along the ship's ribs.

JT's thoughts were also on Monar, Monar and his ability to influence, to convince him to believe they were doing something good for the lower classes. Steal from Chinese overlords to help the British minions.

He stared at his reflection on the glass of the compass rose, "It's not right—you know that. No matter what face you put on it, *it is robbery*."

He looked about, no one heard. Yet, there was something else troubling him. Deeper, darker, Monar. Yes, Monar's *guiding* him, convincing him this was the right thing to do. No, guiding wasn't the word. What was it that he once heard an old, carney Tarot mystic mumble as a patron departed? Soul Stealer? Soul Snatcher? It was something like that. Is that what was happening—could Monar do that? He did have skills, faculties; normal people never even gave thought to. Get away from that, Monar would never do that to him. Yet still, be on your mettle.

So now, he had to keep one eye on Monar and the other on Ealing. For the first time in ages it seemed, JT erupted with a laugh. With one eye on each, how was he ever going to find his *own* way?

And again his mind gyrated. Was all this simply an overactive mind—because of Evelyn? Was he ready for any scheme, any harebrained scheme that came along to get her out of his thoughts and Monar, quite innocently, happened to come along with this plan?

0200. He eased his heading starboard, two points, ordered the forward lookout to stay awake and went back to rummaging—he'd keep his wits around Monar, and never stop thinking of Evelyn.

He sensed a shift in the wind from the east. Strange, he thought. A squall coming from the east, onshore, pushing heavy black clouds, weather billows ahead of it. If he didn't know better it could be…no that was doubtful. Monar said the hurricane or what the east called the typhoon season didn't even begin until late October and this was only July. It's a squall he thought, yet as a precaution gave orders to shorten sail and reef the top-gallants. They'd be well up the Pearl River before any difficult weather hit—at least he thought that. Then again, he didn't know Asian weather.

JT tapped the barometer, the 'sorcerer's' mercury had lowered. His concern increasing, he turned the helm over to the second mate and walked to the taffrail. If there'd been daylight, he'd have seen it more quickly; the waves, formerly rolling west, were now breaking east into west. The sea was being drawn away from shore!

A depression had formed in the Sulu Sea in the Western Pacific Ocean and, racing eastward, rotated into an early tropical typhoon that gathered fury each league before thundering into the South China Sea.

JT felt it coming in his bones, "Chief! Call the men to quarters! Men aloft! Into the yards—reef all sail! Tell Chief Engineer to raise steam and await further orders. Send men down to secure any cargo from shifting and get lifelines up."

The Chief had barely time to shout 'Aye, aye, Captain' and for JT to bring the *Raven* into the wind when the unseen storm struck, shook *Raven* the like a ragdoll and staggered her dead in her tracks. Men, scarcely awake, ran topside and were scattered along the deck, clutching for any fixed object at hand as the clipper yawed side to side. The wind rose to a screech, tearing at their clothing as they struggled into the rigging against the sting of the rain.

Monar stumbled from below, "How bad is it?"

"We'll be lucky not to lose more than sails! Tell the Chief to cut away anything they can't reef, then go forward…I'm blind, can't see afore in this blasted torrent…whosever's there tell them to time our rise to cut away the jib and flying jib." JT turned to the helmsman, "I'll take the wheel. There's smoke from the stack, use the speaking tube to order the engineer for steam and full revs."

JT could feel each time the bow went under and see the mass of seething foam pouring over the foredeck, "Master Gunner! Double lash the guns and the gun ports! Three ports…broken loose…we're taking in damn heavy seas. Get the pump gangs working...if you haven't already."

The *Raven* started to yaw more heavily while her beak thrust deep into each towering sea, to rise, shake the rollers off and plunge again. The masts and yards held fast but rapidly stripped bare. What couldn't be reefed was cut away or left tattered canvas—the deck littered with sheets, rigging, fractured wood and struggling men as wave after wave cleared the gunwales of the vessel and surged into every fractured hatch and vent.

The storm raged into the night and JT could feel the ship heavy on the wheel and knew water was rising in the bilge, making the *Raven* sluggish. Flashes of lightening defined the masts and rigging swaying, unearthly phantoms in each lightening flash, while fearsome seas mounted high above the flanks of the ship, then crashed down onto her deck.

Controlling his nerves and with Monar helping against the tug of the wheel and rudder, JT watched the crew. Showing dread, they wondered their fate, yet stood fast. They'd seen storms before, truly not this appalling, but they knew *Raven* was a stout ship.

At 0600, squinting into the breaking waves, Monar pointed out a vessel coming abaft the stern. Through the sheets of rain, they saw the ship was dismasted, on her beam ends, driven forward by the gusts and current.

"We can't help her, Monar—she's adrift. If we come about…we could broach in a trough…we've taken so much water on...the *Raven* wouldn't...right herself with all the iron and water we're carrying. I've my crew to think..."

JT stopped himself, looking to his men. Anxiety enveloped them, yet they were transfixed on the derelict.

"All right then damn it, I'll try for her lee!"

Monar took JT's shoulder, motioning to the ship, a whaler, whose name they could read, *The Loyal Friend,* out of New Bedford, Mass. Her deck awash, barren of life and dory's, the main and foremasts trailed in the water, and each thunderous wave was dragging her down by the head.

They tried time and time again yet it was futile. The menacing squalls seemed to increase.

"Tell the men to keep an eye peeled for any life and I'll give her another go."

Yet before he could, the sea poured into her breached hatches. *The Loyal Friend* foundered and slipped under.

An opaque gale-slashed sky exposed an uncertain dawn with still no letup to the ocean's wrath. Their existence came down to maintaining steerageway and seamen knowing survival depended on keeping the pumps from jamming, the Captain's seamanship, a sturdy ship and—prayers.

And still the storm raged on unrelenting until Monar, who'd never witnessed such a gale, was compelled to shout out to JT, "Do you think we can make it?"

"Of course. We're doing all right."

"You're serious?"

"No."

Monar let out a roar that boomed above the thundering sea. The sailors, many superstitious and wary of Monar's aura to begin with, thought he was challenging the gods and became alarmed. Then, when his roar was repeated, it seemed more like laughter. Why not laugh? They took up the sound, laughing like fools at the sea and her gods and, hanging on, strove to redouble their efforts.

The result was they fell to their knees exhausted, rolled near lifeless in the scuppers, and crawled delirious where they labored. There was little more they could do.

At 1400 hours, the god's found their efforts amusing and rewarded them.

The typhoon lost its temper and became tiresome of its rage. The gale waned, the seas eased into great swells. The *Raven* and her crew had withstood and won through. Many other ships in the typhoon's crazed path never found port.

Walking among the crew, JT gave encouragement and listened to extraordinary tales of heroism and survival from ordinary seamen. He left open the slop chest so they could replace their lost belongings.

Still, there were seven fewer seamen aboard, seven good men lost to the storm. Four swept overboard. Two died from heart attacks and one drowned while working a pump in the bilge. Added to those, were numerous fractures and other injuries. Although Lord Warfield, an old seadog himself, had seen fit to write loss of life and permanent injury clauses into their contracts, at present this was little comfort to the remaining crew.

JT estimated their ship had been forced south by east and therefore decided to steer north by northwest until finding a landmark. As fate would have it, the first land mass recognized was Hainan Island. This meant that from the point and the time the typhoon struck, they had been driven one hundred miles south and east toward the Philippines.

Directing the *Raven* for the Pearl River and Canton under power allowed time for the men to work on damage repair, laying and resetting the shrouds, running new line and mounting spare canvas. And rest, they needed rest.

When there was a breather, a minor question arose between JT and Monar. Where had Ashley Ealing, Black Moon's company Resident, been during the storm?

Neither had seen him and JT sent a deckhand down to Ealing's cabin to check on him.

"Said he's seasick, Cap'n, but said he worked the pumps in the storm—so he said."

As he turned away, a smirk on the seadog's face was caught by Monar, "Why the look, sailor?"

"Not a thing, Mr. Monar, sir. I meant nothing…"

JT took charge, "You were asked a question, Cole."

"Well, Cap'n Graves, it would seem to me Mr. Ealing's got Cape Horn fever, you know—a shirker. I worked the pumps below his cabin I did, when I went topside I left seaman Kayne at the pump. I'd not seen Mr. Ealing and now he looks just kind of, you know, bored, not weary or bone tired like the rest of us bloody bastards—excuse me, Captain. And Kayne's gone and drowned he did, Sir, so we can't ask him."

"I know he has, I don't need reminding. And Cole, I know it wasn't easy, working the pump with the ship yawing as she was—good job, it will be remembered."

JT dismissed the smiling man with a caution not to spread rumors and looked to Monar, "What do you think?"

"Well, that certainly muddies the water, doesn't it? Still, I've seen Ealing get seasick before and a lot of men were during the storm. But if he didn't lift a finger to help, and now somehow that's tied in with Kayne's death, what does that make him?"

"You mean added to Warfield's warning, our concern and distrust, the possibility he could be a liar, coward, laggard, shirker and an accomplice to murder…"

Monar had to laugh, "Enough! Let's not take chances, let me throw the Cape Horn shirker overboard."

Slapping him on the shoulder, JT walked off, "You know, my friend, I never know whether you're jesting or not. But if you *are* serious—no, at least for now.

"I hope I don't have to say you'll be sorry, Captain. And just for the ship's log, I was serious."

JT ignored him, "One other thing, splice the main brace. Two tots of rum for the men—and us."

After seeing to the men, JT broached another subject, "Tell me, have you ever thought about after, I mean after we pull off this escapade, what we're going to do?"

"Well now, I suppose that depends, doesn't it? If we get off Scot-free, there shouldn't be any change. If we're caught, our lives will be decided for us—no decision to make. But the third possibility is if…"

"That's the one I want to discuss. Say we pull it off and not caught, but the Chinese know who we are?"

"And that *if*, JT, is the big question. What will the Chinese do if? Me, I think they'll come after us."

"I'd put money on it. Do you think Warfield has given thought to that?"

Monar gave a wry smile, "How could he not? But look JT, we're committed so we live with it. Here, have another drink; that will solve all concerns."

With little coal remaining in her lockers, along with jury-rigged sails, the *Raven* passed between the islands of Macau; of late secured by the Portuguese and then the now British controlled Fragrant Harbor—Hong Kong.

Devastation everywhere greeted them. The harbor reminded JT of the gaunt ribs of fourteen Graves' ships that died in Havana Harbor during the '46 hurricane. He shook the memory and pitied the farmers and workers picking through the wreckage of sampans, bamboo rafts and other floating platforms that were once their homes. JT was particularly struck by the destruction of the Chinese junks crushed together. They were war Junks, Monar pointed out and motioned to three still in fair condition. Like Monar on his first trip to Canton, JT was astonished by the sheer size of the vessels—more so when informed they could each carry four or five hundred warriors.

After the mouth of Zhu Jiang, the Pearl River, they picked up a British river pilot where the tributary's east section of the river forked and then steamed the *Raven* up bound on the main tributary to Canton with Tiantang Mountain—the Peak of Paradise—visible if they cared to look, off in the distance.

The pilot, Jock MacLeod, was chatty, pointing out the Chinese Execution Grounds to starboard—the partners kept their thoughts to themselves—then the Honan section with the Women's Temple to port. Reason for needing the pilot was clear when the island of Dutch Folly and its following footsteps of rock trailed off upriver yet the *Raven*, under power, avoided them readily. Next came factories along the starboard side of the river, many of them Black Moon buildings, after that the Custom House and at last, the docks.

Six European ships, five British and one American, that had weathered the storm far better than the Chinese built ships, were tied off along makeshift piers. JT made a mental note to visit the American vessel and hear the latest news from the States.

Mr. Yin, the customs agent in Canton waddled down the wharf, his ankle length, silken hanfu failing to disguise the corpulent body within. Ashley Ealing had not come on deck, so Monar, who remembered Yin from the previous trip, greeted him.

"Mr. Yin, looks like you went through the same Typhoon as we did."

"Yes, we not bad like north. Peking and coast wicked bad, feel naughty devil's breath. You ship not look too bad."

"No, we're all right, bit of a mess. It was harder on the men than the ship. We're going to need sail-makers, spars, line, and other stuff; otherwise we're all right, although we lost seven men."

"Seven men, is easy. We have plenty; we lose men, no problem. It is learn build like English, our problem."

Yin then dismissed the subject, "You have money?"

"Yes, but not yours this time. Lord Warfield is paying in gold and silver. But he wanted you to have this."

A small sack divulged several gold sovereigns, enough to keep the frugal Mr. Yin secure for weeks.

Still, he was angry, wanting more. However, he was alone, and didn't know what this giant standing here with a bolo in his boot might do, "Why you no trade O?"

"The Afghans, Russians and Brits had a battle up in the Khyber Pass. Lord Warfield's army helped the Brits win but the opium consignment was lost."

All fabricated, but Yin had no way of proving it. "We'll resume our usual arrangement the next trip."

Mollified, Yin acquiesced, "With money you go British Consulate and Chinese Customs. They in city. You need pass, I make one. Foreigners no allowed in city."

"What, no foreigners are allowed inside the city?"

"Only to factories. Trouble not have pass to city."

"Then how did I enter without a pass when I was here the last time?"

"Sleeping Dragon rickshaw is pass."

"Archie Feng has that much power?"

"No…fear. You stop rickshaw, you die."

Monar was amazed. No authority dared to stop a Sleeping Dragon rickshaw. A regime within a regime. Monar didn't pursue it, "Don't I need Warfield's Resident, Ealing to go to the Consulate or Customs with me."

"No need Resident."

Ealing had said they did—another mark against him.

Yin looked about furtively, then whispered to Monar, "You see coolie there? You wave him, Dragon Leader Feng come to here."

"Feng will come *here*?"

Yin bobbed his head, continuing, "Here pass to enter city. First you see Mr. Feng, then go British and Customs."

"I've a friend I want to take with me; he's a very important person."

Yin shrugged his shoulders in the international motion of who cares, crossed out 1 on the pass, replaced it with 2 and left with his small, valued bag.

Waving to the coolie, Monar went below to find JT, "Guess who's going to visit us?"

"The Queen of England."

"Not quite, but someone more important around here, the Leader of the Sleeping Dragon Society, Archibald Feng Yün-shan is going to pay us a visit."

JT eyes widened, "How come? You told me his place was an armed camp, thugs everywhere."

"Don't ask me. It's odd, but let's get the *Raven* shipshape and the men into whites. Our Chief Petty Officer, Winslow is former RN; he'll know what to do. We'll do it up Bristol fashion. But remember, be careful around Archie."

When Feng arrived, born on a palanquin by four of his thugs and a retinue of twenty more, he appeared impressive—and impressed at being piped aboard.

"Ah, my friend Monar, back again. So good to see you once more. I trust the typhoon did not cause too much trouble and," Archie looked about, "I thank you for this show of respect, which of course I deserve."

"How could I do otherwise, Archie? After the way you treated me at your home."

Both men smiled at the recollection. At that meeting Archie stated, without equivocation, he could have Monar killed any time he felt like it.

"Ah yes, but I did not know you other than some association with Lord Warfield, so I had to be sure of you. Still, let us not talk of old times, only the new. Is there somewhere we can speak privately? But first, where is Warfield's Resident, Ealing?"

"He's still seasick below, we had quite a storm."

"I see. Please see to it he is not within earshot when we meet, will you?"

Still another negative comment concerning Ealing.

Monar put it aside for the moment, introducing JT, "Archibald Feng Yün-shan, this is Captain John Thomas Graves, the designer and owner of his ship the *Raven*."

They shook hands while Archie took in the ship, "The waters of the Zhi Jiang are graced with her majesty, Captain Graves. Would you consider selling her?"

"Afraid not, Mr. Feng. She's my pride and joy."

"I could have you killed and take her, you know."

Time ticked, no one moved or spoke. Monar waited to see how JT would respond.

He turned to Chief Mate Winslow, "Mr. Winslow, pipe the men to General Quarters *and* Battle Stations."

The sudden activity stunned Archie as seamen rushed to their stations. Twenty-four gun ports opened, the guns run out, muskets handed to the men who awaited further orders. Archie was speechless at the suddenness of it all. Ashore, his thugs moved restlessly.

JT held up his hand for the next signal and glared at Feng, "At the moment, do you want to try to follow through on your words, Mr. Feng?"

Archie kept his composure, "I now see how you came about your surname, Captain *Graves*."

Considering the man and circumstances, it was a disarming response. Nevertheless, under his breath, Archie made a vow to never again permit his words to ensnare him with this captain. And one thing more, it will be more than simply happenstance when somewhere, sometime—he'd find revenge for this humiliation.

Monar was troubled by JT's overreaction to Feng's remark. In the past, when Feng told Monar he could kill him, Monar calmly ignored the comment and a civility between them developed. Here, as far as Feng knew, JT had mustered the whole crew to prepare for battle. It was an inauspicious start. JT exhibited an immaturity to the Leader of the Sleeping Dragons and Monar quite rightfully read the undercurrent that simmered in Feng's eyes.

"Gentlemen," Monar offered, "We have an important mission ahead of us and Warfield will be angry should any quarrel interfere with our task."

Whispering to JT that he should dismiss the men and then see to it that Ashley Ealing was not within earshot of their meeting, Monar led Feng to the captain's cabin.

"That aggressive, bloody-minded person is your partner, Monar? He should watch his tongue and be careful over who he encounters."

Monar knew he had to defuse Feng to prevent the confrontation going any further, "I know, I know, Archie. He's young, from the States, new to this. In America, when a man feels threatened, he attacks. No thought, it's in their blood. Remember they're an upstart country; they don't know the art of diplomacy. To him, you threatened him; it really was surprising he didn't pounce on you."

"You're serious? He would not have survived."

Monar suspected Feng had more than clothes under his robe and felt it time to set the rules, "Archie, both of you were wrong, you shouldn't have threatened him, he shouldn't have responded as he did. With that said, John Thomas is my partner and friend. You are a business arrangement. I don't want trouble. If there is, you'll have to go through me. Is that clear?"

Monar was laying down the law, Feng didn't like it, "You are quite clear, Monar. If there is trouble, I will go through you."

Ignoring the innuendo Monar searched out JT, finding he had sent Ealing topside, "Get one thing clear; I'm speaking to you as a partner here. We're not about to start a war over a personal threat. We *are* here to get tea shrubs and get the hell away…"

"Listen to me Monar; I did all this for show. I was making a point. That person can't go around threatening to kill white people any time he feels like it and I don't think he'll do it again becau…"

Stopping JT in mid-word, Monar mulled over his statement but still felt the need to be clear, "First of all, he did not say he was going to kill you, he said he *could*. That's his way, to find how a person reacts. And you? You *reacted* all right—like you were going to blow up Canton, the docks, junks, Chinamen and start an all-out American, Chinese war! For Christ's sake, JT, that's not the brass ring. Remember the damn tea! We use whoever we have to, in this case Feng. I told you to be careful around him and you ignored that. You make him your enemy and you won't stand a chance with the kind of people he has surrounding him. So keep your wits about you when we go in the cabin, act like a damn accomplice, not his enemy."

Civility danced a fine line between them. While they reviewed the chart, Feng's mind kept straying—it was amusing to think of the ways he could have this upstart captain killed, all of them pleasant.

JT found the plan fairly straightforward; except for one concern. "Why do we dock at this Liaoyuancun? Why not Nangangcun?

Patronizingly, Feng answered, "Because my dear Captain Graves, Nangangcun is too shallow for your draft plus the dock burned. We would have to go back and forth with boats to carry the shrubs. Liaoyuancun has a dock and deep water. Nangangcun would be stupid, my young boy."

Monar interposed between the two, "That makes sense, JT, so what's the problem?"

"For Christ's sake, Monar, look at the chart. It's further into the bay, almost to the entrance to this Quinglan Harbor. If we're spotted by the Chinese navy, we're in a trap without much maneuvering room."

JT glared at Feng, "My Chief Petty Officer saw that and you're trying to tell me you don't see it too, Feng?"

The innuendo hung there until Monar settled the matter, "Archie, before we go in there, we scan the area, you're to be aboard the *Raven* the minute we dock, is that clear? If you're not, we'll drop our lines and be gone."

Feng did see the problem and their resolve, "Oh, I'm to be taken hostage? Think for a moment both of you. Your goal is to get the shrubs; my goal is Lord Warfield's offer. That offer gives me a life in India away from the scum of this country and my waiting for—what is the British expression—the other shoe to drop—on me?"

"What are you talking about; I thought you have the protection of the Canton Director."

"Canton fell to the Ming right after you left earlier this year. I tell you Monar, the Manchus and Qing's Celestial Dynasty are gone; it fell when the Emperor abdicated and my protector went down to death with it. Now, there is the Second Ming Dynasty with a child, Zhu Chongqing as Emperor. But he is nothing more than a figurehead. The country was planned to be ruled by the British system, but now it's the communists who are as ruthless as the Qing gaining control. They will soon come for me; it is a matter of time only."

"So," Monar was still wary, "you've got nowhere to go but with us."

Feng agreed, yet JT was indifferent, "Just as long as you're on the *Raven* when we moor. I'll chance the rest."

One week to the goal. The railroad rails had already been offloaded in Bombay; so in Canton, into the empty hold they took on a cargo of porcelain, lacquer-ware, tea in tins and filled the coal bunkers. This took two days and while the loading proceeded, Chinese sail-makers were fashioning twelve new canvas sails to replace those shredded in the typhoon and the crew finished putting the *Raven* shipshape.

After paying the port tax and stopping at the British Consulate, JT and Monar took advantage of their down time during the packing to visit the sole American vessel at the berths. The ship, the *Siasconset's Pride,* formerly a whaler, was out of Nantucket, or 'Sconset', as Obed Pierce, the Captain of the *Pride* called his hometown.

Nantucket, Pierce stated, was vanishing as a whaling port. Her harbor too shallow for larger ships and the inferno that destroyed her harbor-front in '46 proved a funeral pyre. By the hundreds, sailors fled the island for New Bedford's growing importance in the hunt for the Royal Fish.

"And afore I forgets, Captain Graves," began Captain Pierce, opening a copy of his Nantucket newspaper, "look here in my '48 Inquirer and Mirror from last year. It says if you haven't shipped to ports in the Western States in some while, be sure to avoid San Francisco. It says Polk, the damn fool, when he was President tells everyone there's a gold strike north in California and that triggers crews into jumping ship. Off they go, heading for those mountains leaving scores of ships swinging at their anchor cables."

You're serious? What are the ship owners doing about it?"

"Well, that's a bit tricky, ain't it? What can they do? They's in a fine pickle. No crew is no ship and no money. And not that it helps, but at least Polk's gone and good old General Zack Scott has took up them reins, for all the goods it'll do us. They's always landlubbers or thieves."

JT shook his head, "Well, I shan't be heading to California in any case, but where are you going tied up here with no whales?"

"Me? Why I've found meself new cargo. Three-hundred Chinese laborers, I got me for ballast. Farmhands they is for Hawaii and the railroad planned in our US. She's to come from eastern states all the way to San Francisco."

"But you said you'd lose you crew there as well."

"That's true, so I drop the coolies off at Santa Cruz, they can walk some ninety miles to the city from there. My crewmen? Well thet're wet foot sailors, wouldn't go walk a mile on land. No sir, not even if their life was on it."

Captain Pierce stopped speaking of this when a tall man approached, accompanied by a shorter, stocky person. The taller of the two men spoke up, "That's right; the captain makes money once again off the backs of the poor, workhorse coolie."

Pierce grimaced, irritated, "Captain Graves, this here Englishman is Montgomery Martin, former Treasurer of Hong Kong and self-appointed moral compass for the China Brits. He prefers slavery over these here opium eaters, opining that opium takes people minds, slavery doesn't. This other fellow is a newspaper reporter—another one of those 'Curse the exploiters of the people types'.

"Gentlemen, this's another American sea captain, name of Graves, from that right pretty clipper over there."

JT stood up and shook hands with Martin and the other man whose first name was Karl. JT missed his last. It was Karl who initiated another conversation, "I live in England, Mr. Graves. You're American, yet that ship is flying the Union Jack, how does that come about? Your country was at war with the British not that long past."

The comment, while not spoken sharply, caused wariness as JT responded, "Past long enough to be over, so what's so odd about that? I'm an American employed by the Black Moon Line. You can see her pennant."

Montgomery Martin broke in, "Ah my, yes, the ubiquitous Lord Warfield Blackwood Bunting's shipping line. You see Captain Pierce; the British East India Company grows opium in Afghanistan, but to keep their hands clean, uses private shipping lines, such as Lord Warfield's Black Moon ships to transport it to China. And, it looks that Warfield must be doing quite very well when I see that quality of ship sailing merrily around the ocean."

Monar had not been acknowledged by Captain Pierce or either man—it was as if he wasn't there. Annoyed with the three men, he wondered how JT would handle the exchange. It turned out JT's bile had risen, "Number one, Martin, the *Raven* is not Warfield's ship, she's mine and my friend here. Number two, my payment here is in silver, legal and so she's not simply sailing merrily around the ocean."

Martin wasn't contrite, "In silver, not opium? There's a change. Still, he's a bit touchy, don't you think, Karl?"

Martin reintroduced his companion, "Mr. Graves, my friend Karl Marx is a journalist for the New York Daily Tribune. Karl's done an exposé on the British in India and their despicable treatment of the natives. He's here in China now handing out his Manifesto to the poor working coolies."

"I'm not defending the English whether they are or are not exploiting India or China, but it was going to happen no matter who did it and do you think the 'coolies', as you so carelessly call them, would be better off under the Russian Czar, or Dutch, France or any of the other country?"

Then JT decided to defend the British, "Will your exposé include the facts that the Brit's have improved health and irrigation, stopped slavery, and they're building railroads? That they're trying to prevent wives from committing settee? If you don't know, that's immolating themselves on their husband's funeral pyre. The Brits also send the brightest children to England and educate them to become leaders for their country…"

Marx interrupted, "You have only partial truth there. English education benefits the English, it help Indians become little gentlemen to run the country the British way."

"Yes, you're right, but they're also broken the Maharaja's hold on the land and beginning to crack the damn caste system that keeps the peasants in the dark ages."

Amazed at the response, Monar didn't know JT's knowledge came from Chief Petty Officer Winslow and the values he imparted on British rule, pro and con, during the voyage from England.

Marx's short fuse started to ignite over this unknown *sailor* taking exception to his words, "You're simply picking a few examples. Take your country and the South's slaves and the North's child workers, what is your excuse there?"

"Poor attempt, Marx, when you can't argue points, change the subject. I have no excuse for our poor. Yet at least they have the chance to improve. We can only hope change will come for them, but change takes time."

Marx attacked the response, "Tell that to the people who are living through that right now. It's time for them to unite to throw off the oppression of Yankee and the Crown's Imperialism; take power into their own hands."

JT saw the intrigue behind the words, "And of course *you* intend to be the leader of this mob, correct, Mr. Marx?"

He denied the accusation vehemently, but his face gave away he was caught. Martin was strangely tight-lipped.

Monar saw another side of JT, or rather a new side. On edge yes, yet he seemed calm, knowledgeable, using words instead of anger to make his points. Monar saw he was controlling his temper and smiled.

Then, before Marx could respond, JT took the two men to task. Nodding toward Monar, "Let me see, is this an example of rudeness, or your concern for others?"

They were confused, "Come now you two, it's quite difficult not to notice there's a giant man here and yet you ignore him; don't give him the least common courtesy. Why—because he's black? Doesn't that make him one of your unwashed, but now he's not worthy of notice? Simply used for your so called exposé? Yet he could best you in wisdom and wealth and common sense."

Turning to Captain Pierce, JT had nothing but distain, "This is your ship, Captain, I'll not say more other than you're involved with strange bedfellows."

Montgomery Martin finally spoke up, reproving JT, "You should talk, being a Yankee slaver…"

He got no further in his slur. Monar was in front of him, towering over him, warning, "Take that back or you'll wish you had."

"I…I—wasn't he the slaver from Salem…in the States?"

"That was the father, John Thomas had nothing to do with it—now, swallow those words."

The menace was undoubtedly physical. Captain Pierce thought to interfere; the evil in Monar's eyes glared *do not*. Martin had no choice, "Then I apologize to Graves."

"That's *Captain* Graves."

"I apologize; I was in error…Captain Graves."

The dory back to the *Raven* allowed time for JT and Monar to discuss the meeting although their intention was to leave port immediately—Montgomery Martin, using his former title of Treasurer of Hong Kong could surely cause trouble over Monar's—a Negro man's—threat. The conversation fell to Martin's accusation of JT being a slaver.

"Look, JT, there's always going to be someone who'll know about your father and blame you, there's no getting away from…"

"Let it go, Monar, I've let myself dwell on it too long, it's a sad fact. Fools like those two are only rabble-rousers, trying to agitate the people. In one way that's good—if it's for the people—but them? Not so. I will admit I was on the edge."

"Well, let me ask you about that restraint, JT. Where did that come from? You seemed familiar with everything they were going to say before they said it and you refuted or deflected every remark. What's come over you? From what's happened in the past, you'd have blown a gasket."

"You're right, I would have. But I had a good tutor on the trip from England. Chief Mate Winslow took me in hand—after I got my problems with Evelyn somewhat in perspective—and worked with me. Turns out he was a senior instructor at the Royal Naval College at Greenwich, instructing in gunnery and arbitration—sort of both sides of the discipline he said. It was prior knowledge, having the facts that changed me." Then JT laughed, "And you—you were all steamed up like I normally would have been."

"I was—I admit it. And prior to that spat and while you were berating them I glanced through this Communist Manifesto he wrote with someone named Engels. They want to take all the people's money, put it into one pot and then dole it out to the have-nots. At least it seems that way to me with that 'from each who have it—to each who don't'-muck. Doesn't say much else."

"Doesn't mention them and their gang taking their cut between the have and have not's?"

"Can't find that information here."

With no mourning, the little book fell into the harbor.

4

15 August 1849. The sea between Canton and Hainan.

IT HAD NOT BEEN AN AUSPICIOUS beginning for the theft of the tea shrubs. When JT and Monar had returned from the confrontation on the *Siasconset's Pride*, Ashley Ealing was not to be found. Maddened, Monar checked with Mr. Yin, who claimed, whether truthfully or not was unknown, he had seen nothing, knew nothing.

As a last resort, Mr. Yin was given money to deliver a sealed warning to Archibald Feng. The hope was his Sleeping Dragon cohorts could track Ealing down with, unsaid, a full expectation of what would follow.

Still, there was no choice; they had to assume Ealing knew their goal and Mr. Yin could not, or would not, deliver the warning to Feng. It was also assumed Ealing would make contact with the new Manchu government. How long before he reached a deal with them was another unknown. And, added to this, Montgomery Martin was almost certain to cause them trouble in an act of revenge.

They had worn out what little welcome they'd had and were forced to detail their plan to a fascinated Winslow, who then and there enlisted, simply for the challenge it presented. The slumbering war horse in him awakened.

After that, a major decision was hastily decided. It was time to run. The on-loading was stopped; the crew hurried about making the *Raven* ready for sea in record time. Jock MacLeod, the pilot, was found, and though a bit tipsy, an additional fee convinced him to navigate the Pearl River at night. Unobserved, they reached Macau and the open sea.

«»

Night, the last night before reaching the coastal village of Liaoyuancun and the tea plants. It proved to be a time for thought. JT had retired to his cabin early to be rested for the coming day, knowing that as much as they could plan, all was in order, except the critical unknown of Ashley Ealing. The crew, informed of their Captain's intentions, were in agreement and accorded incremental wages.

It took some swallowing of pride, but on his own accord, JT decided that should a naval confrontation with Chinese war junks prove unavoidable, then for that period, he would relinquish command of the *Raven* to Chief Petty Officer Adam Winslow.

Other than pride, it wasn't a hard decision. JT was the accomplished captain of a merchant ship. Winslow was a former Captain in the RN with battle experience and, although harsh with the crew at times and running a tight ship, they nonetheless would follow him without question.

.

This night, JT slouched in his chair until, in due course, memories of his father once again drifted into his mind. The captain's lantern flickered with a silvery glow, mirrored off the silver ribbon of the *Raven's* wake. This glow, seen and ignored countless times past, unexpectedly beguiled JT this time. He felt peculiar, the only word he could apply to his unease. It wasn't the coming day that disturbed. It was rather more an insight, a fleeting glimpse into his future. This awareness arose from the passion of his tutor, the Chief Petty Officer. Winslow caused him to *think,* whether it made sense or not.

Winslow's comment of 'Life is what happens to you' and then followed it with 'Or is what you happen to do in life?' The first, submissive. The other, imaginative. Don't just let things just happen to you, Winslow stressed, create your particular vision of life, your mark.

Yes, in his few years he had done well, yet his future was at issue. It had to be more than one day following another, yet how do you consciously know?

A mind of muddled thoughts, flowed, drifted, ever shifting, altering, tumbling, mystified. There must be more. *His mark*—those were the words Winslow spoke—decide. His mark in this life. His honor for his heirs, the generations to come. Think of your father, once a decent man, now a stigma on the family's once great chronicle. JT must change that. Honor must return.

His own rueful laugh didn't surprise him in the least.

Honor. For here he sat, enmeshed in Warfield and Monar's scheme. With little thought he had fallen in with their game. Game? Of course, that was all this was to Warfield, the Grand Game. Just like the Brit and the Russki—each cabal trying to one-up the other. On a smaller scale, true, but that was the world ingrained in Warfield. And now JT mused, it was too late to stop this folly. Still, it could be justified by remembering the Chinese surely deserved it. Depriving the humble Brit of a modest mug of warm tea was just plain wickedness. That would surely be his rationalization.

However, the difference now? It's the end of his playing the Game. Whether Warfield or Monar liked it or not. From this point forward, the shame of his father and the Graves name must be cleansed with honor. It was his obligation to his heirs. *His heirs?* That sudden thought brought remorse that as quickly vanished for *she* came to him with an urgency he'd never known. His future unfolded, *Evelyn*. He snuffed out the lantern, sitting in moonlight.

A knock on his door. At this late hour, baring a major setback, it could be only one person, "Come in, Monar."

He entered, looking about, "I heard you mumbling and there wasn't a light creeping under your door. It's 0200, can't you sleep?"

"I'm fine, just talking to myself—or at least I thought I was until you heard me."

"Didn't make out the words, nor listen long. You look like there's something troubling you."

"Well, perhaps I may be premature but… but after this is over with and we've given the plants to Warfield, I'm returning to England."

"That comes without surprise. Evelyn?"

"Yes, I won't go on without knowing if…"

"You know in your heart she'll be there."

"God, Monar, I hope you're right."

"I am, so I'll leave you to your thoughts."

He turned to leave, "Hold on there, Monar. If you have another moment from your nomadic wanderings, there's something else."

"I thought there might be."

"A while back I was pondering if there was a God and if there is, do you think my father received redemption? You know how he suffered for his sins about the Negro slaves. I forget the name of that parson from the Essex Street Church, the one you took to the grave. He interceded with God for father; do you think his prayers might have helped?"

Monar recalled that night. The parson refusing to go until he was threatened within an inch of his life and, after the gravesite benediction, Monar sent the frightened creature scurrying terrified across the church grounds clad only in a mud spattered nightgown.

"That withered old twig, JT? All I know is that by the time I brought up the demons from hell and kicked him off the coach he knew he had ridden with the devil. Still, he did give you father one hell of a eulogy—if that helps you."

It was an amusing picture yet the subject caused JT to ask, "But do you think there's a god or some sort of all-knowing someone who might forgive father?"

"We come from different backgrounds, JT. What I think won't fit with your past."

"That's just it—do *you* think there's some god?"

"JT, the one good thing Ian MacPherson did was to educate me. Of course he did it for the wrong reason; to prove black people could never be as smart as whites..."

"So at least he did *that* for you."

"Unintentionally, because it turned out I proved his theory wrong. But yes, without quibbling, he did give me an education and, to try to answer your question, part of that schooling was the edification of God. The Christian God as only the Church of

England, in her outposts in the thankless back waters of the Caribbean, can beat, or rather whip, it into our thick black skulls."

"I getting the feeling it didn't stick."

"It stuck all right—in my craw."

"So we come back to my question; what did you come up with to replace the white man's God?"

"I cannot explain him, or perhaps her, or perhaps *it*. I don't know what. On top of that, there's *things* a white man can't understand, it's not in their narration, their history. I'm sorry, but that includes you. When I asked the missionaries what came before God, I was told God always was, and that's when they lost me. I cannot grasp that thought without being befuddled. No, no, no. It's something I'm unable to get my brain around. I'm not *that* clever."

"So you can't help me?"

"No, and I don't want to and then again, why should I? You've got to find what's out there on your own…or not find him…" he laughed, "or her, or *it*."

The *Raven* rounded the point, moving further into Gaolong Bay. Keeping the telescope close to his eye, JT scanned along the shoreline past Nangangcun to Liaoyuancun. He could make out people milling about a number of wagons and no other activity.

Chief Mate Winslow approached, "You were right about having to moor in here rather than Nangangcum, Captain. The Point blocks our line of sight to the northeast and that's where the wind is coming from. Any ships up there will have with the wind abaft and we're blind about what's going on past that Point. When we tie off we should hurry a lookout up there as soon as possible."

"My thought exactly. I saw some horses by those wagons; get one of your best riders up there on the quick. As soon as we tie off, my thought is to reef sail and bring our steam up."

"That's certainly for the best, Captain. If this *is* a trap, power is the only thing that can save us."

In the middle of a group of people on the dock stood Archie Feng, his arms outstretched, a relieved smile creasing his craggy face. The *Raven* touched her rubbing rail to the wharf and tied off, then two gangways were quickly lowered.

Archie Feng straightaway ordered the coolies to take up their bamboo poles and start carrying the tea plants, two at a time, aboard. He was the first to board, followed by three women, five children and six burley men. JT allowed the women and was ready for the men. A prearranged signal from JT brought twelve armed sailors to confront the group.

"Flat out, Feng, no men! And who the devil's the rest of these people?"

Feng was furious, but JT would not be dissuaded and the men were forced ashore. The women, Feng insisted were his wives and the children, his. No choice, JT let them stay.

Monar interposed between Feng, JT and Winslow. "Where do we stand, Archie, did you get our note about Ealing jumping ship from the *Raven*?"

Feng was dumbfounded, "What are you saying? He's not with you and you don't know where he is?"

Their faces gave the answer. Monar shouted to the crew to hurry on the coolies while JT and Winslow kept the telescope on the Point.

Feng, appalled at the news, directed his contempt at JT and Monar. He then counted out coins, put them in a small sack and called to one of the men forced off the ship. JT watched closely while the man listened intently before placing his hand on Feng's heart, mumbled a response, caught up the sack and melted into the throng.

Feng moved to the stern where JT and Winslow took turns watching the Point, "I saw you watching me, Captain Graves. Why didn't you watch Ealing instead? You should have, although now it's too late to correct your blunder…"

Knowing the mistake was his, JT could only listen while Feng continued, "I have sent a man to kill Ealing."

JT blanched, "Just like that? You don't know for sure if he did anything."

Feng angrily laid it out, "That Ealing stole away is enough. And before this day is out I'm sure his guilt will be born out —thanks to your blunder."

"You think that thug you gave the money to will follow through instead of just taking the money and leave?"

Feng grinned wickedly, "He is a loyal warrior of the Sleeping Dragon, but more, he is my son. I have honored him by giving him a mission. If he must, he will give his life to kill Ealing. If not, his wife and family will die..."

Chief Mate Winslow grabbed JT's arm, "Look!"

Through the scope, JT watched as their lookout raced from the Point, whipping the horse for all it was worth. He turned to Winslow, "I think our worst fear has come true."

"Sure looks to be the case, Captain. When our man reaches us, we'll find out just how true."

"Four ships. Four Chinese War Junks loaded to the gills with Chinks—three miles off under full sail!" was the breathless report.

Less than an hour. JT turned over command to now Acting Captain Winslow who ordered steam up, on-loading to cease, and gangways removed. He then went among his crew ordering them to battle stations. Past training and memories of service in the Royal Navy became rote once more as men moved through their old habitual routines.

With the mooring lines cast off, the *Raven* eased away from the dock to allow her to come about. At his juncture, the first of the War Junks appeared past the point, soon followed by the other three.

Captain Winslow calmly walked the deck speaking in a low voice. Gun ports open, cannon readied and rolled out, young powder monkeys moving about, shells stacked—the ship was ready, the men calm yet edgy at the same time.

Winslow moved to the helm where the chart of Gaolong Bay was spread and called to JT to join him.

"The information here is quite sketchy. I recall there are reefs south, along with shelving that's not marked. We can't take the chance going that…"

From the spotter, "Captain, Sir, one of the enemy vessels has hove to close to shore and looks like some sort of chain is being laid out from the following vessel. The other three are continuing southeast."

"Very good. Now then JT, this will be their plan. They want to link the four ships together with heavy chain and then draw their net tight, toward land. If we try to run the chain, that will pull their ships and all their manpower into us and it will be all over. Remember, They don't care how many men they lose; only that they have enough."

"Then what do we do to stop them?"

Winslow looked to the lead enemy, estimating her speed fewer than five knots and ordered the helmsman to increase revolutions and intersect the vessel.

Satisfied after looking once more at the chart, he answered JT, "It's really quite straightforward. They're still mired in old school Asian warfare and don't grasp the significance of steam. Right here is where we would normally move south at four times their speed with infinitely more maneuverability and be gone. But, we're coming up on slack tide and with reefs and shelving to concern us we're going to have to cut it close."

"Which means?"

"Which means we have to slip past that lead vessel and the only way to do that is to stop her and give us room and the only way to stop her is to…"

"Rockets, Captain!"

The Chinese rocket launchers were more or less aimed at the ship and a torrent of rockets streamed from their vessels. Sparkling, roaring, they flared over, behind and onto the ship. Yet with the *Raven* coming head on to the rockets; few hit and were quickly extinguished with water or shoveled overboard.

While JT and Monar were shocked at the onslaught, Winslow was watchful but not overly concerned, "I saw rockets farther north, when I was on HMS *Nemesis* in the Anson Bay battle. They're completely erratic and mostly for fright. Nevertheless, if they hit sails they can be a major problem, that's why I kept ours furled."

Winslow left them, saying it was time to act. He gauged the distance from the *Raven* to the enemy.

"Helmsman…hard to starboard…Gunner's Mate, as soon as we're parallel watch the roll…then fire as you bear."

The Captain's timing was perfect, for after the *Raven* rolled to starboard and then righted to an even keel, every cannon was bearing. The thunderous tumult as each of the port twelve cannon, belched flame, and discharged exploding shell that disintegrated the side of the War Junk. Her starboard freeboard took the brunt and crumbled in a violent inferno, followed instantly by her rocket magazine detonating. An immense flash and roar momentarily blinded and deafened the *Raven's* crew while debris fell about them.

Through the flame Captain Winslow saw the stricken vessel go dead in the water, burning furiously. She would soon go under and once they were clear of her bow he ordered full port rudder, all ahead full.

The other Chinese War Junks, avoiding the stricken wreck and the mass of men in the water, dropped the chain and attempted to prolong the chase. In the end they fired off rockets that hurtled in the general direction of the *Raven* but fell short and unscathed, she sailed into the South China Sea.

Most of the crew shouted approval; the sailors knew this captain's reputation and although relieved and giving tribute to him, there was, nevertheless, something adverse going on. Monar noticed it in the crew, or more specifically a few of the old salts were muted in their support. He heard the whispered word 'needless', this despite their belief in Winslow's ability.

The *Raven*, now back in the hands of Captain Graves, sailed on, the tension gone. Yet Monar remained troubled by the word 'needless'.

He was not yet a captain, nor had he ever commanded a steam vessel, still, the men, a few of the men, were quietly bothered over something unknown and his attempt to casually gain the reason for the whispered word met with stony silence.

They cleared the northern end of the Strait of Malacca after easily outrunning three pirate craft and at long last a normalcy returned. Soon, they would haul northeast for Madras and Lord Warfield and although twenty tea plants were abandoned on the wharf at Nangangcum, two hundred and twenty-four plants were aboard.

After clearing between the chain of the Andaman and Nicobar Islands, and with only open water ahead, Monar felt it was time to speak with JT about the damn word 'needless' that kept coming into his head.

It turned out JT had heard the word 'unnecessary', in an aside from the third mate to another sailor and certainly a word with similar meaning. It also turned out JT had, he felt, come close to the answer but tried to ignore the implications.

It came down to the matter of timing and why Acting Captain Winslow didn't keep on with more dispatch once the lookout had warned them. Yes, he was quick enough to stop the on-loading, remove the gangways and cast off, but after that decision, the ship's headway seemed to go at a snail's pace. Coming about, the modest increase of revolutions and the painfully measured approach to run parallel to the War Junk was suspect. At the time, JT thought Winslow was timing the junk's painfully slow rate to get ahead and clear to open water. Yet in hindsight, Winslow appeared to be gauging the junk's momentum for another reason; so that at the last minute he could claim that due to reefs they had to turn closer to the vessel and give her a broadside to stop her from trapping them. At that time, yes, most everyone felt that although it was a near thing, they had slipped the trap before it could be sprung.

Since then however, looking at the chart showed that even at mean low tide there had been water enough under them to feel secure and outrun the War Junk.

So what did this reduce to? Did Winslow intentionally create a condition whereby he could be a hero once again? However a greater concern arose; had he misjudged, everyone on board was placed in jeopardy for what—heroics? The odds now appeared that way, which led to the question—*what if*? What if his timing was wrong? What if the gunnery not on the mark and the ships collided allowing three or four hundred Chinese to charge aboard against sixty retired RN sailors.

JT and Monar stared at each other; memories struck them simultaneously, this could have equaled their fearsome clash with the Barbary corsairs in the Mediterranean Sea last year. A near thing then, was it a near thing now?

They were becoming angry at Winslow over what could have ensued, yet what was there to do? Face down the former captain; try to prove him knowingly, dangerously deceitful? Only JT had the qualifications to judge the sequence of events and question the failure to use the *Raven's* superior speed. Yet, in any discussion Winslow could raise some naval code of combat directive, and whether true or invented, JT would have to defer.

In the end, they decided to say nothing. It was done, over with, they'd never know, at least they thought that—if only for a while.

Archie Feng had gone up to Winslow after the *Raven* had cleared into the South China Sea following the truncated battle in Gaolong Bay and appeared to recognize him from the past. Neither JT nor Monar were going to ask Feng of it, but when the ship was nearing Madras they noticed Feng chatting up Winslow once more. It was a cause for concern, Feng a known scoundrel and Winslow, which of course included the crew, were picked by Warfield and Warfield was not around.

To answer the question of the chats, Monar and JT casually asked Feng to the captain's quarters. At the first query from Monar,

Feng started laughing until he saw the two men were serious and he set them straight. It seemed the Chief Petty Officer's name was not Adam Winslow but Harry Scrimshaw, at one time a lieutenant in Her Majesty's Royal Navy. A *cashiered* lieutenant to be specific. At the raised eyebrows, Feng, initially resistant, finally decided to tell them the tale of Adam Winslow, or Harry Scrimshaw.

"I didn't recognize him at first, I only knew him as Lieutenant Scrimshaw, a RN Officer. Far too many years ago I was the captain of an Indiaman—that's a merchant ship made in India, if you didn't know—and in a convoy of ten ships. We were attacked by Frenchy out of Ile de France. "There were five French warships and three British. The British, under command of a spineless officer name of Payne, put up a sham resistance and signaled us to scatter. Scatter? For Christ's sake, an Indiaman doesn't do five-six knots with the wind howling up her backside—and this fool tells us to scatter. With only four eighteen-pounders each of us were sitting ducks, ripe for the plucking. We looked back, there's only a single British warship, turned out to be HMS *India*, sailing around behind us putting up a hell of a show."

"The other Brit warships ran and *India* was fighting them off?"

"Not just fighting them off, she sent one off aflame and another dismasted. We were cheering them on. Well, that was last we saw of the battle other than that night we could see two fires off in the distance. We figured one was the *India*, but no one caught up with us and ten ships and two Brit warships made sail to Cape Comorin.

Three days later we were still jeering the two RN ships that ran when into the harbor comes a hulk that didn't have any reason to be afloat. It was *India* with half a mast and mostly charred wood. Half the crew dead and the rest looked like they had no right to be alive."

"You're telling us Winslow, I mean this Scrimshaw, was in that crew?"

"Not just in it Monar, he took command. Seems the *India's* captain had a heart attack with Frenchy's first salvo so Scrimshaw takes charge and caused such a mêlée we were able to escape. Anyway, we treated your Chief Petty Officer like a Raj; nothing was too good for him and we thought he was going to head up the Queen's Navy someday. But that God damned, son of a bitch Palmer, the bastard who told us to scatter—he puts Scrimshaw up on charges that he disobeyed a direct command!"

JT was infuriated, "How could that happen? Scrimshaw could have claimed *he* wasn't given the command, his captain was, and get out of the charge that way."

"Don't ask me about that, but he didn't, and remember, Palmer wanted what occurred squashed and of course he has connections in England, family of naval officers back to William of Normandy or some such God sanctified person. Anyway, the Admiralty, neglecting the fact Scrimshaw and *HM India* saved ten merchant ships, says he can retire without charges and half pension—he was only a lieutenant remember—or face an inquiry. Everyone knew that would be a sham."

"So he retired?"

"Without prejudice, meaning nothing on his record."

"Wasn't that good of them."

Monar was curious, "You followed this, Archie?"

"I did, seeing I was one of the ships saved. I set up a fund for Scrimshaw with the other ships and Lord Warfield asked me to find out the truth before he hired him. In fact, that was the first time I did something for the Lord."

"Really? Scrimshaw has worked for Warfield ever since that time?"

"Yes, and he told me Lord Warfield specifically asked him to be Chief Petty on the *Raven*—because he had guts. So, some advice, if you're thinking of doing what I think, whether he was right or wrong, don't make fools of yourselves. Lord Warfield will tell you where to get off."

Monar changed the subject, "Archie, you said you were a merchant captain at one time, how did you wind up as…ah…with the position you had?"

"How? Really quite simply. I learned it's absurd to go contrary to one's instincts."

"Meaning?"

"Meaning that if you can be more evil than the person in your way—then be so. Evil pays Monar, and I think you know precisely what I mean—not like this straight and narrow friend of yours here."

«◊»

The massive expanse of Fort Saint George broadened in front of them as they played out the anchor line. This was the origin of the English footprint in India in the 1600s. An oddly inappropriate area, it developed into White Town due to the Maharajah only allowing the buildings to be painted white, and now, not surprisingly, comprised mainly of white, Protestant, English. After this town, there followed Black Town, for all others, including non-British Europeans.

The two towns and surrounding lands eventually became known as Madras and though fought over and conquered at times, somehow once again, Britain prevailed.

There being no harbor or wharf, to reach the beach required cargo and people to surf ashore in large, high bow and stern craft called massulahs. They appeared as oversized dories, each needing eight to ten rowers to manage it.

JT and Monar were deciding who should go ashore when Monar spotted the *Argus* moored not far from them in Madras Roads. The *Argus* was the Black Moon packet ship Monar had sent to wait for Lord Warfield at the Red Sea port of Suez. This evidently meant Warfield was here and so they, along with Archie Feng and Scrimshaw surfed ashore—right to the feet of Lord Warfield awaiting them.

When an aide had spotted the *Raven* dropping anchor, he ran to Government House inside Fort George where Lord Warfield was holding a conference with members of the East India Company and the Madras Governor General.

On hearing the news, he suspended the meeting and hurried to the beach just as the massulah deposited the members of the *Raven* past the surf.

The success of the venture was of great pleasure to Warfield and after making arrangements to see Feng and Scrimshaw later, he took JT and Monar back to the Government House. They passed under the imposing flagpole with the Union Jack ensconced on Indian soil—India's soil, where The Jack fluttered imperially.

After revelation and raised eyebrows of the members present on being introduced as two of Warfield's future 'key partners', JT and Monar sat in the rear of the room.

Warfield held court, discussing problems with the 1833 act and Parliament's attempt to enforce its efforts to supervise the officers of the BEIC. It was a creeping attempt, difficult to stop. But, he roared, "It will not happen! They won't tell us what is good for us in India *or for India*!"

To a round of applause, Warfield promised that when he returned to England, anyone who tried to interfere with the Company would be stifled. He ordered each Director present to outline letters to their managers in England targeting Members Parliament and he would sign and deliver them personally and intimidate any MP as needed.

Lord Warfield was well-ordered, methodical in his presentation. He controlled the floor in a disciplined manner, no one questioned or took exception, and when he informed each person the year would be the most lucrative in the history of the Company, a deafening applause erupted.

JT and Monar were spellbound at the power of the man and presentation, although in truth, JT's emotions were compromised, tempered by the memory Warfield brought forth of Evelyn. He waited patiently to ask of her.

The conference ended with Warfield stating there would be refreshments served and all should attend.

Expansive as he approached, Warfield held sway, “Well gentlemen, I hope you are happy with what you’re heard and I couldn’t be more pleased with the both of you.”

Before JT could speak, Warfield turned to Monar, “When we were on the beach, Archie whispered something about Ashley Ealing. Could you enlighten me further…oh, damn, I forgot! There’s another person in the atrium I want here. JT, could you go over to that door there, make my apology and ask them to join us?”

It wasn’t what JT wanted, but there was no choice.

The room was shaded, shadowy, making him squint.

“Hello, John Thomas.”

“My God…Evelyn.”

5

28 September 1849 Fort Saint George.

EVELYN WOULD NOT HEAR of having JT court her. She stated they wanted to be engaged forthwith. So that, when Warfield's consort, Lillian Fields arrived with Evelyn still adamant, Warfield announced it to the group.

"I am most pleased to announce the engagement of my daughter and only child to Captain John Thomas Graves who is from the United States. Yes, I know, an American. Nevertheless, he's willing to let our country's bygones be bygones and I will not hold the War of 1812 against him."

The group laughed as expected and Warfield called JT, to his embarrassment, to stand beside him.

"JT, as he is known to his friends, has had my trust and friendship ever since he came to my daughter's aid in a time of deep sorrow when she lost her packet ship *Black Watch* off New York in the States, not to mention later incidents even more extreme. But, it is more than this; let me be brief by simply stating, that of more importance, my daughter loves him, and that's enough for me."

The gathering continued in high spirits. Though it was Warfield who noticed Monar was happy…yet saddened. He realized what that meant to the black man—and the import it carried.

Insisting that JT stay and meet with the people there, Warfield told him the welfare of his crew would be seen to.

They were put in excellent quarters in White Town, ordered to stay away from Black Town and, under the threat of harsh reprimand, to say nothing of their cargo. Warfield kept them under surveillance to be sure.

Unfortunately for the engaged couple, they became *the* social event of the year. Their appearance gave notice of the hierarchy's social and political eminence and demanded by every Rajah and Nabob. Whether party or excursion, each host attempted to outdo the previous. Government outings, elephant junkets to visit Mujuk Empire ruins and Maharajas exposing their unbelievable wealth. Gifts of pearl necklaces, ruby rings, silken robes spun with gold thread, silver urns inlaid with gold Buddha's, elephants and monkeys as well as myriads of charming smaller gifts given by the populace.

By the end of the second week, another week continuously filled with croquet, cricket, polo and lawn and estate parties, it became obvious the English colony was attempting to turn India into England and succeeding. Unfortunately, they couldn't stop the monsoon rains or hide squalor as the grand tour went from one social to the next.

Yet nothing could interfere with the Nabob's desires.

Torchlight festivities, Indian musicians, dancers, illuminated processions and banquets long into each night continued until they called a close to it all, or at least an easing off of the affairs. All of it was not what they expected or wanted.

Evelyn recognized these extravagant shows were for her father; an attempt to keep or court favor and as courteously as feasible, she brought a cessation to the proceedings. In England, she was used to these activities, but knew her decision would do much to help JT's liberty.

They preferred a small chapel wedding, and despite Warfield's desire to have a grand moment for his only child, he relented. Quietly, late one night, they woke the Master of Fort Saint George's, Saint Mary's Church, who performed a chapel service. Of course, Monar was Best Man; Lily, Maid of Honor and Lord Warfield Bunting gave his daughter, Evelyn Kathryn Bunting to Captain John Thomas Graves.

Those in attendance, the Marquee of Dalhousie, Governor General of India, James Andrew Broun-Ramsey, also the Maharaja of Chingle put, the Maharaja of Tamil Nadu and the Acting

Governor for the powerful British East India Company. Sir Henry Dickinson.

This elitist group agreed to an impromptu meeting back at Government House inside Fort St. George and while Evelyn, Lily, JT and Monar sat conversing at a table, Warfield and the select faction held court in another room.

This meeting was cordial, like old friends chancing to see one another after too long a separation, they spoke of their youth, and the years before the stresses of age and privilege found them.

This was also an opportunity, opportunity to speak seriously of the present, the *now* of their lives and their obligations to India, England, and the populous of both.

Although not having supreme powers, the actions of these four men nevertheless affected the well-being and prosperity —or not— of millions.

Broun-Ramsey was the first to broach a rather touchy subject to Warfield. Touchy, as it could soon vex them all.

"I understand, Warfield, you have received the Rights of Diwani to collect revenues in the Bengal. What is your intention in doing this?"

"First, James, it will be a modest tax to improve the substructure of the Bengal, such as roads, hospitals and the rest. You well know the whole blasted area is a muddle."

"*All* of the income will go to this?"

"Of course not, I'm going to support the Imperial Cadet Corps, the Indian Princes Corps and the Sepoy. There's also few other ideas I have in mind."

"Ideas that will also help *you*?"

Warfield voice went flat, "Of course they will. It will also help to keep peace in the region. Just as your Direct Rule and British Domination helps to keep the peace."

The two Maharajas said nothing, listening carefully; Warfield's tone had an edge. With little finesse to his words; he was telling the Governor General of India that what he, Lord Warfield, did in the

Bengal was his business, his business alone and he would brook no interference.

One other crucial element of the discussion the Maharajas perceived was it was the future of *their* country being discussed, discussed by Englishmen—foreigners.

Sir Henry, Acting Governor of the BEIC spoke up, changing the subject, “I say, put the Direct Rule act aside. What are we all to make of the Caste Disabilities Removal Act? Will that pass next year?”

This Proposal, being forced on the Brahman, the highest Hindus caste, would make all castes including the ‘untouchables’ equal in the eyes of British Law.

The Maharajas were immediately incensed. How could the British coerce them into this? People were not equally born and they refused to believe otherwise. To imply anything else was insanity and worse, shameful. The British should know, look at their country; class discord was rife throughout the strata of British society and why, the Maharajas insisted, must they do what the British do not?

At this heated moment, an Indian woman slipped across the room, her gold embroidered, red sari arrayed across one shoulder streamed behind as she knelt alongside the Maharaja of Tamil Nadu.

The Englishmen, mesmerized, then beguiled by the woman’s black diamond eyes, rose ineptly to their feet while the Maharaja, emitting a weary smile, looked lovingly to the woman and then the others, “My English friends, this is my daughter, Princess Amala. I apologize for her intrusion upon the business of men. Unfortunately, the blame settles to me. I should have found a worthy husband before allowing her to stay in Delhi and be English schooled to take up the discourteous ways of your women. Now she has a difficult mind to restrain yet I admit she is the vitality behind my lands. Be that as it may, Amala Singh, this is…”

Her voice was pure English with a remaining trace of Hindi. The men hung on her every word, “Rude is not to be my meaning and please excuse that in me which my father calls dis-courteous. Yet, I have come to take him. He is unwell and he denies to much his unwellness."

The men stumbled over themselves showing concern and Warfield, though mesmerized like the others, still managed one lucid thought—Monar.

The departure of the Maharaja and his daughter was cause for the group to take their leave. Warfield went back to the others and sent word for Harry Scrimshaw and Archie Feng to come to Government House. Until then, the social part of the evening continued. Warfield apologized for detaining the newly married couple, but he knew they would be gone for a week or more and there were thoughts and questions needing responses.

When the two men arrived and congratulated the couple, the women excused themselves.

"Now, to begin." Warfield began formally, "JT, due to your being unavailable for the next week or so, I want your permission to have First Officer Scrimshaw and Archie take the *Raven* and offload the tea plants and get them planted as soon as possible."

It was more an instruction than request, but JT knew if he decided against someone else sailing the *Raven* then he would have to take her to Calcutta now, as the plants would be in jeopardy of dying. Besides, that was no way to begin a honeymoon. He nodded.

"Good, now Monar. You'll start on this plan. I'm going to make an offer to Maharaja Singh of Tamil Nadu to help improve his tea plantation. He produces an alleged Oolong, but it's poor quality leaf for the lowest caste in India and we can improve his quality by grafting the cuttings of our plant stems to his. It will take four to five years, but that's a damn sight better than twenty years from seed and I hope that explains the necessity of thievery. It's not the best conditions here in the south, but with our cuttings and better care and an expert I'll supply, we'll do all right. I'll give Singh forty-five plants and we'll work out a percentage. But, the tea will be called Warfield's Superior Tamil Nadu Blend— that is if it passes our taste testing. If it does, I'll bring it to Europe. Is that clear?"

Monar was unsure, "Your expert better be good because I know nothing about tea, and to be honest, I don't think much of it."

"You don't have to like it, just learn what goes into the processes of growing, harvesting and shipping it. Oh, one more thing, I'm pretty sure you'll have to work with Singh's only child, his unmarried daughter, Princess Amala. The old man's not well so she'll become Maharini if he goes. Make sure to get on her good side."

Monar was vexed, "You're putting me ashore to get on the good side of some old maid Indian woman?"

JT and Archie couldn't help but laugh at Monar's predicament. Warfield simply shrugged and did his best to prevent a smile; he felt his ruse was as good as any the Greek poet Menander could have devised.

"Next on my agenda is security. Archie, what's your thought on Ashley Ealing—anything new?"

"I pledged my son to eliminate him. If my son is alive, Ealing will be dead."

"That I understand and that's all well and good. Ealing's death, however, does not solve our problem. We must assume he's told the Chinese everything; the ship's name, the captain and that *I'm* behind the tea theft. So the fact is none of us, including JT and the *Raven*, are ever to enter Chinese waters again. Yet, there is a greater concern and that's Chinese thugs. You can bet the Chinese will find where *Raven* went through their spies. So…"

These thought's had already entered the minds of those present; they waited for Warfield's resolutions.

"…minus the forty-five for Monar, the story will be I'm sending *Raven* to Calcutta with the plants. Instead, she will meet up with the *Argus,* just north; off the coast of Vishakhapatnam and the plants will be transferred to that ship and delivered to the southernmost mouth of the Ganges, well below Calcutta. Then, along with Archie, they'll be taken inland and then north to my plantation on the Upper Gangetic Plain, near the Yamuna River.

"Once the transfer to the *Argus* is completed, the *Raven* will return to Madras, any spy will know she would not have had time to reach Calcutta and return, so any thugs will search in vain along the coast. After that, I'll finish my business and head home with Lily, Evelyn and JT."

Archie was the first to speak, "Lord Warfield, that's a good plan but my concern is this is a lot of handling, watering and a long time for the plants to be in root balls..."

"I know, yet there's nothing to be done for it. Muddle through the best you can. Now, let us finish about the Chinese. Ealing's defection was unfortunate and I think that no matter how we try to hide our tracks they'll at least track us to Madras and conceivably up to the Bengal. I had already planned to have protectors patrolling your plantation so this will cause an increase in better quality and *armed* sentries. So Monar, you had better plan for the same."

Monar was pensive, "I agree with you on the sentries, Warfield. But one thing bothers me as well. You suspected Ealing of something foul all along. Why didn't you tell us what you suspected and we would have been more on guard."

Warfield didn't like being second guessed—mostly due to his being conscious of the good possibility he was remiss in his obligation to his captains.

He took his time answering, "There wasn't any one specific item I could put my finger on. It was my instinct saying there was dishonesty in his activities. India and China are notorious for corruption. You have to pay dearly to get anything done with their governments and you fall into it."

JT couldn't resist commenting, "Do you mean like paying Mr. Yin in silver or gold?"

If Warfield saw the insinuation, he hid it, "That's the point I'm coming to. Yes, I expect to pay Mr. Yin a certain inducement, but I don't expect my *Resident* to take his own percentage from that before it's given to Yin."

JT took it all in, 'The bribes, the bribes, the bribes' he thought. 'Warfield bribed Yin, Yin bribed the government, Ealing took his share of the bribe, the east was infamous for buying off or taking bribes. Was anyone clean in this, especially when the whole sordid story of bribery was compounded by opium? And we steal tea plants, so we're as guilty as well, yet it's *Ealing* who should die?'

"Enough!"

Warfield, Monar and Archie were brought up short. Uttered without thought, JT was as startled as the others. He apologized, mumbling he would speak to Warfield later.

The outburst pretty much ended the meeting and after a few more questions and responses, the gathering concluded, while Warfield asked JT to stay, "All right, get it out on the table. What's your problem with all this?"

"I'm sorry for blurting out like that, sir. It's just that it seems so…so wrong, so offensive. We steal; we bribe. Yet blame Ealing for being false and kill *him*. I come from an old Yankee family. We were straight-laced, so to speak. We didn't steal or bribe or anything like that. We were uncomplicated, nothing disreputable. A handshake was our honor. That's the life I led right up until my father…well my father…he became a slaver to save our home and he died from shame. Warfield, his death changed my life. I'm certainly not an innocent in the world, but living this incessant deception and double-dealing is not…it's not me."

"Then tell me, what is the real you?"

He fumbled, then spoke up, "I hope the real me is what Evelyn sees. An honest, intelligent, unpolished sea captain who has the brains and drive to work and live a pleasant life with my wife and kids. You've offered me a management position and as soon as I learn the ropes, I'll work into it, as long as I can get to sea at times. But this constant duplicity …this trickery is not me."

Staring at JT for so long he became uncomfortable, Warfield finally relented, "Very well, JT. If that is your choice then so be it. When we return to England, my wedding present will be a home. You have your ship; I'll get you cargo wherever you want to go with or without Evelyn. And when you think you're ready you can grow into the company's management, but remember, I'm getting on."

They shook hands, Warfield knew that meant more to JT than himself, "Now get going JT, it's past time you get on with your honeymoon. But one more thing, go and check out the *Raven*; have it in your mind she's in good hands."

The suggestion was solely to get JT out of the way for a short time. Warfield left Government House and went straight to where his daughter was waiting.

She was surprised, "Father? I was expecting JT, where are you keeping him?"

"My fault, dear. We had a few items to go over before you both left and he wanted to check out the *Raven* as I'm allowing Scrimshaw and Archie Feng to take it north."

"*You're* allowing? I thought it was JT's ship."

"Sorry, yes, you're right. JT's allowing them to take the *Raven*. But put that aside for the moment because I don't have much time to mention something before he comes."

Evelyn was suspicious and careful. What could be bothering her father? "Go ahead then, what in the devil is so important to discuss on my *wedding* night for God's sake?"

If Warfield was embarrassed, it didn't show, "As you know, JT's not too adroit in stating things but he's informed me he wants a quiet life with you, sailing, children and work. He's not looking to grow…or a challenge."

"And…?"

"What do you mean *and*? If I recall, you were always after excitement, to travel, to sail away. Do you really believe you can forsake all that and settle down to marriage and motherhood in some country cottage?"

Evelyn came to her father, putting her arms around his neck, "Times change, father. I've changed. I think what he's after is marvelous. He sacrificed his ship for me in the Crimea and against those corsairs in the Med he fought for *my* life, not his. That's enough for one life don't you think? And now that he wants…" She hesitated, seeing the passion die in her father's eyes, read through his words.

"Father, Not everyone has your passion, your need to," She couldn't find the word, "I don't know how to say it—your *intensity* to strive for some unspoken goal. You're like so many of your friends, *driven.* I know England's future is people like you carrying the Empire onward, but I will tell you this—don't try to mold JT in your image. You have Monar if you want to attempt that. You must understand; he is my husband, *mine,* and we will go our way. If he chooses to work for Black Moon, of course that's acceptable, but I know him and you must realize—as much as I love you, I don't want him to become you."

Warfield wasn't about to give up, "It doesn't make sense—going counter to his best interests."

Evelyn led him to the door, "Father, maybe someday it will make sense to you, but my husband will be here shortly. So thank you for all you've done, but quite frankly, when he arrives, I don't want you here."

When at last they were alone, their minds and bodies melded. The terrors of the past faded from them, their future held infinite promise. Yet, none of this mattered. No one entered their world; for this moment in time, they were the only couple in creation. Together, together. They had dreamed of it and were now ready for anything the world had in store—so long as they shared it.

«»

In the week, Evelyn and JT spent together exploring the ruins of Fort Wandiwash and ancient ruins, one other affair arose.

After the proper prologue, Monar presented himself to the estate of the Maharaja of Tamil Nadu. Since, Monar was informed, the Maharaja was not well at present, he would be attended shortly by the Maharaja's daughter, Princess Amala Singh.

Monar waited, inwardly fuming. Blast it, Warfield had been right; the daughter would be in charge of the process. The daughter, Monar fixated on as an old maid, and, he feared, would not even know English.

An old woman arrived. Monar's worst thoughts reared their ugly heads—until he was informed the Princess would receive him on the veranda.

Leaving the cool darkened rooms into sunlit parklands, he blinked while escorted through arboreal grounds to the Princess. She sat within a pergola, her deep blue sari, woven with gold and silver strands, gathered around her. She looked up while he drew near; a light smile caused her eyes to sparkle, to complement the smile. He felt as if her whole being shimmered in the filtered sunlight.

Lured on by the fragrance of spice, she spoke and he heard not a word, only the warmest melody.

She repeated herself, "I requested as to if you are fine this day…Mr. Monar."

Delight blended into enchantment, "Please Miss, I mean Princess, I'm, that is…I was not expecting…"

She held a finger to her lips, "Please, sir, find your words for a time. I will wait for you to find them. While you do, sit there, to where I may view your person."

She waited, her eyes and smile holding him, "If you please, Mr. Monar sir, is this your first or second name?"

Taking a deep breath, Monar tried to make sense, "It is my only name, Princess. I am neither a mister nor a sir, it is simply Monar."

"Oh, my goodness gracious, that must not be. It is rude of me to say only Monar, or to bring you to somebody's awareness by only Monar. No, that will not do. I will give thought of another, to add a further name. Only, of course, if it may meet with your pleased reception."

If he was thinking at all, Monar knew any name she offered would meet with his 'pleased reception'.

Princess Amala brightened, “I fear I am not rightly thinking or to be well mannered. My father, the Ruler, would dislike my lack of it. May I offer to you a cup of tea?”

Monar nodded and the Princess waved her hand. From the corner of his eye, he saw movement behind a latticed wall and two giggling, lovely young women came forth with a tray holding a teapot, cozy, cups and sweets.

Monar couldn’t help a smile; the giggling women revealed he was not quite alone with the Princess.

They toured the land in an open carriage, followed by another containing four men. The Princess spoke of their farms, not knowing the acreage of the domain under cultivation—no one did, she said. There were cattle, pottery sheds, an indigo factory for extracting blue dye, jewelry creating, spice production, cotton fields vanishing off into the distance supplying some of the plantation’s cloth spinning shops for poorer quality textiles and finally, five square miles of tea plants. According to the type of tea plant, condition, and aging, they grew Black, Oolong, Green—non-oxidized and the sweetest she said—and a rare White tea.

It turned out Warfield sent an expert along with the tea plants and both had arrived ahead of Monar. They watched the expert whip-graft some of the planting stems to crossbreed the Chinese to Indian plants. It soon became boring. To them, anything other than the two of them would.

Walking between the rows, the Princess put her arm through Monar’s. He strolled in a pleasant daze.

“Is this to be proper? I have seen English ladies to do this when they stroll a man by Polo pony.”

“It’s not at all improper. It’s very nice and certainly very ladylike. Tell me, where did you learn English?”

“The English School, in Delhi. They teach fine manners, to be as they say, ladylike and vi…vidacious.”

Monar smiled at her distortion. I don’t think you had to be taught that. You’re a Princess; I’d easily believe vivacious came to you quite naturally.”

She returned the smile, making no response. Nevertheless, unanticipated emotions chilled him when she smiled. A strange sensation coursed through his body, followed by a marvel he'd never known. Was that true? He felt this emotion *had* been known before. Yet when, how? When did he know this, in what other of his worlds…?

He stopped, mystified. She seemed to be waiting—what did she know? He no longer asked, for somehow he knew the emotion was inexplicable, beyond his awareness.

He tried to speak, yet found his feelings would not become words. Even though in shadows, her face held a magical luminosity when her hand went to his lips, "I know you wonder. Do not," she murmured, "It is written. We are predestined to be as one. I knew as you appeared to me."

A lovely lilting laugh, "Yet it took you until now to find that. My name is Amala; I have awaited you to thirty years age. In your tongue, my name means clean, pure. I will come to you in that manner. Alas, my father, for he is to die. He is great Maharaja, whose fathers, fathers, fathers, grandfather were Maharajas back to the time of Great Lord Shiva. Even English know he is great ruler and does works great to his people's name. We, as well, will do great things as he before us."

Monar could tell Amala had rehearsed her words and said nothing, nothing until he focused on her next words.

"When my father, the Ruler, passages to Yama, the Lord of all Death, I will weep for him until he shall reach Svargam; that is your heaven. I will then turn to become Maharini. Then you, my beloved, will become Hindi and my mate and be avowed Prince Monar and have the two names.

'But I ask to you one thing. Not long past there is tales that come to my ear—a huge phantom, a spirit it may be, my people hear, that moves through shadows of the Fort Saint George and White Town and Black Town. This phantom brings frights and worry. If you know of this spirit, please make that it is to stop. My people, they come to fear."

6

The Decade That Followed. 1850 through 1860.

FOR EVELYN AND JT, the decade was, far and away, lived enjoyably. Born to them were three children, two boys, definitely from the Graves side of the family. After the boys there followed a striking, winsome girl, Victoria, the diminutive, very essence of Evelyn. When Evelyn and JT found time without the children, they sailed on excursions with cargo to various ports along the European coast. Once the children were old enough, oceans and destinations around the world were reached and treasured. The single odd thing was that when in New York, Charleston or other ports in the States, JT thought of going farther north, to Boston or Salem, yet never made the effort.

He learned, secured, and extended the once jumbled domain of Lord Warfield to where there were no major ports that did not find the Black Moon burgee fluttering at their wharfs. He removed and stored twenty of the twenty-four of the *Raven's* cannon to reduce weight and increase speed and when sailing with Evelyn, without their children, they did not close their eyes to any adventure. The *Raven's* Captain, with a cargo of Lord Bunting's Supreme Black Tea from Warfield's India plantations would, given the opportunity around Calcutta or Madras, accept challenges from other tea clippers such as the S*outhern Cross, Rainbow or British Pride*, in races around the Horn to London.

On other occasions, which found Monar aboard—without his wife who was prone to seasickness—transporting his Prince Monar's Superior Green Tea, when they raced in fair competition, they never lost to the famous tea clippers *Ariel, Great Republic or Sovereign of the Seas*.

After each feat, a great reunion would be held at Blackwood Abbey for all contestants. It wasn't the finish that mattered; it was the thrill of the race, the companionship that inspired all of the great clipper captains. Yet everyone knew, though aging, *Raven* was still the quickest ship afloat.

Evelyn loved their life together as much as JT. Whether at sea, at home, or with the children, she helped plan and direct business ventures with JT and Warfield and relaxed in sailing ventures around the Isle of Wight or the Continent. She never thought to question her life or want to change. Life was lived to the fullest; they knew it and loved it.

Like the others, Lord Warfield aged over these ten years. Still, it remained unquestioned that Black Moon was his and his to guide. Most of the company's moves were profitable and legal, while those steps with questionable motives were discreetly obscured under false entries that burdened clerks under reams of paperwork.

Aside from legitimate and illegitimate exercises, among his good works, Warfield built clinics for the indigent, fought for shorter work hours for women and children, instituted sanitation programs and the elimination of flogging in both the navy and merchant fleet.

Still, every step the Lord of Blackwood Abbey made solidified his vast enterprises of companies and shipping alliances. Steel mills, railroads, shipyards, hundreds of consumer stores across the world, scores of ships and vast tea plantations were under his control and through him John Thomas grew in ability, influence and wealth. As for Prince Monar, between the hoard he held from Ian MacPherson's death in Barbados, his holdings in tea production through Warfield's percentages and being married to Amala and her fortune, he was easily deemed India's wealthiest Black Raj.

For the first six years of their marriage, Prince Monar and the Maharini Amala, in between having four boys, fought against the encroachment into the Maharini's Tamil Nadu territories by the British East India Company.

As an intermediary, Warfield endeavored to convince Monar it would be for the best to let the BEIC run the region. By allowing that, the BEIC, through Warfield, offered Monar and Amala a worry free life of vast wealth.

He should have known better regarding Monar, and learned better when confronting the Maharini.

With the couple's refusal, and with Warfield's knowledge, if not blessing, the next BEIC foray into Tamil Nadu lowlands comprised a squadron of the 23rd Madras Light Sowar Cavalry and three-hundred Maratha Sepoy foot soldiers. The incursion ended in their unforeseen Battle of the Arkonam Valley Gorge, wherein the Sepoy, misled by BEIC officers into an ambuscade, were hopelessly entrapped. The ensuing parley the Sepoy, in their shame, were only too willing to kill their officers, yet dissuaded by Tamil Nadu General, Prince Monar's benevolence.

This skirmish and other unrest across central and northern India concerned the Crown enough to consider governing the BEIC and discussed the dissolution of the Company. Yet Warfield's disquiet for his India holdings was unfounded for the present; however, the era of the new British Raj, indorsed by the Crown would eventually come.

It was however, during the time of the Battle of the Arkonam Valley Gorge, that Lord Warfield considered Monar's ambush and the bloody nose he'd given the BEIC quite amusing. With few dead, Warfield felt it was really nothing to get unduly bothered about and truthfully, it was something *he* would have loved to have achieved.

There were no hard feelings between the two men. To the contrary, Warfield found that when there were more nefarious schemes in the wind, he had a kindred spirit.

For all of them, the years passed agreeably; they sailed on with little concern, although they did keep up with world events to how it might matter or impose on their world.

1853 caused a latent stir of pride in JT to learn the American Commodore Perry, had dropped anchor with three other warships in a Japanese harbor of Uraga, near Edo, to compel foreigner trade with the Tokugawa Shôgunate.

In '54, when the Crimean War between England and Russia at long last erupted, it brought unwanted memories to Evelyn, JT and Monar. They relived the loss of the *Golden Raven* to the Russian warship *Ghazna*, and later their barely escaping with their lives in the Mediterranean thanks to the US Navy warship, *Cumberland.*

The 2nd Opium War between England and China in 1856 caused additional concern to Warfield, yet they all were relieved that Chinese thugs never assailed them or their plantations. There was curiosity whether Archie Feng had prevented that, although he never said. There was still concern over Ashley Ealing or Archie's son surfacing again.

In 1857, the simmering pot of Indian unrest with the BEIC boiled over—and justifiably so. The Sepoy Mutiny, known as the Great Rebellion started in Meerut, on the Upper Gangetic Plain, and spread to Cowpore, Lucklow and further, even to Delhi. Sepoy and civilians alike rose against the British and specifically the East India Company in a rage that continued unabated into 1858 before quelled. The British Parliament took control of the BEIC, yet Warfield's tea plantations and eastern shipping holdings remained safe. He was, it should be remembered, a Member of Parliament.

In 1859, slavery was the topic from America with the four-week-old news of the hanging of John Brown for treason. Slavery was a disquiet to JT because of his father's involvement and death directly from the aftermath. Slavery had long been eliminated in England. It was the terrible narration of pro and anti-slavery gangs along the American southland and western states, and the worrisome upwelling of threats from the South to secede, that distressed those in England. The more slavery came to the fore, the more JT recognized he was still American—a North American.

1860 closed and a new decade, a decade of calamity began.

7

20 March 1861 Blackwood Abbey, Portsmouth, England.

LORD WARFIELD LOOKED UP from his *Lloyd's Weekly*, "I see here that Lincoln chap is now President of your country with some chap called Hamlin as Vice President, JT and not a single Southern state voted for them. It says here they voted for two other people, Breckinridge and Bell. What do you think of that?"

JT stopped his cloud watching and stretched, it had been a busy two months. "I don't really know much about him other than he was a next to nothing Senator from Illinois and on the fence about slavery. Just coming back from Portugal, I haven't really kept up with news from the States, other than the slavery question over there, but obviously the South being against him will be troublesome."

"Troublesome? That's the least of it. You probably don't know seven States have voted for secession and more joining. In these past two months over there the South formed a Confederate Constitution with a Jefferson Davis as President. I'm telling you, JT, your country could slip into civil war if both parties don't step back and think this over."

Handing JT the paper, Warfield's comments continued, "In my view, the only chance of saving the situation is that Lincoln said he's not in favor of slavery but has no plans to end it. Yet then he turns around and said he won't allow the South to secede. He's right on that score, he surely isn't going to go down in history as the President who split the country into two countries."

JT read further, "I see the South has grabbed some Union forts except for Fort Sumter in South Carolina. If they try to take it by force, I think that will be the match in the tinder box. To me, they're already over the brink and irrational. Compared to the South, the North is an industrial giant. All they have is their cotton industry. I doubt there's even one rifle made down there. But more to the point, why would anyone, anyone other than slave holders, go to war over slavery? Doesn't make sense."

"No JT, it doesn't. But let me posit you this; when people are told what they can and can't do, especially you Americans, aren't there always firebrands rousting them on? People are predictable; get their hackles up—throw sense out the window with the bath water."

"You really think war could happen?"

"Show me the choice. The South is intractable. They think this Lincoln chap is a rudderless, indecisive country bumpkin. My opinion is he'll let them think that until he finally slams his fist down and then there'll be hell to pay for the South. Till then, leaders on both sides should be locked up in Bedlam because they're letting this blasted fervor create its own momentum."

Evelyn entered the room, "You think war, father?"

"Hasn't anyone noticed? The *USS Star of the West* was fired on by the Confederates back in January and since then they've seized all sorts of military property. I'm preparing for trouble. After JT left for Portugal I sent every available Black Moon merchant ship to Savannah to load cotton."

JT took note, "I looked at the shipping forms when I got back and saw you even sent some of them empty and I planned to ask why, but you've answered my question. It's obvious now; King Cotton is the South's sole cash crop and if there's war, the Union will blockade the ports, that's what you're saying isn't it? That will cripple them economically. Stop them getting income and stop any supplies from reaching them. So, you're after cotton before that happens. Damn it, Warfield, no wonder you got where you are. But thinking about it, you're helping the South, aren't you?"

Warfield turned self-righteous, "Well let's remember something, JT, there isn't a war right *now*, is there?"

JT knew he still had a lot to learn. Predict events and use them to your advantage—another Warfield lesson. Yet two other thoughts surfaced. If we could see what will happen, why on earth couldn't the Southern gentry? JT recalled the old adage, 'Pride goeth before the fall'. Yes, he reasoned, with their pride that could be just what happens.

His other thought? To him, Lincoln was unknown and untested. Yet JT was a Northerner, living in England or not. If war should break out, he saw no way to stay out of it.

On 12 April, 1861, Confederate cannon blasted segments of Fort Sumter to rubble and a tattered stars and stripes was hauled down. Declared or not, the fratricidal American Civil War had begun.

«»

She could see it in his eyes. Feel his mind in turmoil. She waited, waited for him to tell her. Eventually, it came out.

"You're troubled about me I know, Evelyn and now I want *your* thoughts on my dilemma."

"You mean the war, don't you?"

"Yes."

"And you want to go."

"God, don't ever think that, far from it. It's that I have an obligation to my country."

"Like that obligation way back to your Savannah Belle? Sorry JT; that's unfair—it's just that I'm upset."

"I know you are. Back then I was some kind of fool, this is for my honor. I've tried to avoid it Eve—I just can't."

"I knew this was coming and I'd lined up all sorts of reasons to make you stay. But watching you all these years I know there are some things you have to do, no matter how it goes against the grain. You're no longer a young man, but you're still an obstinate cuss John Thomas. Despite that—and don't give me that look—I want you to know I'm one-hundred percent against you going. But you're *my* obstinate cuss of a husband, so I have to be ninety-nine percent behind you."

Warfield took a different tactic when JT and Evelyn went to speak with him, "Look at it this way, JT, yes, the South took over a number of installations and few Revenue Cutters, but those are nearly their entire navy. They did that earlier, when Lincoln was trying to prevent a war. Now that it seems South has started it, the divided Yankee's will unite behind Lincoln and that will untie the military. And remember, the North *has* a full-fledged navy. My contacts say the war will be over in a few months, maybe even weeks. Look, why not see who's got the cards, then see if you feel obliged to go."

JT gave the suggestion thought, looking to Evelyn, "Tell you what. I'll delay two or three months. It would take me at least one month to get the *Raven* fitted out, the guns remounted and the engines rebuilt. If things don't look like they're settling down by then, well, then I'll go."

"Fair enough," was Warfield's response, "but I want to make one thing clear-cut. My heart is with the South and not solely because of the cotton—it's her underdog status. In spite of this, I'll stay out of it because her slavery stance is not acceptable and I think England will feel that way too."

Lord Warfield was correct in assuming the North would initiate a blockade of Southern ports in an attempt to strangle the Confederacy. Yet it was far easier to say, than do. To cover more than three thousand miles of the South's coastline with its rivers, inlets, channels and seaports would necessitate the entire US Navy and then some.

In blockading the obvious ports, other ships had to cover the hidden bayous and secreted havens day and night. A major task lay ahead if it was to be done right. Not only ships and trained crews, but *fast,* armed steamships, would be needed to overtake the swift blockade runners.

Although JT followed the war events, he went about his work efficiently for the next two months, adjusting shipping schedules, cargos, and harbors to counter the dilemma of a nation at war with itself. Ships carrying cargo for Australia and India were ordered to return with cotton, even though inferior quality and any blockade runners with cotton from America were indeed welcome. England, as Warfield also expected, remained neutral, yet along with France, leaned toward the South despite her slavery stance.

In the two months from the start of the Rebellion and President Lincoln issuing the order to blockade the South, both sides were active. The Union burned most of the Gosport Navy Yard and five warships—one being the *Merrimack*—at Norfolk, Virginia to prevent their takeover.

The USS *Saratoga* captured the slave ship *Nightingale* with 961 slaves aboard. The *USS Cumberland* captured the ships *CSS Young America,* the *Mary and Virginia,* the *Theresa* and the munitions carrying vessel *George M Smith.* And still no war was declared.

USS Naval requisitions for ships capable of mounting nine-inch pivot cannon were given out to various shipyards and numerous private steamships were armed and commissioned to seize Southern shipping. The plan spread.

The Confederacy, along with taking over the gutted Gosport US Naval Yard, captured the US Steamer *Star of the West* and a goodly number of northern ships. They welcomed four more states to the Confederacy as well but, at about the same time, they found not one of their cargo ships going to or from Europe were safe.

Then, President Lincoln's blockade proclamation—considered the official beginning of the Civil War—was printed in the London papers, placing the South in desperate circumstances on the ocean. Her agents, sent to England to purchase iron steam ships and armaments, were, with few exceptions, thwarted by the thin iron hulls of British merchant ships not built for battle and then Queen Victoria's proclamation of England's neutrality.

After minor skirmishers in western Virginia, the first crucial *land* conflict began on 21 July, 1861 in eastern Virginia with the clash between the Union Army of Northeastern Virginia and the Confederate Army of the Potomac in the First Battle of Bull Run, not far from the city of Washington.

In their conceit, the Washington gentry considered the battle to be some sort of enjoyable excursion, and this led to men in carriages and women twirling parasols, strolling with their beaus, while they awaited the Union troops thrashing of the Rebels to put an end to the Rebellion.

It was true the clash did become a near thing for the South, and would have spelled disaster were it not for the timely arrival of Confederate General J E Johnson's force.

The scale was tipped in favor of the South, and the Yankee gentry's smug, rather pleasant excursion turned to pandemonium when civilians and soldiers stampeded toward the suddenly dubious security of Washington's ramparts.

The day became the North's lament, triumph for the South.

This historic land battle awakened both Northern and Southern leaders to one stark fact; the war was going to be long. Long and bloody.

«»

August 1861

With no actual navy, the South could only resort to blockade-runners, privateers, and commerce raiders. Whether they were successful or lost, these Southern raiders captured dozens of unarmed merchant vessels and kept the American Navy committed to preventing the losses. The Navy had other undertakings as well, including blockading, continuing the bombardment of Rebel forts along the eastern seaboard and moving US soldiers to countless land skirmishes.

Then, the Union Navy captured the North Carolina forts of Hatteras and Clark. Those forts had protected the Hatteras Inlet and given Southern raiders and blockade-runners security inside the barrier islands and reefs. This Union victory sealed off Pamlico and Albemarle Sounds, thereby eliminating what little there was of North Carolina's Navy and any threat to Union shipping from the

Sounds. Following that battle, the Navy also acquired a supply repository for squadrons further south and yet, of even more import, it meant the first victory of the North's Navy *and*, the regaining of United States territory. In the land war however, the news was stark. Union forces were stymied.

In England, JT took it all in, although at best the news was three to four weeks old. Still, he had made the decision to leave, or rather return to the States, and offer his services.

Evelyn understood. She didn't like it, but she knew that what he called his obligation; was actually his attempt to redeem his family's honor after his father's fall into hell. In JT's halting manner, he tried his best to convey this to Evelyn. If, by serving to help end slavery, he could in some way counter the mark his father had given their name—Slaver Graves.

Their children didn't fully understand the concern at his leave taking. They were accustomed to his travels, yet this time they were old enough to feel tautness, the anxiety of their parents and so held to the background as father said goodbye to their mother.

Even at their parting, JT still tried to explain, until she halted him, "John Thomas, please—don't give me this story of truth or right or honor. I know what's inside you, driving you. You're taking on the sins of your father and I can't convince you otherwise. I must admit, deep inside, I'm proud you feel that way and if it was not for the children, you couldn't keep me from going with you…"

She started to choke up, "So I'm taking the children and leaving right now so you can be the dedicated captain of this expatriate crew you've cobbled together. See Warfield before you leave. Oh, one thing more, don't get into the troubles we had at Crimea or off Morocco. You get hurt and you'll come home to one angry wife."

A quick kiss on his cheek and she was gone before he could hold her.

Warfield came up, trying to fill the void, "I've done my best to convince you to stay, JT, so I'll not waste my breath. Now then, what's your plan?"

"Pretty straightforward. I spoke with your contact, Foreign Secretary Russell and he said I'm not breaking British Law, at least according to your Prime Minister, Lord Palmerston…"

Warfield interrupted, "I'd be cautious regarding what Secretary Russell tells you, he can be rather cavalier with facts if he chooses. But if Palmerston blesses it, I'll assume you're all right. What did Adams, the US Minister, say?"

"He said British Minister, Bruce, is doing all he can to keep the South from getting ships in England and for me to contact a Captain Du Pont at the Washington Navy Yard. Adams heard how fast the *Raven* is and gave me a letter for Du Pont about her and another letter for the US Secretary of the Navy, Gideon Welles, recommending me and the *Raven.* I want to thank you for this, Warfield; I know how you feel about the South."

"Yes, but that's all well and good now, isn't it? Yet when you think of it, if that damn Atlantic cable hadn't split again, we'd be more up to date on what's going on over there. But whatever, the main thing is you return healthy and sound. By the by, I've sent a letter to Monar, asking if he and his family would come here to help for the few months you'll be gone. That will benefit him in seeing the overall company picture too."

"Do you think he'll come?"

"Don't know. From what I've heard, he has a well-run operation over there and I've guaranteed no Indian or British interference in the Maharini's Tamil Nadu region."

JT smiled, Warfield still had the right contacts, even though the British Government had taken over the BEIC.

The lines holding the *Raven* to an English pier were cast off although steam pressure was not brought up. Sensing the offshore breeze, JT ordered all sail unfurled to Chief Petty Officer Harry Scrimshaw, and he of the tea theft passed the word. Without assistance from a tug, a gamble, the *Raven* edged away from the wharf. He knew his ship. The wheel eased over. She caught the air. Just as he had done years past in Salem Massachusetts with the old, still lamented, *Golden Raven*, he let the sails billow. By the harbor's mouth, again as back in Salem, dock men and bystanders stood in awe and stared and dreamed and in time would remember her. For it was the last they would ever see of the *Raven*.

Time was nearing the end of the pure sail era. Steam power would now challenge the oceans. Choosing between them was left to the eye and mind of the beholder.

«»

The man sitting behind the desk was an old navy sea dog. Bewhiskered, the thoughtful face with creases from scowling at charts was reserved as he read the letter from the American Minister to England, Charles Francis Adams.

Rear Admiral Samuel Du Pont, former President of the Navy Board and chief strategist for blockading the South, was also in charge of the overall coastal war.

"This information from Adams regarding you and your ship is quite impressive. He writes of the sea trials you had years ago on the Solent. Still think you've the fastest ship in the world?"

Not knowing that information was in the letter, JT was caught off guard, "Well sir, over the last ten years I haven't kept up with the latest in hull and power plant development, but I still think it would take one hell of a ship to stay with her, power and or sail."

"Very good then. I'm only now back from fleet operations at Port Royal Sound and I've been designated Squadron Commander for another naval operation with the army along the coast. That means you won't be in my command until you've finished training to become a Reserve Naval Officer. Don't worry yourself, for you it will be abbreviated, we need every fast ship and experienced captain we can get for blockade duty."

JT was pleased, "Thank you sir, I was hoping I could be of service. Tell me, quite a few in my crew are Americans who were living in England. Some of them returned to help the Union and would like to serve with my ship, could that be arranged?"

“Seeing as I’m shipping out soon, that will be up to the Commander of this Navy Yard. I don’t see a problem with that but…” Du Pont made a wry smile, “but between us sea dogs, Commander Dahlgren is a dry foot sailor, never gets much water under him, so I can’t speak for him. In fairness, he is developing much better ordinance. He invented the Dahlgren rifled cannon and howitzers that are probably the best in the world.”

Du Pont made another crooked smile, “And of course, Dahlgren has Lincoln’s ear and that surely doesn’t hurt his career. I’m sure he’ll be only too happy to inform you of all this and more, so take some of it with a grain of salt—I’ll leave you with that.”

The Commander of the Washington Navy Yard, US Naval Officer John Dahlgren, had little time for a merchant captain. A *civilian* ship captain did not interest the Commandant and he abruptly handed off JT to Captain Silas Stringham. Captain Stringham was a tall man with a short temper and irascible, yet JT couldn’t have asked for a more able officer to serve under.

In the action securing the Oregon Inlet from the Confederate forces by a combined navy, army effort, Captain Stringham excelled by teaching his own navy the value of steam power and the exercise of accurate firing while ships were underway. By forcing through the Outer Banks, the North controlled the Pamlico Sound and initiated the domination of the Albemarle Sound and the coast of North Carolina. This had given the Navy storm-safe harbors.

Unfortunately, for Captain Stringham, Du Pont’s exploits in the Port Royal Sound engagement overshadowed the Hatteras victory and now, Du Pont passing off John Thomas to him compounded Stringham’s annoyance.

His mood only changed when asking if this *merchant* captain in front of him had seen action. He was confident the answer would be an embarrassed ‘no’.

“Yes, Sir, I have.”

“Oh, and where might that have been?”

"I lost my ship against the Russian warship *Ghazna* in the Crimea and fought in two other actions off Morocco, one where we were saved by the *USS Cumberland*."

The words Morocco and *Cumberland* brought Stringham forward in his seat, "Really, Morocco? When were you there?"

"Back in '49. I was in an armed British merchant ship; we were close hauled in light air, never had the weather gauge and being boarded by a horde of Barbary pirates when the *Cumberland* saved us by a whisker."

Stringham came alive, "Well I'll be damned. I was there in '14 with Decatur's Squadron during the Barbary Wars, helped take an Algerine frigate. Christ, if you don't bring back good memories."

JT remained silent while the Captain mused, "And you were up in the Black Sea as well. Seems you've had water under you I haven't. You'll have to tell me about it. But right now, what can you do for the Union and what can I do to help you do it? By the way, do you know that your same *Cumberland* is in our blockade? She's captained by Flag Officer Pendergrass now, captured a few rebel ships carrying munitions, coal, and cotton—she's doing her duty."

Captain Stringham's memories helped JT, but he could see the captain was pondering something as he spoke, "Graves…Graves, seems I recall that name for some reason. Where were you from in the States?"

"Salem, father, and grandfather were captains also."

Stringham's eyes narrowed in thought. JT saw the questioning look and began to speak, "Sir, I want to help the Union in any way I can. I've a good, fast ship and…"

Holding up a hand, Captain Stringham waved him quiet, "I have no interest in your *father's* past, only yours. Come, I want to see this ship that's alleged to be so quick.

«»

Captain Stringham walked along the wharf from the *Raven's* stem to her stern. Once aboard, he went to the taffrail and sighted along the gunwale to the bowsprit.

"You say this ship's sharp bow line was built to your design, *twelve* years ago?"

"Yes, sir, on the Thames."

"Well, all I can say is you were six or seven years ahead of your time. Even today, few carry her line. She's elegant! It's that simple. I believe you when you said there are few to match her. What does she have for power?"

"Twin Napier's, shaft horsepower upgraded to four-hundred fifty each and rebuilt with new copper boilers."

Stringham nodded, smiling, "She will prove to be a blockade runner's nemesis. That is once we replace most of those cannon with two Dahlgren pivot guns."

JT almost snapped his neck turning to Captain Stringham, "Remove my cannon? I don't follow you, why wouldn't I need them?"

"You may know ships, Captain, but obviously you've not kept up with armament in the past ten years. Your cannon are not rifled, that means they're not too accurate. Secondly, as I said, we'll replace them with two pivot guns. I see you're still befuddled, come with me."

Further along the wharf was moored the USS *Pawnee,* a sail and steam powered sloop. As he stepped aboard, JT was taken by the size of two huge cannon, each amid ship, fore and aft on the ship's centerline.

"What you see here Captain Graves are heavy pivot cannon. These are nine-inch Dahlgrens, solid shot or shell guns. The reason they are called pivot guns is simple. The gun carriage is mounted on that flat steel rail running down the centerline deck of the ship."

JT began to follow the concept, "So each gun can run about half the length of the ship more or less and then…?"

"And then, you see those curved rails to port and starboard? They allow the guns to slide from the centerline to either gunnel and from there the guns themselves can swivel in a 90-degree arc. Hence, pivot guns."

"This is something I've never heard of, and the size is remarkable. What's their range?"

"This one is a 34 pounder exploding shell. So, she'll throw shell over 3,400 yards—with some accuracy."

"Two miles?"

"Correct, with your ship, a bow chaser, and this main battery," Stringham fixed his eyes on JT, "if any blockade runner slips away, we'll know who to blame."

"Point well taken and I accept the challenge, Captain. What comes next?"

"I'm recommending you for Reserve Lieutenant in the United States Navy. Let me know who in your crew you want and your second officer and I'll handle the rest. Oh, and I'll also give you the two best gun crews available."

The RMS *Britannica*, a Black Moon Royal Mail Ship was in the Washington Naval Yard for coaling and this gave JT an opportunity to mail Evelyn a letter. This missive proved to be the first of dozens she received and they would follow a strict form. The loved her. He missed her and the children. Then his activities followed and lastly, he loved her.

The *Britannica* had sailed from Southampton to Bermuda, to Washington. Her run would continue to New York, then Halifax, Nova Scotia, and finally on back to Southampton. Each letter would arrive weeks after written.

Commander John G. Goss was the epitome of an officer class that ailed the wartime Union Navy. Conceited, an ego beyond his capabilities and a personality that disguised his incompetence enabled him to baffle his superiors and hide his faults by riding on the backs of his subordinates.

When the war was brewing, the need for forward thinking naval officer's left the Navy with no other recourse to prove an officers worth than by having them prevent Southern privateers from preying on northern shipping.

From shore duty, Commander Goss went to sea and proved afflicted with a slight problem of over-cautiousness and a serious question of ineptitude bordering on farce.

On the night of 18 April 1861, while covering the lighthouse tender USS *Buchanan* off the Virginian coast, Commander Goss stood well off from the *Buchanan* and allowed her to be boarded by a Southern gunboat crew and taken to Richmond with the tender's crew as prisoners.

At the Naval Board enquiry in May, the Commander insisted he had not been informed in writing there was an official Declaration of War between the Union and the Confederate States.

In truth, he was correct. The actual start of the war, that is, the *legal* start of the war, was considered President Lincoln's order to blockade the southern ports. And that happened 19 April, the next day, *after* the *Buchanan's* humiliating capture.

Nevertheless, Goss was found blameworthy in the lesser charges of misconstruing an order and dereliction of duty by his failure to, at the very least; interpose his ship between the *Buchanan* and the now defined Rebels.

In the end, Goss retained his rank, but banished to shore duty—in this case, instructing in the Naval Code of Conduct for new officers at the Navy Yard.

Instruct he did, and with vengeance. The proper form of addressing a senior officer, the proper form of saluting, the meaning of 'aye, aye' the first 'aye' meaning I heard, Sir, the second 'aye' meaning the order would be carried out, Sir. Further tutoring included signal systems, manning of vessels in reserve, active and combat, victual inspection, seaman's health, water quality, more health, firing salutes and the list went on, not once, but repeated over and again. The infamous *Aye, Aye* became the common response to all comments when new, off duty officers met at mess.

When JT requested an appointment with Flag Officer Stringham, Goss laughing told him that, "*Mister* Stringham had resigned his commission in a snit over his treatment after forcing the Oregon Inlet at Hatteras."

Actually, Stringham's actions at the Inlet were questioned for his not bringing his vessels closer to the forts. Later, it was found the water was too shallow and that he had been ordered to return to Fort Monroe immediately.

Stringham however, maddened that his judgment was questioned, requested to be relieved of command. He never left the service and, to sooth his fevered brow, was promoted to the rank of Rear Admiral in 1862.

Sadly, none of this helped JT break free from Commander Goss and his interminable training until an unidentified note was found under his door that brought the quandary to a head. The unsigned missive, apparently from a person with select knowledge, stated that Goss's intention was to 'delay John Thomas' training long enough for the naval brass to question his competence and seek permission, to lease or *commandeer* the *Raven* with a replacement Commander'.

Attached, was a copy of Goss's request for transfer to sea duty and proposing his command of the *Raven*—if the Navy should so decide.

JT's first reaction was rage. His next reaction was to challenge Goss in person. The final reaction he took was to forward the pages to Silas Stringham, asking his advice.

When the letter reached Stringham, he in turn forwarded it to Flag Officer, A. Hull Foote with pointed comments on Goss and advocating John Graves as Reserve Lieutenant and that revised armament be approved to convert the fast clipper *Raven* for blockade duty.

F O Foote demanded the release; Goss was dropped from training instructor and dropped further down to Boston Navy Yard's Stores and Supply Division. There were few steps left to reach the bottom of the officer ladder.

JT was freed; still, he was later to have contact with Goss in the most hostile fashion.

«»

8 December 1861, Blackwood Abbey

Winter had settled in at Portsmouth. Mild enough to keep the shipping channels open, there was, nevertheless, anxiety. As Warfield and others predicted, it didn't take long for cotton to become in short supply. Now it became a question of priorities. Evelyn and Lily saw it wearing on him.

"Father, There's really nothing you can do."

"I know, we're reaching that point, yet it's getting worse. Up in Stalybridge, outside Manchester, I've had to discharge a thousand people at the mills and at least another two thousand more are going to be sacked. The workers at Bayley's Mills are talking strike again—fools. Things are bad enough without those damned radicals Engle and Marx spewing out that dead fool Frenchman Fourier's clap-trap."

"What can you do? You've had soup kitchens set up; you're not collecting rents and you're getting coal over from Newcastle for those on the dole."

"Evelyn, you know nothing's ever enough, in fact you've told me that yourself. Especially now when none of the other owners are lifting a finger to help. Not Bayley, Gordon, none of them. I'm telling you, there's going to be riots if something isn't done, and that something is getting the blasted American Rebellion over with and get cotton."

"Well, don't have a heart attack over it. There's not a thing you can do."

"You think not, do you? Well, if England isn't going to get involved, I'm going to."

"What do you have up your sleeve?"

"Nothing to bother your pretty little head about. Monar will be here not too long from now and we'll put our heads together and come up with a plan."

"You two? Ah, I see, another nest of bandits arising."

"Evelyn," Warfield appearing terribly wounded, "how hurtful of you. What kind of daughter are you to imply your father's a bandit?"

Lily smiled toward the two of them, "Yes Evelyn, what kind of daughter indeed, would ever imply that?"

The kind of father that Evelyn was alluding to was deep in thought on how he could acquire cotton from America. He knew the South was desperate for the material of war and would, in return, supply vast quantities of cotton that he, and all mill owners, were in desperate need. Warfield had swift cargo schooners and, although not having the capacity of a merchantman, they could run the gauntlet of lumbering Northern warships. But not all Union ships were lumbering and he expected the *Raven* to be one of the best of that class. That was why, with a few government officials connivance, Warfield had invested in another ship with Laird & Son, Birkenhead, on the Mersey River. A ship up to the task.

Then, the exploit of a US navy ship gave him pause.

The *USS San Jacinto* halted the British Royal Mail Ship *Trent* off Cuba, then seized and removed two Confederate emissaries bound for England and France. This act instantly caused an international brouhaha. The *Trent* Affair triggered a faction of hot-headed British politicians and their associates to become quite heated over the perceived affront to England's rights on the high seas and wanted England to do more than simply posture. Schemes however, slowed during the year, then quelled. It was pointed out by Prime Minister Palmerston that forty percent of England's corn and wheat came from the US. The implication being that any politicians wishing to antagonize starving British hordes, hordes that would indeed arise from conflict with America, were welcome to tender a proposal for war in their name.

Although England did send ten thousand troops to eastern Canada, and involved themselves with all sort leaderless military pursuits, the Union did not consider any covert or even overt enough to respond in kind.

So despite all her posturing, in the end England remained neutral, much to the South's chagrin.

The Cotton Famine however, stilled the mills and stalked England's laboring class for the next four years.

«»

1 February 1862, a Hill Station in Visakhapatnam, India

They were in sanctuary, beneath a relief of Maurya Samrat.

"He was exalted man, Monar, an emperor of all, most of India. You could be, you and sons, our sons."

"Amala, I have all I want now. In fact, far more than I need and I'll bet I'm happier than this Samrat fellow was."

"If you feel this, tell to me again, why is need to go to England?"

"I told you before, it's not a *need* in that sense of the word, nor *must* I go. It's an obligation I have to Warfield and not because he's my employer. He's my friend and helped me to succeed and, I'll remind you once more, he connived my meeting with you."

The Maharini mused for a moment, "Con-nived? This means in English he is sneak?"

Monar could not hold back a laugh, "Sort of, yes. But in our case, a good sneak."

Monar had written Warfield that he was coming to England with his family. This was before Amala had agreed and the time for her answer was getting short.

She was swaying his way and now he mentioned his final effort, "Amala, listen carefully to me. Someday, India must be ruled by the Indian people. I want our sons to be more than Indian Princes under British benevolence—that's only another word for dominance. I want our sons to be leaders, influential leaders to reveal how England gets more out of India than she gives. Simply because the British Government is benevolent, doesn't mean the Queen will always be that way for India. If we educate our children in England for two or three years, they will learn how the Brits govern and also learn how to beat them at their own game."

It was Amala's turn to laugh, "You mean con-nive the British, like Lord Warfield is to con-nive you and then you con-nive me?"

Monar glanced at her sideways, she never was one to be duped in English or Hindi, "Rather like that, yes."

In the end, Amala agreed to spend at least to two years in England and the children would stay three, or perhaps more. That would require more discussion.

Monar was sure Warfield was hatching some plan that would involve cotton, his realizing there wasn't enough quality cotton coming from Australia or India to run the mills. This much Monar knew for a fact. However, if Warfield's plan involved blockade runners, there was a problem, a personal and moral problem, rearing its ugly head.

In order to get cotton, Warfield would have to supply some type of war material to the South, a South that was fighting for independence—and, to keep slavery.

Monar stared at the dilemma. Yes, the South said they were fighting for states' rights; at least that is the rallying to arms call from the plantation owners. But it came down to their wanting slavery continued, so how could he justify helping them? England and France had eliminated slavery. Not child labor and work hours, true, but at least it was a start. Yet half the United States, the most enlightened country the world had ever known, condoned it.

Monar had never been an abolitionist, he still wasn't. He had simply thought of it, what few times he gave it thought, as a way of life that every black man—if he hadn't the wherewithal, money or ability to escape—had to bear in a white world or even tan or yellow worlds. Arabia, India, Chinese, black Africa, all had slaves in one form or another, but England was doing their best to stop it.

Monar was baffled, "What in this God blasted creation is the matter with the South?"

Although the newspapers and letters he received were weeks to months old and biased from the writer's proclivities, by reading between the lines Monar recognized the North hadn't gone to war to end slavery. Lincoln's singular goal was preservation of the Union. It was clear, at least in 1861, that if he could have done this by the acquiescence of slavery in slave states, without question he would have.

There were however, the radical southern fire-eaters. Those representatives, knowing they were in the minority, felt it was time to bloody the northern Abolitionists noses once and for all to stop the endless infringement on the South's God given rights—at least they thought that.

And then, Monar was ready to throw up his hands in disgust at the next article, an article stating that despite the Abolitionists, there was an immense anti-negro stance by the majority of northern people. They wanted slave's to be restricted to the states that already had them; they *did not* want to end slavery. If slaves were freed, they believed those former slaves would flood into *white* territories by the thousands and that would be intolerable.

Monar twisted up the newspaper, "A scourge on both North and South. I'm damned if I'll follow JT's northern path. I have no loyalty to either side in this dog fight."

He was close to cancelling his journey, but his loyalty to Warfield, and the likelihood of excitement held sway once again.

8

29 February, 1862 twenty miles east of Oregon Inlet

THE BLOCKADE RUNNER *ROYAL GEORGE* was a fast sloop and it took the *Raven* three hours to catch up within two miles of her. Reserve Lieutenant Graves called Captain when aboard his ship, had a shot fired from his bow chaser that proved he was within range, but her captain ignored the warning and tried to run down wind for the open sea.

As the gun crew waited patiently, JT eased the *Raven's* course to port and allow the nine-inch pivot gun to bear. "At your pleasure, gunner."

A few moments later the cannon roared and recoiled, the sailors moving to the rail. The exploding shell exploding just forward of amid-ship, blew a gaping hole in her decking and shattered her mizzenmast. The schooner struck her colors, the Stars and Bars and hove too while the *Raven*, her cannon still trained, came alongside.

Chief Petty Officer and Senior Gunner, Harry Scrimshaw came to the helm, "That's the seventh one, Captain. Two Brits coming in, five like this one, running out."

"Right on, Harry, between helping bombard those tin-pot forts on Roanoke Island and catching Rebel ships, we've been busy these two months."

"You know. Speaking of Roanoke, it makes you wonder how a gang of fools, so ready to start a war didn't look around and say, 'You know something? We're dependent on the sea and *we don't have a navy!*'"

"Harry, they don't have an industry either. Didn't matter to them. Shows what happens when firebrands get in charge. But then again you must admit, even though you were in the Royal Navy, you never saw an armada that size going up the Sound after Roanoke."

"Honestly? In the past I have, still it was impressive. I heard Flag Officer Goldsborough had a hundred-seventy big guns."

"Yes, and thirteen-thousand troops—for one little island. Yet it opened the way into Albemarle Sound."

Easing alongside the schooner JT glanced at her downcast captain who knew he had lost his cargo and his vessel. JT felt sorry for the man. He had gambled everything and lost everything, a cargo of cotton and his schooner, the *Royal George*, probably his most prized possession. By the ship's name, he was doubtlessly British.

JT turned back to his Chief Petty Officer, "Tell me something Harry, I mean about these Brit blockade runners. How you feel about capturing your own countrymen and putting them in the brig."

Harry shrugged, "We all take chances, Cap. The poor sod lost, but least he won't dance a jig on the end of a line. A little brig time and he'll most likely be paroled and try again—or not. I'm indifferent when a person is stupid."

"I suppose. Well, take and armed crew aboard and check the cargo's safe. I imagine its cotton. Find out what they brought in. Then clear away that mast. We'll land her at Stumpy Point and be back out again."

With the crew disarmed and under detention, an understaffed crew sailed the *Royal George* beside the *Raven*. The voyage to the Oregon Inlet gave JT time to assess his crew. Captain Stringham had done what he said he would; two nine-inch pivot guns, two experienced gun crews and the new sailors either experienced or eager to learn. Importantly, Harry Scrimshaw was second in command and the men required little more to mesh together and Scrimshaw made short work of that as JT insisted.

One of the things JT also smiled at was the paradox of the officer's 'rite of passage'. He was a *reserve* officer. The regular service officers, ones who came up through the ranks from years of dedication to the navy and their craft, looked down their noses at reserve officers as nobodies; certainly not the equal of regular navy officers.

Now however, another layer had been added—the Annapolis Naval Officer. This officer felt superior to any naval person not a graduate of the Academy and who found it difficult to be subordinate to non-academy senior officers despite their having authentic campaign experience from the wars of 1812 and the Barbary Coast corsairs.

Nonetheless, the good-old-boy network served the graduates well in this Civil War as the older Rear-Admirals and Captains were retired or eased into less significant missions and The Academy's former cadets took command.

JT saw this, yet other than feeling sad for a number of the aging officers, he knew it wouldn't affect him. After his commitment to the North it would be back to hearth and kin in England...and Evelyn.

The majority of American, English, French and southern blockade-runners were chased, caught or sunk. One after another Confederate fortresses and batteries fell. Hatteras, Clark, Henry, Barstow, St. Simons, Jekyll, Walker, Beauregard, Donaldson, Thomson, Macon and Pulaski were invested and lost. With the exception of the forts at Charleston, South Carolina, the false belief of impregnable granite citadels, supremely guarding river approaches had vanished into rubble. Steam, rifled cannon, and shells ruled.

At sea it was only a few of the Rebel privateers who found success. A patchwork of converted Confederate steamships like the *CSS Sumter, Florida* and *Savannah* were armed and wreaked havoc on unprotected northern shipping. These attacks brought needed supplies and did cause northern shipping costs and insurances to sharply climb. Overall losses however, meant little to the North's war effort as each day the noose tightened around southern ports and rivers. Next, would come the Navy's move up the watercourses. From the mouths of the southern rivers they'd deliver the Union Army deep into the heart of the Confederacy.

Unrealized at the time, yet of utmost importance to the Union, was her navy's shocking successes forestalled foreign nations from recognizing or supplying little more than token aid to the South.

Still to come however, were a few surprises for the North from the Rebel's Pandora's Jar of cleverness.

«»

The captain and crew of the *Raven* were weary. JT felt the strain coursing through himself, his officers and men. In three continuous months at sea, they had captured fourteen blockade runners, two of which fought back before striking their colors. It was the schooner *New Cairo* that caused the deaths of three of the ship's crew, with four wounded and the *Raven* herself sustaining battle damage.

When coming up on the schooner, an incoming privateer, her captain lowered her flag, at the time believed a capitulation. Suddenly, within thirty yards, the flag fell, the side of her cabin dropped, exposing a cannon that fired a full charge of chain shot. Three of the *Raven's* gun crew were killed and then, realizing there were not enough damage, the *New Cairo's* white flag raised, trying to surrender yet again.

Incensed, JT facetiously asked his Chief if he saw any flag. Harry Scrimshaw shook his head and the jeering from the privateer *New Cairo* dissolved in an explosion at near pointblank range from the *Raven's* great pivot gun.

The shell shredded the gunwale and exploded amidships, strewing the deck with wood and bodies. Her skipper and ten men were killed and although incensed at the time, JT was later placated when it was found the *New Cairo's* captain was not from the Confederate Navy, only someone greedy enough to try and make money off war.

When the schooner was finally boarded, four thousand rifles of various calibers and muskets were found in her hold. It was a sign, even in this early stage of the war—the South was desperate for arms.

7 March, 1862

The USS *Raven,* dispatched to Hampton Roads, Virginia, to assist in the blockade of Chesapeake Bay and the James River, passed under the guns of Fortress Monroe. The clipper was then ordered by a naval navigator to moor between the US warships *Roanoke* and *Minnesota* east of Newport News Point. Once there, orders stated her captain could stand down and await further orders.

Fortress Monroe, which had known the engineering skill of a young US Army Lieutenant, R E Lee, was the largest stone fortress in the US and positioned on Old Point Comfort. Known as the Gibraltar of Chesapeake Bay, Monroe was continuously held by Union forces and thus protected the staging area for the Union blockade despite the South's control of the southern shore at Sewell's Point.

On the morning of the eighth, learning that the USS *Cumberland* was on station somewhat west of Newport News Point, JT left Scrimshaw in command and had a naval captain's barge take him to that vessel. Luckily, as it turned out for JT, the master of the barge said he would wait.

Receiving permission to board, JT was met by the *Cumberland's* Chief Petty Officer, who asked courteously for the reason for his visit. The answer given, the Chief sent for the senior officer aboard.

"I'm Lieutenant Morris, Lieutenant Graves. I'm very sorry, but Captain Radford is in conference at Fort Monroe. Is there something I can help you with?"

"To be perfectly honest, Lieutenant, I'm on sort of a memories visit. In September of '48, I was on a British ship called the *Vixen* attacked by corsairs off Morocco. That ship had aboard a woman captain whom I loved dearly and who later became my wife. If it hadn't been for the arrival of the *Cumberland,* I wouldn't be standing here today recalling it all. There was a frightening time on the *Vixen's* deck; she was God awful hacked up back then. A lot of blood drained into the scuppers that day, we lost a lot of crew."

Morris was engrossed, "Back in '48 you say? My word, the *Cumberland* was only six years old then, although in truth, her keel was actually laid down in '24 so that makes her an old lady. When you knew her, she was a Raritan class frigate. She's down to a Sloop-of-War now, fifty-four guns, getting long of tooth I'm afraid, even though she's been reworked and gunned heavier. She's still a good old lady though, at least good enough for blockading Johnny Reb—like she did up at Hatteras."

JT smiled inwardly. The lieutenant was clearly a dyed-in-the-wool, wet-foot sailor who thought his ship more than just a machine. Here was a kinship, JT felt the same.

They walked the deck, JT explaining his singular clashes with the privateers' right up to the arrival of the *Cumberland.* They then discussed the pivot guns on the *Raven*, after which the lieutenant explained the recent modifications to the ship as they went along the guns that included twenty-two, type IX Dahlgren rifled 9" artillery, plus other armament. The *Raven's* two, type IX cannon paled in comparison.

Trying to get a feel of the disposition of the blockading ships, JT asked why the *Cumberland* was so westerly of the blockade, actually on the James River according to JT's chart. The lieutenant was ambiguous.

"Scuttlebutt has it that the Rebels built some special kind of ship out of the hull of the USS *Merrimack.* We'd burned the *Merri* to the waterline and she sank after we idiotically abandoned the Gosport Navy Yard almost intact due to Commodore McCauley's blunder. Johnny Reb raised the hull and made her into what's called an ironclad, iron to the gunwales, least it's what our spy's say."

"I haven't heard a thing about this, anything more?"

"Sure is, she's called the *Virginia* now and they're planning to break our blockade here and protect Richmond as well as Norfolk. There's not a chance in hell, but Flag Officer Goldsborough knows his stuff and doesn't discount anything. My guess is we'll attack the Gosport Yard before the Reb's finish her, but till then here we stand, watch and wait. It's boring us to death, but that's the order so what can we do?"

After noon, JT was back on the steam barge as she pulled away from the *Cumberland.* He saw the warship's lookout frantically pointing toward the mouth of the Elizabeth River. Taking his binoculars, JT could make out a Union gunboat and past her, in the distance, something moving down the channel. He could only describe it as a roof, a long roof, floating down the river toward the line of Union warships.

The 'roof' came into focus and a funnel, sticking from the steeped roof could be seen belching spark laden black smoke. This freak, this so-called ship, was the reason for the *Cumberland's* sentinel duty. Struck dumb for a moment, JT realized this was the *Virginia*, the South's armored beast, the North's fear.

The steam barge's captain hurriedly steered away from the direction the CSS *Virginia* was headed and allowed his boat to drift south, near the Middle Ground Shoals in Hampton Roads to decide which way to escape. JT felt time had slowed watching the drama unfold. A Union gunboat, named *Zouave,* began firing one of her two-30 pounder Parrott rifles until a signal raised from the *Cumberland* recalled her. The signal was none too soon for the *Zouave* found herself straddled by shot from the battery at Newport News, the *Virginia*, her escorts and Union warships.

The South's new warship fired a broadside into the *Congress* while the *Zouave*, still in the fight, fired back and made to take the stricken *Congress* in tow, but she grounded and *Zouave's* luck finally ran out when headed for the *Minnesota*. Struck by shots that crippled her rudder post, she still struggled to reach that warship until saved by a Union ship, where she licked her wounds beside the *Minnesota*.

The master of the two-hundred-twenty-seven foot ironclad CSS *Virginia* was Commander Franklyn Buchanan. When he met up with a squadron of five James River Confederacy warships, he was more intent on urging the most out of the faulty and underpowered engines restored from the scuttled *Merrimack.* Struggling with the handling of the monster caused by the new topside weight of twenty-four inches of oak and four inches of armor plate—he found all of it was fighting him for control.

This expedition was to be an under-way drill to work out those operating difficulties and, if feasible, attack the blockaders. He headed into the Roads at full speed of five knots and there, before him, laid the wooden Union warships *Cumberland, Congress, Minnesota, St. Laurence* and *Roanoke* and an unknown clipper ship of no interest to him.

The Union warships proved too treasured an opportunity to miss, even though the *Virginia's* seven and nine inch Brooke and Dahlgren cannon had yet to be fired.

Confederate Commander Buchanan was 'old navy', adjudged the 'Old Man' of the US Annapolis Naval Academy. Despite this, he had handed in his resignation from US Navy and became a Commodore in the CSS Navy.

Ordering his three-hundred man crew to battle stations, he mostly ignored the *Zouave* and directed his ship toward the *Cumberland,* although taking broadsides from the awakened *Congress.* With neither ship having steam power they remained stock-still, but they and the shore batteries opened fire. Dozens of shot and shell flew and struck the *Virginia* only to hurdle away or explode harmlessly off the ship. Her gun ports opened and a volley of shells smothered and shattered the *Congress*' gun deck. Wounded men screamed and died. Those still alive stayed to the guns.

The *Virginia* then turned and plowed her four-foot iron ram into the *Cumberland's* starboard planking, ripping a gaping and mortal fissure in her side. As the ram was extracted it broke off, but the *Cumberland* was left dying to begin her death throes. Still her sailors continued to fire her cannon until she, they and her flag went under.

JT looked on stunned; the deck he recently trod and owed his life to from the past was gone, sunken, and scores of sailors, sailors he had only recently nodded goodbye to were dead. It gripped at his heart—he had to get to his ship, he *must* get back and somehow fight this monster!

The barge master argued there was no safe passage to the *Raven*. The direct way, by the North Channel, would mean fetching their vessel up around the Middle Ground shoals, thereby closer to the *Virginia's* guns and place her within easy range. Going by South Channel, down around the shoals was definitely no choice as it was longer and Rebel cannon Sewell's Point could reach them. JT, however, was intense, shouting they, like the *Zouave*, were small fry; the enemy was after bigger fish and that forced the issue. The barge master, with pressure the safety valve could barely sustain, took the northern channel without being challenged.

Chief Petty Officer Scrimshaw, on board the *Raven*, seeing the horror to the west and that JT would be able to reach the *Raven*, brought steam up by the time the captain climbed through the gunwale and ordered battle stations.

While this was going on, more ravage ensued. Despite the loss of the *Virginia's* ram, Buchanan went after the stricken *Congress* for she grounded trying to escape. Unable to reach the wooden Union ship due to the *Virginia's* twenty-two foot draft, she devastated the *Congress* by massed cannon fire and compelled her to surrender. Trying to secure his prize, the *Virginia's* captain, and sailors on both sides, were wounded from Union sharpshooters. The *Congress* was set ablaze by *Virginia's* red hot cannonballs.

Next in the Confederate sights was the *Minnesota*. Although steam powered, she had run aground trying to come about and made an easy target.

In spite of Camp Butler's shore batteries on Newport News Point having caused negligible damage to the *Virginia's* armor, the cannon fire did manage to weaken several of her plates. In addition to this was three more Federal steam warships entering Hampton Roads to join the fray. The loss the Confederate's ram continued the inflow of water at the bow and all this gave second thoughts to prolonging the assault. It was imperative the unwieldy *Virginia* not be entrapped if the South hoped to break the blockade. Acting

Captain, Lieutenant Catesby, replacing Buchanan due to his wound, decided discretion should follow valor and the *Virginia* struggled against the ebbing tide to withdraw to the lee of Confederate controlled Sewell's Point and the protection of those batteries.

Earlier, during the shelling of the *Congress*, JT thought he might catch the *Virginia* or possibly her supporting ships and started to give chase. Hailed by the lead Union ship, the *Raven* was ordered to return to her mooring, the last comment through the ship's speaking trumpet was '…what would you do with her if you caught her?' followed by nervous laughter.

As it turned out, no Federal ship pursued the *Virginia*. Two-hundred, sixty-one Union sailors had died.

Captain's assembly, Hampton Roads, night of the battle.
With the continued absence of Flag Officer Goldsborough, Commander of the North Atlantic Blockading Squadron,

Captain John Marston of the USS *Roanoke*, took Command.

The *Roanoke* was the last of the warships to run aground in the battle with the *Virginia* and Marston held a hasty meeting of ship's senior officers to deliberate on the greatest loss of life the Navy had ever suffered in one battle in its history. Captain Marston did not pull any punches.

The mood was black, "Gentlemen, this disaster will go down in naval history. This can't be said any other way and I will not whitewash it to Flag Officer Goldsborough in my report. We were caught with our collective pants around our ankles and if we don't turn this around we might just as well set sail into tomorrow's sunrise. As you're well aware, the F O left a fixed battle plan; surround the *Virginia*, pound her in a cross-fire and beat her to pieces."

The officers were confounded. It was true they had been surprised, yet there had been no word from Union spies the *Virginia* was anywhere near completion. The warships, Marston said, were properly stationed; the sentinels, *Zouave* and *Cumberland,* alert and ready. What happened was a superb stroke with a never before seen unstoppable force. Now, they wondered, were these comments being made now by the Captain in Command the start of laying the blame?

Captain Marston read their minds, "This is not the initiation of a Captain's Mast. I don't find any facts to support dereliction of duty. We were trying to save our ships and at the same time fight off the *Virginia*."

Not quite true, yet the situation could not have been saved, even by the perfect execution of the FO's plan—at least not without steam warships and an ironclad or two.

The Captain continued, "Now then, put all this aside. The ship we've hoped for should arrive tonight."

A spontaneous cheer erupted, but JT was left in the dark. Captain Marston saw him for the first time.

"Ah, I spy the newest addition to our blockade. Not the nicest reception for you I must say. Men, this is Reserve Lieutenant, John Graves, the captain of that slippery looking clipper *Raven*. Graves, I hope we will meet up to your expectations. I hear your *Raven* is the fastest vessel we have on this coast and that you and she performed quite well in hounding down every privateer you chased. That's quite a record. Welcome to the Blockader's Club. Oh, and I would caution you to think twice before charging off again to accost the *Virginia*. It was I who *suggested* you return to your mooring. What on earth were you thinking?"

"To be honest, Sir, initially it was just my reaction to the battle. Then I saw the *Virginia's* bow and stern were low and flat and it would be easy for the *Raven* to catch her and perhaps carry up on her and cause enough to swamp her."

Worden mulled that over, "Not a bad idea, but I think you'd be better served to have an iron stem and tactics to avoid the *Virginia's* guns, although I will say you're apparently not lacking in verve."

There was good-natured laughter all around and JT responded in kind, "Then let me thank you, Sir, for stopping me. One other thing I'd like to mention Sir, is the actions of the tug *Zouave* and her crew. Her Master's name is Henry Reaney. If anyone had verve it was him, and if anyone comes out of this with a medal, it should be him."

Marston lifted his glass, "Well then, to the Master and crew of the *Zouave*. I'll see what we can do for him. But I don't see anyone coming out of this fiasco with a medal."

At this time Captain Marston called for a respectful silence in memory of the loss of their comrades, estimated at two-hundred-forty sailors. The moment was a sobering reminder of what the next day could very well bring.

Outside, in the late evening, there was an upsurge of shouting, shouting that soon faded. Marston smiled, "I think the response to our friend the *Virginia* has arrived."

They went to the topside rail where their pleasure abruptly ceased. Staring down, was a vessel as uniquely appalling—in its own form—as the *Virginia,* and the exact opposite in structure. The *Virginia* was massive, a dominant force. Compared to her, this was a tragically stunted curiosity—was this *thing* their savior? Even the ship they were on towered over the one below—and where on earth were her cannon?

By the light of torches, the officers and men looked upon one-hundred, eighty feet of flat decking less than two feet above the water. How could she be seaworthy? The *Virginia* had at least ten cannon, this vessel showed none. Her deck held one main object, a circular iron barbican, a turret about nine feet tall. Could she be only a ram?

The men were shocked and some muttering. It was agreed by most the thing looked like a damned shingle with a can on it, to others it more resembled a cheese box.

In truth, she did have a short funnel and a low pilot house—yet little else.

Captain Marston, as befuddled as the rest, quieted the men and called for the ship's captain and senior officers to present at his quarters.

Lieutenant, John Worden, Captain of the vessel arrived and introduced his Lieutenant, Samuel Greene, and Master, Louis Stodder, then waited for the present Senior Officer of the Blockade to speak.

Marston began cordially, “And how was your trip?”

The response was not encouraging, “Not too good, Captain. We were being towed by a sea-going tug from Hampton Roads when the weather worsened, the turret leaked, shutting down our fans and, well, to keep this short, we almost foundered. I know this doesn’t give anyone a feeling of security, but the *Monitor* was designed for river combat only and I’m sure you know Hatteras weather.”

Marston did know, of more importance was what this new type of ship, the *Monitor* could do, “So, Worden, tell us about your ship, mainly I want to know her firepower.”

“Certainly Sir. The turret you saw is twenty-six feet across, nine feet high and holds two eleven inch Dahlgren smoothbore cann…”

Every Union officer was upset. Marston in the lead, “Excuse my interruption. Two guns? That’s all?”

“Yes Sir. You see, the turret revolves lock to lock in twenty-two seconds and…”

“What are you talking about, the turret revolves?”

“That is correct, Sir. It’s a totally new concept for the Navy. We can direct our two guns anywhere we want—except forward—no matter which way the ship is heading. The guns turn, the ship doesn’t have to.”

Worden saw no one there had the slightest concept of the theory so he continued, “Sir, the deck is iron plate, the turret has iron plate up to eight inches. The gun ports are closed when the guns are being loaded—the turret turns to the target—the position of the *ship* doesn’t matter, the ports open, the gun runs out, fires, recoils, the port closes, time and again. No more trying to align the ship for a broadside. And remember, the turret is round; extremely difficult to hit directly. She is a solid gun platform.”

The captain of the *Monitor* was making sense and the radical concept quickly sank in. Still, shortcomings were there, mainly to the functionality of the turret, but Worden saw no sense in mentioning them.

Marston went back a pace, "So, I gather Command knows about the *Virginia*?"

"Yes, our spies gave us a pretty good idea of her."

"And you think you can whip her?"

The *Monitor's* captain hesitated for a moment and Marston objected, "You show doubt, lieutenant."

Captain Worden chose his words carefully, "Sir, I firmly believe we can stop her from doing damage. Whipping her is another question. Let me explain. Please remember, this ship was built in a hundred days and we didn't have time to test our solid shot powder charges against iron plate. Then the *Monitor's* inventor, John Ericsson, said he had concerns about using a thirty-pound charge in the turret. If it caused a gun explosion, the turret would be wrecked—to say nothing of eighteen men there—so we've stayed with fifteen-pound charges—its hope for the best and my crew and I have no qualms."

A sobering moment. Yet Worden seemed confident and putting damper on the moment was the last thing the men wanted to do.

It was Worden's next remark that stupefied them.

"So now tell me, have you had any sightings of the *Virginia* yet?"

The officers felt ridiculous. Captain Worden had not been informed of what had taken place in Hampton Roads.

Given orders to be on standby at 0500 the following morning, the captain's returned to their ships. All captains understood that should the next day go amiss, and the *Virginia* gain the upper hand, the remaining Union warships were to revert to Flag Officer Goldsborough initial order to catch the Rebel ship in a crossfire, or ram her, or otherwise find some means to disable her—no matter the cost.

There was concern the enemy might try to board the open deck of the *Monitor* and throw explosives into the gun ports as they opened. To counteract that possibility, the Raven, being the fastest ship, was to race forward with grapeshot in both cannon and clear the *Monitor's* deck.

Worden's comment of, '…best you be quick and be gone…' met with nervous laughter all around.

That night, the *Raven* was made ready. Each man knew his duty. JT and Chief Scrimshaw were confident in their crew.

Remaining on the top deck alone, excepting the Watch, JT looked off to the grounded and still burning *Congress*. He had a few minutes to muse over ships, cannon and the Union Navy. Warships were evolving, and dramatically. True, not *sailing* craft. Omitting steam power, the *Raven* was still one of the most advanced. Yet it seemed he had only blinked and when he refocused, there were steam-powered ships everywhere, some *without* sails! Steam had become so reliable that given enough strategic coaling depots the vessels roamed in calms and storm wherever and whenever they pleased. The new Navy had also embraced the novel shallow draft, twin screw engine, Pook Turtles, or more decorously, *City* Class river gunboats designed by James Eads. These were far and away the most formidable gun batteries afloat. Still, JT hesitated calling them ships. Their angled ironclad sides, designed to deflect shell, enclosed as many as fourteen formidable cannon from bow to stern. Their ugly, twin funnels spewed spark and smoke, a signal of the arrival of lurid, angry gods. Yet he knew, be they ships or floating repugnant fortresses, there was no way the *Raven,* despite her speed and pivot guns, could contest them. And now, another advance in war; this *Monitor* Class, river boats with gun turrets for shallows like the *City* class boats and virtually impregnable floating fortresses.

Starting below, JT knew all the captains in this fleet were once true wind sailors, 'Salt Water Gentlemen' they fancied themselves, who nevertheless felt the only saving grace, if it could be called such, was that the iron-clad turtles were top-heavy and could never endure a difficult sea as true ships could. Yet the other, more imperative point was for now at least, they were Union ships, not Rebel.

He blew out the lantern, dropped onto his bunk fully clothed, finishing up his thoughts. Added to the powerful iron-clads, and monitors, were rams and mobile mortar rafts. Whereas the Union Army was battered and reeling with few successes, the Union Navy, especially during these first two years of the war, had become virtually unstoppable, pounding the Southern fortifications to rubble with rifled guns. However, was the *Virginia* a game changer?

He dozed off thinking of Evelyn and his children.

Later that night a massive explosion startled him awake. The fire on the *Congress* reached her powder magazine. An ill-omen to the coming day.

The sounds of naval men preparing for war barely carried across the bay. Shouts, line running through block and tackle, coal shoveled into the gaping mouths of hungry boilers, steam hissing, nervous laughter—all were muffled by a dense fog that slouched across the bay.

At 0800, the fog dissipated. The *Virginia* and her escort moved from Sewell's Point, the plan was to finish off the stranded *Minnesota,* then turn against the other warships.

Steaming toward the wounded ship, the Confederates were abruptly wary, for out from the *Minnesota's* shadow came the oddest warship they had ever seen. Nevertheless, odd or not, the *Virginia* came on looking for a fight.

Two gladiators, the warships circled, firing their major weapons. Again and again the circle widened to a hundred yards and contracted to but a few yards. Solid shot from the *Monitor* slammed onto and flew off the *Virginia's* iron plates while most of *Virginia's* shells missed the flat hulled Union vessel or impacted and exploded off her turret.

The salvos were mostly at close range, many times the gladiators battered together, while blasting off a constant rate of fire. At those collisions, JT's *Raven* moved within a hundred yards, ready to fire if the *Monitor* was boarded, at the same time he kept a wary eye on the other Rebel vessels.

The battle raged, yet neither side gained an advantage. The *Virginia* continued unrelenting gunfire while struggling with the ponderous handling and laborious turning pace of the vessel.

The *Monitor's* turret became faulty, refusing to stop revolving on command. To compensate, the crew let it continue to revolve and fired her guns as they came to bear.

With little apparent damage to the *Virginia*, the *Monitor's* gun crew cursed the smaller powder charges they had to use. They also cursed, with even more zeal, each time a shell impacted the turret and rivets tore loose and careened around the room.

After the vessel's fifth collision, once when the *Virginia* attempted to ram, her bow began to take on water yet again, not serious enough to retire, but causing concern.

Long into the encounter a shell exploded near the *Monitor's* pilothouse, blinding Lieutenant Worden and injuring others causing the ship to withdraw to shallower water to treat the men and transfer munitions to the turret.

Seeing the Union vessel reposition, the *Virginia* returned to bombard the *Minnesota* and set her afire.

As this transpired, Lieutenant Greene, of the *Monitor*, took over command from the sightless Worden. At first unsure of his next action, Greene quickly assessed the damage to his ship and, though only one of his two guns remained operational, he decided to return to the clash.

During the time of the *Monitor's* breaking off the confrontation, *Virginia* had run aground, freed herself and headed up the Elizabeth River toward Norfolk, the captain believing the *Monitor* had withdrawn from the battle.

It was over. The first battle of ironclads lasted more than two hours, two hours of incessant conflict. Incredibly, no one was killed. Both the South and North considered it a victory.

Overall it was judged a draw, yet the South's attempt to break the blockade failed—the North's grip maintained.

On 11 April, both ships tried to lure the other into a trap, but other than a few pointless shelling back and forth, neither ship ever fought another ship again. The *Virginia* was eventually burned to prevent capture; the *Monitor,* after complete refurbishing, upgrades and some river action, floundered and sank in a storm off Hatteras.

After the summary from the engagement, the world's navies were implicit in averring two foremost realities must be faced. Every wooden warship would soon be obsolete, and Ericsson's revolving turret was the future of naval warfare.

Captain Dahlgren said it succinctly, "The reign of iron has begun…"[24]

«»

JT was irritated, irritated mostly with himself. During the battle and even afterward, he found within him a compulsive instinct to attack the *Virginia*. Anger had gripped him; go after the enemy, force the *Raven* over that ship and plunge the hated monstrosity into the deep. At the time, at the peak of his barely withheld fury, he was actually preparing to do just that; sacrifice his ship and men—until Harry Scrimshaw gripped him, forcing him away from the object of his hate.

"Don't do that, Captain! This is between two causes. Those other Southern ships aren't interfering, nor should you. The age of chivalry isn't dead."

"Chivalry? When men are out there *dying*?"

---

[24] For further information on this battle and the sea change in the thinking of the world navies see: Wikipedia-USS Monitor, CSS Virginia, Battle of Hampton Roads. And, *Civil War Naval Chronology* 1861-1865 or, US Naval History Division of the Navy Department, Washington.1971.

Though his Chief chose not to answer, JT was made to think, something was happening inside, he *must* suppress his anger and control himself in front of the crew.

Scrimshaw could see JT falter, "I know how you feel, Captain, believe me! I'd go to hell with you if I thought you were right—but *you're wrong!*"

And unfortunately at that time, JT's mind was taken off an image he would later recall.

Following the battle and during the summaries made by Captain Marston at the Captain's conference, Captain Graves was commended for his attention to carrying out the order to prevent the *Monitor* from being boarded. No such attempt was made; nevertheless, Marston still gave credit to Graves' service. JT now recalled and related the image he saw during the battle. That the *Virginia,* after firing off the great number of shells, became more buoyant in the water and her iron sheathing exposed the hull, normally below the waterline. If the *Monitor's* crew had noticed that fact and her guns could depress lower and struck below the *Virginia's* plating, would the tide have turned? He passed his memo on.

Marston, as Second in Command at Hampton Roads, sent his report of the battle to Naval Secretary Welles. Welles in turn, presented the events at the Roads to Present Lincoln and telegraphed the Commandant of the Washington Navy Yard in, John Dahlgren.

Yet Marston wasn't sure who would inform Goldsborough, Commander of the North Atlantic Blockade Squadron, and nominally in charge at Hampton Roads.

Marston surmised the Commander should be on the USS *Mohican* somewhere between Hatteras and the Virginia Peninsular. As Chief of the Navy's element in the joint amphibious assault on New Berm, North Carolina, Goldsborough, with Brigadier General, Burnside, would expect someone to report and would want it delivered swiftly. The obvious choice was the *Raven* and soon she and her crew were on their way north through the deepening aquamarine waters of the Gulf Stream while JT was forced into deep introspection.

Why had he been so hell bent on destroying the *Virginia*? Or contrariwise, was it that the ship was merely symbolic—a symbol of the South and her slavery?

Whatever it was, whatever the cause, it was a sign of his physically wearying, wearying from taking blockade runner's ships, destroying what was once a legitimate livelihood in their ill-advised, dim-witted war that had now driven them to desperation. Then again, was there the older, simpler, side of war—greed.

Or, JT wondered, was there more wrong with him than physical, could there truly be a mental strain coursing through him? The question was not long in manifesting.

JT eventually found Flag Officer Goldsborough with Commander Rowan aboard the USS *Delaware* on the Neuse River below New Berm. Delivering the report of the standoff at Hampton Roads, the FO only nodded, noncommittal; the New Berm assault was occupying his mind and the Roads stalemate could wait. The implications of ironclad warfare would later receive his full attention.

After thanking the Captain of the *Raven* for the report, Goldsborough stated he doubted any blockade runners would have knowledge of the battle or the assault on New Berm and it was therefore likely they would persist in trying to land supplies somewhere along the coast.

JT was ordered to midpoint on Shackleford Banks, close to Fort Macon, the severely damaged former Southern fortress once guarding Beaufort and Morehead City. Now in Union hands, the fort was becoming a supply port and coaling station for Union warships.

The *Raven's* watch reach was north along the Core Banks of the barrier cut to Portsmouth Island and south to Cape Garteret. There were other Union warships patrolling in the area, and JT understood he was not to consider every sail raised was an enemy.

Before Fort Macon had fallen, the blockade runner CSS *Nashville*, a side-wheeler, had amazingly slipped in and out of an inlet near the fort without being caught. Due to this knowledge, JT made the decision to concentrate a league or two off that Bogue Banks inlet.

In the next two weeks, they caught up with, and captured two incoming schooners, one carrying potassium nitrate, used for making explosives, and the other schooner filled to her scuppers with provisions.

Both vessels were taken without violence, and the *Raven's* crew, although militarily correct; found it difficult to swallow the privateer's contempt, bordering on hatred, for them. The Southerners, realizing the crew's naval restraint, took full advantage of the circumstances until a few heads were bloodied by belaying pins before reaching Fort Macon's brig. JT, with his Chief's tacit concurrence, did not place any man on report.

«»

5 May 1862. Off Salter Path, the Bogue Banks.

"We've raised a sail, Captain."

Harry Scrimshaw, Chief and Master Gunner stuck his head into the captain's quarters and waited.

"What do you make of her, Harry?"

The lookout had sighted a sail coming toward them from the south, and as the ship loomed into view, she eased the helm to come up on the *Raven's* starboard.

"She must be one of our side-wheelers out of Wilmington, Captain. Barely a wisp of smoke from her funnel, so she's not under power and they're beginning to reef sail."

The *Raven* had been north, above Harker's Island and had started her southern run on the hunt for privateers. The fact that this ship's side-paddles were stationary and she was reefing sail likely meant a Union vessel as the North, for all practical purposes, owned these waters and their ships were often passing each other.

"They're probably like us, getting bored on patrol and want to jaw for a while and see if we've had any recent news on Richmond."

"Makes sense, Cap. You coming topside?"

"Be up in a minute. Keep an eye peeled on her, she's a long way from home unless she's on courier duty. Keep steam up, but shut down the revs and turn out the starboard gun crew—never can be too cautious."

The side-wheeler, her paddles stopped, had her main and mizzen sails shortened and it wasn't long before her name could read. The USS *Boston*, her Union flag snapping at the mainmast, looked to be heavy in the water.

The *Boston* spilled the wind from the sails that hadn't been reefed and with her two paddle-wheels stationary, her momentum was dying.

The *Raven* could barely keep steerageway as they came closer to her starboard rail.

A person shouted through the horn and waved, "Ho, the USS *Raven*, how are you?"

JT and Scrimshaw looked at each other, something wasn't quite right. The greeting was unusual, not *navy*. JT smelled fumes, coal smoke. He knew the wind was offshore, blowing across the *Boston* to windward and then across the *Raven.* Being upwind from his own ship's funnel, he shouldn't smell smoke.

Suddenly, he understood, "Everyone down, now! Helm! Sheer off; give me full power, now! Gunner—fire!"

Though not too late, it was bad enough. The gun ports of the *Boston* were forced open by the mouths of two cannon and those two cannon erupted chain and grapeshot shattering the *Raven's* freeboard and sending a torrent of scrap iron fragments across the top deck to slash down six sailors not quick enough to heed their captain's shout.

The crew of the pivot gun was wounded to a man. Scrimshaw, as gun captain, had been hunched down sighting the cannon and that luck blocked him from the fragments.

He rolled upright to see the *Boston's* paddlewheels suddenly thrashing the water into froth as the ship thrust into the sea while her sails rapidly unfurled, spread and caught the following wind.

He had also seen JT struck by something and stumble as he reached the unmanned wheel. The helmsman was wounded; the wheel spinning erratically as power began to turn the propellers. Scrimshaw reached JT, whose blond hair was turning red.

"Captain—you all right?"

"I…I don't know yet. Grab the wheel…get us under control…are *you* all right?"

Scrimshaw, uninjured, managed to stop the wheel as the ship's doctor appeared.

JT fought to get his wits together, "Stop the bleeding! All right, that's good enough…see to the others."

There was a sense of organized chaos; separating dead from wounded, serious wounds from slightly, marines helping the sailors as much as possible—and their captain shouting orders—one was to set all sail.

Yet JT's main intent, his only thought, was to catch the *Boston*. There would be retribution for the deceitful act—and revenge for his men.

The *Boston* had a significant head start and as the chase began JT and Scrimshaw relived the scene.

JT, feeling his head would split, wouldn't allow the doctor to give him morphine, saying he needed to be alert.

"That bastard pulled the wool over our eyes, Harry, completely fooled us, coming up like that so innocently, dead paddlewheels, reefed sails, that God damned USS *Boston* and flag…we've done this too much, got lax."

"Possibly, but they used chain and grapeshot, Captain! Why not exploding shells at our waterline instead?"

"I imagine because that's all they had and that tells me they're not Confederate Navy—didn't have proper weaponry. They figured they couldn't get past us, so cripple us and run for it. Clever captain—but not clever enough."

"One thing I don't fathom though, how did they get steam up so fast? No sooner did they fire on us than the paddles were digging in."

"That, my friend, is how I knew something was wrong; I smelled coal smoke without seeing it."

To Scrimshaw's blank look, JT explained, "Come on, Harry, anthracite, anthracite coal! Almost smokeless. That was why you only saw a wisp of smoke and thought her boilers were down."

Scrimshaw slouched, "Then it was my fault, my fault, God damn me!"

"Don't take the world on your shoulders, Harry. We were hoodwinked by a bastardly son-of-a-bitch, but we're going to make him pay dearly."

"You think we can catch them before the Sound?"

JT turned away from him, gritting his teeth, "I know the *Raven* will catch her, I'm not sure I will."

With that, the Captain went down on his knees.

The *Raven* ran with the wind at her back, unleashed. It was as if she were herself wounded and turning on her attacker. Harry Scrimshaw, acting as Captain while JT fought to recover, was stunned at feeling ship's power as she thundered after the prey. To Harry, it was as if he was trying to control a thousand horses, horses running amuck but with but one single mind—faster, go faster!

He couldn't stop her; the men saw it and looked about in disbelief. No one had gone this pace; no ship in the world had hurled the sea away, smashed into, crushed the waves with such force. They were sure the *Raven* would either break apart or sail herself under. Strong men became helpless, grabbing for something to hold onto.

Struggling to his feet, JT took the wheel, ignoring the pain as best he could. He reveled running before the wind. Man and ship fused, the *Raven* felt his hands take her and obeyed his voice—all would be well, she would go faster.

The *Boston* was barred from the inlet. There was nowhere to go and hide. Further north would take her into Union territory, south or east; she had to face the *Raven*. She was in an open ocean, yet trapped like a rat. The only question was how the rat would react, give up, or fight it out. JT wasn't about to wait. Standing off at one mile, the ship's pivot gun fired a thirty-eight pound shell that tore off the *Boston's* bowsprit and exploded not ten feet off the bow.

Her flag came down, a white sheet replaced it but not before another shell shattered her foredeck. Now you son-of-a-bitch, JT thought, retribution.

The Captain of Marines took charge, "Kneel in the middle of your deck, hands over your heads. Face away from us. One move and my marines will cut every one of you bastards down. If I see a whiff of smoke from that stack my cannon will blow a hole below your waterline and we will sail off."

No one on the *Raven* thought that would happen, yet everyone on the *Boston* thought it would.

His head throbbing, JT jumped onto the enemy's deck, ignoring a sharp pain in his head as marines disarmed the crew and began to move about the ship. The ship's captain wasn't in sight.

"Where's your captain?"

No one answered. It was the most repugnant crew JT had ever encountered and he knew power was all they would respond to. His pain made him squint against the sun as he pulled out his Navy Colt. Pointing it at the first man, "Where's your captain?"

The man's sneer angered JT. He lowered his pistol, "Your captain killed six of my men, understand you mean nothing to me."

With no response, a bullet struck the man's thigh and he fell screaming. JT stopped the ship's doctor from interfering. Turning the revolver to the sailor's other leg, he quickly pointed out the captain.

There are people who have the look of an innocent, but are malevolent. Then again, there are people who look malevolent and truly are. Captain Matt Volker was one of those who fit the latter right down to greasy hair and facial scars—not simply one, but three.

"You filthy scum, you have broken every law of common decency. I'll see you hang."

Spitting on the wounded sailor as he was carried off, the captain was as surly as he looked, "Don't make me laugh. You've no idea how often fools like you have told me that. They're dead, I'm still here. We've a long sea ahead."

"Just keep believing that and…"

The Captain of Marines came up to JT, "Captain, it's best you come with me."

Curious, JT went to a forward hatch where a marine opened it. A stench, a vile, horrid, nauseating stench flooded out of the hold. JT twisted away. The foul odor, combined with the sickening feeling from his wounds, staggered him.

The marine captain held him, "Are you all right, Captain Graves?"

JT couldn't function, couldn't answer. A slaver, the *Boston* was a slaver! Then, the other blow struck. The memory of his father, his own father having been a slaver slashed at his nerves and his brain.

Holding his breath, JT looked down into the hold to the sight of writhing, whimpering, filthy, black humanity. His mind barely functioned. The horror stunned.

His father had done this same vicious cruelty to others of God's souls. How, how in hell's name *could* he?

And now, JT grasped the reason his father had gone mad; any person with one shred of decency would.

Thoughts of his father dissolved; some infinite, guiding strength that had controlled him unraveled. He returned to Captain Volker, who broke into a smile.

"What's the matter, captain? Seen ghosts? Of course they must have been black ghosts down there if…"

Volker read the wrath in JT's eyes, "Now hold on…"

The Navy Colt fired, driving a red hole, deep into the captain's chest. Volker was right, he wouldn't hang.

Time and motion froze, except eyes that blinked, staring at JT. He had shot down and killed, an unarmed man.

At last, after the longest minute anyone there had lived, JT spoke to the Captain of Marines, "You can write that up in your report, Captain."

"Yes, Sir, I will, just as it happened. Captain Volker lunged at you, you were delirious with your wound; there was no choice other than to shoot the attacker down."

JT couldn't help a weak smile, "Thank you for that, Captain, but don't, for your sake. This will get out."

He called on all his strength to speak to his Chief, "Do what we can for those poor souls below and give them all our food and then chain the *Boston's* crew in their place. Set up a prize crew… and…let me think…yes, fix a course for…for…Beaufort."

He began to fail, "Harry…you know what to do, I'll be in my cabin…and Harry…thanks..."

He made it to the bulkhead hatch before they saw the red stream trickling down the back of his neck. He staggered through his cabin door before they caught up and helped him onto his bunk face down. Whatever had struck him; had caught the back of his head as well.

9

1 June, 1862

3 WEEKS AFTER THE INCIDENT with the USS *Boston*. The Naval Board called a preliminary briefing to discover the facts of the encounter and ascertain any culpability in the death of the Captain of the *Boston*. It was only recently the ship was found to be the privateer *Warlock*, out of Guinea with, originally, 687 slaves, and the captain, for some foolish reason, bound for St. Augustine, Florida. *Warlock/Boston* had been chased north by five separate Union ships, none of which could catch her, that is until she chanced on the *Raven*. At the time of her capture, her hull contained 407 barely living slaves of whom another 43 died after their rescue.

The more the facts unfolded, the more the testimony revealed, the more the *Raven* captain's wound entered the picture. The Navy, rightfully, intended to bury the matter.

The story however, was dribbling out and the Navy did not want their northern captains shot arbitrary for it was felt implicit southern retaliation would surely follow.

In their wisdom, the Navy ordered the *Raven* and crew to the Charleston Navy Yard in Boston for ship refit once the USS *Tioga*, a new side-wheel steam gunboat left the dry dock. Captain Graves had by then been placed on the deactivated reserve officer's index until further notification. All parties assumed that 'further notification' for active duty would never come for Captain Graves.

JT accepted the Navy's decision. Capturing the slaver had torn something out of him and that, coupled with spasmodic headaches plaguing him, made him content to rest and take up smoking a pipe again to help ease the pain.

Still being an officer of the Union Navy meant he couldn't arbitrarily return to England, so he decided to return to Salem and *Seaward*. Salem would be his home until he was reactivated, which was highly doubtful, or discharged.

With the *Raven* in Boston's Charleston dry-dock, the sailors and marines were generally left to their own devices and, JT, knowing *Seaward* would be in desperate need of repairs, offered to have Harry Scrimshaw pick fifteen of the crew to work for additional pay at *Seaward.*

The sailors were informed of the ill-will of the Salem populace. They, including Chief Scrimshaw, were shocked over the foul deed of JT's father and because of him, they would not be welcome in the town. Indifference was the response; they could take whatever the town folk gave out and it was settled.

When returning to *Seaward*, JT wasn't surprised at its sore condition, the men however were. First, at the extent of the estate, secondly, the unkempt grounds and buildings.

The property's guards were to leave until recalled and the men set about making the home livable while JT went down to Pickman's Wharf to find his friend.

Jim Pickman saw him first, "Damn, JT, but you're a sight to make eyes sore!"

"And you look at least twenty years older—and glasses—gad, you make me feel like a kid again!"

It was enough to renew their friendship even after ten years and Jim Pickman filled in on Salem's past years.

JT's mother had died, that much Pickman had learned, and JT wasn't shocked. She had departed when her husband, JT's father, was found to be a slaver and never returned. Jason Graves, JT's older brother, at no time found his senses from being held a chained prisoner of foul-minded Salem men. He'd been sent, hidden away, in the White Mountains. JT decided to leave him to his peace.

Fighting back the memories, JT tried to change the topic, asking about Pickman's life for the past ten years.

"The war is making things slow, JT. I've lost three ships to Rebel raiders. If it wasn't for government contracts, we'd be hard put upon. Me, I managed to stay single, didn't have your way with the women. You married yet?"

"You bet, over ten years now. Wonderful English girl I miss something awful, and three kids, good kids."

"So, where are they, am I going to meet them?"

"Not a chance. They're safe and back in England."

"Then why aren't you heading there?"

"I'm Naval Reserve on detached medical leave."

"I can believe that, you surely look like something the cat dragged home. What happened?"

"Chunk of wood conked me alongside the head."

"Sorry. So you came back to fight for the Union, good for you. I tried, but my eyes are failing, so I do what I can—you know, keep a low profit margin. You staying?"

"Well, I am at least until they release me or use me and I hope release me. What can I expect from the town? Is there going to be trouble—you know, because of father?"

"I don't think so. We've got some of those Wide Awake Cadets and a few of Ellsworth's wounded Zouaves' hanging around. I'll tell them you're a wounded Union naval hero and no one will come looking for trouble."

"I don't have the foggiest who you're talking about."

"Sorry, I forgot, you weren't around here. Ellsworth was the leader of a bunch of gussied up men called Zouaves. He was a little guy. First man killed in the war at Rebel held Alexandria, in Virginia. Actually, he was assassinated. It got everyone riled and there's talk even Lincoln cried. Then his Zouave's got mangled bad at Bull Run. A few are in town."

"People think it's a game, Jim, too bad. But on that other thing you mentioned. I'll let bygones-be-bygones about father being killed by that damn cannon, but if anyone gets in a scrape with my men, they'll be in serious trouble."

"JT, that was a few bad apples and they died. Hey, where's that big black fella you had with you back then?"

JT couldn't help a laugh, "That big black fella is now married to a Maharini in India, that's a female Maharaja, and he's a prince, filthy rich, four boys and happy as can be."

"That's great. I sure didn't think he'd be one to mess around with. Lot of rumors swirling about him being a wrathful poltergeist after dark. No one proved anything, yet those murders way down at Fort Warren sure were strange."

Only nodding, JT was noncommittal. He knew all about those unsolved murders. He was there; rescuing his brother Jason, and had killed two of the three kidnappers.

Jim didn't notice the silence, his thoughts had gone on to another question, "Oh, while I think of it JT—your schooner. I've maintained the *Ocean Pearl* and worked her. Do you want her back?"

"No, but I'll ask to use her if my head gets straight."

Pickman began to say something else, hesitated, then remained close-mouthed. JT had not mentioned going to his father's grave so Pickman stopped from saying what happened there—knowing the rage it would cause.

They were saying goodbye when JT had one more thought, "Jimmy, before I forget, don't think I'm a hero or tell people I am. It's only a depressing job. We destroy people's livelihood, some of them good people led astray by charlatans with glib tongues. I've lost twelve men so far because of those frauds and it's the men I've lost who are the hero's—so don't put me in with them, I don't deserve it—all right?"

«»

Two pleasant summer months slipped by. *Seaward* was restored, the townsfolk, though sullen, thought better than to cause trouble with so many sailors constantly around and others coming and going. JT's headaches faded, it seemed the rest was what he needed to find his course once more. The pipe, and what he put in it relaxed him, even just watching the smoke curl.

While the *Raven* was being overhauled, he relished sailing the *Ocean Pearl,* along the rocky coves of the North Shore, enjoying his sailor's gossip. It rejuvenated the men and made them even more of a unit that JT knew he would miss.

He fully expected to be discharged. The naval war for the Union was going well. One after another, Rebel, French and British blockade runners were being caught. Union gunboat flotillas roamed almost at will along Confederate rivers, whether capturing New Orleans and on up the Mississippi, or forcing their way along the Elizabeth and James Rivers.

Next came the surrender of Memphis, Tennessee, the destruction of the Confederate River Defense Fleet on the upper Mississippi by Navy Captain Montgomery's Union gunboats and following that, the investment of Vicksburg.

Confederate General R E Lee complained to the South's President Davis of his army's inability to move along Southern shores or rivers was specifically due to the Union Navy. Only the Union Army's setback at the Battle of Malvern stopped the North's onslaught.

With the exception of the southern fighting soldier, no one expected the rebellion to last much longer and JT, with his medical leave, saw no reason for the US Navy to prolong keeping a reserve captain. He looked forward to returning to England and his family and had no regrets that he was getting out of it. Yet, the wait pained him.

Dearest Evelyn,

as always I hope you are well. I don't mind telling you once again I'm hurting without you, although I must admit, the headaches have become less frequent & the scar on the side of my head has been covered by my hair growing back. But, now, with all my idleness I have even more time to ache for you. I remember so clearly when we met-so long ago. You were so worn & sad at the loss of the Black Watch & the loss of your friends. It was at that very moment I knew I loved you. I know after all our 'spats' & my foolishness you find that hard to believe, but yes, at that very moment you became my life.

I want you here. Although that is impossible, it doesn't stop me from wanting you here. The problem being that I don't know if I would be 'here' or where. Still, this endless waiting for my discharge tempts me to simply sail off once the Raven is ready.

So, we both wait, hopefully not too much longer. On minor matters, the weather here is cooling, the people in Salem are 'behaved' (I'll explain that when I see you) & my sailors seem content to wait out the war right here. We're guessing by the end of the year that Johnny Reb will see the error of his ways & end the bloodshed.

My best to Warfield & Lily, love to our children & did I mention I want you here? As you asked, I'll write again in two days-I have the time now.

My Love, Captain J.T & Raven Friday 5 Sept. '62 (For your journal)

«◊»

So the weeks passed agreeably, although the waiting for his discharge remained interminable, he knew it could have been worse, he was alive and had all his senses and limbs and his wife loved him. He did, however, have a minor dent in his temple to show for his efforts.

Tuesday, 7 October, 1862

Ultimately, on that crisp Indian summer day, a letter arrived from the Navy Department. JT was pleased —that is until he read it. He was to report to the Commandant of the Charlestown Navy Yard, Boston, on 29 October.

His reaction? He and Harry Scrimshaw read a dozen issues into it, none of them good.

Waiting in the corridor of the Commandant's bureau, JT and Harry stared at the pattern of anchors woven into the carpet. They had deliberated incessantly over the letter's intent without deciphering it, so their only recourse now was to stare at the carpet and wait.

Flag Officer Silas Stringham started to pass them and stopped, recognizing JT.

"Ah, you're looking a little older, Captain Graves."

JT felt the fool, "I apologize, Sir. I was a thousand miles away. It took a moment to place you."

"No need to apologize, Graves, my mind does the same. Who is this with you?"

"My Chief Petty Officer, Harry Scrimshaw, Sir."

Flag Officer Stringham, ever observant and blunt, studied Scrimshaw carefully, "Chief Petty, eh? You look to be a little old for that rank, Scrimshaw; there's probably quite a story somewhere in your service record. But never mind. Come into my office, We've serious work ahead."

They settled in front of an expanded chart of the Atlantic Ocean, marked with Xs and Os. Stringham began.

"Firstly, Graves, how's the head? I hear you took quite a knock; you must have, going off the deep end like that to shoot some filthy slaver trying to jump you. That would be enough to infuriate anyone in your condition."

"The head's all right now, Sir. Just a bit sore."

He said nothing further and Stringham nearly smiled over the shooting before he continued, "Since I'm somewhat responsible for your naval rank, Captain, I've followed your activities; you've done an excellent job, equal to anyone. Flag Officer's DuPont and Goldsboro both agreed to give the go ahead for what we have in mind because of you."

"And what might that be, Sir?"

"In good time, all in good time. I don't think you noticed I called you, *Captain*."

JT had missed the designate, "Captain, Sir?"

"Correct, Reserve Captain, for a mission well done, and actually needed for your next assignment."

Intrigued, JT could only respond, "Thank you, Sir. And my Chief and men?"

Stringham glanced to Scrimshaw, "As far as your Chief here goes, Captain, we'll discuss him later. Your men will receive commendations from Secretary Welles, just what that means I'm not sure, but since they've had quite a few weeks away from the war I think that time will mean more to them than any citation."

JT knew that as fact. Weeks at *Seaward* were working wonders for them.

Stringham ordered coffee and at the same time, JT noticed the F O spoke a while longer to the officer in the outside cubicle.

Stringham began the background to his plan, "Despite our best efforts, we're having the devil of a time ridding ourselves of the Confederate raiders. Have you heard of the CSS *Nashville, Sumter* or the *Florida*?"

"We've heard scuttlebutt, Sir. That they'd struck in the southern Atlantic, Caribe, Gulf of Mexico and a bit of a ruckus here."

"Well, here's an update. The *Nashville* was one of ours but when the war broke out, her captain thoughtlessly entered Charleston and was snared. The Reb's eventually renamed her *Rattlesnake*, and she was very successful as a blockade runner until destroyed by our *Montauk*. The CSS *Florida* was built in England, damn them, ran us ragged catching commerce ships until we caught her and burned her to the waterline."

JT and his Chief wondered why the history lesson on Confederate raiders and noted the F O had not, at least as yet, mentioned this *Sumter*.

He read their minds, "I've saved the CSS *Sumter* for last because she was the most successful of them all. Escaped our blockades twice and captured at least eighteen of our merchant ships and cargos. We finally bottled her up in Gibraltar solely because her boilers gave out. She's been refitted and renamed and in Rebel service as the *Gibraltar of Liverpool,* with a different captain. But it's not her; it's her former captain I want to discuss. His name is Raphael Semmes and when Commander of the *Sumter*, aside from the shipping loss, for six damn months, we had to divert blockade ships to catch her. Gentlemen, we now know Semmes is on the loose again with another raider and, I might add, Graves, with the connivance once more of the British Government."

JT couldn't prevent a comment, "Believe me, Sir; I have nothing to do with this."

They had a good laugh until the F O brought JT up short, "You may have more to do with it than you know, Graves. Your father in law is Lord Bunting and he owns Black Moon Shipping Lines, is that not so?"

Taken completely unprepared, JT could only nod. Scrimshaw, as confused, waited.

"I'll start to enlighten you, Captain. There's a shipbuilding company in Birkenhead, England, across the Mersey River from Liverpool. The company's called Laird and Son. They built a ship under a number only-290. We thought she was built solely for private interests until our federal agents there suspected a ruse and found the South was deeply involved. But, either the Crown authorities were asleep, or, in connivance, because no matter how we tried to stop the project, it would seem that at the last second, when the authorities said they went to prevent 290 from sailing, the wharf was empty and she had disappeared. At the time, our USS *Tuscarora* was at Southampton and our agent sent her to intercept 290, but the attempt failed. That was July 29th, this year."

Stringham called for more coffee and allowed time for his two officers to digest this information. As he stirred his coffee with cream, he watched JT begin to follow the thread of the story.

"So where is the 290 now, Sir?"

"Ah, that is what the entire United States Navy wants to know, Captain. But let me finish the story. Ultimately, through some English sailors who returned to Birkenhead after 290's escape, we tracked her, now dubbed *Enrica,* to Terceira Island in the Azores. That's where the ship was provisioned, coaled, mounted armaments and added crew from a supply ship out of a southern state called the *Agrippina.* And now we find that ship the Brits built is a Southern raider renamed the CSS *Alabama*, with the same Raphael Semmes, from the *Sumter,* now a Captain and raising hell up and down the European Atlantic, north at New England and then down into the West Indies."

At last it was evident to JT and Scrimshaw, "And you want the *Raven* to catch her."

The F O didn't answer at first, summoning the correct or suitable answer, "Gentlemen, yes. However, we don't quite know how to get what we want. Of course we want the *Alabama* destroyed, run aground, burned, disabled, or anything else to put a stop to the destruction. Frankly, this one ship will not be a deciding factor of the war, but she is a damnable thorn in our side and gives the South heart, which is something we *don't* want. Still, to be honest with you, you'd be looking for the proverbial needle in the haystack and up against a formidable, well-armed vessel, captained by an extremely experienced captain…"

It was Scrimshaw's turn to comment, "You sure don't 'paint the lily'…Sir."

"And I see you know Salisbury from Shakespeare's, *King John*, but no, I don't intend to 'add another hue to the rainbow' to gild this up, Scrimshaw. Yet I *do* want you to be fully aware to the situation."

JT was in the dark as to the banter of his Chief and the Flag Officer, yet mindful of the point being made.

"I know nothing of that Salisbury and little of Shakespeare, but if I follow this, you're giving it to us straight and asking us to volunteer."

The F O smiled, "Not yet, just hear me out. Graves, we've checked on you even more and want your experience around the British Isles and the European coast and, I suspect your Chief's knowledge is as good. We will also supply a flotilla of three or four warships but, I believe one of the positives here to be the *Raven's* speed and maneuverability. We've spoken with Laird, *Alabama's* builder and in his *estimate*, since they didn't have time for sea trials, is she'll reach plus fifteen knots and she's a single screw. I've heard you're better than that, are you?"

At last, something positive, "Yes, Sir. The *Raven* will clear twenty knots under sail and is twin screw, much more maneuverable, so that's a plus. If we can find that *Alabama* we can sure catch her—after that, who knows…?

Stringham brought up the flotilla again, but JT wasn't in favor, "A flotilla wouldn't be able to keep our pace, they'd hold us back. What we'd need is a supply ship, times and places, and ports, ports where we could receive supplies and information."

"Still, Graves, from our intelligence you may be out gunned and that causes me concern."

"Not to be argumentative, Sir, but we have a faster, more maneuverable ship with two long range, rifled cannon and I don't expect to get into any short range battle like there was at Hampton Roads."

"Hampton was a dust up. Then you're volunteering?"

JT knew his Chief was in, "We are, yes, Sir. But I'll have to ask my crew."

"That's excellent, thank you both. And now, Captain Graves, I've two more items before we get into the logistics of the chase. The first is Captain Rafael Semmes. He was a decorated Northern Naval Officer, Mexican war. He is a gentleman, a southern gentleman in the best sense, honorable, brave, upright and intelligent. At this moment, I believe there has not been one death attributed to him despite all the ships he's captured. He paroles Northern officers, is correct to his prisoners, courteous to the ladies and, more importantly, he is idolized in the South. Due to this, the

Union does not want him dead and become a martyr. His dying would only inflame the South and instill revenge to a fever pitch and truthfully our, that is our Union Armies, are not doing as well as our navy…"

JT couldn't resist, "So, if I hear this correctly, you want us to find the *Alabama*, destroy her, and yet be sure to prevent her captain getting killed."

Dismissive of the Union's wishes, the F O agreed, "Precisely, and we would prefer he not wind up with a devilish patch over one eye either."

F O Stringham laughed at his own comment, agreeing the limitations the Navy Board tried to impose were outrageous. He then turned to Chief Scrimshaw, "Chief, along with the coffee I also received a bit of information on your history from one of my people who knew of you. Seems that instead of a medal, the Admiralty labeled you the scapegoat. If you'd like to apply for a commission here, I'm sure we would be receptive."

Scrimshaw didn't give the offer a moment's thought, "Thank you, Sir. But I think I'll stay with Captain Graves —It seems I need constant supervision and the pay is better."

From the laughs at this comment, especially from the more reserved Stringham, the three men were becoming colleagues with one goal. JT and Scrimshaw appreciated that F O would go to extremes making the venture succeed.

Then JT remembered, "Sir, you said you had *two* items to discuss."

True, two items. You recall I previously mentioned your father in law, Lord Bunting?"

Leaning forward, to hear more clearly, the two men waited while Stringham went on, "Well, for your information, your father in law is a major investor in the CSS *Alabama*."

7 November, 1862

The Navy's wished the *Raven* off as soon as possible. JT left his Chief to supervise provisioning the ship for the long voyage ahead and at Salem, as those at the navy yard, the sailors voted unanimously to stay with the ship and when the *Raven* sailed up from Boston, all was ready.

Seaward was boarded up, guards reemployed and JT met with his friend Jim Pickman at the wharf for another leave-taking, “One other favor, if you will, Jimmy.”

“Of course, JT, name it.”

“I’d like to borrow your carriage. I wasn’t going to do this, for obvious reasons, but I’ve decided to run up to my father’s grave—you know, to see if I can find some rest about him.”

Pickman sucked in a deep in-breath, JT couldn’t help see it, “What’s that for, Jim, what’s wrong with that?”

“Christ, JT, I had hoped you’d leave before you decided to go there. It’s something you shouldn’t….”

“I’m not following you—what’s wrong?”

“JT, please, don’t ask—just go away, leave.”

“If you don’t tell me what’s going on, I’ll *walk* up there if I have to.”

“Please, JT, don’t.”

He started to walk, “Wait, I’ll tell you. Damn, damn, damn. It was…three, four years past, some drunken, stupid men—and I’ll admit women too…well…they went and dug up your father’s grave…and…”

Hands becoming fists, JT jammed them into his pockets, “And? And what? Where’s my father?”

“JT, I’m sorry, it was too late when I found…”

“*Just tell me!*”

“Dogs, dogs and foxes…there’s nothing left.”

JT’s next words were lifeless; the sound a person would use to describe barely, only scarcely controlled fury. He called over to Scrimshaw telling him to make sure all of the men were aboard and bring steam up.

Climbing the catwalk he shouted to Jim Pickman, “You can tell this to the people around here. John Thomas Graves’ has a duty to his country and his family's honor, but if I ever return, God protect this town, because I'm going to bring the devil's wrath down on it."

Chief Scrimshaw came up; sensing something wicked had been done.

JT remained tense, "Take her out Chief, and point her for England, I'll be in my cabin and don't roust me unless all hell breaks loose."

Dog's gnawing on his father's bones. The very thought, terribly unwanted, forced its way into his brain and lingered. The image ravaged all rationality. He hoped the memory would pass, yet until then he would suffer.

Suddenly, his anger welled and near burst, revealing a collision of wills. That one day there would come revenge, became undeniable. Till then however, he must, *must* do his duty to oath and country.

Evelyn. Evelyn. Her face replaced the other images. His love for her wiped away all pain—except the pain of being without her.

She is his one constant against all the evil he felt around him. To see her again and the vile acts of the war, the deaths, the townspeople and the dogs would diminish. To reach England and Evelyn was to save him. She and only she is his deliverance. My heart, my heart breaks, my wife….

Coming on deck at 0200 he felt more resolved. Keep steady, these troubles will be weathered if he stayed the course and believe this war will be over soon.

The mid-November air was now brisk, the Gulf Stream's silver, well-worn trail and full moon glided the *Raven* along.

Lighting his pipe, JT saw Chief Scrimshaw had the night watch, "How goes the watch, Harry?"

"Quite well, Captain. She enjoys being free to stretch herself like the greyhound she is."

"Aye, free, that she loves. We've put a lot of water past her stern these past months."

The Chief didn't answer, sensing JT wanted to talk. He waited.

"I apologize for coming up short with you last evening, Chief."

“No need, Cap, something set you off. Happens to all of us at times.”

“I guess. But I shouldn’t, it’s unprofessional and won’t happen again. At least I expect it won’t.”

“May I ask the reason?”

JT mulled the question, not really wanting to bring it all back, yet it was still there, “Yes, of course you can. I’ll tell you, but I don’t wish to continue it afterwards. A while ago you learned my father was a slaver. When you heard me shouting at Jim Pickman, it was in response to him telling me some of the people in Salem had dug up my father’s bones and given them to the dogs.”

Scrimshaw visualized the act, taking a moment to respond, “Captain, say the word and I’ll come about and gladly give Salem a whiff of gunpowder.”

A grim laugh, “Thanks for that, some other time perhaps. Look Harry, Let’s lighten this up. Fill me in, anything special happen at the Navy Yard? How’s it going with F O Stringham?”

“He’s good with us, Sir, and everything worked out perfectly with him. Then when the supply officer, a Captain Goss, knew you needed the supplies, he couldn’t be more forthcoming. Had everything packed aboard in two...”

JT was straightaway alert, “Goss, Goss? You’re saying Goss *helped* you when he knew it was for me?”

“Absolutely, JT. Couldn’t be of more help.”

JT was immediately suspicious, “Goss was my pain in the arse instructor, your Goss is not the one I know Harry. I want all the provisions checked this morning, first light and that means all—meat, produce, everything he touched. He’s either had a change of heart, which I seriously doubt, or he’s up to something. If we find rancid food I’ll make him eat it.”

“Why would you suspect that, JT?”

The story was told of Goss’ effort to acquire the *Raven* from JT, after which Scrimshaw was just as suspicious and carried out the order to the letter.

The voyage was actually pleasant, although JT was impatient to reach Portsmouth. The weather held; the crew efficient in their combat drills and resumed their former accuracy in their range finding and firing. The Chief, to avert the possibility of moisture existing in the older cloth powder charges, used most up in target exercises and saved the replacement powder charges and exploding shells. There could be no slipups, their lives depended on that.

«»

Slipping south below Ireland brought a warmth to JT, he knew his way by sight then and, once into the Solent, it was furl sails, bring steam up for Portsmouth. He planned two days with Evelyn before starting the hunt for the *Alabama*.

Soon, soon, Evelyn we'll be together.

At the eastern end of the Solent, there arose before them a sea of masts. Scores of sailing and steam ships lay haphazardly at anchor.

His crew, amazed at the sight, watched as the *Raven* was flagged down and wallowed in the wake of an armed Coastal Watch steam tug. A sign, printed in large letters hung from the shrouds and a shock—CHOLERA.

JT, completely baffled, listened as the officer on the small picket ship called up through a voice hailer.

"You and your crew, Captain, are forbidden to enter this harbor. We have a serious outbreak of cholera and the cities are quarantined."

This was wholly unacceptable and JT could only question, "I thought it was proven that cholera was not airborne, that water borne…"

He was stopped by the officer, "What you think versus what the Government believes is of no import to me, sir. The Great Stink of '54, that foul air from India, has returned once again, so we're told to quarantine the ports and we do as we're told. You're in the American Navy, you, at the very least should understand that."

"Then how long do you expect this to last?"

The answer was not encouraging, "Hard to say, could be a week, could be a month, could be more. Some of these other chaps have been here over two weeks all ready. Might I suggest you go on to the Continent, Sir?"

Fumbling for an answer to this, "My wife lives in Portsmouth, are there other ports we could tie off?"

"Sorry about your wife sir, but there's cholera in most of the cities all around the coast, Liverpool, Bristol, Dover and Deal over in Kent, London, Newcastle, they're all closed, quarantined, even Belfast, Ireland. You might find berth up at Perth, in Scotland, but you're a US Naval Captain and I don't know their regulations on American warships…Sir."

At a loss, as he had a mission and little time to waste, JT asked if he could send a message ashore.

"I'm afraid not, sir, or I'd be doing that all day for the others. And please don't think of rowing ashore after dark, the army has sentinels along the water's edge."

JT had thought of that very move but decided against it, "Don't concern yourself over that. A United States Naval Officer doesn't give up his ship; you should know that after losing two wars with us—if you recall."

The officer in the tug knew he'd been chastised and JT decided to play his ace, "The message is for my father in law, Lord Warfield Blackwood Bunting."

Distinctly reversing his attitude, the officer quickly said he'd be pleased to wait for the message.

JT kept his ingrained anger over the delay from Evelyn and wrote instead of how he had hoped to surprise her and their love and hope to meet soon. Not just for a brief reunion, but he wrote of some future time when they'll be together for the rest of their lives and he would never let war interfere again. He wanted to express more of his emotions, yet held them until he saw her.

Folding the note, he wrote Evelyn on the front but addressed the envelope to Lord W B Bunting. He wrote nothing to Warfield directly. He wanted to be face-to-face when the confrontation began over Warfield's being an investor in the commerce raider, *Alabama.*

For better than two days he waited for a response that failed to arrive. Frustrated, he knew time was against him. Other ships were now mooring to seaward and would box the *Raven* in.

No longer a choice, he must put to sea. It was precisely when he ordered steam up that the Coastal Watch vessel hove to alongside. The same Ensign handed JT's letter back to him unopened. He provided a confused explanation that a maid at Lord Warfield's home said she didn't know where the Lord was for he and 'the ladies' left a week previous for an unclear destination and that the maid would not be responsible for the letter.

The Ensign then pushed off, leaving JT at a total loss. With no alternative, he hauled anchor and got on with his mission, planning to return from the search of the European sea lanes in a month, probably more.

«»

The Raven sailed a zig-zag course south from France, Spain and the Azores—where the *Alabama* originally left for her raiding—and on past the Madeira and Canary Islands.

Off the coast of Guinea they captured the slaver *Hobgoblin*, out of Georgia. JT controlled thoughts of his father and with some difficulty took the slaves and her crew to Liberia, the slave refuge, giving both to the authorities there.

The *Raven* then plotted the trade routes from Spain down to the Cape of Good Hope and returned, raising a goodly number of sail, but the *Alabama* was not to be found.

After more than two months the coast of England was still closed and they moored at Cherbourg in France. There, the freak chance to find the *Alabama* at last occurred.

Chief Scrimshaw had gone ashore for provisions and, after a long time, returned quite agitated.

"JT, quick, see that brig over there?"

Following to where the Chief pointed, JT saw a well-worn, yet shipshape vessel, then looked back to his Chief.

"So, what about her, Chief?"

"Do you remember the name Stringham mentioned of the *Alabama's* support vessel?"

"Not really…" JT shook his head, 'Grip, Agripa..?"

"That's it! *Agrippina*! That's her—right there!"

It took JT less than a second to appreciate the ramifications, "Where she goes, we find the *Alabama*."

"You've hit the nail right on the head. But now listen to what I found out. I followed some of her sailors to a pub and they were talking about how they were leaving at dawn to meet a *friend* who had been visiting New England and the West Indies."

JT's mind was racing, "Christ, Harry! While we've been chasing waves along the sea lanes of Europe and Africa, the *Alabama*—it's got to be the *Alabama*—was capturing shipping along the east coast and Caribe!"

He was angry, but of more importance now was how to catch the quarry?

"Did you find out anything more, Harry? I don't see how we can follow her."

"Nothing clear, they mostly kept their voices down. The only thing else is possibly the word Curveau."

"Curveau? Spell it out; you make it sound like a French wine. Is that a place?"

Scrimshaw threw up his hands, "How do I know how to spell it or if it's a place? I'm only a lowly Chief. You're the Captain; you should be able to figure it out from here."

JT laughed, "Then as Captain, I'm ordering you to get out charts for the whole Atlantic and we start hunting for this Curveau."

For the next hour they poured over charts with no success until a feeling came over JT; the *Agrippina* would meet somewhere both ships knew and trusted. They turned their search to the Portuguese

Azores, where the *Alabama* was first equipped and armed. Their search ended.

Well northwest of the main island, Terceira, was an insignificant dot on the chart—spelled Corvo, not Curveau. JT knew in his bones the *Alabama* would come full circle to the Azores, and he also knew the *Raven* must beat the *Agrippina* there so that it wouldn't be two ships against one.

Thinking the *Alabama* would be to the lee of Corvo, the *Raven,* under full sail went in directly from the north east and, as he looked through the binoculars to about five miles out, there she sat—the *Alabama*. He sized her up to be about the same length as the *Raven*, over two hundred feet, more beamy, heavy weaponry, clean line, barely a trace of smoke from her stack and significantly, men running to their stations.

"Chief, Send a round from the bow chaser in her direction, let her know we're not friendly and have our battle ensign run up. We'll see how this Captain Semmes reacts."

JT was performing an honorable ritual, waiting for the *Alabama* to recover from surprise and prepare for battle, which her sailors did with amazing quickness.

They viewed her closely, "Looks like she's going to live up to her reputation, Captain."

"Surely does. Well, in another mile or two I'm going to come about counterclockwise. From what we've been told, we'll have speed and maneuverability over her. If she's aggressive, like I expect, she'll come at us bow on. If she does, she'll try to try for a broadside and I'll do a tight, fast turn to larboard, cut across her bow at about one mile and you rake her coming bow on. Sound right, Chief?"

"Aye, aye, Captain. Slightly chancy but first-rate."

"See to the guns—good luck and God speed you."

The *Alabama* did not come directly on; unexpectedly, she slipped to the east under steam and started to standoff from the *Raven* so that both ships were now formed into a circular path, one hundred and eighty degrees apart, about three miles distant across the breadth. This meant for a long range battle that JT preferred as the *Alabama* had far more short range guns.

Ranging fire commenced from rifled cannons and for thirty minutes near misses, some extremely near—soaking both crews—continued as the circle contracted to two miles. The difficulty in ranging was that the ships were underway firing at another ship that was underway.

Still barely off Corvo, for a while, both captains sought for an opening.

JT saw his chance. When the *Alabama* swung near the island, she turned slightly in to the circle away from the shore. Guessing there could be shallows their captain had to avoid, JT quickly reasoned he could come about, cut off the *Alabama's* turn and force her bow on to him at less than a mile. He made his decision.

He shouted to the powder monkey and had the boy tell the Gunnery Officer, to bring both cannon to port. That shifted the weight balance and JT had to be careful turning.

The *Raven* heeled heavily into a tight turn that shocked the *Alabama's* captain who instantly saw the difficult position he'd been driven into. The ruse worked. JT's severe turn and the shore prevented the enemy ship from sheering off. The *Alabama* was forced to come bow on to face the *Raven's* broadside.

The Chief was electrified by the move, knowing two exploding shells would blow the bow off the *Alabama* before she could sheer away; he sighted on her bow and as the *Raven* righted, quickly fired off the first cannon, then directly touched off the second.

The incredible happened. The first shell didn't explode, barely damaging the *Alabama's* bow strakes. The *Raven's* second cannon misfired, the shell not reaching fifty yards before dropping into the water to explode.

A disaster for the *Raven* was unfolding.

Instantly grasping the crisis and his cannon still being reloaded, JT threw the rudder over to and shouted into the speaking tube to the engine room for both engines full ahead.

He watched helplessly as the *Alabama,* basically undamaged, was now able to turn the tables and pass the *Raven's* stern and lay a broadside into her. Hurried, many of the shells missed, but enough projectiles blew apart the *Raven's* stern, shattered the two eighteen pound stern guns and, most seriously, jamming the rudder full over.

The *Alabama's* crew saw the damage to the *Raven* was fatal and on their captain's orders, stood down from the guns to watch the drama end. They saw the clipper taking in severe water at the stern, and locked in a turn that would take her a mile or more out to sea and then loop her back—in all likelihood to crash on the shore.

However, at the apex of the *Raven's* circle the watchers noticed the pressure on her steam boilers was blown off, the lines and sheets holding her sails cut away and boats lowered. Finally, her colors handed down.

Captain Semmes surveyed the situation from his *Alabama*. The *Raven* was going to be scuttled in deep water.

"Shouldn't we get over there and try to save her, Captain? She's a mighty fine looking ship."

"That she is, lieutenant, mighty fine and I'd have liked to get those guns, the South needs them. But that captain knows what he's about and I'd wager he has bombs along her skeg, ready for any move we'd made to do that."

What happened? With frustration welling up, JT couldn't comprehend how moisture seeped into the gunpowder contaminating it. Yet there was no time to think of that. The stern was destroyed; water pouring in, the rudder jammed, the linkage broken, not to mention the Confederate raider lurking, waiting. There was nothing to be done for it. JT couldn't chance having the ship somehow saved to become another raider or the guns removed. They blew off the steam, cut the lines and set the bombs. The men were warned not to give out information and sent to quickly collect their important belongings before taking to the boats.

No one reproached their captain. He had the *Alabama* in a perfect position to destroy her. They knew the fault lay with the gunpowder.

The *Alabama's* crew watched the *Raven's* masts shudder, the ship tremble, and smoke belch from her open hatches. The last dory, carrying her captain and chief pulled clear. The fastest ship in the world emitted a forgiving sigh and slipped beneath the warm, calm waters.

JT climbed the *Alabama's* Jacob's ladder and stepped on to the deck. Although seething, he outwardly kept his face blank even as the Confederate sailor's stood to attention and saluted him. All he could do was return the salute.

Captain Raphael Semmes stepped forward and offered his hand. Confused, JT accepted it while stating that he had no sword to surrender, for he was only a reserve officer and not supplied with one.

Captain Semmes gave a half-smile, turned to his 1st Lieutenant and Executive Officer, John Kell, saying to see to the welfare of the *Raven's* crew, and took JT to his cabin.

"I know this must be a difficult time for you, so I thought this would give you a quiet moment, Captain…?"

"Graves…John Graves"

"And I am Raphael Semmes, Captain of the CSS *Alabama.* You and your crew are now prisoners of the Confederate States of America."

JT nodded and Captain Semmes continued, "Now, with formalities observed, may I offer you a drink?"

"No…no thank you…I don't think so, Captain."

"Very well then. First, let me say we were initially lax when my lookout spotted sail. We thought you were our supply ship until we saw your ship's hull was all black without our supply ship's yellow rub rail. You came as quite a shock and I thank you for the caveat of alerting me. It's a pleasure to find a gentleman at sea. I'll also readily admit you certainly gave me the fright of my life when you somehow wore your ship about and crossed my bow. I never expected your vessel to maneuver with such alacrity or, I might add, that there was any ship that could turn that sharply or a captain with the nerve to attempt it, unbalanced as she was with both Dahlgren's to port."

JT remembered the praise Flag Officer Stringham bestowed when speaking of the *Alabama's* Captain and now he was beginning to discern the reason. Captain Semmes then stunned JT with his next comment.

"Of course we both know the tables would have been reversed if someone hadn't contaminated your powder. Have you found the culprit, or is it too soon? "

"It wasn't contaminated, it was moisture."

"I find that doubtful, Captain, *exceedingly* doubtful."

JT was trying to think the remark through when a knock at the cabin door took Captain Semmes' attention, "Captain, the *Agrippina's* hove into view."

"Excellent. As soon as she's alongside, tell Captain McQueen I want to see him in my cabin. And begin the transfer at once. We don't want to remain here any longer than necessary. Captain Graves here might have friends, and I'm sure he's not going to tell us if that is so."

Alexander McQueen, the British Captain of the CSS *Agrippina,* entered with a worried expression, "Raphael, good to see you're all right. Your Exec, Kell, told me about your little skirmish with this chap here."

"Little skirmish may be what my Exec thinks it, but *little* it was not, believe me. If it wasn't for luck and corrupted powder you'd have sailed right into this chap's incredible clipper ship and wound up another of his prizes."

"Clipper you say, Raphael?" Captain McQueen stared hard at JT, "Your ship might have been the *Raven* by any chance?"

Captain Semmes was surprised; JT was not. Captain McQueen explained, "Raphael, when we were coaling that ship was tied off across the wharf from us at Cherbourg. She was something to see, all spit and polish, beautiful line. But what really gets to me is, I left Cherbourg before him and bent on all sail to arrive here and I knew the compass headings, yet his ship beat me. How in hell I don't know. It's too bad you couldn't have captured her intact, she must have been damn fast."

Semmes laughed, "Capture her? We're damn lucky it wasn't us who went the deep six. Still, there's a more important point here, Alexander, how did Captain Graves know where I was? I mean, your ship and this man were at the same dock, same time and somehow he finds out where I am and then beats you here—how?"

McQueen was flustered and shrugged, "I'll find out."

They looked to JT. However, he decided answering one question would lead to many more, so remained quiet.

Semmes' didn't need to be told. Sailors on a night's leave; a tavern along the dock, loud voices. The result?

Captain McQueen indicated he wanted to see Semmes alone and both men went topside. It was an opportune time to look about the captain's cabin, but JT felt Semmes was not the type to inadvertently leave information about and it really wasn't honorable. Also, what could JT do with it?

Now that he had a chance to think, his time was occupied over the loss of the *Raven* and that there may be a saboteur who ruined the powder. Awakened to that possibility by Semmes, it became clear. Someone on the *Raven* must have done it, but who would have the time—or worse, why would someone want to? The single, farfetched possibility? He had an English crew and one of them might favor the South. He was angry with himself at the thought. Don't even think it; it couldn't be a crew member.

The idea struck him; the questions he should be asking are when could it happen, how, and why? Climbing topside, he caught Semmes' eye, signaling he wanted to speak to his Chief and got a nod in return.

"Chief, on this damn powder thing, we had no problem with misfires during gunnery practice, correct?"

"Correct, even with the old powder packs."

"And when did we start using the new packs?"

"Let me see. I randomly checked for dryness and weight at Boston, three other times during our cruise—it's in my Log—and at Cherbourg…"

"No, I mean when did we start firing them off?"

"I'm really not sure. It would have been recently because it caught my eye seeing the Boston Yard stencils. I kept them separate until we used up the old New York packs. Look, JT, I've been thinking along those same lines about the powder, but the packs were dry, no water stains on the canvas or tampering. I don't see how anyone could have contaminated those packs, I simply don't see it!"

"All right and I agree. It was the powder packs, but we have no way of proving that because they're on the bottom of the sea. And we agree no one had the opportunity to ruin them or wanted to. Maybe the powder monkey…"

JT stopped talking, Scrimshaw heard him mumble under his breath…'son of a bitch'.

"What is it, JT?"

"Don't you see? It *is* the packs—but it wasn't anyone *on* the *Raven* who salted them—it was the supply officer at the Boston Navy Yard! Goss! Captain Goss, don't you see?"

"You can't mean that, JT."

"Of course I do, Harry. I told you! In New York he was the one I caught trying to steal the *Raven* from me. I reported him and he was bumped down to supply officer at the New York Yard and then dumped in Boston. You saw him! You said he couldn't be more helpful. Damn—damn him all to hell!"

Semmes saw JT getting hot under the collar and motioned for the two men to go below. They were sitting, still cursing, in front of the captain's writing desk when Semmes, finished with Captain McQueen, returned.

"Now then gentlemen, what was that row over?"

"Captain Semmes, this is my friend and Chief, Harry Scrimshaw. The row you saw was over the powder."

The story evolved, expanded, and clarified. Captain Semmes listened and said nothing until JT finished.

"I have no doubt that is true, an appalling tale and I understand the anger, both of you. But mainly for you, Captain Graves, since I've only now learned the *Raven* was your own personal ship. That must make it doubly painful. However, I see no redress for you, at least for the present. In other times you would have been given the right to confront this Goss person and get satisfaction."

They were sure Captain Semmes was leading to somewhere they didn't want to go, "Yes, other times that are now long gone. Captain Graves, I've been informed by Captain McQueen that you are even more than appears on the surface. McQueen had been in the States meeting with our navy, after-which he slipped out of Charleston, and communed, with our contacts in England and France before proceeding here."

JT and the Chief remained in the dark but felt Semmes was not one to wander too far off focus.

"What I'm getting at in a roundabout fashion is that normally under the present conditions you and your crew, considering there have been no violations of international sea laws, would be released on conditional parole. In this case however, we find Scrimshaw and your crew are British subjects and, as the Confederate Government seeks better relations with England, we will parole them in England…"

JT spoke up, "How can you do that? The ports are closed due to cholera."

"We have our English Friends of the Confederacy, Captain and they have ways. Now to continue. Once you and your crew are transferred to the *Agrippina*, the *Alabama* will leave. When the *Agrippina* reaches our English port, Captain McQueen will release your crew and Chief Scrimshaw, under parole—meaning they will not aid in the war again.

"Now parole is truly a joke on both sides. Once a person is released on parole, they're soon back in the thick of the war, nevertheless, both sides turn a blind eye to it.

"And finally about you, Captain Graves. Captain McQueen had reports informing our captains that some Union blockading ships have made a name for themselves by being constant nemesis' for blockade runners. USS *Augusta, Rhode Island, Itasca, Pursuit* and your *Raven*, have made it quite difficult to obtain supplies and have reached our top archenemy list. In other words, Captain Graves, you will not be released under parole."

"Sir, my wife, and children live in England; I give you my word I will not…"

Semmes held up his hand for JT to stop, "I didn't know you had people there. I'm sorry. Nevertheless, this decision is not in my hands. The captains on this list…" Semmes read from it, "Captains Parrott, Graves, Trenchard, Caldwell and others, if captured, are *not* to be given parole."

There was no recourse. Captain Semmes left to supervise the on-loading while JT and Scrimshaw informed their crew of the decision and recommended they take the offered parole.

When JT abandoned the *Raven*, he had taken the satchel carrying currency including the wages, which he now doled out among the crew. Along with the satchel, he removed some personal belongings and the Ship's Log. He soon cursed himself for not leaving the Log with the *Raven*. Once Captain Semmes' started through JT's possessions, for which he had every right, the Log became the focal point.

Semmes scanned the *Raven's* Log and read a history of capture after capture of Confederate and British blockade runners: New Berm/Schooner *Elizabeth*, incoming/rice for Charleston…the Bogue Banks/Sloop/CSS *New Cairo*/South/ from England /arms / munitions/ skirmish /3 crew dead/10 *New Cairo* dead …Sloop *Boston/*Cape Lookout/slaver fired on *Raven*/captain killed…Off Folly Island/Brig/*Wondrous/* tobacco & cotton for England/brought in rifles ….Schooner/ *Royal George*/Oregon Inlet/cotton for England/trying to bring in heavy cannon boring machinery…Brig/*Peggy O...*

Semmes put the Log down. Eighteen ships captured in all, to say nothing of the periods when the *Raven* shelled confederate shore emplacements. In essence, Semmes' been reading a textbook of the Union plan 'Anaconda', it was an example of the General in Chief, Winfield Scott's, 'Great Snake' agenda strangling Confederacy into collapse.

Moreover, Semmes' thought, Graves had even taken on a Confederate warship, the CSS *New Cairo* and won out.

True, the *Cairo* was a converted commercial side-wheeler, but still, she was armed with two rifled Brooke cannon and that victory alone eliminated any thought Captain Semmes might have considered giving Captain Graves a parole. There was definitely no question—the Captain was a prisoner and would be sent to the South on the *Agrippina* along with the other prisoners the *Alabama* had collected on her voyage of destruction.

It was ironic, the fact not lost on JT. The CSS *Agrippina* moored off Boston, but it was Boston, England. Another bit of irony was that at this very place, English Pilgrims, seeking freedom, took ship to eventually reach the New World. Now a Confederate ship was depositing her prisoners ashore and giving them *their* freedom—in England.

From the Azores to Boston, JT had worked out a plan. Lord Warfield was Chief Scrimshaw's employer through Black Moon Shipping, so JT told the Chief to report everything from the activities of the *Raven* right to her loss from the guns of the CSS *Alabama*.

JT had been told by F O Stringham it was Warfield's money that funded the raider and destroyed the *Raven.* JT felt like adding his anger until deciding to say nothing until one day meeting his father in law face to face. That *that* was going to be difficult, was a huge understatement, considering Evelyn was his daughter.

Over the two weeks voyage to England, JT had written a lengthy letter that Harry Scrimshaw was to deliver to Evelyn. JT's heart spilled out on every page. The loneliness, hurt, dreams, and hopes for their future lives. Helping their children and their grandchildren grow. He had faith he would escape and they would grow old together. Trust me, he said, I'll be there as certain as our love.

«»

18 March 1863. Blackwood Abbey.

"My name is Harry Scrimshaw. Lord Bunting's my employer in the Black Moon Shipping Line and I request to speak with him."

Leading Scrimshaw into a small antechamber off the main hallway, the butler asked him to please sit down and he would see if the Lord was available.

A few minutes passed quietly before two young boys entered, observing Scrimshaw. Curious, the older of the boys asked, "I live here with my grandfather and this is my younger brother. Whom might you be, sir?"

From their faces, Scrimshaw knew exactly who they were, "My name is Harry Scrimshaw, and I'll bet your last names are Graves."

Both boys were surprised, "How do you know that?"

"I'm a friend of your father's and I've a letter here he wanted me to give to your mother."

"The youngest looked upset, "Mother's not here."

Scrimshaw smiled to himself at the boy's serious face, "Oh, too bad. Do you know when she'll be back?"

The oldest stood in front of his brother. Tears formed, "Our mother will not be back, sir. She's in heaven."

Scrimshaw's jaw went slack but he had no time to comprehend the boy's statement. A large black man appeared, seemingly from nowhere, his face severe, "Boys, please go back to what you were doing."

When they were out of sight, he turned menacingly on Scrimshaw, "Now, who in the devil are you to question these boys?"

JT had spoken of Monar, and this, Scrimshaw knew, would be he. Still, the man was big and angry and Harry was careful, "I was

Captain Graves Chief on the *Raven*. He asked me to come here and report to Lord Warfield the latest information and give Lady Evelyn a letter from him. What on earth has happened? Did the boy mean what he said?"

Monar softened; his voice became brittle, "I'm sorry, any stranger asking questions is not welcome here. You're an exception, of course. What happened to Evelyn is still hard to accept. As JT must have mentioned a number of times she…she was…there was no one like her…"

He glowered at the Chief, choking out the words, "There was cholera; she was in the village… helping. Some ass drank from her water jar and refilled it with water from the community pump. Evelyn and Vicky...Victoria, drank from it…and…there was no excuse for him not knowing that water's the killer."

"Victoria was their daughter?"

"Yes, she died as well. They were gone…gone in two days. Evelyn fought to see JT. That was a month ago."

"My God, we were here before that, we couldn't get ashore because the ports were closed. JT will—I don't think he'll be able to live through this. He's on edge now; this could send him over..."

"What do you mean, Chief—what do you know?"

Scrimshaw couldn't see where to begin and so a troubling, disjointed narration ensued. From catching blockade runners, the deaths of twelve crewmen, the tension at Hampton Roads, JT's wounds, learning of his father's bones scattered to the dogs, tracking down the *Alabama,* the defective powder and finally, the loss of the *Raven* and that JT was a prisoner on the *Agrippina,* heading for the South.

Monar shook his head at the litany of misfortunes.

"We didn't know the *Raven* was lost. Christ, that's a God awful blow to him for sure. It's nothing like what has happened here; nevertheless I can imagine the loss to JT."

He leaned over and shook Scrimshaw's hand, "My name is Monar. I assume you've been through it too, Chief. Although you seem to be taking it fairly well."

"My name is Harry, Mister Monar, and it's easier when you're not in charge, it's not your ship, you're not a prisoner and it was not your wife."

Monar nodded, "And none of the losses will matter when he finds out Evelyn and the child died from stupidity."

"What happened to that fool?"

"He disappeared."

Looking to Monar, Scrimshaw quickly gathered the fool would never reappear and moved the subject, "I thought the butler was going to get Lord Warfield?"

"I interrupted him. I wanted to check you out first. You can't imagine how deeply Warfield has taken the loss. She was his only child. The only person who kept him alive over this is Lily, she's his lover and best friend."

"JT told me you and Lord Warfield are confidants."

"I'm more an alter ego. When Warfield has an inspiration that may not pass some legalities, he asks me and I seldom find it a problem."

"Then to be forthcoming…Monar, I've done some deeds for Lord Warfield that I think you will approve of."

"I'm pleased to hear that. As you're speaking, I'm thinking we've got to find a way to free JT. That is, if you're game to try."

"I'm on parole; nevertheless I hoped you'd feel that way and I'll do my part in whatever scheme you suggest."

"Chief, Let's make this a joint effort and win or lose there'll be a well-earned, enjoyable retirement for you."

"Fair enough, but not necessary. While I think of it, there's one problem with Lord Warfield that bothered JT and me. Warfield financed that commerce raider that wound up destroying the *Raven*—why?"

Monar was shamed, "It didn't start out that way. I admit we helped finance her, but to be a blockade runner. We were as snookered as the British Government and we didn't know of it for months, until rumors became fact. When she left here, we were told she was a blockade runner called the *Enrica.* Privately, Harry, and believe me—James Bulloch, the Confederate purchasing agent and the other persons who hoodwinked us will not see one cent of the *Alabama's* loot. And, we'll see that the *Raven* is replaced at their expense."

It was time to meet Warfield. Monar had warned Scrimshaw that the man was distressed; sadness had enveloped him. Sadness that Monar had seen before in the jungles of the Caribe, a sadness never to pass, sadness that oppressed the mind and overlay every thought and breath.

Warfield's pain lessened only when he worked, immersing in the everyday minutia of running an empire. Yet his drive was hard fought. Each day was difficult; each day brought more dependency on Monar and Lily. Not being the sort of person who would take his own life, Warfield was now indifferent to it, offering as little resistance as Lily would permit. He needed a goal, some important goal.

On first seeing Scrimshaw, Warfield's memory seemed clear when the two men joined him and Lily.

"My word! Hello, Harry Scrimshaw. I heard it might be you out there. It's been some time since I asked you to find a crew for Captain Graves."

Despite the forewarning, Harry was taken aback. The Lord of Blackwood was physically failing despite all effort.

"Harry, you remember Lilian Fields from the past. Back when you and I were conniving to give Graves, the best crew money could buy. He's my son in law you must know…"

Warfield stopped, distressed. Scrimshaw picked up the story, "I surely do, Lord Warfield. And I remember how you saved me from being on the beach for the rest of my life. If it wasn't for you, I'd…"

Warfield waved a hand, "Don't. Those old naval hard arses sitting on…fools were old and… and no..."

He lost his train of thought, "How come *you're* here?

Where's JT…and Evelyn? I mean…"

Warfield got to his feet; Lily called to the butler and told him to take the master to his office. She then returned to Monar and Scrimshaw.

"Harry, I know something of your efforts and that you were with JT. You're back now, without JT. What has happened?"

"We lost the *Raven* to the *Alabama*, Lily. JT's a prisoner on another ship heading for the Rebel States."

"I knew investing in that damn ship would bring trouble. Is there any way of intercepting her?"

"No, too much of a head start."

Lily was intense now, "The loss of Evelyn and Vicky has broken our hearts, Harry. We need to get JT back. Monar sent his wife and children home last week and he's to follow her soon. So, I'm asking you, is there anything *you* can do to rescue JT?"

Monar interposed, "Lily, Harry and I've already made a pact on that. I'll write Amala, tell her the problem."

Pleased, Lily was frank, "Thank you both. I'll speak for Warfield. Whatever you want, whatever the cost. Money, ships, men, it's all yours. Warfield needs JT back, we all do. Go get him, no matter how."

Mentally thanking Scrimshaw over and over, Monar set to work. He'd been stymied, lost at Blackwood Abbey. The loss of Evelyn, so sudden and unexpectedly, had left him pained. He loved her. There was no release from the hurt and he felt desperation, a need to lash out. Even drowning that fool in the water that caused her death wasn't enough. There was no escaping the mental ache tearing at him.

He hid it from all around him until Lily chanced upon him in tears and deduced the depth of his loss. She suspected there was a hidden love there all along and in fact had envisioned that Evelyn, in the past, may very well have harbored the same emotions toward Monar.

When Evelyn and Victoria died so horribly, Warfield withdrew to some extent from reality. This left Lily isolated and it was only by finding Monar alone that evening and so lost, was she able to release her own hurt. More than once, their tears fell and mingled. Neither felt embarrassed or foolish, yet it was not spoken of, for neither Warfield nor the Maharani Amala would understand.

There was one clue to where the *Agrippina* was heading in the South and it was hoped to be an important one. When Scrimshaw was being put ashore with his crew along the English coast, he'd overheard one word between Semmes and McQueen. *Savannah*. It was the only start they had.

A fast, armed steam schooner, renamed *Redux* and a daring crew, many from the *Raven*, were hired. The plan was to become a blockade-runner bringing in medical supplies into Savannah. After that, there was no plan.

On the last evening before leaving, they learned the cholera ban on the ports had been lifted. Monar and Scrimshaw sat about still grieving with the family when the butler announced there was a weird Chinaman at the door.

Yet before they could even think to respond, in swept Archibald Feng Yün-shan, Leader of the Empire of the Sleeping Dragon who took their disbelief to the extreme—followed closely by shock and shudders.

10

25 March 1863, aboard the South's ship CSS *Agrippina.*

Having more or less the run of the ship, excepting the chart room, JT roamed. He tried to fight off the thoughts his mind kept summoning as it swept violently between anger and hurt. He had been so close to seeing Evelyn twice, yet at both times prevented. First it was cholera, then the damn Rebel's deciding he was too dangerous to be set free.

Hell, he thought, he would gladly fight to *avoid* the war. He'd had enough of it and enough of fighting it too. Just give him Evelyn, his children and home and he'd evade any attempt to make him fight again. He ached seemingly everywhere. His head, stomach, heart…

"Captain Graves, or should I say John Thomas, do you remember me?"

Startled, JT squinted into the sun and saw a tall, blond lieutenant in Confederate Navy gray smiling at him.

"I'm sorry, can't say that I do."

"I guess I'm being unfair, it's been over ten years, I'm Logan Carlton. You knew my sister, Charlee."

"Well for Christ's sake, of course! Excuse me for not recognizing you—but you *have* changed."

JT's mind raced. Logan, the immature, older brother of Charlee…they were at loggerheads at first, but then again he did seem to turn around and they parted more or less on friendly terms.

"I see you're trying to place me so I'll help. You saved me from getting killed by showing the futility of a duel I challenged you to and somehow you saved my life and honor at the same time."

"Yes, that comes back and also that you worked as a deck hand for me and we then took my schooner along the Gulf Stream to see if you liked sailing. That was it; you could get into the Naval

Academy and wanted to see if you would like the sea. Looks like it worked out."

Logan was embarrassed, 'Well sir, I spent four years at the US Naval School and came out an ensign, serviced mostly at sea, which I prefer, and well, as you can see, I resigned my commission and went with Georgia when she seceded, I'm up for commodore in the CSS and my own ship after this voyage…I'm sorry we've become adversaries."

For a moment JT had forgotten that, but saw no reason to let it matter at the moment, "Let's forget that for now, Logan. Tell me, how's your family? Father, Mother, the girls? Hope the war hasn't…well, you know…"

"I understand, sir. The war has changed everything of course. Father is a Colonel in the Georgia Volunteers, mother and my youngest sister Elizabeth have gone to Richmond and Charlee, I know that's who you want to know about—well, she's still at what's left of Hammersmith, although she's not the same."

"What do you mean, what's left of Hammersmith and Charlee's not the same?"

"When Fort Pulaski was shelled into submission, it opened the river for the Yankees to go upriver after Savannah at any time. I was at sea then and father was away with the Georgia Volunteers, so that left Charlee alone at Hammersmith with only a few of the house niggers, the rest had run off thinking Yankee soldiers would come free them.

Everyone thought the Yankee's would push up river, so white trash started ransacking the river houses. They ransacked our house until they started upstairs and Charlee shot two of them with father's hunting guns, the rest took flight after burning down a part of the house."

"Charlee did that? Good for her! But where the devil was her husband?"

"Ah yes, Stewart Edward James, the fifth Earl of DunDonald. We knew the very minute she returned to Hammersmith married to that dunderhead that he was after her money. Well, father immediately went to our attorney, tied up her trust until she was thirty and told DunDonald he could start working as a clerk on the plantation."

"Huh, did Charlee tell you I saw her in London?"

"Yes, and I apologize for her. She had told me of the promise you two had made and then for her to show up with her fiancé must have been a terrible shock for you. She said you ran off and she felt badly for you."

It *was* a shock for JT, a pleasant shock. Her breaking their promise allowed JT to pursue Evelyn. JT did not mention that in response, instead asking, "As I say, where was her husband when she was fighting off those thugs?"

"The Earl? Once our secession began, he said he had to head back to protect England. Said he had no choice, it was on their family crest, England First, or some such cockamamie thing. Didn't ask Charlee to go with him and I don't think she would have, even if he had asked."

"That's too bad, Logan. Were there any children?"

"No, thank goodness. How about you, you married?"

"Yes, three children. Hope to get back to them and my wife…someday."

"I'm glad for you." Logan looked about, began to walk away and spoke quietly, "Maybe I can help you see that day."

Night and the CSS *Agrippina,* under bare poles, ghosted under steam along the northern shore of Big Tybee Island. The former Confederate Fort Pulaski on Cockspur Island lay a colossal ruin, and the eleven Union batteries that destroyed her were now silent and mostly abandoned with barely a token Union presence.

They could breathe easier on the Rebel ship for the blockading Union warships mostly guarded the northern main channel of the Savannah River, knowing no ship of any draft could reach the city by the South Channel.

Under the shell pocked and shattered ramparts of Pulaski they moved into Confederate territory as the US Army found no strategic value for capturing the City of Savannah. With the blockade, the city was finished as a port.

The *Agrippina's* aim was not to be Savannah, but makeshift wharfs along the shore of Queens Island, a vast marshland beside the Savannah River beneath Long Island.

A minor Rebel compound had been set up there as a way station to receive prisoners from the commerce raiders before taking them on to the prison at Andersonville.

The station would also receive supplies and munitions floated in on the Wilmington Narrows and carted across the marshlands to the river. This was done to protect Savannah from Union spies reporting the city was a base for supplying blockade runners and raise the possibility of Union warships moving upriver to bombard the city.

For all his former enmity toward JT, The Master of the *Agrippina*, Alexander McQueen, had eased his assessment of the prisoner. Watching JT from a distance the captain could see the man was troubled, grappling with his demons, his lips moving subconsciously, seemingly arguing with the devil within and then, at times, quite suddenly doubling over in apparent pain. McQueen at first thought JT had a back problem until he realized it was his throat that ached and put the pain down to ulcers triggered by the circumstances.

Due to this, Executive Officer Logan Carlton, after explaining JT's ties to Hammersmith and Logan's sister, asked that JT be allowed to travel with him to the home. The captain relented, with provisions; the prisoner was an officer and required to take an oath he would not try to escape and, whenever Logan encountered a senior officer, JT was to be handcuffed to Logan. This JT readily agreed to.

The *Agrippina* was laying over for, at most three weeks, so Logan and JT were to be back in one week. As Hammersmith was only ten miles away, that would not be considered a hardship. The final order was that, should the guards arrive to take JT to the officer's prison at Salisbury, word would be sent to Logan and he was to return directly.

«»

Harry Scrimshaw, Captain of the fast schooner *Redux*, stared into the murkiness of the squall blackening sky. The schooner was under shortened sail and steam. Twenty miles east of the Savannah Rivers mouth he looked through the telescope to barely make out the blockading Union warship *Morning Light.* Guarding the North Channel, getting past the ship was only way to reach Savannah and begin their search.

Harry waited in anticipation of the squall rising to the east, behind him, and when it struck the *Redux* would be in the middle of it in a daring sprint past the Union ship.

Until then, Harry glanced past his crew to his two cohorts. Monar, the one man he would want with him and Archibald Feng the very *last* man he would want.

Archie Feng. Scrimshaw couldn't help shake his head remembering when the Brit Chinaman strutted into Blackwood Abbey like it was his and Warfield, Warfield of all people, came alive and welcomed him like a lost brother!

Feng had come, he declared, because he was bored with his wives, children and being a wealthy land owner. So, when word came his 'good friend' Monar had gone to England, Archie had to follow. And then, when Warfield mentioned JT was a prisoner and of the attempt to save him Feng insisted of joining. Not, he assured them, because he liked JT, but because he wanted in on the hunt.

Monar though, felt it might be a good idea. Feng was a martial arts master coupled with being the Leader of the Sleeping Dragon Society, and who knew what they were going to face. Warfield and even Lily were all for it as well so, in essence, Scrimshaw had no say in the matter other than refusing to go—and *that* wasn't about to happen.

Now, with the squall soon to be on them, Scrimshaw didn't mind Feng being there. The stories he recounted of his encounters, his dynamism and power, some of it confirmed by Monar, made the Chinaman an asset in any battle. Although the last tale he told, of Feng's son poisoning Warfield's former China Resident, Ashley Ealing, made Monar smile and Scrimshaw cringe, yet he didn't speak up.

The squall was merciless torrent, what Scrimshaw hoped. Feng was stoic and Monar kept a death grip on the rail. If the steam failed, they would broach and be swamped.

At one point, they could make out the *Morning Light* taking on so much water Scrimshaw was afraid he would have to go to her assistance, but she finally reached the lee between Turtle and Jone's Island while the *Redux* surfed into the North Channel of the Savannah River unscathed. After that, it was a simple matter to slip past battered Fort Pulaski and the Union guns on Bird Island.

Harry never mentioned it—his crew knew—if the Union ship foundered, his honor was to go to her aid. What would Archie have done to stop that? Scrimshaw was wary.

The Confederate gunboat *Josiah Bell* obstructed the *Redux's* passage, but after ascertaining she carried medical supplies for the Confederacy, helped guide her over the shoals and shifting sandbars to Savannah.

They were greeted warmly by the insubstantial military forces guarding the city, especially so when Scrimshaw announced the supplies were from the British Friends of the Confederacy in good will. The nerve of running the blockade was an honor to them and wherever they went in the city, they were feted—even the strange and ominous Chinaman and the large and ominous Negro.

They were at a loss after the futility of searching the docks without finding the *Agrippina.* Scrimshaw resorted to offhandedly mentioning to the dock master he had a friend on that ship who said he might be in Savannah around now.

The dock master frowned, "Your friend misled you, sir and he should be more careful in what he says. The *Agrippina* never comes into the city, too many Union spies."

He looked about; no one was in earshot, "Seeing you're a Friend of the South I'll tell you—she docks at some wharfs down on Queens Island. She's there now taking on stores for her next excursion."

As casually as he could sound, Scrimshaw asked, "God, I'd like to see him. Any chance I could drop down there, just to say hello?"

"Not a sinner's chance in heaven. There's islands and sand bars that block any sailing route from Savannah to Queens. You'd be better using a dory, but guards would pick you off afore you'd reached half-way. Folks around the *Agrippina* don't cotton to strangers, but some of her crew come up here, you might try asking them about your friend."

With a slightly suspicious edge to his words, the man advised, "Otherwise, best you let it go."

Since Monar must pretend to be Scrimshaw's slave, he couldn't wander around freely asking questions of the Negros. Archie Feng however, searched out the small Chinese contingent living along the inland fringe of the city.

Although not knowing Feng, they were well aware of the Sleeping Dragon Society and submitted when he ordered them to find the Yankee prisoner and not say a word. Archie knew the old saw 'a needle in a haystack', yet the way things were heading, he saw no other likelihood.

«»

Hammersmith, the once beautiful southern estate nestled grandly alongside the Savannah River was now a refuge of memories for Charlee Carlton. Yet even the memories were contrived, façades to conceal the disintegration of her life. She vividly recalled the balls, suitors; her marriage into British nobility. Yet abandonment by her husband, war, the damage to Hammersmith by southern scoundrels, her shooting them and the fire were now repressed episodes.

Lieutenant Carlton warned JT on the miasmas possessing his sister. Even so, the actuality of seeing her again was difficult. The pretty, willful girl who captivated him a dozen years past had vanished. What remained was a languid, diminished woman, determined not to tolerate the present engulfing her—not knowing it already had.

One of the three house Negros lingering on—lingering simply as there was nowhere else to go without being drafted by the Rebels to build earthworks—led Logan and JT through the stark home to the once fashionable drawing room to see the Lady of the House.

"Lieutenant Logan, dear, so good of you and a friend to stop by, although, please, you should have forewarned me. We weren't prepared to entertain guests."

"Forgive me Charlee, but I've brought an old friend of yours. Captain John Thomas Graves, may I reacquaint you with Lady Charlene Lee Carlton?"

JT stepped forward, smiling, shocked, looking into glazed eyes. Eyes that held no hint of recognizing him.

"Hello, Charlee, remember me, JT?"

A quizzical, difficult smile, "Charlee? My word, Captain Graves is it? It's been ages, literally ages since I've been called by that and I only allow Logan to do so. I would ask that you please address me by Lady DunDonald or My Lady Charlene, if you'd please be so kind."

This was going to be too much for JT, but before he could respond, Charlee spoke up to her brother.

"Logan dear, on the credenza is a letter for father."

Logan picked up the envelope, "It's not to father, it's to mother...from her cousin."

"Bobby E?" she turned to JT, "He's a General you know, for the Confederacy. My middle name is Lee, after him that was the lee in Charlee. He's quite important."

JT began to see that Charlee kept certain facts straight, although mentioning Robert E. Lee as simply 'quite important' was a considerable understatement.

Opening the letter, Logan froze at the first words, 'With my deepest sympathy….'

Logan excused himself, going into another room, leaving JT and Charlee alone to chat. The longest fifteen minutes of small talk JT ever spent then ensued until Logan called him aside.

"Our father died at a nothing place called Kellysville, along the Rappahannock. He was leading a cavalry charge against an overwhelming force of Union infantry."

"I'm sorry, Logan. I remember him, a gentleman and fair to me."

"He thought the world of you, JT. Especially when you found a way to save my worthless hide."

"I'm glad I did, your mother and Charlee will need you even more now."

"Oh, God, that's right. I'll have to go up to Savannah and break the news to mother and my other sister. JT, please find a negro, tell them to have Old Apollo come see me."

By the time Apollo arrived, Logan had a note written to Captain McQueen explaining the loss of his father and a request for him to go on to Savannah to see his mother. The note also stated that Logan would wait and should the request not be approved, please inform Apollo.

On the front of the envelope he wrote 'Captain McQueen' and Old Apollo was on his way by mule.

As Charlee began conjuring thoughts of an autumn ball with one of the negresses, JT left the room for the rest of the evening to avoid her and her ramblings.

He was dozing on a divan when Logan roughly woke him and pushed a shotgun onto his hands, signaling him to follow. They went through the parlor where the few remaining Carlton Negros were huddled.

"Torches down the road, JT." Logan turned the oil lamp low and the two men slipped out into the night.

"There's been torches seen in the woods at the far end of the cotton. But they've been put out. By the way, your gun is loaded with double shot."

"What's your plan? This is a big house to cover for two people. Are there any other houses or friends near?"

Logan was calm, "No, Just us. I don't like it, they may be foragers or deserters, neither way, I don't like it and this damn cloudy night doesn't help."

"What's the best way to come at us?"

"Down the road, the rest is cotton fields or marsh."

"Where's Charlee?"

"In the house, with two of father's hunting guns."

"All right then, let's get on the offence. We'll spread out on either side of the road and head down it. First sound we hear, we start blasting away."

Logan laughed, "Nothing like a straightforward plan, here's a few more shells."

Fifty yards along Logan signaled to squat down. There were voices down the road, one louder than the others, giving orders.

"Deserters, JT, could have arms, could get messy."

"I say take it to them before they come at us."

"All right then, I guess about ten or a dozen. They're on the right side of the road by that biggest tree."

"You shoot just to the left of it, I'll take the right."

With that they stood, aimed and fired, reloaded and fired again. Screams filled the stillness. Birds woke and took flight, animals screeched and ran. Men fell dead and men stumbled down the road. The quiet returned. Birds roosted, animals nested and five deserters lay forever silent.

Charlee was elated, wished she were out there with them. Logan was quiet; JT could see he was bothered by the night.

In the morning, Logan had the slaves dig the graves while he took their identification tags and then presided over a service.

When they were alone, JT offered his thoughts, "You had no choice, Logan. You know a warning shot would only have alerted them and then they would have taken us."

Nodding, Logan looked across the untended cotton fields, "Did you ever think that by standing up for your God given rights, your states' rights, you'd come to killing your own people? Those deserters were people, probably trying to get back home, worn out, sick of fighting. Knowing if they were caught they'd be hung by their own kind. Lincoln has done this to us, JT, brought us to killing our own, just so he can keep the Union intact, not for the negro. How many more will die for that?"

JT made no response and Logan spoke into the night more than to JT, "Georgia sowed its own destruction. We were the first you know. Secession! Father and I were in the vanguard, damn fools that we were. And now I can see the inevitable, hope, sweat, and determination are useless against the Union's mills and manufacturing. They are determined to crush us under a mass of men and machinery. The South's valor and passion are being humbled under the weight of ships and cannon. So now father is dead, Charlee's not quite right, our slaves gone, the fields are barren and Hammersmith is-well, I guess our Hammersmith will fall to rot as well. Just as I fear the South will."

"Logan…I don't want to get into who started the war and why, but I have to say this, I think slavery is wrong …and…and well I'm sorry it couldn't have been worked out before it came to war."

Wandering off, the shotgun on his shoulder, Logan thought was to react with anger, yet he held his tongue and said nothing more.

Old Apollo returned with new orders for Logan. He was not surprised at his new rank of Commander for it was expected. Still, one packet contained his new shoulder straps with two woven gold stars on each and made him catch his breath.

He read the orders in increased astonishment. Gone was all his despondency, he became a changed person.

"My God, Navy Secretary Mallory has given me the CSS *Georgia*! The *Georgia* will be a commerce raider and my next command! This is unbelievable; she was built in England as another *Virginia* and earmarked for Captain Maury. My guess is he and Mallory had another falling out, so now she's rechristened as the *Georgia* and I've got her! This is what I've trained for, to be in the fight, not second in command on a supply ship."

JT shook his head listening to Logan. He was resurrected, back in the fight—as if one ship would reverse the incoming tide swamping the South. Commander Logan Carleton had reverted to just another young, flag waving hothead, impatient to get his hands on the foe and save the South's honor and, of course, slavery along with it.

The other packet revealed the CSN Jack or, as Logan preferred, the Stainless Banner from its pure white field and small Stars and Bars stripes in the corner. He placed it over the front of the divan, stood to attention, and saluted it.

Standing outside, glancing out over the wasted fields, JT didn't know what to think. Logan had instantly relapsed to a zealous southern hawk, so where did this leave JT? He soon had the answer.

"JT, I'm embarrassed over my comments regarding the future of the South. I fear it was a moment's weakness brought on by being overtired. It won't happen again. As far as our relationship, I assume you will keep to your word and we can proceed in a gentlemanly manner until we part. I have read the rest of my orders. I'm to hand you over to the military in Savannah, then be in Richmond in three weeks before going to Brest, France and my command."

JT's heart sank. Somehow, he'd hoped for a different outcome, but the true outcome was becoming too clear.

Logan hadn't finished, "However, my orders don't say *when* to hand you over, and I would like you to accompany me when I go to see my mother and tell her the sad news on father. Charlee wouldn't leave the house, so you could help me here—you once met mother and she liked you. But one thing must be understood, once we reach

Savannah, I'll have to handcuff you. Take that blue coat off before the townsfolk lynch you. I'll give you one of father's jackets."

«»

Since Savannah was blockaded, Scrimshaw reasoned that any sailors arriving in town would be from the *Agrippina.* This meant he hung out sipping beer after beer hour after hour along the dockside taverns until sailors arriving soon proved out his reasoning. The problem was no matter how circuitous his questions, they said they brought no prisoners to Savannah because they dropped off the lot of them in England 'cause they was only a bunch of worthless lime suckers.'

Admirably, Scrimshaw kept his thoughts to himself and discussed the problem with Archie and Monar.

JT had been a prisoner on the *Agrippina* when Scrimshaw left that ship and another sailor stated the ship hadn't stopped at any port. So, the discussion came down to one of three possibilities. JT had escaped, doubtful. JT had died, possible. Or, JT was still on the *Agrippina*. If so, why?

They had learned Savannah was an intermediate station for Union prisoners heading to either Andersonville or Salisbury prisoner of war camps, so what to do next?

Without conviction, they decided to take shifts keeping watch on the military compound and the hours passed miserably without value for four days.

It was Scrimshaw's shift when one of Archie Feng's coolies came to their hotel with the key. Archie had informed the city's Chinese dockworkers, servants, field slaves, and gardeners who they were to be on the lookout for and it seemed this carriage driver had taken a naval officer and civilian to a river home. The Chinese driver did not think much about it until seeing the men were handcuffed together and just before the door, the handcuffs were removed.

The coolie left a companion to keep watch and raced to tell Archie, who was moody, angry over their lack of success, but Monar saw the coolie frantically running toward them and knew they had found John Thomas.

Archie stopped Monar from contacting Scrimshaw for they saw there was going to be foul work ahead and Harry Scrimshaw was not the kind to stand aside to allow it.

"We're agreed then, Monar my friend?"

"Yes, so let us get to it, there's no time to waste."

Leaving a note to Harry stating they decided to hunt about some more before relieving him, they took an enclosed cab and, with the coolies, waited up the road.

Later that evening a gas lamp flared in the home and a short time later, the front door opened, spilling light across the entry, silhouetting three people. The men in the cab became tense. Two people started down the steps until one turned and went back for a few words with what they took to be woman remaining at the entry. That was important to Monar and Feng; it showed that as men went down the walk to stand by the curb, they weren't handcuffed.

"I'm not going to replace the handcuffs JT, because if we don't hail a hansom soon, we'll walk and talk, be our last chance. This moon reminds me of back at Hammersmith in the past, how we loved it. By the by, thank you for helping there, I think mother will survive and my telling her I've shore duty will give her peace about me."

"Well, with your sister Jo run off to Richmond after some sailor, I think you're pretty much all she has now."

Logan hailed the cab as it moved toward them and told JT that he would do whatever possible to help him.

Monar, peeking through the curtain, confirmed it was JT and their brutally simple plan began.

The driver nodded to the waiting men and pulled up. JT opened the door and awkwardly stepped up into the cab as Logan grasped the cab's side to follow.

JT felt someone in the darkened cab yank him inside and let out a shout—then went numb as his head thudded against the far side of the cab.

Logan, transfixed for a moment by the shout, looked up into a black wrathful face and two massive hands reached out and heaved him bodily onto the cab's floor.

Logan's last effort was to struggle. His last sight, a moonlit glint of steel. His last sensation, pain.

Slowly feeling the jostling of the cab and regaining his senses, JT saw Logan on the floor, then Monar and, of all people, Archie Feng sitting across from him. His mind finally grasped the two men were his saviors and he gripped their hands without anyone uttering a word.

Before he could speak, the JT's tension broke in a series of coughs, growing into a racking pain as he tried to stop. Finally easing, he took a cloth from his pocket and wiped his nose and mouth and shoved it away again.

Through bleary eyes he focused, "Thank you…the both of…you. You've saved me from…from prison."

Monar suspected something else was causing his distress as well, but let it slide, "Don't thank us yet, JT. We've still got to get out of here."

JT glanced at the prostrate Logan on the floor, "How long do you think he'll be out?"

Despite Monar's glaring at him through the dark, Archie wouldn't prevent a horselaugh, "*Out*? That's one Southerner who's *out* all right—for good!"

Stunned, JT could barely find his words, "You killed him?" It took only a second to realize, "You intended to kill him from the start didn't you, both of you? He wasn't a bad person! Why, why…?"

Monar could see Archie getting angry enough to kill someone else, "JT, shut up. What else was there for it? For Christ's sake—think. What else could we do—knock him over the head and when he woke have him raise the alarm?"

"I know, I know, but something..."

Yet as JT anger lessened and thought of it, Logan being out of the way solved a number of problems. JT was free to escape. There was a good chance that Captain McQueen had not informed the Savannah military about JT.

If so, no one was going to look for Logan, or JT, for at least three weeks and even then, Logan might be considered a deserter. In the meantime, no alarm would be issued and to JT, that meant he could keep his hopes of escape alive and seeing Evelyn again.

The Chinese clique in Savannah was given a sizable amount for their assistance and in disposing of Logan Carlton's body. After that, JT was genially welcomed back by the crew and immediate plans were set in place to leave port unannounced. The river pilot said it was against his better judgment but, after threats and now flush with British gold coin, he amiably guided the ship as she drifted out onto the current, raised steam and headed down river.

Union blockaders worked on the premise there were no blockade-runners left inland, so most eyes, when open, were turned seaward.

Now was the time; between the false light of early dawn and the tired eyes of the lookouts awaiting the Change of Watch, who could blame them if, when the schooner *Redux* crashed through the surf of the Savannah River under a full head of steam, nothing more than a nod was made of the smudge of soot seen on the horizon.

They'd been riding the Gulf Stream for two days and no one said a word about the problem. He had to be told. But how and who? They understood JT wasn't well; the flecks of blood seen on the cloth when he coughed made that apparent.

He counted the days until returning to England and Evelyn. She dominated his mind and they now realized all that kept him going. To take that away from him was heartless, for how much more could he take? Yet, they couldn't go on letting him think he was going to see her again. They couldn't do that...

Scrimshaw laid it out, "We can't go on like this— we're caught in a cleft stick..."

Archie Feng looked to Monar, "What's that mean, cleft stick?"

Monar shrugged, "I haven't the slightest idea. Harry, what in hell are you talking about, speak English!"

"I am speaking English. It's a simple term to say we're in a bastardly situation here. We can't go on *not* telling JT what has happened in England and it doesn't seem we can build up enough courage to tell him—a cleft stick."

"Then for Christ's sake say that, don't pull that peer of the realm crap English on us, make believe we're simply a couple of old lower class Limeys."

Scrimshaw felt awkward, didn't know if they were serious or not and made a decision, "I'll tell him."

Monar stopped him, "Thank you, Harry, but no. It should be me—who else?"

He tried to think of how to tell him, how do you tell a person, a friend, his wife is dead? There was no calm or painless manner and Monar gave up searching.

"JT, there's something I must to bring up; I should have spoken to you before."

"I know, I know. I've been wondering how long it was going to take you."

"You know? I don't think we're talking about the same thing."

"I think we are, Monar. You're concerned about Scrimshaw's resentment over your killing Logan. Well, I want you to know that I don't think it was necessary either. Convenient? Yes, Necessary? No. But I was the one you saved so I can't say too much about whether…"

Monar stopped him and was about to speak when JT took on another coughing spell. When he finished and caught his breath, Monar could barely speak, "JT, it's not that. Get that out of your mind and listen to what I say, this is more serious than any of that."

JT could see by Monar's passion it was, and shivered, "Then go on, Monar."

“Scrimshaw told me that when you were given the commission to find the *Alabama*, you brought the *Raven* to Portsmouth, but you couldn’t dock because of the cholera epidemic—remember?”

JT had not the slightest idea of where Monar was leading, “Of course, I may not be well, but I’ve not lost my memory. Get to the point, Monar, please.”

Monar lowered his head, closing his eyes, “JT, Evelyn was helping the sick then and she, well, she drank some of the water…

“My God, Monar, what are you saying…?”

Monar was silent, unable to speak. He heard a sigh, yet no further sound and raised his head. Dismayed yet unsurprised, he looked into JT’s eyes. A candle once burned there, a bright shimmering candle. It had sputtered, died, and left JT’s mind in shadow, and despair.

“Thank you, Monar. I…I never this. I’m going to my bunk, I need time to…to I don’t know what…”

«»

The *Redux* had shut down the steam power to conserve coal and she silently swept into dawn with only the hurry of water past her hull and the rising sun inflaming her sails.

Monar had not slept and held the helm, squinting at the compass when JT came up through the hatchway.

“I’d like you to come about, Monar.”

“What are you saying, JT?”

“Monar, you’re the Captain. I’m asking you to bring the ship about.”

“To what course, JT?”

“By a heading of due east, I would estimate we’re two days at best out from Cape Cod. If I’m not on deck, let me know when you raise Provincetown Light.”

“And the next heading, JT?”

“You must know…Salem.”

"How can you go there for Christ's sake? They hate your father, you and everyone else. Come to England. Warfield and Lily want you back. Your *children* are there for you. You're not thinking straight, JT."

"I want to go to Salem, Monar, I really have no choice. Will you do what I ask?"

Monar shouted, "Coming about!" He spun the wheel, knowing there really was no choice.

Harry Scrimshaw, resting in his bunk, felt the ship altering course and came topside, "What's happening, why the course change?"

Monar pointed to JT, standing by the taffrail, looking at their wake, "He wants to go to Salem; my guess is he plans to die there."

"What are you talking about? Be serious, Monar, he actually thinks he's going to die?"

"Yes."

"Why?"

"Why? Have you seen him, heard him? He's good reason to think that."

"That could mean any number of things. He might only have pustules of the lungs or bronchitis or something. We should get him to a good English doctor—in London."

"Harry, this is something he must grapple with alone. You cannot invade his instincts or approach to his problem. I think he's right."

Archie Feng had come up and listened while Monar continued, "There's no compassion left in him. He never had the chance to hold her, say goodbye. She was his life, his *life*. With her gone, his became meaningless, not even the children can help. If we had told him little Victoria died as well, who knows what he might have done?"

Archie was uncompromising, "He's too weak, better he died back there, before he knew about his wife."

Scrimshaw was disturbed by the comment; Monar thought it more profound, "Perhaps you're right, Archie. But weak—I don't believe so. There's a reason he wants to go back to Salem. Just what, I'm not sure, but now with her gone, there's something else, something hidden that keeps him wanting to live—that's not weakness."

Archie rubbed an amulet around his neck, "You raise a good point. But, if you are right, then Graves becomes an uncertain person, because you're talking about revenge. So then the question becomes, revenge on whom?"

"I guess we'll find out in good time, Archie. And whatever or whoever it is, I'll help him."

11

6 July 1863 The Graves' wharfs, Salem

Standing on the ship's gangplank, JT glanced along the wharfs lining the waterfront, then to the warehouses behind. The Pickman's and Graves' still owned most of the harbor front, yet now the Graves warehouses and docks hiding the shore stood empty, the decaying wharfs and buildings no more than shadows of the once eminent Graves domain.

All they built, all they were, had crumpled; rotted from within like the wooden pilings and planks he stood upon. He wasn't sick enough not to grasp what happened.

It was all too confusing for Harry Scrimshaw. The change of course to Salem and then, when they docked, the decision that when the *Redux* was replenished, Harry was to take her back to England without JT, Monar and Archie Feng.

Harry was the odd man out and protested, saying that Archie should go, but when JT indicated the necessity of Harry's journey, he grudgingly complied. One of the matters Scrimshaw had to attend to was the fact that the Union Navy probably had no idea the *Raven* was sunk or JT was a prisoner or even that the English crew was paroled in England. Scrimshaw was to report all this to the American Consul in London, but *not* report JT was rescued and in Salem.

Those of the crew wanting to return to England would do so with Harry Scrimshaw on the *Redux*. The remaining crew in Salem would perform whatever work JT specified and he estimated the work to be done would take around one month. After completed, Archie, Monar and the remaining crew would take leave for England with the old schooner, *Ocean Pearl*.

The letter Scrimshaw would to deliver to Warfield was a justification of the reasons JT decided to stay in the States.

He wasn't well enough to travel, it said, and didn't expect to improve. He hoped Lily and Warfield would take care of the children as their own and reminding Warfield he now had two grandsons to follow in his footsteps and a granddaughter to spoil. JT further stated that Monar and Archie would return after they helped complete a few issues needing attention.

Harry Scrimshaw, the letter continued, would be an excellent replacement for JT, and it was hoped Warfield would consider that.

Finally, he managed a last few words for them.

And now, Lily & Warfield,

I have come to accept the truth. The loss of Evelyn has overwhelmed any wish for life. That must have overcome you both as well, yet somehow you have the strength to carry on that is not within me, & in truth, with my illness, I do not wish it to.

I thank you for the trust & love you gave me, but

I cannot return & continue, always waiting for a past that can't ever return.

I am sorry that I am unable to say to you what is deep in my heart—& that is for the best.

To only pleasant memories, John Thomas

7.7.'63

Note-I have only now received the Herald, a Boston newspaper. It repeats telegraph reports that on 7.5, at a town called Gettysburg in Pennsylvania, the Union defeated the South's General Lee. It is thought to be a turning point for the war. Can peace & reunion be far behind? Let us hope.

As Scrimshaw left soon after my writing this, you may be the first in England to know.

JT

«»

At long last, too long actually, Monar talked JT into seeing a doctor, or rather having a doctor come to him. In agreeing, JT had a request of the two men.

"I want you to know the other reason I packed Scrimshaw off to England. He would not approve of what I need done, so he would be in the way. You know I'm not well and because of that there are things I cannot do without your help. So, I'm imposing on you. First, I'm asking you to find a way to bring Captain Goss, who I know diluted my gunpowder, to *Seaward*."

Archie Feng was all for the escapade after learning of a sizeable Chinese community centered on Beach Street in the South End of Boston. As he did in Savannah, Archie undertook to employ the coolie and find a scheme whereby Goss could be spirited out of the Boston Navy Yard in Charlestown and up to Salem.

To begin, Archie dressed conspicuously in his black robe and stood by the China Gate. Motionless, his eyes took in the scene until they settled on one person. A watchman, what American Chinese called a 'looksee', tried to blend into the mass while keeping an eye on the black robed man.

Archie moved through the people and faced the looksee, asking softly yet forcibly, "You Tong man?"

The man wasn't overly startled, "Who you to ask?"

Archie exposed the Dragon amulet around his neck.

"I am Feng Yün-shan that is who. Do not chance being impudent. I wish to be taken to your elder."

They strode down meandering backstreets until he was asked to wait and looked about where sunlight seldom entered and trash seldom removed. Noting the pathway name as Alley Street, Archie laughed to himself, 'better to be called Filthy Alley.'

A door opened. Archie adjusted the dagger enfolded in his robe and entered into an opulent, yet windowless room, reeking of opium and the fumes of whale oil lanterns.

A voice from behind a screen spoke English with a Fuzhou Dialect, “Say to me who look to find me.”

With luck, Archie would follow the dialect, “I am Yün-shan Feng, Leader of the Empire of the Sleeping Dragon Society.”

“I know of Dragon. You are not Tong?”

“I am nobler than common, dirty Tong and will lower myself no longer to converse with a screen.”

There followed silence, after which, “We are careful of enemies. If you not, come, speak of why you seek me.”

Seated on a pillow, a beaker of tea already there, Archie courteously waited for the withered Elder to speak.

“I am Wah Yee, Superior Elder of the Chinese Fraternal Society of Boston. I know of the Sleeping Dragon from my years in Fuzhou and absorbed English from Methodist Missionaries. I fled after English started new war to take from us what is ours.”

“And you came to Boston?”

“Not first. Came to what Spanish call Angel City, work on train road, then friend have me come to here. Here I raise to Elder. Why come you and to seek Chinese Elder?”

Archie decided to tell it his way, “I have a friend who is sick, sick to dying. His father before him was wronged by the people of his village and now their wish is to destroy his home and make him despair forever. He wishes to leave a bitter taste for the village to choke on.”

A thought struck Archie, “Think of him like you. British drove you out of your town like he is being driven out of his. Probably you would have craved to destroy something of the British.”

It wasn’t the best of analogies but Wah Yee understood, nodding in agreement, “What is it you wish?”

“Nothing at the moment, but when the time comes, I will need wagons and men, perhaps as many as fifteen wagons and twenty men. I will pay well for both.”

Wah Lee closed his eyes to the offer and instead asked, “This to destroy one home?”

“Wah Yee, it is a *big* house, of granite.”

“And not under…hand…underhanded?”

“Perhaps.”

Wah Yee smiled, “We have no like of these imperial people, but not wish you to kill Yankee soldier.”

“Not a one.”

While Archie Feng was dealing with the Elder, Monar, following another of JT’s requests, directed the crew to begin work on the laborious task of digging under various foundation supports of *Seaward.*

Once that task had begun, Monar and two seamen paid a visit one August night to the Boston office of Doctor Charles C. Crowninshield.

Of that meeting all the doctor recalled was a large black man’s growl, “Come with us, the Captain wants you.”

Befuddled, and no recourse allowed, the doctor was bundled into a coach and off to where he knew not—until, on a paint splashed granite column he read, *Seaward.*

Now apprehensive, the doctor knew the name to be the home of the notorious slaver Captain Richard Graves.

Drawn along marbled floors and fresco laden walls, Monar then pushed the anxious doctor through a doorway that locked behind, leaving him in a great room. The room, pervaded by the odor of tobacco and sea, was where he faced a tired and visibly ill, Captain John Thomas Graves.

After an acrimonious beginning on JT’s part, the doctor conceded that in London, he studied the branch of medicine, oncology, that dealt with cancers and yes, he was forced into admitting, it would appear JT had advanced throat cancer.

The doctor also found that JT well knew this, and the illness was not the real reason for his being there, but rather the Captain wanted to talk. Confounded, over the following weeks, Crowninshield began rendering the Captain’s life.

Until just before the doctor finally left *Seaward*, JT refused any medication so that his recollections would be true—as true, that was to say, as *he* saw the truth.

As this transpired, Archie Feng had made inroads into the capture of Captain Goss. The navy yard utilized outside civilians to do service work and Chinese labor, being the lowest end of the wage scale, received most of the work. Money the laborers received from Archie helped develop more loyalty to the Empire of the Sleeping Dragon than to a country that thought them barely above the level of a beast of burden. This outlook answered Archie Feng's needs.

Goss, it was learned, lived off-base and alone on Tremont Street, which led into Boston's Scollay Square. By having diverse coolies follow him, they found their mark had a regimen of walking from Tremont to Court Street and then to the Square. There he favored Vaudeville shows at the Old Howard Theatre and the freaks or curiosities in Austin & Stone's Dime Museum. Goss would wander in there for an hour, after which he would hop a streetcar to his apartment.

At night, an area off the Square offered the exact setting the conspirators wished; numerous side streets and alleys that posed opportunities to seize Goss quickly, thump him over the head and be gone.

When it should be done, however, was a bone of contention between Archie and Monar. They both endorsed the motive behind JT's hate of Goss; the faulty gunpowder caused the failed attempt to capture the *Alabama* and that, followed by the loss of the *Raven* and JT's imprisonment would furnish *any* person with enough hatred.

The two men agreed Goss should die—for any of those reasons—but Archie thought JT was becoming mentally detached and too physically weak and he would probably verbally punish Goss, then let him go. Or, JT would decide that since no one died—only his ship—from the encounter with the *Alabama*, treachery wasn't sufficient reason to kill him. Then yet again, would JT think it better to give him over to the naval authorities and let them decide? Problem with that was JT didn't want the Navy to know where he was.

Minor dissension then came down to Archie wanting to either kidnap Goss, let him see JT and then kill him, or simply kill him. Monar's view was to let JT have the chance and if he didn't kill Goss, they would then do it—but at least give JT the opportunity to revenge the past.

They settled at last on Monar's scheme and Goss, being a creature of habit, proved a simple mark. After three nights of selecting the proper locale, Archie and two coolies were secreted within a wagon in the shadows of an alley. All then required was for Monar to catch up with Goss from behind and pitch him into the waiting arms of the darkness. It transpired according to plan.

Watching one startled passerby run off frightened witless, Monar entered the alley to see Goss trussed up and dumped into the already moving wagon. He strolled back to the street; there was no commotion—not too surprising. To begin with, the district hadn't a wholesome reputation.

With a flash of insight, Monar saw that dead, Goss only gave JT revenge. Alive, he could be of value. They needed a source for gunpowder; the hated man was supply officer at the Navy Yard. For once, it came about that… hate, fate, and need intermingled to resolve equivalent problems.

All they had to do now was convince him he was kidnapped to prove they were dangerous people who wanted gunpowder, not to kill him.

As it turned out, the easiest way to induce him was with life's prime motivator—money. Goss found it irresistible, the main reason being he couldn't hold on to it.

Unknown to his kidnappers, each hour he visited the Museum was spent losing his money at the craps table or blackjack. And that money came from selling supplies out the back door of the Military Stores & Supply Warehouse.

Quite easily, they convinced Goss that by taking him prisoner it was merely their way of letting him know they were serious war profiteers and not men to fool with. But if he wanted to make money, go along with them.

Archie and Monar claimed they were hired to work the quarries down in Quincy, but the shortage of black powder was putting them out of business and as they had money up front, they could pay top dollar.

To begin with, Goss doubted their story and he balked when they mentioned gunpowder and primer cord. He balked only because gunpowder was needed by the US military—there was a war on he reminded them—and it was difficult to come by. Plying him with cash helped.

Gunpowder, or more commonly, black powder, was made utilizing diverse compounds including corned powder, sulfur, graphite, and potassium nitrate—generally referred to as saltpetre. It was saltpetre, made from bat or bird guano, that became a not too reliable resource for both sides as the war progressed.

In far worse straits to obtain potassium nitrate however, was the South, and they were forced into diverse techniques to cope, improvising with dissimilar mixtures of manure, mortar, urine, ash, straw and other compounds, not all successful. Saltpetre became the critical compound to the output of Southern powder mills like Sycamore and the Confederate Gun Powder Company. Yet the shortage of the compound in the Northern mills of DuPont and Hazard Company, though significant, barely hampered their production. In other words, Goss could supply gunpowder.

The previous month, officials of the Boston Navy Yard received orders to expect delivery of material for the re-equipment of more blockading ships. The plot began to jell.

The navy resupply storehouses at New York, Washington and Hatteras were at their peak and it was about time, the Navy implied, for Boston to pick up the pace.

Remembering this, Goss realized provisions of all sorts would soon be streaming in and a component of those provisions was black powder—for which he had a buyer.

There was one problem; his new purchasers were specific; they would use the powder as it came in. He didn't know this wasn't true; it was Scrimshaw wanting Goss to think that to prevent him from 'thinning' it with beach sand or some such silt.

Well, Goss felt, it simply meant supplying other warships with ever so slightly 'altered' powder.

«»

Monar was still pondering how, even though gunpowder would be made available, enough of it could be secretly transported to *Seaward* when Archie came through the door. Hearing the problem, he smugly provided the answer to Monar's bafflement. His agreement with the Chinese stated that whenever Archie Feng needed something moved, the Chinese would be organized, and at reasonable cost.

Goss had it worked out, although he swallowed hard when they told him they wanted twenty twenty-five pound kegs, one fifty pound keg, and hundreds of feet of slow-burn primer cord. Well paid for his effort, he found a way.

JT knew little of the intrigues and the plotting going on for him. Even if he had known, there was nothing he could do to either change or improve the proceedings.

He was dying. Though everyone kept up the pretense otherwise, it was inescapable—he was dying.

Yet he wasn't quite ready to die. Although hoping there be a God, and desperately wanting to see Evelyn in the afterlife, he had to confront Captain Goss and exact revenge for the *Raven* and, if there be time before his clock ran down, to track those who desecrated father's grave.

Asking his lifelong friend Jim Pickman to visit, JT did his best to convince him it was only a severe infection and soon, following Doctor Crowninshield curing him, he would head back to England. So, JT stated, he needed his schooner, the *Ocean Pearl* returned.

Of course Jim agreed, even while doubting JT's feeble attempt to make their goodbye temporary, Pickman continued the pretense in the same vein.

The pretense stayed and they kept their farewell lighthearted and Pickman hid his sorrow. JT, once more alone in the barren great room, sought to release his physical and emotional pain at seeing his childhood friend gone.

He lit his pipe. Soon the pungent aroma of opium eddied about the room and his brain. "Evelyn, hope my honor here is repaid soon and God takes me to see you happy. Then He can send me to hell if He wishes."

Goss received word. The munitions shipment was arriving at the Old Colony Railroad Yard. It was the shipment's delivery to the Navy Yard where he and Archie had worked out a plan. Under the guise of concern for civilian safety, the route would be circuitous, kept well away from heavily populated areas, yet promisingly close to an old warehouse.

With the time and location arranged, a coolie was sent to inform the Elder Wah Yee, that Archie would be there the next day. Archie was uneasy about giving fore-notice of his arrival and, as his custom, prepared for any difficulty.

The looksee wasn't at the China Gate, in his stead, two burley Chinese who Archie accepted to be hatchet men.

"Come with us, we will take you to Wah Yee."

"Where is the looksee from before?"

"With Wah Yee. Looksee told us look for you."

The room was unchanged. the odors, the screen at the end of the room. Appearing untroubled, Archie knew something was wrong; he was a cauldron about to boil over.

The two hatchet men, one to each side of him, stood unmoving. They didn't worry Archie in the least. His focus was on the unknown behind the screen.

He assumed the silence was to unnerve him and decided to force the issue, "Well, let's get this over with."

The screen slid aside. Archie took it all in at a glance. A fat oriental stranger, smiling. The looksee, battered, at his feet. The Elder, bloodied, tied to his chair.

The man to Archie's left moved. Instinct and reflexes in Archie awakened. He kicked out to his left striking the man's groin, then spiraling to the right, the thug's knife was barely out when Archie's blade buried in his throat.

Whirling about, Archie saw no further threat, only the stranger who moved closer to the Elder, a knife held to his throat.

Calmly moving to the hatchet man still bent over from the kick, Archie drove his knee up into the thug's jaw, snapping his neck. Only then did Archie look back to the man and smiled, "I am Yün-Shan Feng, Leader of the Empire of the Sleeping Dragon Society, you are a cur dog's issue and have come here unwisely."

Perturbed, the man forced a smile, "I am Chen Qian, Leader of New York, Bo Sin Seer Tong."

"You should have stayed there. Here you will die."

"Your talk is meaningless; you have no arrows for your bow or hatchet men to back your hollow words."

Mistaking Archie's blank expression, Chen Qian went on boastfully, "Sleeping Dragon is no longer asleep. He *dead*! Qing Dynasty dead. Your thieves, your power—dead, just as you will be! Second Ming Dynasty now rules with Emperor Zhu Chongqing. Now you know, old fool."

"Zhu is child, ruled by reeking Communists, worse than British. You will find that out. No, not true; you will be dead, more dead than you say Sleeping Dragon."

"You lie from fright. You try to waste time, old fool. To kill me, Elder will die first and you not do that."

"If Elder Yee dies, that is his fate. I will find another Elder. You should think more of how you might live."

Chen Qian knew that *was* becoming a problem. He'd stumbled into this plan by accident and tried to turn it to his profit. Not realizing the dominion of his adversary and scarcely managing to disguise the shock of the sudden death of his thugs, he was in trouble—especially if this person didn't care if the Elder died. He hoped he had one card.

"You want him live, I let him live—and I live."

Archie smiled, "That is up to how bad Elder is hurt."

"He not bad, just slapped up a little."

"And the looksee man?"

"Maybe a little more. It his fault, would not tell us about you—at first. But he worth nothing."

Archie was waiting, waiting for an opening. Already Chen Qian had unintentionally lowered the knife.

"You make deal, big dragon leader?"

"Maybe. Pickup looksee, let me see he's alive."

"Why you care? He nothing."

"I want to kill him myself for telling you of me."

Chen Qian gave a nervous laugh, He was running out of options, "I trust you, I show you he live."

Waiting, in his robe Archie firmly held between his thumb and forefinger a shurken, the star-shaped, steel throwing weapon used by Sleeping Dragon men.

Watching Archie closely, Chen sheathed his knife to bend over and pull the beaten man upright. For one moment, Chen took his eye off Archie and he saw his chance, his hand flew out and hurled the shurken. Chen looked up and tried to avoid it, yet the shurken nicked his neck.

He dropped the looksee, felt blood on his neck, and grabbed his knife. Holding Elder Yee by his queue, Chen was ready to slit the old man's throat. He leered at Archie.

"You missed great leader! Why you not move,—you failed. Why you no plead for old man? You think I die from little nick? I show you big nick if you not let me leave."

Archie still did not move to save the Elder, "You frozen…scared for this old Elder…great…leader? You too…afraid…afraid to help Elder…?"

"No Chen Qian, I'm waiting for you to die."

"Die? Ha! From…little…little…cut?"

The knife clattered to the floor, Chen went to his knees. Coming up to him, Archie couldn't be more pleased.

"Yes, this old fool gave you little cut with a lot of venom—stupid little boy." Archie made sure the man died.

«»

It required ten wagons and fifteen coolie teamsters to on-load the munitions from the Old Colony freight cars. By travelling the oddly designated route past the warehouse, there were few vantage points from where a person had the opportunity to take notice of coolie's hurriedly reaching under tarpaulins and 'lighten' each wagon by two, twenty-five pound kegs. The last wagon, with fifty pound kegs, would be shy only one then it reached the Navy Yard.

Though a verified tally of the containers was kept leaving Old Colony's Rail Yard, Goss personally took the count at the Navy Yard and the numbers certainly matched.

From the warehouse, the stolen kegs were then shipped in small quantities to Salem with no difficulty.

He wanted to destroy *Seaward*. JT's plan was to undermine the main loadbearing supports of the structure, place gunpowder around them and bring down the entire building.

Unfortunately, it turned out that Grandfather and father built a fortress on the grounds. So to accomplish that task would take an unreasonable length of time and the year was getting on. They wanted the *Ocean Pearl* to clear the harbor before any suspicions of the populace arose.

The crew had come to understand JT wanted the manse destroyed. The why? They didn't know, only that he did and they wanted to be away. It became apparent the long task of undermining was impossibility and now they decided to place the powder kegs throughout the rooms and unite them all with primer cord.

One last keg, the fifty pounder, Monar carried into the great room, set down carefully and noted the imprint on the cover, **E I DuPont de Nemours Co Wilmington Del**

Delaware, Monar thought, sitting on the keg waiting for JT to arrive. Delaware to Boston by rail. It was amazing he thought, that Rebel Calvary hadn't raided into Delaware and struck the DuPont black powder mill—or at least tried.

He didn't give further thought to that possibility for it was time, actually far past time, to settle their plans.

Entering, and seeing Monar on the keg, JT vainly sought to retain his composure but the hurt was constant, compounded by his difficulty to speak for extended periods and even then, speech was pained.

"I won't ask how you are, JT, That's fairly obvious and I won't want to keep from your opium longer than necessary. But, my friend, there are dreadful things we finally have to discuss."

At JT's nod, Monar came straight to the point, "You won't be coming with us, will you?"

A nod and whisper, "You knew I…wouldn't."

"It was unspoken, but yes. So, I'm guessing you intend to sit on this keg, light the primer cord and blow *Seaward* and you to kingdom come."

"JT strained to laugh, "Something like that… yes…and the docks…warehouses."

It pained Monar to hear him and he asked, "What do you want me to do about the stupid men and women who desecrated your father's grave?"

"Too late to do anything now…forget them. They shamed themselves, let them…live…with what happens."

"In truth, I have, JT. And it was past time you did. What about Goss?"

JT reached into his greatcoat, the house was cooling with the weather, "Here, post before…before you…sail."

The letter was in an open envelope addressed to the US Navy Department, attention to Flag Officer Stringham.

Monar read the letter exposing Captain Goss to the loss of the *Raven* and the theft of naval property, to wit, munitions of war that were the cause of the damage—yet to be done at Salem.

Monar didn't try to prevent a smile, "Well, that should cook his goose and it satisfies me, although Archie will be unhappy."

"Poor Archie…can't have…everything."

Memories filled the silent room. Monar had first come here with Richard Graves, the father and then met JT. It was a difficult time; for the father had been devolving into insanity from becoming a slaver to save *Seaward*.

JT's father had earlier befriended Monar, a former slave, and he in turn, defended the father against JT's condemnation. It took understanding and time before JT and Monar became friends, very close friends.

"A lot of memories here, JT. You must feel the ghosts even more than I do."

"Since you put it…like ghosts, yes. But…family ghosts…drifting…coming, then going"

JT shook off unwanted recollections, "When will you…finish?"

"Every room is set, we just have to run the primer here and set the charges at the wharfs and warehouses."

"How long…?"

"A day, two at most."

"Please hurry. I…don't have…time…much left."

The physical pain within JT had overcome any hate for others. Those men and women who had dug his father's bones up were not forgiven, they were not worthy of his hate or even revenge any longer. Goss? In the past JT would have been pitiless in destroying him. Now, let the Navy do what they will, JT washed his hands of it with the letter.

Monar had seen the transformation. When they first met, JT was an innocent, unable to comprehend or accept his father's fall into slavery. Later, too much later, after the father went mad from his own conflict of the terrible deed, JT finally at least accepted why—but it was far too late.

Evelyn had changed him. Not that specific tragedy, yet she had made him aware of so many things, ideas in life to live for that he never considered. With her, he grew to become a man. With her gone, life became the absence of significance. He was not sad about dying, not in the least.

Then again, he wasn't content to let the cancer take him, for it would incapacitate him too long, meaning others would have to care for him and he decided it was better all round to die his way. Besides, he had once promised to let the town feel his wrath—it was that simple.

Doctor Crowninshield was dismissed even though he offered to stay JT didn't want anyone in the house. The doctor left a packet of opium; gathered a thousand disjointed notes, nodded goodbye.

Archie Feng, true to his own aberrant code, thought more of JT for planning this act of seppuku—likened to a Japanese Hara-Kiri—than for anything else JT had done in his life. Although he still had doubt JT would go through with it.

«»

9.5.'63 Salem Harbor

Carriage borne, wrapped in a blanket, JT sat by the wharf watching as the men prepared the *Ocean Pearl* for the long sea voyage. The schooner was father's and long of tooth now, he recollected, she dated back to 1817, older than he.

A brisk offshore breeze snapped at the jib as the main and mizzen sails were unfurled, allowed to luff. Bow and stern lines held on dock cleats by crewmen.

There had been no goodbyes; JT and Monar knew that anything more said would twist their emotions past some unknown breaking point.

At various moments, the crewmen would wave, now knowing the reason their captain would not be with them, and those waves were final salutes to their skipper.

JT smelled the wooden planks, soaked down with turpentine and he looked along the wharf, seeing the two powder kegs nestled against the row of warehouses.

He nodded to Monar, who reached down, struck a match to a primer cord hidden beneath the planks.

Monar turned, saluted JT, then hastened to the schooner as, freed of her bonds, her propeller's bit the water.

Twenty minutes. Twenty minutes their tests showed the burning primer would take to reach the kegs.

JT turned his back to the ship and sea. The carriage ride to *Seaward* was tiring and there, he struggled to unhitch the horse and slap its rump. The animal was hired from a stable in Marblehead, the next town south and he knew the horse wouldn't stop running until it reached stable and oats.

The *Ocean Pearl* cleared the harbor in fifteen minutes.

Alone, Monar stood by the narrowed stern of the schooner, waiting, pensive. He had sanctioned JT's decision and on his own had gone to the desecrated grave of his friend and JT's father. There he had filled the shallow depression and realigned the small broken headstone and slipped a slight sheet of paper under its corner.

666, the number of the beast, 'death to all who disturb this earth' was written for white people to fear and Monar had added his own Caribe devil, 'La Diablesse'.

At the rail, only the deep, whispering water listened to Monar's sorrow, "Well, Captain Richard, first I lost you, and now your son. I cannot weep any longer. I hope you both meet, for he has forgiven you, as did I long before. Someday in hell we three will meet again."

Staying at the rail, no one saw his eyes well up.

JT slouched in his father's broken chair in the great room. Swallowing was barely possible now, although that problem and the pain were overcome by the quantity of opium the doctor had left with him. He smiled at the thought; opium, opium and China and Warfield and Monar and, at last, he settled on Evelyn. Strange, that the opium never stopped that ache. If only he had stayed in England.

That 'if only' seared, tormented his brain. He left England and her to selfishly try and redeem his family's honor—something no one cared a fig about—and caused her death. It would not have happened. She would not have died. He knew he could never live with the memory he had caused her death. If only…

The smoke from his pipe curled, spiraled into fascinating, phantasmal shapes. His mind lost focus.

Explosions…ah yes, gunpowder. The warehouses… wharfs….all afire…calm down now…don't waste…time thinking of *Seaward*…or Salem. Only dream of her.

He lit the primer cord from his pipe.

HOUSE OF GRAVES

BOOK III

Am I the sea…
  or a sea monster ¿
    Job 7:12

CHAPTER ONE

November, 1863, Blackwood Abbey, England.

THE DAY HIS ONLY CHILD Evelyn, had died, Sir Warfield Blackwood Bunting's response shadowed his personality. Disbelief and sorrow followed by his order demanding God return his daughter. It wasn't right Evelyn was taken he clearly stated; she died from cholera, helping the poor and sick. *It was not right*, Warfield reasserted times beyond count. Still, when God did not so much as acknowledge his request with even a nod, much less see fit to obey the demand, Warfield cursed Him, then wept and had a *mild* stroke—if such there be.

His second *mild* stroke ensued the following day upon learning Victoria, his only granddaughter, died shortly after her mother—cholera being indiscriminate. No tears remained in Warfield and he was left to hate God—a hatred, strangely, that kept him alive during the rites and double interment.

Still, it wasn't until Warfield appallingly cried, 'God damn you God' that his lover, Lily, put her hand to his mouth and told him to hush, "Don't go on cursing God like this, Warfield. Stop, now!"

"Why shouldn't I curse him? We thank him when things go right; when he performs miracles don't we praise him? To me, when he's wrong *he* should be tormented, as he's tormenting me now."

Then he met the hurt in Lily's eyes as well, and fell silent, suppressed his words and hid within his own counsel.

These twin tragedies occurred back in February of this year, 1863, and left Warfield with his mind weary, his heart broken.

His hate lessened, as do most profound emotions, but there continued an intense argument with the Lord over His judgment. He allowed them to die. There would never be a justification. None whatsoever, and Warfield retained an eternal distaste for the Lord and His teachings and so concluded it was ridiculous to accept Him and His principles. Warfield, a man with near infinite power in England coupled with ambiguous ethics, was left empty, empty except for the love of Lillian Fields—Lily, his solitary constant in a tempestuous and driven life.

If one was given to such beliefs, Lily was a saint in waiting and, more than likely, would go straight to heaven when she died for accepting Warfield for who he was and remained all these years. Admitting love can be quite blind, she knew he loved and needed her despite the turmoil he caused and the power he exercised. He was a creator of empires and gave but little thought to mere people.

At long length Warfield's anger abated somewhat, and though it would have been hopeless to ask him to reconsider his feelings about the Lord, he nevertheless did ease up on Him…*somewhat.*

«◊»

Reading Dante's Inferno in his Abbey's atrium he focused on Dante's concept of hell being depicted as Nine Circles of Suffering. Warfield then fixated on Dante's fifth Circle wherein there was no joy to be found in God. *No joy to be found in God.* Exactly, he thought, and his anger grew yet again. He tossed the volume aside and turned to reading articles in the Times of London, there to find a listing of the American Civil War battles. To be sure, that was not soothing either. The horrific sum of casualties on land and sea swelled until even he, the old warhorse, was baffled, what on earth was America doing he wondered…trying to commit suicide?

"Damn, Lily, we all thought that once the Northerners blockaded all the South's ports the war would soon be over, but by Christ, they're still going at each other tooth and nail."

She nodded; at least he'd found something else to grouse over.

Warfield read on until another article caught his eye, "I'll be damned. Lily, could you get Harry? He's in my office, muddling over something or other. I want to show him this article."

When she left, Warfield resumed reading, finding still more to discuss with Harry Scrimshaw, his company manager, right hand man, and friend.

"You wanted to see me, Warfield?"

"I did—you read in the Times about the Rebel ship, *Alabama*?"

Scrimshaw hadn't, and hearing again the name of the Confederate commerce raider sent a shiver through his system.

"Well, Harry, it says here she's gone, sunk off Cherbourg by a Union warship called the *Kearsarge*. Her Captain escaped in a privately owned ship, the *Greyhound*. Wasn't *Alabama* the warship that sank JT's *Raven* off the Azores?"

It was true and it was bitter; Warfield wasn't thinking straight, age making him forgetful. He should have recognized it was still painful and would always be for Harry. Especially so, considering Warfield's own son in law, John Thomas Graves, Captain of the *Raven,* had challenged the *Alabama,* outmaneuvered and trapped her. It was only from corrupted gunpowder that he was prevented from sinking the Rebel ship—and suffered the loss of his *Raven*.

"Yes, that was the ship. Far as I'm concerned, it's proper she's gone and good riddance. JT will be pleased about it too."

By now, Warfield had remembered. Harry had been First Mate on the *Raven*. But Warfield, never given to embarrassment, went on to another article, "Did you know the USS *Housatonic*?"

With Scrimshaw's dutiful comment that she was one of the warships blockading Charleston when the *Raven* was on patrol off shore down there, Warfield went on, "Well get ready for this, she became the first ship to be sunk be a torpedo."

"Not so, Warfield. A few have sunk from torpedoes in that endless American war."

"I've not made myself clear; she was torpedoed by a submersible ship—an *underwater* ship. It says right here, a ship called the *Huntley*. Or rather *was* the *Huntley*. They think she sank and her crew went with her."

Startled, Scrimshaw took the offered paper from Warfield, but before he could read the article, they were interrupted when Lily stepped in to let them know word was received an American schooner, the *Ocean Pearl,* had tied off at Warfield's wharf in Gosport, Portsmouth Harbor. Two men, by the names of Archibald Feng and Monar had requested to see him.

Warfield was overjoyed and present concerns put aside for the moment. However, conflicting emotions arose. His son in law, John Thomas Graves, the husband of his late daughter, who Warfield hoped would be with them, was not mentioned.

After ordering the messenger to bring the two men up to the Abbey immediately, Warfield turned to Harry Scrimshaw who had initially been with John Thomas, Archie Feng and Prince Monar in Salem Massachusetts. Could Harry supply an answer to his concern, "What do you think, Harry? Archie and Monar are back, but it sounds like JT isn't with them."

"I'm not too surprised, Sir. As I told you, JT was quite ill when he asked me to return here and tell you about the loss of the *Raven,* and give over two letters he wanted delivered to you and…and Evelyn. You said in the letter he wrote you that he didn't think he'd be able to return."

"I know Harry, and I've never read JT's letter to my daughter. But his two sons are here and he couldn't have known his daughter Victoria had…left us. How could he turn his back on them—really, in all creation, how could he?"

"I guess we'll just have to be patient and wait to find out."

Indeed, they waited, but not patiently.

Their two friends alighted from the Hansom cab. Monar, parent's unknown, former slave in Barbados and now *Prince* Monar, six foot, five inch, exceedingly wealthy black man, married to an Indian Maharani with tea, cotton, silk, spice, and indigo estates. He'd been John Thomas' best friend for years.

The other person arriving was Archibald Feng Yün-shan. His mother was a Church of England missionary and father, formerly Han Imperial Commissioner of the Kwangtung District, China. Archie, the bastard son of the two is, or was, Leader of the Empire of the Sleeping Dragon Society, the Society rumored to have been destroyed by the Qing Emperor when the Qing Dynasty usurped the Ming. The loss of Archie's personal empire however, had yet to be proven. Both men are ostensibly employed by Warfield, as was Harry Scrimshaw, himself the cashiered, but heroic Captain of the Royal Navy. Equated with the three other men, Harry would be considered the sole honest or moral person there. Still, to be fair, the others did have some sort of individual code of honor—yet a code not appreciated by the enlightened society of the British Empire. Nevertheless, there was no mistake the men, though each intelligent and aggressive in their own right, owed their successes and wealth to the patronage of Lord Warfield Bunting.

The reunion was bittersweet. Warfield, Lily, and Harry were pleased to see their visitors although the men were not quickly forthcoming to the main question and the troubles of the reunion soon quieted by thoughts of those who now lingered only in memory. Evelyn and her young daughter were sorely missed. And John Thomas Graves?

Warfield could no longer wait, "Well, have it out you two, where's my son in law?"

Monar and Archie knew this would be asked and it was simply stated, "He's dead, Warfield."

The anguish spread across Warfield's face like a wave, his next question shouted out, "For Christ's sake, why did he leave in the first place? Everything he wanted was here!"

Monar knew, "No, not everything, Warfield. His honor was back there. He couldn't help himself. Atone for his father's sin of being a slaver. Fight for the Union; restore the family name for his sons. That was JT; would you think otherwise of him?"

There was no need to tell Warfield how sorry they were, although, in truth, Archie was somewhat indifferent and at first went along with Monar to save further upset to Warfield and Lily.

Warfield, denying the possibility of JT's death until now could only stare, then ask, "Then how, it wasn't the war, was it?"

It was left up to Monar to carefully explain, "No, it wasn't. He had throat cancer, Warfield. Could barely speak. The doctor said there was nothing to be done. He'd have never made it here."

Archie wasn't going to let JT's death go so banally, "He blew himself up, Warfield. That's right. Himself and half the bloody Salem Town along with him."

At their listener's alarm and looking daggers at Archie, Monar knew it would have come out in due course and turned to those who were dumbfounded, "It wasn't that bad. Look, let me justify what happened to him. Everyone here knows JT's father was a slaver—only *once* true—but a slaver. Yet his father was my friend and when I heard what his town did to him, I would have done the same as JT if it had been…"

Warfield interrupted, "I guess I should have faced up to the probability of him being gone. It's a terrible tragedy on top of our losses, but to blow himself up along with a village, isn't it a bit much to imply you'd do the same?"

"It wasn't the village he destroyed, Warfield; it was the property he owned, the wharfs, warehouses and his estate *Seaward*. He wasn't going to leave that village anything of value."

"To me, knowing JT, it's difficult to believe he would do that and putting that aside, where on earth could he get that much explosive during their Civil War?"

Archie was tired of their being defensive, "It was easy. We bought gunpowder off a corrupt US Navy supply officer named Goss. He sold us twenty-25 pound kegs of it along with a 50-pound keg too. JT actually got a receipt from the fool and this was the very damn bastard who salted the *Raven's* gunpowder and allowed the *Alabama* sink her."

Archie smiled while the others were stunned, leaving Scrimshaw to question, "I'll always remember that debacle, Archie. What did JT do to get even with him?"

"I was in favor of tying him on one of the kegs, but JT was real sick by then and couldn't hate anymore, so he said no, he'd just report the theft to the naval authorities along with the signed receipt and let them handle it. It should have been done it my way."

Scrimshaw went on, "Yet the rest of it, you helped him?"

"Damn right I did. We all helped him and it was glorious. Listen to me damn it, JT was near death, understand? It was his way of going out with revenge on the people there for what they did to his father and brother. And it was magnificent! It was dazzling! I'll tell you—night vanished! We were three miles offshore and the whole harbor and then his home up on the hill lit up and exploded. By God, Warfield, JT did get his revenge."

Lily couldn't help probe into JT's rage, "Angry, yes, but was that enough to justify damaging a village?"

Monar added to the story, "Lily, you simply don't understand *hate*. Back when they found out JT's father had been a slaver; they kidnapped his brother Jason, chained him in a dungeon on George's Island in Boston Harbor. We killed three of them when we rescued him, but he was dotty, belonged in Bedlam. Then townsfolk drove his mother off. JT never found her and we heard she was dead…"

"I agree they were a nasty bunch…"

"Please Warfield, let me finish. A gang from town got together and shelled—that's right—actually shelled the Graves' home with an old 24 pounder and killed his father."

That brought additional shock and Monar made one last remark, "And when we were there last, JT was told another drunken bunch dug up his father's grave and threw his bones to the dogs!"

Even Archie Feng was speechless on hearing that happened.

At first no one said a word until Warfield, certainly having a temperament in favor of dispensing retribution asked, "For Christ's sake, what the devil kind of a place is this Salem?"

"Very religious in fact, Warfield. And back a ways in their religious beliefs, they *hung* twenty girls or women they said proved to be witches. They flaunt it! I was offered a tour of Ledge Hill, for money of course. I believe they call themselves Witch Village, something idiotic like that. I'm telling you they're unbelievable, with no sense of shame for their past from what I can see, none." They took it all in, knowing Monar would never spin such a yarn. At last, they grasped the motivation behind JT's retribution. Yet vengeance was now secondary. It was the end of the Graves line except for two young boys left without parents.

And unfortunately, those two young boys, having overheard, had run off. The adults, so taken by the tale, had forgotten the boys were there. Lily chased after them while Warfield's disgust with Salem continued. He looked to Monar, "Another thing on the subject of religion, you were a slave in Barbados, weren't you?"

With Monar's nod, Warfield went on, "Well, I was reading some old Guardian news records the other day and I came upon the fact that when England ended slavery, she had to pay out £20 million in compensation and £8 million went to the Society for the Propagation of the Gospel. Now it seemed one of the Society's officers was England's own Archbishop of York and *this* may surprise you—they owned two slave plantations in your Barbados."

Monar could only shrug, "Does that surprise you Warfield? It doesn't surprise me. What of it? The bible itself condoned slavery and other than some white people, most don't mind it."

"You're right, so £8 million compensation went to the Church of England. But at least the States will finish a war ending it."

"We'll see…" But Monar's thoughts reverted to Barbados, his enslavement there and his vicious owner and how he killed him in revenge. Then, without qualm, he took the man's wealth, using it for himself and John Thomas. True, what led up to the killing wasn't quite that simplistic or undeserved, yet it was how it all worked out.

Well, Monar mused, that was one slave owner who wouldn't be receiving any compensation from the British. He then handed Warfield a large sealed envelope.

"JT gave it to me before we left Salem, said to give it to you."

Warfield was upset, "Thank you. I'll open it when I'm alone."

2

20 November, 1863 Blackwood Abbey

"LILY, I'M SORRY, BUT THIS is the way it's going to be."

"Warfield, please think it through."

"Do you believe I would come to this decision lightly, *without* thinking? I love the boys too, but you're coddling them and they're so wrapped up in themselves, they'll never be normal. That's not a pleasing thought for either of us. We all feel the loss and I'll never be the same either, but at their age it can become deep-seated and they'll never grow to become normal men. Believe me, I know."

"God, Warfield, they're only eight and ten. To throw them into an alien world after what has happened is…"

"Please Lily, I've talked to Doctor Strauss, and he feels it will be for the best as well. Remember, it won't be all at once. I'll make Monar and Archie their guardians and…"

"Archie? For God's sake, Warfield, I can accept Monar to a point, but Archie? The man's just shy of being the devil's proxy and you know it! You expect *him* to bring the boys up to be normal?"

"Lily, listen. Let me tell you a little story about growing up…and I guess it's about time you knew."

His eyes darkened, his mind raced back. Warfield began his story, "My given name that is my *real* given name, is Brodie. In Irish Gaelic that means *from the ditch*, in my case it meant from the mines. My father's surname was Woodman, my mother's Rice. We lived in Newcastle on Tyne, a coal mining family, and I mean we were coal *miners*, not coal mine *owners* or merchants. It was a hard, miserable, God awful, thankless life. Down into the mines before dawn, out after dusk, not seeing the sun except for Sundays…"

Stopping, he saw the coal dust, the dead canaries, the donkeys.

Lily broke into his thoughts, "I always knew there was something back there, Warfield. When you slept, I'd watch you struggling with your past and its evils. But awake, you always kept it behind a mask."

"Well, I promise I won't now. So, the day I left, actually ran away, was a Sunday morning and the mine owner rambled by, his four-in-hand white horses scattering children and told the foreman we had to work that afternoon to make up some supposed quota we hadn't kept to. I was twelve so that included me. I took up my lunch bucket and started for the mine. When I got to the mine head, stopped in front of me was an old donkey pulling a mine trolley up from below. Blind as a bat he was. The poor dear thing was blind from never seeing the sun and *I myself* only saw it for one day a week. Right there and then I was struck dumb. *Now* that's called an epiphany—that was going to be me! I looked into that donkey's blind eyes and went daft in my head. Lily, I went into shock! I knew I'd die if I went down that bloody mine one more time."

Warfield was getting upset, the very thing the doctor wanted prevented. Lily put her hand on his sleeve, 'Go easy, dear, you've been under a great strain and..."

"I want you to know this, why I'm the way I am and don't worry, I won't fly off the handle."

She wasn't at all sure of that, but wanted to know his story, "So you ran away?"

"Dropped my bucket right there and walked off. Said not one word to a soul, not even family. But halfway down the hill the mine owner's toffee-nosed son caught me up with his horse and smacked my noggin with his crop. Even at thirteen, I was a good size and I pulled him off his high horse I did and thrashed him good. Let out a lot of steam I did, but after that I knew they wouldn't rest until they caught me so it was into the woods until I reached the sea..."

"Weren't you afraid? I mean you left on the spur of the moment, no plan, no money, or direction and now they'll be after you and charge you for assault."

"Assault? With them I'd never have got to trial. But afraid? No, I was always planning something and too damn young to be afraid.

"Concerned, yes, but I had direction, a bit of a plan at least. Get to the harbor, find a ship and sail the seas. And that's what happened."

"And you changed your name, why?"

"Well, the mine owner's family held power over the coast and I knew they'd be after me, so I took my first name as Warfield because it sounded brawny—I was thirteen remember. Then the merchant ship I crewed on had a true captain and a remarkable man name of Aclair Bunting. He'd lost his son, and took me under his wing so I took his surname and eventually I chose Blackwood, the name of the coalmine, for a middle name. My parents didn't bother to baptize me so I added that to never forget where I came from."

"After all these years together, Brodie—no baptized name—Woodman, you're suddenly very forthcoming, may I ask the reason?"

"You may."

"And the reason is...?"

"I'm asking you to marry me."

Lily was flummoxed, knocked for six. She knew Warfield loved her but…he was already married. He read her eyes, "My wife died the beginning of this year, Lily. You were in Spain and I was getting ready to write you and settle the estate I let her use outside Paris when…well, when my daughter and little Vicky…"

Lily came to him, "I understand, dear, let's sit over there in the sun. First, it goes without question that yes, I will marry you. Secondly, I'll go along with your plan for the boys, of course not approvingly, but…"

The proposal for the two boys that upset Lily was due to its profound concept. In the months after their mother and little sister's death, the boys had withdrawn into themselves. Only Lily had been allowed in and nothing was bringing them out, so after Monar and Archie returned, Warfield had spoken with them about his decision and with their concurrence, he had only Lily to convince.

Monar was to take his three boys out of their English schools and take them, the Graves' boys, and Archie back to India. Once there and settled in, the oldest of the Graves boys, Mark John, aged ten, would then carry on to the Bengal with Archie to live with his three wives and children, two girls and three boys. The younger Graves boy, Collie Thomas, eight, would live with Monar, his wife and three boys in the Tamil Nadu Region, southeast of Madras.

It was felt within these gregarious groups of children the Graves boys would break out of their shells—if simply to survive. What goals they wanted *after* they survived was up to them.

The Graves' boys, taken from their schooling at Saint Paul's in London, and Monar's three boys, removed from Harrow, soon met. There were no screams or fisticuffs between them and though limited mutual interests occurred, it was nevertheless considered an overwhelming success.

«»

By the light of the fireplace, with decisions made, Warfield once again unfolded the letter Monar gave him. JT's cramped handwriting, scrawled across the pages, revealed the pain the writer went through to give words to his concerns.

Warfield - by now, you're told what happened and why, so there is no need for me to explain myself. After the loss of Evelyn, I died long before the cancer and even thoughts of our children could not end my sorrow. In truth, I look forward without fear as I despise living as I am and the town in which I lived and now die.

You are stronger than me, and I know you will bring Mark, Collie and darling Victoria up to have the best lives...

Warfield's eyes filled once again. John Thomas was at least saved from the knowledge his daughter Vicky had died from cholera immediately after Evelyn.

...so I give them to you and Lily with my blessing. Bring them up as proud men and women, American and English.

And now, to business. On a separate piece of paper is the name and address of my friend James Pickman. I have passed this information on to him. Trust him. The interest on the funds and securities in the Massachusetts Bank in Boston will continue funding the lands of Seaward for decades. I had planned to keep this land and funds for Evelyn and our children to do with whatever they wished. Now, it's for the children, once they are old enough to learn the Graves' history to make their decision. The second envelope is for you or Monar to give to them when they are considered old enough to judge. It is my version of telling them the history of their grandfather-on the Graves side of course-and the stories, good and bad, they don't know. My hope is that they return to the Graves' home, although after what I do here it's doubtful there will be much left, yet they may find some 'feeling' here-though certainly not love from the townsfolk.

It has taken me 3 days to get this down and I am weary. I have to end now. May God go with you, Lily, and my children.

John Thomas Graves, Salem, Mass. 1863

3

15 January, 1864 Blackwood Abbey

WARFIELD KEPT HIS EMOTIONS under a tight leash as he laid out his new plans for the company to Monar, Archie Feng and Harry Scrimshaw.

"Now hear me out. There are writing pads and pens here. You're welcome to ask questions at the end, but save them until I'm finished.

My first point is this. The American Civil War continues and it seems that fact isn't going to change despite the Union success at Chickamauga and the blockade. That war will prove a disaster for them, at least for the foreseeable future and without their cotton, extremely hurtful to us. However, we really don't have to look far for Britain to find a positive factor of their war, and that brings me to my second point."

His listeners glanced to each other, wondering about the positive factor for England in America's Civil War.

"While the United States continues their death spiral and other countries bumble about, this industrial revolution of ours has reinvented England. From railroad steam engines, iron bridges, iron and steam ships, mills, mechanical looms to a standing army and warships that control and govern the sea lanes of the world, England rules. And by this I mean we're also going to teach the heathens how to rule as we do—with a just, but firm hand from the Queen to her benighted people across the globe."

Here Warfield, who seldom laughed now, laughed at own his imperious words. "This may sound overly blunt gentlemen, yet either consciously or otherwise, our government will and should embrace our imperial future to an even greater extent. *Think of this*! We control most of India, Ceylon and the coast of China including Hong Kong. We have Canada, South Africa, Australia New

Zealand, and all of the East and West Indies we want, and before I die I'll bet we'll hold influence over the Greater Indies as well. Add to these our outposts and strategic supply bases in Singapore, Malta, Gibraltar, Gold Coast, South Africa…"

Warfield stopped mid-sentence. He'd made his point. To continue would only squander his energies. Time for specifics.

He inhaled heavily, a brief moment to gather his thrust. It was the old Warfield they listened to, an imperialist missionary's zeal, overflowing with the certitude of his principles.

"With our remarkable Queen, Victoria almost a recluse after Albert's death, now this two years past, our government leaders feel, and rightfully so, that our form of administration and faith in our Christian God—however misplaced—should be the path for every embryonic nation. There is no country to even think of contesting us. Not Russia, France, and certainly not Belgian's Leopold and his too gruesome exploits in the Congo. In other words, the sea is ours and the sea is commerce and commerce means domination of the world. This is Pax Britannica, men, British Peace, whether they like it or not, and the clever shall benefit."

He sat back, appraising each one. His account pleased Scrimshaw, interested Monar, and alerted Archie. It was obvious Warfield was starting to think limitless thoughts of *Empire* yet again. Still, another emotion caught their attention; each of them would be involved, and when Warfield thought on a grand scale he electrified the air.

Another round of drink was ordered and after the servant was out of earshot he laid out the specifics.

"I'll start with China. Even after all these years, as long as the Qing holds sway, our littler caper acquiring the tea shrubs will prevent the Black Moon Line from ever being allowed back into China. China is a great commercial shortfall for us, although I'm sure Monar and Archie are all right with that considering the income from your India tea plantations."

The two men agreed. Prince Monar's Superior Oolong tea and spices and Archie's Supreme Darjeeling Black Dragon Tea were best sellers in Warfield's seven hundred Shoppes throughout England, Europe, Australia and the few in the US. And, since Warfield created the dynamic tea market by bringing the cost of tea down to the masses, he received his share.

"Nevertheless, I want China back. I plan to compensate our loss of trade with them by creating a new merchant shipping company called the Blue Diamond Line which will be registered under Harry Scrimshaw…"

Harry knew nothing of this and it showed.

"…as he won't be known there. So he'll be free to hire Residents in Hong Kong, the mainland, the Philippines and for any other islands he decides on in the South Pacific. And note this; I'm sure the Fiji Archipelago will come under our sphere because nobody else seems to covet it and after that we'll absorb Indonesia. This is what I mean by the Greater Indies, Harry, you've done yeoman service for me, and you'll own thirty percent of the stock, answerable solely to me. Monar and Archie will acquire seven percent each. I'll fill you all in later, but at first Black Moon will lease twenty ships gratis to Diamond giving it a profit margin that will make its bottom line glow when it's time for investors."

Scrimshaw was, as expected, dumbfounded. Warfield had made him wealthy in a few sentences.

"I'll also give you names of people who will help and inform you of the conditions in China. It looks as though the Qing will finish off the Taiping Rebellion by the end of this year—with the help of the British and Chinese Gordon of course. Tell me Archie, what does that mean for you with the Qing firmly in charge?"

Archie shrugged, "I'll give Harry some names to help him as well. After that, we'll have to see what Harry sniffs out."

"Well, we'll hope for the best for you, Archie. Now, for you and Monar. I can't envision the two of you sitting back in your rocking chairs, smoking pipes and watching your boys and my grandchildren become wastrels. What I do want is what I'd have liked to do—open up Japan for the Black Moon. Of course it won't be easy, but I'm sure twenty percent ownership each to you with seven percent earmarked for Harry to back you will give incentive."

Both men were surprised and pleased; it would be a challenging gambit as they thought there was, at best, hard feelings between British and Japanese relations.

Warfield read their minds, "I know, I know, we Brits got our arses kicked by supporting the Tokugawa Shogunate's open door policy against Emperor Kōmei. That sticks in my craw too—yet we had little choice. But by God we're going to get our share of the trade no matter what the cost. England's flag and my burgee will be intertwined with Japan's before I'm finished."

Appearing on top of his game despite the tragedies, Warfield filled his mind with the latest news and laid plans to take advantage of any possibilities. This was one of the peculiar and dynamic traits in him. From the time his wife left him with a young daughter thirty-five years past, he masked, buried his emotions to every dark event by immersing in work. This trait had saved his sanity—such as now. As much as he wanted to hunch over and cry, his backbone was straight, his eyes dry, his mind determined.

"Now, remember the framework we'll work within. The French and Dutch are of no concern. Although the American's have serious inroads in Japan, they've given over their lead there to us—at least until their civil war is over. So for now England remains dominant, and keeps us as the greatest empire the world has known.

Now, whatever cost, I want Black Moon to help Blue Diamond get China back and dancing to our tune. Then Japan will follow. Remember, we have the hammer, we own the seas. It's our time!

Think of what I'm saying and comprehend it. We have a free hand in world trade. The only thing to stop us is our own boundaries—and I don't have any. And you men best not either."

He folded his hands, resting his chin on his thumbs, hesitant, yet now was the moment to tell them, "I had planned to ease back and turn most all of this over to John Thomas and Evelyn. I need not say more on my emotions of their loss other than I now have only my two grandchildren left to receive all I've built. They will, but only on Mark's twenty-second year. This is a multi-year plan we're embarking on. Combined, you three will have forty-nine percent of everything under my corporate patronage. In ten years I may be gone or doddering, but you will be even wealthier and in your late fifties and *then,* by that time you'll be ready to sit on your combined butts and fill your grandchildren's ears with breathtaking and ridiculous fiction of battles fought and won."

Warfield usually found it useless explaining his moves, content to let them play out to eventually become evident to less elevated entrepreneurs—but not this time.

"At present, as I said, none of you are ready for the rocking chair and that's why I'm placing my grandchildren in your hands. You're to bring then up as men, not the weak-willed, worthless dilettantes I see so many of in today's England living off their parent's labors. Our future leaders will come from the young men we send to our colonies to learn, to grow, use their heads and acquire leadership—meaning to take risks, calculated risks. Whether my boys start working in the fields or cabin boys or powder monkeys, I'm placing one undertaking on the three of you; make my grandchildren worthy of their inheritance. Well, that's it!"

So they could relax before dinner, Warfield personally escorted each to their rooms. Monar and Archie soon found his motives were ulterior, to be kept from Scrimshaw.

"I've every confidence in Harry's ability and that he won't be manipulated into irresponsible moves with those shifty Chinese warlords. My problem with him is that he's too much of a straight arrow, too ethical for my liking and what I have planned. We all know that the Japanese are connivers, slippery as Moray eels and just as predatory. Quite simply that's why they're being referred to more and more, along with the Chinese of course, as the Yellow Peril. So we've got to be just as coercing, even more so."

Monar and Archie smiled, it was clear Warfield wanted cutthroat commerce, "You've got to stay alert to each offer and don't trust in any written document because they'll worm out of it and their courts—as pathetic they are—will always rape us. In other words, don't make yourself vulnerable. If a deal starts to go sour, get what you can out of it, cut your losses, and if you can, hurt them as you exit. Don't chase after a crooked Nippon deal. Remember, I'll back your moves no matter what. So, good luck."

Warfield started down the corridor to the conservatory, stopping at a mirror. Eyes are old, he thought. Tired, hair grayer, thinner. Damn. Still, keep up the pretense; make them believe their greatness is yet to come.

He entered the conservatory, the winter sun warming him. Still, he shivered; his grandson's shadows crossing his grave.

Lily looked up, a question framing her face, "What is it, Warfield, are you chilly?"

"No…I really don't know. I'm all right, just a strange feeling. I'm all right now."

He dropped into a chair. What he said wasn't quite true; he knew there was an inertia he couldn't shake. Despite the positive comments from the doctors, the apathy he fought to shake still clung. Was it disenchantment? There shouldn't be, he'd achieved far more than mere men could even dream. Yet there it hung. Disenchantment. His dream for Evelyn and John Thomas gone. So, think about the sons.

"Tell me Lily, have you decided on a date?"

She was startled, as was he, "Date? You mean our marriage?"

Surprised he had mentioned it, Warfield recovered quickly, "Of course, have you? Set a date I mean."

"Not as yet, dear. I don't want a fuss. I thought we'd wait. You know, wait until the boys have left and we'd be more settled and then have a small, quiet service. It wouldn't be right after all that's happened. That would be best, don't you think?"

Warfield squinted through the window, simply nodding.

"You look tired, have a headache, dear? I'll get some aspirin."

"Don't bother yourself; it's not something aspirins can cure, and I've got some serious thinking to do about Harry."

He shaped his thoughts, writing them down as they formed. An hour later, he sealed them in an envelope, wrote *Monar/Archie, Read on arrival in Japan,* and placed it in his pocket.

4

22 March, 1864. Aboard Archie Feng's Blackwall Frigate *Devon*

They rounded the 'corner' at Cape Aqulhas, the boney headland of South Africa and, fitted out with new, smooth copper sheathing below her waterline, she rushed into the flow known as the Agulhas' Return Current, picked up the Southeast Trade Winds and parted the raging seas into the Roaring Forties.

For something to while away the time Monar plotted point to point course bearings for each leg and divided each leg into time value. Then he bet Archie and Scrimshaw he'd be within a twelve hour period reaching Madras—baring a typhoon that is. Archie, of course, smiled to himself, he'd see to it who would win.

"We've made good time, Archie; Warfield fitted out a fine ship to give you. Too bad that damn canal isn't finished over in Egypt."

"True, but I'll bet the French won't finish there. And the *Devon* isn't a gift. Warfield owed me a ship. I got him tea shrubs; that was our deal, so when he said *Devon* was laid down a Blackwall frigate, like the Royal Navy's warships, not like a clipper, I preferred the large tonnage capacity and cabin space."

Monar didn't respond. The mere mention of a clipper was all it took to entwine him in memories of the *Raven*, John Thomas and Evelyn. Yet in truth, he didn't need his memory tormented. With their two boys aboard along with his three boys, he had to well hide his feelings.

The Graves' children had come out of their shell somewhat—they had to, to endure. That and their duties aboard ship were obligatory, so there was no slacking off for man or boy and all the boys learned to respond as fast as their legs could carry them.

Archie was officially Captain, he was qualified and, after all, it was his ship, so that made Monar and Harry Scrimshaw, both qualified master mariners, simply supercargo, although they did spell Archie at the wheel and for Watches.

Standing evening Watch, Monar stared down the centerline at the ship, weapons, and crew. Once again, Warfield's handpicked sailors, efficiently going about their diverse duties, met his eye. She was a fine, armed frigate and well sorted. Not the *Raven* to be sure, then again, no other ship was. *Raven* was one of a kind, never to be equaled. Yet now, what did it matter? That magnificent clipper, all two hundred-twenty feet of her and her two great guns rot and rust beneath the sea off Corvo, the Azores, her stern shattered from the guns of the CSS *Alabama.* So what difference did it make?

He spit downwind, absentmindedly checked for luff in the topsails, and revisited more pleasant thoughts. He would soon be with his wife Amala, the Maharani of Tamil Nadu. They would be whole again once he and their children returned to her at last. Then, after a while, she would listen to his tale of Evelyn and John Thomas and understand his hurt and help him heal.

Heedless of the dying sun's kiss of the horizon, Archie Feng thought of home as well. Not the home he now had in India's Bengal, but *the* home—and of more importance—*the* power he once wielded in Canton, China. Was his Sleeping Dragon Society destroyed by the Manchu Qing's Heavenly Kingdom's resurgence?

The Qing's imperial Army, under Zeng Guofan had broken the twin threats of the Taiping Rebellion and the Hui Revolt. It was the bloodiest revolt up to that time—wars even America's Civil War couldn't begin holding a candle too in savagery or deaths. The Qing reclaimed Canton and Archie had to know if his Sleeping Dragon survived. If so, his vengeance on enemies, real or perceived, would be swift—swift and merciless.

Of Archie Feng's desire to return to China, Warfield knew nothing. Although knowing Archie, Warfield should have thought of that. It shouldn't matter, other than Archie's goal could possibly interfere with Warfield's agenda.

«»

20 May 1864. On to Madras & Tamil Nadu

Under sail east of Madagascar, next came Reunion Island and Mauritius, then northeast through the Palk Strait between India and Ceylon. They at last entered the Bay of Bengal, the last leg of their five month voyage.

The *Devon's* anchors splashed into the waters off Madras, the original British holding in India. Monar won his bet as to their arrival time with two hours to spare. Archie, to his own amazement had decided not to try and dupe Monar with headings or drift.

With no port at Madras, massulahs, similar to large, oversized whaling dories, each manned by a crew of eight men, surfed them ashore. Being English, the crew was billeted in White City, while Monar, Scrimshaw, Archie and the four children were ensconced in Lord Warfield's suite of rooms in Fort Saint George.

During the voyage, the men had finalized their plans for China and Japan. Scrimshaw would administer business in China with the new, in name only, Blue Diamond Industries and be liaison and backup for Black Moon when opening trade with Japan.

Before starting, Archie and Monar would visit their homes for a month and, hopefully, convince their wives—in Archie's case, three—that their benefactor, Warfield, needed their expertise for Japan. In truth, neither man knew anything about Japan or needed further income, for each was wealthy. However, their wealth was due to Warfield, and they felt obligated. Yet even more, Archie and Monar wanted the challenge of the chase, to fulfill their endless restiveness for adventure. That aside, both men sent word ahead to prepare their wives.

Planning to meet Archie in Madras in a month, Monar bid his farewells a day later and headed for Tamil Nadu with the four boys. Archie decided to stay for two days in White City, after which he would leave with Mark Graves and the *Devon* for Calcutta and on to his estate in the Bengal.

Harry Scrimshaw acquired a Black Moon ship, exchanged its burgee for a new Blue Diamond burgee and headed for Canton, China to find Warfield's Chinese contacts and locate any remaining members of Archie's Sleeping Dragon Society.

1 June 1864. Tamil Nadu. The estate of Maharini Amala Singh

The homecoming was weighed with India formality. Laborer's and families lined the entrance and roadway to the domain, respectfully waiting as Monar and Collie Graves arrived at the entrance.

Collie's eyes widened as, cantering toward them were one hundred red coated, Tamil Nadu Brahman Lancers, a detachment of the estate's private army. They, in turn, were followed by three floral bedecked and robed, silver tusked elephants bearing gold trimmed howdahs, the first of which held musician's beating enthusiastically on timpani's and rattles and cymbals and blowing into serpentine horns. Monar realized the second elephant's howdah, which was empty, was for his three children and Collie, and ordered them to behave as princes should. They should only wave. The time for greeting their mother was later, in privacy.

The clamor died as the last elephant, caparisoned with silver-laced robes with faceplate and howdah inlaid with golden images of tigers and monkeys came forward. The mahout had the beast kneel and a silken parasol lifted to reveal the Maharini Amala Singh aglow in the evening sunlight. Monar felt his heart expand, incapable of speech as she smiled and then, his being so tall, without aid he swung up into the howdah. A formal cheek kiss followed and Amala made him to sit before he hugged her—which would be considered quite indecent.

"You have been long away, my husband." She breathed.

"It was not my wish my love. There are sad events to forget. I would not have been gone from you this long, if not for them."

She took his hand, "You will converse them to me in a while."

The caravan wound its way through twelve miles of the domain's parklands to celebrate the return of the Prince. The verges of the pathway laden with trays of Cham Cham, Chhena Gaja and Poda and sweets of Malapur and coconut Burfi, all for the people to enjoy and take for those who could not attend.

The young boy, Collie Graves—encircled by Monar's and Amala's three boys and riding a great Indian elephant, saw the adulation the people had for Monar and the Maharani—was spellbound. Collie had already become secure and now, for an hour or two at a time, he found he was not thinking of his mother or father.

«»

At last, home, was Monar's sole thought. Home with his wife and children. Once a slave in Barbados, now a Prince in India, there remained nothing more he needed or wished but to love his life, his wife and children and oversee their estate and people. Yet, there remained Warfield and the obligation to him that still must be honored. Yet, for a while ready to relax with Amala and the children. There was, however, a minor irritation for Amala which also made her pleased the Prince, or, as their servant's preferred, the Black Raj, was back to assert absolute discipline over the estate and its operation. Although Amala had done an admirable oversight and even though a Maharini, she was still an Indian woman and, in the eyes of powerful British men, not qualified to order British Officers about. This was India. To the British, only Memsahibs, British women, should have such privilege. The Maharini did, however, manage to hold her own with the British, asked nothing of them and independently ruled Tamil Nadu without interference.

She did, nevertheless, ask Monar to correct one bothersome man. It appeared a certain Rodney Laurence Connell, Captain, 5th Surrey, of the Queen's Own Indian Brãhmana Sowar Calvary Regiment—he smartly proclaimed—was recently making an annoyance of himself by stopping by unannounced stating his intention to patrol the estate whenever he chose. This being unquestionably improper and precluded by Crown protocol, did not seem to bother 5th Surrey's Captain Connell.

The Maharini had had enough of this popinjay and about to order him off the Domain and damn what the British thought, when word was received her husband had arrived at Madras. As Amala felt her husband would likely relish dressing down any haughty British officer, she decided to wait.

On the start of Captain's next patrol with five Sepoy, he was a touch taken aback when the Master of the estate filled the doorway then came down the steps. Taking hold of the horse's bridal, Monar told the Captain to come with him. Led away from his patrol and with no recourse, Connell quickly sought a means to take charge of the sudden confrontation and unsnapped his revolver's holster from the saddle pommel.

Noting the move and leery of the Captain in general, Monar took no chances. The Captain's revolver being on the far side, Monar pulled the man's foot out of the stirrup and pushed up on the boot, shoving the man, weapon, and all, off the saddle, dumping him onto the ground.

While the horse reared back and trotted off to the security of the other horses, the Captain, recovering his wits, grabbed for his weapon. Monar's heel crushed the man's hand.

Pulling the officer up by the shoulders, Monar appraised the man's Pinfire revolver, noting it was stamped Hill, London. Almost, but not quite the quality of an American Colt, he thought, while clearing its cartridges, then shoved it back into the holster.

''You know, Captain, there really was no need of this. I took you out of sight of your Sepoy for a private chat."

The Captain, gritting through the pain, was angry, "Private chat? I'll have you up on charges you bloody, arrogant bastard!"

Monar only smiled, angering, then muddling Captain Connell further, "And just why the bleeding devil for a private *chat?"*

"I wanted to tell you that I resent you annoying my wife and if you enter our *private* lands again without permission, I will break the neck supporting your stupid brains."

"Your wife? So then, you *are* Prince Monar and I'll be sure to state your name when I charge you."

"Please do. And if the guards let you in to see Billy Denison, be sure and tell him I said hello and as soon as I find time I'll stop in for a chat about our next tiger hunt."

Monar deliberately mentioned the name and watched Connell, only recently posted to India, display unease at the casual mention of the Governor of Madras as *Billy*. Connell began to catch a glimpse the realm he had entered and, it now becoming quite clear, the power of this man whom everyone seemed to admire.

The entire matter had begun rather harmlessly. Captain Connell, on hearing of the loveliness of the Maharini Amala and the verity of her returning from England—alone, without her husband or children he noted—was too much to resist.

So he, without informing his commanding officer, decided to enter the lands of the Maharini of Tamil Nadu under the guise of duty, a Crown officer had the right to enter any Indian territory.

It hadn't gone well from the start. The Maharini was not some wilting, submissive Indian female and she, in truth, was utterly commanding and yet more pointedly, utterly beautiful. A combination—to a man of Connell's mindset—irresistible.

In his conceit, he actually thought he was doing rather well; the Maharini had not ordered him off her property or reported him.

And then, this day he arrived to be confronted by a giant of a man, visibly her husband, and angry. Now all Connell had to show for it was a dusty uniform, empty revolver and injured hand.

There being no chance of preserving pride in departure. Grim, the Captain walked back to retrieve his horse from the straight-faced Sepoy, retraced his course, never again to journey it.

Watching the Captain and Sepoy canter off, Monar had remained unmoving, his mind and perception elsewhere. He was aware someone was watching, someone listening, someone hidden.

Collie Graves, seeing him from a window ran up, but Monar held a finger to his mouth signaling him to be still. The boy froze, wide-eyed. They waited. A branch moved behind them in the undergrowth.

Without turning, Monar spoke, "Whoever you are, it's best you come out, or my bolo is coming in."

A moment's pause. Then a rather high pitched voice responded, "You have eyes in back of head, handsome, black Prince Monar?"

Monar relaxed, "I said let me see who my admirer is…and I mean now!"

"It appears patience not to be one of your qualities, my Prince."

The bushes parted and Monar turned to see a withered crone, bent with age, a weathered face reminding him of furrowed ground.

"Now don't you wish you did not ask me to come out? And the white boy is not one of yours."

She had a mostly toothless, yet impish grin and Monar could not help but smile, "Well, my Lady of the Wood, you are right, the boy is the son of past friends. But how do you know my name and who are you to enter into the Maharini's grounds uninvited?"

"To answer your first question first, I have often heard your name and followed you when you slip from the manor at night. Yet then you left for England. Now you return to wander our dark land again, never leaving a footprint or seen by others. Even tiger does not see or smell you. You become a spirit at night without form…"

Collie Graves became both frightened and fascinated, as Monar responded, "I have many times felt some presence and wondered what… But wait—that means you wander at night also, so *you* tell me, why is that so?"

"Perhaps for the same reason as you. So you tell, why?"

For some unfathomed reason Monar felt compelled to answer, "I have always roamed the night, I don't know why, some instinct."

"You do not know my Prince, so I will reveal. It is from somewhere shadowy, far past. Shiva made you from tiger to human and our dark predecessors reach out to you again from your past."

Monar would have none of it and did not want Collie absorbing mystical concepts, "Let's change course here. Who are you, why do you come to be here and try to pester me?"

She gave a crooked grin, "Pester you? I am Princess Jyoti Bijral and can pester any and all I wish. Still, that tells you nothing. If you want to know of my right to be here, come with me for I will tell you a tale of this living skeleton in the forest and give you a warning. For we well know the branch did not move, yet you sensed it—did you not?"

For Monar, it was too good an offer to miss and though Princess Bijral did not wish the boy along, she led them over a path, used by tigers and she until, though still in Tamil Nadu, they were two miles deeper into near virgin jungle.

Turning past an immense Banyan tree they barely found, through vine and root, the contour of a small, weathered temple. Only sagged netting covered the doorway and roots, though hacked away in some areas, still snaked through fractured windows.

An old table, rotted wicker couch, scores of mildewed books, and a hammock completed the items of the three rooms. There was a fireplace weakly smoldering and Jyoti Bijral brought it to life with dried palms to ease the dampness.

Young Collie Graves was puzzled, "You live *here*? Why?"

"Behave, Collie. I'm sure the Princess will tell us."

Jyoti Bijral sat cross-legged by the fire and, by its quivering light spun her tale; her aging face glistened from the glow.

"I was born in Sangur. In the Punjab. The land of five rivers. My father was a Maharajah, though not wealthy. He had eight girls; I was the oldest and first Princess, so first in line. But then was born a son and I was without value, in the way. Father was poor so I was taken out of the English School at twelve and sold to an agent who said he would find me a proper, well-bred mate…or so was the fable he uttered."

Monar knew quite well about people being sold, he was one of them in America. Collie, however, was shocked, “You were sold? People sold their own children?”

“Yes, Collie, it happens often. But hush, let her continue.”

“Thank you, my Prince Monar. It came about the agent decided to keep me for his own self for then was I beautiful and, as the boy is here, I will not unfold the happenings. I lived the life of enslavement for my sins. For years we travelled the trading routes east on the Grand Trunk Road. From Peshawar in Punjab, through Lahore, Delhi to Calcutta then down the eastern coast buying and selling people and trinkets. After the hated years through Orissa and many more endless dirty towns we came into Cuddalore and French Pondicherry, south from the British in Madras.

“It was there Hindu God Shiva and wife Parvati agreed I had suffered enough for I had secretly learned Hindi to honor Shiva.”

“You weren’t Hindu? What were you then?”

“I was Sikh, from the north and east, I spoke Punjabi. Sikh not good as Hindi. First Mughal people try to kill us and then British finally fight us into obedience.”

Monar also knew about some not being as good as another, but only a crooked smile was glimpsed as the Princess moved on.

“It was there Lord Shiva spoke and made me to wash in the Gingee River and find a ribbon for my hair and pinch my cheeks pink and stand in the bazaar. I did as He ordered and waited. The purpose of why I was to do this was there; a great man with golden skin and dark eyes stood glowering at me from his palkhi. I shivered and thanked Shiva. The man ordered his servants to bring me to him and he asked who was I. Surprised Shiva had not told him; I nonetheless spoke in my finest Hindi.

“I am Princess Jyoti Bijral, my lord.”

“Princess? You speak Hindi yet not Hindu, are you Ghumiar?”

“No my Lord, I said, I not Muslim. I Sikh, from north and east. Again I thought it odd Lord Shiva did not mention to him this fact before we met, but I dared not question.”

“What brings you to Pondicherry, My lovely Princess Bijral?”

"My agent brought me here for a reason, I answered."

"Agent? Ah, then a slave you are?"

"Now, yes. Yet my father was Maharajah like you, but poor."

"You know I am Maharaja—how?"

"Lord Shiva told me, and you and your finery prove that to be true. The Maharaja smiled and made gesture to Shiva, then ask where my agent is and to bring him. I did such and my agent strutted as if a prince himself."

"He was asked, 'Your price?'"

"He lied. 'My Lord, She is not sale, for very dear to me is she. But if she were…she would be very expensive.'"

"My Lord asked one more time, 'Name a price or I will have you whipped out of the village without her or single rupee.'"

"With that, he ordered me to follow behind and left a servant to haggle with my agent. Forty years ago that will be—until he passaged to Yama and Svargam."

The story became all too clear to Monar, "And he built you this temple and you became his mistress and…"

"Yes, and he schooled me and loved me and Shiva made us happy when together. Even though I was only Sikh."

Monar continued, "And he was Maharaja Gupta Singh, my wife's father."

"That is true…my Prince."

5

MONAR LEANED BESIDE the flaring palms in the fireplace. It took a moment or two for the ramifications to sink in.

Amala was born within the time of her father's affair with this woman and, imagination abruptly running away with him, he saw a likeness in the nose or lips or the way she smiled or the tilt of her head—a tilt *was* one of Amala's mannerisms.

He shook his head to rid the thoughts, yet Jyoti Bijral had read them, "Your beliefs waver, your wisdom falters Prince Monar. You question? Do not; I speak true, your Amala is not mine."

"I did fear to go further, Princess."

"Then trust my words—as Baptist teachers say to do."

Collie failed to follow that thread of their conversation. Then again, he somewhat understood the difficulties this could bring if the information of another woman became general knowledge. Although Maharajas are subject to few rules, it would become fodder for gossip and the Maharini Amala would dislike the implication.

Monar was sensitive to that which led to another line of questions, "What do you want? Of course I can give you funds to return home to…"

"Home? Is there other home for me? No, only here, near my Lord Gupta. I will die as quietly as you wish and until then only ask, as before, that some fruits be placed by my temple now and then as did my Lord before he passed from me. No meat, tigers will sense and no longer be my friends or let me sleep peacefully."

"I will see to that, Princess. And we will speak again, but now, the mention of tigers reminds me the boy and I should retrace our steps before dusk, when the cats wake."

"You will have no trouble, my Prince, be sheltered in this. Yet when we met I mentioned two things. One, the skeleton in the forest will surely be me someday soon. The other I mentioned was for to warn, and I warn you there are Dacoits who prowl and wait on the western paths of Tamil Nadu."

"I have not the slightest idea what you're talking about. Dacoits? What or who are Dacoits?"

"I regret reverting to my Punjabi tongue of Saugor and Nerbudda, where Decoits start centuries past. In English, the word means bandit or thief. Possibly you know them as the English call them—Thuggee. And death comes with them. Many years past I saw the prison in Jubbulpore, in the Madayha Pradesh region where Decoits, Thuggee were kept or hung."

"I'm sorry, I don't know Decoit or Thuggee, please explain."

"I do that so. Thuggee were here long, very long before British coming to India. I not speak of them more before you ask the British of them—and soon. I will tell then of the night I follow overseer of Indigo sheds. I know Thuggee not ended, at least on your pathways. Please, go now, do not tell British why you ask, for they will swarm over your land and one cannot catch Thuggee that way."

She said nothing more, leaving Monar and Collie to question her words as they followed the faded track back to the estate.

Monar was severe in speaking to Collie, "Until I decide whether or not to mention this woman to Amala, you are to say not a word of this to anyone—is that understood?"

"Yes, sir, but don't you think we should do something for her? She's so alone."

3 July, 1864, Shimla, Nepal. Summer capital of British India.
John Laird Lawrence, 1st Baron Lawrence, Viceroy and Governor General of India, responded negatively to Prince Monar's request for permission to visit and query the Superintendent of the Thagi Dafar—the Thuggee Bureau in Jubbulpore—about the long past Thuggee menace. After considerable confusion, caused in part by Monar's obfuscation for the reason he wanted this information, he

was informed his travelling northeast to Rawalpindi District for information would be a waste. If he still desired the material, seek assistance in his own back yard. Sir James Denison, Governor of Madras, could supply someone well versed in Thuggee history.

After the fact, Monar realized he should have simply lied and stated he'd just heard the word Thuggee and was curious and the British would have passed it off. But now, the Governor of Madras became involved and eventually in this roundabout way Monar was introduced to an aging, spindly Hindu priest named Rajiv Acharya.

Although Monar was unaware at first, Rajiv Acharya was the ideal person, for in his younger years he'd been attached to an Indian Civil Division headed up by a Captain Sleeman.

"Captain Sleeman was a forceful and driven man, Prince Monar. He savaged the Thuggee without sorrow, without regret."

"Then tell me from the beginning what is Thuggee—wait, before we talk, what allegiance do you have to this Captain Sleeman I've heard about—or the British Government?"

The priest was caught by surprise, "You have only little knowledge of Captain or Thuggee?"

"Scarcely any. The issue only came up of late."

"I see. Then to answer your questions, I once swore allegiance to great Queen Victoria, for I was what British call Sowar, a Madras light cavalry soldier for British in the 5th Bombay Army. I was not Sepoy; you should know Sepoy are only native *foot* soldiers, cannot be cavalry. But why do you ask who my allegiance is to now?"

"I want my curiosity to remain private from Sleeman and the Brits. I'll give my reason if you agree."

"As long as agreement is not harmful to India and you..." Monar understood and Acharya smiled, "...know I would never sever my allegiance to Major-General Sleeman. When I knew him yes, he was a Captain, but a god to me and many others. He spent his life in India helping kill Thuggee. Unhappily, he was Major-General on his way to England with hope to regain his health. Yet he reached no further than Ceylon, the island off our southern coast. He was buried at sea. That was '56. I pray forever to his memory."

Monar couldn't help think that here was a Hindu priest honoring and devoted to a foreign military man whose country dominated India. Why was this so? The reason wasn't long in emerging.

The old priest faltered, then continued, "I honor him with tears for what he and British did to help eliminate sati—you may know it as suttee, the dreadful deed of widows throwing themselves on their husband's funeral pyres. Yet for even more he is honored for ceasing filthy Thuggee terror, and so too should all people of India."

"Then please, Rajiv sir, continue with your story."

"Not my story, Prince Monar, but India's. First you must recognize India is a land of many paths, pathways that cross this land north, east, south, west and many, many thousands of travelers tread those paths at all times. For ages there were hearsays of people who never reach or not return from these travels, people who were swallowed up, vanish, never to be seen again by their families—never."

At this point, Acharya handed Monar a book, "It would be too long to give the history, so I will lend you this book, *Confessions of a Thug* by an Englishman name of Philip Taylor."

Monar opened the cover, noting it was published in 1839 and well thumbed through.

"Study this Prince Monar, it tells the filth of clans whose only joys were in killing people who did nothing more wrong than have the misfortune of meeting these impure filth on the paths of India. These Thuggee killed in the name of Kali, the Black Mother, visage of the Goddess Durga, and gloried in the garroting of countless thousands. It is said two million innocent souls are buried under India's paths. Do not, do not doubt this is true."

Monar was startled at the numbers and as he stared at the book, the priest became agitated. Monar began to see there was more to his story, "You knew someone involved, Acharya?"

"My wife and two baby daughters…they were coming to see me when I was in garrison with the British Bombay Army along the Sutlej River in Firozpur District. They never appeared to me."

The priest turned away, Monar caught snippets of a prayer.

"Two years later I heard of Captain Sleeman, who was to begin to track down Thags, that means thief in Hindi and British changed it to Thuggee, where your English word thug comes from. I volunteered for revenge and I am Rajput caste—only we and Brahman can be Sowar, British Indian Army cavalry. At that time, in '35, Captain Sleeman had caught one important Thuggee, Syeed Amir Ali—he is in that book—and to save his life he led us to endless graves and told us all. For over twenty years we hunted down thousands of Thuggee to hang or be jailed for life. Still, I have yet to have enough revenge for my wife and daughters."

Monar listened and then isolated on one remark, "You say Sleeman caught one and from there it led to all the rest?"

Rajiv Acharya stared fixedly on his listener. He was no fool and quickly caught the motive behind Monar's question, "Yes. And now you do not believe they are gone, do you Prince Monar?"

There was nothing for it now but to confess, "I've obviously blundered about the purpose of my inquiry. The answer is I have reason to believe they are not gone."

Rajiv smiled, "That would upset the British. They desire to believe otherwise and would dislike to be hearing otherwise. Do not worry: I will not spoil their beliefs that they have ended Thuggee. And if that is the goal you are bent upon, I will help."

The old soldier is still in the hunt, Monar thought, "Do you know an old woman called Jyoti Bihar?"

"The Princess, Bihar? Ah yes, of course I do, yet I become startled you do as well."

"She spoke to me about Thuggee and said she followed the number one man of our Indigo production and knows he is one."

"If Jyoti showed herself to tell you it must be true. She has given you the key to help eliminate them—at least here."

"Then I would ask your assistance in ending this problem."

"You will have it, but you must believe that Thuggee worship the death goddess Kali and can only be halted by death. For Kali stood upon the good God Shiva and she is as black as you and the creator and destroyer, and Thuggee kill in her blessing."

"Then I have no difficulty with killing Kali, Thuggee or any other of your murdering gods."

Rajiv couldn't prevent his comment, "Of course you have no difficulty with death. It is in your blood, you English. You and your Royal Indian Hunting Society. "British love the hunt, either the Bengal Tiger or people it does not matter—you love the *hunt*."

Monar had to grin, "Me? You think I'm British? That's a first. Let me tell you, I'm not British."

"Then the British have rubbed off on you."

6

The previous May 1864, Galactic Plain above Calcutta, Bengal
ARCHIE FENG WAS RECONCILED to the disaster he found. Over a year had passed from the time he'd chosen to accompany Monar to the United States to find John Thomas Graves. And then, after leaving Monar in Madras, he traversed the Ganges Delta and tied off the *Devon* beside Fort William, west of Calcutta. There, he learned a cyclone had struck the previous year leaving Calcutta in chaos along with the loss of their fishing fleet and more than seventy-thousand Bengalis.

Once returning to his plantation estate in Bengal, Archie had to imagine the scope of the devastation for it was clear his wives, children, and laborers had achieved immense reconstruction. The houses and buildings were rebuilt and cultivated acres cleared. Even so, the tea shrubs, an estimated third of them, were obliterated.

He acknowledged his family's efforts simply by an approving nod and began to plan further rebuilding of the estate and its income. Archie wasn't destitute by any stretch of the imagination. Still, once someone with his temperament attains a tangible gold based objective and then have it disrupted, any wound is deep. The storm was an affront and Archie took affronts personally and often.

In the course of recounting his travails in England and the United States, Archie explained the presence of ten-year-old Mark Graves and made it clear to the three wives that the boy was not to be doted on, simply treated firmly as their other children—perhaps slightly less.

One positive aspect of his return was the presence of Archie's oldest and favorite son, Peter Feng Yū-shan. It had been twelve years since they'd seen each other. That occasion was during the theft of the tea plants, when Archie dispatched Peter to kill Ashly Ealing, the erstwhile China Resident for Warfield's Black Moon

Line. Ealing had changed his allegiance to the Qing and exposed that a theft of tea shrubs was near. If it hadn't been for Harry Scrimshaw's adroit handling of the clipper ship *Raven*, they would never have evaded the four Chinese war junks. For that, Archie wanted the traitor Ealing, dead.

"You're certain you killed him, Peter?"

"Never more sure, father. He never saw the dart coming."

"Too bad, I would have liked him to know he was going to die and that it was from me."

Feeling shamed, Peter sought to cheer Archie, "The other news is that your Sleeping Dragon Society still exists."

Animated then depressed, Archie only said, "The Dragon still exists? There can only be rickety old men left after all these years."

"Not true, sir. Jing Joeng kept them together and a goodly number of their sons have been initiated."

Peter omitted mentioning that Jing had done very well with the Society and it was decidedly improbable he would return the Dragon to his father's charge. Not knowing Archie's desire for China, Peter erroneously thought his omission would be harmless.

When a runner brought a telegraph dispatch up from the British station in Calcutta, it was the first any of them knew information could be transferred by a wire and that fact took some convincing.

At length persuaded, Archie read and frowned at the short missive until he began to realize that—as other people could read the message—the words were couched. He worked it out. *Problem* meant trouble; *strangers* meant unwanted outsiders and the last words, *when come,* translated to as soon as you can get down here!

The quickest way—although quickest was a relative term—was by train. After sending a response to Madras, Archie, his son Peter and the Graves boy, Mark, were on their way south in a jammed well over capacity Warfield Engine Company built steam train, rolling on Manchester steel rails supplied by Warfield Mills.

«»

The stratagem to the destruction of the Kali worshiping Thuggee was formed in a private room in the estate of the Maharini. Present were Archie Feng, his son Peter, Princess Jyoti Bihar, the Rajput priest, and former Sowar, Rajiv Acharya, along with ten handpicked Rajput Lancers from the estate and their leader, Prince Monar.

After introductions among the disparate group, Monar dispensed with any extraneous talk, "You are all volunteers. For this hunt, you have sworn yourselves to secrecy; you owe allegiance to no one other than this group. Not the British, Indian Police or the Maharini, all of whom I have intentionally kept in the dark in case they would resist this—or our efforts go awry."

There were no dissenters. Now was the time to entrust them with the first step he and Archie had taken—although it was actually a disastrous misstep.

"One night before Archie Feng got down from his estate, Princess Jyoti and I trailed Akhil Chakraborty, the supervisor of the drying sheds here along the path to…"

Jyoti spoke up, "I swear Prince Monar can see in the dark. I simply went along. Chakraborty never saw us, but Prince Monar had no trouble following him. Believe me; I swear a mystique enfolds our Prince. He told me to hide behind him when a tiger crossed in front of us. Tiger looked right down the path and never saw or sensed us! He stared but never saw…"

Monar quieted her, "Please, Princess, we'll get off the subject if you tell stories like this."

"May be story, my Prince, yet true…"

Monar moved on with his information, "About three miles from here, Chakraborty met with around ten people I will call them Thugs, for I believe they to be so after hearing some of them speak, which Jyoti translated for me."

Jyoti Bihar confirmed what she heard, "Chakraborty was the leader. He spoke of a wealthy caravan and that it would pass through Bengaluru on the trail to the railroad spur at Kanchipuram and then, I think, to Madras.

The priest asked, "When?"

"That, we couldn't hear."

Monar was left to resume, "We kept a very close watch on Chakraborty and when Archie arrived I filled him in and we cornered the bastard and faced him down. That's just before our plans went to all to hell."

Monar held their attention, hanging on his next words, "He admitted everything. He was a Thuggee leader and they were going to assault the travelers. He said there was a fork in the road before the rail spur for the Government Steam Train and that's where travelers rest. The Thuggee plan to attack right there as it was close to the railroad's main line and the caravan would be relaxed, feeling safe."

Nirav Devi, Captain of Prince Monar's Lancers, thought forward, "Then all we have to do is know what caravan and when."

With a straight face, Monar explained, "That's why I said our plans went to hell. While questioning Chakraborty, he pulled out a knife and we had no choice but to kill him."

Most everyone let out a groan, everyone excepting Monar and Archie who knew what really happened, and Princess Jyoti who, watching through a window, saw an irate Archie stab Chakraborty. The only knife there was Archie's and now she comprehended the sudden killing was because they couldn't get the answer of *when* so the Thuggee held no further value.

Jyoti had then seen the men carry the body into the jungle and watched Monar walk off incensed with Archie apparently uncaring.

Captain Devi had a solution, "Prince Monar, I have contacts in the British Territorial Police south of us. If there's a valuable caravan coming north, they're usually notified. I'll find out without causing a red flag with the British or Indian Police."

"Then we will wait for your findings and this will be all for now. Plan so that you can be ready in short order. But one more thing, Chakraborty admitted to killing thirty-seven people and told us of Thugs who had killed over four or five hundred. Hard to believe, I know, but our priest here, Rajiv Acharya, worked with the

Suppression of the Thuggee Bureau and confirms this to be true. So keep in mind, we're dealing with killers and unless I miss my guess, there's going to be trouble."

The priest asked the group be named the Hindi word, Angreji, the nearest in English pronunciation, Avengers—and that was agreed.

Now, with only Archie remaining, Monar's displeasure with Archie's knifing of Chakraborty was still a sore point.

Archie, as expected, wasn't contrite. "Look Monar, you asked me down here to help. You yourself said we wouldn't get anything more out of him so what were you going to do with him? You couldn't have given him over to the British because that would let the cat out of the bag, wouldn't it? Could you keep him a prisoner here? How? I solved what to do with him. He was a murderer and now he rots in the jungle. I've done you a favor, so what is your problem?"

Monar should have half-expected Archie to do something to Chakraborty. After all, at one time, Archie was the chief assassin for the governor of Canton. Yet, as callous as Archie's act was, Monar had to own up to the fact Archie was right. Two years before, he had done the same thing; coldheartedly knifed a decent Southern naval officer to help John Thomas escape from Savanna, and *that* death saved a lot of bother too.

"All right, Archie, I'll concede it was convenient, but Christ…."

Archie started to leave, then turned on his heel, his face severe, "Listen to me Monar, You're not thinking ahead. You talk of trouble. Trouble? I think there's a better word. How about *bloodbath*? Because that's what we're coming to. You know that. And isn't that why you asked me down here? Well, tell me—isn't it?"

"I asked you down here to help, Archie, because you're reliable and that's what…"

"Reliable for what, to kill people? That's a lot of bodies, even for me. Look, Monar, you've got blinders on. Chakraborty won't be there to meet these Thugs, so they'll probably be on guard. But say we charge in there and confront *more* than ten people. Fine, I have no trouble with that either, but trouble isn't the right word to use."

Archie stopped, perplexed, "So then tell me what do we do with the ones we catch…?" But he'd already guessed the answer.

Monar was blunt, "I'm expecting them all to put up a fight."

"That's what I deduced as I spoke. So, fine with me."

"All right then, we're in agreement."

"One more thing, Prince Monar, do we bring the boys?"

"No. Too young and we're also charged with keeping them alive. If something goes wrong, it could be a disaster. We'll take them when we go to Japan, that will be risky enough so let it go at that. Anyway, this mess looks like it will take a while to resolve. I'll send a note to Harry on the next ship to Canton letting him know we might be a month behind schedule getting there. He can telegraph Warfield and let him know."

"Telegraph? From what I've learned, that's hit or miss, and from there to England? Part way by ship, part way through half a dozen countries in between?"

"I know, but still quicker than by all ship. Nonetheless, I'll send a message by clipper as well."

Archie laughed, "Good that will only take three or four months. Send it by way of Egypt."

"That alleged waterway isn't anywhere near finished."

"Jesus, Monar, I know that! Have a Black Moon ship take the message to Suez, then overland by rail to Alexandria and find another Moon ship to England—simple. Just remember, Warfield's not going to like it one bit," Archie chuckled, "and tell him I said a warm hello and we'll get his trinkets delivered, I'm sure he'll appreciate that."

When Archie brought Mark with him to see his brother Collie, the Graves' boys talked themselves out about their father and mother. For all that, they were changing. The life being led now was supplanting their past. Once again, it seemed Warfield was right about sending them away. As with most children, the boys were acclimating. They were two of the Chosen Few learning of British administration, good and bad, in another dominated country.

Their teachers were likewise outsiders and also open-minded, ready to adapt, learn, and even openly criticize both the British and Maharajas in equal measure. The boys idolized their mentors, Archie and Monar and, through them, they were too soon becoming young men.

Hindi and Punjabi were languages the boys undertook and, like most children, were quick to adapt. Their childhood had flown; a thing of the past. Still, it was the past they wanted to know about when they approached Monar with serious demeanors.

Mark, at ten years old, took the lead, "Prince Monar, I…"

"Since when have you decided to address me as *Prince* Monar, Mark? Monar is quite enough for you and Collie."

"Well then sir, Collie and I want to discuss something in real seriousness and we wanted to be sort of formal, you know, so that you would treat us as adults in a conversation with you."

Monar had never seen such solemn faces on the boys and responded to their formality, "Then we will discuss whatever subject you wish as adults. What do you wish to discuss?"

Mark looked to his brother, Collie, who urged him on.

"Well sir, when we were on the *Devon* coming here, we wanted to ask you about our parents, but you seemed to ignore us and even now you seem…well…"

Both boys' eyes glistened. Monar knew exactly what was meant. He had not ignored them; rather he tried to avoid them. On the *Devon*, the loss of his best friend, their father, and memories of their mother was too fresh and the children prevented those wounds from healing. Now, it was clear he had hurt them, hurt them enough so that no matter how difficult, they had to broach their feelings.

"Come here, both of you, sit beside me. It's evident now that I was only thinking of myself and that you hurt as well. You see, I loved your mother…" he quickly added, "and your father, very much. Each time I saw you it distressed me—took me back to them.

I should have known their loss affected you as much as it did me. Now, you've brought this up it shows I have no excuse, I recognize my feelings for them affected my manners with you both. I love you as much as my own sons and sometime in the not too distant future I will tell you about them. Never forget that, no matter what."

"And one more question, are we Americans or Englishmen?"

"After I tell their story, it will be for you to decide."

«»

1 July 1864, Blackwood Abbey

STRIKE THE BLASTED HAMMER RED! If you want a bleeding thing done right, by bloody hell, you've got to go do it yourself!

Ah, thought Lily, at last we're getting back to some kind of normalcy. Still, he should settle down, "What's wrong now, dear?

"My so called *partners* have managed to mess with my timetable. This damn telegraph from Scrimshaw says Monar and Archie have something more important to do. They'll be a month—and sure as hell that will stretch to two—before they get underway with their junket to Japan. *Junket* he calls it! And *Trinkets*! It's iron and steel products and other merchandise to show what we can supply, for Christ's sake!"

"Well for *your* sake settle down, Warfield. Did he say why?"

"Nothing other than Scrimshaw is in China and they're delayed going there and then on to Japan. No reason."

"Well perhaps the reason is touchy and telegraph messages aren't particularly private you know."

"I know, I know. But the American war is being won by the North. When that's done their commercial fleet will be free from the South's raiders and the competition will be fierce. This is why I wanted to get the jump on them, not shillyshally around in India."

"I'm sure they're not simply shillyshallying around. There must be a good reason, Brodie."

Lily, when Warfield got overwrought, now called Warfield by his actual given name as it always brought a smile…as now.

“Damn it Lily, I’m trying to be serious here.”

Warfield’s fuming eased and he went back to trying to re-decipher the telegram while Lily went off and made him a cup of tea. She shouldn’t have left him to muse alone, for when she returned Warfield’s mind was made up.

“Lily, I’m going to India!”

“What? That’s a lot of rot and you know it! But if you dare, then I’m going too, and that’s that!”

“No you’re not. Someone has to stay and run the company.”

“Blast you Brodie or Warfield or whatever your name is!”

Warfield turned the table on her, “Lily, for *your* sake, don’t get all upset. You know in your heart there’s no one else who can do anything as well as you.”

“Well I just might just find someone, and damn quick!”

Lily sat silent when Warfield left the room; he needs something to do she thought. Yet it’s more than that, he’s trying to hide it, but he’s becoming somewhat bitter. The loss of Evelyn is eating into him, making him…

She could only revert to the word, *bitter*.

«»

The previous 20 June 1864 Tamil Nadu highland’s jungle

IT HAD BEEN A BLOODBATH. Archie Feng’s prediction had proven dreadfully accurate. Bodies lay about; the stench of gunpowder draping the fetid air. Few sounds were heard other than the gasps of exhausted men or the softer whimper of men suffering.

Archie, getting off his knees, reloaded his revolver, said, “Shut the hell up!” And shot the three wounded Thugs. No one intervened.

Bloodied and failing, the Rajiput Priest Rajav Acharya was smiling, cradled in Monar’s arms, “Do not be sad my Prince. Be pleased for me. The Avengers have fulfilled my need for revenge on the Thuggee for my…beloved wife and daughters…now the Great God Shiva will take me to them…so I die joyful and go to…and go…”

Laying the priest down, Monar wiped his face on his sleeve and took it all in. Twenty-five bodies, twenty-two Thuggee and three lancers lay grotesquely on the red soaked soil. There were no captives; Monar thought that perhaps four or five attackers had escaped, but did not go after them.

It was hard for him to relive the conflict. The priest had said that in the past, Thuggee infiltrated caravans and then, at night, they would use scarfs to garrote the people, primarily for the joy of killing. So the shock had been absolute when Monar, Archie and Peter, ahead of group, rounded a turn in the path—away from the designated site—and inadvertently stumbled upon the Thugs as they were organizing for the following night's ambuscade of the caravan.

There were close to thirty of them and seeing only three men against them, with little thought, they attacked. With khukuris, the curved Nepali knife, the Thugs shrieked and rushed the three men.

Having no idea the strangers were experienced and well-armed with revolvers and knives, the Thuggee rushed headlong into a fusillade which, though it appallingly decimated them, their onslaught was only slowed, not broken.

Braving the surge, then having to fall back, Monar, Archie and Peter fired until their revolvers were empty, then slashed with bolos. Peter went down. Archie, a cut and bleeding demon, slashed and screamed insanely, standing over his son until he cut the arm off one assailant and the boy regained his stance, All the while Monar, lacerated across the chest and arm, hacked his bolo at the band of onrushing Thuggee.

At that insane peak, the lancers caught up and rushed recklessly into the crazed Thuggee, overwhelming them with gunfire, sabers and khuhuris. A barbaric, bloody minute later, the battle was over.

Realizing the serious wounds some of his lancers had received, not to mention his own, Monar checked with Captain Devi and, finding him the lesser injured, sent him with two other men back to their base camp. Devi was to get their horses and two wagons narrow enough to traverse the constricted paths as well as more bandage and water. It was a good six miles, so it would be some time before they returned and Monar looked to his wounded men then, noticing Peter Feng was not to sight, asked Archie about him.

"He went after the filth who escaped."

"Why did you let him? He'd been sliced on the arm."

"It wasn't bad and he wanted to make it up to us for falling."

"Falling? For Christ's sake, that was a big man, he bowled Peter over, but he got up again to fight and we did give them a thrashing."

"Almost, yet not complete, Monar, some are left. But you still don't understand. Far more than his arm, his pride is pained, as it should be. I didn't tell you he was going because you would have sent lancers with him. This is something he had to do by himself."

"Archie, it isn't right sending him."

Calling his two least wounded men, Monar sent them to overtake Peter and if possible save him before further loss ensued. Monar was left with the disturbing fact that only three wounded men, Archie, and he were left at present and, for that matter, both he and Archie were wounded. If there were more Thuggee…He hastily reloaded their revolvers.

By midafternoon, they were relieved to hear hoof beats, many hooves, pounding toward the bend in the path. Camels cleared the bend and thirty cavalry lancers, led by the Maharini Amala of Tamil Nadu, rushed headlong into the clearing.

Even through his pain, Monar quickly saw that once the Maharini saw him alive, she gasped and…became angry.

She tapped the neck of her camel and it knelt, allowing her to slide off and survey the carnage for a few moments. Her orders started. Lancers were to collect the knives and garroting scarves and throw the dead Thuggee into the jungle. Then, when the wagons arrived, place the wounded lancers and their three dead mates in them. There was a doctor with her who quickly headed for Monar but Amala ordered him to see to the others first. There was no question the Maharini was in charge. Monar watched as she ordered men to loosen the soil with the camels and the sweep it with palms to hide the blood and any sign of struggle.

Archie started to laugh, “We should have had her with us, she’d have done a damn sight better than we did.”

Wordless, Monar and Archie stared, never having seen Amala so forceful and sure of her orders. Neither the blood nor the bodies upset her and the lancers were quick to respond to each command.

Nudging Monar, Archie pointed to the last wagon that arrived and there, sitting upright, as a princess should—was Jyoti Bihar.

Monar was stunned. Amala knew the Princess? What in the devil was going on?

Her orders given, Amala took bandages from the doctor and came up to Monar, a fixed smile formed, “Archie, go have the doctor clean you up. My husband, the Prince, I will attend.”

Preventing even the slightest grin, Archie murmured, “I’m sure you will Madame, I’m sure you will.”

Monar started to speak, but Amala held up her hand as she knelt and opened her husband’s blood-soaked shirt. The slash, although not deep, carved almost a foot across his chest.

“A little deeper and we would be throwing you into the jungle with the others.”

“You’re right, I’m lucky he had a shorter arm than I.”

“You attempt to making humor of this? It is without humor.”

She took a bottle from her sari and splashed it across his chest causing him to wince.

“Does it hurt my husband? Big strong hero that are you to make the face from splash of healing water?”

“Look, Amala, I can explain this whole thing. I didn’t want you involved in case something went wrong and…”

“Do not express reason, Prince Monar. You hide that from me behind your back and it now becomes too late to your front. Jyoti told your plans for even she knew then to be without sense…”

Monar became defensive, “Then why didn’t she say something to me back then?”

"Why? Because you are male prince. What woman would say to male prince *you are without slightest sense*?"

Monar couldn't help blurt out, "Well you're doing a bloody damn good job of it!"

She wiped the wound dry and pressed cotton cloth to it, "So unlike you to use the bad English of the British."

"Amala, please tell me how you came to be here. No, first tell me how you know about Jyoti Bihar."

"Now that your needs become less, I will explain. Princess Bihar was my father's lady friend and…"

"You knew *that*, Amala?"

"My husband, you erupt my speaking. Of course I know of her. My mother as well also. My father the Maharaja had that right and he only kept but only one beside my mother."

"If that was your father's right and your father cared for her, then why do you let her live in poverty?"

"That was her to choose. If ask by her, I would aid. She has not. I would not shame her to offer. Yet you do not follow our ways and we are away from how I came to here."

Confounded, Monar could only nod and Amala went on, "It would be that Jyoti could not be quiet about your senses and made herself aware to me and then spoke of much foolishness. I became…became *mystified* of you…not wanting to question your ways—but fearing. I could not wait more at last and chased you here…" Amala eyes began to well up, "please, tell me why this unruliness in you has happened?"

Improper in public, Monar encircled her in this arms and she nestled there, "I only wanted to protect your name if things went wrong and well…I made a mistake."

"I look here and see how true that to be. My father was a great lord and won many battles, that is why death take place sometime. I saw them before with him. He lived to one rule; he said *for certain have more senses and more men than your enemy*."

Actually, that was two rules, but Monar didn't mention it.

Jyoti Bihar came over, “I hope you are well, Prince Monar I beg you accept this poor Sikh’s plea to forgive for my not having sense either, and coming here with the Maharini, Amala.”

“I do not think I have any choice in the matter.”

Lacking contrition, an unseen, furtive smile flitted past Princess Jyoti lips.

Peter Feng was carried back that afternoon. Monar’s lancers found him and two Thuggee, dead along the path.

Archie spoke with the lancers first and then went to his son. He was saddened; Peter was his first child and, as such, his favorite. His death caused Archie unspoken grief.

Giving Archie time alone with his son, Monar went to the lancers who found Peter and asked what Archie wanted from them. *Did he die worthy,* Archie wanted to know they said, and they told him *yes*. He must have faced at least three Thugs as two were dead and there appeared to be some blood spots trailing off up the path.

“We are saddened with you, Archie Feng.” The Maharini Singh startled him by touching his shoulder.

At a loss for once, he stammered his thanks and then saw Monar standing to her side, “Archie, I feel guilty that he died in this fiasco.”

Archie began to gather his wits, “This was no fiasco, Monar. We set out to kill Thuggee and we did. Not the way we planned, true, but most plans get muddled anyway. If one Thug escaped, that is good. He will warn others never to come here again. Some of our people died, we had to expect that. I wish I was taken in place of my son, but the gods, in their boredom, do this trickery…”

He was fumbling and knew it. They waited; seeing there was more he wanted to say.

“Maharini Singh, this is your land. I ask to have my son buried there, where carcasses of the Thuggee have been thrown…”

Monar questioned him, “Are you sure Archie? Not on your lands in the Bengal?”

"I am sure. In the life beyond, I want my son to chase and torment these scum through the eternal underworld."

Archie's son was buried there. Perhaps he did just that.

7

November, 1864. The shore of Madras

RAIN LADEN, DISMAL CLOUDS of the winter monsoons saturated the lands of Andhra Pradesh and Tamil Nadu. Despite the rain being a yearly blessing for India's rice bowl, it got on the nerves of the sailors rowing provisions through the surf to the Blackwall Frigate, *Devon*, moored offshore.

By this time, Archie Feng had been to his estate in the Bengal, justified and deified their son to his number one wife and given orders to improve the estate. Then he had taken his fourteen year old son, Matthew Feng Yün-shan, and sailed the *Devon* south to Madras. Leaving Calcutta, the prime auction city for opium, he saw the American Clipper, *Witch of the Waves* moored, taking on supplies for New York, and passed another American ship, a sharp clipper named *Boston Light* heading north.

Warfield's wrong, Archie thought, if he thinks the damn Americans are not involved over here. His concern was reinforced when—letting out the chain line's rode for his anchor to bite—he lay to port from the *Snow Squall,* another small, quick extreme clipper from America.

"This damn area is going to be an American lake if British merchants don't wake up, Matthew."

Monar had healed well during the interval Archie was gone. The ministrations of Amala the reason and during that time she had scrutinized the Thuggee battle. For the populace of Tamil Nadu, she wove it into a crusade against evil. Monar became the idol of the land and though the British caught quite a whiff that something had happened, they held their noses and diverted their eyes and no inquiry or reprimand ensued.

The Maharini and Prince, along with the Mark and Collie Graves waited for the *Devon's* longboat to ride the surf in one more time and take the men to the next venture, the unknowns of Japan.

The night before Amala had given Monar her thoughts on his travails. It was one thing after another she said. From being a slave to battling slaves on the Clipper *Lawrence Pike*, then clashes with Barbary Corsairs and a Russian Warship in the Crimea.

She continued, reminding him of the list; stealing tea shrubs in China, his leading and winning the Battle of Arkonam Pass and the rescue of John Thomas in the States. There were skirmishes he omitted; yet now she simply asked if he hadn't enough excitement and that she lived for the day when he returned for the last time. At forty-seven, she said, he'd come close to death enough times. Perhaps he had slowed…if only a bit…and she worried.

"This could very well be my last, long voyage Amala; it becomes harder each time to leave you. More so now with John Thomas and Evelyn gone and England so far."

"That sounds well to my ears. Still, behind your eyes mystery comes to make you wander dark places. Yet I have never gone far. I do not understand how my God lets you stay this way and me to wait for you to stop…for me."

"Yet if your Great God, Mahadeva or Shiva, had you like the sea, do not doubt I would take you with me."

"There must be reason He does not wish me to go, but gives Mark and brother Collie to wanting to."

"Amala, remember, their mother and father were born to the sea, like fish. For them it's only natural, inborn, to want to go."

The *Devon's* dory slid up the beach and was turned, waiting, the Graves' boys helped aboard. Monar's cheek was touched by Amala's lips, "I must tell you, Prince Monar, my husband, I pray to Mahadeva and Shiva, who are one, to make this voyage to be your last forever."

Monar smiled though a chill ran through him. His *last* voyage? That was not quite the way her English should put it.

«»

November, 1864, On the *Devon*, standing off Hainan Island, China

Regimentation. Repetition. Memorization. Rote. To most sailors this outgoing journey was simply their rough way of life when at sea. To the three boys yes, it was certainly that, yet importantly it was more. They were crew now, doing crew work, swearing crew words. Certainly not giving orders or climbing to the topsails, or reefing in storms or matters such as that, but they had learned to scramble up and down ratlines, supply powder charges during gunnery drills, take and deliver orders quickly and efficiently. After that came lessons and a myriad of other duties.

At night, lying exhausted in their hammocks, they whispered among themselves how good they were getting. Old sea dogs now, they laughed. Formal schooling was gone for good—at least hoped.

Mark, Collie and Matthew, Archie's son, were where they wanted to be: encircled in the majesty of the sea, the coarseness of the crew, and being part of both. They were destined for it.

As children would stare at gods, they watched Archie and Prince Monar when they plotted courses, felt the wind, read the sky, shot the sun and stars with the mysteries of the sextant, turned the hourglass, called out numbers, latitudes, and longitudes—and they listened to the sea as she seethed along the hull. It was fascinating to them; they wanted to learn, and learn they would—in time…

The weeks passed. India left in their wake along with the Sea of Bengal and its islands, then Sumatra, Malaysia, Singapore, Vietnam until, at length, the South China Sea parted, inviting the *Devon.*

The island of Hainan, off to port, caught Monar and Archie's eye and they silently recalled the theft of the tea shrubs. Yet Monar recollected more. The shrubs yes, but also John Thomas, Harry Scrimshaw and the four Chinese war junks trying to entrap them.

There were over a thousand Chinese warriors screaming for their heads, and Scrimshaw, calmly maneuvering the old *Raven*.

At the last minute, he gave the lead junk a broadside and the *Raven* was away, making their escape from hundreds of rockets chasing their wake. There were rousing recollections to, yet too soon to delve into them or bring them up with JT's children.

Pointing up for Hong Kong and Zhu Jiang, the Pearl River, they were hailed by the American clipper *Water Witch* and the Chinese steam clipper *Ly-ee-moon,* both well known to Archie as opium clippers. As the three ships wallowed in the swells of the China Sea, the *Water Witch's* Captain used his speaking horn to warn of, "*Chinese junks,*" he said; "*off Macao, loaded to the gills with pirates, so look out for the slant-eyed, yellow skin bastards.*"

With the young boys enthused over the possibility of meeting up with actual brigands, the *Devon* got underway once more, while Archie and Monar settled on a strategy. From this point on until the Pearl River's mouth, any approaching junks would be met with an aggressive show of force; gun ports open with guns run out, primed and gunners attending them.

At this time, the Black Moon burgee was replaced with Scrimshaw's new Blue Diamond pennant. It would be unseemly to fly the colors of the firm that once stole the best Chinese tea shrubs.

The show of force worked. Before they passed between the islands of Macao and Hong Kong, a few junks approached, but if pirates, they sheared off once they looked down the barrels of the *Devon's* sixteen cannon and the eyes of a vigilant crew.

Jock MacLeod, the British river pilot who guided the *Raven* up to Canton years past, came aboard and was not fooled by the burgee once he saw Monar. But he laughed it off.

"Still not welcome in China, Mr. Monar? Pity. You and the Black Moon Line certainly caused a row—what was it—ten, twelve years ago when you stole those shrubs? And believe me, Chinese don't forget. It's still a festering blister with the Qing. So you had better make yourself about ten inches shorter and white."

MacLeod laughed at his own words, not knowing Archie Feng was all for silencing him. But Monar, against that, turned to the pilot, about to reproach him when MacLeod again spoke up, "I'll be damned! As I live and breathe, Archie Feng Yūn-shan. We all thought you to be dead. And as I think of it, you'd be best to keep yourself unseen too."

Archie barely controlled his temper, "You think the Qing will really bother about us?"

"I sure do. But you should worry more about your old Sleeping Dragon gang. Jing Joeng runs it now and it's sure as the devil he won't like you coming back and think to take over again."

Archie, initially cautious about the Qing, was now even more on edge and needed information, "What do you know of the Dragon and Jing?"

"Hell, Archie, Jing is top dog Dragon Leader now, runs Sleeping Dragon like you and even bigger. Him and Governor Po-Kuei fit like hand in a glove. Anyone even blinks sideways at the Gov, Jing sees to it they never blink again—and that means the protection swindle Jing rules has no problem from the law."

"I want you to give Jing a message."

"Me? Hell no I won't. I'm not going to get in the middle of you two. Christ, I might as well kiss my arse goodbye. Anyway, since you're flying the Blue Diamond Line burgee I assume you're going to see Scrimshaw. Just look around his dock, there's always a Dragon lackey or two hanging around who will carry a message."

At that moment, MacLeod had another question for Monar, "Say, what happened to that big, blond chap you used to hang around with—weren't you two partners?"

Archie answered for a silent Monar, "That fellow died in the American Civil War—don't go on about it."

Of twelve ships tied off along the docks, five were outsized four stick barks from the US. Despite their war, American's were still in the game. Blue Diamond merchantmen there were also loading or unloading and word was sent to Harry Scrimshaw about the *Devon* tying off. Jock MacLeod shouted good luck and swung aboard the three stick American schooner *Neptune* heading downriver.

After Harry Scrimshaw arrived and handshakes all around, Archie and Monar began justifying their tardy arrival. Listening to their tale of the Thuggee, all Scrimshaw could do was shake his head in amazement. How many times, he wondered, would these two men dodge the Grim Reaper's scythe? And shortly, they'd be heading for Japan, a country even more withdrawn into the stealthy shadows than China. Harry wondered how they would end up.

«»

Once they were out of earshot of others and could speak openly, Scrimshaw was frank in his assessment of the state of affairs regarding the Blue Diamond and Qing's China. In few words, he was wary he said, as other tidings crept into his review. Watchful, he disclosed, and apprehensive of the Qing, their governor and the undisguised rudeness of Canton's port authorities.

"They're letting us trade here, yet I'm telling you both, my feeling is they seriously doubt the story Warfield thought up that the three of us had broken away from him and started another shipping line. We've got to stay careful and on our toes."

"Well that's a bugger, Harry. Blast it! But when you look back on it, how stupid did we think the Qing was? Warfield spun an exciting web and we jumped into it."

Monar looked to Archie, who continued the thought, "True, but if we're in the web, then why haven't they grabbed you?"

"Two things, I think. One is I'm paying in silver, that the Governor Po-Kuei likes and two is he's under the thumb of Emperor Muzong so my guess is they're waiting, waiting to see what evolves over the next few weeks."

"You mean like us showing up?"

"That could be it. But Archie, I had no way of warning you, especially when I had no idea when you'd show up."

"That was just an observation, Harry, not an accusation."

"Then I'll accept it as such Archie, and I've news for *you*—not good either—on your Sleeping Dragon and Jing…"

"Jock MacLeod filled me in about him being the leader of the Dragon now. Anything else?"

"Probably not then. Except that rumor has it he's an extremely dangerous person to have as an enemy, so it's better you kept a low visibility. Oh, and he has an estate up the Pearl River. But yesterday I heard he's at your old place. That's where he stays when in town."

"My place—he's using *my* place?"

"Just when he's in Canton—again, from scuttlebutt."

Monar wanted Archie off the topic, "Tell us what you've found out about Japan, Harry."

"Well, I think Warfield might have painted a bit too rosy a picture there as well. Because if you're looking for a challenge, it's Japan, don't doubt that. I've a man to steer you on their customs and other knowledge. I'll get him here tomorrow. So until then, let's hold off my assessment, it's getting too late."

Midnight, dockside near the *Devon*.
The shadow moved again. The shadow became a form. The form became a man slinking away from the *Devon*. With the silent grace of a panther, the shadow's hunter slipped up and hissed,

"*Archieee…*"

Archie Feng jumped straight up, every nerve in his skin crawling. Instinctively he reached for his knife, but his hand was locked in an unyielding grip.

"*Jesus Christ*, Archie, ease off—it's me, Monar."

"*Monar*! God damn you—don't you ever sleep? You could have given me the death and here I am simply getting some air."

"Don't hand me that getting some air guff. You think I don't know where you're heading at this hour?"

Archie was unrepentant, "Well, are you going to try and stop me or help? Because you're going to have one hell of a time of it if you try to stop me."

"Damn you, Archie! All right then, what's your plan?"

"Find Jing and kill him."

"Hell of a plan. No wonder I constantly check your course headings at sea."

"You should—But are you in?"

"Do you at least have an idea of how to get there?"

"Of course. We'll walk the wharfs until we find a sampan. It's a shorter trip by river and it brings us in the back way."

They soon found a sampan with a lone boatman and at the point of a knife he was quickly rowing the side channels to the main waterway. The night was uncommonly warm, the water sluggish, a few lanterns giving but a smidgen of light to find their way. Yet Archie recalled each bend, building, and byway until they at last neared their goal. The sampan owner, utterly lost, tied off at an abandoned warehouse and when his back was turned, Archie hit him with a wooden oarlock.

"What in hell are you doing, Archie?"

"We can't let him go, can we? You want me to kill him instead?" Archie pushed money into the man's pants.

They worked along the catwalks until Archie pointed to a building, its second floor window alight from whale oil lamps. Monar had been to the building years past to meet Archie, but he didn't recognize it for he had come in the front. He did recall seeing the wharf and, as before, there were two men loafing in the dark, half asleep. Monar pulled back.

"There are two men on the dock."

"You're sure? Archie whispered, "I can't see them, how the devil do you know they're there?"

"Trust me, Archie, two men, in the corner, under the stairs. They're not alert. I doubt anyone's warned them you're around."

"We can avoid them. These buildings are attached and we can reach the second floor going into this one here. It looks abandoned and there's a locked doorway on the second floor into that room."

"Tell me the layout, I only remember coming up the trapdoor to one large room."

"There's four rooms. The one you know, one for guards, one was mine and my wives' sleeping area and the servant's quarters."

They crept up the stairs to the second level in the dark, Monar carefully guiding Archie past rubbish littering the floor. A thin spill of light seen through the wall drew Archie to it.

"I never knew this hole was here. Damn it, did others know of this before? Christ! I'll…"

"Quiet. How many people do you see and what's your plan?"

"There's six I can make out. My guess is they're elders, I think I recognize two or three. Damn, they're sure older. That bastard Jing is holding court. It will be his last…"

Monar interrupted again, "So tell me—what's your plan?"

"You have a weapon, Monar?"

"No, just my bolo."

"Christ! You wander all over hell at night without a revolver? Here, take mine. Now, I recall this door is nothing special, so I'll smash through it and kill Jing—you keep out of sight—if anyone puts up a fight, shoot them."

"If I've got the gun, how are you going to kill Jing?"

"I'll use to the old, dependable Chinese method. It will build my mystique."

"Your mystique? Don't make me laugh."

Archie smirked, "Why not? Someday they'll be scribbling verse about me and about this night. So, you ready?

"Gad, Archie. You sure are full of yourself! And yes, I'm as ready as I'm going to be…"

"Then you stay in the shadows. And don't forget those two on the wharf, because they'll come charging up those stairs—and from the guard room too."

Leader Jing Joene was haranguing the elders to increase their tithes to him from his protection swindle when a courier came into the room and handed Jing a note. Jing's eyes enlarged, rage filled his mind.

Archibald Feng Yün-shan on board Devon in Canton

Jing froze, but the warning was worthless. No sooner were the words comprehended than Archie burst through the splintering door. His monstrous scream froze everyone for the moment he needed to throw his star shaped, steel shuriken at Jing's body.

Incredibly, Archie's quarry reacted too quickly, pulling the courier in front of him to take the impact of the shuriken in the back of his neck. The four elders fled to the side of the room, one losing a geta, a wooden cog, in his rush while another elder poised his knife to throw it at Archie. A gunshot from behind the splintered doorway threw him against the wall. While Archie and Jing stared at each other, pounding feet heard on the stairs proved to be the two guards coming up through the trap door. Twice again, the revolver detonated from the doorway, dropping one guard on the floor while the other pitched back down and thump onto the wharf.

Jing had depended on the guards and was now uncertain of his next move. Screams from the women's room filled the chamber. Monar appeared, holding the gun toward Jing, shocking the group while he moved to check the other rooms. Except for the women, the rooms were empty and strangely, no lookouts came from the front of the building. Monar watched Archie and Jing carefully, then opened the women's door and told them to shut up. The sight of a black monster filling the doorway convinced them that truly was the thing to do.

Monar turned the revolver toward Jing. Archie shook his head; Monar seeing Archie had something stupid in mind.

"Archie, if you're thinking of fighting him, you're not young enough. You're a toothless tiger and this guy looks to be twice as big and half as old."

"For Christ's sake, Monar! Are you trying to talk me in or out of this?"

"I'm simply stating the truth. You're making a mistake."

"Me? Make a mistake? Well, now you've talked me into it."

There began the oddest ritual Monar had ever seen. Each man chose an elder who agreed to whatever was said and then went to the opposite ends of the room. The elders presented their swords to the combatants. Wishing Archie luck, the elder then proceeded to the center of the room, signaling for the combatants to approach.

Archie took a moment to come up to Monar, "This is a short Kan dao sword with a two-sided blade. Our combat will be Yang Tai Chi. That means nothing to you so you'll get an education. Anyway, I'll try to finish him quickly, I'm getting old."

"*Now* you decide that! Why don't I just shoot the bastard?"

"Too late for that, honor must be preserved, if not, my reputation will tarnish. But," Archie whispered, "whatever happens, I would like to believe he never walks out of here."

"Don't fret about that. You lose, I'm probably dead to."

Archie laughed, "That's true…" and looked weary walking to the center of the room; Monar hoped it was a ploy. The two elders stood between them, murmuring the code of honor. Archie and Jing took five steps backward. The elders stepped away.

There began a series of body turns, pirouettes, whirls—all the while the short swords spun and flashed in specific sequences of flowing arm and wrist movements. They halted and Jing removed his apricot dragon robe with its dragonhead embroidery.

Archie taunted him, "I was hoping you would do that; when I put it on, I don't want your dried blood on it."

"Any blood, Feng Yün-shan, will be yours and *I* shall not mind in the least—I've many more robes."

Realizing these were taunting japes to an opponent, Monar waited. The talk ceased. The deadly game began as the men circled...ever closer. Jing rushed forward, his sword slashing left, then high, then right and low. Archie deflected, parried, his blade relentlessly ringing against Jing's. Jing's blade swung a tight arc, Archie blocked it and his counter arc was barely evaded by Jing, whose thrust found air, yet his blade still fended off Archie's lunge.

The men separated, repositioned, planning the next assault or response. Archie attacked with a coordinated set of strikes from his left, then slashing right with thrusts blocked by Jing's blade, close, yet never touching his opponent.

Abruptly, Jing shifted sword hands and launched a sustained counterattack and that trickery kept Archie off balance, constantly defending against the multiple shifts of the Tai Chi Master.

Monar was stunned, glad he had a revolver. He could have never withstood either opponent. It was a humbling thought, and he knew this art must be learned —for surely it was art, deadly or not.

Archie was tiring, aging quickly. Jing saw it and bided his time, just wear him down. Stressed, Archie knew he was weakening—yet during Jing arrogantly changing sword hands, he saw a chance.

When the four elders had rushed to the far wall to avoid the gunfire, one of them lost a geta, and that wooden cog became Archie's plan. But it must happen quickly. He had to guide Jing to it, his only hope being Jing's single-minded intent to force Archie into parrying incessantly, force him to tire. Then Jing would toy with him, torment with a dozen wounds, ridicule and leisurely kill.

Feigning attacks, turning Jing to deflect a thrust, Archie struggled to manipulate the conflict across the floor without Jing grasping his plan. And Jing took no notice; his focus being that Archie's will was fading along with his strength, with only his memory serving to call up waning skills to withstand the onslaught.

Archie's moment came. Switching his sword hand puzzled Jing for a moment and although he warded off the multiple blows and nicked Archie across the chest, Jing pranced too quickly to the side, stepped on the wooden cog, and rolled his ankle over. Pain shot up his leg and—desperate to save his balance—his sword hand and arm went down. He saw the arc of Archie's blade and knew he was helpless to impede it.

The short blade scored him from groin to collarbone.

Jing stammered, then fell to the floor; his anger streaming out with his blood. Confused, he watched an exhausted Archie barely able to stand, "So, Feng Yün-shan, why do you not kill me?"

"That has already been done, Jing Joeng."

Archie kicked Jing's sword away, leaned over on his own sword, and, with thumb and forefinger, closed Jing's eyes.

Monar came to support a weary Archie, but he refused help.

"I saw what you were up to Archie. What's all this talk of honor? Wasn't that a bit ah…debatable?"

"Honor is not considered where my life is at risk. He was clumsy. Now, give me my revolver, I've other scores to settle."

Archie lurched over to the elder who gave Jing his sword, "I heard you tell Jing to tire me out."

Archie put the barrel to his chest, pulled the trigger. After that, he went to another elder, "You tried to warn Jing over the geta."

That person dead, he put on the apricot, Sleeping Dragon Robe.

Archie demanded absolute obeisance and silence from the remaining elders about the night's incident and gave orders to have a rickshaw at the *Devon* on the morn.

The guards who were at the front of the building had fled from the first sounds of gunfire, knowing that daggers couldn't combat guns, and now Monar and Archie rode toward the ship in a two-person rickshaw. Archie had barely the strength to tell the remaining elders to have all leaders and elders present at the house the next evening, without giving any reason. "Any absent elders," he said, "would be tracked down." No need to finish the sentence.

"I'm sore, Monar, and I admit it, sore and old. I couldn't go through that again, and I don't want to."

"That was a dumb challenge and you lucked out."

"I know, but as my missionary mother said, 'pride goes before a fall'. I had to do it or I wouldn't stand a chance regaining the Dragon."

"You still have to go up against the Governor of Canton."

"I already have a plan for him."

"Really? Then let me hear it."

"All in good time my friend, all in good time."

They rode on in silence, Monar knowing Archie wanted, or rather needed, to quiet his mind in that inexplicable Zen discipline his Oriental mind conjured when seeking for the Truth of this night…the absolute crux—its *meaning*. Archie had no doubt he was chosen, a singular presence for this time and place. He was spirit more than creature. Tonight was proof once again. He knew his Dragon Saint, shén long bi hu, had provided the geta.

With Archie enfolded in his spell, Monar considered his own impressions of the night. He could only think that Archie was lucky, or made his own luck. Whichever, the man had some sort of guiding star over him. Still, he should take care, that slight slice across his chest should be a warning; even stars die.

The other musing that seeped past a reluctant mind was Monar's realization he'd known fright. The fright that Archie was going to die. That Jing would cripple him and slowly carve him up. At the time, Monar felt his revolver elevate toward Jing. Damn any honor he thought. His finger had tightened on the trigger; the sole hesitation came from seeing the shoe and following Archie's treachery to its end.

Monar shook his head. He cared too much for this damn half Chinese, half-English assassin.

"My son, Matthew is going to become Dragon Leader while we're off in Japan."

Dropping the comment so matter-of-factly, Monar couldn't believe he heard correctly.

"What the devil are you saying? That's throwing Matt to the wolves, Archie, he's only fourteen—they'll eat him alive."

"You have no faith in my son?"

"Of course I do, but Christ, Archie, he's *fourteen*, a boy."

"He's more than that; he is Archibald Feng Yün-shan's son and I will instruct him in his duties."

Archie went on to explain the scheme of his plan and though Monar remained doubtful, it *could* happen and Archie was resolute.

«»

The meeting with the elders and leaders of the Sleeping Dragon Society convened. Archie swaggered in, more bluster than confidence and looked about severely. A wave of shock engulfed the meeting. The former Leader, the Founder of the Sleeping

Dragon had returned! Delight and anger churned then boiled as senior members, with their bodyguards, readied for an all-out Tong bloodbath to begin. Stepping into the tension, Archie allowed none of it, ordering the member's guards to leave. Finding some confrontation to his order, he took out his revolver and short sword.

"You will obey, *now*!"

He stared the group down; glaring at the one person he thought would give the most resistance. Begrudgingly, the man told his guard to wait outside and the other's hastily followed suit. Archie now knew his main adversary and planned accordingly.

"All of you older elders here know me, my name, and my repute. For those too young to know or think to be indifferent to me, I will inform you once and warn you—take to heart what I say.

I am Archibald Feng Yün-shan. *The* founder of The Empire of the Sleeping Dragon Society. Do not so much as smirk, you younger ones for I am protected by Shi-shin who's image is of dragon riding tortoise, and intent is that of the Black Warrior…"

The younger locale leaders stared at Monar and stopped smiling.

"…and the name Feng, the mark of the Phoenix…"

Mixing myth and his own creativity, Archie played his listeners, "And, for you who do not understand, last night I rose as a Phoenix, and *slew the false leader who thought he could take that which was mine!*"

His shout reverberated about the room and the realization sank in. Jing Joene was dead—the Dragon's Founder had returned!

For the most part, those present were in agreement or unconcerned and that was enough for Archie to feel secure in advancing to the next step of his plan, "I will name five elders from among you as advisors and counsellors to my leadership."

Archie then went on to name three elders who were present the previous night and two additional from the current group.

Surprised that one of the two he picked was the most obviously disapproving person there, Monar knew Archie always had his reasons and this could be one from the old adages—*always keep your enemies close, in that way you know what they are up to*.

Archie then dazed them, “I will be absent yet again for a while and my son, Matthew Feng Yūn-shan will assume the leadership.”

Though astonished, the members accepted the declaration, knowing nothing of the son and thinking he would be necessary merely as a figurehead; Archie would still hold the power.

“Yes, he is young, yet he speaks and writes both Mandarin and Cantonese and also English and much of Japan Hihongo—how many of you can say that?”

It was safe to say, no one knew any language other than Cantonese. Even Archie, despite his English mother’s teaching, did not know Mandarin or Japanese.

To reinforce his son’s age, Archie also reminded them that when the Heavenly Kingdom’s, Hong Xiuquan, abdicated to his son, Tianguifu, during the Taiping Rebellion, that that boy was only fifteen. Archie purposely omitted the disaster which followed.

He then quickly went on about the member’s tithe to the Dragon would not be increased or enforced for two months—which instantly won them over—and all disputes would be adjudicated fairly by the elders without bias. Archie then undertook other matters bothering the members.

With questions answered acceptably, the meeting ended, Archie asking the five elders to go into private discussion with him. He heard all their grievances out with apparent solutions, excepting resistance of one, Lio Zongtang, from the member assembly.

That resistance had to be resolved, so Archie whispered to the man, that if he would go along, he would make him an individual proposition. After the elder agreed, obviously thinking of personal gain, they met privately on the wharf. It took but a moment for the assassin in Archie to thrust a dagger under the man’s ribs into his heart. He helped the gasping man to the edge of the wharf and gave him a shove.

His blade rinsed, Archie recalled this being somewhere around the twelfth time the river had washed away any difficulty.

At the follow-up meeting, Archie mentioned that elder Lio Zongtang had decided to retire to Nepal. When no one questioned, Archie's next assertion was that, Lio and former Leader Jing's assets would be turned over to the Dragon's new Leader, Matthew Feng-Yūn Shan.

To smooth over any problem with the Manchu Qing's Canton Governor, Po-Kuei, the tithe the Sleeping Dragon paid him was raised by half. Archie knew his trade and that person's weaknesses would secure his son's station. There were certainly enough merchants and wealthy Chinese needing protection from roving gangs, such as the Dragon's. Then again, he'd see to it that all but one gang vanished.

When Monar brought up the subject of the retiring Lio Zongtang, Archie was not evasive. Lio, he said, would have been a constant thorn to Matthew's position. And now it was convenient, with only four elders, any decision ending in a tie would be decided by his son. Once again, all Monar was left with was the uncomfortable feeling that although Archie was all too ready to kill anyone, it always seemed justified, expedient and, in the long run, to sadly make sense.

Harry Scrimshaw, kept in the dark on the bloodletting within the Sleeping Dragon, began to recognize there were fewer demands, in fact no demands occurred, and that all of the Qing's port authorities became quite courteous to him and his employees. Harry didn't ask why, assumed this was due to Archie, and simply appreciated that fact.

When Monar and Archie came to understand the pressure that Harry had been operating under they began to recognize his value.

The Taiping Rebellion was only now ending with a postulation of twenty million dead. The Dugan Revolt, started two years previously along the Yellow River by the Hui and other Muslin factions, had spilled over into western China. Aside from the horrendous slaughter of entire cities, both revolts had devastated the thriving commercial industry and basic operational functions of entire regions were shattered. Chaos ensued, thousands more died.

Into all this, Scrimshaw struggled to build on the bones of the blacklisted Black Moon Shipping as well as the added pressure from competing countries from around the world.

Yet in the end, it was the vast poppy fields held by Warfield's private army in Afghanistan, their control of the Khyber Pass and the legalization of the opium trade—forced on the Chinese by the British government—that kept a monopoly that for all appearances would allow the Blue Diamond Line to eventually flourish. As long that is, as pockets of costly kimonos were lined with coin. It was the same theme sung to the same tune. The unrelenting opium trade would continue to rear its ugly head. And, once again Archie Feng's connivance with Canton's Governor would, ultimately, find the restart Warfield's grip on commerce along the China coast.

«»

"Jae Gae is not a person to easily describe." Harry Scrimshaw warned Monar, Archie and the children before the man arrived. At four foot, two inches, one hundred twenty-five pounds of bulging muscle, people found the man difficult to ignore—despite how they tried. Yet more than size, his face, a face that drew eyes unwillingly to it, virtually defied description. It could not be written off simply as dreadfully broken.

"It's more than that." Scrimshaw said, "If you manage to look deeper, you'll see it's scarred, beaten countless times I think, until all that survives is distorted into a dreadful facade, out from which one dark eye glares at you—quite like an unbalanced Cyclops."

Scrimshaw had found the man when asking about for someone who knew Japan, its people, their business practices and was fluent in English and the Japanese language, known as Nihongo.

Those were difficult requirements, but Scrimshaw found Gae a more than ideal candidate—apart from his appearance.

Harry thought he had done well describing Jae Gae while the man rolled bandy-legged up the gangway and sustained his rolling gait toward his welcoming quintet.

"I forgot to mention he was bowlegged too, Monar."

Monar tried not to laugh, "True, still you did a good to excellent report on the face."

Jae Gae looked up at Monar, a crevice of a mouth opened, "If you're making fun of me, you black, oversized oaf, you'll find trouble."

Monar took a gamble, "No, sir, I'm smiling it Harry's description of you—he left out the bandy-legged part."

The crevice opened more, a low rumble taken as a laugh was released, and "Sounds like Mr. Scrimshaw tried to be kind."

And with that start, they asked, and then listened to Jae Gae weave, with, amazingly, an Irish brogue, a cruel saga, seldom told.

"I believe I was born in Gwangju, southwest Korea, the Jeolla Region called the three Kingdoms. I was found along the Gwangju River by an old farmer looking for a stray goat and found me, just like Moses—at least that's what he said. He told me he thought I was thrown in the river because I was so misshapen. It was pretty obvious to him that no one in their right mind would want to be burdened with someone so crippled they couldn't even work in the fields. And, in truth, the more I learned from him it was obvious that *he* wasn't in his right mind. He was an old holy man and said I was his cross to bear, that I was his affliction and penitence for losing faith in Buddhism, Catholicism, Shamanism and lastly Cheondoism. Yet he stayed with Cheondoism because he said they don't believe in an afterlife, so, there was no devil to bedevil him in death."

Laughing at some vague memory, Gae continued, "Although he was not a mean man, he could do mean things. For years I slept in the barn like any other animal, which wasn't too bad especially in the winter when the animals gave off heat. But mainly I had to sort of hop and slither about on all fours doing my chores until I learned to walk on my—as you said—bandy legs…"

"How old were you then, when you learned to walk?"

"I *think* around twelve, I've never had a birthday to know and I think I'm probably fifty by now, maybe more."

"How did you learn all that you have?"

"Ah, therein is another tale. Sunday I could go to the Catholic school run by Korean nuns and an American priest, his name was Duffy, Father Colin Duffy and he taught me English—or should I say American—with, I didn't know it then, this Irish brogue. He was brilliant, wasted there in that school most of his life, but he became my god. He loved me and when he saw that I, for some strange reason, had a quirk for languages, he gave me books and more books. I think I was born to highbrow, scholarly people who had sinned and some nasty god punished them with me…"

The offhanded remark was curious and Collie Graves, though young, saw the flaw in the statement, "But, sir, why should God punish *you*? You weren't to blame."

Gae stared so long and hard at Collie he appeared frozen in time, "You are very profound, my fledgling. Why indeed? I must rethink my thoughts on nasty gods yet again."

Monar was proud of Collie. The boy, not yet ten, had asked a shrewd question and not flinched from Gae's frown.

Mark, Collie's older brother had waited patiently while listening to Gae, yet he couldn't refrain from asking the question everyone wanted answered, "Tell me, Mr. Gae, sir, were you born with that face too?"

Monar was uncomfortable; Archie simply curious, but Gae expected the query, "No, and I'll be brief. My owner sold me to a man owning a group of performers who traveled Asia and I was made the freak in the show. Over the following years we toured in China, Manchuria and all through islands of Japan. That's where I learned the languages and even dialects. Then, one night I thoughtlessly spoke up about the owner taking his whip to the bears. The whip had a small metal barb on the tip and he turned it on me, I fainted so don't know how many times he whipped me. That was when my face was shredded and I lost an eye."

They were all angry and Archie spoke for all, "I hope you got even with the bastard!"

"Unfortunately, no. The people were afraid of being out of work, so they paid a laborer to take me back to Father Duffy. I did hear sometime later that they got the owner drunk and left him in with the bears. But I doubted that as then they would have been out of a job—wouldn't they now? But it was comfortable thinking it.

And now, gentlemen, with that recited, Mr. Scrimshaw told me you wanted a translator for Nippon, so who are you and what is it you want from me…I mean…more than is spoken?"

They explained what they needed from Jae Gae. Someone who could translate; who knew the Japanese processes required for trade and, as importantly, the Japanese mind and the meaning behind their words and who was not afraid to speak up, or when to play a mute.

"All right then, I won't bother you with the spectacular history of the former Hermit Kingdom; you can read that somewhere else if you care to. I'll simply state that Nippon, or as you call it, Japan—the entire nation is of one mind—insular. They were forced to let the foreign barbarian enter and most of Nippon still resent the barbarian and that unquestionably means *your* presence. The white race has interfered with the Emperor and the Shogun's vision of Nippon versus a coarse and detestable world."

Jae continued, "Actually, the steps to that happening were the Portuguese, then Jesuit missionaries and a few American whalers in trouble. Yet the major problem began—for the Japanese that is—ten or twelve years back when that American Navy Commodore, Perry, and his Black Warships thrust their way into the harbor of Edo—you know it as Tokio—and forced a treaty down their throats. That's my short version. There were some battles with western weapons in there, but Perry was the major reason for what has followed."

Here, looking to Scrimshaw for support, Gae explained that he was in Manchuria in '63 and the first part of this year in China, so he didn't have the whole story of what followed.

Harry picked up the story, “From what I’ve learned, there’s been unrest for years between the Tokugawa Shogunate—that’s Japan’s leadership—and westerners. From this, Emperor Kōmei suddenly issued an Imperial decree, a sonnō jōi, in the middle of last year ordering the ‘expulsion of the barbarians’.

While they absorbed his words, Scrimshaw looked to his notes and then continued, “When I was in Shanghai, I spoke with a Captain Simon Cooper of the Merchant ship *SS Pembroke*. He told me that what he found out later was some Japanese Lord decided to take matters in his own hands and fired on his ship when she was at anchor below Japanese gun emplacements at the Shimonoseki Straits. I’ve since found out it was a Lord Takachika of the Chōshū Domain who ordered it. After the battering of the *Pembroke*, it snowballed into a real donnybrook.”

Monar was getting impatient, “So get to the point, what does all this mean as far as it affects us?”

“Listen, it’s important you know what you’re heading into.”

This time it was Archie, laughing, “Monar—let him have his say, the sooner he’s done, the sooner we’re gone. So be a good bloke and get on with it, Harry.”

Harry did not to take the good-natured joshing well, looking back at his notes, “Look, I’ve broken my butt to get this information and you’re going to hear it, like it or not! Now, it was after the *Pembroke* and a French navy steamer was fired on when a Dutch warship called *Medusa* was pounded badly. Anyway—long story hopefully short enough for you—a minor naval battle started when a US Naval ship and a French Naval ship joined in. That became a diplomatic nightmare for the west and it went on for months. Japanese gangs destroyed churches, factories, and shipping, including the US Consulate offices in Tokio. Finally, we Brits had enough of it and decided on a show of force. Unfortunately, the French fleet was bogged down trying to keep Maximilian on the Mexican throne, so they weren’t much help. The Americans? Well, they’re in that horrific civil war of theirs, so it fell on us to do something. The Royal Navy scraped together fifteen ships and a regiment from Hong Kong, the French added two ships and after a two day battle in the strait between Honshū and Kyūshū—just this past September in fact—the Chōshū forces, the same ones who pushed to *expel the barbarians* in the first place—and other rebels, including some Prince of Nagato, were badly beaten and gave way.

"So that revolt is wrapped up. And I think it means you should be at least *tolerated* there and Gae with his contacts will help. But, a word of warning, expect angry rabble-rousers in their own land. In other words don't let your guard down."

Archie was the first to respond, "God, don't tell me you've finally finished?"

Harry was now irritated, "Yes, damn it! Warfield told me to help you and it's taken me weeks to get this information while I'm trying to build—or should I say rebuild—Warfield's business here!"

Archie replied in kind, "What do you want, Harry? A thank you? Look, I'd bet I've done more for your business by buying off Governor Po-Kuei than you have in all the time you've been plodding around under a bogus burgee. Trying to start a straightforward business deal with Po-Kuei is worthless. This is all about graft for Christ sake! You slip them a little, you get a lot. Get that through your thick skull 'cause if you don't you'll be useless to Warfield here. He knows it; we know it, it's time you knew it!"

Archie was too blunt and Scrimshaw, now doing a slow burn, turned to Monar, but found no backing there. Gae and the children had sat back, listening, trying to show no emotion.

"All right, Archie, you've had your say, now I'll have mine! I'm sick of the way *you* do business too. Someone angers you—or is simply in the way—you kill them. You *kill* them! You think I'm blind to what's going on! For God's sake, *what's wrong* with you?"

Tactless, Archie retorted, "I'm thinking that's not such a bad idea right now, because your saintliness is sticking in my craw."

Into this dodgy situation Monar moved between them, not saying a word at first, letting their words fade, then speaking, "I'm not going to be the mediator between you two…" as he said it, he wondered if indeed that *was* Warfield's plan all along "…over your

God damn petty squabbles. Warfield gave us a job to do, so let's get to it. Harry, do you have any more information for us?"

"Other than discussing Gae's contacts in Japan with you, no."

"We can do that when we're underway. That's it, we go!"

At the time, Scrimshaw was so angry he forgot to mention the Anglo-Satsuma war in 1863, the Hamagun Gate war in 1864, or the constant assassinations that continued against all Europeans. They should be made aware of this. Not that it would have made a difference to Archie Feng—he ignored warnings, he was sacred.

«»

1 January 1866 New Year's Day, on the *Devon*

Another day under power as they had glided north by east between the Chinese Mainland and the island of Formosa. Twice, they out-sailed Mandarin Chinese brigands who kept firing off dozens of short range cannonballs and rockets. Archie knew the shooting was simply for effect. The brigands would never dare try an actual contest with a Blackwall frigate. But Archie also knew they would return to Canton or Shanghai and report the destruction of still another opium carrying, barbarian ship. Everyone in government was in on the hoax, rewards made, funds would fade away and everyone would appear vindicated—they were doing their best to reduce the opium trade. At the last sham assault, Archie had half a mind to come about and challenge them, yet why? He'd have done the same in their position. Everyone needs their rice bowl. Such was China under the thumb of the European.

The *Devon* eased northeast into the Japanese Ryukyu Island chain, and passed into the North Philippine Sea between the small, volcanic island of Iwo-Tori-Shima and the largest island in the chain, Okinawa-shima. Now, it was north past the grander southern island of Kiūshiū where the Aso-san Volcano on that island smoldered, laying a light coat of ash on the deck of the *Devon*. The next goal was the main Japanese island, Honshu, and then to Edo, the city known to the west as Tokio.

«»

Jae Gae was blunt. Previously he had people to help all along the Tokio Bay docks and hopefully, they may still be there. His concern was months that had passed and even though Japanese were patient, there was a limit, so Gae wished, more than hoped, they would still be around to aid them.

Added to his unease, he had left Japan before their civil war blazed and finally weakened, so there again, malcontents were common and he had no idea how many of his contacts survived.

Gae did manage to fill in blanks in Scrimshaw's lecture and told them American's had been quite active in Japanese trade to the point that there was a Japanese Embassy in the States since 1860. Also, one had been in London from '62, when England and Japan had signed the London Protocol. That protocol acknowledged there would be resistance by the Imperial Court and the population to the opening of certain ports to foreigners. 'Resistance' was the couched term for outright hatred of the foreigner by the majority of Japanese.

Still, Archie was indifferent to Gae's news. The British had the same problem with India and China, he said, and they simply bullied their way in and took over. Gae thought Archie's response—if he continued on that course—would be met with forces he'd never even heard of. The Shinobi, a sect begun in China centuries ago, had journeyed to Japan. China knew them as Nin sha and now, in Japan, what few English had heard of them, knew them as *Ninja*, unseen spies or secret mercenaries dating before the time of feudal Japan. If Archie angered the wrong people enough, well…

Gae knew he was going to have to inform Monar of this sect, its danger and power to them and then hope they could instill some sense into Archie's intransigence. His belief in himself was frightening. His conviction he could sail his own course was a deterrent in negotiating with the Japanese. It was not that Gae worried about Archie; it was the trouble he could cause for them all *before* he was humbled—or worse.

«»

The island of Oshima, with its Mount Mihara, passed to port; the white capped sea of Sagmi Bay gave way to the unruffled Uraga Channel. Gae pointed to the twelve-thousand foot, snowcapped peak of Mount Fiji-san to their north, then pointed to the lifeless volcano mounts of Tanzawa, Ashitawa and others stretching off to the northeast. At last, into the channels mouth. Tokio beckoned.

Sails reefed, her Union Jack and Black Moon burgee snapping on mastheads, the *Devon* powered into the vastness of Tokio Bay. Then, easing away to starboard as Gae directed, she moored off five western vessels along the village port of Ichihara.

Jae Gae thought it best to go ashore alone to assess the situation and answer one important question. Who had the power?

For two perturbing hours, Archie and Monar fretted and, while noticing the other moored ships had only the Port Watch aboard, they took turns with the spyglass, scanning along the landscape.

It was time, they both decided, to open Warfield's letter, ***Open When Reaching Japan.*** The precise, brief message was an order meant for them alone, not Scrimshaw, not any other persons.

If Scrimshaw has done his job, you should have a well-informed person. It is your call; give the 'main cargo' to the group most likely to win the empire. However, and this is important—somehow track down a Japanese Naval Captain, Eiji Himura. I met him in Portsmouth in '62 and he thinks along our lines. Unless I'm dreadfully wrong, he's our man. Warfield

They were not surprised. Warfield long knew there was unrest and revolt in Japan and the letter stated he wanted them to gamble on the victor. And that was who—this Himura? It was a huge burden placed on them. If they were correct, riches for those who assisted the victor would unfold, if wrong; cut your losses and run was Warfield's motto. For no matter what, he'd still be wealthy. Still, how the devil were they to find this Captain?

Nonetheless, Archie and Monar accepted the challenge. Warfield was rubbing off on them, they felt the passion. And for that damnable passion, squash your opponent. But did they have Warfield's gut intuition? Gae had some idea of the difficulties ahead, yet Monar and Archie—and in truth Warfield—had little inkling of the task ahead. Japan was a powerful, secretive world. Yet she was still another world at war within and, given the amount of English blood spent in India and China, would Japan prove even more difficult to dominate?

A vessel, obviously Japanese Navy by her flag, was glimpsed under steam approaching and, coming abreast, reversed engine to lay to alongside. Curiosity and concern were relieved when Gae was seen among the ship's sailors waving across at the *Devon*.

He was lifted aboard and helped to stand, "Well, I'm honored. You're making me feel like an important person. To what I do owe to such distinct service?"

Monar had to grin, "Well, Jae, we're only now realizing you're our only contact with the inside world around here."

Archie looked over the gunwale, "You got someone waiting for you over there?"

Gae hadn't forgotten, "Yes, it is a friend, an important friend. He is Captain Himura Eiji, and remember, it is the same here as in China: the surname is first, the given name is second…"

Monar and Archie traded glances. Himura. That was the name in Warfield's letter to them, Eiji Himura. They couldn't help wonder what the chances of this happening were.

Gae continued, "…so refer to him as Captain Himura. He is Samurai and one of the Shoguns of the Chōshū Han."

"We're not following you, Gae."

Mark Graves stepped forward, "I can tell you! Samurai means military warrior, Shogun means he is military commander and Han means Domain or region. Isn't that right Mr. Gae?"

"Very good, Mark. And in its entirety I think that means he could be very important to us. He asks to come aboard to look over the *Devon*. I suggest we do not keep him waiting any longer."

Although the *Devon* was a Frigate laid down along Royal Navy lines at Blackwall, on the Thames River, she was not Royal Navy so no formal piping aboard was conducted.

Captain Himura understood this as he was welcomed aboard with the best of manners while Gae introduced Archie Feng, Prince Monar and the boys, all of whom nodded and his shook hand. True, this was not prescribed courtesy, yet Himura bore about him an air of decorum, not unfriendly, simply more reserved as he bowed slightly to each.

"Had you raised a clipper ship called the *Houqua* out of Yokohama?" Himura soon asked, "She sailed from there last year and hasn't been heard of since. My son is a mid-shipman on her and she should have returned by now."

They had no knowledge of the *Houqua* and Monar noticed that Himura seemed to know the answer before Gae told him. Perhaps, Monar thought, the Japanese captain saw the look on his face or, contrariwise, did the captain understand English? That would make it best to watch one's words.

He was shown about the ship, impressed by her overall construction, crew, and armament…especially her armament.

Complimenting Archie, *Devon's* captain, Himura then smiled at Monar and, with English more correct than either Archie or Monar spoke, asked if the three men and the children would be available for dinner this evening. Without question, they would make themselves available.

Himura issued a limited pass allowing the *Devon's* crew to have shore leave, yet confining and warning them to stay in a specific, conscribed area in Ichihara. His five guests were then assisted to the steam warship *Karin Maru*. The ship, Himura informed, was the first Japanese warship to be schooner rigged with the added advantage of steam power through a single screw. Made in the Netherlands, he said, and delivered eight years past, in 1857.

It came about that Captain Himura knew southern England quite well; after leaving the Dutch Naval Training Center at Tsukiji, he received advanced command tutoring at the Royal Naval College in Dartmouth, County Devon, England. Devon, which improbably happened to be the name of Archie's ship.

Himura laughed when mentioning the training there. As recently as 1863, when he was present, the college consisted of two moored hulks, HMS *Britannia* and HMS *Hindustan*. Certainly not the proper billet for a Japanese Navy Captain and Shogun in the Chōshū Domain. Nevertheless, he said, a great deal was learned.

Gae winced nervously. In the past, Himura's Chōshū Clan was in league with the Emperor's effort to expel the barbarians. The very Clan soundly beaten by British warships massively shelling Chōshū shore batteries. This was back in '63, when Himura said he was in England and, at the moment, he appeared comfortable conversing under a British flag and British company burgee. Gae unware the British changed allegiances to support the two clans, wisely decided to wait and see what unfolded.

The *Karin Maru* docked at the naval base in Ichihara and, while riding in an open coach bundled against the cold, Gae introduced Mark and Collie to Himura. As they were children, Gae inadvertently omitted their last name and Himura became confused, wondering about the two children. Apparently, crew members, he thought, so why were they here? They were white. Archie was Chinese and Monar assuredly black, certainly not their children. Himura decided to hide his curiosity, but not ignore them.

While Gae pointed out the sights, Captain Himura Eiji switched his curiosity from the boys to the *Devon.* Why were she and her men in Japan and asked about her cargo. Before they arrived at Himura's home, Monar only went so far as mentioning they carried examples of steel train rail, iron plating, lathes and wanted to present a viable proposal to the government for a contract for the first Japanese railroad system.

At the entrance to Edo Castle, his hilltop estate, they passed four expressionless samurai guards and once inside five geisha's attended to their every need. The food was strange to them, but editable, although difficult to eat with chopsticks. Laughter ensued and continued until knives, forks and spoons were supplied.

After the men retired to another room and geisha stayed to amuse the boys, Monar asked the question, "Do you know a gentleman by the name of Lord Warfield Bunting?"

Humira sat back, hands folded, eyes lidded. Finally, he answered the question with a question, "Why do you ask?"

"Well, as strange as it may sound, this meeting is a fluke to say the least. We have a letter from Warfield suggesting we find and meet with you, and we didn't know how or where to begin, and then suddenly there you are out of the blue."

"If you've a letter from Warfield mentioning me, then you must have the weapons."

Both men couldn't mask their unease. Gae, on the other hand, was confounded and couldn't mask it.

Himura was amused, "Gentlemen, I can see by your faces that two of you know what rests in your cargo hold and one does not."

Their silence answering for them, Himura settled back and explained the circumstances surrounding his knowledge, "I met Lord Warfield when I was enrolled at the Naval School I previously mentioned in Dartmouth. In fact, he sought me out, we met a number of times at his Blackwood Abbey, and although he spoke of you and your endeavors, we never chanced to meet. I somehow think he wanted it that way. Yet he also mentioned a Captain John Graves who married his daughter, Evelyn. Is he retired with her, no longer with you in your adventures?"

The moment he spoke, the look on their faces made Himura regret his words. It was left to Monar to speak up, "Evelyn, and her baby Vicky died of cholera. John Thomas died during the American Civil War.

Placing his head in his hands, Himura was humbled, "There are times when one should reason things through before speaking words that become the cause of sorrow. Please, I ask that you will forgive my thoughtlessness."

"It was thoughtless of *us*; you would have had no way of knowing what occurred in England or that these two boys with us are John Thomas and Evelyn Graves' children. So, there is nothing to forgive. Please, just go on with your meeting with Warfield."

Himura maintained his composure and straightened, "I am sorry for what has occurred to sadden many people. Yes, about those meetings. Lord Warfield and I discussed the, ah, *condition*, of Japan back then and about its future. We saw eye to eye—as you British say, and agreed Japan had no choice but to open itself to the west. It was then we recognized we could help each other. The problem was I was in England when my Clan, the Chōshū and the Satsuma moved before getting the facts and sided with Emperor Kōmei to expel the Barbarians. The British bloodied our noses badly by our failure to look at both sides of the same coin.

Himura went on, "Nippon is an oligarchy and Emperor Kōmei our religious and political leader, right, or wrong, so it is written. However, the House of Tokugawa, his military Shogunate, is an autocracy, a dictatorship, and he has become more powerful than the Emperor, despite being the rightful ruler of Japan."

Monar was curious, "How could that happen?"

"You are surprised? Isn't the American President subject to the powerful people in his country and government, or the Queen of England subject to formidable people behind the throne? How many times have English Kings been constrained or overthrown or beheaded?"

"I'm not really caught up on beheadings or leadership, but in a way I suppose you've a point. Yet is it that clear-cut here?"

"Yes, and if Warfield sent you to find me, I will be most frank. He knows we intend to bring down the Tokugawa Shogunate. To do this, Sagiō of the Satsuma Domain and Kido, of my Chōshū Domain, are uniting. Lord Warfield is championing our cause in England and will help us reach our ambitions. Your cargo is solely the initial step. If your Lord Warfield continues to support us he will benefit from that kindness. So, make no mistake, there will be battles, yes, and it may take years, yes, but we will restore the Meiji to power. Trust me on this—that we will do!"

8

26 March, 1866. The mountain castle of Samurai Kido Takayosi
"I CAN NO LONGER STAND that damn interfering Chinaman!"

Satsuma Clan's true Leader, Takamori, nodded in agreement with Takayosi, the army commander of the Chōshū Clan.

"So what is your proposal?"

Takayosi turned and stared blankly at Jae Gae who raised his hands in supplication, "It is not for me to propose. If you wish divine punishment, I am here to obey that I am ordered."

"Yet you agree with us this Archie Feng Yūn-shan transcends that of a frenzied typhoon?"

"Yes, my Lord. He is that many times over. Yet I ask that you please keep in mind we have another to consider. His friend, and our friend, Prince Monar speaks for Lord Warfield and could wreak havoc on the future well-being of your Domains if there is any suspicion we contemplate a covert endeavor affecting Feng."

"Yet Prince Monar agrees this Feng causes us dilemmas."

"That is yes. And he has done his best to stop the man's brazen insolence to our leaders. My personal thought on the matter is that Feng believes he has become immortal, impervious from mere humans. I also think, despite his being half English, that he considers the Japanese to be inferior to the Chinese."

"He will learn that error in his judgement *if* he lives long enough to be taught, which, as we speak, is the question."

Sagio Takayosi was cautious, "We must not speak too freely or be careless. Prince Monar is desirable to our plans and as Gae now warns, there cannot be even the minutest risk of him to become wary for what must be done. We must rid ourselves of this disrespectful beetle. Now, I voice to you outright, my Chōshū Domain will no longer accept that Chinaman's insolence and his impeding of our endeavors. Tell me, and speak true, Gae, do you see Prince Monar ever obstructing the Chinaman's affronts?"

"I fear he will not. He says little, yet knows Archie Feng thinks he is fleckless and has become a loose cannon to our strategies."

"I have not heard that term, yet it is understood. Do you know what we are asking you? It is a hazard for Samurai to be involved."

"Yes, my Lords. I do understand, with regret."

"Regret will be enough confirmation of your penitence."

It was true. Archie Feng had been a thorn in Monar's side from the moment he stepped ashore in Japan and acted the conqueror. If it hadn't been the Japanese leaders respect for Monar, Archie would have been driven away long before. However, they had let their anger fester until it was too late to simply rid Japan of him. He had to forfeit his life, he'd become an insult to the Bushido Code of the Warrior, the Samurai.

Samurai, the warrior class, were feared by the common people; nevertheless they still retained a strict code of honor—however flawed to westerners. Eliminating Archie would normally be a simple matter, but Samurai could not be straightforward in this. Any hint the two Clans were behind the deed would anger Prince Monar, and through him, Warfield Bunting, the clan's patron.

It was left to Gae to be the messenger to a clandestine, furtive realm—the way of Ninjutsu—the Ninja. Ninja were markedly dissimilar from Samurai. Slowly evolving centuries past from Chinese peasants and priests joining together for self-protection against marauders, Ninja, through time, transformed. Now devolved into paid predators, they were assassins, spies, hiding in the shadows, without a civilized, moral dogmata. They would covertly strike any person, by any means—of course for a fee.

By 1800, and the Tokugawa Shogunate, Ninja and its ancient, enigmatic history had near vanished in the mists of remembrance.

In Gae's opinion, their history verified they should be left in the mists for what they were. Yet recently, signs they had seemingly resurfaced appeared and whether the Tokugawan Domain's leader,

Iemochi, had any hand in this or not, Gae had no idea. Still, and suspiciously, he felt it was Captain Eiji Humira who slipped surreptitiously into his room and left a missive—or rather, a note and sealed sack stating where and when to wait—this very evening.

It was a night for Ninja. The damp vapor from the bay gave way to murky swirls around the rickshaw, shrouding the runner and Gae as they travelled through the sleeping, tomb-like village.

Gae had to stifle his fears. The Shimaana-jina Shinto Shrine, the note read. This midnight. Cross over the bridge in front. Lean on the left entry post. Face away from the shrine's entrance. Wait.

He was to have the rickshaw runner stay fifty yards back down the road, the note finished. The only other instructions were to write the quarry's name, his location, the time required for his death and, finally, he was to supply this information and the payment in the cloth sack.

Gae leaned against the post straining under the tension. He was a strong, little man yet knew he would stand no chance in the dark and stopped wondering who had supplied his instructions and well knew querying could easily make *him* the next recipient. And, as he gave it further thought, he may be on a list that could further isolate the originators from the deed.

The other problem was that, if Monar found out what was to happen, there would be the devil to pay. Gae shivered. The thought was as terrifying as the all-enveloping dampness.

Well, he justified, if Feng hadn't been so damn annoyingly meddlesome, none of this would have been necessa…

Shadows entangled in shadows moved about, alarming him. Scarcely formed, faces obscured under peasant straw sunhats, were close. A hand, grime covered, reached out. Fear gripped him. What if these were robbers, not his…

"Ninjutsu."

He sighed in relief; recognized the dialect of Kōga, the idiom correct. He handed over the cloth bag and note and rushed—as well as Gae's bandy legs could rush—back to the safety of the rickshaw.

«»

At the private dock of the Chōshū Clan, under cover of the same dark that enclosed Gae, the *Devon* disgorged an amazing array of armament. Fifteen hundred British Enfield rifles, one hundred-thousand bullets, twenty, thirty-four pounder howitzers, five-thousand exploding shells, keg after keg of gun powder and—leave it to Warfield—his friendship with Edward Vickers, the steel magnate, allowed him to acquire five new, rapid fire weapons, unheard of in Asia, Maxim machineguns.

Among other products, aside from the clandestine cargo, were sections of railroad track from Vickers & Sons Steel in Sheffield and two downsized models of Hunset-Vickers locomotive steam engines from Manchester as well as lathes and water powered industrial equipment and tooling.

Monar was glad to be rid of the cargo before any opposing forces got wind of the weapons. It also assured negotiations for developing Japan's first railroad system would supersede efforts of the United States. This would be a major feather for Warfield's prestige and lead to iron bridge construction, stations, and every other related product. And there was the tea. Supplied from India, rather than China, Warfield's highly profitable product would eventually take over the Japanese marketplace as he had planned long past.

As icing on the cake, the *Devon's* return cargo would consist primarily of raw silk, lacquerware, and Japanning—becoming the rage in England, along with copper and pottery.

Despite Monar's conciliations, Archie, for some unfathomable reason continued on his harmful course. Nothing and no one pleased him or was beyond his complaint. At last, it came to a head, Monar reached his limit, "I'm no longer putting up with the trouble you're causing, Archie. I'm at wit's end. This is the last time I'm going to ask—what in bloody *hell* is wrong with you?"

Archie frowned, yet continued his indifference to Monar's frustration. He wasn't about to answer. The truth, a truth he would never admit, was he felt slighted—the lesser person. Monar set the agenda. Whereas Archie simply felt an underling to Monar and subservient to the Japanese. He appealed to no one. When he spoke of his Empire of the Sleeping Dragon they were vaguely amused, yet chiefly disinterested. For a man with his conceit, being overlooked throughout the negotiations was demeaning.

To compensate for the slight, Archie found fault in every discussion of the give and take necessary with the Japanese. Monar, meanwhile, intent on his own efforts saw him only as a problem, not thinking of the cause. "Look, Archie, would you rather go back to China, find out how your son Matt is doing? Because that's what I'm recommending."

"No I don't wish to go back. Are you trying to get rid of me? You're the boss here now, too big for your boots? Don't need me?"

"Christ, Archie! That's not it at all and you know it! But if you're going to remain hostile to them and don't tell me what your problems are with the agreement, perhaps it's best for all of us if you leave."

That exchange turned out to be Monar's last attempt to draw Archie out; but the effort was met with defiance. Turning on his heel, Archie Feng picked up a bottle of Saki and walked off the *Devon* without another word.

Managing to shut Archie from his mind, Monar went back to studying the last proposal from a Japanese industrial group. It gave Warfield's company sole rights to the development of the projected Honshu Rail Road System and included first options for the rest of the island chain. This secret covenant included a cost plus segment, heavily structured in Warfield's favor, and was to take effect 1 May, 1866. Importantly, on Warfield's insistence through Monar, it thwarted the only other serious competitor—the United States.

Acting as Warfield's agent in Japan, Monar signed the covenant and Jae Gae delivered it to the new offices of the Honshu

RRS. A major factor for the pact was that Monar was black. The Japanese didn't have to negotiate with the despised white man.

Heading for the docks the next morning, Japanese fishermen found Archie face down in a slum lane. They considered him simply another dead drunk except for his clothes. There were clues to expose what came to pass, the shattered Saké bottle, blood pooled about in the dirt and streaked down the side of an abandoned building. It told the tale of a ferocious mêlée and more stains of darkened blood straggled away off into an alley. Another clue revealed when turning over Archie's body; a gore saturated, short-sword handle gripped in his hand, the blade nowhere to be found.

Later, authorities following the trail of the dried blood into the alley found two other bodies, apparently dragged there and abandoned. Both were male, black clad, one with a straw sunhat flattened under his head. Another attacker was forever silent from a short-sword blade jammed between his ribs. Leading from those cadavers, other spots of blackened, crusted blood led further into the alleyway before being lost.

Gae hid his guilt well, his loyalty was to Japan not Archie—a half-Chinaman he never liked from the very beginning. Whether or not Captain Humira felt any complicity, outwardly he displayed only remorse. It was left to the two Graves children to fight back tears; they had liked Archie and would miss him.

The agency handling the crime was indifferent; murders of barbarians were expected and, for that matter, easily tolerated. The only possible interest with them in this instance was they thought the barbarian's attackers acted viciously and, quite remarkably, paid dearly with two dead and at least one other wounded.

Then there was Monar, and Monar went silent. Only when asked what to do with the body did Monar respond, "Clean him up, put on new clothes and seal him in a lead casket."

Other than this, Monar seemed struck mute when learning of the brutishness of Archie's death. He sat in his cabin for hours drinking from a bottle of Scotch and tried to come to grips with the fact Archie was dead. The man was imperishable, Monar thought. To survive other assassins—both government and slum lords—to create the Sleeping Dragon Society, and to kill anyone who opposed it, that was Archie. Yes, he did kill without qualm. Yet, the next thing you knew he'd decide to go off to America with Monar to help rescue John Thomas Graves…when he didn't even *like* JT. The man was unfathomable. Add this to his struggle recovering the Sleeping Dragon from Jing—despite the odds. That was pure Archie. Trickery and death always enjoyed following him around.

Monar took another swig from the bottle and then saw Archie's throwing shuriken, and pistol on the bunk. He shook his head sadly. Archie was so angry when he left he'd forgotten them. It was not like him to forget. His dumb rage cost him his life.

Staring up through the hatch into the starless night, Monar started piecing together the scene. It was easy to think that Archie, in his black mood, probably drunk on Saki, had offended some natives and, to cap it, being a foreign barbarian as well, they waited for him in that alley. It must have been shocking to the muggers when they took him on. Two of them dead, at least one more wounded. All the same, when his short sword snapped—and without his forgotten weapons—Archie was unable to withstand the onslaught. And of course Archie would never run.

Monar tried to blink away the image, but it stayed too long. Yet the more he thought of it, he didn't blame himself. Archie, when one gave thought to it, created his own dark future. He went out of his way to court conflict. Then at last, aggressiveness and old age didn't fit together. His ending was written long ago.

Next came a truth Monar tried to push away. Just as Archie killed people to rid a problem, so too did Archie's death rid Monar.

Monar never gave the first thought that Archie's death had been bought and paid for by people around him.

Although he didn't know until a short time later, when he put his hand on Archie Feng Yün-shan's lead-lined, casket, Monar was on the brink of a decision that would change his course forever.

«»

Eiji Humira was confounded, not wanting to believe his ears.

"What are you saying Monar-san, what does this mean?"

"I said I'm going to take Archie's casket to China, or perhaps on to India. I'm leaving for home, Eiji, and won't return."

"But what of our plans, Prince Monar? There will be battles ahead to free Japan and open us to the West! This is for you and Lord Warfield as well."

"Himura, listen to me. You and your Clans can do this on your own. The rest was all Lord Warfield's plan, to get a foot in the door—your door. Archie and I went along with it as an obligation to Warfield for all he'd done for us. But Archie went and got killed, God bloody it, and something in me died with him. We were going to be two old men with our children, meeting to muse on our pasts now and then. That's gone for him and what I've realized now is that Warfield was using us to achieve *his* vision—not mine, not *yours*. I want to take Archie home to his son or his wife, and then I want to go home to my wife and children. It hit me; I don't want more worlds to win for Warfield. I'm sure he'll find someone to help you, Eiji—someone who still has worlds to conquer."

"I'm disappointed my friend, yet I must face what I saw in your eyes when Archie Feng died. I see your feelings are not here so we will thank you for that you have done to help…"

Eiji hesitant, then asked, "The boys, Lord Warfield's grandsons, you will take them back to him?"

"I haven't thought that far ahead, I'll see them to India at least, then contact Warfield by telegraph as to what he wants done."

"Monar, I have not wanted to bother you with this during these times and Feng's death, but I've word the clipper ship *Houqua* is believed to have gone down with no survivors…"

"You're saying your only son is gone…?"

"Yes, my wife and I will have to accept his passing. This is why I mentioned the boys. If you think they could stay here a while…to help her…well…"

"I can't do that, I'm sorry. They are not mine to give, or loan. Also remember, Eiji, even though young, they are still barbarians to many Japanese. And after what happen to Archie, it would be dangerous to…"

"Yes, of course. You make your point; we've seen Ninjutsu are treacherous. It was just a hope of my wife…you see, she loves them. Even in this short time, we both do."

With Archie's loss and his concern for Humira, Monar didn't notice Jae Gae hadn't been around and no one brought up that fact.

"I'm very sorry, Eiji, I can't do as you wish."

«»

30 May, 1866. The *Devon* entering Canton's Pearl River.
During the voyage back to China, Monar had spent too much time in the darkened bowels of the ship staring at Archie Feng's casket. His mind during these stays often lapsed, returning to the words of Eiji Humira. He said, '*You make your point; we've seen Ninjutsu are treacherous.*'

Why, why did Eiji say *Ninjutsu*? No one else uttered that word.

The words lodged in Monar's memory, at first overlooked, now come forth repeatedly—*Ninja.* Eiji said *Ninjutsu, same thing*. Were Archie's killers *Ninja*? Had Eiji slipped up, *knew* it was the shadow warriors? No one else said that word, not the fishermen, or the Tokio authorities, no one.

Did Gae know of this? Then again, where was Gae when he left Japan? Nowhere around. Not even there to say goodbye. Why not? Gae disliked Archie, and once spoke of Ninja. And others, others were angered by him as well. Was Archie's behavior enough for them to feel *that* insulted—so much as to hire Ninja? Of *course* they were! Even he, Monar had been angry with Archie, and Japanese are quick to feel affronted and even quicker to retaliate. It was becoming too clear, too damn clear.

Monar placed his hand on the casket. He felt physical pain. Not the common physical throbbing of a wound, but the profound ache of loss, of irrevocable leave-taking. When one came right down to it, Archie and he had an unspoken accord, an accord now severed, gone. In truth, the two *were* comrades; they had shared conflicts, each depending on the other. But Monar had failed him because of this, this stab in the back from supposed friends. It must be true.

Monar's curses boomed off the ship's ribs and beams to echo then perish in the clammy gloom of the bilge. Curses, yet they carried little hint for vengeance.

The path had forked away from Warfield's goal, "I'm sorry, Archie, you were wrong, but the greater wrong is they were cowards not giving you a chance. They live without honor. Yet it's no use, I can't go on this way, the constant passion for home, the constant battles to get there. Our paths have to part. I'm past revenge, Archie. I'm getting old and must turn my back to you. Too afraid to lose what I have I guess. I want my wife and children and peace. I..."

Monar faltered, leaned back on the bunk, knowing that even as he spoke the words, if Eiji Humira or Jae Gae ever crossed his path, there would be punishment. Still he pondered, was it them, was it true? No thought was given that now, Gae may be on a list as well.

Leaving the casket, determined to put Archie's death aside, Monar's eyes caught the two Graves boys readying for their dawn duties. From the depressing bilge to dawn, from sadness to a smile when Monar recalled how in Japan, the geisha had so beguiled the boys it took a week to get their minds back to the fact they were again part of the *Devon's* crew.

Well, Monar thought, mourning and revenge must pass. It was time to look forward to a securer life. No—a *better* life for all of us.

Between Macau and Hong Kong they picked up the aging river pilot, Jock MacLeod and steamed upriver for Canton. Harry Scrimshaw and Matthew Feng Yün-shan had to be told of Archie.

Jock MacLeod was a little older, yet remained the teller of tales, spinner of gossip and fount of information, although his first words were to question, “Where’s Archie Feng?”

Monar knew how to answer, “He’s still in Japan, holding down the fort so to speak.”

“Too bad, I wanted to tell him about his son Matthew.”

“What about him—he’s all right?”

“Right as rain, he is. Got everyone hopping and running a tight ship. ‘Course, you bet the fear of Archie returning and cause more bodies floating in the river keeps everyone in line.”

That was the very reason Monar didn’t reveal Archie’s death and before the crew went ashore they’d been told keep quiet under of pain of being left on the beach—without ship or funds.

Jock prattled on without another thought of Archie, “So, what’s things like in Goddamn them all to hell Nippon land?”

“Actually damn near perfect. We’ve had everything go our way and couldn’t ask for more.”

“The devil you say! Blimey, up there with them slant eyed Nips? No one survives that bunch of cutthroat, bloody evil spirits.”

Jock MacLeod was spot on to Monar and he struggled to keep a straight face, “Well all I can say is we did. Now, what’s new around here?”

“If you noticed, there were no pirates coming in, were there?”

“That’s right, what happened?”

“Prince Gong made short work of them and a little uprising up in Fujian. He’s showed everyone who’s the top Chinese dog now.”

“What about Po-kuei?”

“The Governor? Hell bells, young Matthew Feng Yün-shan has him so loaded down with British silver he jingles when he walks.”

Monar was surprised, “So Matt’s doing all right then?”

“All right? I guess you could say that. An apple doesn’t fall far from the tree. Branched out he has; warehouses and honest shops now. Bought or has taken over one way or the other real lawful businesses, selling and buying goods. Course he stills got his protection thugs on the side. But now he works with Chinese,

Japanese, American and British businessmen. They want something done, they all come to him. Rumor has it Po-kuei is somewhere in the game and he must be; no one interferes with Matthew Feng. And between you, me and the lamp post, I also hear he's starting to disband the Sleeping Dragon…"

MacLeod went sotto voce, "…so I'll bet there'll be one hell of a row when Archie comes to take it back and finds it's not there. That Dragon gang was the only mark Archie ever made in this backwater of the world and I can see him getting livid, son or not."

Jock MacLeod is truly a gossip monger, was Monar's first thought, but in truth he could easily see that MacLeod would have been right—had Archie been alive.

Monar was also struck by MacLeod's remark that the Sleeping Dragon was Archie's only mark in the world. Strange, he thought. Archie's image of himself was that he was immortal, that his mystique would cause epics to be written about him. Yet here he was, in a lead-lined casket in a reeking bilge and MacLeod basically saying Archie's headstone won't even state he was the founder of the Sleeping Dragon.

So much for fame and you're dead a long time, was Monar's epitaph for him, and it served to reinforce his decision. "Well Jock, I say keep this damn fame stuff. Give me a long life with my family and die old in my bed."

The meeting with Harry Scrimshaw went smoothly. He was surprised at Archie death and still more so that his body was in the hold of the *Devon.* Nonetheless that was Monar's decision to make and Harry simply shrugged and changed the subject. Business was progressing quite well and Scrimshaw gave credit where credit was due. Matthew Feng kept Governor Po-kuei as well as Prince Gong silent concerning the Blue Diamond fronting for Black Moon Shipping. Whatever the arrangements in Canton were, Matthew had worked them out to Blue Diamond's advantage. As Jock had said; an apple doesn't fall far from the tree.

Yet Harry was sure, "Have no doubt, Monar, the threat of Archie returning keeps the Sleeping Dragon in line. If they found he was in a casket in the bilge, there would be serious trouble."

Monar rubbed his forehead, "Christ, here I thought I was doing a good deed, and now…well to hell with it! I'll see what Matt wants to do before I do anything."

Matthew Feng pondered the dilemma, then made two specific points, "Drop him in the ocean and don't say a word of it!"

"Damn it, Matt! What about your mother, or his other wives?"

"You don't understand. Not one of them could stand him. There won't be any tears shed there, or with me either, believe me."

Matthew gave it more thought, "After my brother Peter was killed fighting those Thuggee with you and father, I became next in line to inherit the whole kit and boodle—but my heart is here, where I've everything I want. I'll have a document notarized stating the estate in the Bengal belongs to his wives. I do not want to see any of them again and that includes my mother. And this will wash my hands of it. Let the black art witches fight it out among themselves."

"It's up to you, but you're sure—you're secure enough here?"

"Yes, by the time anyone finds out father won't return—if they ever do—I'll stay in control of what's left of the Dragon until I discard it, plain and simple. My new business operations will be more important by then. But until I do, I'll see to it that no one will survive if they try to take over. So to answer your question, I'll never go back to India. Father felt home was here and I also. Yet there's one more thing, Prince Monar. The *Devon* was a gift from Lord Warfield to my father. Is that not so?"

"Yes. I'll turn it over to you, but you will have to take the casket with her…"

"Please, stop right there, Prince Monar. I want nothing more to do with the sea and that includes the *Devon.* So, here's my offer. You take her and leave for India, on the way drop my father in the ocean. That really would save a lot of bother all around."

A ship Monar wanted; a body he didn't. It all it came down to that.

2 July, 1866. Government House, Madras, India

AFTER ARRIVING IN MADRAS and finding Warfield and Lily there, Monar described to the incidents leading to Archie Feng's death and waited for a response. Not knowing him well, Lily was properly troubled, mainly for Warfield. Truly saddened, Warfield had known and fought with and against Archie for years. Yet with his passing another facet, another prized phase of his past was gone. He felt older from it yet said nothing. The loss still showed and even now, sitting in his suite with Monar and a few of the Black Moon Empire's Asian officers, he remained mostly silent.

Nevertheless, it was time to discuss the successes and losses of the Japanese venture with the officers and Monar's information on the death of Archie Feng met minimal concern to those present. Most didn't know of him, and the few who did kept any negative thoughts to themselves. They knew Warfield's regard for the former leader of the Sleeping Dragon.

The men's interest rose only when Monar linked the state of rebellion in Japan with Black Moon Shipping and they agreed that yes, Warfield's stake in backing the Satsuma and Chōshū Domains to win out over the Tokugawa Shogunate was a gamble. Yet it was also agreed that if—a considerable if—the armaments aided Emperor Kōmei's return to certain and undeniable power, the gamble would be well worth the cost of men and effort.

A westernized Japan would bring tremendous returns to England and Warfield and his officers were pleased Monar had acquitted himself so well. To return with agreements for railroad locomotives, passenger and freight cars, rail track and the associated equipment of bridges, controls, stations and on and on was indeed a positive win for Warfield.

Time and again they raised toasts to Prince Monar, and thought he was going to do it all and run it all. That was their assumption right up until the moment he figuratively threw cold water on their plans. Although he had informed Warfield, the other men were shocked; Monar announced he was retiring to Tamil Nadu, his wife and children.

There were regrets and denials from all, but they fell on deaf ears and what had promised to be a gala fete, slipped into a funereal dirge of sincere regrets and half-hearted good lucks.

Amidst the near empty room, puddled champagne and broken glasses, Lord Warfield, admittedly in his cups, continued to stare at Monar in persistent bafflement.

"Monar, my boy—no one but Warfield would dare call him 'boy', but Monar knew the lord meant it more as *son*—I give up, I finally give up. With Archie gone, you could have had most all of Japan, a slice of China, India and every tin pot volcano spitting country in the Pacific Rim; including Australia, in fact I'd give you a piece of the newly reunited States…"

He trailed off, "I know, I know you won't agree. But you know something? I now regret ever proposing you meet Amala, big regret…"

Monar, not particularly sober himself, shook his head, "No you don't. You're glad you did and I'm glad you did and she's glad you did and listening to you, I think you're tipsy as a lord, my Lord…" He laughed aloud, "I've always wanted to say that to you my Lord…tipsy as a Lord, my Lord…"

Lily Bunting and the Maharini Amala Singh entered, took one look, smiling at the two men.

"Warfield," Lily started, "You're too old to be out on the town at this hour. For heaven's sake, it's nine-thirty."

Warfield stood, "You've ruined all my fun, Mrs. Lillian Bunting. But as always and again, once again, you are right…Good night to all…Oh, and I suppose you're going to say the same thing to him, aren't you, Amala?"

"I would never *say* to my husband advice, my Lord Warfield. I will say I do *suggest* things to him that at times he accepts."

Monar rose, unsteady, another thought coming to mind, “You know something, Warfield? As I now think of it…think of it, you never did tell me how Archie bested…you way back, way back…before I knew you, you said he bested you...”

Warfield thought, “Yes, yes, you…are right. Never did tell. But then, if he didn’t tell, well then I’m the…only one left to tell and you…can’t trick me into it because now I would lie. SO!…I never will be…tattletale…”

Monar wrote to Archie Feng’s widows as Matthew Feng had requested. Aside from informing them that Archie had died and been put to rest at sea, and the mention that Mark Graves would not be returning. The envelope contained notification of Matthew Feng’s release of any claim on the Bengal estate or its lands.

Then came the principal subject—the children. What to do about the children? After much thought and conversation among the adults and the boys, Mark and Collie, it was decided. They should return to England—England and British schooling and life.

It had been a difficult decision. The boys would deeply miss Monar, Amala and their children. Conversely, Warfield was their blood, their grandfather, and Lily helped them through the terrible loss of their mother, father and little sister.

Monar’s concern centered on the boys falling under Warfield’s spell. It had happened to Monar, John Thomas, Archie and Scrimshaw. Now, John Thomas Graves and Archie Feng Yün-shan were dead and Harry caught up in the scheming and riddle of Manchu China.

Lily, however, privately told Monar that she felt Warfield, although talking a good game, had in fact considerably slowed and seemed content to let the company managers run their separate domains under a light touch of his control. Warfield’s being away from England this long was an example.

Before their return to England, Monar knew chances were he may never see the boys again. It was time to tell them the tale of their father.

"I met your grandfather—that is on your father's side—in Barbados. I found it was a very difficult time for him. He was a wealthy man who had lost everything when a hurricane destroyed all but one of his sailing ships and he was on the verge of losing his estate in Salem, Massachusetts. I was a slave…" The boys went wide-eyed, that was unknown to them, "…and a boss of slaves and my owner, a man named Ian MacPherson, a truly vile person, made a devil's deal with your grandfather to transport slaves from Africa to Barbados…"

"Grandfather was a slaver?"

Nodding, Monar held up his hand, "Now listen, there's a lot in what I tell that will provoke you to speak. But you can't keep interrupting each time. So just keep quiet and listen. Then I'll answer your questions when I've finished, all right?"

They agreed and waited. Monar took another sip from his drink, "Yes. Your grandfather was a slaver. Once. Just once he lost his moral compass and, solely to save home and family, he faulted. And don't think there weren't other supposedly moral, church going and wealthy citizens in the States and England who didn't do the same thing for money—only difference was they didn't get their hands dirty—so that made it all right. Another difference was Richard Graves died in shame, killed by some gang who thought he should pay and they killed him by firing a cannon at his home…"

The boys were of two minds; their grandfather felt shamed in his act, only once true, yet nevertheless a slaver, something they would never do and they wondered where their father was when all this was happening.

Guessing that, Monar told them their father, JT, was working an old schooner when they met and the two just sort of teamed up—no need to tell them of JT's infatuation with another woman, his disillusionment with his father, or how Monar came into so much money—Monar simply spoke of their pact to form a business partnership. He did tell them of how he and John Thomas met the boy's mother when in distress after losing her ship, crew, and friends to a fog shrouded, rogue wave off New York, and thrilled them about battles with their mother and father against a massive Russian Warship in the Crimea and Barbary Pirates in the Med. They were spellbound with Monar's stories and he enhanced their father's heroism in the American Civil War and the sea battle with the *Alabama.* Finally, he felt enough had been said and told them a grand love story between JT and their mother. How they fell in love, married and had the boys. Monar hid his feelings for their mother, nor would he mention her lost feelings toward him.

Still, there wasn't any way to bring a happy ending to his story.

9

The years that followed. From 1866. Blackwood Abbey

WARFIELD DIED IN 1873, one year after the Suez Canal opened. The Canal shortened distance and time, helping grow the company even wealthier. It was said Warfield worked himself to death to forget Evelyn. That very well may have been, for all his accomplishments he was never able to free himself from her memory, and though he knew she didn't haunt him, he did continue in her embrace. Despite that, with Lily always beside him, he remained in love with her and a sharp businessman to the very end.

He finally profited from Japan's civil war in 1868 when the Chōshū and Satsuma Clans crushed the Tokugawa Shogunate, to give Emperor Komei full power in the country. That upheaval brought Lord Warfield the approval of his Japanese railroad contracts and the locomotive *Iron Duke* had her first run from Yokahama to Tokio in the same year. Added to this, in one year, Warfield transshipped through Standard Oil in America 200,000 five gallon tins of coal oil—kerosene—to Japan alone.

He intently followed the strife-full years that brought battle and conflict for Britain in Africa and Abyssinia. Spain was enduring a Ten Year War of rebellion in Cuba to remain in control of her colony, and a dozen other countries fought with a dozen other.

Emotions he had controlled when younger exposed with age. He wept on learning Harry Scrimshaw, while touring for markets to expand The Company, had been killed by Spaniard Mestizos on Luzon in the Philippines.

Yet it was America of the future that most concerned Warfield. Their civil war had ended and the Southern Confederate States were welcomed back into the Union. Ulysses S. Grant became President and from that crux, America grew at a quickened pace. The country bonded the Atlantic and Pacific Oceans and in a world where oceanic commerce now dominated, she challenged England on every sea and in every port.

Throughout the 1860s and into the 1870s, rebellion became a constant between countries. Russia against Turkey, France confronted Germany, revolution in Spain, Former US General George Custer and his troop died on the western plains. The US still fought the Apache and British General 'Chinese' Gordon was killed by Mahdi forces in Khartoum. His death was eventually avenged by Lord Kitchener and, more importantly, each battle England won brought her the Sudan, Egypt and, the ultimate prize, the Empire took control of the Suez Canal.

Yet despite it all, progress was as relentless as war. The 600 year Shogun stranglehold ended in Japan; Nobel invented dynamite for construction; the Suez Canal had opened; the telephone was patented; and in 1867, with 'Seward's Folly', the United States bought Alaska from Russia for a pittance. Then, at last, a railroad spanned the county. America's manifest destiny was in her grip. Only the indigenous Indian slowed, yet did not stop, her destiny.

Monar ignored the western world as he and the Maharini aged gently in Tamil Nadu, content in their world. As his family grew he ordered his older his boys to England for schooling. Monar insisted they be immersed in the British monetary, economic, and schooling systems. He knew someday India must demand her own potential—freedom—and needed Indian leaders prepared to guide her future without British rule, although using her systems. With the Maharini's blessing, Jyoti Bihar was given a bungalow and servants considerate to her status as a Princess.

Monar, truly a man without a country until he made India his, stayed in touch with Warfield to the very end and his power became such he became the first non-British, nonwhite person to own a suite in Madras' English Only White City. Warfield had given Monar his former suite and Monar had a plaque stating, *Truly Great men Live The Life They Seek*, placed there in Lord Warfield's honor.

And the years happened.

June, 1873 Portsmouth, England

Collie Graves handed the post letter from India to his brother Mark. As Mark, at age nineteen was two years older than Collie, giving him the letter was a token offering of respect when they received one of Monar's missives. Collie didn't mind doing this in the least, as Mark was succinct in summarizing information to their essentials—just as he had been at Harrow. Mark always isolated on the pertinent, the relevant of their courses and discarded the superfluous. And the beauty of this to Collie was Mark passed this knowledge onto this brother, saving him countless hours of research. Mark never gave his brother specific information, he simply indicated where or how to find it.

Prince Monar's letter was brief, almost harsh. His boys had returned from Eton College as men, inspired men, Monar wrote. He would have to reclaim them to their Indian traditions and then moderate and prepare them for the struggle ahead against their British masters.

Although he thanked them for their friendship with his children, it was clear that Monar was gone from them, Mark and Collie were British subjects to the core, and there were no longer grounds for agreement. They wished him the best, but their friend and his family had left their sphere and their lives.

Lily, on the other hand, was content to leave the sea. She had cosseted herself in a handsome cottage on Blackwood Abbey's point overlooking the bay. With age, she preferred the quiet life after the tumultuous 'time of Warfield'. Now she favored stepping out on the town for dinner or a play with friends, watching the boys become men, listening to their stories, and living with her memories. She still remained the figurehead of the empire—and comptroller—until Mark turned twenty-one and would then took charge.

Collie was a natural born sailor and taught seamanship to Mark every chance they got away from schooling. It would seem seawater ran in their veins, that the souls of their father and mother's love of the sea lived within them, unknowingly, without thought.

Though certainly not wastrels, Mark and Collie lived the good life at the Abbey. After leaving the cloistered halls of Eton with honors, they were destined to assume control of Warfield's empire in two years. They both absorbed Company intelligence three days a week in preparation and Collie spent additional time in studies through Eton Masters. Yet until the day came when their lives would become forever entwined with the Company, they found time for athletics, society, girls, and sailing, not necessarily in that order.

So it would seem outlandish to think that in one brief sailing excursion from Portsmouth to the Isle of Wight, their lives would be forever changed.

It was then they met up with the extraordinary sight of a man swimming along through the salty waters of the Solent without—at least apparently—the slightest care. After spilling the wind from their schooner's mainsail and letting the jib luff, they drifted up to him and fell into laughter as the chap spoke up.

"I say, you blokes do know you're in my way, don't you?"

"In your way?" Collie failed to keep a straight face, "Why we thought it best throw you a lifeline. Where on earth are you headed?"

"You ask where on earth? Well actually, only to Ryde Village on Wight. It's just two miles from Gilkicker Fort, on the Point back over there."

"Well, it's more like three miles and do you know the Solent has four tidal patterns? Your jaunt with the current running east through Spithead right now could wind you up in the Channel, the way you were going."

"And, one supposes, that wouldn't be good?"

"Quite unhealthy, quite. Why don't you pop aboard and have a smoke and warm up."

"Only if you have a tall scotch with soda as well, this flaming water *is* a trifle chilly. Permission to come aboard?"

"Friends call me Trevor and seeing as you chaps have saved me a cold swim, and kindly loaned me this fine robe and have this lovely bottle of Bunnahabhain single malt, I'll lower my normal standoffishness and allow you to call me Trevor."

The sailors sized Trevor up, rather outgoing, seemed not quite British, angular, yet obviously in excellent condition with a severe shoulder scar. After first name introductions they had to inquire, "What were you doing out here or more to the point, *why*?"

"Why? Quite that simple really, wanted to see if I could."

They continued being amused, "If you'd please excuse our smiles we'd say at this point you were rather, ah, flogging about."

"Oh, not at all. Actually I was simply stretching."

"If you stretched much longer, you'd have drifted off to the coast of France, heading for Spain or Holland."

"That wouldn't have been so bad; I've friends all along the coast."

"I don't think they would have been too happy seeing you wash up on shore, whale belly white and with barnacles."

Trevor laughed, "No trouble with that score, I'm well protected."

He showed them a finely wrought, gold neckless chain, holding a small medallion. After failing to make sense of the worn, embossed figure, they questioned its significance.

"Fortuna. Goddess of chance, fate and luck. A woman I loved gave me it years ago. Trouble is we both didn't know Fortuna's luck can be good or bad. Still, so far mostly good, such as now."

As he replaced the pendant into the robe, they again noticed the lengthy ridge across his shoulder, "That's quite a scar you have there, Trevor."

"What? Oh that. Got it back a bit–some stupid little war."

"You were in the Military? Is that where you got the scar?"

"I was once at Sandhurst, but left in '68. Picked up the scar a little later, in the bloody hot Sudan."

Trevor shifted the subject, "So, now you know all about me," They found that doubtful, "how about telling me about yourselves?"

Mark looked to Collie, “Nothing as exciting as that we’re afraid. We’re only now finished University and looking about for a year. Perhaps our only bit of interest is we’ve been in India and China and Japan and we’re thinking seriously of a trip to America. You see our father was American and we’ve never been there to see his home.”

As Mark gave it thought to what he said, he was right, “Nothing exciting—damn it.”

Yet Trevor found America of interest, “Good for you, I’m pretty much a dullard about the States and yet I shouldn’t be.”

He looked up thoughtfully at the mainmast, “I’m only now noticing the Royal Yacht Squadron and the Black Moon burgees. Are you going to enter the Cowe’s Cup Regatta or do you work for the Warfield Bunting line? Rather upper crust to me, aren’t they—or you?”

They appeared hesitant, but Collie took the bait, chuckling, “Yes, they are uppity, quite so. Well, you see, actually we’re honorary members of the Royal Squadron as Lord Warfield was a member and he was our grandfather. Perhaps you knew him?”

Trevor scowled, pensive at the information, “No, unfortunately. However, my stepfather spoke of him in glowing terms, well back that is. Said he was the greatest buccaneer of them all. Or perhaps I’m out of line here.”

Trevor appeared more curious than contrite, but the brothers didn’t seem to mind.

Mark steered clear of the words *stepfather* and filled the void, “Grandfather was more of a risk taker, a shrewd risk taker. He took chances where others were afraid and won far more times than failing. Still, like others, he had sadness in this life, yet he also had verve. To do what others didn’t dare.”

“Verve? I suppose that would be the best all-round word. Yet then again, I still lean to buccaneer as more apropos, much more encompassing. How about we settle on Gentleman Buccaneer with verve for Lord Warfield?”

Before they had a chance to respond, Trevor was curious, "Tell me, is it possible your last name is Graves?"

They weren't too surprised, it was common knowledge they were Lord Warfield's grandchildren. Yet to guess their last name was odd.

"You seem to have more knowledge than most, Trevor."

The boys could see Trevor working out something and when he first spoke they were baffled.

"I'll give you a name; see if it evokes any memories. The name is *Scrimshaw*. Ring a bell?"

It took but a moment, "Scrimshaw? Are you related to *Harry* Scrimshaw, his brother?"

With a jaunty air, Trevor responded, "Please, I'm not that old. I'm his bastard son."

After their shock, the story of Trevor's knowledge of the name was candid. He was given away as a baby and that was all he knew or ever asked about—other than learning his father's name was Harry Scrimshaw.

The bare bones of Trevor's story, most of which he was not completely aware, was of interest. Before he was born, his father, a naval officer, was cashiered, driven from the Royal Navy on false charges. Then, there was an unforeseen child with a Scottish Laird's daughter who rejected the baby for he would reduce her marriage potential. On learning of Harry being cashiered, Lord Warfield hired him. As a six month old baby, Trevor wound up with a wealthy childless couple Warfield knew who loved and nurtured him. He also wound up with a new surname, St. George. Obviously Trevor had no remembrance of his real father *or* mother and quite strangely never asked who they were. For some innate reason known solely to him, he did not wish to meet either of them.

Only once, when Harry Scrimshaw was killed in the Philippines, did Warfield thoughtlessly link Trevor to his Father.

No longer ignorant of whom his father was, Trevor did inquire further, but ignored the information until this present meeting.

"Do you know anything of Harry or how our father's met, Trevor, or what occurred?"

"Little, other than they met through Warfield and my father died in the Philippines. Not much more than that."

"My word, you've missed a lot about him. There were battles, but of course, those were before we were born. A friend of ours, Prince Monar, told us stories about a Russian battleship and Barbary Pirates and your father told us about that famous Rebel ship *Alabama* sinking our father's ship *Raven.* In fact, your father was the ship's Captain when they stole a lot tea plants in China and he was in the American Civil War too. Sounds all quite exciting doesn't it? At least when I say it. Wish we had written down their histories, but you know, we were young, didn't give much thought to it back then. Sure regret that now. Yet we knew your father quite well. He was Captain on some of our voyages to India and…"

Trevor interrupted Mark, "That's quite all right, you can save it for later, right now we'd better pay attention to mooring."

They found clothes to fit Trevor and off they went to their favorite Ryde pub where the Guinness Stout was good and plentiful and the banter was ceaseless and filled with laughter. Toasts to Trevor's savior's and toasts to Trevor's debatable derring-do in attempting to swim from Fort Gilkicker to Ryde and how in the devil did he plan to get back.

"When we were young, we called it Cowlicker Point, we always thought the people there were so old they were Roman cow herders."

The three men found that particularly humorous. Trevor, however, perceived a sturdy fellow—perhaps in his cups also—who did not agree.

The man started to rise. Trevor was on his feet reaching for the man's wrist in the blink of an eye.

His face grim, Trevor whispered, "Please excuse us, sir. We were a bit raucous. No insult meant about the Point and I ask you to be a good chap and sit back down and keep your Dutch courage in check. If we continue to disparage that pleasant area you have the right to ask us to stop. Fair enough?"

Trevor had gripped the man's wrist so that his thumb pressed on the tendon and overstressed the wrist's radial nerve.

The man, in acute pain and shocked he'd been overpowered so easily, decided to agree and sat back down.

The two Graves men, momentarily distracted, barely noticed Trevor over speaking to the man and then casually return and order another round of drinks and one for the stranger.

"You know that chap?"

"Thought so, but no, my mistake. By the way, this is on you."

The three chatted and imbibed so long it was questionable to even think of sailing back to Portsmouth that night. No reason to either, they thought and the decision made, they overnighted on their schooner and returned to the mainland the next morning.

It was decided they should meet again and Mark said they'd be in touch with Trevor about meeting next week at the Fighting Pigs Public House. Trevor was dropped off in only his bathing suit at the Coast Guard Watch House.

"Oh, by the bye, Trevor, whom should we ask for when we call for you?"

"Trevor Falcon Sheffield-St. Cloud, if you'd be so kind."

At dinner that evening, when Lily mentioned their absence the previous night, Mark mentioned their coming upon a swimmer in the Solent heading for the Isle of Wight from the mainland.

"The Solent?" was Lily's response, "Whoever would be so foolish to be swimming there should be grabbed by the scruff of the neck and told he was an asinine fool!"

Mark thought her reaction droll, "I would normally agree but strangely enough, the chap seemed quite normal and pleasant. His name is Trevor Sheffield-St. Cloud. How's that, impressed?"

Lily *wasn't* impressed, "Did he tell you who he really was?"

It was obvious she knew him, or of him, "You mean about his being Harry Scrimshaw's son?"

She was startled, "So, the two of you now know about Harry."

"Why do you seem bothered about this, Lily? Obviously you knew about him. It isn't like he was the black sheep of our family."

"It's not that at all. It's not who he is or his background; I should say it's rather more like *what* he is."

"We don't understand, Lily. We had a grand time with him, struck us as a good chap. Sense of humor, friendly, couldn't ask for a more pleasant companio…"

"I know, I've heard all of this from Warfield who chose to close his eyes to the man's reputation."

"And by that you mean…?

"The man's a cad—and I don't only mean with women. There's been rumors about his clubbing about, gambling, other things…"

"Lily, this is not like you, listening to gossip."

"Gossip? Well…perhaps. Yet it is known that there are one or two Lords, members of Brooks' Club up in London whom are interested in speaking to him about his gambling ethics and womanizing with at least two the member's wives. Why they haven't called him out on it is beyond me. He's also believed to have frittered his way through most of his inheritance."

Although this information intrigued Mark and Collie they did their best not to let on. Mark only mentioned that Trevor didn't strike them that way, that he was merely good company, someone they expected to meet up with again.

"Well I've given you fair warning about the fellow. If you both insist on contacting him again that is your business. But mark my words, there's something more to him than meets the eye. And one more thing, what on earth is a man in his late thirties doing hanging about with you two young men?"

Her question went unanswered and as Lily did not volunteer further information, the subject was closed.

And so began an extended relationship with Trevor Falcon Sheffield-St. Cloud, a name created mostly out of thin air by the bastard son of Harry Scrimshaw, and a woman of considerable prestige. As he grew, the boy simply liked the names Trevor and Falcon. And then, the boy became a thirty-seven year old angular, striking chap. That aside, he was a charming, courageous, adventurous, manipulator extraordinaire…to the point of being duplicitous to whomever didn't know the real man.

When speaking to other persons who knew Trevor, the Graves' men found an ambiguous reputation preceded him. Still, the dubious facets of his persona were cloaked with a gracious, cordial style that captivated any audience. Trevor had a manner which made one think they were best of friends; they felt flattered by his undivided attention and gave off the appearance no one else had his ear. Due to this, his faults were ignored, or forgotten, or forgiven.

The two Graves men certainly felt this way. They were fascinated by Trevor's charisma. His cavalier boldness with women, his unique gregariousness with men and also quite apparent, his indifference to expenditures—whether his or whomever—made him an assured focus when entering any room.

The singular oddity was Trevor's ability to disappear for a few days, weeks or a month and more at a time. Whenever queried on it, he would pass it off with some nonchalant remark such as 'Oh, just visiting on the continent' or 'up to see the Crystal Palace in London.' Other occasions he would facetiously mention he had 'dropped in on Victoria for the weekend'—which they felt was a way of jesting about the Queen, and nothing more was thought of it.

In his suite of rooms on Fort Lane, Trevor settled into his wingback chair and closed his eyes. His most recent departure from Portsmouth had brought issues to a head. Once more into the breach he mused. He knew, well knew, he was getting too old and knocked about for this line of work. A spear wound in his thigh from Ivory Coast black slavers, when only his American Smith and Wesson revolver saved him by killing the spear man and the one coming on. Another painful memory was the Ottoman Sudanese attack on his brigade and a club shattering his shoulder. Then there was the relentless attacks of those damned Melevi Dervishes and…

There were too many wounds that still bothered and restricted his agility, and the reason for the swim was to force him to exercise.

Shaking the thoughts off as ramblings of a thirty-seven year old rapidly aging man, he poured twelve year old Dewar and Sons Scotch into a tumbler and went to his window. The view overlooking Clayhall Road past the Royal Cemetery to Stoke Lake went unnoticed; there were other concerns of more importance.

His thoughts wandered. Absent friends. Close friends from the old Egypt, Sudan, Ottoman Empire days. His last two companions were recently gone, gone together this very year; Not in the heat of battle which would have been acceptable, but nonsensically on the Royal Mail Ship, *Atlantic*, off Nova Scotia, along with five-hundred, forty-five others. He'd planned to travel with them but found himself involved with some woman and begged off. One never knew when or how they'd go, did they? And if anyone should have gone before now, it was he. Yet he was still alive and that meant, among other things, he still had problems. Quite simply, money. Enough to pay off his debts, to retire, have women, an estate and happiness. When one came down to it, it really became quite simple, didn't it? Yet enough money eluded him.

Trevor Falcon St. Cloud's personal history—as far as he had revealed to Mark and Collie was true–simply incomplete. He was Harry Scrimshaw's bastard son and he had been to Sandhurst, The Royal Military Academy. Still, in attempting to be accurate, even that was a bit misleading. While still relatively young, he attended the Advanced College Class at Sandhurst and there became noted for his unique tutorials to undergraduates. St. Cloud's outspoken comments on British military methods—primarily the dearth of espionage as an essential instrument in military planning, evolved into the principle doctrine of his thesis. Still, as Sandhurst was old school military, the establishment argued against his theories for clandestine activities by reasoning, 'the very *thought* that men of honor would rummage through another's mail is repugnant'.

Nevertheless, St. Cloud's writings were respected by forward thinking officers and remembered for his quickly circumscribed booklet by the British Government Secrets Act, *Principles of Political and Military Covert Methodology.*

It was following one of Trevor's seminars that a tall, elegantly dressed, aristocrat introduced himself and transformed Trevor from an academic into a man of action, and he welcomed the change.

Prince Albert, formerly of Sax-Cobourg-Gotha and at the time, Prince Consort, Queen Victoria's husband, was impressed by this speaker and his concepts. It wasn't long before St. Cloud found himself practicing what he preached by being sent on various covert undertakings to the Middle East. The young subaltern from Sandhurst became a successful agent in the subterfuge of undermining the Ottoman Empire's influence in Egypt and Sudan.

Wounds received from those shadowy years required his return to England and his reward was the appointment as Aide for Near Eastern Affairs to Prince Albert. It being unseemly for a Prince to have a mere subaltern as an aide, Trevor was fitted with a major's trappings and a yearly stipend for that position and his past successes in the near east.

Trevor's reputation was enhanced further during the Trent Affair in the American Civil War. The Union Gunboat *San Jacinto* boarded the British vessel *Trent* and removed two Confederate diplomats heading for England to attempt King Cotton Diplomacy with the Crown. This boarding of a neutral's vessel caused England and the United States to issue strongly worded dispatches that reached to a breaking point close to war. The British were on the edge of recognizing the Confederacy.

Prince Albert's decision to try and moderate the next official British response to the Union was supported by Trevor. In fact, his interception of severely worded Foreign Office dispatches *before* they reached the Americans, and his subsequent 'softening' of their language became the key to both sides backing away from severing diplomatic relations.

Albert's private attempt to bring St. Cloud a knighthood for his successful efforts in the Trent Affair and other Crown services ended only when the Prince Consort sickened and died, allegedly of typhoid fever the following month.

The death of Prince Albert left St. Cloud without supporters in the dog eat dog epoch of the combative internal and foreign British relationships. In those days he'd displayed an abrasive, irascible personality and became even more critical of ineffectual tacticians throughout Government. That left him without a benefactor and a dwindling income which in turn made it impossible to support his desired lifestyle. To offset this—and international intrigue being his talent—he shrewdly put himself out for hire on the 'campus'.

«»

Trevor made a scotch and water, his thoughts turned to the agreement he'd made with his sponsor. That actually wasn't quite true. In truth, he'd made separate agreements with two sponsors, British and American. And this is where he walked a tightrope. It was imperative to keep the British ignorant of his American contact.

Strangely, his two sponsors were after the same goal–Cuba, yet for far different reasons. Initially, the issue of Cuba had begun from Trevor being approached secretly by four wealthy British Parliamentarians wishing to 'tweak the nose of America's Uncle Sam' or so they said, by staging a coup on an island in the Caribbean. They led Trevor to believe they simply wanted to 'tweak the nose' by defying the US's 'Hands Off' Monroe Doctrine of 1823. He'd not believed their story, but went along at first.

When they alluded to the large island of Spanish Cuba, Trevor was quick to deduce the four men were, in reality, after that island's industries. Still, when one gave it thought, a coup wasn't too outlandish. Cuba was five years into a war pitting its upper class merchants and native Creoles against their Spanish masters. Slaves and peons were brought in on the revolt simply to do most of the fighting and were soon being slaughtered wholesale.

Spain had lost her massive holdings on the mainland of North America to France in 1800 and only two years later, France sold that land to the United States in the huge 1803 Louisiana Purchase for a total of $11,000,000, plus a debt forgiveness of $4,000,000. This left Spain out in the cold with no holdings on the American Continent, empty coffers, and only Cuba of any value in the Caribe. She determined to hold on to it, rebellion, or no rebellion.
His four British sponsors knew he'd done the Crown's work in the Near East and hired him to do the same in Cuba. Through him, they expected to gain control of the sugarcane and tobacco fields and their production—commerce that would return those men millions and Trevor would be well compensated for the mission's success. The scheme to seize Cuba and how Trevor St. Cloud conceived the implementation of it, would eventually involve clandestine traits he well knew, even an attempt to mislead the Royal Navy.

With conceit in his ability, Trevor laid out the strategy. After five years the revolt in Cuba had stalled. His strategies were insert men and arms on the north coast, east of Havana and thrust south to split the island's Spanish defenders. After isolating each—as the British had done back in the 1700s—he would then follow up by sending a clandestine report to the Royal Navy that British subjects were in danger. He believed the arrival of the RN would resurrect the Rebels faltering hopes; reinvigorate their cause and his force would attack, first east, then west to win the revolution. At that point, Trevor would then wash his hands of it. That was all he promised. Win the revolt. With the Rebels victorious, but leaderless, his investors could install their own proxies. He'd be gone before England and the United States met to discuss the ramifications.

Trevor would be well paid by the sponsors, true. Yet as he saw it, that wasn't enough. It was the even better prospect of wealth within the Cuban mission *if* he could pull off the *American* segment of the agreement. And he intended to do just that and damn the chances.

«»

His deliberations next carried him to Blackwood Abbey and how he could use the Graves' men. They could unwittingly help, not the least of that help being the swift *Argus*.

Both backers of his missions to Cuba insisted he take action. Either begin or return his advance funds. Both stated it was *imperative to get started on the quick*. There was a fair to good chance of success, although as importantly, it must be covert. Trevor must be cautious in covering all tracks and not imperil any of his conspirators.

Actually, he had already decided to act. He had stalled his British investors for there'd been a problem securing the one person he needed. That one person held the key to the private side deal with the US senator—and that one person had recently surfaced.

So, one way or the other, Cuba was the end game. A victorious rebellion followed by a fruitful money-spinning deal with the senator. It was a neat package and juggling act, yet not one above Trevor's talents. Ship, men, munitions, strategy, timing and the means to bring it together, thanks to the largess of the British group and their belief he would see them the victor in Cuba. It had taken him three years for all the pieces to jell into a cohesive design. The game would be played by Trevor's rules and only he knew them.

«»

To start the chess game, it took but little coaxing of his two unsuspecting pawns, the Graves men, to join his gambit once the concept of a trip to America was presented. After all, their great grandfather, grandfather and Father, John Thomas Graves, came from there—Salem, Massachusetts, to be exact. Collie's obligation to University was ending and they had longed for that trip to happen. The Graves lineage would come full circle, and to them, having Trevor St. Cloud along capped the venture. It was vital to disguise his reason for going and that Mark and Collie kept unaware of his goal until he decided the time was right—if ever.

By early August 1873, preparations had progressed rapidly. The handsome, new, twin screw Black Moon three stick schooner, *Argus*, named for the builder of *Argo,* a ship of Greek mythology, was readied. Trevor and Mark were nearly ready, crew on call. Collie, however, was hesitant. His alleged reason being he wanted to finish reading for his Major, World Economics–and expectantly, receive a First before leaving.

Mark, like Trevor, was anxious to be gone and found this a questionable excuse until, speaking some mutual friends, he found there was a certain Miss Elizabeth, who was apparently, a striking, vibrant lass evidently holding a certain sway over his brother.

Faced with making a choice, Collie decided to have Trevor and Mark going on ahead, while he would finish his 'commitments' and meet them in Salem by the middle or late September. Their contact there would be Mr. James Pickman, once their father's friend, if still alive. It wasn't in Trevor's schedule for him or Mark to still be in Salem by late September, although he kept that thought unsaid.

Since the others did not know his reputation preceded him, Trevor felt it important to keep a facade of simply being a companion to the brothers. Someone who would help them visit their father's home and tour the East Coast for possible investments. His planned response to questions that could arise in their travels was that, as they could not find acceptable venture possibilities in the North, they'd investigate the slow recovery from the Civil War in the Southern states and any potential there. The first important stopover Trevor needed was not far from Washington. He knew Florida could be another objective, and then the near certainty of northwest Cuba. Cuba being both investor's and Trevor's ultimate goal. And when the plan unfolded, a fast steam-powered schooner, fitting his anticipation of need and speed, was required. The *Argus* would meet both requirements.

10

24 September, 1873. Latitude 42.412 Longitude 68.305
The schooner *Argus*

"WELL, MARK, IT WON'T BE LONG NOW before we sight land, your father's land—and yours, for that matter."

Trevor St. Cloud watched Mark carefully; there was no apparent reaction to his remark so he returned to deciding at this late date whether to change his mind and reveal his true scheme.

Mark had unexpectedly, and most conveniently for Trevor, mentioned he still had two or more years before he and Collie attained control of their grandfather's empire. But more than the delay, the work that lay ahead keeping that empire together seemed overwhelming and it was distasteful to him to even to think of the challenge. But Warfield's will was specific that either Mark and or Collie must take actual charge. Otherwise, they would not inherit the company. The upshot to Trevor being that Mark wanted to make the most of the remaining two years before his life changed, but he would have to mind his spending until then. In few words, Mark truly wanted Trevor's lifestyle, not Warfield's work ethic.

Watching Mark's reaction to certain comments about money, freedom and women, convinced Trevor to play up that quality of his life, real and imagined. He enhanced stories, mentioned important people who knew him, wealthy friends, the carefree existence, foreign lands, exciting, exotic women wherever he went.

Mark took it all in. This is what he wanted, that was the way of life he dreamed of. Let Collie be the levelheaded one. Let Collie be the worker drone grandfather Warfield wanted. That was not the life for Mark.

Combined with this information, Trevor found it would be too difficult to go where he needed without having to justify each reason to Mark. Trevor needed a subordinate. Mark was the obvious choice, and once knowing his weaknesses, the decision was made. Invite him in as a partner in the intrigue. Dangle the vison of millions in front of him. And all that was expected to earn it was the use of the *Argus* for a month or two or three. There would be so much of a return for the time involved, that when the moment came for Mark to take the reins of Warfield's empire, he could easily afford to sell off control to Collie. Such were the dreams Trevor would have to spin. And spin he did.

The *Argus* rose and heaved, carving the moon tipped waves. The waves slipped along each side to rejoin in the ship's wake time after countless time the sea went past endlessly until soon they would sight land. Now was the time, before landfall, Trevor felt, to set the hook, join Mark to the plan.

In the Captain's snug quarters, Trevor watched the gimballed arc of the oil lamp as it moved against the motion of the ship. Trevor, with prudence behind him, decided to dispense with any further subterfuge and go straight out for his goal.

"God, Trevor! You startled me. Why on earth are you hiding here in the dark?"

"Well, I'm not exactly hiding, I just wanted to have a private meeting without anyone about, but I'm sure with that shout you've woken most of the crew."

"Sorry. But you did startle me you know."

"Yes, yet I certainly didn't expect quite such a reaction."

Mark composed himself, embarrassed, "What…I mean *why* a private meeting?"

"Check outside the hatch for anyone about, then close it and come near me so I can speak quietly."

Doing as he was told, Mark waited; silently questioning Trevor's cautioned approach.

"Mark, I've given this a lot of thought and I feel that I should level with you on one of the reasons I've gone on this trip with you. Beside enjoying your company and helping in any way I can, there is a major request I've been asked to do for a leading US Senator."

It was not only an American representative but members of *British* Parliament as well who made the offers. That Trevor had accepted both for different reasons was omitted.

Yet Mark didn't doubt Trevor and was impressed that a US Senator had turned to him for help and listened intently as Trevor mixed fact and fiction to weave Mark into his web of deceit.

"Around three years ago I was in the States on a private matter for the Crown when I was approached by a southern leader who was once a Rebel during their Civil War and had now become US Senator. Needless to say, he was still angry about the South losing the war and southerners being shunted aside as lepers in the senate. Knowing me to be a Brit, and my importance in the *Trent* Affair—which went against the wishes of the Confederacy I might add—he nevertheless sounded me out, because I had a reputation of getting things done no matter how…should I say, devious. Anyway, he offered me a sum to find a way to…"

Here Trevor stopped, ready for Mark's reaction to his next words. "…steal *Cuba*."

The words had the desired effect. Mark's eyes widened; his mind uncomprehending, "What the devil are you talking about Trevor? Steal Cuba—what does that mean?"

"Of course I don't mean steal in the literal sense. I mean the States have their eyes on the Cuban war between the Creoles and the Spanish that's been going on since '68. So now would be a good time to make Cuba a protectorate of the US. They haven't because wounds aren't healed enough from the Civil War to go and start another one. So there's a chance we, being British, could take it for England."

"But why does this Southern Senator want England to get it?"

"He wants to make the Northern majority in the Senate look like fools by letting another country or faction slip in and take Cuba without the American Government knowing a damn thing about it."

"And you can do that? How, that's possible?"

"Mark, I did stuff like it in the Sudan and there it was even more farfetched than here. As far as how? I laid it all out to my people over the past years. Ships, soldiers, rifles, cannon, bombs, you name it, I've assembled this from all over the Carib through contacts and associates. I've planned the landing, targets, uniting with the rebels fighting there now and frankly, the assassinations of key Spanish leaders. We'll split the island, take Havana and the Spanish military supplies there and after that we'll free the slaves and have an army of fighters ready for revenge."

Trevor breathed, "And, there's plenty of money to go around."

He then cleared his throat and continued, "Mark, we Brits took Cojimar and Havana from the Spanish in the 1760s, but after that we negotiated our occupation there for Spanish Florida. We'll take Cuba again before I'm finished and this time we'll keep it."

"The British Government is in on this?"

"Yes, right from the beginning. I'll explain everything later."

Mark was taken in by the half-truths and outright fabrications. It was exciting to him. Something to be a part of. What a story he'd have to tell. Still, one thing came to him. "It sounds great, but chancy, Trevor, and it also sounds costly. Where's all the money you say we'll need to do this coming from?"

The money was coming from both British and American investors, but Trevor couldn't tell Mark that, "My friend, that will be between me and the people I spoke about. For now, however, just digest what I told you and make a firm decision. There's more, far more to the story, but I won't say anything further. I'll get your commitment, or not, later. Yet, I want to warn you, if you say yes, there's no going back on your decision."

It was getting tricky; Trevor had to keep the players straight.

Mark was chasing after the golden ring. Trevor made it sound exciting and maybe a bit risky. Even if the story was only half true, it was just for up to three months. And what difference did three months make in the grand scheme of things? He didn't want to miss out on the excitement. Even a bit of risk with Trevor would be exciting. And, if Trevor's other ruses were successful, this would reach all the papers in England. He'd be famous and have plenty of money in his pocket. Wouldn't his old school chums be jealous! Mark couldn't wait for the rest of the story.

At Race Point on Provincetown, Cape Cod's 'hook', they sighted the stone tower light and noted a steel structure rising to replace it. Then, seeing Wood End and Long Point Lighthouses, they made a course correction and pointed up north, north by west. With all sails furled they powered into Cape Cod Bay, picking their way lighthouse to lighthouse. Past Boston Lighthouse, Grave's Ledge Light, Egg Rock, and Marblehead Neck Light, until at last, the two-year-old Derby Wharf Light Station off Salem's breakwater was sighted.

The *Argus* wallowed in the swells as Captain Joshua Wilkes reviewed a copy of John Thomas Graves' letter to Warfield Bunting. Written so long ago, it was given to Monar before John Thomas, dying of cancer, blew up his estate *Seaward,* his docks and himself.

Reading the letter their contact, if he could be found, was a James Pickman. They motored up the channel formed by the breakwater and there, in bold lettering over warehouses along the lengthy wharf proclaimed, J. PICKMAN. Trevor, Mark and Captain Wilkes couldn't help laugh—so much for the problem of tracking down James Pickman.

They tied off; trying out their sea legs along the wharf as two old salts lounged on a bench admiring the *Argus*. A young man, partially crippled, limped along the planks, "This is a private dock for Pickman shipping clients only. Can I help you?"

"We have business with Mister Pickman."

"Well, Pickman's my name, but I figures you mean dad, I'll fetch him up."

Trevor shook his head, watching the abrupt youth negotiate the gaps in the planking, "Too bad, to be so young and so crippled, wonder what happened?"

Captain Wilkes offered an opinion. “Could be shark, swapped his leg for a log. Happens in these along these ports when the water warms and sharks follow bait fish north.”

In a short time, James ‘Jimmy’ Pickman, in his 50’s and JT’s former youthful friend was seen coming along the wharf, matching his pace to his son’s. He came up and, while introducing himself, stared curiously at Mark. Before anyone could begin to speak, Pickman said, “You’re JT—John Thomas Graves’ son—or I’m a hoss’s ass.”

Mark was stunned, “I look that much like my father?”

“Younger, aye, yet you be JT’s spittin image. And if you’re anything like him, then you’re to be most welcome here, if only to me and my wife.”

A pleasant meeting carried on into the afternoon. Jimmy Pickman told the crew where to wet their whistles and took the three travelers on a brief tour before asking Mark if he would like to see the Graves’ property on the bluff.

The land was encircled with rusted wire fencing and Pickman admitted that although the area should have been guarded as Mark’s father designated, there was really little left to guard so why spend the money. Let people go there to picnic, see the view and catch the salt air and forget the fearsome explosions that night so long past.

As it was actually Mark and Collie’s land, Pickman was quite honest in that he had not followed their father’s instructions or spent more of the Trust money than necessary and they would find everything in order. Mark found no cause to question Pickman’s decisions; his father’s orders had long since been pointless.

Moving further up the hill, the full extent of the damage revealed. Mark’s father, with kegs of gunpowder, had quite destroyed the once handsome, granite estate. That gunpowder he had acquired from a corrupt naval supply officer. And that same officer had previously supplied contaminated powder which caused JT to lose the *Raven* to the Rebel ship *Alabama* so long ago.

Ten years, it had been ten years since *Seaward* was destroyed. Not a wall remained upright, hardly one granite block stood on another. Weeds and small pines and oaks sprouted in the indentation of the foundation and amid a crazy quilt of stone spread along the bluff. Charred timbers remained, mostly hidden among the weeds.

Pickman was quick to point out that such was the massive explosive force that fragments of granite came down on the town. The Graves' wharfs and warehouses shared the same fate. And, although no one was killed, a few were injured and a goodly number of roofs damaged.

"The Night of the Hurling Boulders they call it—a night no one would ever forget." He added.

Mark walked off alone. The other two men left him to his thoughts. This land was his father, grandfather, and great grandfather's. Now his and Collie's.

He had expected a chill, some emotion to bare itself. Yet there was nothing. He had never lived here, had never seen it or even seen America. He was an Englishman and this entire site meant little more than it was pretty. Yet the destruction in which his father perished held no sentimentality. Mark had over-romanticized the thought of his father…and Salem.

Trevor read the disenchantment in Mark's face, "Not what you hoped, is it? Thought there'd be some great emotion, a thrill running through you about finding your father's memory here didn't you?"

"I did—yes. I've thought of him and Salem for years. It was thoughts of this place and finding something of him—but he's not here. Back then, he left us to come over here and fight in the Civil War. But was simply that, wasn't it? He left us for the war. Left us and mother for good…never came back…killed himself here."

"Now you see why I don't want to know of *my* father. I never found him anywhere either. Mark, we create myths of them out of pipedreams. Myths from dreams. We put them on pedestals, create an aura, and then find our imaginings are nothing more than what you see around here…silent, lifeless ruins."

"You're right, Trevor. No reason to wait here longer for Collie."

Trevor took a carriage to Boston for the day to telegraph his contact in Washington, while Mark supervised the provisioning.

They spent the night as guests of the Pickman's. Katherine Pickman was a taciturn sort of woman, affable enough, yet with little to add to Jim Pickman's stories of Salem, Mark's father or the area. The young Pickman boy, Caleb, was their fourth child they learned, the others dead from childbirth, the Civil War and disease. He did not eat with them. He was self-conscious of his injuries they mentioned, his leg gone from the knee and the restrictive use of his gnarled fingers on his right hand made him awkward.

The boy, they were told, was a wild youth and had gone off to find his fortune in the west, away from parents. He made his way as far as California the previous year via the Transcontinental Railroad and been caught up in the Modoc War. He was shot in the leg and then captured by Modoc Indians at the beginning of their war with the US Army. They had finished crushing the fingers on one hand when a rescue party saved him from further physical pain, although his leg had to be removed. He returned home a beaten, brooding young man, just two years younger than Mark, yet withdrawn from the world. Although mentally, the Pickman's confided, he was smart, they had never expected him to become so dreadfully remote.

Mark felt awkward, they'd no hope for their last child, "I wouldn't know what, but is there anything we could do to help him find something?"

Jim Pickman was candid, "Not really, he resents his fate; he resents not being able to do more. I have him organizing my bookkeeping here, still, it's difficult. We can only hope the years will settle his mind. Hope God shows a way to…you know…give him peace, a future…"

There was a pause until Katherine Pickman, her voice pleading, spoke up, "You wish to help? Take him with you. Help him find his own path in this world."

«»

The chill of an October morning along the coast of New England found the *Argus* off Cape Cod's Nantucket. Coursing south, they hugged the coast to avoid the north flowing and swift Gulf Stream while Trevor mentioned the Stream was the old homeward bound boulevard for the Spanish West Indies treasure fleets. Yes, he thought, Spanish Gold, but forget them, think of other gold.

A note had been left with the Pickman's for Collie Graves explaining the early departure was to beat the New England winter. They would contact him by telegraph through to the Pickman's.

With Captain Wilkes at the helm, the crew busy, and their new crewmember Caleb Pickman making the Ship's Log legible, Trevor laid out a chart on the Captain's table. Then, alone with an impatient Mark, he revealed the rest of the plan.

"Mark, I'll come to *our* main goal. What I told you so far is true, that is as far as it goes. But what we're really after is *gold*—buried Rebel gold."

Mark was at a loss, had not the slightest idea of the import of Trevor's words. If he had known beforehand, he might have, just might, have thought twice.

11

Early October, 1873. The Argus.
TREVOR FALCON ST. CLOUD spun a tale of intrigue.

"I first heard of this story when I was in Washington three years ago. At the time there was nothing I could do about it as it was just a story of some missing gold being buried somewhere in some parish in Georgia. The true story of it was sparse and as I was under contract to the Prince Consort, all I could do was tell my contact in Washington to keep an eye out for more. Then, two years later, the one person alive who knew the story—the complete and *real* story that is—surfaced in Washington and spoke to my contact. My man swears by this fellow and his story fits into place with other evidence that's since been accumulated."

Mark was impatient, yet he knew Trevor had to present in his own fashion, so waited.

"What happened was that towards the end of the American Civil War, the South's President Davis had to move his government and Treasury out of Richmond, the South's Capital to avoid being captured. By Treasury, I mean hard currency. In other words, they had to remove all the silver, gold ingots and coin the Rebels held in Virginia out of the path of the Union forces before they broke through General Lee's lines. It seems Lee managed to hold long enough for two trains to leave; the first one carried the gold with guards, and the second held what was left of the Confederate Government. The first train, with the gold, is the one we'll follow."

Mark was held spellbound while Trevor poured whisky into a glass, making him wait.

"Ah, that's good. Now, where was I?" He looked to his notes, "Ah yes, the gold train. A Lieutenant William Parker from the Rebel Navy was put in charge. In charge, but all he had for guards were naval cadets—some hardly into their teens. That's how desperate they were. Anyway, both trains reached the end of the line at Danville, Virginia. The gold and records were put in a dozen wagons and they headed for the former US Mint in Charlotte, North Carolina. But they found the Union Calvary was already there and this is where the whole escape and the truth of what happened next went to hell. Now, *most* of the wagons carrying gold and whatever else got away, although later they were captured by the Union."

Trevor became forceful, "Mark, all this is *fact!* Up to this point, there was no question of what took place. Since then however, all sorts of stories have made the rounds about one gold wagon and that gold had been buried everywhere, and my people have had to track down most every damn false lead. I said *most* of the wagons were captured because we now know what happened. And how? We now have a *witness* who knows where that missing gold wound up!"

Trevor could bring words alive, the image filling Mark's mind.

"As most of the trip was done at night, one of the cadets, a fifteen year old midshipman, was ordered to count the wagons every ten minutes and he said, in fact swears, he counted *thirteen* wagons each time and when they turned off before getting to Charlotte, he and a Confederate Chief Petty Officer went with one *another way*."

Mark was intense, "But can you believe him? Just one person?"

"Yes, because we researched and found no count was made when the gold was transferred from the train other than this kid and there were only *twelve* wagons when the Union caught them and…"

"But *one* midshipman, that's pretty thin to hang your hat on…"

"Hold your horses there, Mark. Hear me out, then see if you have any doubts."

Trevor, not expecting skepticism, was getting angry. Mark must be convinced because, frankly, there was no letting him back out.

"Look, Mark, the *good* part is there *is* only one witness and his story rings true. Let me finish, you'll see why."

Mark nodded in agreement and Trevor went on, "The other leader of those wagons was that Chief Petty Officer named Robert Hogan and Hogan, it turned out, had enough of the sea war, and saw a great way to get out of it. He sure was a conniver, let me tell you. When that Lieutenant Parker went off for a meeting with the officials to decide what to do next once they knew where the Yankees were, Hogan started swapping silver bars for gold ingots from other wagons. No one knew why and anyway, if they did, there was no one with rank to stop him. When he thought he had enough, he grabbed our witness—to help drive the wagon I guess—and took off east before Parker came back."

"Parker didn't chase after him when he returned?"

"Don't know if he did or not. But our midshipman said things were in a horrible muddle. They were worried sick about the Yankee Calvary; the cadets were panicky, no officers…my guess is Parker couldn't chase after him and leave the rest to wait—and perhaps they'd run off with more of the gold too."

"I can see where that could happen. Yet what a chance that Hogan was taking. So what happened next?"

"Well, our midshipman said they went through God's hell. People evacuating, panic everywhere, houses burning, deserter's robbing. Now this Hogan was a big man and had two Navy Colts sticking out of his belt that made sure everyone kept clear of him. Anyway, he said they must have gone two hundred miles before skirting above marshland he later found was called the Great Dismal Swamp and they made it near the coast at an inlet called Lynnhaven Bay. It took over six weeks along rutted roads with horses and wagon breaking down and he named a lot of tin-pot towns along the way like Ebony, Gasburg, Dahlia. Those were places known only to locals, something no average person ever heard of and I tested him with a map. The few towns he remembered were bang on."

It was beginning to sound legitimate to Mark, and he didn't question further, seeing Trevor had well researched the story. Although he wondered why this witness, this midshipman, name wasn't stated.

Trevor continued, "Well, it turns out Hogan had a method to his madness. He'd been stationed at Norfolk on the *CSS Raleigh* when they had that ironclad battle down there and he knew the area and people. He tracked down an old mate, some shrimp and sponge captain name of…ah, hell's bells…I forget. Whatever, they made a deal. Tell you what…I'm tired. When we meet the Washington people involved, I'll let the chap who was there relate the rest."

"You mean the witness? What's his name? You never told me."

"I didn't? Well, it's not in my nature to be *too* forthcoming. Yet seeing you're my partner…his name is Noah Benjamin, the son of Judah Benjamin, who at that time was Secretary of State for the Confederates."

Surprised and pleased now that someone of real importance was enmeshed in this venture, Mark was impressed, "You mean this Benjamin chap is aboard on this?"

"Just the son. His father was there with the wagons, yes, but he went with the larger group including Vice President Stephens and some other nabobs. They all got caught up by Union soldiers. All except Judah, the father that is. He got away somehow and made it to England. If memory serves, he's a barrister there, at least I think. Son doesn't like him for leaving and never spoke to him again. Oh, and bye the bye, the Union forces found seven hundred thousand dollars' worth of gold bars and gold coin on those wagons—even *after* some Rebel and Union stragglers raided them—so you can imagine how much Hogan got away with."

"What's your guess, Trevor, how much do you think there is?"

"I'm thinking…five million in American, good chance more."

"My word! That's a lot of money."

"Right you are. And after we pay twenty or thirty thousand to Noah and take care of two or three others we'll split, I'd say, four and a quarter million plus. Of course my share will be more than yours, but you'll be able to live pretty high off the hog don't you think? Especially when you can buy a mansion and a massive piece of land in the South now for thirty thousand. And remember, no obligation to do anything you don't want to, plus sell your share of Warfield's empire to your brother for more if you feel like it."

Mark smiled, nodding. Anything. No obligation to do *anything*. Live like Trevor, on the cusp of life. That certainly beat the future he saw ahead managing Warfield's shipping and Shoppes and all the other tentacle's the company owned. And, if he needed more money, like Trevor said, he could always sell off his share to Collie. What a life lie ahead! And in sight—only three or four more months Trevor said! Mark never for one moment pondered why, why Trevor was being so generous—because all Mark provided was a ship. Still, he also said, they were *friends*...

«»

They powered up Chesapeake Bay and, when Trevor ordered, the *Argus* was eased up to a fisherman's shanty in Herring Bay, across from Deale, Maryland and east of Washington. Captain Wilkes and the crew were allowed to go ashore but to stay close. As it was nothing but a dreary backwater, the crew was not about to wander.

They waited. All Trevor said was the rendezvous with the key people was to be here, so they waited, isolated and waited.

After five days of swatting sandflies and mosquitos, two strangers approached. Trevor became leery. He should have known one of the men approaching but didn't. As he stepped to the gunwale, Mark was startled to see a Colt revolver jammed under the belt at Trevor's back.

"We come bearing information on Cuba."

Trevor relaxed somewhat, "Come aboard—but I was expecting the Senator and Noah."

The men laughed until one spoke, "Senator Acton is nervous, decided to be hands-off. I'm his agent, Dupree, and this *is* Noah, only with a beard and taller. You haven't seen him for three years."

Although all the men were courteous at first, it was not a social meeting; there was business to be conducted. Noah was now a twenty-three year old insecure man and, after a few cordial remarks, the men huddled in the Master's cabin. At Trevor's suggestion, Noah filled in the rest of the tale for Mark.

"Well, Trevor said he brought you up to as far as Chief Hogan ordering me to guide the wagon, and the trip to the coast. That was hell, believe me. I was only fifteen—still wet behind the ears and he was my Chief. Anyway, when we got to Lynnhaven, he fell in with an old navy friend, some Indian guy name of Olan Chappa. My Chief tells Chappa what we've got in the wagon and he goes crazy, whopping it up and jumping all around like he *was* some kind of crazy Indian on a warpath. Seems he was into the corn whisky and Chief smacks him around until he quiets down a bit and they make a deal.

"Turns out the Indian, Chappa, was a sponge and crab fisherman. But more to our needs, he'd run cotton, guns and anything else you wanted snuck through the Union sea blockade. He was a real sleazy character, but I was afraid to say that 'cause he was just what the Chief wanted."

Curious, Mark asked, "Run the blockade? Where the devil did Hogan intend to go?"

"Why…Cuba. You didn't know?"

Mark felt the fool. Of course—Cuba wasn't in rebellion back then so they were to take the Rebel gold to Cuba! And that explained why Trevor wanted to help the revolution against the Spanish in Cuba. It soon became so apparent. For a cover! While the revolutionists were fighting to free their country from Spain, Trevor would steal the gold.

Mark struggled with the ethics of the situation. It became clear Trevor was using the uprising for his gain. Then again, why not? He didn't start the uprising; by supplying munitions and soldiers, it helped the peon. They would never get this help without him. So, why shouldn't Trevor and he, after all it *was* his ship—make money? It wasn't like the gold was being taken from those peons; it wasn't theirs in the first place! He saw everyone was staring at him, "Well then, if the gold's in Cuba, let's weigh anchor!"

Mark wasn't privy to the truth behind the revolution. It wasn't the poor peon or the slave, who started the revolt. They were being used as cannon fodder by affluent Creole natives and Cuban planters, both of whom instigated an uprising among the masses by having them think they would free Cuba from the Spanish yoke. Instigated by a wealthy sugar plantation owner, Señor Carlos Manuel Céspedes, the uprising began five years prior, in 1868. Cuban Independence was proclaimed in an effort to reduce the rising costs of taxes for the slave-holding planters in the eastern region of the country. Added to the unrest, the Cuban Creole elites made demands for tariff reform and equality with their Spanish aristocrats. Not the slightest concern for the peon was heard.

Mark knew nothing of this and went blithely on, taking what he heard as gospel. The peon would win, and he and Trevor would free the poor and be famous and rich and live happily ever after.

Noah Benjamin's story of his time with Chief Hagan continued.

A moonless night he said, shrouded in downpours, the *Swordfish* with only a three man crew, piloted by Chappa's expertise, cleared one of the inlets.

"Straight out, He whispered to the helm, "no lights, no noise. Don't hug the coast, that's where the stinking Yankee's shallow water ships anchor, afraid of deep water under them they are."

After Noah's trials reaching the coast, he recalled the Gulf Stream's testy manner didn't seem to matter in the least.

They reached the coastal port of Càrdenas in the Province of Matanzas, Cuba, east of Havana without problem and tracked down Tomas Martinez, another Civil War smuggler Chappa knew.

Cuba was under the thumb of the Spanish and if they heard of the gold they would simply shoot the thieves and take it. Knowing this, Hogan, Chappa and Martinez agreed to bury the gold until they found a willing and secret foundry to melt down the gold coin and re-stamp the ingots and then sneak it back out of the country to Europe. Overall it could take a year and they swore, swore to wait in the name of the Patron Saint of Cuba, La Virgen de la Caridad del Cobre. It was at one of her secluded, hallowed and near forgotten groves where they carried uncounted ingot after ingot and bury it behind her stone effigy.

Noah then recounted how Hogan had second thoughts. Well recognizing how his own devious mind worked, in short order he started back to the site with Chappa. Hogan didn't want Noah left free, so he was taken along, yet for some strange reason given one of Hogan's Colts. The act proved prescient. For drawing near in a downpour, they came upon Martinez, just starting to dig furiously.

Noah recited the scene in a stupor. The rain, the rain he said. Martinez in shock seeing Hogan. Hogan, furious, shoots him. Chappa, angry at Hogan for killing his friend, draws his knife, Hogan laughed, 'haven't you heard never bring a knife to a gun fight?' turned his Colt on Chappa. Yet Hogan shouldn't have taken the time to laugh—for Chappa's knife struck Hogan in the neck. Then, Martinez still alive, managed to scream and stagger toward Noah with yet another knife. Though frightened, Noah doesn't take time to shout or hesitate. He lifts the Colt in two hands and pulls the trigger. The rain became torrential and veiled the dig.

Noah finished his tale. For all his youth and fright at the time, he had the presence of mind to drag the corpses well into the jungle and saw the rain would hide the scene by the shrine. Sneaking back to the ship there was another shock. He found the partners had killed the three crewmembers. Less to split the loot Noah felt was the reason and grasped he would have soon followed. Not knowing how to run the boiler or to sail, he cursed himself for his ignorance, after which he then located a small amount of money in the men's belongings and fled on foot to Havana. Once there he found a Confederate blockade running ship captain willing to drop him at the Chesapeake for the few coins he had and performing crew work. After they slipped past the Union patrol ships he made his way to Washington. At last, at wit's end he tracked down an old Union friend of his father in the Senate, disclosed his tale and told 'to keep quiet, everything will work out and you'll be well taken care of'.

Mark was the only listener who hadn't heard the story and fittingly shocked. The gold had taken on a bloody history.

"Mark, I wanted you to hear this," Trevor began, "because you must come to grips with the seriousness of our voyage. This is no jaunt to scoop the gold and hightail it out of Cuba. You're aware a rebellions going on there and we may very well come up against treacherous people. All of us must be prepared for whatever happens. You've said you've shot pheasant in the past, well, if it comes to a shooting war, I hope you were good at it. One thing more, the Captain, and crew know nothing of our goal, or the gold. They think we're strictly helping the Revolutionaries."

Mark tried to keep a grim face, and simply nodded. But, all eyes were on him. He felt an inward tremor, no turning back. He soon understood they'd never let him leave. He knew too much now. A jolt pulsed in him and numbness overcame his thoughts.

"Don't worry about me Trevor, or any of you. If the time comes, I'll hold up my end of the bargain."

There was much more to Trevor's plan. He had been assured by his backers in the British Parliament that Prime Minister Gladstone was out of favor, weakened, and would lose power by the end of the year. This meant he wouldn't be a factor when Trevor's British backers tested American's Monroe Doctrine of America for Americans. That is *if* Trevor could succeed in manipulating Cuba's persisting revolt against Spain to England's advantage. Through their clique at the Admiralty's Naval Board, once a coded message from St. Cloud was received by the British West Indies Squadron in Jamaica, warships would be dispatched to Havana Harbor as a show of force for the Rebels. The belief then was the Spanish resolve to fight on against an apparent de facto British takeover would end their domination. If Trevor's plan succeeded, Britain would expose the Monroe Doctrine's vulnerability, add Cuba and her sugar and tobacco industry to her chain of islands intensify her domination of dozens of Caribbean islands, and, tweak the nose of the Americans.

It was a grand scheme if Trevor could pull it all off and there was a very good possibly he could. If so, and enhanced with the other prospect of securing the gold, his financial future was assured.

Senator's Acton's aide, Paul-Henri Dupree, waited until Noah's story finished, then began the intelligence Trevor needed, "As you directed, we secured the former Confederate side-wheeler *Virginius* that was laid up in Kingston, Jamaica and hired that former Rebel navy Captain Fry you recommended for command. Fry said the ship needed repairs to her boilers and while this was being done, he recruited a new crew of fifty Americans and Brits. He also said he's received your payment including the amount for the hundred foreign mercenaries you contracted for from Alfaro. They have arrived and when the crew got suspicious the soldiers kept them in line without too…"

Unknown to Dupree or Senator Acton, all this had been done with British investor's money and, realizing Mark could inadvertently mention who was paying for all this, Trevor diverted that possibility by interrupting, "Look, Dupree, don't bother me with trivialities. Where is the *Virginius* now, does she have the munitions and when do we rendezvous off Cárdenas? That's all I want to know."

Dupree, his sallow face showing annoyance, "Just wait. I'll get to that after I finish my repo…"

Trevor was on his feet in an instant. He grabbed Dupree by his shirt and lifted him bodily out of the chair. Dupree was no light weight, so Noah, Mark and most especially Dupree were shocked by the suddenness of Trevor's strength and temper.

"You'll answer me when *I ask*—not when you're ready—and I won't ask you again!"

Shoving the shaken man back into his chair, Trevor's anger escalated, "Do you understand me—you God damn Cajun clown?"

"Yes…Yes…I…I…"

"Then answer me!"

The poor fellow had forgotten the questions and fumbled answering, "Yes, yes…well, the *Virginius* is at sea, it…it loaded on the munitions in Haiti…and…and what else did you want to know?"

"Christ, man! When is she due off Cuba—off Cárdenas?"

"Oh…this month…the end of this month, October."

"Damn it! We're not far from that now! We can't have that ship drifting about waiting for us! They'd be sitting ducks. Mark, get Wilkes and the crew aboard, there's not a minute to waste. Dupree, what's the signal when we sight the *Virginius*?"

"I...I don't recall."

"*Christ*! You're useless. Get off this ship."

"But…but I'm supposed to go with you. Senator Acton wants me to secure his share…his percentage when you find the gold."

Trevor was furious, towering over Dupree, "Get this straight because it will only be said once. *I* take the chances and *I* decide how the gold gets divided! Is that clear? Because it better be!"

Dupree wavered, "Acton will be furious!"

"You think I care? Let him! What's he going to do—report me? That would be a laugh! Report me to who? He's in deeper than me, because *I'm* not a senator. If the US government finds out he's aware of a plan to attack Cuba, which in essence means attacking Spain, and said nothing about it because he's a secret deal to steal Confederate gold—actually that's US American gold now, isn't it—there'd be hell to pay. You go back and ask him if he thinks ten years in your federal prison sounds about right."

Dupree responded, "So you say the Senator gets *nothing*?"

"I'm saying I'll see what I have to go through. Then he'll get what I think is fair."

"What *you* think…"

"This isn't open for discussion, get off this ship!"

Trevor started for him. Dupree went for the gangway.

As Captain Wilkes set the crew to work, he was left with no question of who was in charge. Trevor's voice was energetic, "Get those damn boilers fired up and bend on all sail—for *Cuba!*"

The *Argus* had the bone in her teeth as she sliced the waves, plunging through the north flowing Gulf Stream and into the open sea. Trevor held on to a taut line, braced against the sloped deck, the sheer strake inches above the thundering sea racing past. He was as restless and alive as the ship; the game was on once again, no more of that damnable waiting. Now, now the plan was evolving, the quarry within grasp. Meet up with the *Virginius*, fire up the rebellion, send the Rebels into battle, make the Royal Navy believe there were British subjects in danger and have them come to the rescue, all guns blazing.

Perhaps though, he mused, there could be little need for them. He found his principal task was to use his troops to drive everyone away from Cárdenas. After that, he could simply find the gold and be gone. And, should the revolution succeed? Well then, icing on the cake, so much more income from the Brits.

He ceased woolgathering. Right now, it was imperative to concentrate. First rendezvous with the *Virginius*—keep the revolt going, add even more fire to it!

«»

Noah Benjamin and Caleb Pickman wedged themselves on the deck between the angled hatch and the gunwale, chilled by the spray, yet enjoying the sea rushing past.

At first, Noah thought Caleb cold, withdrawn, but that was until he found the boy simply ashamed of his lost leg and misshapen fingers. Yet in the nights they spent chatting in their hammocks Caleb had gradually come out of his self-imposed exile and, being asked, related his tale of stupidity.

"I left home," he said, "cause I thought there was somethin more than stuck in a village up in New England. I'd read about the California gold rush in Coloma back there in the fifties and I thought, sure, it may all be panned out, but there could be more further north. Well, I sure was stupid because California was one hell of a long way's off and most everyone who didn't strike it in 'round Coloma had my same thinkin. It took weeks and weeks, but I kept trudgin 'til I was told don't go no further. There were some kind of fightin in Oregon Territory between the US Army and some Modoc Indians up there. They said we were treadin on their sacred

Indian land. The short of this is a bunch of us gold hunters got drunk and into thinkin we could help the Army take the land, so off twenty of us go all stewed to the gills. I didn't even have no gun."

Noah shook his head, "I don't think I could get that drunk."

"Well, I didn't think so nether, but I was and won't never be again. You can take that to the bank."

Caleb looked back at that reckless day, "We were headin on up this blind ravine when they trapped us and took their God damn good time shootin us down. Everyone but me were killed. I got shot in the leg and I found out after some time they'd saw I was unarmed and just plain dumb. They dragged me around some, kicked my bad leg, mashed my fingers with a rifle butt, stuff like that and right then, I figured I was dead, so there's no sense beggin over it so I just stood there, silent like, waitin for a knife to finish me off."

"How *could* you—or anyone—do that? Just stand there?"

"Don't know. It just kinda come over me, like some kind a trance folks talk about. No fear, no nothin. I just thinks—what the hell, just die, get it ta hell over with."

"Damn! Well it's evident they didn't kill you, what happened?"

"So these Indian come dancing 'round to me, I found out their names a while later, first one was Hooker Jim. He stares at me and says 'You crazy or creepy?' somethin along that line, and this other Indian—name of Shack Nasty Jim and another was Boston Charley, don't ask me how they got the names—well, Boston Charley says I'm not crazy, and they get to arguing and decide to take me back to their chief, a Captain Jack and let him decide. All this time I'm seemin numb, like retarded—maybe I was, maybe I'm now—and all the while they're callin each other the names the white man had given, and braggin about them.

"Anyway, they strips the dead, take the weapons and they start to run. Well, I can't run and down I went, face first. So two of them drag me for a while and then two more and on it goes. They rest and eat, I don't. They speak Indian and American of sorts to me. I tried to look glassy eyed, don't says nothin and they laugh and brag to me about their names. They say how bad white men is and I shrug my shoulders and bobbles my head.

"Then, this Captain Jack fella,[25] seems he was their Chief, comes up on a horse and points to the south that somethin is acomin, then sees me, turns to them like 'who the hell is this?' They tell him I'm stupid in the head and he signals them to run off and I was left standin there like a fool and then the Calvary come chargein up like to beat the band…"

Caleb trailed off with a wry smile, "I *was* a fool you know…"

So now, his dreams, dreams and hopes lay shattered. He thinks of nineteen dead miners, he a cripple, his youth wasted and nothing and no one understanding the inner hurt. The never ending *hurt*.

Learning Caleb's struggle helped Noah. When a young midshipman, he too had beheld the murders in Cuba. And even though now twenty-three, he too was troubled and being used by the other men and saw no way out. Trapped, with no help coming from the Calvary or anyone. He had to find the gold for them. For *them*, and perhaps a little something for him to start some sort of life of his own—if he lived through it.

Unhurriedly, unmentioned, a pact forged between the two men. There would come a time when both would look out for the other.

The *Argus* continued to race south. Soon they would reach the waters off northern Cuba–hoping the *Virginius* will be there.

13 November, 1873. Washington

Paul-Henri Dupree hurried along the corridor to the Senator's office. He was thankful to be away from the *Argus* and especially from Trevor St. Cloud. Dupree was sure, St. Cloud was a possessed brute, out for no one but himself and to hell with everyone else. He couldn't wait to tell the Senator about the confrontation.

---

[25] Captain Jack (Modoc Indian Chief, Kintpuash) was hung along with Boston Charley on 10.3.1873 for the killing of US General E R S Canby and two others.

The secretary knew Dupree and went to the Senator's office to announce him and a frantic Senator Andrew Acton shouted past her for him to come in quickly and shut the door.

Hastily Acton asked, "Did my aide catch up with you in time?"

Dupree was confounded, "Aide? *Your* aide? No one caught up to me. I came straight here, haven't spoken with anyone."

Acton sagged in his chair, "Then you haven't heard, don't know what's happened?"

"I have no idea what you're talking about, Senator."

"Here then, sit down. Read it and weep."

A November 12, 1873 edition of the New York Herald was spread out for Dupree:

CUBA.

The Captain and Crew of the Virginius Executed by the Spaniards.

FORTY-NINE PERSONS SHOT TO DEATH
Bloody Scene in Santiago De Cuba

Dupree's face went slack, "What the hell…?"

"Keep reading! It says right there. The *Virginius,* carrying insurgents, which *we* knew about, was heading for Cuba—which some Spanish Voluntary Force found out about—and they intercepted her with a warship called *Tornado.* Caught up to her off Jamaica, almost in British territory. Read! It's right there. The crew was taken to Havana, lined up in the public square and some slaughter house and shot! Shot! Around some fifty people. Captain Fry, the whole crew, and twelve of the rebels—*so far*.

Some Brit ship captain found some guts and said he would blow them all to hell if the Spic's shot more. We've got to cover our asses here Dupree, and hope mud from this doesn't stick to us…"

Continuing to read while the Senator spoke, Dupree asked, "Who's this Franchi Alfaro—the man it says with all the money?"

"St. Cloud had picked him to be the next El Presidente of Cuba. The guy offered a million dollars to ransom himself. Didn't work, they shot him too...Damn, I'm not thinking! If *you* didn't know about the *Virginius,* then St. Cloud doesn't know about her either. I've got to send someone down to warn him."

"Too late for that, senator. They sailed right after I left."

"Christ, what a mess. He could be sailing right into a trap."

"Don't feel sorry for him, he's a bloody cheat and ruffian."

"What makes you say that?"

"He pushed me around when I demanded what your percentage of the gold would be. Said he'd give you what he felt like."

"Did he now? Didn't picture him for that. Well then, perhaps he'll get his comeuppances there. Still, it would have been nice to get that gold. If we keep out of this, maybe we can take another shot at it. But Christ! At all costs, we've got to stay clear right now."

2 December, 1873. The *Argus*, standing off the port of Càrdenas, Matanzas, Cuba.

Keeping watch for the *Virginius*, they reached the village indifferent to a golden dusk settling on the bay. After anchors were set for the night, they were deciding whether to send a dory ashore or wait until dawn. A decision was unnecessary when a native craft was soon seen coming from shore.

Helping the passenger aboard, the man asked for 'Comandante, St. Cloud, Royal Navy'. To raised eyebrows from the crew over his rank, Trevor led his Cuban contact to an isolated area of the ship.

"Well, Perez, what's happened? Heard from the *Virginius*?"

The man, Adan Perez, guessed the *Argus* had been at sea so that that no one aboard had any idea of what had occurred, meaning Trevor would not know of the disaster.

"She capture by Spanish Volunteers, Comandante St. Cloud."

Trevor was struck, "Don't tell me that! Are you sure?"

"Yes, sure, there is no doubt, Comandante. Captain, crew, fifty rebels you hire shot so far."

"God damn it! And the cargo?"

"All gone. I hear they throw everything over side to lighten ship when chased. All over board. Gun, bullet, shell, horse, cannon…"

"Blimey! Two thousand Remington rifles were in her belly!"

Trevor cursed, but he knew cursing wasn't going to help. He had to look ahead, "Have any Spanish forces been *here*?

"Only foul-smelling collector of tax and few others. British warship *Niobe* went Havana when Spain Governor General lock up people off Steamer *City of New York*—he think they part of revolt."

"They weren't."

"That found as true, British say so. They free, *Niobe* sail off."

"What about Alfaro, have you heard?"

"Yes, dead. That too is sure. He try to buy him own self, they not listen—shoot with others. Other thing, Captain of *Tornado* say one hour more of chase *Virginius* be in Jamaica, British waters."

"Blast that God damn Rebel Captain Fry! That was my blunder; I never should have put him in charge. Good Christ, this is ending in absolute chaos."

So, Captain Fry and Franchi Alfaro were dead. Alfaro was Trevor's choice for President of the new Cuban Republic. With him dead, the thought of any Republic died with him. Everything was at an end. Rebels, rifles, cannon, Royal Navy and the plan were swept away in one fell swoop by the Spanish warship, *Tornado*.

Trevor cursed himself. He conceived the exploit and it had gone to hell, finished, a complete disaster. Well now, hold up there, he thought, just wait, that might not be necessarily so. There were two plans, weren't there? This plan, the revolution, has been botched to a fare-thee-well and, the other plan was to steal the gold. Why not carry on with that? There was only one possible hitch.

"Tell me," He asked, "are there any Spanish *military* around."

"No Comandante. Tax people not return for month and most hated Spanish soldados go when ship *Virginius* caught. Only few now here."

There was a chance—an improbable one—but a chance…

«»

5 December, Blackwood Abbey, Portsmouth, England

Dear Brother,

I apologize. I've put off writing because the news keeps piling up, one good thing after another.

First, and of course most important to me, I'm married! And no, I didn't have to. My wife's name is Mary Elizabeth Stafford-Bain. Her friends call her Mary, I call her Beth (I'm the only one who does) and she is the most wonderful, smart, (far more than I) beautiful, loving, levelheaded, sensible, (that's redundant) even-tempered, (probably redundant somewhere in there too) and fun-filled Lady I have ever known.

It was the old 'love at first sight' story, I swear, at least on my part. I stayed with my best deportment until she finally responded—and then I reverted to my natural lack of proper deportment—and damned if she didn't still love me!

When I had Beth meet Lily, I was scared to death. You know how she can be—no nonsense—but she fell in love with her too! I'm not even 20 yet and I'm married and we love every minute of it! Can't wait until you meet her.

And speaking about your meeting her, I now segue way into my next subject and I want you to keep an open mind. If I overstep my bounds, remember I'm your brother and can read your thoughts and believe you will like this. Lily, as Executer of Warfield's estate until you turn 22 (and his empire, as you are aware, converts to us) was approached by an American enterprise named the Great Atlantic and Pacific Tea Company or A&P. Their intent was a complete buy-out of Warfield's shipping, shipbuilding, manufacturing (including steel factories, tea plantations, and Warfield's Shoppes to add to their grocery chain!) The offer for all rounded off at around 10,000,000 American dollars!

Lily spoke to me about it, knowing that I'm more 'levelheaded' than you—just kidding, you're not around. I thought the offer interesting, until a representative of a grocer, (that's right, a grocer in Glasgow*) of all places, name of Thomas Lipton (I had him researched, found him somehow quite liquid with wealthy backers) who made a proposition that would return over 12,000,000 American. As you know there is a contingency in Warfield's Will that Lily receive 12% of company net or sale, so she will be quite comfortable–as we would surely be.*

The long and short of it, the A&P finally topped Mr. Lipton (I wasn't sure of him being that liquid anyway) at 14,000,000 and we've signed a Letter of Intent predicated, of course, on your agreement and signature.

Mark, this part is private. I know you were not looking forward to assuming control of Warfield's empire. You want freedom to do as you please. And don't think I blame you for that in any way. To be quite frank, since I've met and married, neither do I want to be another person with the intensity of Warfield. I've found there's another world out there. I don't mean of doing nothing, It's just that Mary's shown me that no matter how great England is, there are other countries, places, people. We know that there are things to explore, somewhere to grow, not stuck in some office, doing bookkeeping, ordering workers about, taking, always taking, never giving—I'm rambling, sorry. Back to the subject—I feel sure you'll agree with this decision. If so, get to wherever there's a telegraph cable station, or whatever they're called and if it's working under the Atlantic (I believe so) wire your YES—or no.

Now, about our travel to America. The winter is frightful here and I do not wish to take Mary on a long trip in rough weather. She is not a sailor (at present) and do not want her to suffer seasickness (I'll tell you why another time). So, we will wait for the spring and when the weather breaks, we'll visit you and father's village.

We look forward to that day. Hope you and Trevor are having great fun carousing throughout America. Knowing Trevor, he will show you how to enjoy life and, if it weren't for Beth, I would be envying you.

Will write again shortly. Perhaps we will have heard from you by then & know when we will be leaving here.

Your Loving Brother, Collie.

"Well, Beth, what did you think of the letter?"

"It's fine. You covered everything quite well. And don't think I was bothered about your saying you would be there if it wasn't for me. For you to be carousing as you put it, in America with an old man is not to my liking. You're far better off here with me…" she laughed… "and don't you forget it!"

"I wouldn't dare, but calling Trevor an old man? My Lord, Trevor's only in his late thirties."

"Nevertheless, it strikes me as odd a man his age would be associating with young men unless there was something more than friendship in it for him."

"When you meet him, I think you'll change your mind. He's a person who's led a life full of excitement and, well, from the moment we met him he's a lodestone; people, men or women are easily attracted to him."

"Collie, I don't want to prejudge the person, and I can see I have, but it seems to me that he rushed Mark off—separating the two of you—off to America on *Mark's* boat with *Mark's* money."

"In hindsight I know how it looks, but at the time we were all for going and really, we haven't heard that anything untoward has happened so far and..."

"And you've heard—exactly what …?"

"Well…nothing…"

"So you're philosophy is, 'No news, is good news.'"

Collie was boxed in, Beth hurried to explain, "Collie, listen. I'm three years older than you, and like Lily, I've viewed life through a distinctly different…ah...prism. You see life as a straight line. You grew up—unusually I admit—but nonetheless structured. And from what Lily tells me, disciplined one way or another by your grandfather, Mr. Warfield, who was admittedly, a dynamic, persuasive, powerful person…"

"But Warfield's dead now, Beth, so there's no…"

"Wait, wait, Collie dear—this is the very point I'm trying to make. Your straight line of life has been broken. There is no Warfield now, only his memory and through Lily. So your mind looks for another strong person to remain on that straight line. And Trevor Falcon St. Cloud fits that need. He's strong, decisive, secretive, been places…"

Beth paused, holding up a hand for Collie not to speak. He could see she was deciding, or rather undecided, on what course to resume on the conversation.

"Collie, in many ways, most ways by far, your thought processes are older than your years, and definitely deeper than I've heard of your brother's. That's why I love you. You have innate intelligence, decency and ability to think things through sensibly. Whether you were at University, or life, or with me–well, you don't change. You're really unique in today's England, you know."

She was redirecting her thoughts to some main point and when she spoke this way, he didn't want to interrupt.

"Having said that, Collie…I have to tell you this, you have a blind spot. So, with the understanding I love you dearly…"

Now he was sure it was something serious.

"You should be made aware of certain *things*, Collie. One day at the Ministry when I had some spare time…" Not quite true, she made the time, "I went through the secured and private records under, 'Prince Albert, subdivision, Stafford-St. Cloud, Trevor Falcon, and it appears his *activities* while acting under Prince Albert's authority—yet unbeknownst to the Prince—were subject to your friend being severely censored *and*, to save embarrassment to the Crown and the Government, these activities were papered over under many layers of obviation to prevent the information becoming public knowledge.

"Now it seems true he gave valued aid in advancing the Crown's position in some regions in the Near East. But, later on, from what I can follow between the censured and obscured lines are the words, ‘questionable’ ‘women’ ‘money’ ‘bribery’ ‘murder’ along with other words of adverse import. When I saw this, I wondered why these words would be left readable and I *think* it’s with an eye to blackmail. That your friend Trevor, if he should ever again attempt to use the Prince Consort’s name—even though he is dead—or the Queen’s name as a reference, this file will be made public and St. Cloud would, in the very least be censured. I also guess there’s an unblemished copy tucked in someone’s memoirs.

“Needless to say Collie, I’d be discharged should it be found I tracked this down and that’s probably the least that would happen.”

Since he was the sole person she would tell, the last statement didn’t bother Collie. Beth, however, for all her intelligence, had unthinkingly caused Collie concern. The information she revealed on Trevor’s questionable moral code was the person his brother was travelling with. Could Trevor, he wondered, possibly be the reason Mark had still not contacted him?

12

10 December, 1873. Aboard the *Argus*

The ship had been laid in stern first to a slimy backwater half a mile east from the town of Càrdenas, Matanzas, Cuba. Covered with foliage from seaward to hide her from any passing craft and from landward from any rare passerby, they felt hidden for the while. Heat hung like a mist and most of the crew—crammed into the confining main cabin to escape the swirl of mosquitos and the stench of putrid vegetation—waited while Trevor laid out the unwelcome choices ahead.

Mark couldn't take it. Despite the moist heat he'd known when living in India for a year in the past, Cuba was too much to take. He'd become used to England with its cooler, dryer clime. This moist air and heat frayed his nerves and simply to flee the cabin, he told Trevor he would go along with whatever was decided.

Mark was disillusioned. What he once thought would be a grand visit to America with Trevor had instead degenerated into his friend being the motivating force engaged in a grand scheme to overthrow the Spanish. That had failed. Damn the whole thing. What a misadventure. Misadventure? No, how about *catastrophe*?

So now Mark brooded over Trevor discussing a dash for gold with the crew. Huddled in a fetid cabin it had come down to that. Mark wanted nothing more than to flee the steaming heat. Take the *Argus*—after all, it was *his*—and sail for home, or at least Salem. Yet, could he? Trevor had picked the crew in England, so it was easy to guess that if a choice were made they would follow him. Trevor was probably making that decision for them right now.

With his first plan in ruin and the possibility of the second plan falling apart, Trevor was compelled into bringing the crew—Captain Wilkes and four sailors—in on the attempt to pilfer the stolen gold. From the start, Captain Wilkes had suspected something wasn't quite above-board. Yet even he was amazed, along with his crew, at the scope of the goal.

Trevor was his usual compelling self, "A little more than a mile away," he whispered, creating an image in their minds, "was a hoard of gold ingots, waiting to be dug up and," he added, "the cache was in a shallow grave—barely any digging needed at all."

Their key was Noah, he said. Noah was there when the gold was buried and knows where it is. All they had to do was dodge any Spanish, if around, or some poor, unarmed natives.

"Whereas," Trevor informed them, "I have rifles stashed in the bilge. But far more than likely we won't even need them."

"So, we just follow Noah. The gold is there for the taking. We'll scoop it up, carry it to the ship and be gone. It's simple…"

The hardest part he said was getting the gold to the ship, "and each man who helps will never go to sea again unless he *wants to!*"

The crew was of one mind, take a stab at it, the gamble was far too good to let pass and Captain Wilkes approved. Furthermore, he'd seen Trevor had tried to put one over on them. Now he's found they were needed so he's come about to run downwind with them. Well, Wilkes resolved, we'll see who controls the wheel at the end.

When Mark left the cabin, he saw Caleb and Noah at the bow, using palm fronds to annoy the flies and mosquitos. They both knew of the meeting and the reason it didn't include them. Noah was to find the gold even if Trevor had to hold a gun to his head—that was a given. And Caleb? Well, he had a crippled leg and hand. Couldn't dig, couldn't carry anything—why should Trevor include him in the split of the loot? Anyway, he'd only been taken along as a favor to the Pickman's, not for any need.

In their growing friendship, Noah had informed Caleb of the gold and both formed misgivings—this plan could meet the same fate as Trevor's last one. Yet before, they were away from the scene of the fiasco. Contrariwise, here on Spanish soil, they were closely immersed in the deed and dire consequences should something go amiss. The consequences of failure here meant death; the *Virginius* had made that exceedingly clear.

Mark couldn't ease their disquiet. In fact, their concern affected him even more. But there was no recourse; he would lose if he opposed Trevor. And truthfully, he didn't dare. Yet Caleb and Noah couldn't understand why Mark hesitated to show his disagreement. Wasn't it his ship, his money? He should be the one who decides.

After a while, Mark screwed up his courage. Trevor must be made to listen. When he finally found Trevor alone, he broached his concerns, "Trevor, we have to discuss your plan."

His mind closed, Trevor didn't want to discuss it, "Mark, what's come over you? You were all for this a few weeks ago and now you've gotten cold feet."

"I was for it, yes. But that was when there was a plan. Now the plan's gone all to hell and you're still…"

Trevor bristled, "Gone to hell? You're talking rubbish! I talked with Perez, and he said there aren't soldiers within ten miles."

"That was five days ago. You don't know if that's true now."

"Well it's true enough for me and we're getting ready!"

"Trevor, you're carried away with your own delusions. Look, your plan was for the revolutionaries to drive away and then chase the Spanish troops so that we had free hand for the gold. But the revolutionaries will go berserk if they show up and find us running off with the gold. To dangerous, Trevor, the plan is shot, gone."

"Not true, because with the Spanish gone the rebel's will chase after them, so that makes us all even up again. And I'll take even odds in this game anytime."

Mark was baffled that Trevor thought this a game, "Well do what you want but find another ship, because I'm not risking the *Argus*. I'm leaving, sailing tomorrow. So find another ship."

"If you're sailing tomorrow, you'll be on a raft with a paddle."

The gauntlet was down and Mark could tell by Trevor's smile he had won. There would be no challenge to his power.

"You know, Mark, you should have a few drinks, screw up some Dutch courage, because you're acting like a scared little girl and really, you deserve a white feather."

Smug, Trevor walked past a speechless Mark and found a sailor, "Perez doesn't know where we moved the ship. Find him and tell him to check there are no Spanish troops anywhere for ten miles. Wait there for him and if the troops are gone find out what he's up to. And be sure not to tell him where we are—understand me? Trust no one and make sure you're not followed when you come back."

Trevor then returned to a sulking Mark, "Look, my friend, you're letting this wait, the bugs and this miserable weather fray your nerves. When we're in Paris with women and Champaign we'll look back on all this and laugh, believe me. It's just tough going right now, but we'll get through it. I've been through far worse, so get your chin off your chest."

With slightly lifted spirits, Mark said he would try. Trevor patted his shoulder and left. He wasn't going to be a problem, Trevor thought, at least until they seized the gold—and then, he better *not* be a problem with the split.

«»

It took two days for the sailor to return with Perez's report and the news was distressing for two reasons. The Spanish military had returned in the belief rebels who were once in league with those captured on the *Virginius* were still about and hiding in the area. Perez heard that any rebels tracked to Matanzas were to be caught and killed. This included anyone sympathetic to their cause.

The second problem was difficult for Taylor to disclose. He returned with a woman who said her life was in danger because she had two brothers with the rebels and Perez had made him take her to the relative safety of the ship.

Trevor was furious. No one was to know where the *Argus* was hidden and Taylor was being roundly cursed until the woman came forward and lowered her shawl.

Trevor gazed with disbelief, "Consuelo…"

"Yes, Trev, once more we have met."

«»

For the first time in his life, Trevor St. Cloud was tongue-tied and befuddled. He stumbled over whatever it was he wanted to say in response and instead took up her hand and kissed it. Then becoming aware all eyes were on them, led her to the bow.

Three years past in Washington, when he was evolving the plan for Cuba with Senator Acton about appropriating the gold, he had met Señorita Consuelo Alazne Abano-Quiñones, one of the rebels seeking help from the US. Consuelo mistakenly thought Trevor was there to help free Cuba and he'd kept her believing that error.

Now, as her dark eyes met his and sent a shiver through him, the pain he'd remembered from that time returned.

They'd commenced an impassioned love affair that lasted but a week—until Consuelo vanished. Trevor had been spellbound and then bewildered. Trying to find her it seemed no one knew where she had gone, whom she met, or even her being in Washington.

Finally, at wit's end, he had to leave, leave with an ache never forgotten. Yet here and now, she stood before him. The emotions he'd known, his fear for her safety back then followed by anger for her leaving were of no matter. She was here.

"Consuelo…"

"Trev, I can give you no sane answers to the question you intend to ask. It is just that I live for Cuba, nothing else…and then I met you. But Cuba cried out for me and I had to be single-minded. I could not face a goodbye with you, my dedication would fail me. Even leaving a note would make me weaken. So I fled and please, do not question more, I ask this of you."

“Then I won’t ask. But you’re here now, what does this mean?”

“I have heard great things of you trying to save my Cuba from the devils from Spain. If you still wish…if you still feel as before…then…then I will not leave you again.”

“Could it be…can we really go back to that time, Consuelo?”

“Of course, my hero,” she looked about, “but surely not here.”

There was silent laughter between them, Trevor could only sigh. She had remembered him. Thank you, God.

And he remembered her down to the minutest detail. They talked and lingered awhile at the bow and were about to return to the group when Trevor’s mind raced with the problems Consuelo now presented. She knew nothing of his scheme for the gold and that Cuba’s freedom alone was his reason for being here. He must be careful with word and deed. His only deceit must be solely that of omission.

He had to warn the men to keep quiet, “Consuelo, let me speak to the crew first. I’ll explain our situation before any of them get outspoken; it’s been a long time since they’ve even seen a woman.”

With the crew informed who Consuelo was and warned any conversation would be over helping the Rebels, Trevor once more spoke with her alone. Now it seemed, her concern was Adan Perez and his becoming suspicious about Trevor remaining in Matanzas and having hidden the *Argus*.

“It may not seem so, but he can be very dangerous, Trev. He has to be, simply to survive the Spanish militia. I am happy you are here, but I too wonder why you stay when the *Virginius* is lost. Do you still look to find a way to help my people?”

To continue the fiction Trevor needed to disguise his reason to remain, “I didn’t tell Perez this, but I have an ace. Actually, another ship is due here shortly with more supplies…”

Consuelo became excited, “It is, Trev? That’s wonderful! But why have you not told Adan. He will be excited as I, we all will be.”

“This must be kept between ourselves Consuelo. I’m not sure I should trust him, so I’m being cautious.”

"But why would you not trust him? When we were together in Washington, you seemed to trust him with the plan to free Cuba. What has happened to change your mind since then?"

Trevor could only say he wasn't sure, simply being cautious.

She accepted the answer, "I must go back soon, Trev."

"But what of your brothers, and the Spanish being after you?"

She laughed, "My God, Trev. You can't see the deception so I could come to you?"

They had to part; she had to find her way back to Cárdenas before nightfall. She assured Trevor that she would circle around and enter the village from the north to disguise where she had been. She was not to say where the *Argus* was moored and simply tell Adan that Trevor was overly afraid a spy would follow him to the ship and report to the Spanish.

She kissed him lightly and promised and they would meet again, as soon as she could slip away.

Breathless, Consuelo hurried back to Perez.

"It is as I thought, Adan—he is after the Confederate gold!"

13

ADAN PEREZ BECAME IRATE. "Everything pointed that way once you reminded me of that meeting in Washington three years ago and the mention of missing gold. Now that his attempt to help the revolution has failed why else would he remain hidden here? I couldn't think of a reason until you mentioned that stolen gold."

"I'm surprised you could forget, Adan. You were the one interviewing those Southern officers about helping our revolt when the subject of that gold came up."

"Getting old I guess, but you're right. Lieutenant Parker–yes, that was his name. He had charge of the wagons when that thief Hogan took off with one loaded with gold and no one ever heard of him or the gold again. But how did you find out this is St. Cloud's intent? I'm sure he didn't come right out with it."

"Of course he didn't. It was two things. When I was in the US capital last month, I met Senator Acton, the one who's involved with St. Cloud in their hoax to free Cuba. He told me they hoped nothing went wrong because there was no follow up. There'd be no more mercenaries, weapons or ships because he couldn't hide any more funds in the Senate. And here was Trev telling me he was waiting for another supply ship to arrive…"

"But what if he financed it on his own, Consuelo? Another support ship I mean, without anyone knowing?"

"When would he have had the time, or get the money? He had very little money when I knew him and I can always tell when he's spinning tales. I knew him quite well, remember?"

"Do not remind me."

"Don't be jealous, Adan. My Trev was a fling, every woman should have one. I came back to you didn't I?"

"Yes…yet be sure you do not have another *fling*. It would be very unhealthy for you and the fling."

She laughed, yet she knew a threat when she heard one—and also knew he would carry one through. She was amazed he hadn't tried before—but she was ever ready should he make any attempt.

"Consuelo, you said there were two things that convinced you, what is the other?"

"Ah, yes. That happened as I was leaving. I overheard some crippled boy there call someone Noah."

"Noah? So?"

"My God, Adan, you're getting *hopeless…*"

With continued his blank look, Consuelo reminded him, "Think back to that Lieutenant Parker. He said that when Hogan took off with the wagon he took a young midshipman with him—think Adan, think—a midshipman by the name of…?"

Perez dredged up the name, "*Noah!* Noah! The son of the South's Secretary of State, Judah Benjamin! You're telling me his son is on board St. Cloud's ship?"

"I'll bet my life on it. He'd be eight or ten years older now, but it's him, it must be him. And, Adan, this means one thing; Noah knows where the gold is buried. I'm sure all Trev is waiting for is the path to be clear—and we'll see to it that the path *is* clear."

"Consuelo, this is wonderful—*you* are wonderful!"

"Just remember that when we get the gold—for Cuba."

Consuelo knew Adan was untrustworthy where the gold was concerned, and expected his next question, "How will we get it? I've not eight or nine men left I can trust in this."

"I'll work that out. But for now get two men you can trust to spy on the ship. I'll tell them where it is. And for God's sake, tell them not to be seen!"

"Why two men?"

"Jesus, Adan! When Trev makes his move for the gold, we need one to follow him and the other to report back that he's on the move and which way they're heading."

Consuelo determined that, as the *Argus* remained hidden close by, the gold was somewhere near Cárdenas and within carrying distance. The simplest way for her to find it, was to let Trevor find it. As he would not come out of hiding until the path was clear, she had to convince him.

«»

Two days later, on Seaman Taylor's next trip to Cárdenas, he was met by Consuelo. She gave him a missive stating the government forces had retreated and Perez had left with his men along with the revolutionaries to fight at Colon. This meant, she wrote, Trevor's concern over Perez spying is unfounded. She continued the farce with a reference to his story of the supply ship and stated there was no one here to interfere when it arrived. Her missive ended with a disarming, "…how soon will they meet again?"

She gambled on Trevor's lust for the gold would prevail over any other lust—at least for the present—and her judgement proved sound. He responded by a message stating he would meet her in two or three days. To her, that meant Trevor would be after the gold and that she needed to ready the ambush, and soon.

Trevor had the men readied. Removed from the bilge were the newest bolt action, Navy Remington rifles with tubular cartridge magazines, along with shovels, machetes and wheelbarrows. He then made sure the rifles were degreased, oiled, loaded and the men were versed in the rifle's action.

Since Trevor considered Caleb of little use he was left on the ship with orders to keep steam up no matter how much fuel he had to burn up. If there was trouble, keeping steam up was imperative.

Noah didn't know what site to start from as the *Argus* was now hidden. This created the need to slip back to their original location nearer Cárdenas' eastern coast as the starting point.

Adan Perez was nowhere to be seen, giving Trevor reassurance, yet he still insisted Noah find the path quickly so they could go on unnoticed. Although Consuelo informed him there were no forces arrayed in the area at present, there was no assurance that information would hold true and he tried to plan forward. First problem he saw was that Noah, the only person who knew where the gold was, had to be in the lead. Lose him and the game was over. That meant there had to be a sailor near each side of him should any enemy make an attack. Noah's protectors were not too keen on that knowledge but it assured they kept a sharp eye on their surroundings. With Mark not too dependable, Trevor's concern persisted. The fact there were but five armed men, including he, to back up the three point men was cause for disquiet.

The path was narrow, barely passable in segments. There wasn't any chance to advance three abreast and little enough room for the wheelbarrows to pass. Perfect for an ambush thought Trevor, but he kept his voice low and steady to ease the men's nerves and at times, Mark's and his own.

Noah was often uncertain, as there were few landmarks. A weathered signpost and then he spied a boulder with a chiseled cross and the convergence of three paths. He recalled the three paths and a seldom-trod pathway that went on erratically for a hundred yards or more through the sugarcane. Wherever he led, the party of gold searchers, racked with apprehension, plodded on uncertainly.

Trevor estimated just under a grueling two miles had been covered. There'd been two villages, but no people. Had the Spaniards driven them all off or killed them? Or was something else going on? Doubts shuddered through his head warning him to take care. There were Flamingos overhead, Hutia rodents and lizards scurried from their path and parrots squawked their dislike of them. Yet, no people. Even if the men were gone, where were the women?

They still kept on silently with no reassuring answers. Soaked in sweat, the humidity clung like lice to them and tension rose. Noah stopped, gaping with recognition. Scarcely seen, worn coral tile crept from a wall of flowering Begonia bushes.

Trevor held up a hand for silence. The creatures around didn't obey and continued their chatter, a good sign he felt.

Their machete's hacked the bushes away, and they stepped into a barely cleared area and found the precast cement, weather-worn statue of Cuba's Our Lady of Charity, the Blessed Virgin Mary, holding the Christ Child.

Noah pointed to the rear of the figurine and the men tore into the ground with shovels. With little resistance, the earth gave up its treasure. Ingot after gold ingot, interspersed with sacks of gold coin, were revealed. The men clawed at the earth, shouting madly. Trevor was in the middle of the pack, shoving them, urging they stop making noise and, in the excitement eased by their exhaustion, the men fell back laughing.

It was a frightening scene and Trevor knew it would take all his goading to control the crew. The strange part was he had picked them—former Royal Navy sailors—for their obedience to orders, yet, the sight of gold in such abundance, had unbalanced them.

Trevor understood the reaction. He too was taken aback by the magnitude of the wealth being spread-out, but quickly sobered by the realization this was the undemanding part. Getting the gold to the ship and then away from the crew's clutches was another matter altogether. Even in this moment of elation he'd become conscious that they were not going to be bought off cheaply. Well, he thought, he'd taken care of dissidents in the Sudan and that should serve as his approach here. No one was going to get his gold, not one soul.

At last he dominated them, ordering quiet and to start moving the ingots to the firm ground of the path and stacked into the wheelbarrows. He soon saw that the weight of the gold, and with only three barrows, two or three exhausting trips would be needed.

Coming up to him, Mark's eyes seemed to glow, "You did it, Trevor, you've done it!"

His nerves frayed, the response was harsh, "I've done nothing! Don't you grasp the situation? Until we get away from Cuba with all this we've accomplished nothing!" Get *away*, that's the goal!"

He also knew, secretly, that as well as this, somehow he had to convince Consuelo to either come away now or wait for him.

Shaking the thought, he decided the best way to proceed. Each man was ordered to carry two sacks of gold coin and following that, he set a rotation schedule for the men to push the barrows.

The column queued up. Noah was told to take two sacks and go on ahead to make sure Caleb had steam up. Next came Mark and Trevor, his eyes darting everywhere. Following them were sailors carrying sacks and alternating as riflemen or pushing wheelbarrows.

Inside of fifteen minutes, the column spread back over a quarter of a mile. Trevor called a halt to allow the stragglers to catch up. Waiting, he found the sounds of the forest no longer existed. Except for the breaths of tired men there was no chatter. The forest creatures were silent. He ordered everyone to stay alert and together as they started off again.

For some unknown reason—if there ever was one—the path meandered through cane-fields and Trevor remembered this would be the place for an ambush as some of the men were often out of his line of sight. He found he was unsure, nerves racing through his body. Why? He'd faced dread before—why was he so damn tense this time? Consuelo said the way was open, no one about. What is it? Did some inner sense doubt…doubt her? Don't even think it…

No, no, it couldn't be that. He was getting old, old, and afraid of his own shadow as they say. Mark said he'd won. If so, is he now afraid of losing what he'd won? But it wasn't true; he hadn't won—not just yet. "Hang on Trevor…" he mumbled under his breath, "show your inner strength! Show…"

He knew the two sounds all too well, the crack of a rifle and a scream… "*Down*! Everyone down, *now*!"

The sound came from the trail behind him, unseen, around a turn. He raced back past two of his riflemen as another rifle report sounded, then another and another! At the turn there was a sailor falling and Trevor saw a wisp of gun smoke rising from the cane field. He emptied his revolver in that direction, reloading while he looked at two men dying and two overturned wheelbarrows.

There were two sailors hunched down, “For Christ’s sake—start firing into the fields! You’ve got the best rifles! Damnit, make some noise; scare the hell out of them, where’s your God damned training? They’re just a bunch of peasants!”

The men obeyed and stood there, firing back, exchanging rifle fire until they went down, torn apart by an hail of enemy gunfire.

Trevor, disbelieving the amount of rifle fire and bullets whining past him, raced back to the front of the column, but there was no front. Captain Joshua Wilkes was dead and Mark lay contorted on the path, blood turning the dirt into red mud.

His eyes glassy, he stared as Trevor knelt beside him.

“How bad is it, Trevor? I really hurt…am I going to…to die?”

“Oh come now, Mark. It’s not as bad as you think my lad. More blood than wound, believe me.”

“What’s going to…to happen to me? I can’t die here…alone…”

“Don’t talk rubbish, you’ll be all right. Nothing’s going stop us. All that shooting you hear is our men driving the peasants…”

“But I’m so sore, cold, weary…I…”

“You’re not…” Trevor saw him grimace, then slip into death’s grip, “Sorry about all this old chap—but I’ve got to go!”

Grabbing Mark’s rifle, he raced for a sharp turn in the pathway. A bullet easily beat him to it, splintering his spine.

More in shock than pain, Trevor dragged himself to the turn. Another bullet spattered dirt in his face, “You think you can…kill me…you blasted dirt farmers?”

He rolled over and fired two shots down the path, rewarded when a man doubled over screaming.

“Scream like…a little girl…you pathetic bastard…you…”

He heard a male voice behind him, but couldn’t turn.

“Mr. Trevor! It’s me, Noah. I heard the shooting and came back. Can I help you? Where’s Mr. Mark and the others?”

"He's dead…all of them dead. Christ...yes, you can help… prop…me against…this tree so, so I can see down…path, give me the rifle..."

"Can't I help get you to the ship?"

"I'm going no…where. No sense now. You get to…*Argus* and…get away. One thing, in Mark…in Mark's sea chest…false… bottom…money… Wait! Take this…"

He fumbled in a pocket, removing what looked like a steel bolt, handing it to a confused Noah.

Trevor forced a crooked smile, "It's the…attach pin for… driveshaft. And…and that woman…on the…*Argus.* If you… see…ever see her again…tell I love, I love her…love..."

Noah hesitated; Trevor tried to tell him to leave, but could only nod his head for him to go. Another bullet tore through to leaves, then another. Trevor pointed the rifle down the path and fired. Noah left him to his fate.

He reached barely twenty yards a before someone stepped onto the path pointing a revolver. He froze as the person moved closer, he recognized the woman, "You're Mr. Trevor's friend! I saw you on the *Argus*, didn't I?"

"Yes, and you are Noah. You led them to the gold. Are you armed?'

"No I'm not. They didn't give me no gun. All they used me for was a guide. But Mr. Trevor gave me a message—for you!"

"Trev's alive? Back there?"

"Right back there, ma'am, by the bend. All the others are dead and I'm sure he's dying too."

She glanced to where Noah pointed, scarcely seeing a form slouched against the tree trunk. A look Noah couldn't fathom masked her face. Was it indifference, concern—he couldn't tell. She turned her dark eyes back to him, "What was his message?"

"He said to tell you he loved you…"

She took a quick breath. Unsought, unwelcome compassion she sought to ignore flickered. She fought past it.

"Anything else?"

Noah saw no sense in divulging information about the money, "No, Ma'am. He just said that and told me to run."

"Where is your crippled friend?"

"He's on the ship. Mr. Trevor told him to keep steam up in case, well, in case we had to skedaddle on out of here."

She didn't suppress the smile, "Skedaddle, eh? Well I think that's a good idea. Get on board and skedaddle out of here—and fast. If you get away before my friends catch up, never set foot in my Cuba again."

"No ma'am, I surely won't."

"And, Noah, leave those two sacks, they look too heavy for you to run with."

Watching him run off, her attention then turned to Trevor. She saw him move and slipped up behind him.

"Trev, it is Consuelo. How badly are you wounded?"

"Consuelo? The Black Foe…is calling me…God…thank you…I thought…I thought I'd never…

His hand flayed erratically trying to wave her on.

She couldn't face him, "I'm near, almost to you."

"Thank God…I…love you Consuelo…"

"I know, and I love you too, my Trev."

"You've…come…here…you gave me…this…"

He held out his medallion of the goddess Fortuna. Choking up, she couldn't take it, "Damn Trev! You were my precious picaro, my rogue. Why did you try to take this gold from my beloved Cuba?"

With no response, she placed her pistol to the back of his head. Through his pain, he felt the slight pressure and knew, "I…I understand…thank you…"

Noah ducked hearing the weapon's report and could barely make out her standing over him. Seeing Perez run up to her with his men he knew what she had done, and why. He ran faster.

She stood with her back to his body, staring into the sugarcane, seeing nothing, feeling drained, "You lied to me Trev, lied. You were after the gold all the time. That gold is for Cuba's freedom, not your women. Now I've had my vengeance. Yet—is it not bitter?"

Adan Perez was angry, "I saw what happened and you may have finished him off, Consuelo, but *I* wounded him."

"You proud of that, Adan? If there'd been a fair fight with him, you'd be laying there, not him. So just shut up. Now we've work to get the gold to General Maceo at Bijaugal. He and Señor Céspedes will buy more weapons for our Mambises to continue the fight."

"Well hold up there, Consuelo. I lost four men here in this battle. I've got their wives and children to think of."

"And I'm supposed to believe that the gold will go to them?"

"Believe what you want, I no longer give a damn. Get out! From here on in *I* take charge of the gold."

He started to walk off. What a fool he was, she thought, to say that and turn his back to her. She called out angrily to him. Twisting to face her, he stared, transfixed at her revolver pointed at his chest.

"You cheating bitch, you wouldn't dare…"

Two shots tore into him.

"That's for Trev. And an angry woman should never be dared, estúpido boy."

Perez's men smirked at her remark. Adan wasn't popular with them and never in their lives would they think to dare her.

She stared at the men, "I'll see to it that the wives and children are taken care of and that you will all receive handouts from this. You have any problems with that?"

With only silence, Consuelo went on, "Bury Trevor over there. The others? We'll take our dead home to their wives. The rest, leave them for the scavengers. And that includes Adan and that fool, Mark something. If you want, a few of you can go chase after the boy I saw get away."

Standing with a rifle, Caleb was shocked as Noah scrambled aboard the *Argus*, "What's up Noah? I heard shots! Where are the others?"

"There are no others, everyone's dead! And we've got to get out of here right now!"

Caleb froze, "Dead? Everyone? Mr. Mark and Mr. Trevor too?"

"Yes, we got the gold—but got ambushed. I'll tell you later! Right now we've got to get the hell out of here! Do you know how to sail this thing?"

Coming out of his muddle, Caleb retorted, "Know how to sail? Christ, Noah! I've been 'round ships since I were a pup! Give me a chart and compass and I'll sail you to kingdom come!"

"To hell with kingdom come, Cal! Stop talking! Get us *out of here now!*"

"All right! Cast off the bowline and clear away those branches hidin us. I'll drop the stern line and be ready to throw her in gear."

Noah recalled the bolt, "Wait—take this! Trevor said it was for the driveshaft."

Puzzled, Caleb took the bolt, "Damn! It's the Clevis pin linkin the gearbox to the propeller shafts. We'd go nowhere without it!"

As he hobbled below to insert the pin and find a cotter pin, Caleb quickly grasped Trevor's thinking—if he didn't go, the *Argus* didn't go. For some reason, the man changed his mind.

Noah's pursuers finally located the narrow track to the ship. Yet he and Caleb were so frantic to get underway—as well as the clatter of the engines building more steam—that the noise their hunters made finding their way along the track was muted. The first they knew of them were two bullets perforating the funnel. Caleb, while shouting to Noah at the bow, took his rifle and dropped behind the taffrail and fired at the three men closing in on them. The first man went down, then the second collapsed, while the third man soon dove into the bushes. Noah rushed the length of the ship, took the rifle and began firing wildly up the path. It kept their attacker hiding in the brush long enough for Caleb to limp to the wheel.

The propellers churned, roiling the water and *Argus* lunged forward and roared out of the backwater and into the open bay, her exhaust bellowing under full throttle. Once out of rifle shot and with no other craft in sight, they finally had a chance to breathe again and backed her down to a cruising pace of six knots.

"That was some shooting you did back there, Caleb!"

"Thanks. Me and dad hunted wild turkey over in Newtown and we never came back emptyhanded. You done right proud yourself!"

"Hell, all I did was wound a couple a trees."

Caleb was jubilant, "Maybe so, but those trees surer the devil were too scared to shoot back—now ain't that not the truth?"

Their raucous hilarity veiled their relief.

When they felt safe Noah told his tale of death, the loss of the Rebel gold and the words and action of Trevor's woman.

"He may have been dying, Caleb but she killed him."

"But if she loved him like you say, how could she?"

"My thought is she knew he couldn't last much longer and she didn't want him to see Perez stand over him and laugh."

"That's too deep for me, Noah. But, if you're right, that's a heck of a way to show love. Anyway, what do you think about Mr. Mark dyin?"

"I was shocked 'cause I liked him. He was weak though, seemed to live in Mr. Trevor's shadow, but he was a decent sort and certainly treated us fairly. It was Mr. Trevor who…"

Caleb interrupted, "Trevor? I think he lived a dark life—he was Mark's devil—and not a too disguised one. You could see him twistin' Mr. Mark in a knot. It was his ship, but he did anythin he was told, so the devil in the shadows won. And then he lost too."

"Mr. Mark must have gone along for the money."

"For the money? Christ, Noah, when he showed up back in Salem, Captain Wilkes told me Mr. Mark was heir to some big company in England, and he was to take control and be worth millions when he turned twenty-two, somethin like another year."

"I never heard that! God damn, Caleb, what a fool he was to fall in with the devil."

"Anyone who deals with the devil is a fool, a *damned* fool."

"Well, Cal, what in hell do we do now? The gold is gone, not that it's a loss for us. Those scallywags would probably a gotten rid of us too, so *we're* more than likely still ahead of the game."

«»

As the day's passed, the sense of loss eased to be replaced by relief and then freedom as Caleb set a course of north, north by a half to pick up the northward flowing Gulf Stream. He felt the tug of home and family. Noah, or the other hand, homeless with his mother gone and estranged from his father, readily welcomed his friend's offer to sail to Salem with him, perhaps to find a new life.

Nonetheless, once Noah remembered the cache of American money at the bottom of Mark's sea chest to enhance their new found freedom, they soon recognized there was no urgency to gain the cold climes of New England's January and February.

The *Argus* moored for a week at Saint Augustine for supplies and after breaks at Savanna, Norfolk and Newport, more than two months drifted by. Between layovers, Caleb spent hours teaching Noah how to work the mainsail and jib and, at the wheel, to point up and close haul into the wind. It was the airstream, Caleb repeated and how to read it across a sail that most fooled novice sailors and Noah, despite his namesake was no exception.

Still, the men—one a crippled young man from the North seeking a purpose for his life and the other, a former Confederate Navy cadet, directionless and alone—found common ground. A love of the sea and their dependence on no one but themselves.

Daybreak, 28 March, 1874. The *Argus* ghosted along through a dissipating fog off Southeast Point, Block Island, Rhode Island. Spring had come early. After hauling anchor from their last mooring, they felt the milder air as the *Argus* stood well off the Point. Next would be north along the Elizabeth Islands, Martha's Vineyard, Nantucket and Race Point on Cape Cod's hook. From there, a leisurely cruise across the bay to the north shore and Salem.

They were proud of themselves; through calm and squall, in day or night, the two had sailed a fifty-foot schooner from Cuba to the waters of Cape Cod Bay. They were two proven old 'Sea Dogs'.

With no plan, yet sure in their minds, they both had grown. Ready to take on whatever life threw at them.

The unlikeliest event anyone could ever have imagined was the twin screw, sleek schooner that arrived in Salem only two days before the *Argus*. They tied off astern that schooner at Caleb father's wharf and read her stern board-*The Warfield B. Bunting*

The name meant nothing to either of them.

14

AT BEST, THE MOOD WAS STILL SOMBER. Seven days after the *Argus* tied off, Elizabeth Graves sat with her husband Collie in the canopy glider on the Pickman's veranda. The evening hosted the warmer onshore breeze that signaled the advent of New England's transformation from the bleak winter to the optimism and stirring hopes of spring.

Elizabeth was trying to bring Collie out of his lassitude from learning of his brother's death when both were startled as two ghostly specters, appearing to glow in the moonlight, slowly moved up the stairs onto the veranda. The shapes were soon revealed as two great, aged mastiffs stood and stared at them. In truth, the dogs had heard them talking and it was the sound of Collie's voice that roused their instincts and caused them to come onto the veranda.

Concerned at the size of the dogs as they came forward, for in fact they were quite large, Beth and Collie's sole comfort was that the dog's tails wagged slowly. Collie held out his hand for the dogs to sniff, which, after doing so and apparently satisfied, they allowed themselves to have their ears scratched and be patted before lying down on each end of the swing.

It seemed a strange occurrence to the couple who now smiled at the incident until Jim Pickman came up with the oddest expression, "I don't believe this. The dogs never leave the horses when they're out at night because of bears, yet here they are with you. Did you call to them? Because believe me, they're not people dogs, quite the opposite in fact."

Both people shook their heads, "We didn't call to them, Jim, we were simply sitting here, and they came up."

"You've not seem them before?"

"No, perhaps they heard our voices and came to check on us. But they've certainly befriended us."

Pickman was baffled, “Then Collie, there’s only one answer and it’s the weirdest thing—these were your father’s dogs.”

Collie was as confounded as Pickman, “That’s difficult to believe. How could they possibly know me for God’s sake?”

“Don’t ask me, but animals can sense things. Collie, this dog here is Golden and that’s Raven. Your father named them after that clipper he loved and they hardly left his side from when he was sick right up until he gave them to me the day before…well …before the explosions. Look, I don’t know your plans, and I’d not like to give them up, but they were your father’s and if you wish they’re yours.”

“Thank you, Jim, but we don’t know what our plans are.”

Seven days passed. A week since they had learned of the death of Mark Graves in Cuba. Before learning of that tragedy, Jim Pickman had mentioned that an uncle of Collie’s, his father’s brother Jason, once lived in the mountains of New Hampshire. Jason had died in a rockslide up in Crawford Notch five years past and left no will. That news hardly disturbed Collie for he hadn’t known he even had an uncle. It was hearing of his brother’s death that was wrenching and the thought that his final resting place was unknown compounded Collie’s loss. Why Mark was in Cuba, or how he died would have to wait. The fact his brother was dead was all that Collie could accept for the present. For now, the reason didn’t matter.

The purpose of Elizabeth and Collie leaving England early was due to Mark’s failure to contact them. Now, to accept his death was a difficult process at best, for the sorrow of acceptance was bitter and learning the cause too harsh to face.

A message had been sent to Lily via the Atlantic Cable telling of Mark’s death and Collie’s decision to accept the offer from the A&P. Following that, the Parson immediately honored Collie’s request for a Service for the Dead. The Parson was the very person from the past whom Monar had so shabbily treated when he withheld a service for John Thomas Graves’ father because he was a slaver. At that time, it was only after Monar threatened to ‘snap his neck like the withered old twig he was', that the Parson changed his mind. And now, perhaps the Parson's quick and positive response to Collie's request was possibly due to noting his last name was Graves and thinking Monar may have returned with him. For whatever reason, the Parson's eulogy was seemingly heartfelt—considering he had never seen or even heard of the deceased.

Collie, after eight days, felt the time had come, it must be done; he had to learn the cause of his brother's death and asked Noah to sit with the group and disclose the events leading to it.

Noah, on his part, knew this moment would come, and in the interval between saying Mark was dead and Collie's request for the reason, Noah had time to reflect. He thought it perhaps better to enhance certain aspects of the tale. This enhancing was not shameful—at least to Noah—it was more a coloring, or enriching, something more than simply stating the bare facts and cause his listeners more pain.

Before Noah began his account, he remembered that no one there, with the exception of Caleb, had the slightest inkling of the twists and turns the tale would take and of more import, no one had the slightest inkling gold was involved.

With Caleb, Mary and Collie Graves and the Pickman's seated, Noah still pondered how, how he should begin, and to start blurted out, "It was all because of the gold, the Rebel gold!"

The general response was as expected. Jim Pickman was the first to question, "What in the devil are you talking about Noah?

"Please, sir," was Noah's response, "I've got to explain in my own way or not at all because it won't make sense otherwise."

With all in agreement, he began.

"In 1865, towards the end of the Civil War, the gold was stolen from the Confederacy. And when it happened,"—according to *Noah's* account—he, "was forced at gunpoint and the threats of the gold thief to kill my mother."

The terror of stealing a gold wagon and the trek to the coast hung on him; hogtied at night—so he claimed—chained to the wagon through the day. The thief meeting a blockade running friend, their escape by slipping past the Union block ships to Cuba. In Cuba, where there was no war then, he was forced to help move and bury the gold and, when the villains had a falling out, he was attacked and involuntary had to shoot the one remaining thief.

Noah was a stranger to the Pickman's, Collie and Mary and yet here he was, relating a confounding tale of theft, deceit, and murder. And this, they began to gather, was merely the beginning.

Once again, fact and fiction blended in Noah's story. His escape to Havana, working a ship home, and was lost in events for years until around 1870, when the US Senator he told the story to remembered him as the sole person who knew of the missing gold.

Noah first met Trevor St. Cloud he said, three years past and at that time it seemed from the bits and pieces he could glean, along with other comments, that St. Cloud was engaged by that Senator to *allegedly* assist the rebels in their War of Liberation in Cuba. Yet when St. Cloud got around to questioning him, "…it was mostly about the missing gold and I sensed his helping the revolution was secondary or a dodge, to conceal the true purpose of the mission."

Mark whispered to Elizabeth, "You were right about Trevor."

"Maybe, but I never dreamed of this sort of thing."

"My brother certainly got taken in."

"And you would have too, Collie–you would have had too."

"Without question, Beth, I readily admit it."

Noah continued and the narrative of deceit unfolded. "It took about three years, until the start of this year '74," he recalled, before St. Cloud returned with his plan to aid the Rebels and, secretly, go after the gold.

"I was taken to Herring Bay, near the coast of Maryland, picked up by Mr. Trevor, Mark, and their crew and from there we all set sail for Cuba. I soon learned that though she was Mr. Mark's ship, Mr. Trevor had handpicked a crew of former Royal Navy sailors and he seemed without doubt in charge. When we reached the coast of Cuba, we got the news that a ship Mr. Trevor was expecting, loaded with Rebels and munitions, had been caught by the Spanish Navy and everyone got shot."

Pickman spoke up, "Was the name of that ship the *Virginius*?"

Noah surprised, nodded yes.

Pickman responded, "I thought so as soon as you spoke of the shootings. It was in the Boston papers. So that was all St. Cloud's doing was it? Well that was a mucked up operation if there ever was one. You know, when St. Cloud was here with Mark you'd never guess what he was up to. He seemed a pleasant person. Worldly, been around, told great stories, kind of a man's man..."

"Well, Mr. Pickman, I guess he was really somebody back some time back. I heard him talking to the captain about him and Prince Albert of England planning some scheme in Egypt..."

Pickman picked up on the comment, "Sure, schemes. One of his schemes just got—I think it was fifty-seven men—shot."

Collie, silent at this exchange until now, broke in, "Was my brother aware of St. Cloud's scheme?"

"Not at first he wasn't, sir. He thought they were going to help the Rebels. But after, when he heard of the gold, he joined in."

"So you say he agreed?"

"Yes, sir. He knew there was a bad war going on down there and by using Mr. Trevor's ships and troops was the way to get both the Spanish soldiers and the rebels away from Matanzas so they could get the gold. But...but..."

"But what?"

"Well, sir, what little I learned of Mr. Mark I liked. Caleb and I both did. We felt that at first your brother was fooled by Mr. Trevor into thinking the expedition was planned to help the peasants in Cuba, but I couldn't say anything to him about what I knew without getting in trouble. Then, well then, when he learned about the gold, well, he got sort of excited. He wanted to do it. But he changed his mind when he heard of the *Virginius* and all the dead Rebels and he wanted out."

"What happened after that?"

"We, me and Caleb I mean, we wanted out too, so we spoke to Mr. Mark and he went to tell Mr. Trevor right out 'she was his ship and he was taking *Argus* and sailing off' and, and…"

"And what? Get it out Noah, what happened then?"

'Well, we overheard a bit of a ruckus sir, the whole crew did. Mr. Mark was told…well he was told something like he'd have to paddle or swim if he wanted to leave."

Collie slumped back into the divan. There was nothing he could articulate. The cause was the word *swim*. It brought back that fateful meeting when he and Mark found Trevor swimming to the Isle of Wight. It all came rushing back.

Mary saw his distress, "Why don't we call it a day, Collie? Noah can finish tomorrow."

He found the words, "No, I don't want to do that. I can't go through this again. "

"All right, then let's all have some libations and ease off for a few minutes."

Noah found time to take Caleb aside and whisper, "I'm going to change things around, Cal."

"Why? What are you changing?"

"You'll see. I just don't look surprised."

When they were reassembled Mary asked Noah if there would be much more to be told.

"I'll try to shorten it up, ma'am."

Collie would have none of it, "No, don't do that. I want to know everything and that will be the end of it. I'll never bring it up again. So, continue."

"Well, sir, it was after Mr. Trevor showed who was the real boss that we eventually holed up in a backwater when word came from a spy. A woman Mr. Trevor someway knew from the past sent word the Spanish militia was gone. To us, that meant we were now free to find the gold. He had wheelbarrows, rifles and ammunition brought up from the cargo hold and I was to lead the way, although it took some time finding the trail. Oh, Caleb was left behind on the ship alone with orders to keep steam up in case of trouble."

"How many of you were there?"

"There were, I believe, seven, eight…"

"You all had rifles?"

"All but me, sir, Mr. Pickman. I wasn't given one."

"Go on then, Noah."

"Well, once I found the trail it was pretty smooth sailing. We found the statue and…"

"Statue?"

"The Patron Saint of Cuba, some woman Saint, that's where we buried the gold. I told you about the other shootings there before."

Collie remained on edge, "All right. You found the statue and I assume the gold."

"Yes, sir. No one else had found it and we started digging. But Mr. Trevor hadn't realized how much was there or how much it weighed. A lot had to be left for later, so we put as much as the three wheelbarrows could hold and started back. Some of us were pushing the barrows or carrying two sacks of gold coins and rifles. That was when Mr. Mark spoke up, saying it was too quiet and warned everyone to stay alert. But it came too late, we were ambushed from both sides right proper we were and it was terrible.

Mr. Graves sir, your brother was a hero. He kept shooting into the sugarcane telling us to forget the gold and get running. Captain Wilkes was shot and then the other sailors too. I was running and saw Mr. Trevor go down. He died as Mr. Mark tried to carry him. I got to a turn in the path and stopped for Mr. Mark to catch up but he was shot real bad in the spine and asked me to prop him up against a tree so he could see down the path and shoot anyone coming after me because no one else was left. He told me to run and I did, but when I looked back I saw that spy woman and all the rest standing around him making sure he was dead and…"

"All right, Noah, that's enough!" Elizabeth Graves had to stop him, "Is there anything else we should know?"

"Sorry Mrs. Graves—about saying that I mean. About the only thing else is how Cal, Caleb here, on the *Argus*, saved us by shooting two men coming after us on the ship and getting us out of there alive with only two bullet holes in our smoke stack—and also sailing us back to here with only me, a landlubber for crew."

They all sat back, each to their own thoughts. Caleb knew Noah had twisted the story to make Mark look the hero to ease Collie's pain. The Pickman's were pleased their son reacted well under the stress. Collie was proud of his brother's exploits in leading the men and trying to save Trevor, despite all the misfortune he brought on all of them. And the highpoint was Mark telling Noah to run to safety while he held off the enemy. In truth, Collie never thought Mark would act that way under pressure and the story filled him with pride. That knowledge warmed him. Yes, Mark was gone from them, but now, somehow, Collie found solace knowing Mark would always be with him.

Elizabeth saw the slight smile that creased Collie's lips. Unspoken, she doubted the story. Farfetched, she felt, too heroic from what she'd heard of Mark. Yet, one never knows. Collie believed it and to her, that was more important than any truth.

The First Cuban War of Liberation lasted ten years, 1868 to 1878. Led vainly at first by Attorney and wealthy landowner, Carlos Manual de Céspedes, he was deposed by the Rebels internecine feuding and later ambushed and killed by Spanish soldiers. From the very beginning the war was a cataclysm for the peon and slave and for those ten years they suffered execution and extermination. The insurrection ended 10 Feb. 1878 with, in essence, nothing gained. The peon still suffered and it wasn't until 1880 that slaves received a 'deferred' freedom.

After a sleepless night, morning found Collie transformed. He couldn't continue his black mood, Elizabeth meant too much to him. He would keep Mark's memory to himself and stop worrying others. The blunders, terrors and deaths had to be buried.

Elizabeth saw the change, "I thought you'd be a bear this morning, you tossed and turned so much all night."

"If you know that, you must have too."

"I did, worrying about you, love."

"Well, I've given a lot of thought to what has happened. I'm going to put things in perspective and go on from here. In fact, I'd like to go see father's old Graves' property—you know the hill where father, grandfather, and great grandfather lived. I know the house is gone, but I'd like to take the dogs and go up there and see the area."

"Do you have something in mind, Collie?"

"Something, Beth? I think so, but certainly nothing I could express. You know me, think before speak."

"That's you for sure, and I'll patiently wait you out."

The chill air was past when they reached the two decayed columns indicating the entrance to *Seaward*. Elizabeth held back.

"What is it, Beth? Aren't you coming with me?"

"Not right now. I've given this some quick thought. I want you to go on alone with the dogs and I'll come up in a bit."

He neared the crest and could see the ruin. Once an immense manor, now only granite blocks. Ancient sentinels safeguarding the remains he felt. Collie's father, John Thomas Graves had died there in the ferocious explosion he himself had ignited in anger over *his* father's death, his wife dying and his own cancer. The dogs, Golden and Raven hadn't been there since before the explosions and they wandered, sniffing here and there until, seemingly bemused, they settled near the old foundation.

Collie shivered when touching a granite slab. Unexpectedly, the hates, lies, truths, power, loves, and stories came alive to him. He summoned them, lived in them, with them, his father, grandfather, and great-grandfather. Stormy, unyielding, proud, Yankee sea captains all, flowed into his veins and through him. Collie Graves wasn't surprised; he was home.

As Elizabeth came up, she knew what transpired and was pleased. The one fault Collie had, she felt, was he had no sense of family, of *home* in him. In England, he had lived with his father and mother only until he was five; the father leaving the family to fight in America's Civil War as atonement for *his* father being a slaver.

Father never returned. This was followed by his mother and sister dying from cholera. Those losses scarred both he and Mark. Warfield and Lily tried to replace their parents and then thought it best to send them to abroad. Taken out of school, Prince Monar and Archie Feng took the brothers to the strange worlds of India and Japan and China. Back once more to England, it was education and preparation for them to govern Warfield's companies. It was not until meeting Elizabeth that he found sanctuary, a well-being he'd never known.

It was Mark's shocking death that unnerved him, yet it was Elizabeth's presence, which stabilized Collie, gave him the courage, the independence, and will to carry on.

Worn photographs Elizabeth had seen of Collie's father showed a striking physical resemblance, but it was his mother's personality that made him who he was.

There were townspeople picnicking in the sun on the seaward side of the slope when Elizabeth had come up to him.

"You want to move here, to live here, don't you?"

"How on earth did you know that, Beth?"

"I knew it this morning. Something told you this was home."

"Yes, I feel that. But you—how do you feel about it?"

"We need our own home. There's no better place than here."

"We've a lot of things to square away if we migrate here."

"You know there's no *if* about it, so don't let that be a bother."

“I want to have a Tudor house built here. What do you think?”“As long as it’s big enough. There won’t be just us and those two old dogs of yours. There will be children too, you know.”

“I know, I’m hoping that too and I can’t wait. Right after I become an American citizen.”

“I thought you just said you couldn’t wait.”

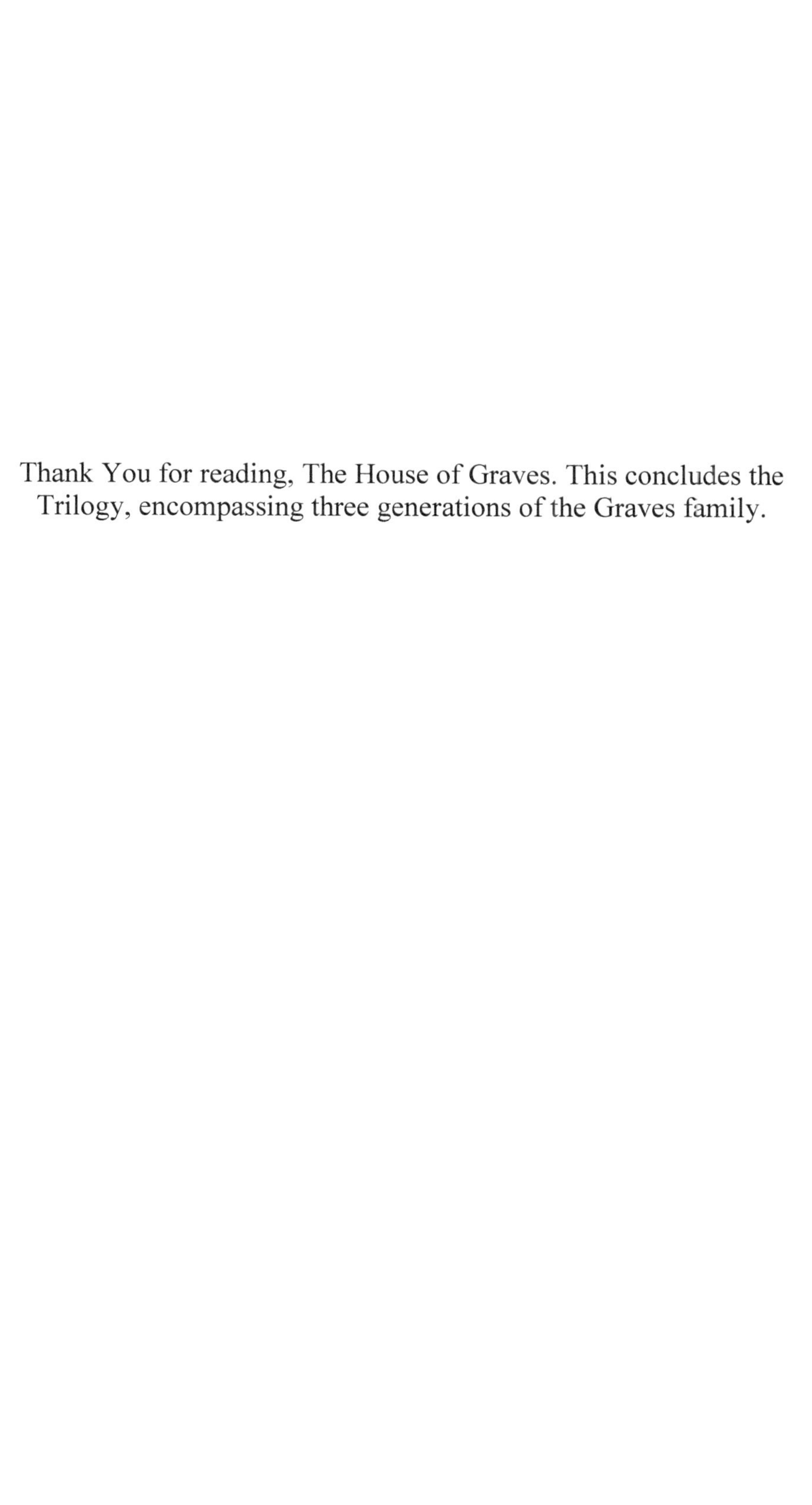

Thank You for reading, The House of Graves. This concludes the Trilogy, encompassing three generations of the Graves family.

EPILOGUE

The Great Atlantic and Pacific Tea company purchased the Warfield Empire and turned Collie Graves into a wealthy young man. Blackwood Abbey was given to Lily Fields Bunting and in her remaining years, her percentage from the transaction easily covered the expenses of living a quiet, comfortable and outgoing life.

Through the A&P, Collie bought the contracts for building ten Warfield's Shoppes along the east coast from New York to Boston and financed them for Caleb and Noah. They were also given the Argus for commuting on the seas they treasured. Laughingly, Collie also gave them two bicycles to reach their Shoppe's after mooring.

Trevor Falcon Stafford-St. Cloud left no will. As his being illegitimate, no one made claim to being his mother, or his child. His blood father, Harry Scrimshaw, had died in the Philippines, also leaving no will. There was some talk much later that a private party, a woman, laid claim to Harry's minor assets. Collie didn't enquire.

The Pickman's, well off themselves, asked for nothing. They did suggest various improvements the town would benefit from and Collie and Jim usually teamed up to assist. The Graves' docks were rebuilt and there Beth and Collie kept a fore and aft masted yawl for day sailing along the rocky north shore. It didn't take long to decide that her bow should be emblazoned the Evelyn & John Thomas.

An oversized Tudor cottage was built on the hill. The twin granite columns were replaced and the SEAWARD sign renewed. Villagers still picnic on the low, sunny, seaward side of the estate.

Elizabeth and Collie Graves? They bought into White Star Line's commerce fleet and sailed the world for pleasure and business on White Star's powerful four sister steamships, Oceanic, Atlantic, Baltic and Republic.

At times, they saw Prince Monar and Maharani Amala, their children and grandchildren. Even into their old age, the Maharini was forever concerned of Monar's roaming the jungles of Tamil Nadu at night. Yet that was he and even the Bengal Tiger gave free passage. Unexpectedly, for all his formidable, wrathful, and daunting life, from slave to absurd wealth and a Prince, he died in bed of old age.

On a positive note, their four sons grew into India's leadership, and with other patriots, stiffened India's backbone in her lengthy fight for self-determination and independence from England.

And the ageless Princess Jyoti Bijral lived on to see most of it.

In the early years, Beth and Collie returned often to England to visit old haunts, see Lily and onetime friends. Yet when Lily died the old haunts meant less, and they and their friends had aged and now dissimilar, changed. Not for the lesser or better, simply …changed.

England, despite her empire encircling the globe, was no longer a home away from home. She was their past, an often pleasant past, yes, but the past, and each time they returned to America and saw the coast of New England, they never failed to smile to each other. The Graves' clan had come full circle–they were home.

During and between those trips, Elizabeth and Collie had four children, Evelyn, Mary, Anna and Christina. The difficult birth of the last girl threatened Elizabeth's health it was decided to have no more children. That decision caused the one regret in their otherwise fulfilled lives—

No son continued their branch of the Graves name.

Perhaps this was just as well.
(There would have been the temptation to delve more.)

REMEMBRANCES

Captain Richard Melville Graves, Book I
Paterfamilias of Graves International Shipping & Whaling Company of Salem, Massachusetts. His fleet of 14 sailing vessels was destroyed at Havana, Cuba during the devastating 1846 Hurricane. He turned to slaving to save his home, but lost his sanity.

Captain Jason Graves, Book I
First son of Richard. Kidnapped in retaliation for his father. He became addled-headed and lived out his years in New Hampshire.

Captain John Thomas (JT) Graves, Book I&II
Second son. The linchpin of this story. His friendships and growth from a modest, gifted sea captain carries his saga from creating the fastest clipper ship in the world on to war, love and more war.

Evelyn Graves, (Bunting) Book I&II
Headstrong, independent, sea captain daughter of Lord Warfield. After many trials and battles at sea and with John Thomas, they eventually marry and have three children.

Prince Monar, Book I, II &III
Former slave in Barbados, he kills his vicious master, joins with John Thomas in adventures from the Russian's Black Sea, the Med's Barbary Pirates to the Civil War. No longer with JT, he marries an Indian Maharini, fights Thuggee in India and opens Japan for Lord Warfield and the British.

Lord Warfield Blackwood Bunting, Book I, II&III
Powerful, at times overbearing, his commercial empire and private army dominates British shipping and the Far East from the opium fields of Afghanistan to India, China and on to Japan.
Ian MacPherson, Book I

Plantation owner, Barbados. Monar's Master in the early years.

Harry Scrimshaw, Book II&III
Falsely cashiered Royal Navy officer. Captained the clipper ship involved in the theft of 250 tea shrubs. Was with John Thomas. Monar and Archie Feng during most of their exploits.

Archibald Feng Yun-Shan Book IIY&III
Leader of the Empire of the Sleeping Dragon. Thought nothing of killing an enemy if he was an inconvenience. Was responsible for stealing the tea shrubs and once saved John Thomas' life even though he cared little for him. Assassinated in Japan

Trevor Falcon Stafford-St. John, Book III
The heroic and self-centered leader who plotted the Cuba venture, bet on it…and caused the death of Mark Graves and his own.

Mark, Collie and Victoria Graves, Book II & III
Children of John Thomas and Evelyn. Victoria died from cholera when a child. Mark died in Cuba, Collie lived into old age.

Noah Benjamin & Caleb Pickman, Book III
Two troubled youths who rose to answer the call when the chips were down…and lived happily ever after.

Edgar Allen Poe, Book II
One splendid night, a Baltimore tavern, and reciting '*The Raven*'.

SHIPS: *Lawrence Pike, Golden Raven, Raven, , King of Edinburgh, Laird of Glasgow, HMS Diligent, Vixen, Black Watch, HMS Rattler, Nightingale, CSS Alabama, Argus, CSS Agrippina, Ocean Pearl, Siaconset's Pride, USS Cumberland, USS San Jacinto, Royal George, USS Monitor, CSS Virginia, USS Roanoke, USS Zouave, USS Congress, USS Minnesota, USS Boston, CSS Florida, HMS Victory, Princess Kathleen,* The Ottoman's Empire's, *Mahmudive,* the Tsar's Warship *Ghazna…*& many more.

BIBLIOGRAPHY

NINJA- Shadow Warrior, John Man James, Morrow 20123

The Tale of the Heike, Royal Tyler, Viking 2012

London and Her People, J. Richardson, Barrick-Jenkens, 1998

Compton's Encyclopedia, 1944

Along the Coast of Essex County, The Junior League of Boston 1970

The History of the American Sailing Ship, H. Chapelle 1935

Ships Through the Ages, D L Lobley, Octopus Books 1972

East Asia, the Great Tradition, Reischaure & Fairbank, Houghton Miffin 1960

Raj, Lawrence James, St. Martin Press 1977

Men and Ships around Cape Horn, Jean Randier, David McKay Company 1969

American Sail, Alexander Laing, Bonanza Books 1961

Seas, Maps and Men, G E R Deacon, General Editor, 1962

1861, Adam Goodheart, Alfred A Knoff, 2011

Great Britain and the Confederate Navy 1862-1865, Frank J Meril, Indiana University Press 1965

Storm over Carolina, R. T. Campbell, Cumberland House 2005

Storm & Conquest, Stephen Taylor, Norton & Company 2008

Voyages, H. Melville, Hallmark Editions 1970

The Alabama, British Neutrality and the American Civil War, Frank Meril, Indiana University Press 2004

Edgar Allen Poe, various books on his life & works.

Heaven's Command, Jan Morris, faber & faber 1979

Google & Wikipedia, general information

Civil War Naval Chronology 1861-1865, US Naval Records

Chart:
C&GS #246 Boston Harbor

Map:
PORTSMOUTH, England. Incl. Portsea, Landport, Gosport
G E Bacon & Co. 1913

About the Author

After a business career as VP/GM of a multi-million-dollar corporation in Boston, the developer of upscale condominiums in the White Mts. of New Hampshire, and the founder of an air purification company in Florida. Now retired, Barry Wood's hobbies include working on his BMW 330 Ci coupe and assisting the ground's crew on his Vero Beach home. Evenings are spent in the lanai discussing golf with Christina, his wife of 35 years and of course there is always the delightful sound of tinkling ice cubes. Serious writing came late, and Barry approaches it on impulse. Fifteen minutes one day, five or six hours the next. Yet when he is alone, writing is not far from the surface. Whether helping with yard work, or awake in bed, he is often visualizing realistic scenes of actual events, or imagining dialogue and interaction between his protagonists and the world around, and research, research, research them. And the process works. Read any one of his novels and you will see why. Barry Wood is a member of the Florida Writer's Association

Other Novels by Barry Wood

MURDERS IN A SMALL TOWN

And

MAN ON THE EDGE

Barry Wood was a finalist in the 2015 Royal Palm Literary Awards for Man on the Edge.

www.ingramcontent.com/pod-product-compliance
Lightning Source LLC
Chambersburg PA
CBHW070824020826
48982CB00014B/450
* 9 7 8 0 9 9 7 1 5 3 0 0 2 *